THE CHEMICKAL MARRIAGE

G.      hlquist is a writer of many talents and virtues, and you underestimate
        peril. His first book was the much-applauded *The Glass Books of the*
        *s.*

*By the same author*

The Glass Books of the Dream Eaters

The Dark Volume

# THE CHEMICKAL MARRIAGE

## G. W. Dahlquist

PENGUIN BOOKS

PENGUIN BOOKS

Published by the Penguin Group
Penguin Books Ltd, 80 Strand, London WC2R 0RL, England
Penguin Group (USA) Inc., 375 Hudson Street, New York, New York 10014, USA
Penguin Group (Canada), 90 Eglinton Avenue East, Suite 700, Toronto, Ontario, Canada M4P 2Y3
(a division of Pearson Penguin Canada Inc.)
Penguin Ireland, 25 St Stephen's Green, Dublin 2, Ireland
(a division of Penguin Books Ltd)
Penguin Group (Australia), 707 Collins Street, Melbourne, Victoria 3008, Australia
(a division of Pearson Australia Group Pty Ltd)
Penguin Books India Pvt Ltd, 11 Community Centre, Panchsheel Park, New Delhi – 110 017, India
Penguin Group (NZ), 67 Apollo Drive, Rosedale, Auckland 0632, New Zealand
(a division of Pearson New Zealand Ltd)
Penguin Books (South Africa) (Pty) Ltd, Block D, Rosebank Office Park,
181 Jan Smuts Avenue, Parktown North, Gauteng 2193, South Africa

Penguin Books Ltd, Registered Offices: 80 Strand, London WC2R 0RL, England

www.penguin.com

First published by Viking 2012
Published in Penguin Books 2013

ISBN: 978-0-670-92166-9

www.greenpenguin.co.uk

MIX
Paper from
responsible sources
FSC
www.fsc.org   FSC™ C018179

Penguin Books is committed to a sustainable
future for our business, our readers and our planet.
This book is made from Forest Stewardship
Council™ certified paper.

ALWAYS LEARNING                    **PEARSON**

# ACKNOWLEDGEMENTS

An ending unravels as much as it knits. This book is indebted to the following, and I am grateful for the chance to thank them:

Ace (PS), Liz Duffy Adams, Danny Baror, Venetia Butterfield, Cupcake@ Casa, Shannon Dailey, Mindy Elliott, Joe@ 23rd, Joseph Goodrich, David Levine, Todd London, MacDowell Colony, Bill Massey, Honor Molloy, Rachel Neuburger, Suki O'Kane, Donna Poppy, Howard Sanders, Jillian Taylor, Anne Washburn, Mark Worthington, Yaddo, Margaret Young.

For Anne, after it all.

# PREFATORY NOTE

*T*he *Chemickal Marriage* finishes a story begun in *The Glass Books of the Dream Eaters* and continued in *The Dark Volume*. However much this present book may stand apart as a discrete narrative, a few notes regarding what has come before may prove useful.

Celeste Temple, a plantation heiress from the West Indies of twenty-five sharp years, her engagement to Roger Bascombe summarily terminated without explanation, found herself in the position, some three days later, of shooting him dead in a sinking dirigible. Mr Bascombe had joined a mysterious cabal (funded jointly by the financier Robert Vandaariff and the munitions magnate Henry Xonck) whose control of the nation was scuttled, along with the dirigible, by the very unlikely alliance of Miss Temple, the criminal assassin Cardinal Chang and Captain-Surgeon Svenson of the Macklenburg Navy, a foreign spy.

When these three escaped the wrecked airship, they thought their enemies vanquished: the Comte d'Orkancz, inventor of the blue glass, had been run through with a sabre; Francis Xonck had been shot; Harald Crabbé had been stabbed; and the Contessa di Lacquer-Sforza had leapt to her death. Betrayed by these supposed underlings, Henry Xonck and Robert Vandaariff had already fallen prey to blue glass, their minds wiped clean, their bodies animal husks.

However, the dying Comte had been alchemically preserved, his memories captured in a glass book by a resilient Francis Xonck, who was unaware of how mortality would taint its contents. Xonck and the Contessa, the latter evidently a swimmer, hurried to recover the threads of their plot, even as Temple, Svenson and Chang raced to forestall them. All parties were met by a new cabal, an alliance of former underlings who understood the power of the blue glass, if not the science behind it, and stood determined to defy their former masters. At the Xonck factory in Parchfeldt, all parties convened for the infusion of the Comte's corrupted memories into the body of Robert Vandaariff, seeking at a stroke to command the one man's science and the other's fortune. Once resurrected, however, the pawn overcame his ignorant masters, deliberately provoking an inferno in which, once more, many lives were lost.

That night Miss Temple escaped the burning factory, only to see Cardinal Chang and Doctor Svenson cut down before her eyes. In the woods, Miss Temple met up with Elöise Dujong, the Doctor's love, and Francesca Trapping, the seven-year-old heir to the Xonck fortune. But the Contessa caught them in the dark, stealing the girl and the dark volume, leaving Elöise dead and Miss Temple only half alive, but determined for revenge.

# ONE

# ANTAGONIST

**M**iss Temple eyed the clock with a characteristic impatience, for she much despised lateness in others. She pulled the green clutch bag onto her lap, aware that sorting its contents had become a ritual, as if she were some old woman with a set of clacking beads.

A purse of money. A notebook and an all-weather pencil. Matches. A beeswax-candle stub. Two handkerchiefs. A sewn cloth pouch of orange metal rings. Opera glasses. A small black revolver whose recoil did not spoil her aim (she had practised on empty bottles in the hotel cellar and could nearly hit them). Ammunition. Gold.

She had paid Pfaff well. If he did not come, she was betrayed. Or – Miss Temple pursed her lips – Mr Pfaff was dead.

Miss Temple cinched the green bag shut. The clock's silver bell chimed the half-hour. She called to her maid: 'Marie, my travelling jacket.'

Five weeks had passed since her return, five weeks spent wholly on revenge.

It had taken Miss Temple two days to regain the city from the wilds of Parchfeldt Park. The Contessa's metal-bound case had not cracked her skull, and the wound on her forehead had eased its throbbing by the time she reached the canal and slept a few hours in the cover of its reeds. Tentative fingers told her the gash had gummed to a tolerable scab, and she walked for hours, dizzied but no longer sickened, to the Parchfeldt railway head, where she finally boarded a coach to Stropping Station, into the heart of the city.

She had gone back to the Hotel Boniface, for her enemies would find her no matter where she hid – she must visit her banker, she must have clothes, she must hire violent men, all of which would draw the notice of any diligent

foe. When she arrived at the hotel's doors, filthy, bloodied and after a fortnight's absence, the staff said nothing apart from a single polite inquiry as
to whether she required a doctor before a bath was drawn or whether, pre-
paratory to either, she might prefer a meal.

She huddled naked in the copper tub until the water went tepid. A maid
stood deferentially in the dressing-room doorway with fresh towels, nervously glancing between the dull face of the soaking woman and the sharp
knife Miss Temple had insisted stay within reach, atop a wooden stool.
Dressed enough to have a doctor examine her, Miss Temple had kept the
weapon in her lap. The white-whiskered man applied a salve and bandage to
her forehead, frowned at the fading weal of a bullet above her ear and left a
powder to aid her sleep. Miss Temple ate two slices of buttered bread, stopping at the first flicker of nausea. She dismissed the maid, locked the
corridor door and wedged it with a chair, did the same for the door of her
chamber and curled into bed, the blade under her pillow like a snake in wait
beneath a stone.

She slept for three hours before her fears rose up to wake her. She lay in
the dark. Chang. Svenson. Elöise. Their deaths could not be undone.

Her survival felt like a betrayal, and every small comfort arrived with a sting.
Yet Miss Temple had withstood such stings all her life. The next morning
she made her first list of everything she ought to do and found herself filling
two diligent pages. She set down the pen and wiped her nose. In truth it was
simpler to keep one's heart a stone. She rang for breakfast and a maid to curl
her hair.

She sent to her aunt in Cap-Rouge, requesting the return of Marie (of her
own two maids, the one who could read), and then spent the day – making a
point to be accompanied by footmen from the Boniface – attending to her
most basic needs: bank, clothes, weapons and, most important of all, news.

She did not fear for her immediate safety. When her train had arrived, the
platforms of Stropping Station were no longer thick with dragoons. Brown-
coated constables had been posted to manage the openly hostile crowds of
travellers, but their only charge was to maintain order, not search for poten-

tial fugitives. Nowhere had she seen posters offering a reward for her capture, or for that of any of her former companions.

She scoured the newspapers, but found only a standard refrain of imminent crises: the Ministries paralysed, the Privy Council in disarray, business at a standstill. For Miss Temple, this was excellent: the more the world was hampered, the freer she would be to act. She sallied out, a hotel footman to either side, gratified by the frayed tempers that seemed to catch at every inconsequential jostle.

Her journey that first morning did not stretch to any destination she might deem provocative – that is, she did not venture near the St Royale Hotel, the Foreign Ministry, Stäelmaere House, the Macklenburg diplomatic compound or the Hadrian Square residence of Colonel and Mrs Trapping. All these places might have become bolt-holes for enemies that still lived. When the Contessa's spies found her at the Boniface, all well and good. She would not be so vulnerable.

And if her other great enemy had survived the destruction at the Parchfeldt factory? Miss Temple had last glimpsed Lord Robert Vandaariff face down in a pool of black slime, about to be swarmed by an angry mob . . . yet had he lived? It would be a fool who assumed otherwise.

Miss Temple paused (the scarlet-coated footmen halted obligingly with her) at the cobbled road's sudden descent, gazing at a district of the city she had never visited. One footman cleared his throat.

'Shall we turn along the avenue, miss?'

Miss Temple strode ahead, down to the river.

Cardinal Chang had mentioned it once, and the detail – a proper name from his secret life – had taken Miss Temple's mind with the attractive force of a silver buckle to a magpie. When she stood in the street outside the Raton Marine, she was unprepared for the surge of tenderness that filled her heart. The tavern lay in a nest of filthy streets, with the buildings to either side tipping like old drunkards. The people in the street, openly staring at the finely dressed young woman with two liveried servants, seemed to Miss Temple like humanity's bilge, beings who could scarcely take two steps without leaving a stain. Yet in this place Cardinal Chang had been *known* – these ruins were his world.

Again the footman cleared his throat.

'Wait here,' said Miss Temple.

A scattering of men sat outside the tavern at small tables – sailors, by the look of them – and Miss Temple passed through to the door without a glance. Inside, she saw the Raton Marine had been fitted out to serve a broad clientele – tables near the windows with light enough to read, and tables in shadows even the brightest morning would not pierce. A staircase led to a balcony lined with rooms for rent, their open doors draped with an oilcloth curtain. Her nostrils flared in imagining the reek.

Perhaps five men looked up from their drinks as she entered. Miss Temple ignored them and approached the barman, who was polishing a bowlful of silver buttons with a rag, depositing each finished button with a *clink* into another bowl.

'Good morning,' said Miss Temple.

The barman did not reply, but met her eyes.

'I have been directed here by Cardinal Chang,' she said. 'I require a competent man not averse to violence – in fact perhaps several – but one to start, as soon as is convenient.'

'Cardinal Chang?'

'Cardinal Chang is dead. If he were not, I should not be here.'

The barman looked past her shoulders at the other men, who had obviously overheard.

'That's hard news.'

Miss Temple shrugged. The barman's gaze flicked at the bandage above her eye.

'You have money, little miss?'

'And I will not be cheated. This is for your *own* time and attention.' Miss Temple set a gold coin on the polished wood. The barman did not touch it. Miss Temple set down a second coin. 'And *this* is for the man *you* would recommend for my business, taking into account that it is Cardinal Chang's business as well. If you knew him –'

'I knew him.'

'Then perhaps you will be happy to see his killer paid in kind. I assure you I am most serious. Have your candidate present this coin at the Hotel Boniface, and ask for Miss Isobel Hastings. If he knows his work, there will be more in its place.'

Miss Temple turned to the door. At one of the tables a man had stood, unshaven, with fingerless gloves.

'How'd he get it, then? The old Cardinal?'

'He was stabbed in the back,' said Miss Temple coldly. 'Good day to you all.'

Two restive days went by before the coin was returned. In that time Miss Temple's headaches had gone, her maid had arrived (bearing a querulous letter from her aunt, thrown away unanswered), and she had begun regular practice with a newly purchased pistol.

The newspapers said nothing of the Duke of Stäelmaere's death, and thus no official appointment of a new head for the Privy Council, though the Council Deputy, a Lord Axewith, had assumed a prominence simply through his regular denials of irregularity. No word of Robert Vandaariff. No word of the Parchfeldt battle. No mention of the Contessa di Lacquer-Sforza. No one called round at the Boniface to arrest Miss Temple. It was as if the Cabal's machinations had never taken place.

Miss Temple had taken another room on a lower floor for business dealings, ignoring the attendant overtones of impropriety. She knew that to the staff of the Hotel Boniface she had become an eccentric, tolerated as long as each breach of decorum was plastered over by cash. Miss Temple did not care. She installed herself on a sofa, the clutch bag on her lap, one hand inside the bag holding her pistol.

A footman knocked to announce a Mr Pfaff. Miss Temple studied the man who entered, and did not offer him a chair.

'Your name is Pfaff?'

'Jack Pfaff. Nicholas suggested I call.'

'Nicholas?'

'At the Rat.'

'*Ah.*'

Jack Pfaff was at most a year older than Miss Temple herself (a ripe, unmarried twenty-five). His clothing had at one time been near to fashion – chequered trousers and an orange woollen coat with square buttons – as if he were a young fop fallen to poor times. Miss Temple knew from his voice that this was not the case, and that the clothes represented an impoverished man's desire to climb.

'You can read? Write?'

'Both, miss, quite tolerably.'

'What weapons do you possess – what *skills*?'

Pfaff reached behind his back and brought out a slim blade. His other hand slipped to an inner pocket and emerged with a set of brass rings across his fingers.

'Those are nothing against a sabre or musket.'

'Am I to fight soldiers, miss?'

'I should hope not, for your sake. Are you *averse* to killing?'

'The law does prohibit the practice, miss.'

'And if a man spat in your face?'

'O goodness, I would step away like a Christian.' Pfaff raised his eyebrows affably. 'Then again, most incidents of face-spitting can be laid to drink. Perhaps it would be more proper to cut a spitting man's throat, to spite the devil inside.'

Miss Temple did not appreciate trifling. 'Why does this Nicholas consider you fit for my employ?'

'I am skilled in opening doors.'

'I requested no *thief*.'

'I speak broadly, miss. I am a man who finds *ways*.'

Miss Temple bit back a tart remark. A man like Pfaff, now unavoidable, must be met with intelligence and a smile.

'Did you know Cardinal Chang?'

'Everyone knew him – he cut a rare figure.'

'You were his friend?'

'He would on occasion allow a fellow to stand him a drink.'

'Why would you do that?'

'You knew him, miss – why would I *not*?' Pfaff smiled evenly, watching her bag and the hand within it. 'Perhaps you'll enlighten me as to the present business.'

'Sit down, Mr Pfaff. Put those things away.'

Pfaff restored the weapons to their places and stepped to an armchair, flipping out his coat-tails before settling. Miss Temple indicated the silver service on a table.

'There is tea, if you would have some. I will explain what I require. And then you – with your *doors* – will suggest how best it can be done.'

Miss Temple soaked again that night in the copper tub, auburn hair dragging like dead weeds across the water. Her thoughts were stalled by fatigue, and the sorrow she strove to avoid loomed near.

She had told Mr Pfaff only enough to start his work, but his mercenary trespass of the roles formerly occupied by Chang and Svenson left Miss Temple feeling their absence. Even more troubling, close conversation with Pfaff had awakened, for the first time since leaving Parchfeldt Park, the spark of Miss Temple's blue glass memories. It was not that Pfaff himself was attractive – on the contrary, she found him repellent, with brown teeth and coarse hair the colour of dung-muddled straw – but the longer he had remained in her physical proximity, the more she felt that dreaded bodily stirring, like a stretch of invisible limbs too long asleep.

In the copper tub, Miss Temple took a deep breath and exhaled slowly, inching herself towards the brink of her fears. In her struggle against the Cabal, she had exposed herself to the contents of two blue glass books. The first had been deliberately compiled by the Contessa di Lacquer-Sforza as an opium den of pleasure and violence. Staring into its swirling depths, Miss Temple had experienced the bright, hot memories of innumerable lives – in *her* thoughts and in *her* limbs – and Miss Temple's literal virtue became a mere scrap of protest before the debauchery she had known. Ever since, this book's contents had lurked beneath her thoughts, and a glimpse of skin or smell of hair, a mere rustle of cloth, could call forth pleasures sharp enough to drop Miss Temple to her knees.

The second book had contained the memories of but a single man, the Comte d'Orkancz, preserved in blue glass by Francis Xonck aboard the sinking airship in the very moment the Comte's life bled away. The great man's mind had been captured, but the contaminating touch of death had corrupted its character, twisting the aesthete's discrimination into a bitter disdain for life. Miss Temple's glimpse of this second book had left her gasping, as if her throat had been coated with rancid tar. Ignorant of the tainted nature of these memories, the remaining factions of the Cabal had convened at the Xonck Armaments works at Parchfeldt and agreed between them to infuse the book's contents into the emptied mind of Robert Vandaariff – hoping at a stroke to regain the Comte's alchemical knowledge for their use as well as take control of Vandaariff's fortune, the largest in the land. Resurrected in Vandaariff's body, the Comte, despite his unbalanced soul, had quickly triumphed over his former servants: Mrs Marchmoor, Francis Xonck, Charlotte Trapping and Alfred Leveret were all dead. Only the Contessa had survived to stand against him . . . only the Contessa and Miss Temple.

At Parchfeldt Miss Temple had received her own revelation. As she walked through the factory, she had suddenly *known* the task of each machine. However poisonous, her touch of the Comte's memories had provided insights into his science. If Robert Vandaariff did still live, it was possible that Miss Temple – throughout her life indifferent to any study – could anticipate the Comte's dire imagination.

Stunned by grief, both books had lain dormant in Miss Temple's mind, just long enough for her to hope they might remain so. But now, prompted by the unsightly yet provocative vision of Pfaff's tongue dabbing at his cup rim for a drop of tea, they had returned. Naked and alone, Miss Temple knew she must make herself mistress of these wells within her, or forever be their slave.

She sank deeper, until the water touched her chin, and extended one leg so her pale foot dangled, dripping. She listened for Marie, heard nothing and settled her hips with a squirm. The fingers of her right hand grazed the hair between her legs, teasing the skin beneath. Miss Temple shut her eyes, willing her thoughts to a place she had never allowed herself, apart from the one impulsive moment in the darkness of Parchfeldt, the rash action she was sure had been the ruin of them all. She had kissed Cardinal Chang. She had felt his lips on hers, had pressed her tongue into his mouth, had thrilled at his firm grip upon her body. Miss Temple's left hand traced circles across her inner thigh as the fingers of her right slipped further down, stroking her arousal to a glow. She frowned against the press of blue glass memories, pursuing her own private need, the slicking quickness beneath her dipping fingers. A flick of bile from the Comte's memories – she swallowed it back and bit her lip, concentrating. Chang had pushed her away, arching his back as the Contessa's blade struck home – she opened her legs to imagine him between them, pulling his sweet weight onto her body. Her thumb swirled a tight circle and she gasped, ignoring another chorus of lurid incident inside her, cleaving again to Cardinal Chang. He had carried her shivering body from the sea after the sunken airship – she sank two fingers deeper still – he had cradled her, nearly naked, white with cold. She pushed her foot against the tub, holding her desire firm, cutting through the noise in her mind like a ship through the foam on the sea. She knew he was dead, even as the remembered strength of his legs drove her deliciously near the breaking of an almost painful wave. She knew she was alone, even as the crest of pleasure finally spilt, flushing her breast like a bird's – opening her heart as it had never been in life, and thrusting it beyond the living world.

She slept more deeply that night, waking after five hours instead of three. With a determined grunt Miss Temple rolled onto her front, face deep in her pillow, her fingers digging beneath her body. This time it was easier to keep the foreign memories away – perfumed seraglio, church confessional, the back of a jouncing wagon – each banished by a fierce deployment of her memories of Chang. When she again lay spent, the pillow moist with her hot breath, Miss Temple began to sob. She wiped her nose on the edge of her pillowcase. Another hour of fitful dozing and she rose, pushing the hair back from her puffy eyes.

She was still at her writing table in her shift when Marie entered hours later, a box tied with ribbon in her arms.

'Sent from downstairs, miss – and just in time for your day . . .'

At Miss Temple's curt nod, the maid set the box on the bed, pulling apart the paper inside to reveal a new pair of ankle boots, the leather dyed dark green. Her old pair had been placed in the wardrobe, split and scuffed by too many perils to name. She hiked up her shift as Marie fitted both feet in turn. Miss Temple flexed each arch and felt the bite of hard, new leather. She crossed to her pillow and flipped it up, revealing the knife. With a satisfying ease the blade slid into the lean sheath the shoemaker had – under protest – stitched inside her right boot. She dropped the shift and caught Marie's troubled expression.

'Stand up, Marie,' she snapped. 'Tea first, then ask what fruit is fresh.'

Mr Pfaff sent four more men to the Boniface for her scrutiny – ex-soldiers, discharged from colonial duty – jobless men inured to following orders and unafraid to fight. As the men stood towering above her in a line, Miss Temple imagined how the Contessa would serve each a special smile, applying a delicate adhesive of desire to their purchased loyalty. Miss Temple was not ugly – if her face was too round, her limbs were well formed and she bore a complete set of bright teeth – but she wanted no piece of these men's desire. She gave them money, her grey eyes coldly fixing theirs as the coins were taken.

With a pang she remembered her pact with the Doctor and the Cardinal. But she did not want to be encumbered – her heart could bear employees, but no longer allies. To Pfaff and his men she was a source of money. They could have no great opinion of her character – and with no ready way to prove herself otherwise, she did her best not to despise them in return.

Three of the new men were sent out of the city to gather news: Mr Ramper to the factory at Parchfeldt, Mr Jaxon to Tarr Manor (whose quarry had provided the Cabal with raw indigo clay) and Mr Ropp to Harschmort House. The fourth and most presentable, Mr Brine – late Corporal Brine, 11th Territorial Fusiliers – Miss Temple kept near her at the Boniface, with the firm provisos that he never enter her private rooms unless requested, nor on any occasion – requested or no – insinuate himself with Marie.

Mr Pfaff himself brought a steady stream of information. The Contessa had not returned to the St Royale. Harald Crabbé's widow still occupied their home, as Roger Bascombe's mother remained sole resident of her son's. The homes of Leveret and Aspiche were quite empty apart from servants. Xonck's rooms had not been touched. Of all the addresses on

Miss Temple's list, only one had received any sort of return. Confirmed by several witnesses, Charles and Ronald Trapping had been delivered home by two uniformed dragoons.

As Pfaff helped himself to a seat, Miss Temple passed him another page from her stack of papers. 'The Comte's house in Plum Court – it appears derelict, but the rear garden held a greenhouse where he worked. Also the art dealer that exhibited the Comte's paintings. And then the Royal Institute. If Vandaariff is alive –' She sighed. 'How can there be *no* word whether the richest man on three continents has died?'

'Soon now,' Pfaff chuckled indulgently. 'Once Mr Ropp returns from Harschmort –'

'The Royal Institute,' continued Miss Temple. 'Since every one of the Comte's laboratories was destroyed, he may have sought other facilities. Also, he will need particular supplies to rebuild – and in such quantities that must reveal the effort.'

'An excellent stratagem.'

'It is, actually,' said Miss Temple.

Pfaff stood with a smile, and called to Mr Brine, who sat impassively on an upholstered stool. 'Keeping the mistress safe, then, Briney?'

To Miss Temple's disgust, both of Mr Brine's cheeks flushed pink.

Cramming her hours with tasks brought welcome exhaustion that served to insulate her grief. In the night she cleaved to Chang, but through her days, passed in a world that so assailed Miss Temple's senses, he was gone. It was a widening divide she fought to ignore.

Mr Ropp did not return. Pfaff speculated the man had received better work elsewhere, or given himself over to drink with his advance wages. When Mr Jaxon delivered his report from Tarr Manor (the house occupied by Roger Bascombe's cousin and her young son, the quarry empty and unguarded), Pfaff sent him – at Miss Temple's insistence – after Ropp to Harschmort, this time with instructions to approach Robert Vandaariff's mansion cautiously on foot, through the dunes.

The longer she waited the more the Boniface felt like a prison. Without revenge to shape her character, doubt gnawed at Miss Temple's mind. Her efforts had been directed against Robert Vandaariff – since, as master of the blue glass, he represented the greatest threat. Yet the Contessa was Miss Temple's primary enemy – her *nemesis* – and had eluded her altogether. The woman had fled Parchfeldt with the glass book that held the Comte's memories. She had also captured young Francesca Trapping. Heiress to the Xonck Armaments fortune, the child offered the Contessa brutal leverage over Vandaariff.

Miss Temple had promised Francesca safety. Would her present efforts prove any less bankrupt?

Miss Temple emerged from the cellar of the Boniface, her gloved hand smelling of gunpowder, and returned to her rooms by way of a rear staircase, ascending just in time to see Mr Pfaff and Mr Ramper, returned from Parchfeldt, proceed rapidly past.

'Tell me *exactly*,' whispered Pfaff. 'And are you sure he was there, not just some mucker from the train?'

Ramper, taller than Pfaff by a good five inches, stopped where he was and leant very close to Pfaff. Pfaff did not flinch.

'He was in a brown coat,' snarled Ramper, 'looked like he'd been living rough – but no poacher, no woodsman and no farmer. He was watching the gate.'

'How do you know he wasn't some gypsy, sniffing out salvage?'

'Why would a gypsy follow me through the woods? Or take the same train?'

'Then why didn't you damn well take him?'

'I thought if I followed him I could find out who he was.'

'*And?*'

'I told you – once I got past the constables –'

'He was gone. *Superb.*'

'No one would go to that ruin without a reason – the *same* damned reason I had.'

Ramper raised a hand to knock on Miss Temple's door, but Pfaff caught it mid-air.

'Not a word,' Pfaff hissed. 'The factory, yes, but not this . . . *figment*. We don't scare the mistress.'

Miss Temple emerged from the stairwell, grinning broadly.

'There you are, Mr Pfaff,' she called. 'And Mr Ramper – how good to see you safely returned.'

Pfaff spun round, his hand darting instinctively behind his coat. He smiled in greeting and stepped aside so Miss Temple might reach her door.

Mr Ramper had not entered the Parchfeldt factory itself. The gate was barred and strongly guarded. The grounds outside were pitted with artillery craters, but he saw no bodies. The white walls were blackened by flame. The machines inside – if they remained – were silent, and the smokestacks on the roof were cold.

Miss Temple asked if he had examined the canal. He had: there was no traffic to be seen. She asked if he entered the woods to the east. Mr Ramper described the shell holes and fallen trees amongst the stone ruins. Without noticeable tightness in her voice, Miss Temple asked if he had found any bodies *there*. Mr Ramper had not.

She poured more tea before turning to Pfaff.

'After a reasonable period of refreshment, of course – I will have Marie fetch brandy – Mr Ramper will direct his efforts to these *machines*. If they have been moved, then surely someone with knowledge of the canals can confirm it. If they have been repaired, then an inquiry to the Xonck Armaments works at Raaxfall may help us, for it is there the Comte's devices were made.'

'The works at Raaxfall are shut down,' said Pfaff. 'Hundreds of men without a wage.'

'Mr Ramper – the men guarding the factory, did they wear green uniforms?'

Ramper looked at Pfaff before responding. 'No, miss. Local men for hire, it seemed.'

'The Xonck factory had its own small army,' Miss Temple explained. 'Perhaps they have accompanied the machines.'

Pfaff considered this, then nodded to Ramper, who stood.

'Do wait for your brandy, Mr Ramper. Mr Pfaff, what of the Royal Insti-tute?'

Pfaff smiled, and rubbed his hands in a gesture Miss Temple was sure he'd copied from the stage. 'No one's let it spill, but there's money in the air. I've found a glassworks by the river, apparently turning away work – I'm off tonight to see why.'

'Then let us speak this evening, when you have returned.'

'I will not return until quite late.'

'No matter.'

'The hotel staff will not admit me.'

'Mr Brine will wait in the lobby – it is the simplest thing.' She turned brightly. 'Mr Ramper, perhaps you will finish this plate of biscuits – one dis-likes their persistence in a room. And, Mr Brine, if you would come with me – I believe Marie has explained there is a fault with the lock on my window.'

Mr Brine obligingly followed Miss Temple to her chamber, pointedly avert-ing his eyes from her bed as he advanced to the window. He turned, his face quite wilfully blank, at the sound of her closing the door behind them.

'There is little time, Mr Brine,' she whispered. 'When Mr Ramper leaves the hotel, I want you to follow him.' Brine opened his mouth to speak, but Miss Temple waved him to silence. 'I am not interested in Mr Ramper. My fear is that his brown-coated man did not lose him at all, but has followed him *here*, and will follow him away. Say nothing to *anyone*. Exit through the rear of the hotel – I will send you on an errand. If Mr Ramper is under scru-tiny, follow this brown-coated person as best you can. Is that clear?'

Brine hesitated.

'Silence is a provocation, Mr Brine.'

'Yes, miss. But what if the fellow wants you? If I'm gone, you'll be alone.'

'Not to worry.' Miss Temple patted her clutch bag with a smile. 'I have only to imagine the man a brown glass bottle and I will pot him square!'

She did not have to fashion an excuse for Mr Brine to leave after all, for when they reappeared Pfaff himself sent Ramper and Brine on their way, expressing a desire to speak to 'the mistress' alone. Once the door closed, Pfaff reached into an inner pocket and removed a green cheroot, wrapped tight as a pencil. He bit off the tip and spat it into his teacup.

'I trust you do not object?'

'As long as you do not foul the floor.'

Pfaff lit the cheroot, puffing until the tip glowed red.

'We have not spoken of Cardinal Chang.'

'Nor will we,' replied Miss Temple.

'If I do not know what he did in your employ, I cannot succeed where he failed –'

'He did not *fail* in my *employ*.'

'However you paint it. The Cardinal's dead. I do not care to join him. If my questions intrude on delicate matters –'

'You overreach yourself, Mr Pfaff.'

'Do I? The Cardinal, this doctor – how many others? You are perilous company, miss, and the less you make it plain, the more I am inclined to *nerves*.'

'You have spent your time investigating *me*,' said Miss Temple with a start, knowing it was true.

'And learnt enough to wonder why a sugar-rich spinster took up with foreigners and killers and disappeared for a fortnight.'

'*Spinster?*'

Pfaff rolled ash onto a white saucer. 'If a woman can look past the Cardinal's scars, what business is that of mine? We all shut our eyes in the dark.'

Miss Temple's voice dropped to an icy snarl. 'I will *tell* you your business, Mr Pfaff – and if I choose to straddle twenty sailors in succession in St Isobel's Square at noon, it is nothing you need note. I have paid you good money. If you think to defy me, or if you think I care a whit about your leers or the threat of scandal, you have made a very grave mistake.'

Only then did Pfaff realize that Miss Temple's hand was in her bag and the bag now tight against his abdomen. Very slowly, he raised both hands and met her eyes. He grinned.

'It seems you've answered me after all, miss. Forgive my presumption – a fellow acquires worries. I understand you now quite well.'

Miss Temple did not shift her bag. 'Then you are for the glassworks?'

'And will send word, however late the hour.'

'I am obliged to you, Mr Pfaff.'

In a show of bravado she dropped her bag onto the side table and snatched the last tea biscuit, snapping it between her teeth. Pfaff took his leave. When she heard the door close, Miss Temple sighed heavily. Her mouth was dry. She spat the biscuit back onto the plate.

Miss Temple looked up at the clock. She still had time. She found Marie in the maid's little room, mending buttons, and explained what to tell Mr Pfaff on the unlikely chance that Miss Temple did not return. When Marie protested this idea, Miss Temple observed that the thread Marie was using did not exactly match the garment. After Marie had promised for the third time to relock and bar the door behind her, Miss Temple tersely allowed that the girl might avail herself of a glass of wine with supper.

The corridor was empty, and Miss Temple met no other guest on her way to the kitchen. Ignoring the looks of the slop boys and tradesmen, she walked to the corner, peered into the street, saw no obvious spy and hurried from the hotel, keeping her head low. At the avenue Miss Temple hailed a carriage. The driver hopped down to help her to her seat and asked her destination.

'The Library.'

Miss Temple had never been in the grand Library before – it held no more natural attraction than a barrelworks – and in its stiff majesty she saw a monument to a high-minded struggle interminably waged by others. She approached a wide wooden counter, behind which stood waxy, bespectacled men whose dark coats were dappled with grey finger-swipes of dust.

'Excuse me,' Miss Temple said. 'I require information.'

A younger archivist stepped to serve her, eyes dipping down the front of her dress. The counter drew a line just below her breasts, making it appear, to Miss Temple's chagrin, that she had jutted herself forward.

'What information is that, my dear?'

'I am searching for a piece of property.'

'Property?' The archivist chuckled. 'You'll want a house agent.'

On his upper lip swelled a pale-tipped pimple. Miss Temple wondered if he would pop it before next shaving, or leave the work to his razor.

'Do you keep property records?'

'By law we collect all manner of records.'

'Including property?'

'Well, depending on what exactly you want to learn –'

'Ownership. Of *property*.'

The archivist grazed her bosom one last time with his eyes and sniffed diffidently.

'Third floor.'

The third-floor clerk was on a ladder when Miss Temple found him, and she pitched her question loud enough to hurry him down in haste to lower her voice. He marched her to a wide case of black leather volumes.

'Here you are. Property registers.' He turned at once to go.

'What am I to do with these?' Miss Temple gave the bookcase an indignant wave. 'There must be hundreds.'

The soft dome of the clerk's head was bare, black hair dense around each ear in vain compensation. His fingers shook – did she smell gin?

'There does happen to be a great *deal* of property, miss. In the world.'

'I do not care for the *world*.'

The clerk bit back a reply. 'Every time property changes hands, there must be a record. They are arranged by district . . .' He looked over his shoulder, longingly, to the ladder.

'Why don't you have properties arranged by the owner's name?'

'You didn't ask for that.'

'I'm asking now.'

'*Those* records are organized for taxation and inheritance.'

She raised an eyebrow. He led the way to another case of black-bound books.

'The letter *p*,' she said, before he could leave.

'The letter *p* encompasses five volumes.' He pointed to the top shelf, high above them both.

'You'll need a ladder,' observed Miss Temple.

*

It had been the Doctor that spurred her thought. Her last vision of Svenson had been in Parchfeldt forest with Mr Phelps, corrupt attaché of the Privy Council, peeling back the Doctor's gashed tunic and attempting to staunch the blood with his own coat. Like everyone else at the Ministry, Phelps had been under the sway of Mrs Marchmoor, her mental predations eroding his health and sanity. At the end he had been set free by Svenson's suicidal duel with Captain Tackham. Phelps had not returned to the Ministry, yet who knew what secrets he possessed? She opened the first of the five volumes and sniffed at the dust. Phelps could also tell her about the Doctor's final moments, when she herself had fled. She thrust the image from her mind and licked her finger. The fragile page caught, leaving a damp mark, and Miss Temple began to work.

After twenty minutes she sat back, noting with displeasure the grime on her fingertips. The sole address for any 'Phelps' was a tannery on the south side of the river. This could not be where a Ministry official *lived*. It had been a fool's errand anyway – how many in the city took rooms, like she herself, at some hotel or block of flats, without leaving any record of ownership? She would delegate the task of finding Phelps to Pfaff. She stood and looked at the scatter of black books, wondering if she was expected to reshelve them, before deciding that was ridiculous.

But then Miss Temple hurried to the ladder and shoved it loudly to the volumes marked *r*. It took her two trips to get them to the table, but only five minutes to find what she wanted. Andrew Rawsbarthe had been Roger Bascombe's direct assistant. Another drone sacrificed by Mrs Marchmoor, Rawsbarthe had perished in Harschmort House. Through Roger, Miss Temple knew that Rawsbarthe was the last of his family, living alone in an inherited house. If Phelps sought a place to hide, there would be few better than the abandoned home of an unmissed subordinate. Miss Temple scribbled the address in her notebook.

The pleasure of her discovery bled easily into confidence and Miss Temple decided to return on foot. Her path kept to avenues lined with banks, trading houses and insurance firms, yet Miss Temple was not large, and the crowded walkways became a gauntlet of bumps and jostles, with never an apology and often an oath. This was the discontent she had seen in the Cir-

cus Garden, but further inflamed. She turned at a knot of men storming out
of the Grain Trust, shouting insults over their shoulders, and was nearly
flattened by two constables swerving towards them, cudgels ready. Chastened, Miss Temple veered to the tea shops of St Vincent's Lane, where one
could always find a carriage. The city felt unmoored, a reactive writhing that
brought to mind only unpleasant visions of beheaded poultry.

As she crossed the lobby, the desk clerk caught her eye and raised an envelope of whorled red paper.

'Not ten minutes ago,' he said.

'Who is it from?' The envelope bore no writing she could see. 'Who
brought it?'

The clerk smiled. 'A little girl. "This is for Miss Celeste Temple," she
said, and so directly! Her hair was near your colour – brighter, though, quite
nearly crimson, and such fair skin. Is she a niece?'

Miss Temple spun behind her, the sudden movement attracting the attention of other guests.

'She is gone.' The clerk was now hesitant. 'Climbed into a handsome
black brougham. Do you not know her?'

'Yes – of course – I did not expect her to arrive so soon. Thank you.'

It had to have been Francesca Trapping. But how could the Contessa be
so confident as to send the child in by herself – was she not afraid the girl
would run? What had been done to her?

Miss Temple walked calmly to the rear stairs, beyond any eyes. She took
out her revolver and began to climb.

The door to her rooms swung silently open at her push before stopping
against the broken leg of the chair Marie had propped against the knob. Miss
Temple glanced at the extra bolt: sheared away.

She eased into the foyer, not daring to breathe, her eyes – and the pistol
barrel – darting at every piece of furniture. The maid's room door was open.
Marie was not there.

To her own bedchamber door a second red envelope had been affixed with
a knife. Miss Temple tugged it free. At the sound, a cry of fear echoed from
within.

'Marie?' Miss Temple called. 'Are you hurt?'

'Mistress? O my heavens! Mistress –'

'Are you *hurt*, Marie?'

'No, mistress – but the noise –'

'Marie, you may come out now. They are gone. You will be safe.'

Miss Temple pushed the front door closed, no longer bothering with the chair. She turned to the sound of her own bolt sliding back and Marie's pale face peeking out.

'We will call for supper,' Miss Temple said. 'And a man to repair our lock. Corporal Brine will be back directly, and I promise, Marie, you will not be left alone again.'

Marie nodded, still not prepared to step into the parlour. Miss Temple followed her maid's gaze to the two red envelopes in her hand.

'What are those?' Marie whispered.

'Someone's mistake.'

The lock had been replaced and Miss Temple's inevitably frank talk with the manager, Mr Stamp, concluded. Stamp's mortification that his hotel had been so effortlessly penetrated by criminals was exactly balanced by his resentment of Miss Temple for having attracted said criminals in the first place, and it had taken all of her tact – never amply on supply – to settle the matter, for she knew his truest wish, finance notwithstanding, was to turn her out. Mr Brine appeared in the door some minutes later, out of breath, for the tale of the attack had reached him in the lobby and he had run all the way up the stairs. After Brine had asked to see for himself that Marie was well – which Miss Temple allowed only on the hope that such attention might persuade the maid that much sooner to effective service – she received his own report, a tale that eased her mind not at all.

He had indeed found the brown-coated man, who had not only eluded Ramper at Stropping, but had looped around and followed Ramper to the Boniface. Upon Ramper's departure, the man had trailed him to Worthing Circle, where Ramper had hired a carriage. The brown-coated man hired a carriage of his own, but Mr Brine had not been able to engage a third carriage in time and had lost his quarry. With a shake of his head – the square nature of which made the gesture more like the swivelling of a wooden block – he described the man as 'weedy and queer', with a large moustache. The brown coat was out of fashion and too large for its wearer.

At this point Mr Brine burst into another apology, but Miss Temple abruptly stood, forcing Brine to stop speaking and rise with her.

'The fault is mine alone, Mr Brine. You warned me. If you would let me know when Mr Pfaff sends word.'

She sat on her bed with the two red squares upon her lap, turning each in her hands for any hint of what they might contain. That the envelopes came from the Contessa seemed clear: the first to trumpet her command of Francesca Trapping, the second to make plain Miss Temple's mortal weakness. Neither fact could be gainsaid. She plucked the knife from her boot and sliced open the first envelope. The red paper was stiffer than it appeared. Inside was only a snip of newsprint, by the typeface recognizably from the *Herald*.

> –grettable Canvases from Paris, whose *Rococo* Opulence languishes in a mire of degenerate Imagination. The largest, abstrusely entitled *The Chemickal Marriage*, happily eschews the odious, irreligious Satire of Mr Veilandt's recent *Annunciation*, but the only Union on display is that of Arrogance and Debauchery. The Composition's Bride, if one can bear to thus describe a Figure so painstakingly degraded

Miss Temple had seen the artist's work and did not dispute the assessment, though she did not know this particular piece. That the decadent artist Oskar Veilandt and the Comte d'Orkancz were one and the same was not widely known, for Veilandt was supposed to have died in Paris some years before. If she could acquire the entire article from the *Herald*, she would certainly learn more.

Miss Temple took up the second envelope, heavier than the first, and cut along its seam. She peeked inside and felt her breath catch. With delicate care she drew the blade around the next two sides, peeling it open as fearfully as if it were a box that held a beating heart.

The envelope had been pinned to the door quite deliberately to avoid damaging the small square of glass it held – no thicker than a wasp's wing, and the colour of indigo ink pooled across white porcelain. She glanced at the door. This had come from the Contessa. The glass might hold anything – degrading, deranging, unthinkable – and to look inside would be as irrevocable as leaping from a rooftop. Her parched throat tasted of black ash . . . the Comte's memories told her that the thinness of the glass allowed only the simplest inscription, that the memory must be brief.

The skin on the back of her neck tingled. Miss Temple forced her eyes around the room, as if cataloguing its reality might give her strength. She looked into the glass.

Two minutes later – she glanced at once to the clock – Miss Temple had pulled her eyes free. Her face was flushed, yet her transit of the glass fragment had not been difficult: the captured memory was but the viewing of a roll of parchment . . . the architectural plan of a building she did not know.

The Contessa had wasted her strategic advantage to acquaint Miss Temple, an *enemy*, with an unhelpful newspaper clipping and an equally pointless map. Obviously each *might* be useful, if she knew what they meant . . . but why would the Contessa di Lacquer-Sforza desire Miss Temple to become even *more* entangled in her business?

Taking into account the curiosity of maids, Miss Temple hid the clipping and glass square beneath a feathered hat she never wore. The red envelopes were left in plain sight on her desktop, each now containing arbitrary swatches of newsprint.

The night brought only a terse note from Mr Pfaff: 'Glassworks engaged, following on.' Because Ramper and Jaxon passed messages through Pfaff, she heard nothing from either man, and Pfaff himself sent no further word that morning nor the next entire day. Miss Temple strode through the hotel, to her meals, to the cellar, even once on a whim to the rooftop in hopes of spying the brown-coated man in the street. She saw nothing, and clumped back to the red-flocked corridor of the topmost floor, where Mr Brine stood waiting.

At her chambers the evening editions had arrived and lay on the sideboard. Miss Temple took the pile in both hands and retreated to her writing desk, holding the papers on her lap without looking at them.

The journey to Harschmort House was a matter of hours by train, somewhat more by coach, and perhaps as much as an entire day on foot. Mr Jaxon had been gone five days, and Mr Ropp above a fortnight. That both had vanished into the mystery of Harschmort confirmed that Robert Vandaariff *had* survived. If the brown-coated man served Vandaariff, did it not mean, upon his trailing Ramper, that Ramper would disappear as well?

The Contessa had found her. She was wasting time. Her enemies were moving.

Miss Temple shoved the papers onto the floor. The sun was setting. She sorted through her bag. She could wait no more.

'Marie, my travelling jacket.'


The maid had been safely installed in the room Miss Temple kept for business, the hotel's footmen within earshot of the door. Miss Temple again left through the kitchens, Mr Brine at her side. With no idea whether they were being watched, she had to assume they were.

The art salon where the Comte's paintings had been shown was locked and its windows dark.

'I don't suppose you can open the door?'

'Not without breaking the glass, miss.'

Miss Temple cupped both hands around her face and pressed her forehead to the cold surface. The gallery walls were bare. She sighed. From her previous visit she knew there was no room for a very large canvas in any case. *The Chemickal Marriage* must be at Harschmort.

She whispered for Brine to look as well. When his face was nearer she spoke evenly and low. 'Behind the gallery agent's desk is a mirror. In that mirror – do not turn, Mr Brine – is a figure crouching in the shadow of that dray-cart. Would that be your brown-coated man?'

Brine sucked breath through his teeth in a hiss.

'Excellent,' said Miss Temple. 'We will walk away without a care. I doubt the man's alone, and until we locate his confederates, we cannot act.'

They kept to well-lit avenues. At the next intersection Mr Brine leant close to whisper: 'If he's got fellows, they haven't shown. If you'll allow me, miss, perhaps we can trap him.'

Brine took her elbow in his massive hand and guided her to a smaller lane of darkened markets, the cobbles strewn with broken boxes, paper and straw. Once around the corner, Brine skilfully folded his own bulk behind three empty barrels. She walked ahead, pulling the pistol from her bag and then making a show of waving into the glass door of a shop, hoping it would appear as if Mr Brine had gone inside and left her waiting.

Silhouetted against the brighter avenue, a figure crept into view . . . head darting to either side like a snake. Miss Temple continued her performance with impatience. The shadow came closer, straight past the barrels . . .

Mr Brine rose, but the brown-coated man was warned by his shadow and avoided the swinging cudgel, fleeing back into the crowds. Miss Temple dashed towards them both, pistol raised, but it was no use. Their quarry had been flushed, and they would not trap him so easily again.

Mr Brine blamed himself bitterly, well past Miss Temple's patience, and she was driven to change the subject, making conversation when she would have preferred to think. They had engaged a carriage and every time the man peered out of the window he was reminded of his failure and began to mutter.

'I say *again*, Mr Brine, it does not signify – indeed, I am happy to be rid of the man, for now we may engage in our true business of the evening.'

Brine kept looking out, his large head mocked by the lace curtains bunched against each ear. Miss Temple cleared her throat. 'Our true business, Mr Brine. Do attend.'

'Beg pardon, miss.'

'There will be ample opportunity to demonstrate your skills. Albermap Crescent, No. 32. As its occupant has died, I shall rely on you to make our entry – preferably nothing to attract the neighbours.'

\*

They left the coach and waited for the sound of hoof beats to fade. No. 32 lay in the centre of the Crescent's arch, and entirely dark.

'I expect there is a servant's entrance,' Miss Temple whispered. 'Less on *view*.'

Mr Brine clutched her arm. The topmost windows had been covered with bare planks, but from one of No. 32's three brick chimneys rose a wisp of curling smoke.

They hurried to the side door. The stones around it were smeared with a grainy paste, like mortar, and Miss Temple looked to see if the house next door was being repaired.

Mr Brine squared one shoulder near the lock and drove the whole of his weight against the door with a resounding crack. Miss Temple shut her eyes and sighed. She followed Mr Brine in and shoved the broken door shut. In the silence of Andrew Rawsbarthe's pantry they waited . . . but no answer came.

She slipped the wax stub from her bag, struck a match and led them to the kitchen proper, the grit on her shoes rasping against the floorboards.

'Do you smell . . . cabbage?' she whispered.

Brine shook his head. Perhaps the ghostly trace lingered from Rawsbarthe's final meal. She motioned Brine on with a nod. They must find the third chimney.

The hearth in the main room was cold, and Mr Brine's index finger drew a line of dust across the sideboard. The front door was locked and barred. The staircase was steep, the wood reflecting the candle like a dark mirror. The old steps creaked, thin complaints at their intrusion. When Miss Temple reached the empty landing, she pointed to the ceiling with her revolver. Brine nodded, his cudgel ready. But the staircase did not continue up. If Mr Phelps was using the house to hide, it must be in an attic . . .

Far below them, quite unmistakably, came the creak of the pantry door. Miss Temple blew out the candle. At once her heart sank. Behind them shone a double line of smeared footprints, glowing palely with the moon. She looked down at her boots and saw them rimed with the mortar from the doorstep – some phosphorescent paste? It had been a snare. Their location would be plotted for the man downstairs as neatly as a map. She desperately scuffed her boots across Rawsbarthe's carpet, then pulled Brine's head to her ear.

'Guard the stairs,' she hissed. 'Surprise him. I will find the way up!'

In Rawsbarthe's wardrobe she pawed through hanging clothes, hoping a ladder might be tucked behind them. Her foot caught on an open trunk and she stumbled full upon it, wrinkling her nose at the iron tang of blood. The trunk held jumbled clothing – impossible to see more without light – but her fingers confirmed, by the amount of stiffened fabric, how very much blood there had been.

She groped across the bedchamber. Her luminous footprints muddled the floor. Between the basin and the bookcase lay three feet of open wall. Miss Temple felt along it until one blind finger found a hole ringed with painted iron. She hooked the ring and pulled. The wall panel popped free on newly oiled hinges.

She dashed back, skidding to a stop in the doorway. Mr Brine lay flat on his face, a pistol barrel hard against the base of his skull. Glaring at Miss Temple was a man whose brown coat was buttoned tight up to his neck.

She heard a breath to her left, in the shadows. She dodged back, just ahead of hands attempting to seize her, and bolted through the opened panel, fumbling for a latch to hold it shut. The first kicks were already cracking the wood as she flung herself up a ladder, climbing with both hands and feet. At the top she bulled through a hanging flap of canvas and sprawled into the sudden brightness of an attic room. By its iron stove stood a tall, thin figure in his stockinged feet, wearing steel-blue uniform trousers and a seaman's woollen jumper. He had not shaved. His right hand gripped a long-barrelled Navy pistol and his left – fingers shaking and skeletal – held an unlit cigarette. Miss Temple screamed.

Doctor Svenson sank to his knees, setting the pistol to the floor and extending both pale hands, speaking gently.

'Celeste . . . my goodness – O my dear girl –'

At the final splintering of the panel below Svenson sharply pitched his voice to her pursuers: 'Stay where you are! It is Celeste Temple! There is no concern, I say – wait there!' He nodded to her, his blue eyes bright. 'Celeste, how have you come here?'

Miss Temple's voice was harsh, her throat choked equally with surprise and rage.

'How have *I* come here? *I*? How are you *alive*? How – without a single *word* – without –' She jabbed her pistol at his own. 'We might have shot one another! I *ought* to have shot you!' Her eyes brimmed hot. 'And just imagine how I would have wept to find you dead *again*!'

Mr Phelps had given her cocoa in a metal mug, but Miss Temple did not intend to drink it. She sat on a wooden chair next to the stove, Svenson – having put on his boots – near her with his own mug. The abashed Mr Brine perched on what was obviously the Doctor's bed, the frame sagging with his weight. On either side of Brine stood Mr Phelps – balding, his watery eyes haunted, yet no longer so openly ill-looking – and a sallow-eyed man introduced as Mr Cunsher, whose voluminous brown coat had been hung on a hook. Without it Cunsher looked like a trim woodland creature, with a woollen waistcoat and patched trousers, all – in contrast to the Doctor – scrupulously clean.

'Celeste,' offered Svenson, after yet another full minute of silence, 'you must believe I wanted nothing more than to speak with you.'

'The Doctor's wounds should have killed him,' explained Phelps. 'He was confined to bed for weeks –'

'I was fortunate in that the sabre cut across the ribs without passing beneath,' said Svenson. 'A prodigious amount of blood lost, but what is blood? Mr Phelps saved my life. He has seen the error of his ways, and we have thrown in together.'

'So I see.'

Svenson sighed hopelessly. 'My dear –'

'If they were followed, we must leave,' muttered Cunsher. He spoke with an accent Miss Temple could not place.

'We were not followed,' Brine protested gruffly.

'Cunsher has been our eyes,' said Phelps.

Miss Temple sniffed. 'He went to Parchfeldt.'

'And he has watched your hotel. Your movements have been observed by our enemies. And your fellows –'

'Have been taken,' said Miss Temple. 'When they went to Harschmort, I know.'

'Celeste,' Svenson's voice was too gentle, 'you have been very brave –'

Miss Temple resisted the urge to fling the cocoa in his face. 'Chang is dead. Elöise is dead. You tell me I am watched, that my efforts have been undermined. If I could find you, are *your* efforts any better? I should not be surprised if the Contessa herself has taken the house next door just to laugh at your useless sneakery.'

No one spoke. Miss Temple saw doubt on Cunsher's face, and disdain on Phelps's. Mr Brine looked at the floor. Doctor Svenson reached towards her, gently pulled away the mug and set it on the floor. Then he took Miss Temple's hands in his own, the fingers long and cold.

'I say you are brave, Celeste, because you *are* – far braver than I. Despair gives a hero's strength to anyone. To be a heroine in *life* is altogether different.'

Miss Temple grudgingly tossed one shoulder. Doctor Svenson looked to the others.

'And I expect she is correct. We should depart at once.'

They walked single file through the houses behind Albermap Crescent, Phelps in the lead, then the Doctor and Miss Temple, Mr Brine at the rear. Mr Cunsher had stayed to feed all evidence of their inhabitation to the stove. He would join them further on.

'Why can we not simply return to the Boniface?' asked Miss Temple.

'Because I do not care to deliver myself into my enemy's hand,' Phelps whispered without turning. He waved them through a battered wrought-iron gate. 'Keep low . . . do not speak . . . with any luck no one will see . . .'

Beyond the gate lay shuttered houses, riven walkways choked with weeds and an open common. Through the darkness Miss Temple perceived a host of canvas tents and winking lanterns, and snatches of talk in other tongues. Svenson took her hand. She wondered if she ought to take Mr Brine's, so no one would be lost, but did not. A dog barked near one of the tents, and a chorus of yaps rose all around. The party broke into a run, outpacing the human calls that followed the dogs, challenges sent out to passing ghosts.

Their way ended at a high stone wall. Phelps began patting at it like a blind man. Miss Temple looked back. The dog had again provoked the chorus of its fellows.

'I expect that's Mr Cunsher,' whispered Brine.

'Who *is* Mr Cunsher?' Miss Temple asked.

'A man known to the Ministry,' said Svenson. 'You would call him a spy.'

'But not from *here*.'

'No more than you or I, which recommends him, this city being a snake-pit . . . '

Miss Temple realized the Doctor had quietly drawn the Naval revolver.

'At last . . . at *last*,' muttered Phelps, and she heard the turn of a key. 'Quickly, inside and up the stairs.'

'A relic of an older time.' Phelps's whisper rebounded off a brick ceiling. He tamped the lamp wick to a lower flame and slid a fluted glass over it. 'A portion of ancient city wall – a tower left to secure river traffic, and then left again as a useful hole for stuffing things and people one's government ought not to have. I learnt of it from the late Colonel Aspiche, who stumbled across it as a subaltern. Once assigned to Palace duties, he sought out the key . . . a key which I took it upon myself to, ah, take.'

'Colonel Aspiche was horrid,' said Miss Temple.

Phelps sighed. 'I am sure you must have found him so – as you must find me. Ambition has made apes of better men, and far worse.'

'How do you *feel*?' asked Miss Temple, not interested in another apology. 'The sickness from the blue glass – has it passed? Are its effects reversed?'

'In the main, though not without cost – I do not think I shall ever sleep the night through without some dream of *her* staining my mind. If Doctor Svenson owes his life to my efforts, I owe my sanity to his.'

Svenson smiled tightly, snapping open his silver case for a cigarette. 'You ask what I have done these weeks, Celeste, apart from tending my own wounds. Do you still have the orange metal rings? Cardinal Chang stuffed a quantity into my pocket – I assume he did the same to you.'

Miss Temple flushed at the memory of Chang's fingers thrusting into the bosom of her dress, for it had become a fixture of her intimate relief. Svenson hesitated at her silence, but then went on. 'The qualities of this orange mineral counter those of the blue glass; thus the rings enabled each of us to resist the powers of Mrs Marchmoor. You will remember the liquid we used to cure Chang's wounds in the airship. I was able to distil a kind of tincture from my supply of rings. Crude, to be sure, yet it minimized the poison in Mr Phelps. With time and proper tools I could do more – if I knew what the alloy *was*, I could do more still.'

He knelt and studied her face. 'The glass woman rummaged in your thoughts too. At the factory, you appeared nearly consumptive . . .'

She turned from his gaze. 'I have made a point since to eat fresh fruit.'

Svenson smiled, and it seemed he might touch her cheek, but instead he stood. His unshaven beard was darker than his hair and gave a masculine cast to his sharp chin that she had not previously discerned. Indeed, standing above her in his boots and rough clothing, the Doctor exuded an altogether disturbing maleness.

He was staring at her. Of course he was – he quite naturally wanted to know everything – but Miss Temple found herself unable to speak. Her cheeks burnt. How could she tell him about Chang? How could she speak about her secret needs? How could she explain the derangement she risked from even his kind hand?

The silence was broken by Mr Brine offering a match for Svenson's unlit cigarette. Mr Phelps shifted the conversation to food, removing from a satchel several meat pies and a green bottle of sweet wine.

Over the meal, Mr Phelps related their own experiences since the Parch- feldt wood. They had joined a ragged party of fleeing men – minions of Mrs Marchmoor who did not question their presence – finally reaching St Porte and a surgeon for Svenson's wounds. Two days by dray-cart had seen them to the city and the refuge of Rawsbarthe's home, where the Doctor fell into a fever. Phelps had risked returning to the Foreign Ministry only once, to find his offices ransacked and abandoned – indeed, like the offices of all senior staff.

'Who is in charge?' asked Miss Temple.

'The Foreign Minister, Lord Mazeby, still lives, but has ever battled dementia – thus Deputy Minister Crabbé's untoward authority. Junior attachés, such as my own aide, Mr Harcourt, have been promoted, but true policy must lie with the Privy Council, or the Crown. The Queen is old, however, and the Duke who ruled the Privy Council dead. A non-entity like Lord Axewith may take his place, but what does that serve? The entire government, and industry as well –'

Miss Temple interrupted to suggest he speak to what she did *not* know already.

In the ensuing pause Doctor Svenson cleared his throat and more fully described Cunsher as an *agent provocateur*, personally loyal to Phelps, who had employed his services abroad. At this, Phelps resumed the tale: while he had seen to the Doctor's recovery – and then the Doctor to his own – Mr Cunsher had set to investigating their enemies. A recitation of Cunsher's discoveries was again interrupted by Miss Temple – she *knew* about the St Royale, and the factory, and the Institute, and –

'But you were unaware of your own danger!' barked Phelps. 'Villains watching your hotel and attacking the men in your employ!'

'*Whose* villains?' asked Miss Temple. 'From the Contessa, or Vandaariff?'

'We suspect the latter,' said Svenson. 'Not even Cunsher can get near Harschmort. It is a rearmed camp. The Cabal spread a story of blood fever to justify Vandaariff's confinement at their hands, and one would expect at least an announcement of recovery, to allow him back into public life – but none has come.'

'What of the Contessa?' asked Miss Temple.

'Nothing,' spat Mr Phelps. 'Not one sign.'

The tower had a primitive barracks, six musty bunks, now echoing with Mr Brine's snores. Miss Temple peered across the room, unable to see whether Svenson and Phelps were asleep, though she assumed they were.

A dream had awoken her. She had been in Harschmort, standing before the Dutch mirror, naked but for a green silk bodice. Someone was watching from behind the glass and she felt a keen pleasure in imagining their hungry eyes as her hands traced the sweep of her white hips. She wondered who it was and turned her buttocks to the glass. Someone she knew? Chang? In delicious provocation, Miss Temple bent forward and reached between her legs . . . and in answer, like delight's inevitable consequence, the room changed. The mirror was gone, revealing the niche behind it and her observer. Stretched upon the velvet chaise was the dead-eyed, grey-skinned corpse of Elöise Dujong.

The threads of sleep slipped away and with them the chill of horror. But, as she stared at the bunk slats above her, bowed against the weight of Mr Brine, Miss Temple felt the dream's hunger remain. Her mouth tasted sour – the wine, along with her own spoilt essence – and she ran her tongue along her teeth in hopes of subduing her desire through disgust. But the urge would not subside. She sucked the inside of one cheek between her teeth and bit hard. The others were too near. They would hear – they would smell –

In an abrupt rustle of petticoats Miss Temple rolled from the bunk and padded to the other room, hugging herself tight at the stove and rocking on cold bare feet. She forced her mind to the dream. What did it mean to bare her lust to Elöise, of all people? Miss Temple was not at heart shamed by her desire, only that so much of what informed it derived from other minds. Was her feeling of debasement more truly a matter of pride?

Elöise had been married. She had loved men – perhaps even the Doctor, in some bare-planked room at the fishing village. At this thought Miss Temple's imagination flared: Svenson's unshaven face kissing the pale skin above Elöise's breasts, her dress pushed up her thighs, his knees bent with effort. Miss Temple whimpered aloud, and in sorrow. In her dream, desire had been grotesque. But that was wrong, and the truth came cruelly in the gaze of care her imagination placed between Elöise and the Doctor, her liquid brown eyes up to his clear blue. Miss Temple wiped her nose with a sniff. What made desire unbearable was love.

She turned at a sound. Doctor Svenson stood in the doorway.

'I heard you rise. Are you well?'

She nodded.

'Aren't you cold?'

'I had a dream.' Miss Temple exhaled with more emotion than she cared for. 'Of Elöise. She was dead.'

Svenson sighed and sat near her in a chair, his hair across his eyes.

'In mine she lives. Small consolation, for I wake to sorrow. Yet my memory retains Elöise Dujong in this world – her smile, her scent, her care. She is that much preserved.'

'Did you love her?' Her back was to the stove, her dress bundled forward so it would not singe.

'Perhaps. The thought is a torment. She did not love me, I know that.'

Miss Temple shook her head. 'But . . . she told me . . .'

'Celeste, I beg you. She made her feelings clear.'

Miss Temple said nothing. The thick stone walls cloaked them in silence.

'You were with Chang?' the Doctor asked. 'At the end?'

Miss Temple nodded.

'The night was chaos. I remember very little after the ridiculous duel –'

'It was not ridiculous,' said Miss Temple. 'It was very brave.'

'I heard you call and guessed something had happened to Chang. I did not know until this night it was the Contessa. Nor that she killed Elöise.'

Svenson had changed, as if the blue of his eyes had been run through a sieve. Again she wondered at his wound – how raw the scar, how long, imagining the blade slicing across the Doctor's nipple –

She whimpered under her breath. Svenson half rose from his seat but she kept him back with a shake of her head and a half-hearted smile. The Doctor watched her with concern.

'I have been quite out of the world,' he said softly. 'You had best tell me what you can.'


Her story poured out, everything that had taken place from the clearing where Elöise had died to Albermap Crescent – Pfaff, the vanishing of Ropp and Jaxon, the red envelopes, the Comte's painting, the scrap of inscribed glass. She said nothing of her own distress, the books roiling inside, her deracinating hunger. She said nothing of Chang. Yet, as she spoke, she found her attention catching on the Doctor's features, the efficient movement of his hands as he smoked, even the new rasp to his voice. She found herself guessing his age – a decade older than she, surely no more than that – his German manners aged him next to a man like Chang, but if one only looked at his face –

Miss Temple started, deep in her own mind. Svenson had stepped closer to the stove and rubbed his hands.

'I am growing cold after all.'

'It *is* cold,' replied Miss Temple, holding out her hands as well. 'Winter is the guest who never leaves – who one finds lurking behind the beer barrel in the kitchen.'

Svenson chuckled, and shook his head. 'To keep your humour, Celeste, after all you've seen.'

'I'm sure I have no humour at all. Speaking one's mind is not wit.'

'My dear, that is wit exactly.'

Miss Temple reddened. When it was clear she had no intention of replying, the Doctor knelt and scooped more coal into the stove.

'Mr Cunsher has not come. He may be hiding, or in pursuit – or taken, in which case we cannot remain here.'

'How will we know which? If we leave, how will we find him?'

'He will find us, do not fear . . .'

'I do not like Mr Cunsher.'

'Upon such men we must rely. How long did it take until you trusted Chang?'

'No time at all. I saw him on the train. I *knew*.'

Svenson met her determined expression, then shrugged. 'Harschmort is too perilous until we know more. Our struggle has become a chess match. We cannot strike at king or queen, but must fence with pawns and hope to force a path. Your Mr Pfaff –'

'Went to a glassworks by the river, which led him somewhere else.'

'And Mr Ramper went to Raaxfall. Phelps and I have hopes to waylay Mr Harcourt as he leaves the Ministry –'

'We should go back to the Boniface,' Miss Temple said. 'As it is watched, my arrival may provoke one of these pawns to action – which you and Mr Phelps can observe. I will be safe with Brine, and with any luck Mr Pfaff will have returned.'

'Spelt out like that, I cannot disagree.'

She smiled. 'Why should you want to?'


Breakfast was quick and cold, well before dawn. Fog clung to the stones. The streets on the far side of the tower were of a piece with the tents on the common they had passed in the night – even at this hour crowded with faces from other lands, tiny shops, carts, mere squares of carpet piled with copper, beadwork, spices, embroidery. Miss Temple found herself next to Mr Phelps. Unable to shed her distrust, yet feeling obliged because of the Doctor's alliance, she did her best to strike up a conversation.

'How strange it must be, Mr Phelps, to be so uprooted from your life.'

The pale man's expression remained wary. 'In truth, I scarcely note it.'

'But your family, your home – are you not missed?'

'The only ones to miss me are already dead.'

Miss Temple felt an impulse to apologize, but repressed it. Behind them Svenson listened to Mr Brine describe his service abroad, apparently spurred on by the dark faces around them.

'When you say "dead", Mr Phelps, do you refer to your former allies – Mrs Marchmoor, Colonel Aspiche and the others?'

Phelps's lips were a thin, whitened line. He gestured at the market stalls. 'Have you spent all your hours in that hotel? Do you not see how we are stared at?'

'I am not unaccustomed to dark faces, Mr Phelps, nor their attention.'

'Have you not perceived the disorder in the streets?'

'Of course I have *perceived* it,' said Miss Temple. 'But disorder and unrest have always been the lot of the unfortunate.'

'Don't be a fool,' Phelps replied under his breath, angry but not wanting to draw attention. 'Everything you see – the fear amongst these colonials, the anger of the displaced workers, the outrage with the banks, our paralysed industry – all of this comes directly from my misguided efforts. And your virtuous ones.'

'I do not understand.'

Phelps exhaled, a chuff of clouded air. She saw the strain in his eyes, a vibration of guilt. He did not like her, she knew, but, more, Phelps did not like himself. She gave the man credit for his awareness of the latter dislike colouring the former – thus the sigh, and an attempt at explanation.

'Those you name as "the Cabal" insinuated themselves into the highest levels of every ministry, the Palace, Admiralty, Army and Privy Council. Even more importantly, through the subversion of men of industry like Robert Vandaariff and Henry Xonck, they influenced mills, banks, shipping lines, railways, a gridwork of influence and power – all of it suborned through their *Process*, and all, on their departure in that dirigible, left awaiting instructions, free will expunged.'

'And I have worked *against* them –'

'Yes, and unintentionally, through your success, delivered the nation from one dilemma to another. When the Cabal's mission to Macklenburg failed and its leaders were undone, this gridwork I describe was left without command, even without sense. Various minions attempted to take the reins – out of ambition, I make no bones, for I was of their number – Mrs Marchmoor and the Colonel, but there were others too with a scrambling knowledge of what plans had been in place. This second crop was defeated at Parchfeldt, as we deserved – but that victory has only allowed the nation's sickness to deepen.'

'What sickness?'

Phelps shook his head. 'The sickness of rule. The Cabal has hollowed out the *rule* of this land like a melon – and what remains? What remains of the *nation*? In governance there is ever but a narrow margin between acceptance and revolt. Quite simply, Miss Temple, that margin is gone.'

'But why should you care?'

Phelps stammered, aghast. 'Because I am guilty. Because others have died without the chance to repent.'

Miss Temple sniffed. 'What does repentance do, save ease a villain's conscience?'

Phelps turned down a lane of smithies, where the air rang with hammers and the breeze was warm. He spoke abruptly, his voice unpleasantly crisp. 'We went back to Parchfeldt. While Cunsher spied out the factory. Did the Doctor tell you? No. It had been weeks – cold, rain – the *wild*. We went back for *her*. We took the body to her uncle's on a cart. Dug a grave in the garden.' He twisted his mouth to a grimace. 'Who'll do that for you or me?'

When Miss Temple spoke her voice was small.

'Did you look for Chang?'

'We did.' Mr Phelps took her hand to cross the busy road. 'Without success.'

Mr Spanning, the assistant manager, was just unlocking the hotel's front door as Miss Temple and Mr Brine arrived. Mr Phelps and the Doctor had gone to secure a carriage and would meet them outside.

'Early morning?' Spanning offered, eyes flitting across their rumpled clothes.

Miss Temple had not forgotten Spanning's willingness to accept the Cabal's money, nor her own threat to set his over-oiled hair aflame. He smoothly preceded them to the desk.

'No messages. So sorry.'

Mr Brine leant over the lip of the desk to look for himself, but Miss Temple was already walking to the stairs.

'Will you want tea?' called Spanning with arch solicitude. 'Brandy?'

By the time Miss Temple reached her own floor the revolver was in her hand. Mr Brine pressed ahead of her with his cudgel. The door was locked as they had left it.

Inside, nothing had been touched. Miss Temple sent Mr Brine downstairs to wake Marie. While he was gone, she retrieved the two red envelopes and their original contents, tucking them carefully into one of her aunt's serial novels (*Susannah, White Ranee of Kaipoor*) to protect the glass. Her eyes caught her old ankle boots. The bold green leather had been chosen out of spite, of course, at the disapproval of Roger Bascombe's cousin. She disliked the memory.

Miss Temple waited for Mr Brine in her parlour, a growing tension in her hips. Why was she alone? Why was she *always* alone?

She shifted and felt the seam of her silk pants pull between her legs. How long before Mr Brine came back? With one hand she bunched up her dress and petticoats so she might slip the other beneath. How close had she come to depravity in the barracks bunk, pleasuring herself in plain view of the Doctor, the noise waking every man in the room? Did she not risk the exact same mortification now, if Brine were to enter with Marie and find her red-faced and gasping? She worked her thumb through the gap in her silk pants and grunted at the spark of contact. And if it was not them entering, but Svenson? She imagined his shock at her brazen need. Was the rest of his skin so pale? She grunted again and shut her eyes, then with a sudden stab of anger pulled her damp hand free.

Was she such an animal?

Anything was possible – it was a lesson her blue glass memories made clear – but because a thing was possible did not mean she ought to want it. She had opened her heart to Chang. It did not signify that he was dead (or that she had only been able to do so *because* he was dead). She exhaled through her nose and rose to wash her hand.

They met the carriage in front of the hotel.

'No word from Mr Pfaff,' Miss Temple said, and handed her aunt's novel to Doctor Svenson, who opened it to reveal the red envelopes. 'You all ought to look into the glass, in case you recognize the building it shows.'

Phelps studied the newspaper clipping. 'Is it worth a stop at the *Herald*? The complete text might tell us where to find the painting, and thus the man.' He saw the glass in Svenson's lap and swallowed with discomfort. 'I will never see that shade of blue without a headache. Are you sure it is safe?'

'Of course I am.'

Svenson looked up from the glass and blinked. 'I have no idea what this is.' He offered the envelope to Mr Brine. 'Just look into it; do not let the experience surprise you.'

'You seemed so sure they are watching us,' said Miss Temple. 'Still, we remain unmolested. Can it be they do not *care*?'

'Perhaps they know where we will go,' offered Svenson.

'But how?' asked Phelps. 'Do we?'

'If they have captured Cunsher or Mr Pfaff, they may know enough. Or' – Svenson flicked a fingernail against the red envelope in his hand – 'they have laid an irresistible path for us to follow.'

Phelps sighed. 'Like visiting the *Herald*.'

Miss Temple turned to Mr Brine, lost in the blue card, and gently tapped his shoulder. Brine started and the envelope slipped off his knees, deftly caught by Doctor Svenson. Brine at once began to apologize.

'There is no harm,' Miss Temple said quickly. 'The blue glass is *immersive*. Did you recognize anything?'

Brine shook his head. Miss Temple wished he might say something clever, feeling that his dull presence reflected on her. Mr Phelps steadied himself to enter the glass. He came out of it moments later with a sneeze – again the Doctor saving the glass from breakage – eyes watering and his nose gone red. Phelps dug for a handkerchief and mopped his face.

'My constitution has been spoilt. Dreadful stuff.' He blew his nose. 'But, no, I've no idea of the place, save to say it looks *large*.'

'Could it be a portion of Harschmort?' asked Miss Temple.

'It could be anything.'

'*Anything* can be anything.' Miss Temple slumped back in her seat, taking in the passing street. 'Why are we riding to the Ministries?'

'We're not,' Phelps protested, 'not *strictly* – yet I had thought, perhaps, if we did waylay Harcourt –'

'Ridiculous,' said Miss Temple. 'I did not spend a miserable night in hiding to deliver myself to Ministry guards. By your own logic, we are in this coach – at liberty – because our enemies allow it. The Contessa has sent these envelopes to spur us to action. That means she must be desperate.'

'If it were so pressing, her hints would be *clearer*.'

'Perhaps they are clearer than we know,' said Svenson. 'A clipping about the Comte's painting and an architectural plan – in glass, which links it too with the Comte. May we suppose the structure is the home of the painting?'

'Then must we visit the *Herald* after all?'

'Possibly,' continued Svenson, 'yet if the Contessa possessed the entire clipping, why send only this part?'

'To force us to visit the newspaper.'

'Or the opposite,' replied Svenson. 'She could have given the whole page. Do you see – in reducing the text she also omits extraneous facts that might distract us.'

'You speak as if she can be trusted!' cried Phelps.

'Never in life, but her actions can be deduced from her appetites, like any predator's.'

Miss Temple plucked the clipping from Mr Brine, who currently held it. She reread the text and then turned it over. At once she snorted with disgust.

'I am an outright ass.' She held the scrap of paper out for them to see. 'Our destination is Raaxfall.'

Phelps gave an exasperated sigh and looked to the Doctor for support. 'That is an advertisement for scalp tonic.'

'*Yes*,' said Miss Temple, 'look at the *words*.'

'Scalp? Tonic?'

'No, no –'

Phelps read aloud. 'New guaranteed formula for medical relief! From Monsieur Henri's Parisian factory! A recipe for healing, restored vitality and new growth!'

Miss Temple stabbed her finger at the paper. 'Factory – medical – formula – healing – new growth! Those words – in reference to the Comte d'Orkancz –'

'But they aren't in reference –'

'*He* is on the other side of the paper! Put them together! It is the Contessa's way!'

Phelps shook his head. 'Even if that is so – which I doubt – how do you possibly reach the conclusion of Raaxfall? If anything "new growth" would point us to a repaired Harschmort, or even back to Parchfeldt!'

Miss Temple swatted the paper again. 'It is obvious! "Monsieur Henri"!'

'"Monsieur Henri"?'

'Henry Xonck!'

'O surely not –'

'Doctor Svenson!'

She shifted to face him, willing her expression to blankness, as if she would accept his impartial verdict. He pursed his lips.

'I would not perceive the interpretation myself –'

'Ha!' cried Phelps.

Svenson was not finished. 'However, the puzzle was not sent for *me* to solve, but to Celeste . . . and the Contessa is one to know her target.'

Miss Temple smiled, but her victory was tempered. Her cleverness had been fitted like a jigsaw piece into her enemy's plan.

Raaxfall emerged as a sooty smear of workers' huts clustered on the river's curl. The banks bristled with an unsavoury dockfront, the wood as black with tar as the water was with filth. Everything in the town seemed blasted and cracked, even the ashen sky. The carriage took them to an inn where the driver might wait as they partook of a meal, it being by then near noon.

'I have entered the Xonck works but once, for a demonstration of a new model carbine for territorial service – there were disagreements on the size of projectile required to stop *native* militia.' Phelps cleared his throat and went on. 'The point being, the works are outside Raaxfall proper, and less a standard mill than a military camp, with discrete workhouses built to protect against inadvertent explosion. At the inn we may find men put out of work who will know more about the present occupation and can show us a less visible approach than the main road.'

Miss Temple felt the grit beneath her boots as she climbed down, aware in this drab town of the colour in her clothes – green boots, dress of pale lavender, violet travelling jacket – and her chestnut hair hanging in curls to either side of her face. Mr Brine's stout wool coat was the colour of dark porter, while Mr Phelps still availed himself of Ministry black. Doctor Svenson was last to appear, once again in the steel-grey greatcoat of the Macklenburg Navy. He stood tall next to Miss Temple, tapping a cigarette on his silver case.

'I thought your coat had been lost,' she said.

'Mr Cunsher was able to liberate a spare from the diplomatic compound – along with my medical bag and my cigarettes.'

'How resourceful.'

'Extremely so. I wonder if we will see him again.'

They were the only patrons at the inn. The luncheon came as bleached of colour as the town – everything boiled to the near edge of paste. The men drank beer, while Miss Temple made do with barley water, impatient at how much time they seemed to be wasting. She stood well before the others had finished.

'I will be outside,' she announced. 'Do take your time.'

'What if you are seen?' asked Mr Brine, a white potato spitted on the tip of his knife like an eye.

'*Seen?*' she replied waspishly. 'We have been here half an hour. *That* cheroot has been smoked.'

Their blunt entry to the town was Mr Phelps's way of disputing her leadership, and the insistence on a meal – though they had not eaten since dawn, and did not know when they might eat again – another way to curb her personal momentum. She stood outside and scanned the dark huts, all scalded brick and planks tarred with paper. The air was crisp in a way she might have enjoyed, save for the metal tang in which all of Raaxfall seemed steeped. She saw where the road stopped at a towered gate, like a castle made of iron instead of stone.

They had asked at the inn after Mr Ramper, but he was not remembered. Who was at the Xonck works? The townspeople did not know. Was anyone there at all? O yes, they saw lights, but could say nothing more.

She looked up and saw doorways around the battered village square now dotted with pale faces. Had they never seen a violet jacket before? Miss Temple walked towards the river. Here too she passed faces, young and old and those aged too soon by work, peering at her and then stepping forward to follow. As the citizens of Raaxfall crept into view, they reminded Miss Temple of rats on a ship, emerging from every possible crevice. She picked her way to an especially long wooden dock, to its very end, ignoring the people behind her – none yet bold enough to follow onto the pier – and gazed over the water.

Just beyond the river's bend was her first glimpse of the Xonck works proper: high loading docks and a canal leading deeper inside. She looked directly below her. Several small oared skiffs had been roped to the pilings.

A skittering *clomp* caused her to spin. The townspeople now formed a wall across the pier. Another *clomp*. A *stone* had been thrown from the crowd. Miss Temple looked with shock into the blanched faces and perceived that she was hated – *hated*. The fact stung like a swinging fist. Her first impulse was to pull out the revolver – but there were a hundred souls before her if there were five, and any such step would justify their rage.

A ripple of bodies burst through the centre of the mob: Doctor Svenson, harried and out of breath, Brine and Phelps close behind.

'Celeste – we did not see you –'

The three men dropped their pace to a rapid walk, aware that the mob was slowly following them onto the planking. Svenson reached her and spoke low.

'Celeste – what has happened? The townspeople –'

'Pish tush,' she managed. 'There are boats below: I suggest we secure one.'

Quite belying his bulky gait on land, Mr Brine swung himself over the pier like an ape, seized a rope and slid into an open skiff. Mr Phelps and Doctor Svenson took out their pistols and at this the mob halted, perhaps thirty yards away.

'Citizens of Raaxfall,' called Phelps, 'we have come to discover why you have been put out of work – why the Xonck factory has barred its doors. We are here in your own interests –'

With his city accent Phelps might as well have been Chinese; nor did the presence of Miss Temple – and a foreign soldier – help to make any credible show. Another rock whipped past Phelps and splashed into the water. Svenson seized Miss Temple with both arms and held her over the edge – she squawked with surprise – where she was caught about the waist and hustled to a seat in the bow.

'The rope, miss.' Brine returned his attention to the pier.

Miss Temple tore at the knot linking the skiff to the pilings. Another rock struck the water, and then three more. Phelps's pistol cracked out as Doctor Svenson dropped into the skiff, the entire craft tipping as his weight came home.

A cry came from above, and Mr Phelps's black hat struck the water, floating like an upturned funereal basket. The man himself lurched into view, blood pouring from his cheek, and stepped into the air. He plunged into the river and came up gasping. Mr Brine extended an oar to his flailing hands, and Svenson snapped off six deliberate shots above them, emptying his revolver, but keeping the mob back from the edge long enough for Brine to gather Phelps and push off.

Brine stroked at the oars to propel them away from the teeming mass that lined the dock. The stones came in a hail, but, barring two that bounced dangerously off the wood, they were only splashed. Phelps slumped between the thwarts, water streaming from his clothes, a handkerchief held against his face. The natives of Raaxfall hooted at their ungainly retreat as if they'd chased a gang of armoured Spaniards off a palm-strewn strand. Phelps shrugged off Svenson's attempt to see the wound and took up an oar, pulling with Brine. The Doctor shifted to the tiller and when enough distance had been gained turned the small skiff east.

No challenge came from the Xonck docks as they neared, fully visible in the afternoon light. The main canal into the works was blocked with a gate of rusted metal bars, like a portcullis sunk into the water. They bobbed before it, unable to see into the shadows beyond. At Svenson's nod the other men pulled to the nearest floating dock. Miss Temple scrambled out with the rope. She looped it around an iron cleat and held it tight until the Doctor could tie a proper knot.

'Here we are,' sighed Mr Phelps. 'Though I confess it seems a wasted journey.' He peered at the lifeless canal.

'How is your face?' Miss Temple did not feel responsible for what had happened at the pier, but nevertheless appreciated Mr Phelps's bravery.

'It will do,' he replied, dabbing with the handkerchief. 'Stoned by an old woman – can you believe it?'

'Can all that truly be a response to no work?' Svenson had opened the cylinder of his revolver, and from a pocket he retrieved a fistful of brass.

'No work in the city anywhere,' offered Mr Brine.

Svenson nodded, slotting in the new shells. 'But when exactly did the Xonck works close?'

'After we returned, some three weeks now.' Phelps patted his coat and looked behind them. 'My weapon is in the river.'

'It cannot be helped,' said Svenson. 'But before this recent stoppage, did not the people of Raaxfall enjoy near total employment? The marriage between a crocodile and the birds that pick its teeth?'

'You can imagine the wages Henry Xonck would pay – they will have no savings to last out one bare week, let alone three.'

The Doctor sighed. 'You are right, of course . . . yet I cannot credit poverty with such an unprovoked attack. On strangers, no less – on a woman!'

'Why should you think it unprovoked?' asked Miss Temple. The three men turned to her in silence. At once she flushed. 'Do not be absurd. I did nothing but stand in the air!'

'Then what do you imply?' asked Phelps.

'I do not know – but perhaps there is more to their discontent than we understand.'

'Perhaps. And perhaps this same mob tore your Mr Ramper to pieces in the street.'

They climbed rusted stairs and met another wall of iron bars. The Xonck works were a honeycomb of huts and roads, bristling with towers and cat-walks. It was divided by earthen redoubts and moats of sickly green liquid and caged blast tunnels, the earth around each entrance black as coal.

'The lock is on the other side,' Svenson said, slapping a wide metal plate. 'Nothing to pick or even to shoot open. We need a field gun.'

'There must be someone within,' observed Phelps.

'No one especially *mindful*,' said Miss Temple. 'We are veritable trades-men at the door.'

'We might climb,' offered Mr Brine, pointing up. The fence was ten feet high, topped with sharp spikes.

'Surely not,' said Phelps.

Miss Temple went onto her toes to peer through the bars. 'Do you see that barge?'

Svenson screwed his monocle in place. 'What about it?'

'Was it not at the Parchfeldt Canal?' she asked. 'I recognize the rings of red paint around the mast.'

'Perhaps it came from Parchfeldt with the machines.'

Miss Temple turned to Phelps. 'From the river here, could one reach the Orange Canal – and Harschmort?'

Phelps nodded. His hair was plastered to his skull, and Miss Temple saw that the man was shivering. 'But if they have gone to so much trouble, where *is* everyone? What is more, if the people of Raaxfall are so exercised against the factory, what has stopped them from storming it? Not their own reticence, I am sure, yet – no, no! What is this?'

His last words were petulantly addressed to Mr Brine, who had nimbly clambered halfway up the fence.

'Mr Brine,' Miss Temple called. 'There are spikes.'

'Not to worry, miss.' Brine gathered himself just beneath the spikes, curling his legs, then recklessly sprung over them, slamming into the other side of the fence with a clang. Miss Temple gasped, for a spike had gouged through his sleeve.

'Not to worry,' he repeated, and lifted the arm free. Brine landed with a solid *thump* on the other side.

'Well *done!*' cried Miss Temple.

'Is there a lock?' called Svenson. 'Can you –'

Before Mr Brine could reply, he was surrounded by a dozen sudden lines of jetting smoke, each lancing towards him with a serpentine hiss. Brine staggered, eyes wide with shock, then toppled off the platform and out of sight.

Miss Temple had the sense not to scream, and instead found that she – like both men – had dropped to her knees.

'What happened?' she whispered. 'Where is he?'

'Is he killed?' asked Phelps.

She quite quickly began to climb, fitting her feet like a ladder.

'Good God!' cried Phelps.

Both men reached for her legs but Miss Temple kicked at their hands.

'He will die if I do not help him.'

'He is dead already!' called Phelps.

'Celeste,' whispered Svenson. She was too high to pull down without causing her harm. 'It is a trap. Think – you render Brine's sacrifice without purpose –'

'But we cannot go back!' she hissed.

'Celeste –'

'*No.*'

'You are being stubborn.'

The fence seemed higher from the top than it had from below. Brine's strategy to reach the other side would not work for her – she'd not the strength, nor would her dress clear. She grasped the base of two spikes and called down.

'You must support my foot.'

'We will not,' answered Phelps.

'It is the simplest thing – one of you climb beneath and let me rest a foot on your shoulder – and then I will step over as if the spikes were daisies.'

'Celeste –'

'Or I shall fling myself like a savage.'

She felt the fence shake and then Svenson was below her, gritting his teeth.

'I will shut my eyes,' he said, then looked up directly beneath her legs and began to stammer. 'For the height, you see – the height –'

'The danger is on the *other* side,' called Phelps. 'You will set off the trap!'

'A moment,' she said to Svenson. 'Let me gather my dress . . .'

Somehow his shyness gave her a confidence she had not had. She raised one knee and slowly settled it on the other side, digging her toes between the bars. The line of spikes ran straight between her legs, but she did not hurry, shifting her grip and gathering the dress to swing her second leg.

The small platform behind the gate floated in a sea of dark space. The only way off it was a ramp – Brine had clearly missed it in his fall – descending into shadow.

'The shooting smoke,' said Svenson. 'It may have been bullets, or darts . . . can you see where they came from?'

Miss Temple eased her body lower. The metal plate that covered the platform . . . it sparkled.

'There is *glass* . . .'

To either side of the gate stood tall, thin posts, each with a vertical line of dark holes, as if they were bird houses, all facing the platform and anyone trying to break in. Miss Temple measured the distance to the ground and the width of the metal plate. She gathered her nerve, quivering like a cat. She flung herself towards the darkness.

'*Celeste!*'

She landed on the ramp and rolled, scrabbling with her hands to stop herself sailing off the edge. She rose with a sudden urgency and scuttled to the top of the ramp.

'Celeste – that was incredibly foolish –'

'Be quiet! You must either climb over after me or hide.'

'Is there no lock?' asked Phelps.

'I cannot reach it without being killed – the metal plate, when one treads upon it, the trap is sprung – you will see for yourself. You must leap past it. The task is nothing, a girl has done it before you. But you must hurry – someone is coming from below!'

Phelps reached her first – spraggling and damp at Miss Temple's feet. He motioned Svenson on with both hands. The Doctor had cleared the spikes with only a minor catch on his greatcoat, but clung uncertainly.

'I do dislike high places,' he muttered.

Beams of light stabbed up at them. Svenson jumped, clearing the metal plate by an inch, and lurched into their arms. Miss Temple put two fingers over his mouth. A voice rose in the darkness, harsh with amusement.

'Look at this one! Right in the chops. You lot see if he's alone . . .'

Their only exit was the ramp, exactly where a gang of men was approaching behind a raised lantern. Miss Temple took hold of her companions, pulling them down.

'Lie flat – do not move,' she whispered. 'Follow when you can!'

She pressed her green bag into Phelps's hand and then started down at a trot. She reached a landing and turned into bright lantern light.

'Where is Mr Brine!' she cried shrilly. 'What has happened? Is he alive?'

The man with the lantern caught her arm with a grip like steel, the light near enough to burn her face.

'What are you doing here?' he snarled. 'How did you pass the gate?'

'I am Miss Isobel Hastings,' she whined. 'What has happened to Mr Brine?'

'He's had a bit of a fall.' The man wore an unbuttoned green tunic, the uniform of the Xonck militia. The others with him were similarly dressed – all sloppy and unshaven.

'My goodness,' cried Miss Temple. 'There are *five* of you, all come to rescue me!'

'Rescue?' scoffed the leader. 'Take her arms.'

Miss Temple cried out as she was seized, doing her best to shove forward. 'I am looking for my – my fiancé – his name is Ramper. He came here, for his work – Mr Brine told me – I paid him to help me –'

'No one comes here, Isobel Hastings.'

'He did! Ned Ramper – a great strapping fellow! What have you done with him?'

The leader looked past Miss Temple, and made to aim the lantern at the ramp above. She kicked his shin.

'Where is he, I say – I insist that you answer –'

The man's backhand struck her face like a whip, and she only kept her feet for being held. The leader marched down the ramp and barked for the others to follow. She could not place her steps. After the first few yards they simply dragged her.

She was dropped to the floor in a cold room fitted with gas lamps.

'That one on the table.'

Men crossed in front of her and carried the deadweight of Mr Brine to a table of stained planks. Brine's eyes were shut and his jaw was mottled and crusted with blue, like a French cheese from a cave.

'And the sweetmeat on the throne.'

Miss Temple rose to her knees. 'I can seat myself –'

The men exchanged a laugh and shoved her into a high-backed seat, made from welded iron pipes and bolted to the floor. A chain was cinched below her breasts and another pulled across her throat. Behind her came the creak of a door.

'Who did you find, Benton?'

The voice was thin, as unhurried as swirling smoke. The lantern man – Benton – immediately dipped his head and backed away, ceding any claim.

'Miss Isobel Hastings, sir. Says Ned Ramper's her fiancé. Came with this great lump to find him.'

'Can she speak?'

'Course she can! I wouldn't – not without your order –'

'No.'

Miss Temple sensed the thin-voiced man behind her, though the chain stopped her from turning. 'Tell me, Isobel. If you will forgive the impropriety.' A finger insinuated itself into a curl of her hair and gave a gentle tug. 'Who is your friend on the table?'

'Mr Brine. Corporal Brine. He is a friend of Ned Ramper.'

'And he led you here? Did you pay him money?'

Miss Temple nodded dumbly.

'Benton?'

'Six silver shillings in his pocket, sir. No one touched it.'

'Does six shillings pay a man to die, I wonder? Would it be enough for you, Benton?'

'Way things are now, sir . . . I'd call it a decent wage.'

'And who paid Ned Ramper, Isobel?'

'Is that important?'

He pulled her hair sharply enough to make her wince.

'Leave what's important to me.'

'A woman. She lives in a hotel. I don't like her.'

'What hotel?'

'Ned would not tell me. He thought I would follow him.'

She felt his breath in her ear. 'But you *did* follow him, didn't you, Isobel? What hotel?'

'She lives at the . . . the St Royale.'

Benton glanced suddenly at the man behind her, but when Miss Temple's captor spoke his voice betrayed no care.

'Did you see this woman yourself?'

Miss Temple nodded again, sniffing. 'She had b-black hair, and a red dress –'

'And this fellow here – *Brine* – she'd hired him as well?'

Miss Temple nodded vigorously. Her captor called softly to Benton.

'Empty his pockets. Show me.'

Benton leapt to the table. Miss Temple quickly counted – there had been five on the ramp . . . here she saw Benton and three more, digging at Brine's clothing like vultures. The fifth man must have gone to collect their master. Was he standing guard at the door behind her? The hand tugged at her hair.

'And what of *your* pockets? Have you no purse or bag?'

'I lost it, climbing over the gate. When Mr Brine fell, I was so frightened –'

'Not so frightened that you died.' He called behind him. 'See if it's there.'

Footsteps signalled the fifth man running for the ramp. Miss Temple's blood froze. If he discovered Svenson and Phelps –

'He had this.' Benton held the clipping from the *Herald*. ' "-grettable Canvases from Paris". Don't know what "-grettable" is, not speaking French.'

The paper was snatched from his hand as Miss Temple's captor stepped forward. She glimpsed only a shining black coat before he was off without a word.

Benton watched him go, his posture lapsing back into feral comfort. He turned to Miss Temple with a satisfied smile.

'Maybe I should search your pockets too . . . every little pocket you possess.'

A footfall in the darkness did not shift his hungry gaze. 'Find her bag, then?' Benton drawled.

'Step away from the woman.'

Doctor Svenson strode into the light, the long Navy revolver in his hand. Benton swore aloud and reached in his tunic. The pistol roared in the echoing room like a cannon and Benton flew back, shirt-front spraying gore. Another shot shattered the leg of a man near the table. Two more, rapidly snapped from Miss Temple's smaller weapon, drilled the back of a fellow dashing for the door. Mr Phelps came forward with Svenson, their guns extended towards the fourth man, his hands in the air.

'Down on the floor,' growled the Doctor. The man hurried to comply, and Mr Phelps bound his limbs. Doctor Svenson looked to the open door, then to Miss Temple.

'Are you hurt?'

Miss Temple shook her head. Her voice was hoarse.

'Is he – is Mr Brine –'

'A moment, Celeste . . .'

Svenson knelt over the man with the shattered leg, then stood and tucked the gun away, stepping clear of the blood.

'It is the artery,' he muttered. 'I meant to wound . . .'

Even as he spoke the heavy breathing fell to silence. Had it been even one minute? The Doctor crossed to the table, saying nothing. Miss Temple cleared her throat to get his attention. She nodded at Benton.

'The key to these chains is in his waistcoat.'

Phelps returned Miss Temple's revolver, with her bag, and helped himself to the unlamented Benton's.

'They will have heard our shots.'

'They may assume their own men did the shooting,' replied Svenson. He turned to Miss Temple. 'We heard some of your interrogation.'

Phelps frowned. 'Their leader's voice – I'm sure I ought to place it, but the circumstances escape me.'

'Whoever he is,' said Svenson, 'they have taken Mr Ramper – and who knows what he told them.'

'It cannot have been much.' Miss Temple straightened her jacket. 'Not if they believed the Contessa to have hired him. But I must look at Mr Brine.'

Svenson stood with her. 'His neck was broken in the fall. It is perhaps –'

'A blessing,' she said. 'I know.'

Blue glass had been driven into Brine's jaw, each spike sending out veins of crystallized destruction, like the limbs of embedded blue spiders. Svenson indicated a spot on Brine's chest, then others on his abdomen and arms. In every case, peeling away his clothing revealed the hard, mottled skein of penetration.

'Glass *bullets*?' whispered Phelps.

Svenson nodded. 'I cannot see the purpose. I doubt they alone would have killed him.'

Miss Temple dug in her bag for a handkerchief and walked to the door. 'We cannot get back over the wall. We must go on.'

'I am sorry for your man, Celeste,' said Svenson. 'He was a brave fellow.'
Miss Temple shrugged, but did not yet face them.

'Brave fellows arrive by the dozen,' she said, 'and fate mows them flat. My own poor crop did not last at all.'


At the end of an echoing tunnel they met a metal door.

'This explains why no one came,' said Svenson, tugging on it. 'Thick steel and entirely locked. We will have to return to see if one of those villains kept a key.'

'Already done,' said Phelps with a smile. 'Courtesy of the late Mr Benton.'
He spread the ring of keys on his palm, selected one and slipped it in. The lock turned. Phelps stepped back and readied his pistol.

'Do we have a plan, as such?'

'Quite,' offered Svenson. 'Discover what Vandaariff has done here – find Mr Ramper – glean what we can about the Contessa – then manage our own escape.'

Miss Temple simply pulled open the door.

If the works above ground were a broken honeycomb, spread before them now was the hive itself: cages of iron, walls of blistered concrete, great furnaces gone cold, assembly tables, dusty vats, and staircases near and far, extending to the shadows.

'Ought we to divide our efforts?' whispered Phelps. 'The ground is so large . . .'

The Doctor shook his head. 'Even separated we could not search it in a week. We have to think: where would they locate themselves – *why* would they? In a foundry? With the ammunition stores? What serves them best?'

Phelps abruptly sneezed. 'I beg your pardons –'

'You have a chill,' muttered Svenson. 'We must find a fire.'

'We must find that *man*. Perhaps if we climb the stairs we may see more.' Phelps sighed and finished his own sentence. 'Or *be* seen and get a bullet. Miss Temple, you have not spoken –'

She was not listening to either man. She had clearly never seen this place before . . . and yet . . .

She opened her bag and removed the glass square. Selecting a row of high columns as a touch point, she looked into the glass. For a moment, as always, her senses swam . . . but then the same columns were there . . . and wide circles that must be the chemical vats . . . and a furnace whose slag she smelt from the door. Still, recognizing the map did not tell her where they ought to go . . .

The Contessa had sent it to *her*. Just as Miss Temple had deciphered the clipping, so she ought to decipher this. The message had been sent some days ago – before Ramper had been taken – it was nothing to do with *now*. The key lay in the past. In the Comte's past . . .

Her throat seized at a rancid nugget of insight from the Comte's memories. She spat onto the ground and shut her eyes, finally managing to swallow.

'The map!' whispered Phelps.

The square of glass lay shattered. Miss Temple wiped her mouth on her sleeve.

'We do not need it. There is a room, fitted for the Comte's research, from when they built his machines. We would have walked right past . . .'

They crouched behind crates stencilled with the Xonck crest. Twice they had heard steps nearby – more fellows in unkempt green – but avoided discovery. Ahead lay a well-lit door that echoed with activity, a guardhouse. Miss Temple pointed to a smaller door half the distance on.

'But it has no guard,' whispered Phelps. 'It seems a disused storeroom.'

She darted out, forcing them to follow. The final yards had her heart in her throat, waiting for the thin-voiced man to appear . . . but then her hand was on the cool brass handle. They slipped inside.

Phelps carefully shut the door and turned the lock, one hand tight across his mouth and nose. Miss Temple crept forward, face pinched against the pungent reek of indigo clay.

Mr Ramper lay on a table, naked and white as chalk. Across his body were craters – each as large and deep as an apple – where both flesh and bone had been scooped away: abdomen, right thigh, left wrist (the hand severed), near the heart, left shoulder, right ear – each cavity offering its own appalling anatomical cross-section.

'The glass bullets,' whispered Svenson. 'All transformed flesh has been removed . . . and, good heavens, preserved.'

She followed his gaze to a row of meticulously labelled jars, each dark with thick liquid in which floated a fist-sized, jagged blue mass. Svenson delicately peeled back one of Ramper's eyelids. The pupil had rolled into his skull, leaving a dead white egg whose veins were shot with blue. Svenson put two fingers to the carotid and stepped away.

'I do not think he died at once.'

'Interrogated?' asked Phelps.

Svenson indicated two of Ramper's open wounds and against her wishes Miss Temple leant forward to look. 'The variance in the clotted blood – the colour. I would hazard that during some of these *excavations* the poor man still lived.'

'And there are more,' said Phelps. 'My God . . . they must be from the town . . . no wonder their rage . . .'

Beyond Ramper lay five men and one woman, naked and despoiled, their discoloured flesh indicating a longer tenure in the room. Miss Temple's eyes drifted to their hands – callused, with broken, dirty nails – and then, despite herself, to their genitals, exposed and mournful. The lone woman's breasts hung flat to either side of her ribs, framing a bloody cave at the base of her sternum.

A rustle of papers startled her. The Doctor stood at a long table piled with bound journals and surgical tools, his face an impassive mask.

'He has documented every step,' said Svenson quietly. 'For weeks. Keeping records . . . every one of these people – each step scrupulously observed.'

Phelps nodded towards Ramper's corpse. 'God forgive me – but does he note anything the poor man might have revealed?'

The Doctor thumbed the notebooks quickly. Phelps glanced to the door. Miss Temple stared at a body whose eye socket was a coagulated well.

'Whatever the Comte's insanity,' muttered Phelps, 'this room cannot explain Vandaariff's occupation of the entire works.'

Svenson turned to Miss Temple, his eyes wide. An open journal lay in his hands.

'What is it? What have you found?'

Instead of answering he marched past her, past the tables, to the cluttered shelves, the journal dropped, both hands pawing the wall.

'Doctor Svenson?' she asked, suddenly afraid.

'What has happened?' hissed Phelps.

The Doctor found the hidden door and pulled it wide. On another table lay a man secured with chains, naked, pale and still. Miss Temple screamed. Cardinal Chang's eyes snapped open.

# TWO

# LAZARUS

When he woke everything had changed. One moment Chang had been face down in the forest, his life bleeding away . . . and the next – a next he frankly did not expect to occur – he was chained to a table, or so he guessed from the iron bite across his chest and waist and around each limb. The coarse planks scratched his back and buttocks. He was naked and quite blind.

A rasping attempt to speak echoed strangely, and he realized his head was encased in metal. He extended his tongue to sketch a rectangular opening, sealed tight. The inner edge was crusted . . . was it porridge? It seemed someone was keeping him alive.

He arched his back, bracing himself for agony. The chains held tight . . . but where was the pain? The wound in his back ought to have killed him – how could it be so neatly healed?

How much time had passed? How had he survived?

He shifted his body against the wood. He retained his limbs, his extremities, but the area where the wound ought to have been was numb. He turned his head and the helmet bit around his neck.

Chang started at a hand on his bare abdomen, a friendly pat. He pulled at the chains and demanded to be freed. The words crashed around his ears, but then the metal plate over his mouth slid open. A wet cloth was shoved inside and his nostrils flooded with the reek of ether.

When he woke again he was lying on his face, neck awkwardly bent by the helmet, something sharp probing his back. He lay still, concealing his wakefulness, until a spike of pain shot the length of his spine, and he gasped aloud. The mouth box was opened, and again came the ether.

He woke and slept in an incessant, arbitrary cycle, always aware of some-one around him, intrusive hands, constant observation. How long had he been here? His existence made no sense. Had he not fouled himself? He could not remember. Or had he died after all – was he in hell?

He blamed such thoughts on the chemical nightmares and strove to con-centrate during each lucid period, to recall the world he'd lost . . . his rooms, the Slavic Baths, the Library and the opium den. The irony did not escape him. Had he finally found the oblivion he had courted for years?

And Celeste? Chang reflected with chagrin on their last minutes in the wood. Like a fool she had kissed him, and like a greater fool he had responded. What had he been thinking – to take her there in the bracken? And then what? He could just imagine the awkward – no, that word was far too weak – the *unconscionable* afterwards: mortification, guilt, stupidity. He'd enough on his conscience. He hoped she had outrun the Contessa, found Svenson, made her escape. He ran his tongue across his lips, remembering the sudden softness of her mouth. And her *hunger*. As a man whose most common intimacies arose from negotiations in a brothel, Chang knew it was Celeste's expression of *need* that had pierced his reason like a nail. But sense had returned. He tried to imagine the two of them strolling together in a street. Even had he desired it – and he was quite sure he did not, for the girl, how-ever beddable, was also wholly absurd – to entertain the idea, in this world, was like planting corn in the snow.

He woke, eyes screwed shut against a painful glare. The helmet had been removed. Chang squinted and saw it on the wall: hammered brass, with two glass eye plates – round, like the eyes of an insect, now painted black. The earpieces and mouth box had likewise been bolted tight. It was a helmet designed to protect the wearer during the smelting of indigo clay.

He was a prisoner of the Comte d'Orkancz, whose rotted mind now lived in the body of Robert Vandaariff. Who else? The others were all dead. Chang had done his best to kill the Comte and failed. His skin went cold. Had he been kept alive only for revenge?

A voice reached him from beyond the glare, soft, chuckling.

'You have been so long away from any light as to be a *mole*.'

Chang blinked and made out a padded chair. In it, business attire shielded by an oilcloth apron, sat Robert Vandaariff.

'You are under my protection.'

Vandaariff used a thin black cane to rise and advanced to the table. His steps were brittle and, as he entered the light, his face revealed new lines of age.

'Reincarnation disagrees with you.' Chang's voice was raw. 'You look like a fishwife's dinner.'

'And *you* have not seen a mirror.'

'Now that I'm awake, might I have my clothes?'

'Are you cold?'

'I am naked.'

'Are you ashamed?' Vandaariff's eyes drifted across Chang's body. 'A handsome man – barring the scars, of course. So *many* scars . . . knives mostly, by the stitching. But your face . . . the damage there is singular – and to most tastes horrifying, I'm sure. The eyes are abnormally sensitive – even when asleep you flinch from a lantern. Do you mind my asking the cause?'

'A riding crop.'

'Viciously applied. How long ago?'

'Where are my clothes?'

'I've no idea. Burnt? No, Cardinal Chang, you remain almost as you were born. For one, to increase the difficulty of slipping away, were you – ever resourceful – to manage it. But, in the main, it makes you easier to *study*.'

'Study how?'

'Such a hopeful question. I will ask one in return, now we are speaking. What do you remember?'

The words hung between them, and Chang knew his inability to recall a thing since the forest was a direct result of something Vandaariff had done. With nothing else to say he could only hope to provoke the man.

'I remember putting a sabre through your guts on the airship.'

'But that was not me at all,' Vandaariff replied mildly. 'That was the poor Comte d'Orkancz. *I* was at Harschmort House, left behind by all my former friends.'

'Left an idiot, you mean. I *saw* you – *him* – and I saw everything at Parch-feldt! How in hell did you survive? That mob was set to tear you to pieces.'

'Very good. The airship *and* the factory. And after that? What, Cardinal Chang, do you remember *next*?'

Chang pulled against the chains and exhaled through his nose.

'If you have done anything to me – I promise you –'

'Done? I have saved your life.'

'Why would you do that?'

'Another excellent question. You are abrim.'

Chang turned at a sound to his left – a panel flush with the wall, swinging clear. A tall man in a shining black coat stepped through, silk rustling against the doorframe. Though he was not old, white hair hung to the man's collar, and his skin was as brown as a Malay sailor's. He sank into a silent bow and then spoke gently, tamed.

'My apologies, my lord . . .'

'Yes?'

'Another incident at the gate. A single man. Not from the town.'

'Not from the town? Gracious, is he alive?'

'He is.' The white-haired man met Chang's gaze without expression.

'Bring him, Mr Foison,' said Vandaariff heartily. 'We will seize the opportunity to learn.'

Foison bowed and left the room. What town? Chang could see nothing to place where he was. If only he were not so *weak*. Through the door came the sounds of men lugging a burden. Vandaariff rubbed his hands as if this bespoke an awaited meal.

'What of the others?' Chang could not help himself. 'Celeste Temple, Svenson, the Contessa?'

'Do you not know?'

'I've asked, haven't I? Tell me, damn you!'

'Why, they are all dead,' answered Vandaariff. Then he smiled. 'That is, dead or entirely mine.'

Chuckling, he limped through the door and pulled it tight. The walls were not so dense as to stop the screams. It was a relief when Foison finally re-entered with the ether and sent Chang to darkness.

*

He was shocked to wakefulness, face down again, by a sudden freeze across his lower back, sharp as an animal's bite.

'Do not *move*,' Vandaariff intoned. 'It will only prolong the struggle.'

'What . . . struggle is that?' gasped Chang, his chin grinding into the planking.

'A struggle of metals.' The chill curled to the base of Chang's spine. 'Alchemy tells us of different metals linked in a lattice of power. The natural blood of your body, Cardinal Chang, is suffused with iron – thus we have begun with a vector of quite traditional *magnetism*.'

'You're insane, mad as a foaming dog.'

'Your body was depleted of course – vital salts, ethereal compounds. After this restoration, the true work may begin . . .'

Just beyond the light stood Foison, silent, white hair glowing in the shadow. The cold seeped past Chang's pelvis to his legs. His teeth were chattering.

'I killed you once. I'll do it again.' Chang could scarcely speak. 'What true work?'

'A cloth in his mouth, Mr Foison. It would be a shame if his shivering broke a tooth.' Vandaariff leant to Chang's ear. 'The true work of heaven, Cardinal.'

Their final conversation had been prefaced by the entrance of Foison. In the man's hand was a ceramic bowl with a wooden spoon sticking out. He saw Chang was awake and set the bowl aside. Inside lay a sickly dollop of grey paste.

'Is that what I've been eating? If you free my hand I could feed myself.'

Foison ignored him, glancing instead to Chang's groin.

'Do you need the bucket?'

'And you're cleaning me as well? I trust the privy-work hasn't spoilt your lovely sleeves.'

Foison only pulled at the chains and, satisfied with their sureness, left the room.

'What about the true work of my supper?' Chang called mockingly.

The cold had left his body eventually, the gradual warming keeping pace until he burnt with fever. This too had passed. His back remained numb around the wound, but Chang no longer felt an invalid's weakness.

Vandaariff hobbled in with the cane, a leather satchel tucked beneath his arm. He set the satchel down and dug a gloved hand inside. Chang heard clicking, like the beads of an abacus, and Vandaariff emerged with a fistful of blue glass cards. He laid them on the table as if he were playing Patience, eyes unpleasantly bright.

'No apron?' Chang asked.

'Not today.'

'Are those for me?'

'You will look into them. I prefer not to prise back your lids, but Foison is within call.'

'What events do they hold? What do you want me to see?'

'Nothing at all,' said Vandaariff. 'I want your body to *feel*.'

The first card plunged Chang into the midst of a rousing country dance, a farm girl to either side. Fiddle music sang in his ears. Vandaariff pulled the card away and he was back in the nasty room, panting, sweat on his limbs.

Vandaariff raised the second card. Chang balanced on the edge of an icy rooftop. Three yards away, across an abyss of five flights, stood the next building. Men ran towards him, shouting, waving clubs. He steeled himself and leapt – and once more Vandaariff pulled the card away. Chang's breath heaved. His body pressed against the chains.

'Who are these people? Whose memories –'

The third card was a banquet. The fourth card a horserace. The fifth a game of whist. In the sixth he strangled a man with a silken rope. In the seventh he lay on a brothel sofa with a thin-limbed whore bouncing energetically above him. Vandaariff pulled the glass away and Chang looked down at his arousal, mortified and angry.

'Enough,' said Vandaariff, smiling. 'Unless you would prefer that last again?'

'Choke on your own blood.'

'An admirable performance. A foundation upon which to build.'

Vandaariff returned the cards to the satchel. He removed a second batch.

These cards were like nothing Chang had ever seen, for they were not *blue* . . . instead, each glinted with different colours. The first was mottled with streaks of red.

'We start with iron.'

The card contained no experience, no memory, no human life. Chang's senses fogged and he gagged at the taste of blood filling his throat. Vandaariff pulled the card away and selected another, greenish and flecked with copper . . .

One after another Chang absorbed their depths. Where before the glass had implanted memories, here the transaction lay beyond his mind, as essential forces passed from the glass to his body. Each time he felt both sickened and more strong, Vandaariff tempering Chang's body like a blacksmith working steel. When the cards were back in the satchel, pain echoed in his bones and knotted his organs. His teeth burnt like coals in a fire. Vandaariff reached into his coat and came out with an eighth card, bright orange. He gripped the back of Chang's head and thrust it before his eyes. Chang arched against an explosion of agony near his spine.

When it was finally taken away, Chang could barely breathe.

'I'm going to cut your throat,' he gasped.

Vandaariff took off his gloves and snapped the satchel closed.

'Three days, Cardinal. In three days you may well do just that thing.'

But the next day he heard voices in the other room. Then the door was flung open by Doctor Svenson, with Celeste Temple screaming like a fool. Svenson leapt to the chains but Chang stopped him with an urgent whisper. 'Where are we? Where is he? Where is his man?'

'The Xonck works at Raaxfall – there are soldiers just outside –'

Another figure in the doorway – was it *Phelps*? 'They have heard – they are coming!'

'Leave the chains!' Chang hissed. 'Against the wall – hide!'

Svenson had already shut the door. The Ministry man pressed himself into the corner. Celeste Temple stood like a stone, staring at Chang's body. Finally she noticed Svenson waving vigorously and dropped under the table. The girl would kill them all.

For a moment he heard nothing . . . then the hidden door swung open, shielding Svenson behind it. No one stepped through. Chang jerked his head as if woken and blinked at the light. He could see Foison's shadow, and a gleam of metal in his hand.

'What now?' Chang called hoarsely. 'Where is your master?'

Foison took a single step into the doorway, offering no clear shot to Svenson or Phelps.

'Where are they?'

'What are you talking about?' Chang cocked his head. 'Has the cat misplaced its mice?'

Chang looked past Foison, hearing more footsteps.

'Benton's dead, sir!' The man was out of breath. 'Everyone but Hennig – two men, he says, with guns – left with the girl!'

'Left where?'

'He didn't see, sir. We're looking everywhere –'

'Bring Hennig. Send word to Lord Vandaariff.'

'But, sir – if we find them – no one need know –'

'If we find them, we will then send word of *that*. Do it *now*.' The man ran off. Throughout their conversation Foison had kept his eyes on Chang, who could not decide whether his captor was Asiatic or, instead, some Lapp or northern Finn.

'There are footprints outside. I came to ask. You might have *heard*.'

'Not a thing,' said Chang.

'You are fortunate they did not find you.'

'Why is that?'

'Because *you* . . . are the property of a jealous, jealous man.'

Foison drove his body hard against the door, slamming it into Svenson, then he spun, whipping the knife in his right hand towards Phelps, who cried out, the bright blade sticking out of his topcoat. Foison slammed the door again, still harder – Chang could see Svenson's legs buckle – and then opened it wide, another knife in his hand, and kicked the still-struggling Doctor in the ribs.

The chain across Chang's chest and arms went slack. Foison turned at the sound, but Chang took hold of the chain and cracked it at Foison like a whip, the last hard link snapping at the man's forehead. Foison sprawled into the wall.

Miss Temple stood, her fingers rapidly working free the other chains, eyes blessedly averted from Chang's body. Svenson was on his knees, an unwieldy Naval revolver jammed into Foison's belly. The white-haired man lay on his back, blood on his face, his teeth bared in pain.

'He has pinned me to the wall,' hissed Phelps, pulling at the knife that held him.

Miss Temple hurried to assist Phelps, who did not seem to be injured. Chang gratefully slipped off the table to crouch near the Doctor.

'We did not expect you,' said Svenson. 'We thought you dead.'

'As I you,' replied Chang.

'These fellows will kill us.'

'They will try.'

Chang slapped Foison across the face, and then wrenched him up by the collar.

'I require your clothes.'

He left the white-haired man his undergarments and boots, for Foison's feet were small. He turned his back on the others to dress. Foison's trousers were black leather, but the white shirt was silk and draped Chang's skin like cool water. Decent once more, he reached for the jacket, but paused at the expression on Svenson's face.

'Dear Lord . . . Cardinal . . .'

'I beg your pardon,' Chang snarled, turning his head. 'I have lost my glasses, I cannot help it if my eyes offend your delicacy –'

'No, no – good heavens, no – your *spine* –'

Both Miss Temple and Phelps stood in shocked silence. It was the last thing Chang wanted to think about. He could move without pain – that was what mattered. He slipped into the coat, a surprisingly good fit, given the discrepancy of shoe size, and jerked his chin at their prisoner.

'Get him on his feet.'

Foison's hands had been tied behind his back. Chang picked up the second knife – Foison's coat still held another pair sheathed within it – and held it flat against the man's throat.

'Must we take him with us?' asked Phelps.

Chang raised a hand for silence, then pointed to the door. At his nod the Doctor pulled it wide, revealing Chang alone in the doorway, Foison before him like a shield.

The clicking of pistol hammers came like a chorus of crickets – at least ten men, standing in the cover of more tables and the colourless corpses they bore.

'If you interfere, he will die.'

'If you touch him, we'll shoot you to pieces,' replied the man to his right, in a green Xonck tunic, three stripes on his sleeve. His revolver pointed straight into Chang's ear.

'Then we understand one another,' said Chang. 'As much as I would enjoy killing this man, in exchange for safe passage, I will not.'

This was the moment. If they had orders to prevent an escape at all costs, the bullets must fly. But Chang did not believe these men possessed such autonomy. Foison ruled them with as tight a hand as Vandaariff ruled him. Chang pressed the blade into his captive's brown throat, against the vein. The Sergeant lowered his pistol and barked at the others. They fell back.

Chang looked at Svenson. He had no idea where they ought to go, yet it was crucial this ignorance not be conveyed to their enemies. But the Doctor turned to Miss Temple. She swallowed with a grimace, and her words came out a croak. 'Follow me. The tunnels.'

Chang kept his face a mask, but marvelled at the size of the factory – furnaces, silos, catwalks, assembly tables, projectile moulds, cooling pools. He walked backwards, holding Foison between them and the gang of soldiers, whose guns still tracked their every move.

Foison did not speak, though his eyes remained fixed on those of his sergeant.

'This coat of yours cannot have come cheap,' Chang whispered. 'I did not think silk wore well enough for the expense.'

'Silk is surprisingly warm,' observed Doctor Svenson. 'The north of China is very frigid.'

Chang ignored the interruption, watching the Sergeant, not ten steps away, and hissed into Foison's ear, 'What will your master say, I wonder?'

'This changes nothing,' replied Foison. 'Three days. You are his branded stock.'

Miss Temple's sharp call stopped Chang's reply. 'We require a *key*.'

A gate of iron bars blocked the tunnel. At Foison's nod, the Sergeant came forward and unlocked the gate. Doctor Svenson held out his hand.

'You shall not follow.'

Again Foison nodded and the Sergeant gave over the keys. They slipped past the bars, and Chang called to the soldiers as Phelps relocked the gate.

'We will leave him further on, unharmed.'

The Sergeant opened his mouth to protest, but Foison shook his head.

Chang continued to walk backwards until the light had gone and their view of the soldiers with it. Then Chang drove a punch into Foison's kidney and forced him to kneel.

'What are you doing?' Svenson whispered.

Chang had the knife at Foison's throat. 'What do you think?'

'You gave your word . . .'

'This man will kill us all. Don't be a fool.'

'If his men find him dead,' hissed Svenson, 'they will hunt us all the more!'

'They are already hunting us. Without their leader, they will hunt us *poorly* –'

'But you have given your word!' whispered Phelps, aghast.

Chang wedged a knee into Foison's back and pushed him face down in the dirt. 'You do not know how he has wronged me.'

'We do not,' said Phelps, 'but you cannot execute a helpless man –'

'He is helpless because we have bested him. Are you an idiot?'

'We have all given our word with yours,' said Svenson. 'I understand your impulse –'

'Sanity is not an *impulse*!'

'What on earth is happening?' asked Miss Temple. She stood beyond the others, sagging against the wall.

'This man must die,' said Chang.

'He cannot,' said Phelps.

Svenson reached over to her. 'Celeste, are you well?'

'Of course I am. Have we not promised to let him live?'

Chang growled with frustration, then impatiently extended his hand to Phelps. 'Give me your damned handkerchief.'

Having stuffed the cloth into Foison's mouth, Chang bound Foison's legs, pulling the knot as tightly as he could.

'This kindness means nothing,' he whispered. 'If I see you again I will kill you.'

Foison remained silent, and Chang resisted a final urge to kill him anyway. He padded on to where he heard the others breathing.

'I cannot see,' he whispered. 'Celeste, do you know where you've led us?'

'Of course.'

'Those men will pursue, and quickly –'

'Yes, but do we seek the canal, or the front gate?'

'Where are we *now*?'

'The blasting tunnels. They run in all directions.'

The girl's assurance frayed Chang's patience. 'How do you *know* this?'

Phelps cleared his throat. 'There was a map of glass, sent by the Contessa –'

'That is not it at *all*,' croaked Miss Temple.

'Perhaps we should press on,' suggested the Doctor.

'If we talk while we are walking, I will lose my way.'

'And our pursuers will hear the echo,' added Phelps.

'Go how you please,' Chang snarled. 'We will follow like blind lambs.'

Chang's poor eyes could discern but shadows in the chiselled ceiling, and he was forced to keep a hand on Mr Phelps's coat-tails, last in line, wincing when his bare feet caught the edges of broken stones.

It was not the reunion he had expected, with Celeste Temple in particular. What in the world was *Phelps* doing here? And why had they stared so at his wound? Svenson was not one to talk – unshaven and more gaunt than ever, the man looked like he'd crawled from a crypt.

Where was Elöise Dujong? Probably somewhere minding the Trapping child . . .

Knowing the others could not see, Chang reached beneath the jacket and under the silk shirt . . . his finger ran across the ridges of a new scar, but from the scar itself he felt no contact. He gently probed . . . below a thin layer of flesh lay something hard.

At the tunnels' end the ground was damp, the gravel sunk with river mud.

'These tunnels would have been used to transport the Comte's machines,' explained Miss Temple. She coughed and then, to Chang's surprise, she actually spat. 'Do excuse me – beyond is the canal, and beyond that our boat, unless someone has sunk it. We can return to the city, or press on to Harschmort.'

'Are we prepared for Harschmort?' asked Svenson. 'Two of your men have disappeared there – Cunsher himself would not risk it.' He turned to Chang. 'And you, Cardinal . . . in all gravity, had I the space and the light to examine –'

'Who is Cunsher?' Chang broke in curtly. 'And what *men*?'

Svenson fell behind and whispered a brief and thoroughly frustrating account of their doings since they had seen him last. However gratifying it was to hear of Tackham's death (and Chang could not help but be impressed by the Doctor's courage), the rest of Svenson's narrative strained any impression of sense – an alliance with Phelps, dependence on this Cunsher, and then acceptance of Miss Temple's own ridiculous scheming. *Jack Pfaff?* And how many others – apparently dead? Arrant foolishness aimed at taking her money and abandoning her to peril when that was gone.

'You had no idea she was pursuing such nonsense?' he asked the Doctor.

'She found *me*. Once I realized – well, the girl is determined.'

'Damned little terrier.'

Svenson smiled. 'A terrier with her teeth around a wolf's leg, I agree. Nevertheless –'

'We're here again.'

'We are. It is a comfort to have you.'

Chang shrugged, knowing he ought to return the sentiment – that it *was* good to have Svenson by his side – but the moment passed. He had scarcely spoken to the Doctor since their sojourn in the fishing village on the Iron Coast and almost laughed to remember how Svenson had been expected to tend any and all ailing goats and pigs.

'And the Contessa?'

For a moment Svenson said nothing. 'Only the two red envelopes. The woman has otherwise vanished, with the book and the child.'

'Rosamonde is the most dangerous of all.'

'So experience would indicate.'

Abruptly Chang realized that the Doctor had said nothing of the person he ought to have mentioned most of all. 'Where is Elöise?'

The question had come without consideration of her absence, and an instant later Chang regretted it.

'Your Rosamonde cut her throat.' Svenson's voice betrayed no emotion. 'Phelps and I went back and made her grave.'

Chang shut his eyes. No words came. 'That was good of you.'

'We looked for you as well.'

He turned to the Doctor, but could not read his expression at all. 'I am happy not to have obliged.'

The Doctor nodded with a wan smile, but took the moment to turn his attention to whatever Phelps was asking Miss Temple. Chang fell back a step and let the conversation end.

They crouched in the shadow of an empty barge. Ahead was the sunken gate to the river. Chang scanned the catwalks and iron towers for any watchman with a carbine.

Miss Temple pointed to a platform just visible beyond the docks. 'That was where we entered,' she said. It was the first time she had addressed him since the tunnels. 'Set with a snare of glass bullets.'

'No guards in sight,' said Phelps. 'Perhaps they have placed their trust in another trap.'

'Or do they wait for another reason?' asked Svenson. 'The Comte's arrival?'

'The Comte is dead,' replied Chang drily. 'He told me so himself.'

Mr Phelps sneezed.

'Are you *wet*?' asked Chang.

Phelps nodded and then shook his head, as if an explanation was beyond him.

'O this waiting is absurd,' snapped Miss Temple, and she marched from cover towards the gate. Chang sprang after, hauling her back. She sputtered with indignation.

'Do not,' he hissed. 'You have no idea –'

'*I* have no idea?'

'Stay *here*.'

Before she could vent another angry syllable he loped down the pier, bare feet slapping the planks. If he could but satisfy himself that the gate was locked . . .

It was nothing but luck that the first shot came an instant before the others could move, and that it missed. At the flat crack of the carbine Chang hurled himself to the side and rolled. A swarm of bullets followed – the new rapid-firing Xonck weapons he'd seen at Parchfeldt. Tar-soaked splinters flew at his eyes. He scrambled behind a windlass wrapped with heavy rope. The slugs tore into the hemp but until the snipers moved he was safe. At the barge, Miss Temple knelt with a hand over her mouth. Svenson and Phelps lay flat, none of them thinking to look where the shots had come from, much less of returning fire.

Not that they would hit a thing – their pistols would be inaccurate at this distance, and the sharpshooters too well placed. Chang looked behind him: a wall he could not climb, a locked gate he could not reach. Now that they had been seen, it was a matter of minutes before a party arrived on foot.

Above, a hemp cable rose from the windlass to a pulley, from which hung a pallet of bound barrels. A chock held the windlass in position. Chang grimaced in advance and bruised his bare foot kicking it free.

The gears flew as the rope whipped upwards, and the pallet of barrels dropped like a thunderbolt. Assuming this would draw all eyes, Chang burst forth, racing for the barge, waving for the others to run. The barrels crashed onto the wharf behind him, and quite suddenly he was lifted off his feet, the entire dockfront shaking. He landed hard, ears ringing, smoking wood all around him, and began to crawl. Svenson pulled him up and they ran. Chang looked back to see a massive column of smoke obscuring the gate and the canal, lit from within by bolts of light, an angry stormcloud brought to ground.

'What on *earth*?' managed Mr Phelps, but no one had the breath to reply. They were running blindly, simply racing down any clear avenue that appeared. Then, looking left, Chang saw a flash of black.

'A tunnel!' he cried, and veered towards it, the others raggedly at his heels. But the tunnel was blocked by an iron grille.

'Shoot the lock!' cried Phelps.

'There *is* no lock,' snarled Chang, who nevertheless dug his fingers into the grille-work and pulled. 'The bars are set into the cement.'

'It is a blast tunnel,' said Svenson, 'for testing explosives. Pull in the centre – better yet, step away.'

Chang realized he had been pulling at the edge of the grille, trying to wrest it from the stone. But the centre of the iron mesh was blackened from who knew how many exhalations of scalding gas. Svenson raised one heavy boot and stamped hard. The bars shook and bent inward. Phelps added his foot to the Doctor's and one corroded joint snapped clean. They kicked again and two more gave way. The Doctor fell to his knees and strained with both hands, bending the damaged metal enough to clear a hole.

'Hurry. Celeste, you are smallest – see if you can fit!'

Miss Temple carefully inserted her head and writhed forward. The cage caught her dress but Svenson disengaged it and she was through.

'It smells dreadful!' she called. Chang crawled in. He knelt alongside Miss Temple, the two of them together for a moment while Svenson and Phelps each insisted the other enter first.

'I was foolish,' she said quietly. 'I'm sorry.'

Chang did not know if she meant having darted forward to the gate on the dock, or their kiss in the Parchfeldt woods. He had never heard Miss Temple apologize for anything.

'What's done is done.' He reached for Svenson's flailing hand.

*

Where Miss Temple passed with a stoop, the men were forced to bend low. Chang called forward irritably, 'Do you know where this takes us?'

'No. Would you prefer we turn back?'

Mr Phelps sneezed. Svenson rummaged in his pockets, and then a wooden match flared. The tunnel, walls blackened and stubbled with chemical residue, receded far beyond the match light's reach. Svenson took the opportunity to light a cigarette, speaking as he puffed the tip to red life.

'The main gates will be guarded, and we are no party to force them.' The match went to his fingertips and Svenson dropped it, the flame winking out mid-fall.

'I should like a pair of *shoes*,' said Chang.

'And I should like to examine your spine,' replied the Doctor.

'Whilst we are being hunted in the dark, I suggest it be postponed.'

'Perhaps we could find that man again,' said Phelps, 'with the white hair –'

'His name is Foison.'

'The thing is, I believe I have seen him before.'

'Why didn't you say so?' snapped Chang.

'I was not sure – and we have been running!'

'*Where* did you see him?' asked Svenson.

'At Harschmort, it must have been – ages ago. Not that he spoke, but when one serves a man of power, as I did the Duke of Staëlmaere, one observes the minions of others.'

'So he was Robert Vandaariff's man?' asked Svenson.

'But Vandaariff's body holds another,' said Miss Temple. 'Robert Vandaariff is gone.'

'Does Mr Foison know that?'

'Why should he care?' asked Miss Temple, crawling on. 'The man is a villain. I think you *should* have killed him. O there now – do you mark it – the air is warmer . . . is there a join with another passage?'

The Doctor lit a second match. Chang turned his eyes from the flare and noticed, above them in the cement, a perforated hatchway.

'Here it is . . .'

He slipped his fingers through the mesh and lifted the hatch from its place, then hauled himself up into darkness, where his bare feet touched cold stone. The Doctor's match died and he lit another. Chang reached to Miss Temple.

'And so Persephone escaped from the underworld . . .'

At this she pursed her lips, but took his hand with both of hers. He lifted her out, then helped Phelps. The Doctor stood in the hatchway, head and shoulders in the room, holding the match aloft. Miss Temple laughed aloud.

'I am a goose! See here!' From her bag she pulled a beeswax stub and gave it to Svenson to light. 'I had forgotten!'

'O for all love,' muttered Phelps sullenly.

Chang shared the sentiment, but was happy enough to see where they were: a square chamber with a stone-flagged floor. At the base of each wall lay a scattering of straw, and bolted into the cement at regular intervals – almost to resemble an art salon – were long rectangles.

Doctor Svenson sniffed the air. 'Vinegar. As if the chamber had been scoured.'

Miss Temple took the candle from him, walking closer to a wall. 'Look at the straw,' she said. 'It has all come out of this burlap sacking . . .'

The scraps of sacking had been painted with crude faces, and within the straw lurked tattered strips of clothing.

'Straw mannequins,' Chang said. 'Test targets . . .' Crossing nearer, he could see the rectangles were of different materials: hammered steel, smelted iron, brass, oak, teak, maple studded with iron nails, each to test an explosive's power. The power of a prototype explosive set off within the chamber – its gasses venting to the tunnel – could be measured against all kinds of surfaces: wood, armour, fabric, even (he imagined a row of hams hanging from hooks) flesh, all from a single blast.

'Take care for your feet,' said Doctor Svenson, joining them. 'Celeste, hold your light closer to the straw.'

She knelt and Chang saw a glimmer near her boot. She gingerly pulled the straw away to reveal a gleaming chip of blue glass. Miss Temple lifted the light to the rectangle above. Its oaken planks bristled with tiny glass splinters, like a cork board stuck with pins. Higher up, still whole, perched a small, spiked blue disc, perhaps the size of a Venetian florin. Chang bunched the silken sleeve over his fingers and tugged the disc free. The edge was sharp and the spikes as regular as a wicked, wheeled spur.

'A projectile?' asked Svenson. 'Grapeshot?'

'But why *blue* glass?' countered Chang. 'A broken gin bottle will cut just as well.'

'What have you found?' called Mr Phelps from across the room, sniffling.

'The poor man needs a fire,' Svenson muttered, before calling back. 'It is blue glass, perhaps part of a weapon.'

'Will they not be searching for us?' Phelps replied. 'Should we not flee?'

Miss Temple plucked the disc from Chang's palm. Before he could protest she raised it up to her eye.

'Celeste!' gasped Svenson. 'Don't be a fool!'

Chang forcibly pulled her arm down, breaking the connection.

Her eyes were wide and her face had flushed – but with *anger*, he realized. Miss Temple thrust the glass back into Chang's hand.

'I saw nothing,' she growled. 'It is not a memory but a feeling. Deeply felt, obliterating *wrath*.'

Chang looked to the shredded straw. 'What does rage matter when the target's cut to ribbons?'

'There is a *door*,' called Mr Phelps thickly. 'I am going *through* it.'

Svenson hurried after Phelps. Chang caught Miss Temple's arm and turned her to him. 'You insist on risking yourself –'

'That is my own business.'

Her cheeks were still red from the glass, and Chang recalled the forest at Parchfeldt. She had been striking his chest in fury before lunging up to kiss him. He imagined slipping a hand through her curls right then and pulling her face to his.

'Impatience gets a person killed,' he said instead. 'And trying to make up for past mistakes only muddles your thinking.'

'*Mistakes?*'

'What of these men you hired, or Jack Pfaff – what of Elöise – what of shooting Roger Bascombe –'

'I should have spared him, then? And the Contessa – shall we spare her as well?'

'Are you coming?' called Doctor Svenson, his words edged with a finite patience.

'You know full well what I refer to,' muttered Chang, wishing he had not said a word.

'An ordnance room,' explained Svenson, indicating the high scaffolds holding kegs of powder. 'The racks allow ventilation – and do you mark the slippers?' A pile of grey felt slippers lay heaped just inside the doorway. 'To cover one's shoes, so there is no chance of a spark from a hobnail – an old habit from ships. And there, do you see?' Svenson pointed to a portion of empty scaffolding against the wall. 'View-holes into the blast chamber, bent like the mirrored periscopes one uses in trench-works, so no random shot can plunge through, yet still allowing the engineers to view the explosion.'

Mr Phelps had rallied, or perhaps was abashed at his show of peevishness. 'These barrels are not yet stored away – if they are newer, might they not hold the explosive we saw at the canal?'

Chang took one of Foison's knives and set to prising the lid from the nearest barrel, grateful for an excuse not to talk. He did not relish companionship for its own sake and often felt, perhaps perversely, that the people one knew best were the most difficult to bear. Over-familiarity with their habits made even the smallest interaction grate, while the obverse notion – of being that much more on view himself – was even worse.

He wedged the knife under the lid and saw Phelps had joined him.

'If it is the same explosive, might the jostling of your knife set it off? It did strike me as especially volatile.'

Chang applied a slow, strong pressure. The edge grudgingly rose until he could fit his fingers beneath and wrench it clear.

'Merciful hell,' muttered Mr Phelps.

Instead of any kind of powder, the barrel was filled with blue glass discs, sharp-spurred, coin-sized ... thousands and thousands of them. Chang scooped up a handful and threw it against the wall, but the discs only shattered. Clearly these new glass weapons were not the source of the explosion on the wharf.

Outside the ordnance chamber was another tunnel laid with rail. Miss Temple screwed up her mouth, as if she'd taken a ladle of fish oil.

Svenson reached out with concern. 'Celeste –'

'Left at the crossroads takes us back to where we found Chang. Right and straight ahead lead to other blasting chambers . . . but I believe I know our exit.'

She glanced at Chang, as if daring him to disagree. When he said nothing, she wheeled away. What had happened to her? Chang could feel Svenson watching him, but he had no desire to speak of what he did not understand.

At the crossroads they entered another blast tunnel proper, the men again reduced to ungainly scuttling. Chang managed to slip ahead of Phelps, but he reduced his pace so the Doctor and Miss Temple were soon some yards ahead. Then Chang stopped altogether.

'Have you hurt your foot?' asked Phelps.

'No. It seemed prudent for us to talk. If you are playing Svenson false I'll cut your throat.'

'I beg your pardon –'

'If you cause harm to Miss Temple I'll hack off your hands.'

'Harm? Have I not shared their peril? Why would I have saved Svenson's life –'

'I have no idea. Didn't he break your arm at the quarry?' Chang clamped a hand around Phelps's wrist. 'You've taken off the plaster, but no doubt the bones remain fragile . . .'

Was it the insistence on sparing Foison that had fired Chang's suspicion? Foison's knife had only pinned Phelps to the wall – on purpose? Had Phelps not delayed them with his snivels and sneezes, perhaps enough to allow recapture? He squeezed. Phelps gasped and tried to pull his arm away.

'Doctor Svenson is a man of principle! In killing Tackham he saved my life as well!'

'Where is the Contessa?'

'If I knew that, I would not be in a stinking tunnel with a madman! I have thrown over my entire life –'

'Why should I trust a man who's done his best to kill me?'

'Because everything has changed!' Phelps hissed. 'The city is in chaos!'

Chang seized the man's damp cravat and twisted the knot against his throat. 'All part of your mistress's plan, I think.'

'Listen to me,' Phelps wheezed, 'I think you *are* a criminal – and that your kind deserves death – but you hardly threaten the *state*. We need you now – as you need me!' Phelps jerked his chin towards Svenson and Miss Temple. 'Do you think *they* know the codes to summon the militia, or can counterfeit diplomatic ciphers? When it comes to the final battle –'

'I will be watching your *every* move.' Chang released his grip and turned after the others . . . half expecting a bullet in his back.

If Chang's bluntness accomplished nothing else, it would make Mr Phelps keen to prove his value, if he was honest – and, if dishonest, that much more likely to misstep, from fear. That he would also hate Chang with a burning fire was neither here nor there.

Miss Temple crouched with Svenson beneath another metal hatchway, waiting for Chang and Phelps to catch up. The Doctor studied Chang's blank expression but said nothing. Phelps only cleared his throat and apologized for keeping them.

'But you've found another room, it seems,' he said. 'How cunning.'

'It is not a room,' whispered Miss Temple, 'but our exit.'

Chang lifted one foot, for the ground was damp. 'You've brought us to a sewer.'

'Try your luck with Mr Foison,' she replied. 'I'm sure he's forgiven everything.'

This time Svenson shifted the metal hatch cover, then pulled himself from sight. A hand came down and Miss Temple went next, then Chang. He emerged into another cement chamber, but one lined with massive cisterns, each with a spigot the width of a 12-pound cannon at its base. He did not bother to assist Phelps.

'They contain different solutions,' Miss Temple explained, her voice thick, 'released into the tunnels to stifle various kinds of explosive residue. The Comte was taken with the . . . engineering.'

'How will that get us out?' asked Phelps, rising stiffly. Miss Temple pointed to the largest cistern of all, filling one corner of the room and reaching near the roof beams.

'Because *that* is full of water – to flush away the other chemicals – and the pipes that feed it run to the canal.'

'I am just beginning to *dry*!' moaned Phelps.

'But Celeste,' said Svenson, 'we have tried the canal – the defences are too strong.'

Miss Temple shook her head impatiently. 'Not the canal gate at the *river*. We have walked entirely beneath the works, *away* from the river and near a spur of the Orange Canal itself, used to ferry goods in the opposite direction, to the Raaxfall railway head. These pipes pass under the border fences to reach the water.'

'You want us to swim through the pipes?' squawked Phelps. 'The plan is blind idiocy!'

Miss Temple was stricken by another fit of choking. It did not stop, and she bent over as if she might be sick. Svenson glared at Phelps, who shrugged and fished out a damp handkerchief to blow his nose. Miss Temple straightened. Her eyes were red and moist.

'There are *valves*,' she rasped. 'The water can be turned off or reversed – they also use the pipes for drainage. It will be noissome, but the distance is not far, and we may pass through.'

'How do we enter?' asked Svenson.

Miss Temple looked to the top of the cistern, high above. 'There is a ladder – it may require a bit of a jump.'

'*Ah*. Perhaps –'

Chang slashed his hand through the air to indicate silence. They followed his gaze to the hatch, which Phelps had not replaced, and the flickers of light that danced in the tunnel beneath.

Chang waved them brusquely to the cistern of water, where Miss Temple told the other two men which valves to close. The squeaking valves were heard in the tunnel: lantern beams stabbed into the chamber. Chang crossed to a smaller cistern, wrenched at the spigot head and leapt clear of a spew of green liquid. The chamber floor was angled exactly for this purpose, and the steaming chemicals gushed straight at the hatch. Chang ran for the ladder. Phelps was in the lead, then Miss Temple, and finally Svenson, climbing with the speed of a tortoise.

Shouts of outrage echoed from the tunnel, then the crack of lantern glass bursting from contact with the liquid. Chang shoved the Doctor's rump without ceremony. A hand rose through the sick green flow and then a gasping, shaking head – one of the Xonck soldiers, more intrepid than the rest. Chang looked up to see Phelps's feet disappearing into a pipe above the cistern pit, Miss Temple right behind, balanced on the slippery rim. Svenson reached the top of the ladder but quailed at the four-foot gap to the pipe.

The soldier hauled himself clear and saw them, his shaven head gleaming green. He aimed a pistol at Chang's back, but the hammer clicked impotently – the chemical wash had done something to the charge. He tried again – more heads rising to the hatch rim – then threw the gun aside and drew a wicked knife. Miss Temple had entered the pipe, but Svenson stood fixed.

'It is just like the gangplank of a ship!' cried Chang.

'I despise gangplanks!' But the Doctor lunged forward. Three reckless storklike steps and he was there, Miss Temple catching his arm.

Chang readied one of Foison's knives. The bald soldier had reached the ladder. Chang considered throwing the knife, but he'd not Foison's skill. Another two men stood at the hatch, pistols snapping without effect. Chang ignored them, waiting for the bald soldier – climbing with one arm, the long knife held upwards. The green liquid had bleached his uniform yellow, and his coat seams split at the effort of his arms. Chang feinted a cut at the climbing man's face, which was aggressively parried – but all Chang sought was blade contact. He deftly turned his wrist so the silver tip of Foison's knife drew a sharp line along the soldier's hand, cutting deep. The long knife leapt from the man's grip. Chang snapped a fist into the soldier's nose, the man's feet went out from under him, and he slid down the rungs. Chang crossed the cistern rim as quick as a cat and was gone.

*

Like fools, the others were waiting in the pipe. He shouted them on, but then caught Svenson's foot and called for a pistol. He could not count on all their pursuers' firearms being disabled. Svenson passed back his revolver. Chang crawled furiously, then turned and aimed for the diminishing circle of light at his heels. He squeezed off four roaring shots and slithered on – the pipe was coated with slime – then turned and fired two more.

The pipe angled abruptly down and Chang slid out of direct range with relief, and just in time, for the metal behind him echoed with gunfire. He pressed himself flat, but the ringing ricochets spent themselves at the turn. He kept crawling. The pipe changed its construction – intrusive ridges where each individual piece had been riveted together. Chang clipped his knees and elbows groping forward.

More shots came from the cistern, but nothing found its mark. Chang feared the other end of their journey. Surely Foison's men knew where the pipes led, and might run over land more quickly than they could crawl like worms. Abruptly Chang's face met the grimy sole of Doctor Svenson's boot. He swore aloud, spitting, and the Doctor's whisper reached him. 'Do you hear it?'

'Hear what?'

'The *water*.'

Chang listened. Of course . . . far more effective than any scramble of men, Foison would simply reverse the valves. He wondered how it had taken them this long to think of it. Chang slapped Svenson's foot.

'Go on, as quickly as you can – we cannot go back!'

'We will drown!'

'And if we go back they will shoot us! For all we know we are near the finish!'

They scuttled like crabs before a looming wave. Chang heard Phelps's cry, though by then the water's rush echoed all around them.

'I am to it! O – the cold – O damnation!'

The icy black water swallowed them all. Chang used the riveted ridges as ladder rungs, hauling himself forward against the current. Again he struck Svenson's boots, and shoved the Doctor to go faster. The pressure in Chang's lungs flowered into pain. He felt a tightness in his ears but pressed on, the idea of drowning like a rat in a drainpipe still worse to bear.

Then Svenson's feet were no longer there, and Chang's fingers found the pipe rim itself. He wriggled his way through and shot for the surface of the canal, breaking into the air with a gasp. The others were bobbing near him, pale and heaving, hair plastered to their heads. Chang spun round, searching the banks for men with carbines.

'We have to go on,' he gasped. 'They will be here.'

'Go where?' called Phelps, teeth chattering. 'Where are we? We shall catch our deaths!'

'This way, sir! There is a rope!'

A crouching man in a long brown coat had appeared on the canal bank, a hat pulled low over his eyes.

'O Mr Cunsher!' exclaimed Phelps. 'Thank God you have found us!'

The small hut felt like a room at the Slavic baths. Their clothing hung on lines and steamed in the heat of a squat metal stove so stuffed with coal that one could not approach within a yard. A separate line had been draped with a sheet from the cabin's cot, and behind lurked Miss Temple, unseen.

Chang wrapped a blanket around himself and cleared his throat, as if the sound might clear his mind. Svenson sat with a mouldy blanket of his own. Phelps had taken the other bedsheet and now stood like a dismal Roman, his bare feet in a pan of hot water.

The strange foreigner had pulled them from the canal and led them pitilessly through brown scrub woodland to a scattering of squat shacks – stonecutters he said – one of which he unlocked with a hook-ended metal pin. Cunsher spoke only to Phelps, gave an occasional respectful nod to Svenson, and ignored Chang and Miss Temple altogether. He had found their carriage in Raaxfall, heard the explosion and observed the movements of guards at the gate, finally deducing that the canal was the only possible exit within his reach. Cunsher then left them, muttering something to his master that Chang had not heard. To Chang, the drainpipe was no sensible option to occur to anyone. He was glad for this second rescue, but trusted the fellow no more than he trusted Phelps.

It was not suspicion that now gnawed his peace of mind. Whatever their danger, Chang found his thoughts quite irresistibly settled on the proximate nudity of the young woman, not ten feet away behind a single pane of threadbare cloth. He could hear her bare feet on the floorboards, the creak of her body on the wooden stool. Were her arms huddled for warmth or modesty – or were they raised to recurl her hair, breasts exposed and high on her slim ribcage? Chang shifted on his own seat, willing his thoughts elsewhere against tumescence. How long had it been since he'd had a woman?

'Are you warm enough, Celeste?' Doctor Svenson called.

'Yes, thank you,' she replied from behind her curtain. 'I trust you will recover?'

'Indeed.' Svenson selected a cigarette from his silver case, a civilized veneer already returned to his voice. 'Though I must admit – when the water rose, my heart was in my throat. You did very well to drive on,' he said to Phelps. 'The slightest hesitation would have done for us all.'

Phelps shuddered. 'It does not bear thinking. Though one begins to understand why men of adventure are so grim.' He made a point of looking at Chang. Chang said nothing, his own gaze taken by the long, livid scar across the Doctor's chest. Svenson inhaled deeply, then thought to offer his silver case to the others.

'Were they not drenched?' asked Chang.

'Ah – it is the *case*, you see.' Svenson snapped the silver case closed so they all might hear the catch of its clasp, then popped it open again. 'Tight as a clam. Will you partake? Tobacco is *highly* restorative.'

'It hurts my eyes,' said Chang.

'Truly? How strange.'

Chang turned the subject before Svenson recalled his earlier keenness to examine him. 'As soon as our clothes are dry, we must move on.'

'We need food,' croaked Phelps, who had accepted Svenson's offer. His words were broken by coughing. 'And rest. And information.'

'But we *have* learnt much,' said Svenson. 'The new explosive, the glass spurs – that they are inscribed with an emotion instead of a memory.'

'We've no idea what that *means*.'

'Not yet, but have you ever eaten hashish?'

'I beg your pardon,' said Phelps.

'I am thinking of the glass – the *anger*, a state of pure emotion –'

'You think the glass contains *hashish*?'

'Not at all. Consider Hassan i-Sabbah and his guild of assassins, who entered a state of deadly single-mindedness under the combined influences of religion and narcotics. Think of the Thuggee cult of India – incense, incantations, *soma* – the principle is the same.'

'Not unlike the Process,' observed Chang.

Phelps managed to exhale without coughing. 'The glass may answer for the narcotic, yet if the spurs hold no memory, where is the instruction? Without *thought*, how can Vandaariff direct those stricken?'

'Perhaps he cannot.' Svenson sighed ruefully. 'Do not forget, the man *believes* his alchemical religion. We mistake him if we seek only reason.'

Chang knew Svenson was right – he had seen the unsettling glow behind Vandaariff's eyes – yet he said nothing about the 'elemental' glass cards, or the too-rapid restoration of his own strength. He ought to have described the whole thing then and there – if there was any man to make sense of things, it was the Doctor – but such disclosure would have led to a public scrutiny of his wound. Chang waited until Svenson put more coal in the stove before carefully stretching the muscles of his lower back. He felt no pain or inhibition of movement. Was it possible that Vandaariff had merely healed him, and that the others had stared only at the vicious nature of the scar?

A faint but high-pitched gasp came from behind Miss Temple's curtain. The three men looked at each other.

'Celeste?' asked Svenson.

'Do go on,' she replied quickly. 'It was but a splinter on my chair.'

Svenson waited, but she said nothing more. 'Are you all right?'

'Goodness, yes. Do not mind me in the least.'

The trousers were not completely dry, but Chang reasoned that wearing them slightly damp would settle the leather more comfortably around his body. To hide his wound from Svenson he made a point of shucking off his blanket with his back to the wall. Tucking in the silk shirt, stained by its time in the canal, he caught a flicker of movement at the edge of the curtain. Had she been peeking? Disliking the entire drift of his thoughts, Chang strode past the others and slipped into the cold afternoon sun.

The hut was surrounded by squat pine trees. Chang did not relish another bare-footed tramp through twigs and stones, but saw no alternative, and so set off, keeping to the mud and dry leaves. As he reached the other huts, he saw one whose door hung open several inches. Smoke rose from the chimney – indeed it now came from several huts, none of which had seemed occupied before – and from inside he could hear footsteps.

Chang snapped his head back from the door at the wheeling movement of a pistol being drawn and the click of its hammer.

'Do not shoot me, Mr Cunsher.'

If Cunsher was in the service of their enemies, this was the perfect opportunity to blow Chang's head off and explain it away as an accident. But the man had already lowered the gun. Chang stepped inside and nodded to the stove.

'Our company does not suit you?'

Cunsher shrugged. His accented speech slipped from his mouth as if each ill-fitting word had been oiled. 'One smoking stove reveals our refuge. Four stoves make a party of stonecutters. *Here* – for you.'

Cunsher tossed a pair of worn black boots in Chang's direction. Chang saw the leather was still good and the soles were sound. He wormed his foot inside one, stepped down on the heel, and then rolled his ankle in a circle.

'It's a damned miracle. Where did you find them? How did you know the size?'

'Your feet of course – and then I have *looked*. Here.' Cunsher took a pair of thin black goggles from a wooden crate. 'Used for blasting. The Doctor related your requirements.'

Chang slipped the goggles on. The lenses were every bit as dark as his habitual glasses, but came edged with leather to block peripheral glare. Already he felt his muscles relaxing.

'Thank you again. I had despaired.'

Cunsher tipped his head. 'And you are dry. The others? We should not wait.'

But Chang subtly shifted his weight so he stood between Cunsher and the door. The man nodded, as if this too was expected, and thrust his hands into the pockets of his coat.

'You do not know me. These enemies are strong – of course.'

'You're Phelps's man.'

Between the thick brim of his hat and the even thicker band of hair below his nose, Cunsher's face was lined and his eyes were as brown and sad as a deer's. 'You are like me, I wonder. We have stories – stories we cannot tell. Your Ministry had business where I lived, a business that in time allowed me to . . . execute a relocation.'

'And you have served Phelps since? Served the Ministry?'

'Not in its most recent campaign – which has assailed you, and whose part in it my employer most earnestly repents. But otherwise. I was abroad.'

'Macklenburg?'

'Vienna. When in time I came back –'

'Phelps was gone.'

'What is *not* gone? All your nation. One has seen such change elsewhere.'

'Because a crust of parasites is getting scraped off the loaf? Worse could happen.'

Cunsher caught a tuft of moustache in his teeth and chewed. 'Parasites, yes. Hate the oppressors, Cardinal Chang – there I am with you. But *fear* the oppressed, especially if they receive a glimpse of freedom. Their strength is, how to say, *untrained.*'

Cunsher reached into the wooden crate and came up with a small cracked teapot in the shape of an apple.

'I had thought to make tea for the young lady,' he said glumly. 'There does not seem now the time.'

His body low, as if he were discerning the way by smell, Cunsher led them to a rutted cart road, and along it to the railway station at Du Conque.

As they waited for the train, Miss Temple stood apart under the station eaves, frowning at a faded schedule posting, for all the world the same insufferable girl who had made Chang and Svenson swear an oath on the roof of the Boniface. Chang found himself annoyed by her standing apart. Did she expect him to make a point of walking over to inquire after her health?

Svenson spoke of the need to search the train for any agents from Raaxfall and Chang grunted his agreement. In the presence of Phelps he could hardly speak freely, though the change in Svenson was clear. The Doctor's starched manner had been leeched by loss to the brittleness of an old man's bones. Quite casually, for he was abashed to realize he had not yet done so, Chang asked the date. Phelps informed him it was the 28th.

Two months since Angelique had died. Chang wondered what would have become of Angelique had she possessed Miss Temple's privilege – then scoffed at his own sense of injustice. Angelique well born would have tolerated his presence even *less*.

The train came at last. When the conductor arrived, Miss Temple opened her clutch bag, speaking tartly to Phelps. 'I assume you have money for yourself and your man. I will pay for the Doctor and Chang.'

Phelps sputtered and felt in his coat pocket for a wallet of wet bills. Miss Temple took her tickets and stuffed them into the clutch bag with her change.

'I am obliged, my dear –' began Svenson, but Chang hooked the Doctor's arm and pulled him out of the compartment.

'Your idea to *search*.'

They need not have bothered. Five carriages found no one from the Xonck Armaments works. At the far end, Svenson stopped for a cigarette.

'As to our return. You have not been in the city. We would do well to avoid the crowds at Stropping.'

'It can be done.'

Svenson nodded, inhaling sharply enough for Chang to hear the burning paper. Chang sighed, feeling obliged and resenting it.

'I did not know about Elöise. I am heartily sorry.'

'We failed her.'

Chang spoke gently. 'She failed herself as well.'

'Is that not exactly when we depend upon our friends?'

The silence hung between them, marked by the rhythm of the train.

'I do not *have* friends, as a rule.'

Svenson shrugged. 'Nor I. Perhaps in that way we fail ourselves.'

'Doctor, that woman –'

'Rosamonde?'

'The Contessa. I promise you. She *will* pay.'

'That is very much my intention.' Svenson dropped the butt and ground it with his boot.


Returning, they met Miss Temple in the corridor, clearly on her way to find them.

'Is anything wrong?' asked Svenson.

'Nothing at all,' she said. 'I mean no disrespect to Mr Phelps and his foreign agent – but – both of you – I thought the three of us might be together. If there are things we ought to say. Aren't there?'

Chang saw Cunsher watching from the far end of the carriage. On being seen, the man retreated.

'What things?' asked Svenson.

'I do not *know*,' she replied. 'But so much has happened and we have not talked.'

'We have *never* talked,' said Chang.

'Of course we have! At the Boniface, and at Harschmort, and on the airship – and then at Parchfeldt –' Her eyes met his and she swallowed, unable to go on. Svenson took Miss Temple's arm and indicated the nearest compartment, which was empty.

She sat in the middle of one side, leaving Chang the choice to sit next to her, which seemed too forward, or opposite – where he installed himself against the window. The choice passed to Svenson, who settled on Chang's side, leaving a seat between them. Miss Temple looked at each man in turn, her face reddening.

She took a deep breath, as if to start again, but only let it out with a slump of her shoulders. Svenson slipped out his silver case.

'Did you not just have one?' asked Chang waspishly.

'They *do* sharpen the mind.' Svenson clicked the case shut and tapped the cigarette three times upon it, but did not light it. He cleared his throat and addressed Miss Temple, far too stiffly. 'Indeed, it *has* been some time since we three were together. All the days with Sorge and Lina – but you were not strictly with us then, were you Celeste?'

'You both *left* me!'

Chang rolled his eyes.

'O I know you had *reasons*,' she added, with an impatience that made Chang smile. She saw the smile and went on with a venom normally reserved for disobedient maids. 'I have said this to the Doctor, but perhaps you will appreciate that I have passed the last five weeks believing you had both been killed through my own foolishness. It was a *terrible* burden.'

'Now we are alive you may unburden yourself, I am sure. Do you wish to dissolve our little covenant and go our separate ways, is that it?'

'*Go?*' She glared at him. 'How? Where? We all heard that white-haired serpent – that you were the *property* of a jealous man. Can *you* walk away? Can the Doctor, after Elöise? Can *I*? Is *that* all you think of me?'

Svenson cleared his throat. 'Celeste –'

'Our agreement *holds*. To the death of the Contessa. To the death of the Comte – whatever body holds him. After these things, I do not care.'

Her last words carried an air of drama, and the men exchanged a tactful glance. Again, Miss Temple reacted with fury.

'Elöise is a corpse because we were not stronger, and both of you – and I – would be rotting too but for blind chance – how many times? I will not have it. Who else will do our work? Who else will stop them?' She flung herself back and appealed to the ceiling. 'O this is not what I wanted to say.'

Chang did not require Svenson's look to know he must say nothing. The Doctor's voice was gentle. 'We have all been frightened –'

'Being frightened is *appalling*,' Miss Temple whispered. 'There is nothing for it but rage, and I am so tired of being angry.' She looked down at her hands, flushing red, though her eyes remained fierce. 'I'm sure it is easy for you to laugh.'

'No, Celeste.'

'I do not believe you. I do not believe either of you.'

Chang jerked his head to Svenson. 'What has *he* done?'

'He is unpleasantly kind. As if I could forget how I have failed – as if I ought to. You have no idea.'

'Idea of *what*?' asked Svenson.

'How late. How late it already is.' Miss Temple abruptly stood, and reached the door before the Doctor had gained his feet.

'Celeste, wait –'

'She has Francesca and the book. *He* has the money to make his madness real.'

But Svenson held out an open hand. 'All that is true. But please . . . what else did you want to say? The three of us. When you say it is "late" –'

'I'm sorry. I would not want to further bruise Mr Phelps's feelings,' said Miss Temple. The door slid shut behind her.

Svenson struck a match and puffed his smoke to life. 'She is agitated.'

This did not strike Chang as worth reply. He recalled the sabre scar across the Doctor's chest and wondered, not for the first time, what truly drove the man.

'Celeste has changed. Her sense – her *moral* sense.'

'Did she tell you this?'

'Of course not. I cannot explain it otherwise. She has ever been collected –'

'Unless she is bursting into tears or a rage, certainly.'

Svenson's tone grew sharp. 'Perhaps you have your own answer.'

'What does *that* mean – why should I?'

'You question my observation – I ask for yours.'

'I've no idea in the slightest!'

Svenson passed the hand with the cigarette over his brow, wreathing his head with smoke.

'We are men. We meet our fate as a duty – as our lot. But her fate surpasses expectation. The book that held the Comte's corrupted mind – it was in Celeste's possession. Did you not wonder how she could guide us through the munitions works?'

'Of course I *wondered*.'

'You did not *ask*.'

'When should I have done so? When the dock was exploding? In the damned pipe?'

'Well, that is why, I think. She has touched that book, gazed inside.'

'Why did you even go to Raaxfall?'

'I told you, Celeste received a map of the works, in glass, from the Contessa.'

'And you *went*! Of all the idiocies —'

'Our journey saved your life.'

'Do you think that is the end of it? What else did you accomplish without understanding? What task did you perform for *her*?'

Svenson rose and stalked from the compartment. Chang suppressed the urge to call the man back. He shut his eyes behind the stonecutter's goggles and settled deeper in his seat.

His thoughts rushed elsewhere, worrying a phrase of Miss Temple's like a sore tooth: 'Whatever body holds him.' She had referred to the Comte, his essence scattered to Vandaariff, a glass book, even part of Miss Temple herself — and as long as that book existed, what prevented his incorporation into one new victim after another? Chang was not concerned with imaginary incarnations. He could think only about himself, chained to the table, suffering the procession of elemental glass cards. No sleep came.

When the train met the tunnels outside Stropping Station, Chang rejoined the others. He was surprised no one had come to fetch him — taking it either as a measure of respect for his ordeal or disapproval of his temper — and so simply stood and faced them, cracking the knuckles of both hands.

'The conductor is gone to the front,' said Phelps.

'Good. As soon as the train stops we will exit through the rear. Follow me. We will cross the tracks and leave the station in secret.'

They waited at the rear of the train. Miss Temple's eyes were red. Chang looked to her right hand and saw the fingertips smeared, as if she had been reading newsprint. A bead of black stained her collar.

The train's brakes seized with a screech and Miss Temple staggered, steadied by Doctor Svenson. Chang peered out of a compartment window. Setting off from the platform at a trot was a squad of brown-coated, truncheon-wielding constables. Across Stropping, similar knots of lawmen prodded passengers into groups, escorting them through the station like criminals.

'Open the door! We will be stopped any second.'

Cunsher, in the lead, called back, 'It is locked!'

Chang rushed into the corridor. 'Kick it open! The place is thick with policemen!'

'Policemen?' cried Phelps. 'But why?'

Chang shouldered through to Cunsher, whose kicks had done nothing. The train gave out the massive hiss of an exhausted dragon. The air was split with police whistles. Svenson pulled them aside and extended the long Navy revolver, firing three rounds point-blank into the lock plate. Chang kicked and the door flew wide. He leapt to the gravel and turned for Miss Temple. A constable shouted to stop. Letting the others come after, Chang raced away, Miss Temple's hand tight in his, headlong for the nearest train.

'Under! Under!' he cried, and dived first. The stones stung his knees and elbows, but Chang rolled out the other side. He caught Miss Temple's shoulders as her head appeared and they were up and scrambling towards another train. Miss Temple held up her dress (the clutch bag leaping about on its strap), all attention focused on keeping her feet.

Out from under the next train, Chang finally looked back: no police in sight. He sighed with relief. If the search had been particular to them, the constables would not have given up so easily. From the number of officers spread across the station floor, he guessed their orders had been limited to managing passengers in general – and to give chase would have meant leaving other travellers with little or no escort. Besides, lacking Chang's knowledge of the remote corners of Stropping, the harried lawmen would assume that any fugitives must return to their cordon sooner or later, when their capture would be far less strenuous.

Svenson slithered from under the last train, smeared with soot.

'You spoke the truth about *unrest*,' Chang called.

'Lovely, isn't it?' huffed Phelps, just behind the Doctor.

'Who could order such measures?'

'Any number of utter fools,' Phelps replied grimly. 'But it means the Privy Council.'

Cunsher emerged after Phelps, holding his soft hat in place as he crawled. Chang took Miss Temple's hand, proud of how well she had managed. Despite her outburst on the train, this was the same Celeste Temple who'd kept her wits on the airship.

'This way. There is a climb.'

The side exit to Helliott Street from the railway tracks had always felt like Chang's private possession, discovered on a pillaged Royal Engineering survey years before and employed sparingly. But now, mounting the metal staircase, his boots scuffed into newspapers, wadded fabric and even empty bottles. Miss Temple pulled her hand free to cover her nose and mouth.

'Are you not choked? The stench is horrid!'

Chang's own sense of smell scarcely existed, but as he squinted above them he perceived a huddled shape blocking the way. He climbed and gingerly extended a toe to the pile of rags. It was a man: small, old, and dead for at least a week.

'Step carefully,' he called behind, and then to Miss Temple, 'I should not let your dress drag.'

Two more corpses cluttered the top of the stairs, propped against the iron door like sacks of grain – women, one gashed across her forehead. The wound had suppurated, and bloomed in death like slashed upholstery. The second woman's face was wrapped in a shawl save for the hanging mouth, showing a line of stumped brown teeth. Chang heaved at the bolt, then kicked the door open. The two bodies toppled into the cold light of Helliott Street. Chang stepped over them onto the cobbles, but as always Helliott Street was abandoned. Cunsher helped him shove the door closed again, sealing the corpses back into their tomb. Chang wiped his hands on Foison's coat and wondered what had happened to his city in so short a time.

'At the end of this street is the Regent's Star,' he explained, 'as nasty a

crossroads as this city holds. Any of its foul lanes will offer rooms to hide . . .'
Miss Temple had been scraping something from her boot, but now looked
up to meet his gaze. 'Unless anyone has another suggestion.'

'As a matter of fact, I do,' she replied. 'I did not think – or rather thought
I could find our enemies only by their own clues – in any event, I am a goose
for not perceiving the significance of my dressmaker, Monsieur Masseé. As
you may imagine, a woman known to have money is besieged like Constanti-
nople: she must submit to this fashion, that fabric, this fringe, or, if you
please, a perfectly unnecessary *toque*. And so used am I to this beseech-
ment, even from dear Monsieur Masseé, that I did not mark a suggestion
some days ago to avail myself of an elegant bolt of fabric sworn to have
arrived straight from Milan. Indeed, I rejected the offer out of hand –
crimson silk is not only beastly expensive, but also unseemly for anyone not
in an Italian opera. And yet I thought only of myself, not of who *would* buy
that rarest, exquisite silk, in that colour, demanding a specific complexion
and temperament.'

She raised her eyebrows expectantly, waiting.

'You think the Contessa desires new dresses?' asked Phelps. 'Now?'

'All *her* things are lost at the St Royale. It was an *entire bolt of cloth*. A
woman of fashion wanting any of it would buy *all* of it, to prevent anyone
*else* from duplicating her prize. We need only find who *did* buy the fabric,
and where it was delivered.'

'So you do not *literally* know where she is?' ventured Svenson.

Miss Temple rolled her eyes. 'Monsieur Masseé's salon is directly down
the Grossmaere. Shall we?'

'Of course not,' broke in Mr Phelps. 'Look at us! We cannot dream to
enter such an emporium – and you yourself could only do so by presuming
upon a very established familiarity. Miss Temple, you have been immersed
in a *canal*. You offer to expose yourself gravely for our benefit, but whatever
information you hope to acquire will be more dearly bought, if not rendered
beyond price, if such bedraggled men as we come with you –'

'Do you think I care for such exposure? I am more than willing to pay for
what I ask.'

'Society is not only a matter of *money*,' said Phelps.

'Of course it is!'

'For all your pride,' Phelps answered harshly, 'Roger Bascombe was not a titled prince. Despite the advantages some wealth may have afforded you, Miss Temple, *real* status is something you have not glimpsed.'

Miss Temple scowled. 'I have never found disdain for money to be a compelling force.'

'Who stands with you now, Celeste?' asked Svenson quietly. 'Are we swayed by your banknotes?'

Miss Temple threw up her hands. 'That is not the same at all!'

'You will be *seen*,' insisted Phelps. 'When all of this is over, if you do expect to retain any place in society –'

'I have no place!' Miss Temple shouted. 'I am a New World savage! And I *expect* this present business to end my life!'

She turned on her heel down the narrow canyon of Helliott Street. The four men avoided each other's gaze, watching her small form diminish.

'Deftly managed all round,' muttered Svenson.

'But the *idea*,' protested Phelps, 'that a ridiculous bolt of *fabric* –'

'Hiding is not about concealment,' said Chang, 'but revelation. A fugitive is given away just like an animal – by instincts that aren't, or can't be, denied. A badger spreads its scent. The Contessa has her finery.'

'I should look in the home of some sympathetic great lady,' agreed Cunsher, 'where the signs you mention may be laid to another's appetite.'

'But she has the child,' said Svenson. 'Francesca Trapping would be a burden.'

Chang shook his head. 'For all we know, the girl is chained in a wardrobe, licking glue from hatboxes to stay alive.'

Phelps wrinkled his nose. 'Cardinal Chang –'

'Licking hatboxes if she's *lucky*.' Chang stepped to Svenson and slapped the dust from his coat. 'Doctor, since your uniform suggests *some* respectability, will you run after Miss Temple so she does not launch on any additional journeys alone? Phelps, I would suggest you visit the offices of the *Herald* and locate the full text of this clipping about the Comte's salon. Mr Cunsher, perhaps you might discover whether any further red envelopes have arrived at the Hotel Boniface. As we near the end of business hours,

I recommend speed. Let us meet in two hours at some public place. St Isobel's statue?'

He turned sharply to leave, but Svenson called behind him, 'What of
you? What will you do?'

'Find a fresh pair of stockings!' Chang shouted back. Under his breath,
he muttered, 'And wrap them tight around Jack Pfaff's neck.'

Ten minutes took Chang to the river. The streets were filled with huddled
figures – men passing bottles, children watching his passage with large eyes,
women with hopes as cold and distant as a star. He assumed these were foreign dregs, washed into the city without language or a trade, but from
snatches of conversation – and cries for money he ignored – he realized they
were displaced citizens, refugees in their own city. Chang increased his pace.
He had no wish for any entanglement, nor for the constables these unfortu-
nates would inevitably attract.

To his right lay a fat Dutch sloop, painted the warm yellow of a ripened
pear. The craft was anchored well out in the river, and on its deck stood
armed men. He had seen such caution before, with especially valuable cargo,
but the sloop was not alone. In fear of pillage, the entire river was choked
with vessels keeping a night-time distance from the bank.

The building on the corner of his own street remained derelict and Chang
entered through an empty window. He drew one of Foison's knives, but
advanced without incident to the roof. He picked his way across four buildings, and dropped in silence to a fifth, landing in a crouch. The windows
around him glowed with candles and lamps, but no sign of habitation came
from his own open casement. Chang gave the window a shove, waited, then
eased himself in. No one. The floor by the window was caked with feathers
and white-streaked filth.

Few objects caught Cardinal Chang's sentiment, and most of those – his
red leather coat, his stick, his books – he had already sacrificed. Within his
genuine regret for their loss, he nevertheless detected a vein of relief . . . the
more of his past that disappeared, the less he felt its cold constraint.

He lit a candle and, scraping the crust from the sill, pushed the window
shut. He quickly stripped off Foison's clothing and laid out his own – red

trousers with a fine black stripe, a black shirt, a fresh black neckcloth and clean stockings. He stood for a moment, exposed to the waist, shaving mirror within reach, but then pulled the fresh shirt on, telling himself he'd neither the light nor time to examine the wound. Cunsher's boots he kept, but availed himself of stockings, a handkerchief, gloves and a spare set of smoked dark glasses. The goggles had been a godsend, but he could not wear them and fight – too much of his vision was blocked off.

He knelt at his battered bureau, pulled the bottom drawer from its slot – a clatter of pocket watches, knives, foreign coins and tattered notebooks – and set it aside, pausing to pluck up an ebony-handled straight razor and drop it into his shirt pocket. He groped into the open hole, face and shoulder pressed to the chest-of-drawers. His fingers found a catch and an inset wooden box popped free: inside were three banknotes, rolled tight as cigarettes. He tucked them next to the razor, one at a time, as if he were loading a carbine, and turned his attention back to the box. Underneath the banknotes was an iron key. Chang pocketed the key, dropped the empty box into its space and shoved the drawer back into the bureau.

He shrugged his way back into Foison's black coat. It *was* warmer than it looked, and remained a trophy after all.

The Babylon lay on the edge of the theatre district proper, convenient to several notorious hotels – no surprise, given that its stock in trade lay less in strictly recognizable plays than in 'historical' pageantry, with the degree of accuracy proportionate to the lewdness of the costumes. The only offering he'd seen – whilst stalking a young viscount whose new title had prompted a naive rejection of past debts – *Shipwreck'd in the Bermudas*, featured sprites of wind and water, strapping seamen, and shapely natives clad in leaves that tended to scatter before the mischief of said sprites. Befitting an institution so shrewdly dedicated to fantasy, the Babylon permitted no crowd of admirers at its stage door – an alley where no money could be made. Instead, its performers escaped the theatre through a passage to the St Eustace Hotel next door, with both champagne and easy rooms in staggering distance, from all of which the owners of the Babylon exacted a share.

The rear door *had* attracted the attention of at least one man of secrecy and cunning. Cardinal Chang strode to it unobserved and opened the lock with his recovered skeleton key, determined to cut Pfaff's throat at the slightest provocation.

It was too early for even the curtain-raising circus acts, but backstage would soon fill with stagehands (often sailors with their knowledge of ropes and comfort with heights) and performers, getting ready for their work. Chang found such entertainments dire. Was there not ample pretence in the world, enough mannered screeching – why should anyone crave *more*? No one in Chang's acquaintance shared his disgust. He knew without discussing the matter that Doctor Svenson admired the theatre greatly – perhaps even the opera, not that the distinction mattered to Chang: the more seriously a thing was taken by its admirers, the more fatuous it undoubtedly was.

The man he pursued loved the theatre above all things. Chang found a wooden ladder, bolted to the wall, climbing in silence above painted flats and hanging velvet to a narrow catwalk. Jack Pfaff adored beauty but lacked the money to join the ogling fools in the St Eustace, settling to be a hungry ghost in the shadows. Past the catwalk was another lock, the opening of which must ruin any hope of surprise. Chang did not need surprise. He turned his key and entered Jack Pfaff's garret.

Mr Pfaff was not home. Chang lit a candle by the sagging bed: peeling walls, empty brown bottles, a rotten, rat-chewn loaf, jars of potted meat and stewed fruits, once sealed with wax, knocked on their sides and gobbled clean, a pewter jug near the bed with an inch of cloudy water. Chang opened Pfaff's wardrobe, an altar of devotion filled with bright trousers, ruffled cuffs, cross-stitched waistcoats and at least eight pairs of shoes, all cracked and worn, yet polished to a shine.

Pushed against the far wall, angled with the slant of the rooftop, was a desk fashioned of wood planks laid across two barrels. A square of newsprint had been spread, and atop it lay an assortment of glass.

Most might have come from a scientist's laboratory – fragile coils to aid condensation, slim spoons and rods – but two pieces caught Chang's eye. The first was broken, but Chang recognized it all the same – a thin bar ending in a curled circle: half of a glass key. The Contessa had described keys that allowed a person safely to examine the contents of a glass book – and then asserted that all such keys had been destroyed. Chang turned the fragment in his hand. The original keys had been made by the Comte from indigo clay. The broken one in his hand was as clear as spring water.

The second piece was more confounding still: a thin rectangle, the twin of the Comte's glass cards, yet so transparent that it might have been cut from a window. Chang held the card to his eye without any effect whatsoever . . . yet its size, like the construction of the key, could be no accident. Someone without a supply of indigo clay was nevertheless learning to make the necessary objects.

The city was full of glassworks large and small – no doubt Pfaff had isolated the proper one after a great deal of legwork. Chang searched the desk, under the newspaper, even lifting the planking to examine the barrels, but found no papers, no list, no helpful notes. Not that note-taking was Pfaff's style. The information would be in his head and nowhere else.

Apart from the wardrobe, Pfaff's possessions were few and without character. Crammed in a box and set on the street, they would denote no particular man. Chang thought of his own rooms, so recently rummaged. His books of poetry might offer a measure of identity – but was a taste for words so different from that for gaudy clothing? Would Pfaff ever come back to his rat's nest above the theatre? Would Chang ever return to his own den? He had longed for his rooms – but the place answered his deeper need no more than a dream. Like a wolf whose forest has been cut down, Chang knew his life had irrevocably changed, that in some profound way it was over. The crime, the corruption, the violence, everything that fed him had only become more virulent. He ought to feel alive, surrounded by dark opportunity. But change was not a force Cardinal Chang enjoyed. He blew out the candle and descended quickly.

As he stepped off the ladder a giggling woman dressed as a shepherdess burst in from the corridor beyond, no doubt accustomed to the always-closed rear door providing a private alcove. She stopped dead – Chang's glasses had slid down his nose – and screamed. Behind her stood a shirtless man in trousers of white fleece – a costumed sheep. The woman screamed again, and Chang's left hand shot out, taking hold of her jaw. He shoved her into the man, throwing them off balance, and swept out the razor. The pair gaped up at him. Chang wheeled away. He strode down the alley, angry at how close he had come to carving them both, his jaw still tight with the desire to have done it.

He had an hour before meeting the others, not that he cared to keep them waiting – but how could he replicate Pfaff's labour in an hour? And where was Pfaff now? Had his investigation taken him too near the Contessa? Did he still trail her or had he been killed? If he had fled, it had not been to his garret. Was there *any* way to guess where the man had gone to ground? One possibility was a brothel. Miss Temple would have advanced him money . . .

He tried the South Quays. Pfaff was not there. Chang spoke to the strong men minding the door and then to the skeletal Mrs Wells, whose surprise at finding Cardinal Chang alive actually distracted her from demanding a fee for their conversation. Back on the foul cobbles of Dagging Lane, Chang frowned. However early the hour, he had never seen the South Quays so quiet – he could not ever remember actually being able to hear the fiddle players scraping away in the main parlour. Was Mrs Wells so worried as to seek goodwill from a villain like Chang? As he could imagine no person of less sentiment than the beak-nosed brothel-mistress, he had to admit the disturbing possibility.

Pfaff could have found a room at any of twenty waterfront inns, but Chang had no more time to search. He made his way from the river, keeping to the wider streets. The narrow alleys remained thick with the disaffected poor, and he'd no care to arouse either their resentment or his own sympathies. Chang stopped abruptly – sympathy and resentment, that was it exactly. Pfaff's pride: he would seek a refuge where he felt *protected*, not anonymous. Chang had not wanted to show his face so soon, but there was one obvious place he could not avoid.

By the time he reached the Raton Marine, mist had risen and the tables outside had been abandoned. Chang pushed his way in and crossed to Nicholas, behind the bar. Both men ignored the sudden rustle of whispers.

'I was told you were dead.'

'An honest mistake.' Chang nodded to the balcony and its rooms for hire. 'Jack Pfaff.'

'Is he not doing your business?'

'The men he hired have been killed. Pfaff has probably joined them.'

'The young woman –'

'Misplaced her trust. She came here for help and found incompetence.'

Nicholas did not reply. Chang knew as well as anyone the degree to which the barman's position rested on his ability to keep secrets, to take no favourites – that the existence of the Raton Marine depended on its being neutral ground.

Chang leant closer and spoke low. 'If Jack Pfaff is dead, his secrets do not matter, but if he is alive, keeping his secrets will quite certainly kill him. He told you – I *know* he told you, Nicholas – not because he asked you to keep his trust, but because he wanted to brag, like an arrogant whelp.'

'You underrate him.'

'He can correct me any time he likes.'

Nicholas met Chang's hard gaze, then reached under the bar and came up with a clear, shining disc the size of a gold piece. The glass had been stamped like a coin with an improbably young portrait of the Queen. On its other side was an elegant scrolling script: 'Sullivar Glassworks, 87 Bankside'. Chang slid it back to the barman.

'How many lives is that, Cardinal?' drawled a voice from the balcony above him. 'Or are you a corpse already?'

Chang ignored the spreading laughter and stepped into the street.

He broke into a jog, hurrying past the ships and the milling dockmen to a wide wooden rampway lined with artisans' stalls. It sloped to the shingle and continued for a quarter of a mile before rising again. Once or twice a year the Bankside would be flooded by tides, but so precious was the land – able to deal directly with the water traffic (and without, it was understood, strict attention to such notions as tariffs) – that no one ever thought to relocate. Remade again and again, Bankside establishments were a weave of wooden shacks, as closely packed as swinging hammocks on the gun deck of a frigate.

The high gate – as a body Bankside merchants secured their borders against thievery – was not yet closed for the night. Chang nodded to the gatekeepers and strolled past. Number 87 was locked. Chang pressed his face to a gap near the gatepost – inside lay an open sandy yard, piled with barrels and bricks and sand. The windows of the shack beyond were dark.

His appearance alone would have caught the attention of the men at the gate, and Chang expected that they were watching him closely. He knew his key would not fit the lock. In a sudden movement Chang braced one foot on the lock and vaulted his body to the top of the fence and then over it. He landed in a crouch and bolted for the door – the guards at the gate would already be running.

The door was locked, but two kicks sheared it wide. Chang swore at the darkness and pulled off his glasses: a smithy – anvils and hammers, a trough and iron tongs – but no occupant. The next room had been fitted with a sky-light to ventilate the heat and stink of molten glass. Long bars of hard, raw glass had been piled across a workbench, ready to be moulded into shape. The furnace bricks were cold.

No sign yet of the guards. Past the furnace was another open yard, chairs and a table cluttered with bottles and cups. In the mud beneath lay a scatter-ing of half-smoked cigarettes, like the shell casings knocked from a revolver. The cigarette butts had been crimped by a holder. Behind another chair lay a ball of waxed paper. Chang pulled it apart to reveal a greasy stain in the centre. He put it to his nose and touched the paper with his tongue. Marzipan.

Across the yard lurked a larger kiln. Inside lay a cracked clay tablet: a mould, the indented shapes now empty, used with extreme heat to temper glass or metal. Each indentation had been for a different-shaped key.

From the front came voices and the rattling of the gate. To either side of the kiln stood a fence separating the glassworks from its neighbours. From the right came the scuttle of poultry. Chang picked up a brick and heaved it over. The crash sparked an cacophony of squawking. He then vaulted the opposite fence, away from his diversion, landing on a pile of grain sacks. At once he continued to the next fence, vaulting it and then three more in turn, meeting only one dog – a speckled hound as surprised by Chang's arrival as he by it – and no human bold enough to interfere. The final leap set him on a stack of wooden crates stuffed with straw. Whether they held exotic fruit, blocks of ice or Dresden figurines, he never knew. He straightened his spectacles and walked without hurry past a family sitting to supper, out the front, and away from the curious crowd converging on the disturbance four doors down.

He did not doubt Pfaff had been there. Was that why it had been abandoned? The crimped cigarettes conjured up the Contessa di Lacquer-Sforza. Was the marzipan a treat to buy Francesca Trapping's good behaviour? Chang was late to meet the others, but even if he'd two more hours to search it hardly mattered – the trail was dead.

He hurried north, slowed by streets crowded not only with the disaffected but also with all sorts of respectable men and women, wreathed in the grim determination of travellers at a railway station. Chang pushed on with an unpleasant foreboding. The crowd's destination was his own.

When he finally reached St Isobel's, Chang had to crane his head to see the saint's statue. Screeching street children dashed across his path, as high-spirited as feral dogs. The crowd around him recoiled – first from the children and then more earnestly from the black coach cracking forward in their wake. The driver lashed his team, threatening the whip to anyone in his way. The coach windows were drawn, but, as it swept by, a curtain's twitch gave a glimpse of the white-powdered wig of a servant. Once the coach was past and the whip out of range, resentment swelled into curses hurled at the driver's receding head. Chang wormed towards the statue, his patience frayed by the press of bodies.

He realized that he was squinting, despite the hour, and looked up. The sky was aglow with torchlight from the rooftops of the Ministries lining the far side of the square. Was there an occasion he had forgotten? A gala for the Queen? The birthday of some inbred relation – perhaps the exact idiot inside the black coach?

'Cardinal Chang!'

Phelps waved his arms above the crush. Cunsher and Svenson stood near with Miss Temple dwarfed between them.

'At last!' called Phelps. 'We had despaired of finding you!'

Chang pushed himself through to meet them. 'What in hell is happening?'

'An announcement from the Palace,' Svenson replied. 'Did you not hear?'

Before Chang could reply that if he had heard he would not have *asked*, Miss Temple touched Chang's arm.

'It is Robert Vandaariff!' she said excitedly. 'He has emerged, and will call on the Queen and Privy Council! Everyone looks to him for rescue! Have you ever seen such a gathering?'

'We have waitied for you,' Phelps yelled above the noise, ' but our thought is to move closer and observe.'

'Perhaps even brave a rear entrance to the Ministries,' added Svenson.

Chang nodded. 'If he meets the Queen, there will be a regiment around them – but, yes, let us try.'

They edged around the great statue, the martyr scoldingly content in her sacrifice. Chang tugged Svenson's sleeve and gestured to Miss Temple, who had taken the Doctor's other hand. Svenson nodded. 'The fabric *was* gone, and all purchased by a single customer.'

'Who?'

'Not who so much as *where*.' Svenson pointed to the row of tall white buildings. 'Sent to the Palace.'

'The *Queen*?'

'Or someone well placed at court.'

'That could be one of five hundred souls.'

'Still, it fits with where we thought the Contessa might be hiding.'

Chang glanced at Miss Temple. 'You were right after all, Celeste.'

'I was indeed.'

It was not a remark Chang had any desire to answer, so he called to Cunsher. 'Did Pfaff leave word at the Boniface?'

Cunsher shook his head.

'The Contessa?'

Cunsher shook his head again.

'Anything?'

'The maid is frightened.'

Before Chang could ask Phelps about the *Herald* clipping, the air was split by the bray of trumpets. Horsemen in bright cuirasses had formed a line between the crowd and the Ministries and pushed forward to clear a lane. Every third horseman had a brass trumpet to his lips, while the men in between rested drawn sabres against one shoulder. The crowd gave way.

Chang searched for some other avenue. He saw the black coach again, in the thick of the crowd, and a figure – only half seen – slipping from it. At once the driver whipped his team into motion. But who had been left behind?

'What is it?' Phelps went to his toes, following Chang's gaze. 'Do you see Vandaariff?'

The trumpets came again and Svenson touched Chang's shoulder. Behind the horsemen came a train of coaches, skirting the square. In an open brougham sat Robert Vandaariff, hatless, waving to the sea of staring faces. Lord Axewith of the Privy Council sat opposite. They swept through the ceremonial iron gate that marked the Palace proper.

'Mr Ropp!'

Miss Temple pointed across the crowd. It took a moment for Chang to place the man she meant – barrel-chested in a black greatcoat. She shouted again, her words lost in the trumpets and the noise. Ropp was Pfaff's man, a former soldier. Had he escaped from Harschmort? Miss Temple pushed towards him. The Doctor tried to catch her hand. Ropp vanished in the shifting crowd, then reappeared. Something was wrong. Ropp walked stiffly, as if his torso were made of steel. Had he been stabbed? Miss Temple hopped up and down, waving. Ropp finally turned to her squeaks. Even at thirty yards Chang was shocked by the man's dull eyes. Ropp tottered and thrust a hand into his topcoat, as if he were clutching a wound.

Chang's mind cleared. The white-wigged figure in the coach had been Foison. The barrels at the Raaxfall dock. The boxed carapace of Ropp's body.

'*For God's sake – get down!*'

Chang tackled Miss Temple, doing his best to cover her body. His ears were split by a deafening roar as a blast of smoke and fire consumed the air. An inhuman high-pitched shrieking, dense as a cloud of arrows, whipped at the crowd, which answered with a chorus of blood-curdling screams. Chang raised his head, glasses askew, ears throbbing. All around them bodies were flattened, pulped, writhing – a perfectly scythed circle of destruction. Where Ropp had stood was a scorched and smoking hole. A grey-haired woman thrashed beside Chang, mouth flecked with foam, a blue glass spur embedded in her eye. As he stared, the white orb filled with indigo and the woman's screams turned from shrill agony to blind wrath.

# THREE

## PALACE

Doctor Svenson's mind was elsewhere. After years of bleak service to the Duchy of Macklenburg, he had glimpsed in Elöise Dujong another possibility – had felt his heart crack into life – only to have that hope laid bare as the groundless optimism of a fool. He blamed no one save himself, mourning Elöise yet allowing no claim to her memory, for he had shamed himself enough as it was. Instead, still haunted and, if he could admit it, stunned, Svenson had thrown himself back into service as soon as his health allowed – assisting Phelps and Cunsher. Now he had been reunited with the quite obviously disturbed Celeste Temple, and the wilfully grim Cardinal Chang, but the company of these comrades reminded him only of what he'd lost. As he stood with his back to the cold stone of St Isobel's statue, he wondered how much of his life had passed without purpose, every abdication punctuated with a crisp bow and a click of his heels?

The Doctor exhaled sharply and shook his head. He had his own discipline, and his own pale fire.

The action saved his life. Svenson heard Chang's warning and at once dropped to the ground, the hail of glass shards screaming past his head.

He staggered up, ears ringing. Next to Chang lay an old woman, one of hundreds brought down. Though never in an outright battle, Svenson had witnessed accidents involving artillery ordnance and seen his share of shredded human beings. St Isobel's Square had been thronged. Svenson stared at the scorched black spot where the bomb had detonated.

All around him, victims struggled with an unholy energy – howling and lashing at whomever they could reach, flailing like horses in a coach collision – unable to rise, unable to comprehend their condition. Chang rolled off Miss Temple, who seemed unharmed. Behind him, Phelps and Cunsher, both alive, wrestled with a man in a blood-spattered waistcoat. The man roared, and, as he twisted the dark stains on his waistcoat cracked and broke apart – the blood from his wounds had congealed into glass. Without a qualm Chang delivered a solid kick to the man's jaw, freeing Phelps and Cunsher. The Doctor read Chang's lips as much as heard his words.

'There is nothing here! Hurry!'

The cavalry sounded their trumpets, at last moving to restore order, and with a dreadful prescience Svenson saw what would happen. He shouted, stumbling in the opposite direction, hauling Miss Temple with him.

'This way! We cannot be caught between!' Chang spun, his expression shot with impatience. Svenson pointed to the advancing horsemen, his own voice strangely far away. 'The glass! The anger!'

The first cobblestone flew from the crowd – hurled by a tottering, blood-swept man – knocking the horsetailed helmet from a rider. A woman, blue-faced and screaming, charged blindly into the advancing line. A trooper reined in his horse, and the animal reared. Any sane person would have fallen back, but these two rushed on, the man catching a hoof in the chest that knocked him flat. The woman cannoned into the horse, scratching with her nails, even biting, until the soldier struck her down with the guard of his sabre. But by then dozens more had attacked the horsemen. The trumpets sounded again, to no effect.

Chang wheeled round and they forced a path away. Behind erupted more screams, shouting, trumpets. A wave of madness had overtaken the entire square. Phelps called to Chang, 'If you had not shouted when you did –'

'We must keep on,' Chang broke in. 'If we can reach the river –'

'Wait,' said Svenson. The ringing would not leave his ears. 'Is this not the opportunity we desired?' He looked to the white buildings of the Ministries and the Palace beyond. 'In this chaos, might we not find an entry – find Vandaariff?'

Chang turned to Phelps. 'Do you know a way?'

Phelps nodded. 'I did not spend my life in that beehive without learning *something* –'

His words were cut off by the crash of gunshots.

'Jesus Lord!' cried Phelps. 'Do they fire on their own people?'

The mob roared in echo of his outrage. The soldiers' reprisals had only provoked the rest of the crowd to action. This would be an out-and-out riot.

Without another word Phelps drove for the Ministries, Cunsher at his heels. Doctor Svenson took Miss Temple's hand, only to notice that Chang had taken her other.

'It was Foison in the coach,' Chang called over the noise. 'They made Ropp into their weapon.'

'But how?' Miss Temple's cheeks were wet with tears. 'What did they *do* to him?'

'The Process!' Svenson shouted. 'Overturning a man's mind is the Comte's first principle.' He flinched at the crash of an ordered volley. The crowd ahead of them roiled and then split before a squadron of black-jacketed lancers, each man's high czapka sporting a single red plume.

'Behind!' yelled Phelps. 'Cross behind!'

The horsemen clattered past – lances menacingly low – and the way was momentarily clear. Phelps dashed forward and they followed at a run. With a shock Svenson saw an entire column of infantry advancing behind the lancers.

'Are they planning to kill *everyone*?' Chang yelled across Miss Temple's head.

Svenson had no reply. Only moments ago a single line of cavalry had seemed an ample expression of force.

A line of constables blocked their final passage to the Ministries. Phelps shouldered his way to the front.

'*Officer!*'

A constable with frightened wide eyes spun to face him, but Phelps retained an official bearing that won the man's attention.

'Why are only you officers posted here? Does no one realize the danger?' Phelps's voice sharpened. 'I am Mr Phelps, attaché to the Privy Council. What provisions have been made for securing the *underpassage*?'

'Underpassage?'

Phelps pointed past to the maze of white buildings. 'To Stäelmaere

House! Through it one can access both the Ministries *and* the Palace. How many men have you posted?'

The constable gaped at Phelps's extended, damning finger. 'Why . . . no men at all.'

'O Lord *above*, man! There is no time!'

Phelps burst through the line of policemen. The constable darted after. 'Wait now, sir – you can't – all these people – you cannot –'

'They are with me!' snapped Phelps. 'And no one will bar my passage until I am personally assured of the Queen's safety!'

'The Queen?'

'Of course the Queen!' Phelps directed the constable's attention to Mr Cunsher. 'This man is a foreign agent in our service. He has information of a plot – a plot employing significant *distraction*, do you understand?'

The constable, for whom Svenson was by now feeling a certain pity, looked helplessly to the square, echoing with screams and gunfire.

'*Exactly*,' said Phelps. 'I only pray we are not too late.'


The constable gamely followed to a cobbled lane descending below Stäelmaere House.

'Down there?' he asked, dismayed by the darkness.

Phelps shouted into the cavern, 'You there! Sentries! Come up!' No soldiers appeared and Phelps snorted with bitter satisfaction. 'It is the grossest oversight.'

'I'll run to the guardhouse –' offered the constable.

Chang caught the constable's arm. 'If the attack has already begun, we will need every man.'

He pulled the constable with them, tightening his grip as the man's countenance betrayed his doubts. They descended to a dank vaulted chamber. Phelps hurried to a heavy wooden door and pulled the knob. It was locked.

'Safe after all,' ventured the constable. 'So . . . all is well?'

Doctor Svenson spoke gently. 'You need not worry. We wish your Queen only long life.' The constable's expression sank further. 'Restored health.' Svenson's words ran dry. 'Dentistry.'

*

Phelps peered at the door's lock while Cunsher and Chang combined to secure the constable: wrists and ankles tied and mouth stuffed with a handkerchief.

'Dentistry?' asked Miss Temple.

Svenson sighed. 'I had the privilege of the royal presence, when the Prince was first received.'

'I suppose one would not see it on the coins.'

'A rotting dockfront hardly inspires monetary confidence.'

'Surely there is carved ivory or porcelain.'

'The monarch lays her trust in the Lord's handiwork,' replied the Doctor.

'One enjoys all manner of advancements not strictly from the Lord.'

'Apparently matters of the body have their own strictures.'

'Surely she styles her hair, and uses soap.'

Svenson tactfully said nothing.

'Royalty are in-bred dogs,' said Chang, joining them, 'yapping, brainless, and fouling any place they can bring their haunches to bear. What is he doing?'

This last was directed at Mr Phelps, but Chang did not wait for an answer, crossing to Phelps and repeating his question directly.

Miss Temple whispered to Svenson, 'It is a pneumatic vestibule.'

'A what?'

'A room that moves up and down. I travelled in it with Mrs Marchmoor and the Duke, and with Mr Phelps.'

'Do you accept his repentance?' asked Svenson quietly.

'I accept his guilt. One does not care why a cart-horse pulls.'

'Chang fears Phelps will betray us. Did you not mark their discussion in the blast tunnel?'

'What discussion?' asked Miss Temple, a bit too loudly.

They turned at the sound of Mr Cunsher clearing his throat. Miss Temple took interruption as censure, and addressed Cunsher directly: 'It is easy to repent when one has *lost*.'

Cunsher studied her face, which Miss Temple bore for perhaps three seconds before returning the stare doubly hard.

'Any luck with the door?' called Doctor Svenson.

'The problem,' Mr Phelps replied, 'is that there is no *lock*.' He nodded at a metal key plate. 'To summon the car, one inserts the key, at which point the vestibule car descends. Only when the car is in place will the door open. Even had we an axe, we could only reach the empty shaftway.'

'Then why did you bring us here?' snarled Chang.

'Because the way is unguarded. The hallways of Stäelmaere House connect to the Palace on one side and to the Ministries on the other. *This* was the private exit for the Duke himself – only his most intimate servants and aides know of it. Once inside we can search for the Comte – for Vandaariff – in any direction.'

'Is there no signal?' asked Miss Temple. 'Some sort of bell?'

'Of course,' huffed Phelps, 'the use of which will alert those inside. We will be taken and killed!'

'Perhaps I do not understand,' Svenson offered. Phelps had so deftly managed the cordon, it was dismaying to see him at such an impasse. 'If we *do* ring the bell –'

'Whoever hears it may well send the car down. But ringing the bell after the Duke's death will spark all kinds of suspicion. The car will rise to a reception of armed men.'

'And that is because we lack a key.'

'Yes. Without a key, it will only return to whoever sent it down. It is a protection against any stranger using it. *With* a key, we could go to any floor without pause –'

'But that could still deliver us to armed men,' said Chang. 'You have no idea.'

'I descended from the Duke's rooms to this sub-basement without stopping,' announced Miss Temple rather unhelpfully.

'We should press on to the river,' muttered Chang.

'I disagree,' replied Svenson. 'The idea to infiltrate is sound, a chink in our opponent's armour.'

'Entering a lion's den does not constitute a *chink*.'

'Then *I* will go,' the Doctor snapped. 'I will go by myself.'

Miss Temple took his arm. 'You will not.'

Chang sighed with impatience. 'Lord above –'

Phelps raised his hands. 'No. I have brought us here – no one else need take the risk. Stand away.'

He pressed a disc set into the keyplate. Somewhere above them echoed a distant trill.

They waited, the sole sound the muffled breath of the constable, which they all chose to ignore. But then came a mechanical *thrum* . . . growing louder.

'Well begun at least,' Phelps said with a brittle smile. '*Someone* is home.'

His relief was cut short by the click of Cunsher pulling back the hammer of his pistol. Svenson dug out his own and soon they all stood in a half-circle, weapons ready. The car descended, settling with a *clank*.

The door opened wide. Beyond an iron grating, the vestibule car was empty. Phelps shoved the grate aside and stepped in.

'I will go where it takes me, and if all is safe return to collect you.'

Chang shook his head. 'All of us together may be able to overcome resistance – if you are taken alone, it will expose everyone.'

'And there is no time,' added Svenson. 'Vandaariff is in the Palace *now*.'

Svenson entered the car and turned, averting his gaze from the figure of the trussed, wriggling constable. Overruled, Phelps slammed the iron gate home and the car rumbled into life. Cunsher took Chang's arm, looking up. 'Count the floors . . .'

They waited, listening. Cunsher nodded at a particularly loud *clank*.

'Do you hear? We have passed the cellars.'

Svenson gripped his revolver. Another *clank*.

'The ground floor,' whispered Phelps. 'Which offers passage to the Ministries.'

'We're still climbing,' said Cunsher. They waited. The cables above them groaned. Another *clank*.

'The first floor.' Phelps nodded to Miss Temple. 'The Duke's chambers.' Another loud *clank*. 'We will reach the second, with passage to the Palace. Of course the corridor leads not to the Palace *proper* – first to suites of older apartments, where no royal has lived these fifty years – but technically speaking –'

'Who will *be* there?' hissed Chang.

'I have told you!' replied Phelps. 'Absolutely anyone!'

The vestibule came to a shuddering halt. The iron gate slid into the wall and a wooden door was before them. Its lock snapped clear. Before the door could be opened from the other side Chang kicked it wide. An elderly man in black livery took the door across his chest and sprawled on the carpet. In a second Chang was above him like a ghoul, his razor against the servant's throat.

'Do not! Do not!' Phelps spoke quickly to the stunned old man. 'Do not cry out – it is your life!'

The servant merely gaped, his webbed old mouth working. 'Mr Phelps . . . you were pronounced a traitor.'

'Nonsense,' said Phelps. 'The Duke is dead and the Queen in danger. The *Queen*, I say, and there is little time . . .'


Svenson inhaled, tasting the dank air of a sickroom. Stäelmaere House had been the glass woman's lair, staining all who came there with decay. The Duke's old serving man showed dark circled eyes, pasty flesh, livid gums – and this after weeks of recovery. Phelps interrogated the servant. Svenson walked to a curtained window at the corridor's end.

'Where are you going?' called Chang.

Svenson did not reply. The corridor was lined with portraits, intolerant beaks above a progression of steadily weaker chins, watery eyes peering out between ridiculous wigs and lace collars as stiff and wide as serving platters – an archive of the Duke's relations, whose exile to the upper floor reflected the degree to which they'd been forgotten. Was there a plainer emblem of mortal doom than the extravagant portrait of an unremembered peer?

The Ministry of War blocked his view of St Isobel's Square, but beyond its slate rooftops echoed regular spatters of musketry. That gunfire continued after the lancers and the column of infantry only confirmed the extent of the uprising, and the savagery employed to put it down.

To his left was a small wooden door. Svenson put an ear against it. Miss Temple motioned to return. Instead, the Doctor carefully turned the knob and eased the door open: a bare landing with a staircase leading down and, unexpectedly, continuing up. Was there a higher floor Phelps had not mentioned? He walked back to the others.

'What did you see?' asked Miss Temple.

'Nothing at all,' he said. 'There is more gunfire in the square.'

'Even better for a distraction,' said Chang, stepping behind Svenson and Miss Temple and herding them along. Chang leant close to Svenson's ear. 'What *did* you see?'

Svenson shook his head. 'Nothing – truly –'

'Then what is *wrong* with you?'

By then they had reached Phelps, who laid a hand on the door behind him and spoke in a nervous rush. 'Stäelmaere House is all but abandoned, under quarantine. The lower floors are a sick ward. The Privy Council has shifted to the Palace, and Axewith and Vandaariff will meet in the Marble Gallery, only a minute's walk from the Queen herself. Axewith must be desperate, practically begging Vandaariff for the money to solve the crisis –'

'But is money the issue?' asked Miss Temple.

'No, which Axewith does not understand. Without sound strategy, Vandaariff's entire treasure is but a bandage on an unstitched wound. The crisis will continue, and Vandaariff has to know it.'

'Then why appear?' asked Chang. 'Why associate himself with Axewith's failure?'

'Perhaps he only seeks an excuse to enter the Palace,' said Cunsher.

At this Phelps opened the door and hurried them through. 'We are now in the Palace. We will *quietly* descend and proceed east – east, I repeat – until the décor changes first to lemon, and then to a *darker* yellow, like the yolk of a freshly poached egg. It is a question of concentric *layers* – ah . . . here is the balcony.'

Svenson forced a yawn in hopes it might end the nagging whine in his ears. He looked at the faded and splitting blue wallpaper. Why had this wing of the Palace been allowed to go to seed? When had its last royal resident died – and was its lack of care an expression of poverty or grief? Svenson found the squalor a comfort.

Phelps started down the staircase and Svenson followed, last in line, the revolver heavy in his hand. His eyes darted along the opposite balconies, recalling a mission to Vienna long ago, a search for documents that had brought him to an abandoned brothel . . . bedsheets spread across a barrel-head, upon which a consumptive whore played cards with a one-legged pensioner –

Phelps hissed from the foot of the stairs and pointed to a heavy door. 'Remember the walls: blue, then lemon –'

'Then a poultry yard, yes,' Chang sighed. 'We have grasped the sequence.'

'It is a precaution if we become separated.'

'We will only become separated if we are seen – and in that case we all know enough to run for our lives.'

It was an ill-timed remark, for as the sour words left the Cardinal's mouth Mr Phelps opened the door. Directly before them stood a detachment of the Palace guard in helmets, doublets and hose – holding *halberds* of all things – and a group of men in black topcoats. One of these, with pale hair and a waxed moustache, yelped in shock, staring at Phelps.

'You!'

'Harcourt!' cried Phelps, but Cunsher lunged at the door and slammed it closed. The door leapt in his hands as the soldiers pushed from the opposite side.

'Run!' shouted Chang, seizing Miss Temple's arm. '*Run!*'

The door was flung wide and an axelike blade shot through, nearly sever-ing Cunsher's arm. The others fled, but Svenson raised the revolver with an unfamiliar coolness and fired into the mass of men. The two in front sprawled, but a guard behind came on, his long weapon aimed at Svenson's chest. A third bullet and this man toppled into the guards behind him.

The fire drew their pursuers, and Svenson retreated up the stairs, hop-ping like a hare as a halberd stabbed through the railing. He fired again, splintering the rail, and scrambled upwards. His companions had vanished. His boot slipped on the carpet. The last of the halberdsmen charged up the staircase. Svenson deliberately squeezed the trigger. The man flew back in a windmill of limbs. No one took his place.

At the top of the staircase Svenson dropped into cover, just ahead of a hail of bullets tearing at the wall – halberds finally succeeded by modern weaponry. Svenson charged back to Stäelmaere House, racing for the pneu-matic vestibule.

It had been called to another floor. He pelted down the corridor to the little door by the window. To go down would only deliver him to his enemies. Svenson took the staircase leading up. The door was unlocked. He tumbled through, shut it behind him and – blessedly – found a key sticking out of the hole. He turned it, heard the sweet sound of a bolt going home and let out a deep, heaving sigh of relief.

His coolness of mind was gone. Svenson's fingers were shaking. He looked down the attic hall, its angled ceiling echoing the rooftop. Twenty yards away, in a flaming silk dress, stood the Contessa di Lacquer-Sforza.

At once the Doctor raised the revolver, aiming for her heart. The hammer snapped on an empty chamber. He squeezed again – nothing. The Contessa stumbled back, lifting her dress with both hands. A rush of hatred enflamed the Doctor's body and he ran at her, already tasting the satisfaction of crack-ing the pistol-butt upon her head.

She ran but he was faster, seizing a fistful of her dress. He pulled hard and she spun towards him, eyes blazing, swinging a small, jewel-encrusted hand-bag. Svenson swore at the stinging impact and launched a roundhouse blow with the pistol-butt that struck her shoulder. The Contessa overbalanced on her heels and fell. Doctor Svenson stood over her, ignoring the blood on his face, and snapped open the cylinder of the revolver. With a flick of his wrist he dumped the spent shells onto the carpet and groped in his pocket for more.

The Contessa dug in her handbag and pulled out a fist wrapped with an iron band from which protruded a vicious sharp steel spike. Svenson retreated two quick steps and slotted another cartridge into place. She strug-gled to her feet, weighing whether to attack him or to flee. He did not care – he would quite happily shoot her in the back. He slammed the cylin-der home, having loaded three shells – more than enough – and extended the weapon.

'If you kill me now you are a fool, Abelard Svenson.' She spoke quickly but without desperation, a statement of fact. 'Without my knowledge you will fail.'

Behind them, the staircase door flew open and two uniformed guards tumbled into the corridor. Svenson spun round and fired twice, the shots roaring in the cramped confines. The Contessa bolted and he dashed after her. At the end of the corridor stood a narrow door. Svenson fired his last bullet and the panel near her head split wide. She slammed it shut but before she could turn the lock he crashed through. She slashed at his throat but the blow went wide. Svenson tackled her to the floor.

'You idiot!' she snarled. 'You *idiot*!' She kicked with both legs, but her dress had caught them up. He dropped the revolver and pinned the spike-hand down. Her other clawed at his face – more scratches, more blood – but he caught that too and slammed it to the carpet. He lay atop her, both of them panting, inches away from one another.

With a shock his gaze found her pale throat, strung with garnets, and then her bosom, heaving with exertion. He lay between her legs. His groin pressed to hers. He met her gaze and swallowed, stupefied.

'The door! The *door*!'

She stabbed her mouth at his nose, teeth flashing, and nearly snapped it off. Svenson rolled back with a cry and the Contessa flew to her knees. But instead of running she leapt for the door and turned the bolt. Had the guards followed? Had he shot them? He did not even care. He fumbled for the pistol. The Contessa faced him with malice and disdain, hair in disarray, breathing hard. The knob was worked roughly from the other side.

She brushed past, but his weakness had broken the spell of hate and he did not attempt to bring her down. Svenson stumbled after the woman he was sworn to kill.

The Contessa obviously knew the Palace. Within seconds, her twisting path had shaken their pursuers. Svenson kept close but never within range of her spike. At last, with an angry snort, she dropped the pretence of ambushing him, and, with this tacit suspension of hostility, they moved still more swiftly. Her movements remained sure – he remembered the woman navigating the forest of Parchfeldt with the same wolf's confidence – and he held himself ready for when she must finally turn and attack. But the Contessa pressed on, glancing only to make certain he followed.

The apartments they passed through were unused, the tattered blue wallpaper familiar from before. Soon they trespassed into occupied (and lemon-papered) rooms, picking past the detritus of the court's poorest relations. More than anything, Doctor Svenson noticed the papers – bundles of correspondence testament to the endless pleading for place and favour that made up life at court. How many days had Svenson stood at the side of Baron von Hoern, as the great man dismissed such petitions as if he brushed tobacco ash off his sleeve.

Had the others been taken? Though Doctor Svenson so often found reason to question his own courage – altitude, women, an especially haughty clerk – he knew his quick work with the pistol had saved their lives. Still, he felt no satisfaction. Other men might perform marvels, but if Svenson possessed a talent, its employment carried no mystery, and was no matter for praise. Stopping the soldiers had been his task, and was scarcely more than a postponement, after all.

They reached an apartment whose wallpaper in the gloomy gaslight suggested a more bilious discharge than Phelps's sunny yolk. Here the Contessa – finally, decisively – turned to face him. He closed the door they had come through. She indicated an empty chair.

Instead of sitting, Doctor Svenson reached into his pocket for more shells and began to reload. The Contessa watched him carefully, then opened her jewelled purse and dropped the spike inside. She snapped the purse shut, ignoring the clicking work of his fingers, and crossed to a small sideboard cluttered with bottles. She pulled the cork from one and poured ruby port into a glass. Svenson closed the recharged cylinder. The Contessa sipped her port.

'You'd have a score of men upon you before my body strikes the floor. We are well inside the Palace.'

'Just above the Marble Gallery, I should guess.'

'Honestly, Doctor, you have pursued me this distance –'

Svenson extended the pistol. 'To hear you *talk*. Do so, madam, or be damned.'

Why did he not pull the trigger? This woman had murdered Elöise.

He watched her breathe. Her complexion had reclaimed its lustre, her violet eyes were as sharp as ever, and yet . . . he thought of his own weeks of healing . . . had the Contessa changed since the disaster at Parchfeldt? He knew her body bore new scars – a wound on her shoulder, another at her thigh. However, just as her wit and grace complemented rather than contradicted a savage heart, Svenson saw her beauty enhanced by these injuries – and wondered at the emotional wounds that had come with each, that lingered within . . .

His eyes dropped to her bosom. He hurriedly raised his gaze, only to meet a contemptuous flip of a smile.

'You are not *all* grief, then.'

Svenson felt his face redden. He shifted the pistol to his left hand and reached for his silver case. 'Whose apartment is this?'

'As long as we are quiet, we will be safe.'

He returned the pistol to his right and aimed it at her heart.

'You will *answer* me, madam.'

'My goodness. Well – we *are* above the Marble Gallery, as you said, in the rooms of Sophia, Princess of Strackenz. Do you know her?'

'Not personally.'

'No? One assumes the German aristocracy to be its own small-minded village, fed by petty rivalry, drunken duels and spouse-breach. Your late master, Karl-Horst von Maasmärck, was especially keen on the latter, with whoever he could entice for two minutes into a closet.'

'Sophia of Strackenz has been exiled these many years.'

'Poor thing. Now that I think of it, arranging for your prince to encounter Sophia would have made for an exquisite wager – he had no end of reckless appetite, and she is an outright hag. Would you be so very kind, while we are waiting?'

He had set a cigarette between his lips. She snapped open her jewelled bag and removed a black lacquered holder. He extended the silver case and the Contessa made her selection, fitting the black-papered tube into the nib.

'You have resupplied yourself with your Russians.'

'You have managed a new dress.'

'Many, many of them – nothing says beggar like fine clothes twice-worn.' She lit her cigarette and exhaled. 'How strong these are.'

'Why Strackenz? She has no sway at court.' Svenson puffed his cigarette to light, then answered his own question. 'And that is the idea itself. Protection from the unloved Sophia provides sanctuary without exposure.' He studied the sparsely furnished room. 'And where are these many, many dresses? Does that explain your presence in the attic of Stäelmaere House – garment storage?'

She sneered through blown smoke. 'And what explains *your* presence? That Oskar comes to the Palace to save the nation? Did you hope to shoot him down?'

'It seemed worth the attempt.'

'*Peh.*'

'Is it coincidence to find you here too, just when Lord Vandaariff has arrived?'

Svenson had taken several steps as he spoke, and he realized she was watching him closely, as if he were near an open flame. He stepped decisively to the high-canopied bed.

'Doctor Svenson –'

Svenson extended the pistol and carefully flipped up the pillows. Underneath lurked a blue glass book, like a cobra at the bottom of a basket.

'Poor Sophia,' he said. 'Does she sink her mind in its depths every night – living glories she'd never know on her own? Does she even bother to eat and bathe?'

The Contessa laughed. 'She was fat to begin with, and never fond of a wash.'

'She will die.'

'Not while I need her.'

Doctor Svenson brought the pistol-butt down with a crack onto the book, starring the thick cover and punching a gritty hole in the centre.

'Hell's damnation!' snarled the Contessa.

Svenson struck the book again, cracking the cover into shards and splitting the layers below. The Contessa spat with fury.

'Doctor! The Princess is an empty-headed, greedy – she is despised – O the waste!'

A final blow broke the book to pieces, like the battered carcass of a horse-shoe crab. Svenson wiped the pistol on the bedlinen.

'You have no idea –'

'But I do – and besides, you have another.'

'I do not!'

'You have the volume tainted by the Comte's own mind. This isn't it – the Princess would be driven mad. This was a book of allurement, a honeyed trap filled with pleasures. With any luck it is the last. And, now we come to the topic, *you* do not look ill – which means you've found a way to consult the Comte's corrupted book without harm. Where is it?'

'Safely stowed.'

'Where is Francesca Trapping?' the Doctor demanded. 'In an attic room with your clothes racks?' He gestured to the shattered book. 'Is *she* enslaved? Have you flooded her mind with wickedness as well?'

'As *well*.' The Contessa laughed. 'As well as Celeste Temple? Tell me, does she tremble? Does she drool? Can you smell her like a barnyard mare?'

Svenson raised the pistol.

'Doctor, if you act the fool we will be taken. They search from room to room – they are not all idiots – we are only safe here a few minutes more.' She reached to what he realized was a second door, painted to appear flush with the wall. 'If I intended to betray you, Doctor, I would not have brought you *here*.' She put her head to the panel, listening. 'Indeed, it did occur to me, while you strove to take my life, that our meeting might well serve us both.'

'How?'

'What do *you* think Oskar will demand, for his money and guns?'

'Whatever it is,' said Svenson, 'Axewith will give it to him.'

'What Oskar wants, Lord Axewith does not have.'

She smiled, allowing Svenson to guess what things – or persons – she meant. From outside came the chime of a silver bell.

'Exactly on time.' The Contessa ground her cigarette on the tabletop. 'If you would just tuck the gun behind your back?'

*

She sailed into a lush corridor ablaze with light. Standing not ten yards away were three men in stiff black topcoats: a pair of Ministry officials and a grey-bearded figure with a blue sash.

'My dear Lord Pont-Joule, what a relief it is to see your face!' the Contessa cried. 'The rumours one hears are frightful! Is Her Majesty safe? Has there truly been violence?'

The blue-sashed lord bowed kindly, but his deep voice rumbled with disapproval. 'Who is the man behind you, madam? Sir – what uniform is that? Whom do you serve? How are you here? Is that *blood* on your face?'

'It is Abelard Svenson!' The Contessa's voice dropped to a whisper. 'Captain-Surgeon of the Macklenburg Navy. Surely you know him – he is a *fugitive!*'

Svenson whipped the pistol from behind his back. The Contessa gave a yelp and leapt to the side of Pont-Joule, who stammered angrily, even as the Ministry men – evidently unarmed – advanced towards the Doctor with earnest, awkward stances copied from boxing matches.

'Now, sir!' cried Pont-Joule. 'That will not do – you must surrender! You cannot escape! You will not harm the lady –'

His next words were lost in a gurgling choke, his stiff white collar dark with spurting blood. Pont-Joule's aides turned in time for the first to take the Contessa's spike into his throat. The second stood in shock, covering his mouth with one hand. The Contessa came for him, but before she could land her blow Svenson struck the man behind the ear. The man arched his back and fell. Without a pause the Contessa knelt down, hiked her dress out of the way and opened his throat with a stroke of her hand.

'Are you a savage?' cried Svenson. 'Dear God –'

'He has seen us both,' she answered flatly. A bead of red had caught her cheek. With a grimace of irritation the Contessa wiped it off with a fingertip, and then impatiently stuck the finger in her mouth. She stepped carefully past the spreading pools and called to Svenson, white-faced, rooted to the spot. 'Pont-Joule is the Queen's Master of Comportment.'

'Comportment?'

'Etiquette and safety – if we are past *him*, we are past the cordon of soldiers, who will now be posted at every exit. But *our* way should be clear – come.'

'Then we cannot escape?'

'O Doctor, for shame! When the cradle waits unguarded at our feet?'

Svenson hurried after her into what could only have been the Marble Gallery – a gaudily elegant chamber draped with crystal. Their footsteps echoed across the chequered parquet floor. They were alone.

'Is it not a lovely room?' the Contessa called, her voice echoing. She spun like a girl, arms outstretched, laughing. Svenson came doggedly after, glancing at the wide chair on a dais that must have once held the Queen. Two more were set near it for Axewith and Vandaariff. Tables were still laden for tea, with plates of thickly iced pink petits fours. The Contessa snatched one up, took a bite with a satisfied growl, then dropped the rest onto the floor, walking on.

In the sickroom of his heart, Doctor Svenson condemned these three new murders . . . but again found himself shrugging off the guilt. The Contessa paused at the double doors, her composed features studying his face. He could imagine how she had seized every chance to flirt with poor Pont-Joule over these past weeks, just to make possible so deft a slaughter. The wall panels framing the door were set with mirrors, but the man reflected there bore scant resemblance to the officer he had once been. This figure was unshaven and hollow-eyed. Even his hair seemed to signal with its lack of colour the weight of withering experience.

It had not been fear that kept him from shooting her in the bedchamber. He knew it was better for anyone who remained in the Doctor's affections that *he* had been the one to collide with the Contessa di Lacquer-Sforza. Phelps or Cunsher would have hesitated and been slain. Miss Temple and Chang would have shown no quarter, killed her or been killed in turn. But their principles were founded on hope, and his reflection showed a man cut free. Svenson admitted expediency. Alone amongst his comrades, he might sacrifice himself – might make such an alliance, murder innocents, sink to unanticipated depths – and so spare them all.

'What a stricken face,' observed the Contessa. 'I tell you we are on the verge of a most profitable collaboration –'

Svenson seized her wrist and pinned her spike-hand against the door. She stared at him, eyes questioning and fierce, but his face was calm – indeed he felt altogether absent from his own body as it moved. Her left fist was ready to swing the jewelled bag. He deliberately shoved the pistol into his belt.

He caressed the soft curve of her jaw. She did not move.

His hand slipped lower, trailing the soft pulse in her throat with a finger-tip, and then with a deliberate slowness slid his outspread palm over her bare collarbone, her bosom, and down her torso, feeling the silk and whalebone, until he reached her thin, cinched waist and the exaggerated sweep of her hips. Still the Contessa said nothing. Svenson sensed the span of her body between his fingers. He moved higher and squeezed again, feeling her ribs beneath the corset.

'There is blood on your face,' she murmured.

'A way of dressing for the occasion.'

He released her and stepped away, pulling the revolver from his belt. The Contessa's voice remained hushed.

'For a moment I feared you might try to kill me . . . and then I understood that you have every intention of doing so. You have changed, Abelard Svenson.'

'Is that so strange?'

'When any man changes there ought to be fireworks.'

'You still have every intention of killing *me*.'

The Contessa extended her left hand, the jewelled bag dangling, running her own fingers – pressing hard, her lips curling into a smile – the exact length of the scar from Tackham's sabre.

'I saw you, you know,' she whispered, 'bleeding on the ground, groaning like the damned . . . I saw you kill him. I thought you would die, just as I thought I had killed Chang. It is not often I underestimate *so* many people.'

'Nor the same people so many times.'

The pressure on his scar was repulsive, but arousing. She lifted her fingers. 'We overreach ourselves.' Her cheeks held a touch of red. 'Whatever your new *provocations*, there remains very much to do.'

At a pillared archway the Contessa raised her hand and they paused, peering into an ancient hall of high tapestries and cold stone walls. A row of tables ran down the centre of the room, arranged with bowls of floating white flowers.

Svenson craned his neck. 'This room seems old – and, judging by the medieval decorations, quite out of fashion and unused.'

'How do you account, then, for the flowers?'

'A floral *penchant* of the Queen?'

The Contessa laughed. 'No, because of the *drains* – the horrible drains! It is a wonder the entire royal household does not perish from disease. This chamber is particularly *fragrant* – but, while relining the pipes with copper would be an unthinkable expense, it is entirely acceptable to spend a colonel's salary every fortnight on fresh flowers.'

'Is this where the Privy Council meets, with Stäelmaere House under quarantine?'

The Contessa shook her head, enjoying her riddle. 'Axewith took the Regent's gatehouse. Because it boasts a *portcullis* – which tells you all you need to know about Lord Axewith. No, Doctor, there is no hope of getting anywhere near Oskar himself – he was always a coward, and he will have soldiers as thick around him as his old bearskin fur. I wonder if he'll get another one? The real Vandaariff would never wear such a thing, but I don't suppose anyone will care.'

'Then where *have* you brought me?'

She pulled Svenson back into hiding. 'We each have our talents, Doctor, and I have brought you where my own may shine. Observe.'

At the head of a cloud of men, all burdened with sheaves of paper, satchels, rolled documents, leather-bound ledgers, strode a thin young man with fair hair, the tips of his moustache waxed to a darker maple: Harcourt, the man they had collided with in the doorway. Svenson knew – from his days recuperating in Rawsbarthe's attic – that Harcourt was an obsequious fellow whose advancement had come from never questioning his superiors' commands, no matter how criminal. With so many riddled by sickness, Harcourt had vaulted to real power. Phelps had taken the news with dismay, but Svenson could see the burden did not weigh lightly on Harcourt's shoulders. The young man's face was haggard, and his voice – rapping out commands to the crowd that clustered behind him like a burlesque of some multi-limbed Hindu deity – reduced to the flat crack of a toad.

'The port master must receive these orders before the tide; requisitions to the mines must not be sent until *after* the morning's trading; these judges called to chambers as soon as the warrants are approved; *local* militias marshalled for property seizure. Disbursements set against the Treasury's reckoning as of *today*, we must draw down to demonstrate our need – Mr Harron, see to it!'

Harcourt swept on to the nest of tables. The Contessa pushed into Svenson as a determined portly figure – the dispatched Mr Harron, with a thick portfolio, each page dangling a ribbon weighted with a blot of wax – hurried by without stopping.

'Will you drink something, Mr Harcourt?' asked one aide, more concerned with an alluring ruby decanter than with property seizures.

'There are hours left in the day,' sniffed Harcourt. 'Send to the kitchens for strong tea. Where is the list from Lord Axewith?'

'It has not yet come, sir.'

'Vandaariff will dictate terms to us all.' Harcourt rubbed his eyes and exhaled. He took up a new stack of documents, at once thrusting a page at another aide. 'Make sure the commanders understand – there is to be no official record of casualties, nor any death benefits charged to the paymaster. They are to draw on Lord Axewith's fund. *Go.*'

The aide bustled out and the next – they were all of an age with Harcourt – stepped up with a ledger and a pen. Harcourt blinked at it, wearily. 'Just remind me?'

'Transport tariffs, sir – to widen the Orange Canal, from the new Parchfeldt spur down to the sea.'

'Ah.' Harcourt scribbled his name but kept the pen, his eyes hovering over the ledger. 'Parchfeldt.'

The young man took his master's hesitation for a chance to speak. 'Do you know how long the quarantine will go on, sir? In Stäelmaere House?'

'Am I in the College of Medicine?'

'Of course not, sir – but you served the Duke, were aide to Mr Phelps –'

'Attend to your canals, Mr Forsett!' Harcourt slapped the ledger shut, nearly upsetting the inkpot. 'What in God's name is keeping Pont-Joule? And where in blazes is that tea?'

But his last words were drained of wrath – indeed, were quite infused with stammering anticipation. The Contessa di Lacquer-Sforza had appeared before him, the red dress shimmering like a gemstone.

'Sweet Christ,' Harcourt croaked. 'To your errands – at once, off with you all!'

'What of your tea?' squeaked Forsett.

'Damn the tea! Drink it yourselves! I must meet with this lady alone!'

Harcourt's officials hurried out, clutching their papers as if fleeing a house fire. Harcourt's attention stayed fixed on the woman, and his lower lip trembled.

'M-my lady . . .'

'I told you I would return, Matthew. You look tired.' The Contessa stood opposite Harcourt, the bowl of white blossoms between them like a ceremonial offering.

'Not at all.' Harcourt's nonchalance was betrayed by the twitching of one eye. The Contessa set her jewelled bag onto the table and snapped it open, extracting a pair of silk gloves dyed to match her dress.

'Such service, to manage a nation at risk,' she said gently. 'Is it truly recognized? Does such sacrifice ever find reward?'

Harcourt swallowed. 'In the absence of other – experienced – Minister Crabbé – with the sickness that has pervaded –'

'That terrible woman . . .' The Contessa shook her head, her gloved fingers *clicking* as they sought inside her bag. 'Can you imagine if anything like her should appear again? Or a score of them at once?'

Harcourt stared at the gleaming blue rectangle the Contessa had extracted.

'This is for you, Matthew . . . for you alone.' She offered her hand across the perfumed bowl and smiled shyly. 'I trust you will not think the less of me.'

Harcourt shook his head, gulped and snatched the glass card. He raised it to his eyes, licking his lips like a hound. His pupils expanded to black balls and his jaw fell slack. Mr Harcourt did not move.

'Come out, Doctor. The fellow is so earnest, it would be a shame not to share his misfortune.'

Svenson felt like a pet who'd been whistled for. 'How long until his people return?'

'We have at least . . . O . . . three minutes?' The Contessa leafed through the papers in Harcourt's portfolio.

'That is no time at all!'

'More than enough . . .'

She pulled a sheet of parchment free, reading it quickly. Harcourt gasped − in pain or ecstasy − but his gaze did not shift. Svenson inched closer, curious as to what held Harcourt in thrall.

'Time, Doctor, *time* . . .'

'What are you hoping to find? You might have waited until he had the news of Vandaariff's demands −'

'I have told you, Doctor, that does not *matter*.'

The Contessa shoved the parchment at Svenson and went back to the portfolio. The page was a list of properties to be temporarily seized by the Crown: railway lines, shipping fleets, mines, refineries, banks, and then, ending the list, at least fifteen different glassworks.

'Glassworks?'

'*Curious*, isn't it?'

'That demand has to come from Vandaariff − it's all been planned in advance.'

The Contessa raised an eyebrow at his slow arrival and continued to sort through the mounds of paper. Harcourt gasped again.

'What is the memory on that card?' Svenson asked her.

'Nothing to concern you . . .'

'It must be extremely alluring.'

'That is the intention −'

'Because he does not wrench himself free. Thus you do not offer him information, but a sensual experience. As this is not your first meeting,

I presume each new card draws him deeper into enslavement. Do you have such a storehouse of them? I assumed they had been lost.'

The Contessa plucked two small pages from a portfolio, folded them to tight strips and slipped each into the bodice of her dress. 'Doctor, you will find a door behind that tapestry – the Turks besieging Vienna. Though if those are Turks I am a Scottish donkey, and if that is Vienna – well, not that it *matters*. The experience of one Florentine winehouse apparently equips a man to describe the world. Still, there is but one thing worse than an artist who has not travelled.'

'The artist who has?'

She laughed. Too aware of his pleasure at sparking her amusement, Svenson lifted the tapestry and found a wooden door. The Contessa plucked the glass card away. Harcourt jackknifed at the waist with a shuddering cry, both hands digging at his groin.

'Until we meet again, Matthew,' she cooed. Svenson ducked to escape Harcourt's eye, but need not have bothered. Harcourt had curled into a grunting, sobbing ball.

As soon as the Contessa closed the door, the light was gone. On instinct, Svenson edged away, to set himself beyond her spike.

'Where *are* you?' she whispered.

'Where are we going?'

'Stop running from me, you fool – there are steps!'

As she spoke, Svenson's right foot skidded into space. He nearly overbalanced, toppling into the darkness, but managed to claw a handhold on the uneven walls. Before he could recover he smelt her perfume, and felt her breath warm at his ear.

'You will break your neck – and we have not even made our bargain.'

'What bargain is that?'

'Go down – carefully, mind – and I will tell you.'

The steps were narrow and worn from a century of footfalls, and his boots slipped more than once. 'Where does this take us? Where in the Palace?'

He felt her whisper on his neck. 'Do you *know* the Palace?'

'Not at all.'

'Then it will be a surprise. Do you like surprises?'

'Not especially.'

'O Doctor – you waste the glory of the world.'

'I shall endeavour to bear it.'

The Contessa nipped Svenson's ear.

At the foot of the stairs his hand found another door, and her whisper reminded him to open it *slowly*. From behind another tapestry they entered a circular room with walls of stone.

'It is a tower,' said Svenson, his voice low with caution.

'Well observed.' The Contessa brushed past – Svenson flinched and brought up an arm – to the room's exit, an open arch that left him feeling nakedly vulnerable. She peered out. Far away were indefinable sounds – trundlings, calls – but nothing near. The Contessa turned and Svenson retreated several steps. She raised an eyebrow at the distance between them and smiled.

'It is the particular character of royal dwelling places to possess such oddities, because they are in a constant state of being rebuilt and then abandoned and then rebuilt again – what was once a castle must become a house, and then with fashion a *different* sort of house. Portions are devoured by fire, or cannon, or rotting time – doors are bricked over with haste, walls no longer connect, and – as you see – whole staircases misplaced without care. The myriad adulteries of a court hang upon such lore – such secrets are guarded, after all. But secret-keepers die and it *can* be possible to have such rooms as this . . . reliably to one's self.'

'Ah.'

'And in answer to your persistent questions. Twenty yards through that wall is the Greenway, and beyond it the river.'

She pointed to a wall upon which hung a wide mirror, the silver spotted with decay. Below the mirror was a divan draped with blankets so tattered as to predate living memory. Svenson sensed a sneeze just looking at them.

'Then we've come quite a distance.'

Further speech died in the Doctor's throat, and he licked his dry lips. There had been ample opportunity to end his life on the dark staircase. What did the Contessa di Lacquer-Sforza possibly *need* that he should still breathe? He nodded deferentially to the woman's bosom. 'You preserved two papers from Harcourt's portfolio.'

'I did indeed. Will you retrieve them?'

'I should prefer you did not mock me, madam.'

'We all *prefer*, Doctor, it does not signify.' She slid two slim fingers beneath her bodice, then drew them out with the papers pinched between. 'I will happily exchange a view of their contents for another cigarette.'

Svenson took the papers and handed the Contessa his case, making sure she was occupied before beginning to read. She exhaled a jet of smoke and then, rolling her eyes at his caution, crossed to the divan, swatted a dusty corner, and sat.

The first document brought a lump to Svenson's throat: a dispatch from the Foreign Ministry's attaché in Macklenburg describing the upheaval in the aftermath of the Crown Prince's death. Konrad, Bishop of Warnemünde – the ailing Duke's brother – was now the power behind the throne, filling vacant positions with his own appointees. Svenson sighed. Konrad had been the Cabal's hidden agent in Macklenburg, enabling their acquisition of lands rich in indigo clay. He refolded the letter with a heavy heart. Had the Cabal reached Macklenburg as intended, Konrad would have remained a strictly managed puppet. In the absence of his masters he had simply adopted their ambitions. Had their success in destroying the dirigible accomplished anything at all?

Svenson read the second document twice, then extended both pages to the Contessa. She nodded without interest to the divan next to her and he dropped them on it, stepping nearer. The second page was the Contessa's death warrant, signed by Matthew Harcourt.

'I thought he was your creature.'

'Serpent's teeth, Doctor – we all have felt them.'

'I am surprised you did not end his life.'

'You do not know what the glass has shown him.' She suddenly chuckled. 'And the perfection of his people returning to find him *thus* – it is a small compensation.'

'His career will be ruined?'

'His career is nothing to me – but his heart, his dreams? Those have been spoilt *forever*.'

Svenson collected his case and lit a smoke of his own. He nodded to the folded paper. 'What will you do?'

'That changes nothing. It has not gone out. And if it had – well, you are a fugitive yourself. If caught, your head will be pickled and sent back to Macklenburg in a cask, evidence of this government's friendship.'

'And what of you?'

'Being a woman, as befits an honourable nation, I will be treated far worse.'

She looked up at him, and then to the archway.

'What is it about an open door that so fires a body for mischief? As simply joyful as a sweet breeze or the embrace of hot water – do you not agree? About open doors, I mean, about their *spark*.'

The Contessa ground her cigarette into the divan and hooked a foot behind the Doctor's knee, pulling until he stood between her legs. She parted his greatcoat with both hands, eyes fixed somewhere near his belt buckle.

'That is an intrusive, large pistol in your belt. Do you mind?'

Before Svenson could reply she had eased the weapon from its place, sliding the long barrel clear, and dropped it atop her papers. He looked into the crease of her white breasts. Perfume rose from her hair. He ought to take hold of her soft neck and squeeze. This woman had killed Elöise. No greater good, no compromise could justify –

The Contessa laid one hand – still in its thin silk glove – flat upon the Doctor's groin, her palm conforming to the stiffening shape beneath. He gasped. She did not look up. Her other hand caressed the outside of his leg. He looked wildly about and saw the jewelled bag, pushed away, the spike inside. Her fingers closed about his length. She dragged along the fabric with her thumbnail. He quickly gripped her hand with his.

'You – *ah* – you mentioned a bargain . . .'

'I did . . . and you never answered me about open doors.'

'Your point seemed indisputable.'

'What a charming thing to say – I appreciate being indisputable . . . most ardently . . .'

She pulled away his hand, taking the cigarette from his fingers. She inhaled once, then flicked it into a corner. As she exhaled, the Contessa unbuckled the Doctor's belt with three sure, unhurried movements. Her fingers returned for a single delicious slow stroke, and then, with the same easy efficiency, set to unbuttoning his trouser-front. Unable to contain himself, Svenson reached down and gently sank his fingers under the Contessa's bodice and corset. For the first time she met his eyes. She smiled, warmly – to his shame the whole of his heart leapt – and shifted her posture to give his hand more room to grope. His fingers went deeper, until the tips curled beneath the curve of her breast, the edge of his hand dragging against the soft stud of her nipple. His other hand smoothed the hair from her eyes with a tenderness at odds with his desire.

With a two-handed wrench the Contessa peeled his trousers to his thighs and then with another ripped open his knitted woollen undersuit, bursting the buttons to his ribcage. She laughed at the flying buttons and then chuckled more deeply – with pleasure and, Svenson wanted to believe, appreciation – at the sight of his arousal. One gloved hand wrapped around his extended flesh, the grip of silk perfectly exquisite. The Contessa coyly bit her lip.

'True bargains are tricky things, Doctor . . . would you not agree?'

'They are the soul of civilized society.'

'Civilization?' Her hand resumed its measured stroke. 'We live in the same riot as old Rome and stinking Egypt . . . my goodness, there it is . . .' Her free hand reached to push aside his underclothes and expose the pink whorl of his scar. 'That you did not die is a miracle.' Her hand slid upwards, and, as she stretched, the Contessa's full mouth came closer to her stroking. 'But *bargains*, Doctor . . . between the likes of us, we have no need for such veneer.'

'What would you offer, then?'

The Contessa grinned at his dry tone. 'Well . . . I *could* give you what I gave Harcourt. The card is in my bag.' She smeared a bead of fluid across the sensitive plumskin with the flat of her thumb and the Doctor hissed with pleasure. 'The experience it holds is singularly transporting . . . if transport is what you want.'

'And if I decline?'

'Then perhaps I could give you the key to Oskar's grand strategy.'

'You know what he plans?'

'I have always known. He is complicated, but still a man.'

As a man well in her power Svenson let this pass. 'And in exchange I would do my best to stop him. Is that why I am alive?'

'O Doctor Svenson,' she cooed disapprovingly, 'we are alive for *pleasure* . . .'

Her head dipped and the Doctor gasped with anticipation of her tongue, but instead he felt only the cool tease of her blown breath. The Contessa rose and with both hands took his greatcoat's lapels and shoved him into her place on the divan. Bared and straining, trousers balled at the knees, with the pistol to one side and her jewelled bag to the other, he looked up at her. The Contessa gathered her dress – revealing her splendid, shapely, stockinged calves – and knelt astride him, her thighs upon his own, the mass of red silk covering his body near to the neck. His stiffness pulled against her petticoats. He gripped her waist.

'This means nothing to you,' he gasped.

'What a ridiculous thing to say.' Her voice was husky and low.

'I remain your enemy.'

'And I may kill you.' She nudged her hips forward, sliding herself along his length. 'Or make you my slave.'

'I would rather die.'

'As if the choice were yours.'

She drew her tongue over the gash below his eye. Svenson shifted his hips, seeking her with a blind nudge, but the Contessa edged away. His hands slid to her buttocks and pulled her closer, encountering another tangled layer of frustrating silk. The Contessa chuckled and raised her face. Too late he saw that she had reached into her bag. Before he could blink her gloved fingers had a blue glass card before his eyes, sticking Svenson as fast as an insect impaled on a board.

*

The Doctor's mind traversed the entire cycle of experience inside the card but without understanding. So immersive were the colours that he lost all sense of space, and so vivid the curving lines and modelled forms that their images vibrated inside his brain, as if they'd been accompanied by silent explosions of gunpowder. More confusing still was the disconnection between the chaotic tableau before him and the still position of his body – and the body of the person from whom the memory originally came, the mind from whom this card had been harvested.

But slowly the space around him cleared . . .

A brightly lit room . . . an enormous room, for the canvas it held was immense.

Another cycle swept by, his attention lost in the details of swirling paint. The back of his mind throbbed with warning. Was this Harcourt's card after all? But no, Harcourt's transfixion had been erotic, and such was not, despite the extreme arousal of only moments before, his present experience. No . . . the emotion here was fear, controlled through great force of will, a deep-rooted dread emanating from the vision before his eyes, and in the sickening realization that far too much of the painting – and thus the intentions of its maker – remained incomprehensible.

This fear was especially strange coming from the body of the Contessa, for the memory came from her mind. However much the painting set the senses ablaze, he could not deny an anxious, thrilling tremor at feeling her body as his own – the weight of her limbs, the lower pivot of gravity, the grip of her corset . . .

The Contessa had learnt to make glass cards herself, from consulting her book. No doubt Harcourt's card was also infused with some incident from her own life. Why had she sacrificed her own memories? Was her desperation so great as to warrant boring these holes into her own existence? Such questions the Doctor could only sketch in the backroom of his thoughts, as the greater part of his attention was devoured by the painted spectacle.

In form, the composition resembled a genealogical chart, centring around the joining of two massive families, each branching out from the wedded pair – parents, uncles, siblings, cousins, all punctuated by children and spouses. The figures stood without strict perspective, like a medieval illuminated manuscript, as if the painting were an archaic commemoration. Svenson felt his throat catch. A wedding.

This was the Comte's canvas, mentioned in the *Herald* . . . what had it been called? *The Chemickal Marriage* . . .

That this was the work of Oskar Veilandt brought the canvas into clearer focus. The obsessively detailed background, which he had taken to be mere decoration, became a weave of letters, numbers and symbols – the alchemical formulae the Comte employed throughout his other work. The figures themselves were as vivid as Veilandt's other paintings – cruelly rendered, faces twisted with need, hands groping for fervent satisfaction . . . but Svenson's gaze could not long alight on any single figure without his head beginning to spin. He knew this was the Contessa's experience, and that his path by definition followed hers.

Still, she had looked again and again, staring hard . . .

And then he knew: it was the paint; or, rather, that the Comte had inset slivers of blue glass within the paint; and sometimes more than slivers – whole tiles, like a mosaic, infused with vivid daubs of memory. The entire surface glittered with sensation, undulated like a heaving sea. The scope was astonishing. How many souls had been dredged to serve the artist's purpose? Who could consume the lacerating whole and retain their sanity? His mind swarmed with alchemical correspondences – did each figure represent a chemical element? A heavenly body? Were they angels? Demons? He saw letters from the Hebrew alphabet, and cards from a gypsy fortune-teller. He saw anatomy – organs, bones, glands, vessels. Again the cycle played through. He felt the Contessa's heroic determination to carve out this very record.

Eventually, Svenson was able to fix his gaze on the central couple, the 'chemickal marriage' itself. Both were innocent in appearance, but their voluptuous physicality betrayed a knowing hunger – there was no doubt of the union's carnal aspect. The Bride wore a dress as thin as a veil, every detail of her body plain. One foot was bare and touched an azure pool (from which Svenson flinched, for it swam with memories), while her other wore an orange slipper with an Arab's curled toe. One hand held a bouquet of glass flowers and the other, balanced on her open palm, a golden ring. Orange hair fell to her bare shoulders. The upper part of her face wore a half-mask upon which had been painted, without question, the exact features of the Contessa. The mouth below the mask smiled demurely, the teeth within bright blue.

The Groom wore an equally diaphanous robe – Svenson was reminded of the initiation garments of those undergoing the Process – his skin as jet black as the Bride's was pale. One foot was buried in the earth up to the ankle, while the other was wrapped in shining steel. In his right hand he held a curved silver blade and in his left a glowing red orb the size of a newborn's skull. His hair, as long as hers, was blue, and, like his mate, the upper portion of his face was masked – a blank mask of white feathers, save the eyes that shone through were bright ovals of glass. Svenson knew that each eye, perhaps more than anywhere else on the canvas, contained charged memories that might make sense of the whole. But the Contessa had not dared to look. The cycle of the card ended, and swept the Doctor helplessly back to its dizzied beginning.

He blinked and saw the tower chamber, the blue card safe in Cardinal Chang's gloved hand. At Chang's side stood Miss Temple, frowning with concern. Doctor Svenson sat up like a yanked puppet, only to find that his clothing had been completely restored. The pistol lay to his side. They stared as if he were mad.

'What has happened?' he asked, his voice cracking.

'What has happened to *you*?' Chang replied.

Svenson turned to the open arch, saw no one beyond it, then pointed vaguely at the tapestry hiding the staircase door. He saw the exasperation in Chang's sneer, and the confusion on Miss Temple's brow. *They* had not done up his trousers. It had been the Contessa. But when? His arousal had passed – he could not suppress a downwards glance – but under what circumstances?

Cardinal Chang held up the blue card. 'Where did you get *this*?'

'The Contessa.' In his companions' presence his complicity with the woman seemed utterly indefensible. 'I met the Contessa –'

'How could you have been such a fool to look into it?'

'I tried to kill her – I failed – somehow we ended up fleeing from the guards –'

Miss Temple took his hand and sat next to him. 'You must tell us everything.' Her gaze caught the glass card in Chang's hand. 'And you must tell us what you saw.'

Doctor Svenson kept the tale decorous, aided by the fact that any impropriety with the Contessa lay beyond their imagination. Whenever his narrative faltered, Miss Temple or Chang would cut in with a question whose answer allowed an elision. Interwoven with their questions were details of their own struggle. Under the cover of Svenson's gunfire they had fled deeper into the Palace. A wave of soldiers had swept each floor, but they managed to hide. When Miss Temple related this last, Svenson was sure he saw her cheeks redden.

'Where did you conceal yourselves?' he asked.

'A wardrobe,' muttered Chang. But Miss Temple, compensating for her blush, seemed determined to dismiss all mystery.

'The trick of it being that a wardrobe *full* of clothing does not allow two people in it, and a wardrobe *without* clothing does not hide them if a diligent searcher opens its door. Further, it does not do at all to heave out half the contents to strike the proper balance – a heap of clothing serving as advertisement for close scrutiny.'

'Quite the puzzle,' offered the Doctor.

Her blush returned.

'We saw nothing of Phelps or Cunsher,' said Chang brusquely, shovelling earth on the subject of wardrobes.

'Nor I,' said Svenson. He described the death of Lord Pont-Joule, the Contessa's enslavement of Princess Sophia and Mr Harcourt, and the two purloined documents.

'And you left her alive.' Chang's voice was flat, as if the fact of Svenson's action was damning enough. 'And she spared *you*. Why?'

'For the same reason she sent the red envelopes to Celeste's hotel. She is not strong enough to defeat the Comte on her own – now that the Comte is Robert Vandaariff.'

'What did she want you to do?' asked Miss Temple.

'I cannot say – yet the answer lies in that bit of glass. Infused with her own memories.'

'Uncharacteristic,' said Chang. 'Such *harvesting* is for the lower orders.'

Svenson nodded. 'There is no way to explain. You must each look into that card.'

Already seated, Miss Temple took the card first. Svenson remained next to her. Though she'd displayed no ill-effects from viewing the glass map, he wanted to be sure that this more potent card did not provoke any. She gasped softly as the cycle completed, but he detected no sudden pallor, no chill upon her skin. Chang watched with a sour expression.

'How long should we allow her to look?'

'Another minute.' Svenson spoke quietly, as if Miss Temple were asleep. 'The level of detail is prodigious, almost impossible to comprehend.'

'What *is* it? You have not said.'

'The Comte's great painting. The one mentioned in the cutting from the *Herald*.'

'That cannot be coincidence. Did Phelps find where it is, where it had been shown?'

'I do not know.'

'He did not tell you?'

'We were distracted by the crowd –'

'But that fact is extremely important! I assume you told him about *your* errands. Was he hiding the information deliberately?'

'No – yes, we did ask him, but he was not – excuse me . . .' Svenson rubbed his eyes.

'What's wrong? Are you sick?'

'In a manner of speaking. It is the glass card – the bodily perspective. One inhabits the Contessa herself.'

Chang took this in, then snorted with a wolfish appreciation.

'Indeed,' said Doctor Svenson drily. 'One is taken aback in unexpected ways.'

Both men turned to Miss Temple. Svenson realized he was staring and cleared his throat. 'The Contessa made a deliberate examination of that man's masterwork – again, one assumes she had a reason.'

'Where is the memory from? Or when? Does she tell us where to find the painting?'

Svenson shook his head. 'The very scale places the execution in the past.

The Comte simply wouldn't have had time in these last months. What's more, as the clipping cites Oskar Veilandt, it more likely dates to before the artist remade himself as the Comte. As to location, that would have to be someplace large.'

'Harschmort?'

'I have to think we would have seen it already – we have walked miles through those halls.' Svenson was painfully aware that only one of Chang's questions had been answered: the Contessa had spared the Doctor's life, for her own reasons . . . but why had Svenson spared hers?

'I assume she cannot hear us,' said Chang.

'I should not think so.'

'You say the Contessa makes her own glass. I agree. She may have made Miss Temple's man Pfaff as much her creature as that Princess.'

'Does Celeste know this?'

'She knows not to trust him. What about you?'

'Me? I should not even recognize the fellow –'

'No. You are continually distracted. Yes, you were injured – and certainly your losses weigh upon you –'

'No, no – I am perfectly able –'

'Able? You left this monstrous woman alive!'

'And my presence of mind with a pistol kept both of you from being taken.'

'Perhaps, but if we cannot rely upon –'

'*Perhaps? Rely?*'

'Do not become agitated –'

'Do not presume to be my master!'

Svenson's words were sharper than he intended, the venting of too many worries, and they echoed off the stone walls. Chang's hands balled into fists – in the silence Svenson could hear the stretching of his leather gloves.

'Cardinal Chang –'

'There is no time for any of this,' Chang announced coldly. 'It must be half nine o'clock. Wake her up.'

Distracted by her experience, Miss Temple did not notice their anger. She insisted that Chang too must look, promising to pull the card away after two minutes. Once he was installed on the divan with the card before his livid eyes, she turned to Doctor Svenson with a shrug.

'Five minutes will do just as well. You are right to say one cannot get one's mind around the painting, if one can even term it that. Beastly thing.'

Svenson studied her face for a toxic reaction. This painting went straight to the Comte's alchemical cosmology, to his *heart*.

'One does not appreciate being stared at,' she told him hoarsely.

'My apologies, my dear – I am worried about you.'

'Do not be.'

'I'm afraid I must. Did you – well, from the Comte, did you recognize the painting?'

'In fact I did not,' she replied, 'or, I did, but not in the detail I should have expected – I should have expected to lose my last meal – but it struck me like the memories of a distant summer. The awareness of being there, but no longer the knowledge.'

'Because the memory comes through the Contessa?'

'Possibly, though I couldn't say why. Perhaps the Comte wasn't himself at the time.'

'You mean opium?'

'I don't mean anything. But I'm sure we will puzzle the matter out. I have a great fondness for reading maps, you know, and you must have experience with codes and ciphers – we are halfway home.'

'It is more than that, Celeste. Think of the thirteen paintings of the Comte's *Annunciation*, and the alchemical recipe they contained for physical transformation. Think of Lydia Vandaariff.'

Svenson recalled the hellish scene in the laboratory at Harschmort: the Comte in a leather apron, cradling a snouted device of polished steel, Karl-Horst von Maasmärck lolling in an armchair, stupid with brandy, and Robert Vandaariff's daughter tied to a bed, a pool of bright blue fluid between her legs. Whether she had been impregnated by the Prince or by the Comte himself barely mattered. Sailing to her wedding in Macklenburg, oblivious to all that had been done, the young woman had grown rapidly more ill, as poisons strove to remake her issue for a madman's dream.

Miss Temple shuddered. 'But it cannot have *worked*. Lydia would not have given birth to . . . to any living . . . I mean – transformed –'

'No,' said Svenson. 'I am sure she would have died. But what is death to the Comte's – now Vandaariff's – madness? And this new painting is more than three times the size of the *Annunciation*. We know it is a recipe for *something*. We must not delude ourselves at how terrible it may be.'

'That is the snap of it,' said Miss Temple. 'Now he has the money.'

'Exactly. His plot with Lydia was done in the shadows, indulged by the others in exchange for what they saw as his *true* work with the blue glass.' Svenson sighed. 'But now, what he only imagined before, he can make real.'

'Or so he believes.' Miss Temple shook her head. Her voice was ragged but firm. 'And where is Francesca Trapping? Has she been harmed?'

Svenson was surprised by the leap in Miss Temple's thought. 'The Contessa would not say. My guess is that the child has been hidden in the Palace, yet with the Contessa's flight I think she must have been moved.'

'Have they enslaved her too?'

'Children are resilient,' said the Doctor, without confidence.

'But she will remember.'

The words carried a quiet gravity. Svenson waited for her to say more. Chang inhaled through his teeth – the cycle of the card coming full circle. The Doctor nearly pulled the card away. He dreaded to receive Miss Temple's confidence, despite his curiosity as to what she might say.

Miss Temple sighed heavily, almost a groan. 'We were together, you know . . . the Contessa and I, in a goods van, from Karthe. I was cold, and so tired.'

'Were you harmed?'

Miss Temple's voice took on a pleading tone. 'I did nothing wrong. She is a wicked woman.'

'Celeste.' Svenson knelt in front of her. 'Elöise told us you had looked into a glass book – Celeste, you cannot blame yourself –'

'Of *course* I can't! I did not ask for this – this – *infestation*! I cannot think! I cannot go two minutes –' Her cheeks went red and she covered her face with both hands. Svenson touched her knee and Miss Temple yelped.

He stood at once, blushing. 'I have *tried*,' she whimpered. 'But even with her – her of all people. She sees through my skin. I cannot *think* but I am overcome. God help me – God help me!'

He had tended her through fever, bathed her, applied poultices, yet, as Miss Temple so boldly revealed herself a creature of appetite, the Doctor felt his view of her could shift. Was he such an ape? Was he so *fragile*? He bit down hard on the inside of his cheek, tasting blood. Miss Temple pulled her hands away and Doctor Svenson saw, without question, her tear-brimmed eyes dart to his groin.

'Chang and yourself – you mentioned a wardrobe – did you –'

'Did we what?' she asked hopelessly.

'Did you see anyone else?'

'In the wardrobe?'

'In the Palace.'

'Hundreds of them! That was why we had to hide!'

'Yes – of course –'

'It was terrible! That tiny space! Do you not *understand*?'

'I do – my poor dear – but – does Chang – I mean to say, did you –'

His gaze slipped to her bosom, and, before he could shift it, she had seen. To Svenson's dismay Miss Temple's expression altered in an instant. Within her undimmed agitation appeared first a flash of unfeigned hunger and directly after a grimace of contempt that shook him to his core. Then her face fell into her hands. Her huddled shoulders shook.

He felt the cold isolation creep back into his bones. The girl was a quivering ruin.

'My dear Celeste. Gather yourself. Say nothing more. We will find the Contessa. We will find the Comte.'

'They think it all a perfect *joke*!'

'That is laughter they will choke on. Be brave still, and wipe your eyes. There is no shame. We must reclaim Cardinal Chang.'

When the card was removed, Chang cursed and set to rubbing his eyes and the skull around them. Svenson heard a new note of hoarseness in Chang's voice, and noted the pallor of his lips, the shine of fluid at his nostrils.

'Are you ill? Is it the card?'

'It is nothing at all.'

'You should let me examine you.'

'We have wasted enough of the evening.'

'You have not *seen* the wound – truly, if you would just –'

'*No.*' Chang slipped his dark glasses back into place. 'I am perfectly well. Certainly compared to either of *you.*'

Despite Chang's bad humour, Svenson was glad for the distraction. Miss Temple had done her best to restore her face, turning away as if to examine the tapestry.

'The floors above are thick with people,' said Chang. 'We cannot hope to pass unseen. That no one has come down and found us is only due to their fear of past contagion.'

'What contagion?' asked Svenson.

'The sickness! The glass woman's legacy!'

'But we are well away from Stäelmaere House, under the Palace – not twenty yards from the river.'

Chang pointed through the archway. 'Twenty yards will take you to the Duke's own cellars.'

'But – but the Contessa told me –'

Chang snorted.

'But why would she lie?'

'To aide her own escape. Or provoke your capture.'

'But you two fled deeper into the Palace,' said Svenson. 'Why come back?'

'We knew no other way out,' Miss Temple said. 'And hoped we might find others in hiding – as we in fact did.'

'Then we may be near Phelps and Cunsher. If they are taken, we must rescue them.'

Chang exhaled with impatience. 'That would be the height of folly. To search means throwing away our own lives and abandoning all hope of stopping Vandaariff and the Contessa. Phelps and Cunsher *know* this.'

Svenson did his best to swallow his irritation, hating how expressing simple decency rendered him, in Chang's eyes, a sentimental fool.

'Well, then, if we search for Vandaariff –'

'Vandaariff is *gone*,' Chang scoffed. 'He only came for his fireworks in the square, and for the pleasure of his hosts' abasement.'

'Then where do we find him?'

'Harschmort. Raaxfall. Setting off another blast in Stropping Station. Anywhere.' Chang jerked his chin at Miss Temple. 'Ask *her*.'

'I have no idea.' Miss Temple spoke quietly, and to his dismay Svenson realized she had just consulted the Comte's tainted memories, surely to compensate for displaying her weakness a moment before. He had told her to be brave, but hadn't intended self-punishment.

Between Chang's distemper and Miss Temple's distress, the Doctor felt it was for him to set their path. But he could not make sense of the most basic facts. *Had* the Contessa left him to be captured? Why reveal the Comte's painting if she simply wanted to see him hang? Svenson fought the urge for a cigarette. What *had* the Contessa told him, exactly? And once the Doctor had eventually wrenched himself from the blue glass card, left to himself, would he not have followed her direction?

'What are you staring at?' Chang asked.

Svenson pointed to the mirror. 'The other side of this wall.'

'I don't understand.'

'Nor I. Follow me.'

The Doctor crossed to the archway. As Chang stood, his boot slid, scraping on the floor. Svenson turned to see him pick something up, and frown.

'Some idiot's button,' muttered Chang, and he threw it away.

There was no other side of the wall they could reach. The corridor ended in a stack of barrels. 'I told you,' said Chang. 'We are in the cellars.'

Svenson frowned. 'She acquainted me with the Comte's painting to provoke some action. Saying I was near the river must have been deliberate, to send me in that direction . . .'

'The woman is a vampire,' said Chang. 'Cruelty for the sake of being cruel.'

'Cruelty would have meant taking my life.'

'If the Contessa was civil it must have galled her terribly,' Miss Temple observed, 'like playing courtesan to a bitter enemy.'

'Wait.' The Doctor pointed. 'Look at the floor.'

Thin lines of grit curved across the tile from beneath the barrels, as if they had been moved. Chang reached for a barrel and Svenson helped him shift it, revealing a metal door set into the stone. Hanging from the knob by a leather loop was a notched brass tube three inches long.

'The pneumatic vestibule,' Svenson said. 'And here is the key.'

Inside the panelled box, Svenson paused. 'Do we follow the Contessa, or escape?'

'She may have returned to the attic, to Francesca,' said Miss Temple.

'We don't know that the child is there,' Chang cautioned. 'I say we descend to where we entered and hope it is not thronged with soldiers.'

Acknowledging this logic, Svenson thrust the key into the slot and stabbed the lowest button on the brass plate. The car vibrated with life. They descended without speaking – all three with weapons ready – but when they heard the tell-tale *clank* the car did not stop.

'I thought we entered directly below the cellars,' said Chang.

'Perhaps we did not pay attention,' said Miss Temple. 'Perhaps it was two stops below.'

'It wasn't.'

'Then there is another floor further below.'

A second *clank* and the car came to a halt. Chang pulled the iron gate open and set his shoulder against the tarnished metal door beyond it.

This was not the underpassage to Stäelmaere House. Instead, they had been delivered to another tunnel, with a tiled floor like a bath house. A single lantern, lit within the hour judging by the level of oil, had been left on the floor. Next to it, like a malicious rose, lay a third red envelope.

It was empty save for a scrap of white tissue, smeared with a scarlet imprint of the Contessa's mouth. Svenson said nothing. Chang scowled with displeasure. Miss Temple put her nose to the tissue, and observed that it smelt of frangipani flowers. They began to walk.

'This cannot have been simple to construct,' said Svenson. 'The digging must have displaced the coach traffic above us for ages –'

'Nothing of the kind has displaced anything,' called Chang, walking in the lead. 'This can only be the old Norwalk.'

This meant nothing to Svenson or Miss Temple. Chang sighed. 'The Norwalk fortifications were dismantled to lay the Seventh Bridge, and the new Customs House.'

'I have been to the Customs House,' said Miss Temple. 'To learn about trade.'

'That does you credit,' said Svenson. 'It is the rare heiress not simply content to spend.'

Miss Temple made a bothered face. 'I did not want to be cheated – sugar-men are famous scoundrels. But, once I was inside, tiresome is not the half of it –'

Chang cleared his throat. They stopped talking. He went on.

'The Norwalk formed one wall of the original Citadel. I would guess this was once a lower catacomb.'

'But why has it been remade?' asked Svenson. 'New tile and fresh paint.'

Chang reached into his coat for his razor. With the handle he scratched a line in the plaster and blew the dust away. 'Replastered these past two months.'

'Before or after the dirigible went into the sea?' asked Svenson.

Chang shrugged. Miss Temple held up the lantern.

'We forget *this*. Someone lit it. We must keep on and make her tell us everything.'


A quarter-mile brought the tunnel's end: a wooden door, and another red envelope left atop its polished handle. Chang tore it open, glanced at the paper and passed it to Svenson with a snort.

*My Dear Doctor,*

*As a man of evident Vitality you would have found this Lair in Time, but Time is no good Friend.*

*The Task is beyond any single Agent.*

*Do not let Love blind your Eyes. Ample Time remains to settle our Account.*

> *RLS*

Miss Temple raised her eyebrows impatiently and Svenson handed the paper to her.

'Why should she mention "love"?' asked Chang.

'I expect she means Elöise,' Svenson replied, wondering if it were true, wondering – despite his surety of the woman's heartlessness – just how the Contessa viewed their encounter. And how did *he* view it? 'She will say anything to mitigate her guilt if she requires our aid.'

Miss Temple thrust the paper back. 'I will not be a party to her bargains.'

'If we find the Contessa,' said Chang, 'no matter where, she is to die.'

Svenson nodded his agreement. It was not that he wanted to spare the Contessa – and he did not, truly – but he saw in his companions' resolve a wilful denial of the fact that their struggle now stretched beyond the individuals who had wronged them. And if he did keep the woman alive to defeat the Comte, would Miss Temple and Chang come to hate him just as much, at the end?

The 'lair' certainly looked to be inhabited by an animal. Clothes, however fine, were strewn across the floor and furniture, unwashed plates and glasses cluttered the worktops, empty bottles had rolled to each corner of the room, a straw mattress had been folded double and shoved against the wall. Despite the Contessa's detritus, it was clear the low stone chamber had been refitted for another purpose. Metal pipes fed into squat brass boxes bolted to the wall. The chamber reeked of indigo clay.

Svenson touched the pipes to gauge their heat, then put his palm against the wall. 'Very cold . . . could that be the river?'

Chang slapped his hand against the wall. 'Of course! I'm a fool – the Seventh Bridge! The turbines!'

'What turbines?' asked Miss Temple. 'You say such things as if one mentions *turbines* over breakfast –'

Chang rode over her words. 'The supports of the bridge contain turbines – it was an idea for flushing sewage –'

'These pipes hold *sewage*?'

'Not at all – the plan was never implemented. But we know Crabbé and

Bascombe plotted against their allies – so of *course* they required their own version of the Comte's workshop. The bridge's turbines, with the force of the river, would serve up enough power to satisfy even these greedy machines.'

'And I assume the Contessa learnt their secret from her spy, Caroline Stearne.' Miss Temple waved the reek from her face. 'But why has she abandoned it?'

'That is the question,' agreed Svenson. 'This night she has given up her refuge at the Palace, and now a quite remarkable laboratory . . .'

'There is the matter of her death warrant,' said Miss Temple.

'It did not appear to trouble her especially.'

'Also, if she lit the lamp and left the envelopes to get us here,' said Chang, 'where did she *go*?'

They did not see any other door. Svenson searched behind the mattress and under the piles of clothing, pausing at a wooden crate. The crate was lined with felt and piled with coils of copper wire. Next to it, in a tangle of black rubber hose, lay a mask, the sort they had all seen before in the operating theatre at Harschmort.

'As we guessed, not only was our view of the painting leached from her own mind, it seems the Contessa did the leaching herself.'

'How can she be sure the machine selects only the memory she desires?' asked Chang. 'Does she not risk its draining everything?'

'Perhaps that is determined by the glass – a small card can contain only so much.' Svenson moved on his knees to one of the brass boxes. It was fitted with a slot in which one might insert an entire glass book, but above this was another, much smaller aperture, just wide enough for a card. 'I agree, however, that to do this alone is insanity. How can she rouse herself to turn off the machine? We have all seen the devastating effects –'

'Did you see them in her?' asked Miss Temple, just a little hopefully. 'Thinning hair? Loosened teeth?'

'Here.' Chang held out a tiny pair of leather gloves, dangling them to show the size. 'The Contessa took precautions after all.'

'They would not fit a monkey,' said Svenson.

'Francesca Trapping,' said Miss Temple.

'The sorceress's familiar.' Chang hoisted himself onto a worktop to sit. 'But I still don't see why she's left the place, nor why she's bothered to lure us here . . .'

His words trailed away. Svenson followed Chang's gaze to a china platter, blackened and split, piled with bits of odd-shaped glass, most of them so dark Svenson had taken them for coal. But now he saw what had caught Chang's eye: in the centre of the platter lay a round ball of glass, the size and colour of a blood orange.

'The painting,' Svenson said. 'The black Groom – in his left hand . . .'

Chang picked up the reddish sphere and held it to the guttering lantern above them.

'It is cracked,' he said, and pushed up his dark glasses.

'Chang, wait –'

Doctor Svenson reached out a warning hand, but Chang had already shut one eye and put the other to the glass.

'Do you see anything?' asked Miss Temple.

Chang did not answer.

'I wonder if it is infused with a memory,' she whispered to Svenson. 'And what could make it *red*?'

'Iron ore, perhaps, though I couldn't speculate why.' Svenson sorted through the remaining pieces on the platter – several were obviously the remnants of other spheres that had broken, but none were of the same deep shade.

'If this *is* indigo clay . . . the refining is not what we have seen. I would guess each piece has been mixed with different compounds – no doubt to alter its alchemical efficacy –'

'Doctor Svenson?'

Miss Temple stared at Chang, who remained gazing into the glass ball, as still as a stone.

Svenson swore in German and rushed to Chang's side. He wrenched the ball from Chang's grip. A warm vibration touched his hand, but nothing that stopped him from setting it back on the platter.

'Is he poisoned?' Miss Temple squeaked. 'Save him!'

Chang's naked eyes stared at nothing. Svenson felt his forehead and his pulse. He tapped Chang's cheek sharply, twice. Nothing. 'His breathing is not strained. It is not a fit . . . Celeste, do you have your rings – the rings of orange metal?'

She rummaged in her clutch bag and came out with a canvas pouch. The Doctor extracted a single ring and – feeling something of a fool – held it close to Chang's eye. Chang did not react. Svenson pressed the whole pouch against Chang's cheek.

Like a wine stain seeping through thick linen, the skin in contact flushed pink, then red, then went purple, like a deepening bruise. Miss Temple shrieked.

'What is happening? Take it away!'

Svenson dropped the pouch. A pattern had been scorched onto Chang's face, the colour of cherry flesh. The Doctor looked hurriedly around him.

'The mattress! We must set him down –'

Miss Temple leapt to the mattress, dragging it close. Svenson lugged Chang off the worktop and they laid him down. Already the scorched ring had faded again to the pink of health. How had the effects reversed so quickly? Svenson seized Chang's shoulder and belt. With a heave he rolled the man over, face down on the mattress.

'What are you doing?'

'Celeste, when you saw Chang's wound, at Raaxfall, did you query your own memories of the Comte?'

She nodded, then choked in the back of her throat. 'I found nothing.'

'As I thought. You see, he is attempting something new. Our friend will not be another Lydia Vandaariff.'

The Doctor lifted Chang's coat. The brief glimpse at Raaxfall had been in poor light.

'Celeste, please look away –'

She shook her head. Svenson raised the silk shirt.

The wound lay to the right of the lumbar vertebra. The original puncture had been enlarged through what looked like at least three different surgeries, expanding the scar to the shape and size of a child's splayed, thumbless hand. The scar tissue was an unsettling vein-blue, with a rough, thickened surface like the hide of a starfish. But it was the flesh *around* the wound that had made them gasp in the wicked room at Raaxfall, and the Doctor winced to see it again. Like dye dropped into a milky basin, virulent streaks of red radiated from the centre, as if signifying a flowering of infection.

'The same colour as the ring against his face,' Miss Temple whispered.

Svenson delicately palpated the discoloured area. The flesh was cold, and beneath it his fingertips met an unnatural resistance.

'Something has been placed inside.'

Her voice was small. 'Will he die?'

'If the Comte had wanted to kill him, he would be dead. We saw the other bodies –'

'Then what has happened? Can you remove it? Why has he collapsed when he was perfectly fine?'

Svenson caught her flailing hand. 'Clearly he was not *fine*. I cannot hope to remove it, even had I the tools. Whatever is *implanted* lies too near the spine. The slightest mistake and he is a cripple.'

'That isn't true!'

'Please, Celeste – you must let me *think* –'

'*But he will die!*'

Svenson looked helplessly around him, searching for any idea. The orange metal had always been effective in reversing the predations of the blue glass, but its application here had worsened Chang's condition . . . could it be as simple as that, a matter of opposites? Svenson crawled to the china platter and pawed through the jumble of glass . . . was all of it so discoloured? He shouted to Miss Temple.

'The card – the blue glass card!'

She dug in her bag and he snatched the card from her grasp, protecting his fingers with his coatsleeve. He rolled Chang onto his back. The man's eyes remained disturbingly open. Svenson dropped to his knees and thrust the card before them.

At first he saw no reaction, his close observation echoed by Miss Temple's silence as she held her breath. But then the pink colour began to drain away. Had that happened when Chang looked into the card, to view the painting? Svenson had no clear memory. Chang's breathing thickened. His skin went paper-white. The blue card made things worse as well. Svenson yanked the card away and heaved a sigh of relief as these latest symptoms too reversed themselves.

'It is not science,' Svenson said helplessly. 'It is not medicine, playing with a life as if it were a cooking pot, adding this and subtracting that. I am sorry, Celeste – desperately sorry –'

He turned, expecting to find a face in tears. But Miss Temple stood at the platter. He saw her hand close around the reddish ball, but he was on his knees, and Chang lay between them. Svenson's reaching arm fell short.

Miss Temple's shoulders heaved with convulsions. He spun her round, tearing the ball from her grasp and hurling it against the wall, where it shattered. Miss Temple's eyes were dead. Black fluid rimmed her mouth.

'Celeste! Celeste – you idiot girl! *Celeste!*'

She did not hear. He eased her down, but her eyes refused to clear. Oily bubbles bloomed between her lips, but he could not make out the words, if words they even were. She arched her back against a bout of choking. Doctor Svenson knelt between his fallen comrades, ridiculous victims, and groaned aloud.

A cupboard door below the worktop popped open, driven by the heel of a diminutive black boot.

He blinked. The cupboards. They had not looked in the cupboards.

She wriggled out legs first, stockings stretched around a colt's knobbed knees, then little hands pulled her body into view. Francesca Trapping stood and brushed at her very rumpled dress in an automatic gesture that had no effect whatsoever. Her red hair was all tangles and snarls, her face unclean.

'You are alive,' Svenson whispered.

Francesca took in Miss Temple and Chang, nodding as if their conditions were steps in a recipe she had memorized.

'There is little time.' Her shrill voice was raw. 'By tomorrow Oskar will have had his way.'

With a shudder Svenson saw the teeth in her mouth had gone grey.

'Francesca . . . what has she done?'

'What was required. What she has done to you.'

# FOUR

# CATACOMB

It had not been her intention to act rashly. But the impulse to snatch up the red ball was a spark of clarity within the riot she had felt since Chang had been recovered. Her delight at his survival, an unexpected flood of joy, had been immediately displaced by a host of clamouring thoughts and images – and none of that turmoil touched the man himself. In the tunnels, on the train, even when Chang held her hand, the *distance* between them was agony. A sea of feeling lay within his heart, she knew, as she knew it held her only hope of peace – yet he remained, as ever, untouchable and withheld.

And so she had entered the red sphere. A frightening energy suffused Miss Temple's mind, as if the glass were reacting *to* her – measuring . . . *examining*. This was not the brutal plunder of a blue glass book, with a victim's mind drained whole. In the red sphere Miss Temple felt her mind being explored like a stretch of uncharted coastline. Unfortunately, the Comte's knowledge provided no more detail beyond another glimpse of the painting, the apple in the Groom's black hand. She was sure this *examination* was but a first step of its function, a preface to some larger task, like a wall being scrubbed before receiving new paint.

And then, quite suddenly, the spell was broken, its work unravelled. This was the flaw in the glass. At once the foul tide in her rose, and her mouth formed words, a last memory. The Comte had whispered in her ear . . . no, not to her, but to Lydia Vandaariff, as his alchemical poisons remade her body. The young woman had been terrified – that had given him pleasure – such fear had seemed *appropriate* . . .

\*

'I do not like her,' said a small rasping voice. 'I should prefer to let her die. She let Elöise die. Elöise loved me. She did nothing. The Contessa did not say *she* would come, or *him*. Just you. We ought to leave them here.'

'You must let me work . . .' muttered Doctor Svenson.

'Why is her mouth black? Has she drunk ink? What is she trying to *say*?'

A damp cloth cooled Miss Temple's face. She rolled her head to the side. The red mist dimmed. Three words congealed inside her mind.

'Flesh of dreams,' Miss Temple croaked. The Doctor wiped her mouth and then held her hair away as she coughed. She saw the mattress, Svenson on his knees, and, behind him, legs dangling from the worktop, an unkempt little girl. Francesca Trapping bore the bitter expression a hungry cat might bestow upon a duck too large to acknowledge its authority.

'Where is Chang?' Miss Temple managed.

'Just behind you,' said Svenson. 'He came to his senses two hours ago – now he sleeps.'

'Two hours? Is he safe? Is he whole?'

'He is – we have been more worried by *you*.'

'I am perfectly fine.'

'You are not. Celeste, my lord, between Chang's wound and your own reckless –'

'What did he see? What did he tell you?'

'Nothing. We did not speak. He did not *want* to speak. Once the danger passed –'

'It was cracked,' said the girl, as if this fact was proof of their collective stupidity. 'Of *course* he woke up.'

Svenson helped Miss Temple to sit. 'I will not chide you. You live, and that is all that matters.'

She looked past him. Chang lay stretched on the floor, hands folded like a statue on an old king's sarcophagus.

'You said something as you woke,' said Svenson.

'The red glass ball was nothing the Comte had made before.' Miss Temple hiccupped wetly. 'But "flesh of dreams" was something he said to Lydia – it came to me now for a reason.'

Svenson sighed. His face was haggard. 'Alchemy is about equivalents – balancing one element with another, transformation through incremental change. The nearest analogy would be symbolic mathematics. The Comte of course transposes chemical compounds with living bodies. But the language operates like a code – and so a phrase like "flesh of dreams" will have an equivalent, opposite concept –'

'The flesh of life,' said Francesca, chewing a thumbnail with her teeth.

'Exactly,' said Svenson. 'And that tells us how he thinks – that the opposite of life is not, as most would have it, death, but dream.'

Miss Temple frowned with distaste. 'Lydia's pregnancy. The flesh of dreams is born from the ashes of the flesh of life.'

'For what purpose?'

'Paradise.'

Svenson snorted. 'And what can that word mean to *that* man?'

Miss Temple was aware of Francesca watching her. How many hours had she been left alone? Francesca's arms were marked with smears of soot . . . or were they bruises? Miss Temple felt a pinch in her throat.

'Is there someplace I might . . . spit?'

'A chamberpot, here – and somewhere is a bit of food, and water –' The Doctor's voice dropped off, in sympathy, as she bent over the chamberpot and let fly.

'There isn't time.' The child's voice was a whine. 'We were waiting for *her*. Now we have to *go*.'

Miss Temple met Francesca's disapproving gaze and held it until the girl turned away. She waited for the girl to look back. When Francesca did so, pressing her lips together at being caught, Miss Temple stared even harder.

'I did not let Elöise die.'

'Celeste – the child is hardly responsible –'

'She needs to know what is right.'

Francesca Trapping muttered to herself. 'I know perfectly well.'

The chamberpot prompted Miss Temple to notice the fullness of her bladder. The single room offered no privacy beyond a meagre half-barrier of cupboards, behind which she would have to crouch, with Svenson only a few feet away hearing all. Instead, she picked up the chamberpot and crossed to the door. On her way, she impulsively took Francesca Trapping's arm in hers. The child squawked in protest.

'We will return directly,' Miss Temple called to Svenson. 'Girls together, don't you know.'

Svenson opened his mouth, coughed instead, and pointed vaguely to Chang.

'Yes – while you – right –'

Miss Temple hauled the squirming girl into the corridor. She dropped the chamberpot with a *clang*. 'Will you go first or me?'

'I will not go at *all*.'

Feeling she must make an example, Miss Temple resentfully hiked up her dress and sat, daring the girl to say one mocking thing. But Francesca only stared. Disliking a silence broken only by the rattle of her own urine, Miss Temple cleared her throat.

'We have been searching for you. You should know that the Doctor was very much in love with Elöise and grieves for her particularly. As do I. We also grieve for your mother, and your father, and your uncle – yes, even him, for his death no doubt has given *you* pain. Your brothers are safe at home.'

'I know how my brothers are.'

'Have you visited them?'

The girl looked away.

'No. Do you see? You *don't* know – you have been *told*. What else have you trusted that woman to say?' Miss Temple stood, rearranging her petti-coats, and indicated the chamberpot. Again the girl shook her head. 'It will be a long journey,' said Miss Temple, annoyed that she had come to parrot every exasperating aunt or guardian she had ever known. With a shrug the girl took her place on the chamberpot, gazing sullenly at a point between her shoes.

'The Contessa sent you to my hotel,' said Miss Temple. 'You did not try to go home.'

'Why should I have done that?'

'Because she is extremely wicked.'

'I think *you're* wicked.'

The retort flung, Francesca squirmed on her seat and said nothing. Francesca's face was naturally pale, but now it was pinched and drawn. Had the girl been eating? Miss Temple imagined the woman flinging scraps at Francesca's feet with an imperious sneer – but then recalled her own experience in the railway car, the Contessa breaking a pie in two, passing bites of a green apple with an insidious amity.

'So the Contessa is your friend,' she said.

Francesca sniffed.

'She is very beautiful.'

'More beautiful than *you*.'

'Of course she is. She is a black-haired angel.'

Francesca looked up warily, as if 'angel' had a meaning she did not expect Miss Temple to know. Miss Temple put one gloved finger beneath Francesca's chin and held her gaze.

'I know it is frightening to be alone, and lonely to be strong. But you are heir to the Trappings, and heir to the Xoncks. You must make up your *own* mind.'

She stepped back and allowed the girl to stand. Francesca did so, the dress still gathered at her spindled thighs. 'There is no water,' she said plaintively.

'I did without water perfectly well,' muttered Miss Temple, but she opened her clutch bag and dug for a handkerchief. With a grunt she tore it in half, then in half again, and held the scrap to Francesca, who snatched it away and hunched to wipe.

'A soldier does not need someone's handkerchief,' observed Miss Temple.

'I am not a soldier.'

Miss Temple took the girl's arm and steered her to the door. 'But you *are*, Francesca. Whether you want to be or not.'

'You are returned, excellent.' Doctor Svenson rose to his feet, working both arms into his greatcoat, a lit cigarette in his mouth. Chang stood across the room. Miss Temple perceived the shift in each man's posture at her entrance. They had been speaking of her. Her sting of resentment was then followed by an inflaming counter-notion, that they had *not* been speaking of her. Instead, at her entrance, they had ceased their discussion of strategies and danger, matters to which she could neither contribute nor need be troubled by.

Despite his crisis Chang seemed every bit as able as before – and far more so than anyone imprisoned for weeks ought to be. One look at Svenson showed the man's exhaustion. That he had been unable to kill the Contessa, of all people, was proof enough. Miss Temple resolved to help him as she could, just as a colder part of her mind marked him down as unreliable.

'How best to return?' asked Svenson. 'The vestibule key allows us some choice –'

'You don't go *that* way.' Francesca marched to the cupboard doors and pulled them wide. Inside was a metal hatch. 'You need a lantern. There are rats.'

Svenson peered down the shaft. 'And where does that – I mean, how far down –'

'To the bridge,' Chang answered. 'The turbines.'

'Ah.'

Miss Temple called to Chang. 'Are you fully recovered?'

Chang spread his arms with a sardonic smile. 'As you find me.'

'Is that all you can say?'

'I looked into something I should not have, like a fool.'

'What did you see?'

'What did *you* see? The Doctor described your ludicrous imitation.'

'I looked in the glass ball to provoke the Comte's memories – to learn how to help you.'

'And in doing so only endangered yourself.'

'But I discovered –'

'What we already know. Vandaariff has made glass with different metals. The red ball figures prominently in his great painting, and thus no doubt is highly charged within his personal cosmology. An alchemical apple of Eden.'

'But you –'

'Yes, *I* have a foreign object near my spine. Apparently.'

'It could kill you!'

'It has not yet.'

'It was the Comte's alchemy that killed Lydia Vandaariff.'

'She was killed by the Contessa.'

'But she would have died – you well know it! He only cared about the thing inside her – his blue abomination –'

'Do you suggest I am with child?'

'Why will you not tell me what you saw?'

Her voice had become too loud, but, instead of matching her, Chang answered softly, 'I do not know, Celeste. Not a memory, not a place, not a person.'

'An *ingredient*,' said Svenson. 'Neither one of you has described the experience as concerning memory – and you have both retained your minds. Logic thus suggests the red glass is not a mechanism for capture but for change. Is that right, Francesca? You did see the Contessa make the ball of red glass, didn't you?'

'She was very angry. The man made a mistake.'

'Mr Sullivar,' said Chang. 'At the glassworks.'

'He stoked the oven too much. The ball cracked and wouldn't work properly.'

'Did she make another?' asked Svenson.

'Didn't need to.' Miss Temple flinched, both at the child's deadened teeth and at the bright gleam in her eyes.

Chang insisted on going first, with the lantern. Once down, he held the light high to guide their descent. Miss Temple bundled her dress and wriggled through the hatchway, aware that Chang's lantern showed him her stock-inged calves – and more, depending on the exact gather of her petticoats. She paused in her climb, ostensibly to make sure of her clutch bag, but in truth to indulge a tremor at prolonging her exposure. She imagined Chang's gaze rising from her legs to her face as she reached the ground, each study-ing the other for a sign of intent. But her nerve failed and she finished facing the brickwork, turning only at Chang's brusque offer to take her hand. She held it out to him and hopped to the tunnel floor. Chang called for Svenson to send the child.

The tunnel was new brick, more secret construction on the part of Harald

Crabbé and Roger Bascombe. Miss Temple walked behind Chang, happy to let Svenson hold Francesca's hand, and wondered when her fiancé, Bascombe, had last walked these halls. Had he still loved her then? Had he ever come from here to her arms, all the more thrilled at keeping his secret?

Brooding on Roger Bascombe made Miss Temple feel foolish. She shifted her attention to Chang, fighting the impulse to reach out and run a finger down his back. She started at a touch on her own shoulder. Svenson indicated a growing rumble in the walls.

'The turbines. We are under the bridge.'

Miss Temple nodded without interest. She had imagined the sound was the river itself, flowing past in the dark, an enormous serpent dragging its scales across the earth.

The iron stairs echoed with their footfalls, and the sound launched flurries of motion above their heads.

'Bats.' Chang aimed the lantern at a niche of cross-braced girders. The little beasts hung in rows, wide-eared, small teeth polished white by darting tongues. Miss Temple had seen bats often, whipping across the veranda at twilight, and these did not disturb her. She enjoyed their little fox faces, and smiled to see such awkward things wheel about so fast.

Francesca stared down through the gaps in the iron staircase. Miss Temple forced herself to remember their first meeting in the corridors of Harschmort. She had tried to be kind, and when she had seen Francesca again at Parchfeldt, had there not been *some* sympathy between them? The child's tangled hair made plain she'd not been cared for. But the Contessa's habitual thoughtlessness hardly explained Francesca's deadened teeth.

Miss Temple did not remember herself at seven years of age with any clarity. Her mother was well dead, of course, but who had been her father's housemistress? There had been nine in turn, and Miss Temple ordered her youth through the prism of their reigns, consorts to a relentless, unfeeling king. At seven the housemistress was most likely Mrs Kallack, a harsh lady whose Alsatian husband had died of fever soon after bringing her to the tropics. Mrs Kallack's success in the house was due to her ability to meet Miss Temple's father with utter subservience, and then, like a two-headed idol, wreak his brutality on the rest of the household. Miss Temple had hated her, and recalled with grim satisfaction when Mrs Kallack was found dead in the fields from heatstroke. She had stood over the body with a gang of housegirls, everyone wondering what could have taken the woman so far from the great house. Mrs Kallack's fingers were red with the clay of the sugar fields, as if she had clawed in the dirt before death, and her false front teeth had come loose in her mouth. One of the housegirls had laughed aloud, and Miss Temple – understanding for perhaps the first time the responsibilities of her station – had kicked the housegirl's shin. Before the young woman could do anything in return – and, luckily, for if she had, it would have meant the skin off her back – her father's overseer arrived with the wagon.

She wondered how Francesca Trapping carried the indigestible knot of her parents' murders. Miss Temple knew she ought to take her hand – especially since Doctor Svenson had all but shut his eyes as they climbed, gripping the rail – but she did not. The child made her angry.

At the top of the staircase they found another metal door, fastened with heavy chain looped round an iron hasp. As they passed through, Chang plucked a tuft of fabric snagged on the hasp's ragged edge: a scrap of wool the colour of an overripened peach. He showed it to Francesca.

'I don't suppose you've ever seen this before?'

She shook her head. Chang flipped the fabric to Miss Temple.

'What is it?' asked Svenson.

'Ask *them*.' Chang stood and walked on.

'It belongs to Jack Pfaff,' Miss Temple said, and then called at Chang's receding back, 'He was charged to investigate the glass – this only suggests he was successful. You are determined to mistrust him!' She held up the scrap of cloth. 'Here is welcome news! Jack Pfaff – in *my* employ – may even now have her at bay!'

Chang turned to face her. 'And where would that be?'

'How should I know? I do not even know where we are!'

'We are on the Contessa's errand,' said Doctor Svenson flatly. 'The Contessa charged Francesca to lead me to a certain place –'

'Then why won't she tell us where?' asked Chang.

'Because I would guess she doesn't know the name. Do you, child?' Francesca shook her head. 'No,' continued Svenson, 'the only way is to get there. The Contessa is nothing if not mercurial – yet perhaps Mr Pfaff has managed to best her after all.'

'Did you *see* Mr Pfaff?' Miss Temple asked the girl. 'What did he do?'

'I can't say,' Francesca replied. 'When he was there she put me in the cupboard.'

The brick passage echoed with a gust of cold wind. Chang crept ahead to an open arch, then waved them forward.

'We've reached the bridge from the northern piling,' he whispered.

Miss Temple clapped a hand across her mouth. 'The entire bridge is swarming with soldiers!'

'Not only the bridge.' At Chang's silent indication she saw the dockside was ringed by soldiers in torchlight. On the river lay ships moored out in the channel, and on their decks stood more men in uniform.

'Then it has begun,' said Svenson. 'Harcourt authorized property seizures across the land, for the public good.'

'Are the people taken as well?' asked Chang. 'Earlier this evening the riverside was thronged with the dispossessed.'

'Perhaps they went to the square,' suggested Svenson.

'Not so many – every damned street was crawling.'

Whatever Chang had seen before, the cobbled riverfront was as well ordered as a military parade ground. Miss Temple picked out officers on horseback, troops mustered into line. The bridge itself bore a cordon at each end, limiting traffic – those few allowed to cross did so between uniformed escorts. Chang spoke to Francesca.

'If we are seen by the soldiers, we will be captured, and *he*' – Chang nodded to Svenson – 'for he has made havoc in the Palace, will be shot. Which direction do we go?'

Francesca pointed to the nearer end of the bridge, back at the heart of the city.

Chang stood. 'Doctor, if you would pass me the lantern.'

'Will it not be seen?'

'Indeed, but there is seen and *seen*, you know.'

They crept after Chang onto the bridge proper. He pointed to a railing ten feet away.

'Go now – as quick as you can, over the side – Celeste, you first.'

Miss Temple did not like to baulk – she knew Chang had chosen her to lead only because he could not ask the height-stricken Doctor or a seven-year-old-girl – but neither did she relish hanging over the edge of such a wicked drop. Nevertheless, she ran as instructed and was rewarded by an iron ladder on the far side of the rail. She climbed down, the dizzying abyss of dark water answered by a small platform five steps below, and smiled at Chang's cunning. A narrow catwalk extended under the bridge all the way to the river wall – to aid repairs, she assumed – which would allow them to pass unseen beneath the sentries. At a tremulous whisper from Francesca, Miss Temple rescaled the ladder and brought the girl down, then helped Svenson, whose passage was every bit as tentative. She heard the crash of breaking glass above them – and then a piercing shout.

'Fire! Fire on the bridge!'

The alarm spread in a roar through the soldiers. Chang vaulted the railing and landed beside them like a cat.

'Go! Go!' he hissed, and drove them on, bent low.

'You *threw* the lantern!' whispered Svenson.

'No drawing moths without a flame, Doctor. Quiet now . . .'

The catwalk dead-ended at the bridge wall, high above the riverfront. The cordon lay right over their heads. The citizens demanding passage had been shouted to silence by the officer in charge.

'A lantern, by God. Get men searching! Enough of this nonsense!'

The officer broke off, railing at someone in the crowd hoping to slip past, and his sergeants began to detail the men to search. Soldiers would appear at the ladder, and on their catwalk, and soon.

'We appear to be trapped,' Svenson whispered, readying his pistol.

Miss Temple hurried to the inner rail. They were no longer above the water, but this meant they faced a prodigious drop to the stone bankside.

What had Chang said about the old Norwalk? That the bridge and the buildings around it had been raised on the foundation of the old fortress . . . she leant over the rail. A firm hand caught her shoulder.

'What are you playing at?' snarled Chang.

'I am looking at the wall. It is your fortress – look for yourself.'

Chang peered over the rail, then whipped off his glasses. 'I can't see a damned thing.'

'There are old windows,' said Miss Temple. 'Or not windows but whatsits – slitty bits of stonework, for arrows – your old fortifications –'

'She's right.' Svenson had taken Chang's place with an uncomfortable swallow. 'But it's yards away – we've no rope, we cannot reach it.'

'Of course we can't reach *that* one,' said Miss Temple.

'Celeste –'

'There is a *line* of them. If they extend away from us, then there must *also* be one directly beneath our feet!'

Miss Temple began to hike up her dress, but Chang thrust her aside and quickly dropped from view, hanging by his arms. At once he came back.

'It is no more than climbing down from a coach. Hand me the child first . . .'

The far end of the catwalk echoed as soldiers landed on the planking. Miss Temple and the others sank to their knees.

'The girl!' hissed Chang, invisible below them. Svenson lifted Francesca over the rail so her legs dangled. The child said nothing, face pinched and white, when Chang's hands shot out and seized her waist. Miss Temple pushed Svenson to the rail and he flung himself over, knobbed fingers squeezed tight. Chang's arms reached for the Doctor's kicking legs.

The soldiers came nearer, playing their lanterns along the girded under-carriage of the bridge. Miss Temple slipped over in silence, sliding down until her hands were out of view, grasping the lowest edge of the catwalk. She hung in place.

Above her lantern light danced across where she'd stood. Sentries patrolled the bankside below. If even one soldier noticed the lights and looked up, she would be found. A gloved hand caught Miss Temple's foot and another her waist, and then both hands squeezed, a sign she should let go. Soldiers stood directly above her. She opened her hands. For an instant it did not seem as if Chang could bear her weight, but then his hands were joined by the Doctor's and she felt herself pulled through a crusted opening of stone.

'It stinks of birds.' Miss Temple rapped her boot against the wall, knocking away the clotted grime. The soldiers had moved on after finding the catwalk empty, and they were able to talk.

'Better birds than vagrant beggers,' replied Chang.

'I would not think a soul has been here since the bridge was built.' Svenson held Miss Temple's beeswax stub above his head and studied the walls. Beyond the windowed crevice lay a wider passage, once used to house sentries. 'Another corpse, architecturally speaking. Do we simply wait here for the bridge to be opened?'

'We could wait eight years,' said Chang. 'They control the entire river.'

'I wonder if Mr Pfaff escaped them,' said Miss Temple. 'Though who knows when he was there. Perhaps he has been captured.'

No one answered her, which Miss Temple found irksome. Francesca Trapping peeked out of the narrow window.

'Come away from there,' Miss Temple said.

Francesca did so, but then walked past Miss Temple to Doctor Svenson and pulled at his arm. 'I am supposed to take you somewhere else.'

Svenson dredged up a smile. 'Then let us see what we can find. The work here was hastily done . . .'

He led her further into the alcove, tapping at the wall, a mixture of old stone and new brick, until the impact of his boot echoed hollowly. He looked to Chang and Miss Temple with a raised eyebrow.

'Perhaps it's a colony of rats,' offered Chang. 'Burrowing out their home.'

Svenson held the light to the join of the floor and the oddly angled wall, then passed the candle to Francesca. He braced his hands against the wall for leverage.

'Steel-toed boots, you know . . .' He kicked and the bricks were driven in, for the mortar was honeycombed with mould. A few more kicks and he was chopping at an opening with his heel. The crusted stones tumbled into the darkness as they came loose, and soon the Doctor had cleared a gap wide enough to writhe through.

Miss Temple wrinkled her nose at the dank air rising from the hole. 'What do you suppose is down there?'

'Apart from rats?' asked Chang.

'I am not frightened of rats.'

'Then you should go first.'

She saw he was smiling, and, though his tone annoyed her, she recognized his teasing as a kindly overture. Why did it seem impossible to have a conversation that did not leave her feeling cross?

'Do not be absurd,' said Doctor Svenson seriously. He dropped to his knees, extending the candle through the hole and then his head. He waved his remaining hand in the air. Chang caught it and, so braced, the Doctor crawled further. Finally Svenson squeezed Chang's hand and Chang pulled him back into view. In the candlelight, the Doctor seemed to have emerged from some fairy portal, aged ten years, his hair floured with cobwebs and brick dust. He brushed it away with a smile.

'If we had not seen Crabbé's tunnel I should not have known what to make of it – but it is indeed another part of the old fortress. Utterly derelict, yet I cannot think but it will take us *somewhere*.'

Svenson insisted on widening the hole for the ladies, prising away what bricks he could without risking the wall's collapse. This done, he led the way – sliding down a slope of rubble to a shallow stone trench. Soon all four of them stood beating dust from their clothes.

'I do not see one rat anywhere,' said Miss Temple.

'I am glad of it,' whispered Francesca.

Chang smiled. 'We can only pray something larger has not eaten them.'

With a disapproving glare the Doctor led them in the direction least cluttered by debris. Miss Temple wondered who had last been in this place – some man-at-arms in polished steel? She felt she ought to have been frightened – outside the candle's meagre glow the passage was pitch black, and the air hung heavy with rot – but her foolishness with the red glass ball seemed long ago, and their escape from the bridge had fuelled her confidence.

'If we do reach the Customs House, I am sure I can find our way, having been inside it.'

Svenson called over Miss Temple's head to Chang, 'What is your guess as to the time?'

'Near sunrise. We may meet porters, but it is unlikely any staff have arrived.'

'The porters will not bother *us*,' announced Miss Temple.

Francesca Trapping shrieked and thrust herself against the Doctor in fear. Miss Temple's heart leapt at the child's cry, but she could not see what had provoked it. She felt Chang at her shoulder and saw the knife in his hand.

Svenson advanced with the candle. Across their path lay a jumble of blackened shapes, bound together by twists of rotting leather.

'Bones,' said the Doctor simply. 'Not old – not ancient – nor would any person be buried in a fortification's corridor.' Svenson studied the squalid heap. 'I make it at least three men . . . but I cannot say what has killed them.'

He lifted the light towards the roof of their tunnel. 'This has been more recently bricked in, of an age with the bridge, I would guess.'

'Deceased labourers.' Chang turned away and spat. 'Their bodies hidden away.'

'Hardly unusual,' said Miss Temple quietly.

'What does that mean?' asked Chang.

'It means people always die doing this work – making things like bridges and spires and railway stations –'

'Or growing sugar cane.'

Miss Temple met Chang's gaze and shrugged. 'People walk on bones every minute of the day.' She leant forward and gave Francesca's arm a friendly squeeze.

They emerged into a basement corridor, startling a round-faced porter with a mop and bucket, his uniform protected by a cotton apron. His expression of surprise vanished abruptly when he saw the dust upon their clothes.

'You were at the cathedral.' His voice was hushed.

'I'm afraid we lost our way,' replied Doctor Svenson.

'Of course you did.' The porter's head bobbed in sympathy, and he pointed behind him. 'It's back through the trading hall. But I didn't think – they're not letting people in, even family. Only from the hospital –'

'I am a physician,' said Svenson quickly.

'O – well then. I'm told the Shipping Board is given over as well – not that there's trading today, nor any shipping –'

The porter hesitated, as if he doubted his licence to say more. His eyes fell to Miss Temple and the girl. 'If you don't mind my speaking, it's no sight for a lady, or a child. No sight for anyone. Straight from hell itself.'

'Thank you for your kindness,' said Miss Temple softly. The porter excused himself, fumbling for words. He hurried away, but not before Miss Temple noticed that the water in his bucket was stained red.


On her visit to the Customs House, Miss Temple had been shown the famous trading hall like a child visiting a grist mill is shown the great wheel. She had dutifully murmured amazement at the clamour around the dais, where busy clerks posted the latest figures in chalk. Her father's agent had escorted her to the firm's own office above the fray, hoping to shed her presence after a single cup of tea, but Miss Temple had insisted on examining every ledger, matching her resolve against that of the crisp-cuffed men forced to attend her. In the end she had affected a grudging satisfaction, aware that reticence and a scowling demeanour were her best defence against thievery. She had decided to get a recommendation from Roger for someone to study her accounts independently. No doubt that person would have been enmeshed with the Cabal, and she shuddered to think how near her holdings had come to being plundered . . .

But now the enormous trading hall was silent. Heatless shafts of morning light fell onto rows and rows of oblong bundles, quite unmistakably human beings, covering the entire floor. At first it seemed the trading hall had been given over as a dormitory for Chang's dispossessed, but then she perceived their utter stillness, the shapeless huddling . . . there had to be *hundreds* . . . hadn't the porter said the Shipping Board had been so consigned as well? He'd said something else . . . the *cathedral* –

Moving through the bodies were several cloaked figures, some standing, some bent low, making observations. Were they Ministry officials? Or perhaps the bereaved searching amongst the dead – only a few let in at a time, out of decency? One figure waved to the others. A lantern was shone on the corpse in question, and a satchel brought forward. The crouching man rifled the bag's contents, but his back was to Miss Temple and she could not see his work.

The crouching figure rose and hobbled along the row of bodies – an elderly man, walking with a cane. He must be a doctor, or a savant from the Royal Society. Surely the authorities had found the glass spurs, but had they placed them as the source of the chaos?

Before Miss Temple could step forward or call out – not that she *would* have called out – Cardinal Chang pulled her from the archway.

'The *scale* of it,' Svenson whispered. Miss Temple assumed he meant the slaughter, but then the Doctor waved back towards the storage room in which they had emerged. 'The bridge closed, the riverfront seized – now the Customs House shut down? *And* the Shipping Board? There are private warehouses that could be guarded to contain rumours, but they use this – by *design*. We know the explosions were deliberate – and now, just as deliberately, the city is strangled to a halt.'

'Axewith and Vandaariff,' said Chang. '*This* is why they met.'

'But *why*?' asked Miss Temple. 'Even if Vandaariff wishes everything in ruins, why should the Privy Council agree to –'

'The oldest lure of all,' said Svenson. 'He has given the Ministry an excuse to expand its power. Whether Axewith is a pliant fool or a knowing rogue scarcely matters. If money cannot move and the streets are filled with soldiers, who can fight him?'

Miss Temple did not understand at all. 'But how does expanding Axewith's power serve Vandaariff? I should think it makes it harder for any villainy to occur. As you say, soldiers on every street corner –'

'But *whose* soldiers?' Svenson asked with a vexing certainty. Miss Temple knew her mind was not strategic – the month after next might as well be Peru – but the Doctor spoke as if the world were a chess game worked out three moves in advance.

Chang eased himself between them, speaking quietly. 'Whether this

carnage justifies the soldiers or conceals their purpose, they *are* in place –
and, especially after the gunplay in the Palace, they reduce *our* efforts to
skulking.'

'As being in hiding has reduced the Contessa's,' added the Doctor, 'and if
we *are* in her position, perhaps we can better understand her own intentions.
Remember, she was in the Palace, but showed no interest in Vandaariff's
meeting with Axewith –'

'All the more reason not to emulate her methods,' replied Miss Temple.

'That she follows a separate path does not make it *wrong*.'

Miss Temple huffed. 'But all that has so exercised you – the soldiers, these
writs, the Ministry – if those have nothing to do with the Contessa, then why
do we speak of her? There are only the three of us – which would you have
us address? Vandaariff, the Ministries or the Contessa?'

Svenson sighed. 'We must address them all. I cannot see which holds the
key.'

'But that is *impossible* –' Miss Temple stopped at a sour exclamation
from Chang. 'What?'

'Keys. I had forgotten. The book that contains the Comte's memories.
The Contessa forged glass keys to read it safely.'

Miss Temple clenched her throat. 'Even with a key that book is deadly.'

'The Contessa is no fool.' Svenson laid a gentle hand on Francesca's shoulder. 'She would recruit an exceptionally brave assistant to do the reading for
her.'

The girl acted as if she did not hear, idly rubbing her shoe against the
floor, proud of her secrets.

The cloaked figures had left the trading hall. At Chang's insistence they
clung to the edge on their own way across, creeping beneath the great chalk-
boards upon which the previous day's figures were still visible. Atop the dais
stood a massive clock, large enough to be seen from the floor. Its ticking
echoed oddly – perhaps the machine contained a double works to prevent
winding down in the midst of trading. To Miss Temple, the doubled ticking
only made clear the narrowness of her luck. But for Chang's swift action in
the square, she might well have lain amongst these anonymous dead.

They were nearly to the other side when Svenson pressed Francesca's hand into Miss Temple's, to the dismay of both.

'A moment. Keep going, I beg you.'

The Doctor dashed through the lanes of bodies to where the party of cloaked men had been. He knelt, lifting the covering from several corpses in turn. Svenson went still, staring down, then hurried to rejoin them.

Chang extended a hand for silence. They had reached the other side, and he cautiously peered into the column-swept portico. Miss Temple detected voices echoing from the front entrance.

She turned to ask what Svenson had seen, but the words died in her throat. From the field of corpses three figures had risen, wrapped in sheets like ghosts on the stage. Then the sheets fell away to reveal three cloaked men, positioned to block any angle of retreat. Beneath their cloaks Miss Temple glimpsed flashes of green. Soldiers from Raaxfall.

A dry chuckle drifted from the portico and from the columns emerged three more soldiers, Mr Foison and the man – the one amused – who'd hobbled with a cane.

'Forgive my little ruse,' called Robert Vandaariff. 'Spirits from beyond! And yet you were fooled – of *course* you were, so inevitable as to be *dull*.' The soldiers with Foison fanned out, blocking their way forward. Chang had a knife in each hand. Miss Temple tugged the revolver from her bag and felt her back touch that of Doctor Svenson, who faced the men behind.

'The corpse I examined,' Svenson whispered, 'the transformed flesh had been removed, for study.'

'For the *future*, Doctor! What convenience to find all three of you at a stroke . . .' But then Vandaariff saw the girl. His voice took on an ugly tremor. 'Sweet hell, the child. Is the Contessa dead?'

'Don't you *want* her dead?' asked Miss Temple.

'Eventually – O everything eventually. And how do *you* do, Cardinal? Counting the hours?' But Vandaariff kept his gaze on Francesca. 'Step away – let me see her. She is mine by rights, legally so. I am chief shareholder of Xonck Armaments and have been named guardian of all three Trapping orphans. Once their uncle Henry succumbs I will adopt them formally. Would you like that, my dear?'

The girl stood as still as a frightened rabbit. Vandaariff's eyes glowed as he appraised her.

'Your father – your true father – was a dear old friend. You have his eyes, and hair – now so wild . . .' Vandaariff stretched out a shaking hand. 'Come to me, Francesca. I know your sacred origins. I know your destiny. You are a princess of heaven. An *angel*.'

He sketched a shape in the air with stiff fingers. Francesca bit her lip. Her reply was faint, but everything the Comte d'Orkancz could have desired.

'An *angel*.'

Miss Temple seized a handful of Francesca's hair with enough force to make the girl gasp, and pressed the pistol to her skull. 'I'll kill her first. And then I'll kill you.'

Francesca squirmed. A glint of metal in Foison's hand showed a palmed throwing knife, but he did not act. The Customs House must have been full of soldiers, like the bridge. But Vandaariff did not summon them.

Keeping hold of the child's hair, Miss Temple suddenly shifted her aim to Vandaariff. The spell was broken. Foison's arm whipped forward. With a sharp ringing the knife was knocked wide by Chang's own flung blade. Doctor Svenson's revolver roared in her ear. Miss Temple squeezed the trigger of her own pistol, aiming at Vandaariff's head, but only plucking his high collar. Before she could fire again, Chang shoved her roughly back and met the charge of Foison's three men with a knife in one hand and his razor in the other.

She collided with Francesca, who fell, causing Miss Temple to sprawl in turn and lose the pistol. Francesca scuttled away. Miss Temple got to her knees, intending to crawl after, but instead tripped one of Foison's soldiers – careening from Chang with a spurting wrist. She whipped the knife from her boot. As the soldier groped for her throat she slashed at his fingers. He rose before her, then arched his back with a scream. Another of Foison's knives had buried itself in the man's body, clearly intended for Miss Temple.

A gunshot made her turn. Doctor Svenson lay on his side, the last cloaked soldier tottering above him with a smoking revolver. Between them crouched Francesca, somehow tangled in a corpse's cover sheet. Miss Temple flung her knife at the cloaked man's face. It struck harmlessly on the shoulder, but caused him to spin, whipping his pistol towards her. The Doctor fired, punching a hole under the man's clean-shaven jaw. Francesca clapped both hands over her ears. Svenson slumped back, clutching his chest.

Two more soldiers lay at Chang's feet, a knife-hilt sticking from one's throat. Chang flicked the blood from his razor and stepped deliberately between Foison and Miss Temple. He snatched up a cloak, twirling it around his wrist. Foison drew two more knives from his silk coat.

The two men advanced with feral precision. It was the first time Miss Temple had seen Chang treat an enemy like an equal, and it frightened her more than anything.

Vandaariff had withdrawn from the mêlée, back to the columns, and now stood waving. Behind him, at last, came the calls of soldiers. She blinked. Vandaariff was waving them *away*.

Because their meeting had been a surprise, she realized, an interruption. Vandaariff's true business in the Customs House could not stand scrutiny – the soldiers would take matters in hand, clear the area, scour the premises for confederates . . .

What if Vandaariff had not come to the trading hall for *bodies* at all? Had his artist's indulgence delayed his departure, after his true errand?

The square. The cathedral. Why not the Customs House too? Vandaariff would know when it would be released for normal work and filled with men – would know to the minute. The doubled ticking –

More voices filled the portico, the soldiers calling out at the sight of the battle. Any moment they must burst forward. Miss Temple saw her own pistol. She snatched it up.

Her shot splintered the wood of the clock case.

'Celeste, what are you doing?'

It was Svenson. Behind her Vandaariff's voice rose to a shriek. She marched closer, for a better shot. Her second bullet missed entirely.

An officer loudly ordered everyone to drop their weapons. Miss Temple extended her arm, imagining the clock a brown glass bottle, and fired.

Blue smoke spat out at the bullet's impact, an instant ahead of the blast, a deafening wall of smoke and debris that choked her breath and blotted out all sight. Miss Temple was lifted off her feet and landed hard. Her last thoughts boiled with unreasoning fury. She wanted nothing more than to blind Robert Vandaariff with her own two thumbs.

She came to her senses at a blaze of agony in her left arm.

'*Pauvre petite*,' said an unpleasant voice. 'You will regret your waking. Hold her, please . . . she may still be subject to the *infusion*.'

Firm hands clamped Miss Temple's shoulders, and above her face loomed Mr Foison, white hair hanging down. Robert Vandaariff stood near in his shirtsleeves, an apron over his clothes. He held a pair of forceps and, as she watched, insinuated their tip into a gash running perhaps four inches along her forearm. She protested, but he only thrust deeper, beneath a crust of blue that sealed one end of the wound. With a wrench that made Miss Temple cry, Vandaariff prised up the crystallized flesh. He tore the patch free with his fingers and dropped it on a plate. Despite the pain, Miss Temple felt her thoughts clear. Vandaariff set the forceps next to a porcelain basin and washed his hands. Next to the basin she saw a lock of auburn hair, quite obviously her own.

'Not a serious wound,' he said. 'Mr Foison is perfectly capable of dressing it. I have done enough for *you*. That you live at all, that I have not melted your soft body for candle fat . . .' He sniffed and reached for a towel. 'It goes against tradition.'

Vandaariff tucked the lock of hair into a pocket, collected his cane and hobbled to a cabinet lined with bottles – but not, she realized, bottles of liquor. He poured out an ugly mixture, like milky weak tea, swirled the glass and drank it off. 'You were only touched the once.' He wiped his mouth with a napkin. 'Your luck persists.'

'You do not have Francesca.' Her voice quavered, for Foison had begun to wrap her arm. Her wool jacket was gone, her dress ash-blackened and tattered.

'Why do you say that?'

'My survival.'

'I suppose you do not care – being so brave – that your friends were blown to rags. Only that you managed to vex *me*.'

Miss Temple's body went cold. 'I do not believe you.'

'By all means, Miss Temple. Believe your *heart*.'

She gasped again as Foison knotted the bandage. He stepped away, and Miss Temple pushed herself up. She lay on a wooden work table in a strange room panelled with polished steel. Had there been time to reach Harschmort?

'But this is your own natural advantage,' Vandaariff went on. 'Celeste Temple acts without the impediment of remorse. Though it *was* clever to realize a device had been set for tomorrow's trading. And decent shooting to strike it.'

'Are you always so generous when you've been bested?'

'Bested? Miss Temple, the bee is but part of the hive, the single piraña one of its school. In the world of men, such multiplication of effort is accomplished by wealth. This is *my* advantage. And when such a device is set off by my *enemies* in the presence of officers of the 8th Fusiliers? At a stroke it is proved that I have nothing to do with such destruction – I was there only to search for a missing old friend, don't you know, arranged as a favour from Lord Axewith. And the blame is laid fully upon the three individuals who have continually thwarted my plans. I could not have asked for more.'

Her throat closed against any reply. Foison coughed into his hand.

'Indeed,' agreed Vandaariff. 'Off with you. But indulge my frailty – you've seen the animal.'

With a cold efficiency, Foison looped her limbs into leather restraints and pulled tight. Then he was gone.

The precaution was hardly necessary. Miss Temple could barely breathe. She saw Svenson clutching his chest and Chang, his back to the blast, unprepared . . . she looked down at her bandaged arm and wilfully clenched her fist. Pain shot up her arm and tears stung her eyes. Vandaariff was lying. She had been kept alive to be ransomed, and only Svenson and Chang would so preserve her. They had escaped with Francesca, Vandaariff's desired prize.

Vandaariff shuffled beyond her view, making a menacing clatter of metal and glass. But, instead of the stink of chemicals or indigo clay, the room was suddenly suffused with the pleasing odour of cooked eggs and melted butter. He returned to his seat with a lacquered tray.

'You have not eaten, I know.' He plucked up a fresh white roll and tore it at the seam, fingers stiff as the talons of a bird. He smeared butter into the bread, then dipped a spoon into a Chinese pot and withdrew a gleaming lump of plum jam. He shook this onto the butter and cut – the shaking knife edge ringing on the plate – a wedge of soft white cheese. The finger's-width of cheese fell off the knife, and with an exasperated grunt Vandaariff smeared it into the roll with a gnarled thumb. He wiped his hand on a napkin and sighed at the effort.

Miss Temple's last meal had been at Raaxfall, and so poor she'd left half on her plate. She watched the tray closely. Her arm throbbed.

'One must eat, you know, for strength.' He swirled the eggs with a fork and raised a quivering morsel, dripping yolk. He swallowed with difficulty, as if it were a mouthful of small bones. He set down the fork and took an awkward bite of the roll. Vandaariff's teeth were not ill favoured for an older man, but his hesitation to bear down made Miss Temple wince that one might break away. Vandaariff chewed, breath flaring his nostrils, and finally forced the bolus through. He wiped his lips and grimaced, dropping the napkin onto the tray.

'Does it not agree?' Miss Temple asked. 'I would have thought you ate for pleasure. Even for *art*. The Comte d'Orkancz told me everything in life came down to art. Then he made me pay for his coffee. I suppose *that* is an art as well.'

An appreciative smile graced his lips. 'Do you not worry for your life?'

'I am alive to be ransomed.'

She could not tell if he laughed at her delusion or at the chance to correct it. 'You are like a fox intent on its prey, never noticing that the forest around her is aflame.'

'I am not. And, if I am, my prey is still *you*.'

'But when you so brightly speak of *ransom*, you should realize that those who might reclaim you do not know to what extent you have been harmed. One bit of glass has scratched your arm – who is to say five more did not scratch your face? What if one exploded straight into your mouth and turned your tongue to stone? You could not tell them what had happened. You could never tell anyone *anything*.' He poked the cane at the hem of her dress and dragged it up above the knee. 'The trick about *art*, Miss Temple, is to understand how each moment is compounded into another, *tempers* another. You see the weakness in my body. I see the fever in yours. Does either one of us see true?'

'I have no fever.'

Vandaariff snorted derisively. 'I could light a match by touching the tip to your skin.'

He flipped the cane in the air and caught the opposite end, then pushed the handle – a smooth brass ball – along her calf.

'What are you doing?'

'Claiming my property.' The brass ball slid up her thigh. Miss Temple squirmed.

'You are vulgar and coarse – and no gentleman!'

'An artist is never a gentleman. And a *lady* ought to be a better liar than you.'

The cane nudged the seam of her silk pants. Miss Temple shrank from its touch.

'You are withered and old! You torment me because you cannot do anything else!'

He turned the brass ball with a delicate, teasing motion, and spoke with an airy distraction. 'If I wanted your submission, I could put a piece of glass before your eyes. If I sought your degradation, I could summon Foison's men to rape you through the afternoon. Do you think I would not dare?'

Miss Temple shook her head quickly. The cane pressed hard against her and she whimpered in fear. Vandaariff tugged her dress above her waist, and then her petticoats. He looked down with a musing expression, as if she were a food locker whose jumbled contents might just constitute a meal. He spread his palm against her pelvis, measuring the soft flare, then pressed down. He took her hips with both hands, hefting her body. His stiff fingers cupped her buttocks and squeezed.

'Wide enough,' he announced, 'should other plans fail and you still live. I do appreciate your spark.' He shoved her petticoats higher.

'I beg you,' she whispered. 'Please –'

'My interest is entirely contingent, I assure you.' He caught the waist of her silk pants and pulled. The silk ripped. He pulled again, with a grunt, and they came away. 'After Rosamonde's book, you are not intact in any *practical* sense of the word. Time enough has passed to show you made no mistakes with young Bascombe. But since then, with your mind so swimming – and I *know* it's swimming, Celeste – have you remained so careful? This last day with Chang . . . more time with the Doctor . . . and how many others have crossed your path at that hotel?' His thumb stroked the curls between her legs. 'Have you surrendered or been strong? Or have you found strength to be something *else*?' He laid his palm above the hair, against her belly, as if to listen through it. 'I prefer to think you failed – the guilt burning even as you've quenched your need, with one of those paid-off soldiers – yes, Mr Ropp behind you, thrusting away. I imagine you soaked in the history of the world, so many generations of mindless rut.' His hand slid lower, his thumb dragging along her folds.

Miss Temple flexed her fist again, but Vandaariff merely took her gasp as a sign of enjoyment.

'What do you *want*?' she pleaded.

'Your confession.' His motions became forceful, his smile more fixed and contemptuous.

'Confess to what?'

'Futility.'

'You are hurting me –'

'Pain is nothing. Desire is nothing.' Vandaariff's lips had stretched with effort, tight across his teeth. 'Trappings of useless vessels . . . flawed from the start . . .'

Miss Temple yelped. Vandaariff raised his fingers, pinching between them three reddish hairs. He flicked them away and plucked again.

'What are you doing! Stop it!' She cried out over her shoulder towards the door: 'Mr Foison!'

'All signs of age must be expunged. Age is corruption, ash, decay –'

'Stop! Mr Foison!'

'The alchemical Bride bears no blemish. She is without colour, holds the moon – she cannot be *marked* –'

His fingers sank into Miss Temple's hair and seized hold, tugging her pubis. She raised her hips to stave off the painful wrench, whimpering –

The door opened behind her. Vandaariff turned, eyes unfocused.

'Lord Robert?'

Vandaariff followed Foison's gaze to Miss Temple's exposed body and released his grip. He wiped his hand across the apron. 'Is there word?'

'Just now, my lord.' Foison extended a folded page to his master. Vandaariff slid a crabbed thumb beneath the wax seal. In her shame Miss Temple did not look at Foison. She stared at Vandaariff, watching the paper tremble with his fingers.

'We will depart at once.'

'Yes, my lord.'

With an easy movement Foison caught the upturned hem of Miss Temple's dress and swept it down, over her legs. Vandaariff stuffed the note into his pocket.

'It plays out exactly to plan.'

'Yes, my lord.'

Vandaariff awkwardly pulled the apron strap over his head. Foison slipped behind to untie the knot, draped the apron on the chair and handed Vandaariff his stick. Vandaariff brought the brass handle to his nose, sniffed, then dabbed his tongue across the ball. He gave a disapproving grimace and hobbled from the room.

As efficiently as he had bound her, Foison released the leather straps. Only after sweeping her legs together could Miss Temple meet his gaze, yet Foison was watchful and withheld. Not unlike Chang, but without Chang's animal temper . . . yet that was not true – they were different animals. Where Chang was a loping cat, Mr Foison was a cold reptile.

'Can you walk?' he asked simply. 'It is only to the coach.'

'And then where?' What she wanted was to curl into a ball.

'Where else?' Foison said, helping her to stand. 'The Contessa.'

They entered a courtyard ringed by tall stone buildings. Miss Temple gazed around her.

'The Royal Institute,' said Foison. 'Lord Vandaariff is a significant patron.'

'I believe the Comte d'Orkancz conducted experiments here, with Doctor Lorenz. Did you know them?'

But Foison's attention was taken by smoke rising in a cloud from what looked like an open cellar door, across the grassy court. Green-coated guards hovered around it with buckets of water and sand. Two black coaches waited under a massive archway. Foison hoisted Miss Temple into the first coach. She slid into place opposite Vandaariff. Foison glanced over his shoulder.

'A moment, Lord Robert –'

'I have no moment. Get in and order the men on.'

'There is a small fire –'

'Let the scholars deal with their fire.'

'Evidently supplies of chemicals have been stored nearby – it will be a matter of minutes to shift them and then attack the blaze. Not doing so risks –'

'Risks *what*?' snapped Vandaariff.

Foison hesitated. 'Why, the Institute itself, my lord.'

'Fascinating.' Vandaariff leant to the open coach door and sniffed. He sat back in his seat. 'Let it burn. I'm done with the place.'

'But Lord Robert –'

'Get *in*, Mr Foison, and order the men on. I have no spare time. Not in this world.'

With a grim expression, Foison shouted to the men to drop their buckets and be about their orders. He swung himself next to Miss Temple and rapped on the roof to set the coach in motion. Vandaariff's seat was piled with the day's newspapers and, already deep in the *Courier*, he did not acknowledge their departure.

The other newspapers announced two more explosions, at the Circus Garden and the White Cathedral, with a death toll of at least a thousand, for each blast had provoked a violent riot. A second headline blamed the disaffected populace of Raaxfall – a man from that distant village was recognized before the Circus Garden blast destroyed him. Miss Temple guessed the man was another of Vandaariff's prisoners, repurposed as a weapon. The Ministry had announced new measures to protect the national interest.

Vandaariff closed the newspaper. If he took any pleasure in his success, his flat interrogation of Foison did not betray it.

'All is prepared?'

'Yes, my lord. The second coach follows. I have instructed the driver to follow the Grossmaere, as it is lined with hussars.'

'Your face is bruised.'

'It is, my lord. Cardinal Chang.'

'I find it ugly.'

'I will strive to avoid further injury.'

Vandaariff paused, measuring possible insolence. 'We have not discussed your failure at the Customs House. Six men, and yourself – against two men and a negligible woman. And how many of your six are of any use to me now?'

'None, my lord. The explosion –'

'I did not ask for excuses.'

'No, my lord.'

'The men are of no account. I must rely upon *you*.'

Vandaariff slipped a finger between the black curtains of the coach window and peered out. Miss Temple knew she should keep silent. But Vandaariff had shamed her, and as she watched him – withered neck and knobbed hands – she felt her hatred rise.

'I saw your painting.' Vandaariff looked up, without expression. 'O I am sorry, I meant to say the *Comte's* painting. I forget of course that the Comte d'Orkancz is dead.'

'He *is* dead,' said Vandaariff.

'And thank *goodness*. What an odious, vulgar, canker-brained, preening madman. Perhaps it's something in your manner that recalls him.'

'Gag her mouth.'

Miss Temple laughed. 'Don't you even want to know *which* painting? Or who showed it to me? You are so very sure of yourself –'

Foison had a cloth between her teeth, but paused at a sign from Vandaariff.

'I have quite a collection of the Comte's works at Harschmort.'

Miss Temple spat the kerchief from her mouth and flexed her jaw.

'Bought for Lydia's wedding – yes, *so* thoughtful. Is it *St Rowena and the Vikings* that shows a rape on a church altar? The Viking *bracing* himself on the crucifix –'

'This was the painting you mean?'

'No, the painting *I* saw was not *at* Harschmort. It was called *The Chemickal Marriage*.'

The smile on Robert Vandaariff's lips became perceptibly more stiff.

'You cannot have seen that painting. It does not exist.'

Miss Temple smirked. 'Perhaps you tried to buy it and were refused! Of course the composition is demented – depicting a marriage, I suppose, but of *symbols*. An *allegory*.' She turned to Foison. 'Allegory is for *donkeys*.'

'That painting was burnt.'

'Was it? Well, it's odd because the Bride in question wears a mask of the Contessa's face. Isn't that strange? The Groom is black as coal, with a red apple in his hand, except it isn't *really* an apple – more like a beating heart, and made entirely of *red glass* –'

Foison pulled the handkerchief tight between her lips. Vandaariff leant closer.

'Sooner than you imagine, Celeste Temple, I will reclaim you, and service *you* on an altar. In that the Comte d'Orkancz had things exactly right!'

Vandaariff sank back. He shut his eyes and reached a shaking hand to Foison.

'The bottle.'

Foison opened a satchel and removed a squat bottle of dark glass. Vandaariff drank, a thin line of milky fluid escaping down his chin. He wiped his face with a black silk handkerchief, folded it over and then mopped his brow.

Composure restored, he addressed her again. 'I have not thanked you for the delivery of such excellent mules, Mr Ropp and Mr Jaxon. Discharged soldiers, they told me – amongst other things. Amongst *every* thing. And Mr Ramper as well – still, even a stricken animal can be used. You must know that from your plantation. Scrape off the meat and burn the bones for fuel. Will you be pleased to see the Contessa?'

Miss Temple made a noise in the back of her mouth.

'Tell her anything you like.' He reached into his coat and came out with another handkerchief, white silk this time. 'But when you have the chance, Miss Temple – and you will, for the Contessa will underestimate you, as she always has – you would serve us all by cutting the lady's skin . . . with *this*.'

In the opened handkerchief lay a blue glass spur. He chuckled, a guttural wheeze, and refolded the handkerchief. His crooked fingers reached across the coach and stuffed it down the bosom of her dress.

'Created expressly for our own shared nemesis. Dig it into her arm, across her lovely neck – wherever is in reach. Then I suggest you *run*.'

The coach came to a halt. She heard the ring of bolts being drawn and the scrape of an iron gate. Vandaariff nodded, and Foison bound Miss Temple's hands.

Her heart went cold. She had not truly believed it until the handkerchief had been tucked into her dress. She was being given to a woman who sought her death. Why not to Chang and Svenson? What could the Contessa offer more precious than Francesca Trapping?

Foison opened the door and leant out to unfold a metal stair-step. Miss Temple drove her bound hands against his back and sent him flying through the door. She hurled herself at Vandaariff, snarling like a dog. Her hands found his throat, the rope between them digging his wattled flesh like a garrotte. He batted weakly at her face. He gaped, eyes wide, tongue protruding . . . and then let out a horrible stuttering gasp. *Laughter*. She met his insane, *encouraging* nod and squeezed as hard as she could –

Foison's strong hands wrenched Miss Temple away and hauled her out of the door. With a snarl of his own he flung her down with enough force to drive the breath from her body. Wet grass and earth were cold against her cheek. She gulped for air. Foison was tending his master. She heaved herself up – only to drop again secured in place. One of Foison's knives – thrown from the coach – pinned her dress to the ground. Before she could yank it free her wrists were caught by a hand in a leather gauntlet. Miss Temple looked up to a semicircle of men in green uniforms.

Foison emerged from the coach and called to the driver, who started his team, turning back the way they'd come. Foison retrieved his blade.

'Make sure of her.'

As they walked Miss Temple's stomach rose. She shut her eyes against the bile in her throat and sucked air through her nostrils.

Something in the smell . . . the Comte had been here before . . .

She took the first statues for more green uniforms, for the stones had been overcome by moss. Soon they appeared in lines between the trees, stained by years of leaf-fall, tipped by sinking earth or knocked headless, even toppled, by falling tree limbs. A cemetery . . .

Miss Temple's nausea sapped any notion of escape, and she followed Foison through the woods and down a proper row of tombs. Even here the stones were cracked and crumbled, swathed in green, the names scarcely legible, abandoned . . . had so many families passed out of time? She turned her attention to the statues: mournful figures, some with wings, some humbly shrouded, facing down in grief or up in supplication. In their hands were open books and closed, torches, laurels, lilies, roses, harps, keys – and on the tombs so many inscriptions, from the Bible or in Greek or Latin.

None of it touched Miss Temple, for she was too near the Comte's estimation of such piety. To his mind, and thus persuasively to hers, such trappings of grief and hope were akin to a toddler's scrawl.

The skin of her elbow stung from her awkward fall, and, unable to reach with her hands, she rubbed it against her stomach. She had risked everything in attacking Vandaariff, but Foison had merely pulled her away. At the Customs House, he had twice sought her life with a thrown blade. She had become a valued commodity.

Beyond a spiked iron gate stretched a dim avenue lined with vaults. The gate stood between Egyptian obelisks, but their plaster had crumbled to reveal red brick, the work of an especially unscrupulous builder.

Foison unlocked the gate. The vaults had no names across their lintels, only metal numbers nailed into the stone. At the avenue's end was a vault with the number 8, deliberately placed sideways. Foison sorted another key, then surveyed the sky above them. Miss Temple was reminded of a snake tasting the air with its tongue.

The vault door scraped open, and from inside the tomb rose a golden light. Someone waited inside.

Foison went first. He'd no weapon ready, nor had he brought a lantern. Miss Temple came next, prodded by a fellow with a cutlass, and then the others in a line. Instead of a horrid vault lined with niches, they entered an anteroom gleaming with blue ceramic tile. The far wall was fashioned like an ancient city gate, with a crenellated top and narrow windows, all aglow.

'The entrance to Babylon,' said Foison, removing her gag. 'The Ishtar Gate.'

'Ah.' In Miss Temple, vanished cultures met a sense of justice as to their vanishing.

'In Ishtar's temple is eternal life.'

A flicker of recognition came from the Comte's memories. Miss Temple tried to place the source . . . was it the light? She saw no candles or lanterns – the golden light came from the other side of the blue wall.

Foison opened the gate with an elaborate key with teeth like a briar's thorns. His men thrust Miss Temple through and slammed the gate. She cried out, naming Foison a coward and his master a degenerate toad. There was no reply. She heard the vault door close, and the cold lock turn.

The tomb was bright without the aid of a single lantern or candle. The floor was copper, polished near to a mirror. She recalled the metal on the walls of Vandaariff's room, and the sheets of steel hanging amongst the machines at Parchfeldt. A thread of bile burnt her throat like an incision and she knew: this interior part of the tomb had been a commission to prove the Comte's abilities – an unknown artist first brought to Vandaariff's attention by a new and intimate adviser, the Contessa di Lacquer-Sforza . . .

Miss Temple held up a hand and waved, making tiny shadows. The decorated ceiling was honeycombed by dozens of shafts that rose high to the surface and drew the sunlight down, directing the beams with mirrors and colouring their glow with glass.

More grimly, however, the shafts meant Miss Temple's earlier assumption had been wrong. No one else had entered the tomb – she *had* been abandoned. She looked for an edge to slice through the cord binding her wrists, but the walls and floor were smooth. The room's only feature was a slab of white marble, carved to depict silken bedclothes pulled open across it.

Two names were carved: Clothilde Vandaariff and, in fresh-cut letters, Lydia Vandaariff. No dates or epigraphs accompanied the names – nor, in the case of Lydia, could the tomb contain a body. Miss Temple wondered if it was her fate to serve as Lydia's proxy.

She sank down against the stone. Her forearm throbbed, and it seemed she had not slept in days. She curled on her side, yet, despite her fatigue, the solitude only gave Miss Temple's mind more opportunity to seethe . . .

When they had collided with Mr Harcourt and the Palace guard, Chang had seized her hand. They did not speak as they fled, but then a reckless turn left them in a dead-end room, with no time to double back.

'The wardrobe,' he hissed, pushing her to it. Chang leapt to a writing desk and dragged it beneath the room's single high window.

'Where are you going?'

'Get in the wardrobe!'

Chang vaulted onto the desk and opened the window. Did he think to draw pursuit away? He hauled himself through to the waist. He held a handful of papers from the desk and flung them out.

'A trail to follow,' he said, jumping down. 'The ledge is wide and the roof is flat – why are you not in the damned closet?'

Chang yanked it open and propelled her into a line of hanging garments.

'There is no *room*!'

The back of the wardrobe had hooks from which cloaks had been hung and Chang shoved her beneath them. Then the doors were shut and he was with her, limbs overlapping, bodies crammed together. Chang squeezed her arm, his words faint as a sigh.

'They are here.'

Miss Temple heard nothing. She had reached to steady herself and taken hold of Chang's belt in the dark. Chang had shifted, settling his weight, and one knee rolled forward, gently, to press between her legs. The corners of her mind began to crawl.

From outside came a scrape of floorboards – someone climbing on the desk. She tightened her grip. She wanted to lean forward and kiss his mouth. She tipped her body against the hardness of his knee. She bit her lip to keep silent.

With another shudder she heard his breath in her ear. 'Do not be afraid . . .'

She almost laughed aloud. He thought she shook with fear. She squeezed his hand. It would be the simplest thing to guide it to her breast.

The door to the wardrobe opened. The hanging clothes were jostled. She went still at the *chok* of a blade thrust home above her head. Another thrust, near her hand – *chok*! – and then a third, piercing the cloak directly between them. The blade was pulled free and the wardrobe door slammed shut.

They waited, Miss Temple at the edge of her control. Chang patted her hand. She rocked her body forward in a last sensual grind before he crawled cautiously out.

'They've gone.'

She pushed the cloaks away, feeling the heat in her face. He reached to extricate her. She did not meet his gaze.

Miss Temple opened her eyes. She jumped up, sure she had heard the jingle of metal.

A key scratched at the lock, slipped in, then turned. Miss Temple crept to the wall. The door swung inwards. She would kick as hard she could, jump through the door –

'I know you are there. Do not attempt to break my head.'

It was a voice she knew. 'Mr Pfaff?'

Jack Pfaff peered around the doorframe. 'As ever.'

Miss Temple restrained herself from rushing to his arms, content to present her still-bound wrists. Pfaff drew a knife and smiled as the cords gave way. Miss Temple began to rub the vivid marks, but Pfaff put his own hands on hers, chafing the skin to life.

'What have they done to you? And your poor arm!'

'It is nothing.' She pulled her hands away, disquieted by a lingering ache from her dream. 'Where have you been? How did you get a key to this awful prison? Who told you I was here?'

'First, we'll make you safe.' Pfaff took Miss Temple's uninjured arm. 'Can you walk?'

'Do not doubt it.' Miss Temple made a point to lift her dress with both hands, despite a stab of pain. 'But you must answer as we go. Where have you *been*?'

'Following the glass, as we agreed.' Pfaff laid a hand against her back, yet such was her relief that she did not slap it away. 'As for the keys to this place, I found them in the outer door, as was arranged.'

'*Arranged?*' Miss Temple spun to face him.

'We're not out of it yet, miss. You must trust me and play along.'

'Play along with what?'

'Kicking and cursing will be enough. I shall take your weight with my other hand, so it will *appear* that I drag you by the hair. Here we go!'

Pfaff shoved the vault door wide. One insolent hand snaked round her waist while the other seized her curls. Before she could protest, Pfaff deftly tripped her ankles, so he entered the lane dragging her behind. She did her genuine best to kick and scratch, and shrieked aloud when – having jostled him off balance – Pfaff did yank her hair so hard she feared it would rip.

He staggered through the Egyptian gate. No black-cloaked men, no green uniforms, only a single coach with a shabby fellow holding the reins.

'There!' Pfaff cried, speaking loudly. 'And I'll have no more of your non-sense!'

He shoved her in the coach. She scrambled onto her back, kicking out. He caught her foot and closed the door. The driver cracked his whip and eased his team forward. Pfaff paused . . . listening . . . then sat back with a smile.

'I think we've done it –'

Her boot landed square on his kneecap. He clutched it with both hands, hissing with pain. 'O! O – damn you to hell!'

'If I had any weapon now you would be dead,' she spat. 'If you ever take such liberties again I will see your back flayed white!'

Pfaff rubbed his knee. 'You're an ungrateful witch. Do you know where we are? How many eyes observe our every move?'

'I will not be *trifled* with.'

'That is no answer!'

'I am not *obliged* to answer. Do you remain in my employ or don't you?'

'I am not in the habit of accepting such abuse from anyone.'

'But you *are* in the habit of flinging a woman without care like a bale of cloth?'

'You've seen worse, I'm sure.'

To these hot words she said nothing, taking the moment to settle her dress. Pfaff smirked at its condition.

'What's he like, anyways?'

'Who?'

'Robert Vandaariff. I once caught a glimpse of his hat, on Race Day at the Circus. Did he mention the Contessa?' His gaze drifted across her body. 'Did he . . . mistreat you?'

'What is that?'

She pointed to a leather notebook poking from Pfaff's orange coat.

'Why, do you know it?'

'Of course I do. You were under the bridge. You took this from Minister Crabbé's laboratory. That notebook belonged to Roger Bascombe.'

'It did indeed. I'll admit, Miss Temple, I only half believed your stories – but now . . .' He broke off with a grin, showing his brown teeth. 'I kept it for you. Don't you want to peek inside?'

'I do not.'

'Liar.' He tossed the notebook onto her lap, then laughed at her discomfort. 'You act like I've given you a scorpion.'

'Where are we going?'

'Come, how *else* could I learn where you were, or collect you without being killed? You thought the glassworks would lead to Vandaariff, but they led to *her*.'

'Why should she want me saved? She hates me.'

'She described you to Vandaariff's messenger as her *intimate*.'

'Nonsense.'

Pfaff gave his own sceptical shrug. 'It saved your life.'

She could not read him – did Pfaff remain her man or not? She did her best to soften her tone. 'Do you know, Mr Pfaff, that every man you hired in my service has been killed?'

'That's a pity. I think Corporal Brine quite liked your maid.'

Perhaps Pfaff never felt sorry about anything. Chang's ill-will for the man stewed inside her. Why had she ever defended him?

'Why was I taken to the Vandaariff crypt?'

'Because it is isolated, I suppose, and easy to observe.'

Miss Temple knew this was wrong, and berated herself for not having examined every inch of the place. But there seemed nothing to find – the Comte had so little expressed himself in its making. If the real Ishtar Gate indeed had blue tile, the Comte's improved *artistic* version would have been made from coal and painted blood red.

'Where are we *going*?'

'Nowhere at all until I'm sure we aren't followed . . .'

Pfaff pressed his face against the window. Miss Temple scooted to the opposite side. She did not recognize these streets.

'Was there a second explosion today? At the Shipping Board?'

'Explosions all over.' Pfaff peered out, distracted. 'Terrible stuff.'

'The blasts are Vandaariff's doing – to provoke unrest. Who knows what he plans next, while you waste our time. Do you?'

Pfaff closed the curtain. 'Do I what?'

'Know where he is!'

'No, miss.'

'And you smile to say it! Of all the imbecilic –' Miss Temple's tirade was cut short by a sharp knock against the coach. 'What was *that*?'

The window near her head was shattered by a fist-sized chunk of brick. She squeaked, flinching from the flying glass. Luckily most was caught by the curtain.

'Perhaps you'd best lie down,' offered Pfaff.

Cries rose around the coach and Miss Temple recalled the faces on the Raaxfall dock. Their driver cracked his whip. The coach broke forward and the shouts began to fade. Pfaff slapped his hands together.

'That should peel them off.'

At the high-pitched cry of distressed horses behind them, Miss Temple peered through the broken window. Another coach had been stopped in the road, surrounded by an angry mob. The blasts had brought the unrest of Raaxfall to the city proper – and Pfaff had exploited the discontent to strip away pursuit. Who knew how close they'd come to harm as well? If the driver had been injured, or a coach wheel snapped . . . she was appalled at the reckless disregard.

'So where are we going *now*?' she demanded.

Pfaff laughed aloud. 'Where else, little mistress? *Home*.'

Pfaff said nothing more, and Miss Temple would not ask. Roger's notebook lay on her lap, but she had no wish to open it until she was alone and unobserved. While it might contain useful information, she did not trust her own reactions. What if there was fawning praise for Caroline Stearne's ankle or her opalescent skin? Opalescent was *exactly* the sort of word Roger would have used.

They arrived at the Hotel Boniface. She gripped the notebook tightly as she climbed down, ignoring Pfaff's outstretched hand. She considered shouting to the footmen, but she'd no firm idea how she stood with the hotel or the law, and further scandal might allow the management finally to expel her. Instead, she advanced to the desk and asked for any messages. There were none, but her asking allowed the clerk to take in the scorch marks on her dress, and her bandaged arm.

'You see what has overtaken me.' Miss Temple swallowed bravely. 'St Isobel's Square . . . I cannot speak of it.' The clerk's suspicion turned to cooing sympathy. For the moment, at least, Miss Temple had outflanked disapproval.

'Very good!' Pfaff chuckled, as they climbed the staircase. But Miss Temple found she actually *was* unsettled – and truly unable to speak of what she had seen in the square and at the Customs House. She had no experience through which to comprehend such carnage. Her eyes began to burn. Why *now*, treading soft familiar carpets, should she weaken? She quickened her pace to keep ahead of Pfaff, so he would not see.

'Are you well?'

'My arm hurts.' They were at the door. Pfaff cut in front and rapped three times. Miss Temple turned to dab her eyes. The door opened to Marie's anxious face.

'O, O *mistress* –'

Miss Temple pushed past – all she wanted was to be alone. 'I will need a wash and new clothes and supper and tea – strong hot tea before anything –'

'Mistress –'

'I am perfectly well, I assure you. I – I –' Miss Temple clutched Roger's notebook and groped for words. 'Marie – Corporal Brine –'

Pfaff easily took Marie's shoulder. 'Briney's all right, Marie – he's with the others, asked we pass along his regards – what about that tea?'

'But – but – *mistress* –'

Disgracefully grateful for Pfaff's imposition, Miss Temple pushed on as if she had not heard. Three steps brought her bedchamber and she shut the door and turned the key. She dropped Roger's notebook on a side table . . . and went ice-still.

The Contessa di Lacquer-Sforza sat on Miss Temple's bed, her cigarette holder smouldering like a stick of Chinese incense. She did not smile.

'Once more, circumstances prevent me from taking your life.' The Contessa savoured the catch of smoke, then spat a blue jet from the corner of her mouth. 'You look a fright.'

Miss Temple retreated to her writing desk. Were there scissors in the drawer?

'Is Mr Pfaff your creature?' Her voice cracked. In shame, she forced it low. 'I saw no scars around his eyes.'

'Not everyone requires the Process – in point of fact almost no one does.'

'But he – for several weeks, I employed –'

The Contessa sighed. 'Do you *still* not understand? The cream of this city *ached* to be chosen for the Comte's machines. Clawed each other like cats for the privilege. Slavery amongst the mighty is simple – one only has to make it *fashion*.'

'Mr Pfaff is no one's idea of *cream*.'

'He is his *own*. Enough – you cannot look like you've been tumbled in a cowshed.' Miss Temple turned to the door. 'Do *not* call your maid. She has been sent away.'

'Sent where?'

'Downstairs for tea or to the surgeon's with a broken jaw – I've no idea. We will pretty you and depart, without incident and without notice.'

'I will not budge.'

The Contessa raised her voice to an authoritative bark. 'Mr Pfaff!'

At once came a sharp yelp of pain from beyond the door, unmistakably from Marie. Miss Temple shot to her feet.

The Contessa spoke swiftly, with annoyance. 'You can do nothing to help her but *obey*.' She tugged the cigarette from its holder and dropped the butt to the floor, snuffing it as she stood.

'Where are we going?'

'Not until you change, Celeste.' For the first time, the Contessa smiled. 'Afterwards, everything. But first you must at least *pretend* to be civilized . . .'

The woman's fingers pulled at the back of her dress, each touch pecking apart Miss Temple's concentration. She had fought at the Customs House, and tried to strangle Vandaariff in his coach, but now it was all she could do to stand.

The Contessa peeled the fabric from Miss Temple's shoulders and then the sleeves over each hand, like a magician extracting two scarves from a hat. The Contessa yanked the dress to the floor. Miss Temple obediently stepped free of the pile.

'What happened to your arm?'

'It was cut by flying glass. At the Customs House.'

'And were you *very* brave?' The Contessa's hand traced its way without hurry around the circuit of Miss Temple's hips.

'Why are you here?' she whined.

'Better to ask why *you* are here,' replied the Contessa.

'This is my room.'

'I thought it belonged to sugar and slaves.'

'Then who owns your suite at the Royale – pulchritude?'

Miss Temple cried out as the caressing hand struck her buttock hard enough to leave a mark. The Contessa crossed to the wardrobe. Miss Temple plucked the Comte's silk handkerchief from her corset, but she'd no time to unwrap the glass spur before the Contessa had returned. Her breath blew warm against Miss Temple's nape.

'You smell like a *pony*.' The Contessa snatched up an amber bottle, Signora Melini's *Mielissima*, and came back with a basin of water. 'Arms *up*.'

Miss Temple complied. The Contessa roughly swabbed Miss Temple's armpits with a cloth, then her bosom and neck, and last, with smaller strokes, the planes of her face. Miss Temple held still, a kitten submitting to the ministrations of its mother's tongue. The Contessa dropped the cloth into the basin. With pursed lips she applied the perfume far more liberally than Miss Temple ever had, under her arms, at her wrists, behind her ears, and then, like a drunken signature to end a night of gambling, dragged the moistened stopper across the nooks of her collarbone. She replaced the stopper and threw the bottle carelessly onto the bed. With a sudden flicker of suspicion, the Contessa thrust a hand down Miss Temple corset, probing for anything hidden, and then swept in either direction, searching beneath each breast. Finding nothing, she pulled her hand free and then bent forward for a last sniff.

'At least no one will take you for an *unperfumed* pony.'

The Contessa snatched up a dress, fluffed it wide and lifted it over Miss Temple's head.

'But that is a dress for mourning –'

Her words were lost in a mass of black crêpe silk. She had worn it but once, for the funeral of Roger's cousin, at the beginning of their courtship. The sudden purchase, entirely for his sake, had pleased her immensely.

'Arms in the sleeves. Be quick about it.'

She realized that the Contessa's dress, which Miss Temple had taken for a dusky violet, was in fact closer to a shimmering charcoal. 'Who has died?'

'O who has not?'

The Contessa cinched the laces with as little regard for comfort as a farmer trussing goats. Her hands darted purposefully, flicking the skirts free of Miss Temple's feet, batting the dress over her petticoats, and alternately tugging down the bodice and lifting her bosom. Throughout it all the silken handkerchief remained in Miss Temple's hand, balled tight.

The Contessa stepped back with a sigh of resignation. 'Your hair would shame a sheepdog. Have you a hat?'

'I dislike hats. If you would allow my maid –'

'No.'

The Contessa took Miss Temple's curls with both hands. They stood near to one another, the Contessa fixed upon her task and Miss Temple, shorter, gazing at the other woman's throat, inches away.

The Contessa frowned. 'With charity, one could say you looked Swiss. But we are already late. What did you make of Oskar? Is he in *health*, Celeste? In his *mind*?'

'We scarcely spoke. I had been injured –'

'Yes, he must have liked that. Probably wanted to eat you whole.'

'Why did you not kill Doctor Svenson?'

'Beg pardon?'

The question had flown from Miss Temple's mouth. 'You left him alive with the glass card.'

'Did I?'

'Half of him wants to die, you know. Because of Elöise. Because of you.'

The Contessa met her censorious gaze and laughed outright, her pleasure the more for being taken unawares. Still smiling, she opened the door and walked out, leaving Pfaff to collect Miss Temple. He hooked her arm with his, but paused at the side table where she'd set Roger's notebook.

'She'll need a bag,' he called. 'It will look odd not to have one.'

The Contessa snorted from the foyer – a judgement on such propriety or, more likely, Miss Temple's taste in bags. Pfaff snatched up a handbag, deftly stuffed the notebook inside and shoved Miss Temple through the door. The Contessa rolled her eyes.

'Jesus Lord.'

Pfaff looked hurt. 'It matches perfectly well.'

'Like a headache matches nausea. Perhaps it will attract sympathy.'

Marie had vanished, and, though Miss Temple considered shouting to the desk clerk for rescue, in the end she allowed herself to be swept into the street. The door to a shining coach was held by a footman in rich livery. Miss Temple climbed up first and took the instant of solitude to return the silk handkerchief to the bosom of her dress. Pfaff installed himself next to her and the Contessa opposite, flouncing her dress with a deliberate thoroughness. Though she carried a black clutch, large enough to keep her cigarette holder, it was of no size for a glass book. Once more Miss Temple wondered where the dark volume had been cached. She cleared her throat.

'That footman's uniform – I mean – are we truly –'

'Celeste,' sighed the Contessa, 'if you can guess, must you *ask*?'

Pfaff only smirked and tugged at the lapels of his coat. Miss Temple could not think what the man seriously hoped to attain. That he had shifted his banner to the Contessa made Pfaff's character more clear – one might as well protest a bee being drawn to a more splendid flower. She recalled Mr Phelps insisting, so rudely, about society's divisions. As deluded as she saw Pfaff to be, so the Contessa saw Miss Temple – and no doubt there were circles where the Contessa appeared a garish *parvenu* . . .

The streets around them clattered with hoof beats. Their coach had attracted an escort of horsemen. Miss Temple stared at the Contessa.

'What *is* it, Celeste?'

'The Vandaariff crypt.'

'Yes?'

'You wanted me to see it.'

'This *insistence* on confronting me with what I already know –'

Miss Temple nodded to Pfaff. 'Does *he* know?'

'Why should I care?'

Pfaff's lips turned in a tolerant smile, as if he saw past the Contessa's disdain. 'I already told her – the tomb is isolated, easy to watch –'

'How did you know I'd been taken?' Miss Temple demanded. 'Was it that Francesca Trapping never appeared with Doctor Svenson?'

'If I cared for the child I should not have left her behind. She is nothing to me. No more than the Doctor.'

'But you spared his life. And have gone to some effort to save mine.'

'None of which, Celeste Temple, changes our *understanding*.'

Despite the Contessa's tone, Miss Temple sat back and grinned, showing her small white teeth. Both Vandaariff and the Contessa had preserved her life when she ought to have been slain, each to employ her against the other. They were fools.

'That's a repellent little smile,' said the Contessa. 'Like a weasel about to suck eggs.'

'I cannot help it,' said Miss Temple. 'I am excited – though you have not told me what I am to do when we arrive.'

'Nothing at all. Remain silent.'

'And if I don't?'

'I will cut your throat and spoil everything. And *then* what will I tell Cardinal Chang?'

The Contessa raised one eyebrow, waiting for her words to penetrate.

'Cardinal Chang?'

'How else do you think you were redeemed? For a chocolate cake?'

'You gave Chang to Vandaariff?'

'When a thing is already owned, one prefers the term "restoration" –'

'But where was he – how did you – he would never –'

'My goodness, we are here. Do try to honour the Cardinal's sacrifice. Remember – respectful silence, humble grief, pliant nubility.'

The Contessa pinched Miss Temple's cheeks to give them colour, then swatted her out onto a walkway of red gravel. The Contessa joined her, taking Miss Temple's hand. Pfaff remained in the coach. A richly uniformed man strode towards them, cradling an enormous busby, as if he'd come from beheading a bear. He clicked his heels and nodded to the Contessa, the gesture as sharp as a hatchet stroke.

'Milady.'

The Contessa sank into an elegant curtsy. 'Colonel Bronque. I apologize for our delay.'

The Colonel scrutinized Miss Temple with an icy scepticism, then ushered them on with a sweep of his gold-encrusted arm.

'If you will. Her Majesty is never one to be kept waiting.'

# FIVE

## RELIQUARY

Chang ignored the gunshots. It was up to Svenson to deal with the men behind them. The slightest break in concentration and Foison would have Chang's life: he could no more heed the commotion around him than a surgeon marked a patient's screams.

The razor was open in Chang's right hand. In his left he held a black cloak, long enough to tangle a blade and which, accurately thrown, could baffle Foison's vision. Foison matched him with two knives, balanced to throw, made for thrust, heavy enough to snap the razor clean. Instead of broad strokes to keep Chang back, Foison would favour point: one blade to entangle Chang's defence, then the other for the kill. Chang's options were more limited. The razor might spill quantities of blood, but to incapacitate a man like Foison the edge must reach his throat. Nothing less would prevent the second knife from stabbing home.

An observer would have sworn that neither man moved, but to Chang it was a flurry of threats and counters signalled in subtle shifts of weight, flexing fingers, pauses of breath. Skill ran second to what advantage could be seized from circumstance: a blade, a chair or a shove down a staircase, Chang hardly cared, and expected the exact lack of courtesy in return. He was no fop to entertain the notion of a *duel*.

Fast as a bullet, Foison moved, a high thrust at Chang's face. Chang whipped the cloak in the air, hoping to catch the knife-tip –

Both men were blown off their feet in the roar of flame and debris, and the whistle of flying glass.

Chang rose and pushed off the cloak that had caught the debris of the blast. Not two yards away, Foison groped for his knives in the smoke. Chang's swinging fist caught him below the eye, and then a merciless kick dropped Foison flat.

Chang's ears rang. The soldiers' shadows already danced in the portico. Any moment the trading hall would be swarmed. A writhing movement at his feet – the kicking legs of Francesca Trapping, her body shielded by the arms and greatcoat of Doctor Svenson. Chang pulled the girl to her feet and raised Svenson by the collar, unsure if the man was alive. The Doctor's hand slapped at Chang's arm and Svenson erupted into a coughing fit, dust caking his face and hair.

Chang did not see Celeste Temple.

All around lay corpses whose white coverings had been blown away by the explosion. With the dust and smoke and so many women and children amongst them, it was impossible to isolate one small body with auburn hair. The fact entered his brain like a bullet. Body. The dead were everywhere. Nothing else moved.

He had failed her. Without further hesitation, Chang sprinted to the nearest archway, the girl beneath one arm and Doctor Svenson hauled along by force.

He kicked out a window, heaved his squirming burdens through, then compelled them the length of the alley to a low brick hut. He knew exactly where they were.

The girl was in tears.

Chang snatched two lanterns, set them alight and crossed to a greasy stone staircase, leading down. He held one out, impatiently, for the Doctor.

'Hold hands, the way is slick.' Chang's voice was hoarse. They kept the wall on their left and the dark, stinking stream to the right, until they reached a place where the steps were relatively clean, and at Chang's gesture the others sat.

'We are in the sewers. We may travel unseen.' Svenson said nothing. The girl shuddered. Chang held the lantern to her face. 'Are you hurt? Can you hear me – your ears?'

Francesca nodded, then shook her head – yes to hearing, no, she was unharmed. Chang looked to Svenson, whose face was still streaked by white dust, and nearly dropped the lantern.

'Good Lord, why did you not speak!'

The bullet hole was singed into the front of Svenson's greatcoat, directly above his heart. Chang tore open the coat . . . but there was no blood. For all their running, Svenson's front ought to have been soaked. With a wince the Doctor extracted his mangled cigarette case, a lead pistol slug flattened into the now misshapen lid. Svenson turned it over so they could all see the opposite side – bulging from the bullet's impact, but never punched through. He worked a handkerchief gingerly under his tunic, pressed it tight against his ribs and then pulled it out to look: a blot of blood the size of a pressed tea rose.

'The rib is cracked – I felt it running – but I am alive when I ought not to be.'

Chang stood. Francesca Trapping's eyes gazed fearfully up to his. Behind him in the dark, the trickle of sewage. He felt the smoke in his lungs, heard its abrasion when he spoke.

'I did not see Celeste. I could not find her.'

Svenson's voice bore the same ragged edge. 'You were occupied with that fellow – you saved us all.'

'No, Doctor, I did *not*.'

'Celeste set off the explosion. She fired into the clock. I don't know how she guessed it held another explosive charge. Who knows how many lives she saved – if it had gone off tomorrow . . .' Svenson placed a filthy hand across his eyes. 'I could only reach the child –'

'I do not blame you.'

'*I* blame myself – quite fiercely. She was . . . Lord . . . a remarkable, brave girl –'

'*I will have that bastard's head.*'

Chang's words echoed down the sewage tunnel. Doctor Svenson struggled to rise, and placed a hand on Chang's shoulder. Chang turned to him.

'Are you well enough to go on?'

'Of course, but –'

Chang pointed to a wooden door above the stairs. 'You will be in the lanes behind the cathedral – the blast there will explain your appearance, and you should be able to walk freely.' He shifted his gaze to Francesca. 'You will take the Doctor where the Contessa asked?'

The child nodded. Chang clasped Svenson's arm and took up the lantern. 'Good luck,' he managed, and strode into the dark. The Doctor called after him.

'Chang! You are needed. You are needed *alive.*'

Chang hurdled the fetid stream in a running leap. They were lost behind him. He increased his pace to a jog, already caught up with all he had set himself to do.

The great Library, like every other civic institution, was shot through with privilege and preference. Inside it lay elaborate niches, like endowed chapels in a cathedral, housing private collections that the Library had managed to wrest from the University or the Royal Institute. Though every niche held one or two bibliographical gemstones, these collections attracted more dust than visitors, access being granted only through referenced application. Chang had learnt of their existence quite by accident, searching for new ways to reach the roof. Instead he had found the hidden wing of the sixth floor, and with it the old Jesuit priest.

The Fluister bequest would never have attracted Chang's interest under normal circumstances. The fancy of an admiral in whom a curiosity for native religions had been instilled by a posting to the Indies, and whose prize money had been lavishly spent on acquiring any volume relating to the aboriginal, esoteric, heretical or obscure – to Chang it was a fortune wasted on nonsense. To the Church, Admiral Fluister's bequest – pointedly made to the public, yet diverted into its present inaccessible location through proper whispers in the proper ears – represented an outright gathering of poisons. Conquering through kindness, the Bishop had offered the services of a learned father to catalogue such a haphazard acquisition. The Library, caring less for knowledge than possession, had naturally accepted, and so Father Locarno had arrived. Ten years at least he had sorted through the Admiral's detritus (it was an open wager amongst the archivists as to when the porters would find Locarno dead) with scarcely a word to anyone, a black-robed spectre shuffling in when the doors opened and out only when the lamps were doused.

In Chang's experience, there were two kinds of priests: those with their own life history, and those who had taken orders straight away. The latter he dismissed out of hand as fools, cowards or zealots. Amongst the former, he granted one might find men whose calling rose from at least some under-standing of the world. In the case of Father Locarno, his nose alone set him in that camp, it having been deliberately removed with a blacksmith's shears. Whether this marked him as a reformed criminal or an honest man whose misfortune had led to a Barbary galley, no one knew. It was enough to specu-late why this weathered Jesuit had been given the task of managing the Fluister bequest – which was to say, Chang wondered how many of the books Father Locarno had secretly amended or destroyed.

He stepped into the Fluister niche. Father Locarno sat, as he ever had in Chang's experience, at a table covered with books and ledgers. His grey hair was bound with a cord, and his spectacles, because of the nose, were held tight by steel loops around each ear. The exposed nasal cavity was unpleas-antly moist.

'Esoteric ritual,' said Chang. 'I have questions and very little time.'

Father Locarno looked up with a keen expression, as if correcting others was a special pleasure. 'There is no knowledge without time.' The Jesuit's voice was strangely pitched, vaguely porcine.

Chang pulled off his gloves, dropping them one at a time on the table. 'It would be more truthful to say there is no knowledge without commerce – so, churchman, I will give you this. The Bishop of Baax-Sonk has not been in his senses since visiting Harschmort House some two months past. Many others share the Bishop's condition – Henry Xonck perhaps the most not-able. It has been ascribed to blood fever. This is a lie.'

Father Locarno studied Chang closely. They had never done business, though surely the priest had heard rumours from the staff.

'Do you offer His Lordship's recovery?'

'No. His Lordship's memories have been harvested into an alchemical receptacle.'

Father Locarno considered this. 'When you say *receptacle* –'

'A glass book. Whatever he knew, any treasured secret he kept, will be known to those who made the book.'

'And who would that be?'

'I would assume the worst. But I should think this much information will allow your superiors to take *some* useful precautions.'

Father Locarno frowned in thought, then nodded, as if to approve at least this much of their transaction. 'I am told you are a criminal.'

'And you are a spy.'

Locarno sniffed with disapproval – an instinctive gesture that flared the open passages on his face. 'I serve only the greater peace. What is your question?'

'What is a chemical marriage?'

'My goodness.' Locarno chuckled. 'Not what I expected . . . not a common topic.'

'Not uncommon in your field of expertise.'

Locarno shrugged. Chang knew the man was now rethinking the Bishop's fate – and every other recent change in the city – in respect to alchemy.

'This blood fever – now Lord Vandaariff has recovered, perhaps His Lordship the Bishop –'

Chang cut in sharply, 'There is no cure. The Bishop is gone. This chemical marriage. What does it mean? Is it real?'

'*Real?*' Locarno settled back in his chair, the better to expound. 'Your *formulation* is naive. It is an esoteric treatise. *The Chemickal Marriage* of Johann Valentin Andreæ is the third of the great Rosicrucian manifestos, dating from 1614 in Württemberg.'

'A manifesto to what purpose?'

'Purpose? What is enlightenment without faith? Power without government? Resurrection without redemption?'

Chang interrupted again. 'I promise you, my interest in this ridiculous treatise is immediate and concrete. Lives depend upon it.'

'*Whose* life?'

Chang resisted the urge to snatch up his penknife and rumble '*Yours*'. Instead he placed both hands on the table and leant forward. 'If I had the time to read the thing, I would. The explosions. The riots. The paralysis of the Ministries. One man is behind it all.'

'What *man*?'

'The Comte d'Orkancz. You may also know him as the painter Oskar Veilandt.'

'I have never heard either name.'

'He is an alchemist.'

Locarno released a puff of disdain through the hole in his face. 'What has he *written*?'

'He has made *paintings* – a painting named for this treatise. I need to know what he intends by it.'

'But that is absurd!' Locarno shook his head. 'These works are all inference and code precisely because such secrets can be perceived only by those who *deserve* the knowledge. Such a treatise may indeed tell a *story*, but its *sense* is more akin to symbolic mathematics.'

Chang nodded, recalling Veilandt's paintings in which shadows and lines were actually densely rendered signs and equations.

'For example, in such works, if one refers to a man, one also means the number 1. The *Adept* will *further* understand that the author *also* refers to what *makes* a man.'

'I'm sorry –'

'For what is man but spirit, body and mind? Which, of course, make the number 3 –'

'So the number 1 and the number 3 are the same –'

'Well, they *can* be. But the triune –'

'What?'

'Triune.'

'What in all hell –'

'Three-parted, for heaven's sake! Body, spirit, mind. That *triune* constitution of Man will *equally* stand for the Nation and the three estates that form it: Church, aristocracy, citizenry. In today's parlance one might substitute government for aristocracy, but the comparison holds. Moreover, the three estates – as every man carries the shadow of sin – necessarily contain their opposite, fallen aspects: the bigotry of the Church, the tyranny of the state and the ignorance of the mob. This duality is precisely why secrecy is of paramount importance in communicating any –'

'This is exactly the nonsense I had hoped to avoid.'

'Then your errand is hopeless.'

'Can you not simply relate the thing as a tale?'

'But it is no *tale*. I do not know how else to put it. Events occur, but without *narrative*. In its place comes only detail, description. If there is a bird, one must know what colour and what species. If there is a palace, how many rooms? If the seventh room, what colour are the walls? If the Executioner's head is placed in a box, what kind of wood –'

'Nevertheless, father, please.'

Father Locarno gave a querulous snort. 'A saintly hermit attends a royal wedding, along with other guests. The guests undergo several trials, and a worthy few are admitted to the mysteries of the wedding. But before the young king and queen can be married, they and the royal party are executed. Then, by way of more rituals and sacrifices, they are miraculously reborn. This journey – the Chemickal Marriage – is emblematic of the joining of intelligence and love through the divine. The Bridegroom is reality, and the Bride – being a woman – is his opposite, the empty vessel who attains perfection through union with that purified essence.'

'What essence?'

'What do you *think*?'

Chang snorted. 'Is it an instruction book for madmen or for a brothel?'

'Those outside the veil rarely perceive –'

'Again, the Bride and Groom. He is also reality and she –'

'Is possibility, fecundity, emptiness. Woman.'

'How bracingly original – fecundity and emptiness at the same time. And this king and queen – the Bride and Groom – are *executed*?'

'By ritual.'

'Then brought back to life?'

'Reborn and redeemed.'

'And what is made, in this spectacular marriage – when these two become one?' Chang's voice became snide. 'Or, excuse me, three – or also six –'

'They make heaven on earth.'

'What does that mean?'

'The restoration of natural law.'

'What does *that* mean?'

It was Locarno's turn to scoff. 'What informs our every dream? The return of Eden.'

In the lowest basement Chang availed himself of a porter's luncheon, trustingly left on a table. He ate standing, and stuffed the last bites into his mouth before lifting the sewage grate with both hands. He emerged some time later in the shadow of St Celia's madhouse. Chang washed his hands and face at its carved fountain – an infant baptized by Forgetfulness and Hope – and slopped water onto each boot, the worse for a second journey underground.

Three streets past St Celia's was Fabrizi's. Chang's visit was brief – and cost the second of his rolled banknotes – but he was once more armed: a stick of ash with iron at the tip and, inside it, a double-edged blade, twelve inches and needle-sharp. Signor Fabrizi himself said nothing with regard to Chang's absence or his present disarray, but Chang knew full well the picture he made. He had seen it himself too many times, men risking all on a last desperate throw – a gamble, it was obvious, they had already lost. If one ever saw them again it was only being pulled from the river, faces as shapeless and swollen as an uncooked loaf.

Before leaving, he had asked Father Locarno if there was anything unique to *The Chemickal Marriage* that might have explained its singular attraction for the Comte.

'The messenger, of course.'

'Of course? Then why not mention this before?'

The priest had huffed. 'You wanted the *story*.'

'What messenger?'

'The hermit is summoned by an angel, whose wings are "filled with eyes" – a reference to Argus, the hundred-eyed watchman slain by Hermes –'

'A reference to what purpose?'

'The messenger – the Virgin – is a figure of vigilance –'

'Wait – the Bride is a multi-eyed virgin who is slain?'

Locarno had shaken his head in exasperation. 'By Virgin I refer to the angel.'

'Not the Bride?'

'Not at all –'

'The Bride is not a virgin?'

'Of *course* she is. But the angel – the *emblematic* Virgin – messenger, summoner – also presides over the executions, the wedding and the rebirth. She is called Virgo Lucifera, and is quite unique to this particular work.'

'Lucifer?'

'Have you no Latin? *Lucifera. Light.* The virgin of enlightenment.'

'A creature of tenderness and mercy, then?'

'On the contrary. Angels have no more emotion than birds of prey. They are creatures of justice, and therefore relentless.'

A covetous pride infused Locarno's speech. Chang turned with a shiver. There was enough cruelty in the world without its being worshipped.

Halfway back to St Celia's was an apothecary's, where Chang purchased a three-penny roll of gauze. As the clerk measured the cloth to cut, Chang's gaze passed across the bottled opiates behind the counter. Any one would exhaust the coins in his pocket, requiring him to use the final banknote. He stuffed the gauze in his pocket and walked out before temptation got the better of him.

He hurried towards the high walls of St Albericht's, a seminary given over to the Church's more worldly concerns: finance, property, diplomatic intrigue. Was the blast at the cathedral damaging enough to force the Archbishop to shift his residence? Chang slipped into the shadows opposite St Albericht's and was gratified by a veritable parade of displaced churchmen.

Something about the look Fabrizi had given Chang – that presentiment of doom – sparked a reckless daring. He emerged behind two black-frocked priests escorting an elderly monsignor in red, a satin toque capping his bald head like a cherry atop a block of ham. Chang stepped hard on one priest's ankle. The man stumbled and when the second priest turned Chang knocked him, arms a-flailing, into the gutter. Chang's arm hooked the Monsignor's neck and dragged him into an alley, out of sight. It took perhaps five seconds to remove the long scarlet coat, and fewer to snatch the wallet beneath it, hanging by a strap across the old man's chest.

He left the Monsignor slumped against the bricks. It was not often that Chang practised open thievery, but he was of the opinion that priests had no possessions themselves, only goods in common. Cardinal Chang, as common as they came, was pleased to liberate his share.

As he rushed on, Chang felt a distracting lightness. Attacking the priests might have been impulsive, but he'd never been truly at risk. No, the sharp edge to his mood was entirely due to *time*, as if death were a destination his nerves already sensed.

He had lost her. Undeserving people had died before – why was she different? Her mulish presence had destroyed his solitude, just as her ignorant ideals had exposed his complacency. The three of them on the Boniface rooftop. Without his realizing, Celeste Temple had come to embody Chang's notion of the future. Not his *own* future so much as the possibility that *someone* might, with all the ridiculous attending symbolism, be saved.

Chang was unable to imagine a *life* beyond this fight.

When the ground began to rise, Chang ducked into a filthy alcove whose use as a privy had overtaken that for assignations. He balled up Foison's silk coat and threw it into the corner. He tucked his glasses inside the fine red coat and did up the buttons to its high collar. He then wound the gauze around his eyes, thinly enough to still see, but so his scars peeked out. He left the alcove and continued with a slower pace, tapping his stick, until he reached the high stone steps. Almost immediately a man in an attorney's robe offered Chang his arm. Chang accepted with a gracious murmur and they climbed together.

The ancient bones of the Marcelline Prison had been laid as an amphitheatre, built with the seats climbing naturally up the slope. The marble had long been stripped away to drape church fronts and country homes. All that remained of the original edifice was an archway carved with masks, jeering and weeping at each soul ferried through.

At the top of the steps Chang thanked the attorney and tapped his way to the guardhouse, introducing himself as Monsignor Lucifera, legate to the Archbishop. As hoped, the warder found it impossible to look away from Chang's bandaged eyes.

'I was at the cathedral. Such destruction cannot, of course, deter my errand. I require a man called Pfaff. Yellow hair, with an ugly orange coat. He will have been taken by your constables at the Seventh Bridge, or near the Palace.'

The warder paused. Chang cocked his head, as if listening for the man's compliance.

'Ah, well, sir –'

'I expect you require a writ.'

'I do, sir, yes. Standard custom –'

'I have lost all such documents, along with my assistant, Father Skoll. Father Skoll's *arms*, you see. Left like the poor doll of a wicked child.'

'How horrid, sir –'

'Thus I lack your *writ*.' Chang could sense a restless line forming behind him, and made a point to speak more lingeringly. 'The document case was in his *hands*, you understand. Shattered altogether. One would have thought poor Skoll a porcupine for the splinters –'

'Jesus Lord –'

'But perhaps you can make it right. Pfaff is a negligible villain, yet important to His Lordship. Do you have him here or not?'

The warder looked helplessly at the growing queue. He pushed the log book to Chang. 'If you would just *sign* . . .'

'How can I sign if I can't see?' mused Chang. Without waiting for an answer he groped broadly for the warder's pen and obligingly scrawled – 'Lucifera' filling half the page.

Chang made his deliberate, tapping way inside, to another warder with another book. The warder ran an ink-stained finger down the page. 'When delivered?'

'Last night,' Chang replied. 'Or early this morning.'

The warder's face settled in a frown. 'We've no such name.'

'Perhaps he gave another.'

'Then he could be anyone. I've five hundred souls in the last twelve hours alone.'

'Where are the men arrested at the Seventh Bridge – or the Palace, or St Isobel's? You *know* the ones I mean. Delivered by the Army.'

The warder consulted his papers. 'Still don't have any man named Pfaff.'

'With a *p*.'

'What?'

'Surely you have those men all rounded into one or two large cells.'

'But how will you know if he's there? You can't see.'

Chang rapped the tip of his stick on the tiles. 'God can always smell a villain.'

Chang had three times been in the Marcelline, on each occasion luckily redeemed before proceedings advanced to outright torture, and it was with a shiver that he descended to the narrow tiers. Chang did not expect the guards to recognize him – the cleric's authority granted him an automatic deference – but a sharp-eyed prisoner might call out anything. If Chang *was* recognized, he had placed himself well beyond hope.

The corridors were slick with filth. Shouts rang out as he passed each cell – pleas for intervention, protests of innocence, cries of illness. He did not respond. The passage ended at a particularly large, iron-bound door. Chang's guide rattled his truncheon across the viewing-hole and shouted that 'any criminal named Pfaff' had ten seconds to make himself known. A chorus of yells came in reply. Without listening, the guard roared that the first man claiming to be Pfaff but found to be an impostor would get forty lashes. The cell went quiet.

'Ask for *Jack* Pfaff,' suggested Chang. He looked at the other cells along the corridor, knowing the guard's voice would carry, and that if Pfaff were elsewhere in the Marcelline he might hear. The guard obligingly bawled it out. There was no response. Despite the increased chance of recognition, Chang had no choice.

'Open the door. Let me in.'

'I can't do that, Father –'

'Obviously the man is hiding. Will you let him make us fools?'

'But –'

'No one will harm me. Tell them that if they try, you will slaughter every man. All will be well – it is a matter of knowing the sinning mind.'

The cell held at least a hundred men, crowded close as in a slave ship. The guard waded in, swinging his truncheon to make room. Chang entered a ring of faces that gleamed with sweat and blood.

Pfaff was not there. These were the refugees Chang had seen in the alleys and along the river – their only sins poverty and bad luck. Most were victims of Vandaariff's weapon, beaten into submission after the glass spurs had set them to a frenzy. Chang doubted half would live the night. He extended his stick to the rear, waving generally – since he could not see – but guiding the guard's attention to where a vaulting arch of brick created a tiny niche.

'Is anyone lurking in the back?'

The guard shouted for the prisoners to shift, striking the hindmost aside with a deep-rooted, casual savagery. A single man lay curled, barely stirring, his face a mask of dried blood.

'Found one,' muttered the guard. 'But I don't –'

'At last,' cried Chang, and turned away. 'That is the fellow. Bring him.'

The guard following with his burden, Chang tapped his way back to the first warder.

'The Archbishop is most deeply obliged. Will I sign your book again?'

'No need!' The warden made note of the prisoner's number, then carefully tore out half the page. 'Your warrant. I am glad to have been of service.'

Chang took the paper and nodded to the slumping man, upright only by the guard's vicious grip. 'I require a coach – and those shackles off. He will do no further harm.'

'But Father –'

'Not to worry. He'll have confession before anything.'

As soon as the coach was in motion, Chang tore the bandage from his head and used it to wipe the blood and grime from Cunsher's face. The cuts above the man's eyes and the bruising around his mouth spoke to a punishing interrogation, but Chang detected no serious wound.

Chang tapped Cunsher across the jaw. Cunsher flinched and rolled away his head. With a sigh, Chang wedged his other hand under Cunsher's topcoat and pinched the muscle running along his left shoulder, very hard. Cunsher's eyes opened and he thrashed against the pain. Chang forced Cunsher's gaze to his.

'Mr Cunsher . . . it is Cardinal Chang. You are safe, but we have little time.'

Cunsher shuddered, and he nodded with recognition. 'Where am I?'

'In a coach. What happened to Phelps?'

'I have no idea. We were taken together, but questioned apart.'

'At the Palace?' Cunsher nodded. 'Then why were you sent to the Marcelline?'

'The officials who took us were fools.' Cunsher probed for loose teeth with his tongue. 'Did you take such trouble to find me?'

'I sought someone else.'

Cunsher shut his eyes. 'That you came at all is luck enough.'

In the minutes it took the coach to reach the Circus Garden, Chang explained what had happened since they had parted, revealing the loss of Celeste Temple only in passing.

'The Doctor goes with the child to the Contessa's rendezvous, but I cannot guess what she has gone to such lengths to show him, save this painting.'

'Has she not already shown you the painting?' asked Cunsher. 'This glass card –'

'But the actual canvas must be the heart of whatever Vandaariff plans.'

Cunsher frowned. 'My being sent to prison shows how low my interrogators set my worth – a foreign tongue is a useful tool to suggest one's idiocy – but it suggests the contrary for poor Phelps.' Cunsher pressed the gauze to his oozing cheekbone. 'Either he remains at the Palace, or he has been given over to Vandaariff. Or – and most likely – he is dead.'

'I am sorry.'

'And I for you. But this is what I wanted to say. Phelps did go to the *Herald* –'

'Did he learn the painting's location?'

'The salon was in Vienna.'

'Vienna?'

'Indeed, and the only reason the *Herald* printed the report was the rather large fire that consumed the entire city block, along with every piece of art in the salon. With regard to Veilandt's *œuvre*, it was not seen as a loss.' Cunsher's puffed lip curled to a wry smile. 'To the *empire*.'

Chang could not believe it. The painting was *gone*? What, then, was the point of the Contessa giving Svenson the glass card?

'Do the others know?' He shook his head, correcting himself. 'Does Svenson?'

'No, Mr Phelps told me as we walked to the fountain. Lord knows where the Doctor truly has been taken.' Cunsher grimaced at his thumbnail, bruised purple, and brought it to his mouth to suck. 'And conditions in the city?'

Chang's reply was swallowed by an oath as the coach came to a sudden halt. He stuck his upper body out of the doorway. The street was a tangle of unmoving coaches. Trumpets clamoured ahead of them, followed by a menacing rush of drums and the crash of stamping boots. Chang ducked back inside, speaking urgently.

'The Army holds the road – we should escape on foot, before there is violence.' Chang leapt down, ignoring the protests of the driver, and extended a hand to Cunsher. 'Can you walk?'

'O yes, since I must. If we are blocked from above the Circus Garden, then this is . . . Moulting Lane? Just so – and if we keep to it as far as the canal –'

But Chang had already set off. The smaller man followed gamely, calling to Chang as they threaded a path through the debris.

'The soldiers are not constables – that is, they do not think of suspects and disguises. The likes of us may escape notice.'

'Unless they have been ordered to detain *everyone*,' replied Chang. 'You know full well how many of the men in your cell were innocent.'

Cunsher looked over his shoulder at another flourish from the trumpets. A gunshot cracked out, then a spatter of five more. Cunsher stumbled into a box of rotten cabbages and came to a stop. The next chorus of trumpets came laced with screams.

'Dear God.'

Chang took Cunsher's arm and hauled him on. 'God is nowhere a part of it.'

The Duke's Canal was a narrow channel of green water, so choked with bridges and scaffolding that it vanished for wide stretches, then tenaciously reappeared, like an elderly aunt determined to survive her younger relations. But the route was bereft of soldiers and, mindful of Cunsher's weakness, Chang spared a moment for a nearby tavern. He bought them each a pint of bitter ale, and pickled eggs from a crock for Cunsher. The small man consumed his meal in silence, sipping the beer and chewing as steadily as a patient mule.

'Were you at the cathedral?'

Chang turned to the tavern's brick hearth, where a grizzled man in shirtsleeves sat with a serving woman. Chang nodded.

'When will it be stopped?' the woman asked. 'Where is the Queen?'

'*Queen?*' The man rumbled. 'Where's the old Duke? He's the one we need! He'd lay 'em down like mowing wheat – damned rebels.'

'A mob went to Raaxfall,' called the barman. 'Burnt the place like a pyre.'

The pensioner at the hearth nodded with grim relish. 'No more than they deserved.'

'Were the rebels from Raaxfall?' asked Chang.

'Of course they were!'

'And yet we are just come from the Circus Garden,' said Chang. 'No one from Raaxfall in sight. Soldiers are shooting folk in the street.'

'Rebels in the Circus Garden?' piped the girl.

'Dig 'em out!' The old man slammed his tankard onto the bench, so the foam slopped over his hand. 'Right into the grave!'

Chang took a pull at his mug. 'And what if they come here?'

'They won't.'

'But if they do?'

The old man pointed at two rust-flecked sabres over the hearth. 'We'll have at 'em.'

'Before or after the soldiers burn the entire street?'

The mood in the tavern went cold in an instant. Chang set down his mug and stood. 'The Duke of Stäelmaere has been dead these two months.'

'How do you know that?' called the barman.

'I saw his rotting corpse.'

'By God – you'll speak with respect!' The old man rose to his feet.

'There's been no announcement,' said the girl. 'No funeral –'

'Where are the funerals for the dead in the Customs House?'

'What kind of priest are you?' growled the barman.

'No kind of priest at all.'

The barman stepped back nervously. Cunsher cleared his throat. He had finished the third egg. Chang set two coins on the counter, and flipped a third to the serving girl on his way to the door.

'If you cannot see who you are fighting, then you ought to *run*.'

'I see no use in scaring these people,' Cunsher observed as they continued along the canal. 'Does one blame sheep for their shyness?'

'If the sheep is a man, I do.'

Cunsher scratched his moustache with a forefinger. 'And if they did rise, like the mob that burnt Raaxfall – would you not despise them just the same?'

They walked on. Chang felt the man's eyes.

'What is it?'

'Your pardon. The scars *are* extraordinary. How are you not blind?'

'A gentle nature preserved me.'

'Everyone is very curious to know what happened. Doctor Svenson and Mr Phelps discussed the matter one evening, in medical terms –' At Chang's silence Cunsher caught himself and bobbed a mute apology. 'You are perhaps curious about my own history. The facts of exile, life left behind –'

'No.'

'No doubt it is a commonplace. How many souls does each of us preserve in memory? And when we pass, how many pass with us, remembered no more?'

'I have no idea,' Chang replied crisply. 'What do you know of the Contessa's patron in the Palace, Sophia of Strackenz?'

Cunsher nodded at the shift in conversation. 'Another commonplace. An impoverished exile with the poor taste to have become unattractive.'

'Nothing more?'

'The Princess is insipid to an exceptional degree.'

Chang frowned. 'The Contessa does not act without reason. She sequestered herself in the Palace while employing the glassworks and Crabbé's laboratory. Now she has abandoned them all – as if an event she had worked for, or awaited, has finally occurred.'

Chang stopped. Cunsher came up to him and stood, breathing hard. When he saw where Chang had brought them, he clucked his tongue.

'You grasp my idea,' offered Chang.

'Quite so. Court society *is* about patronage.'

'And her target's elevation is recent.'

'Brazen, of course, but that is the lady.'

'*Precisamente.*'

Given his appearance, Cunsher offered to remain outside and observe.

'And if you do not reappear, or are exposed?' he asked.

'Escape. Find Svenson. Make your own way to Harschmort and put a bullet in Vandaariff's brain.'

Cunsher twitched his moustache in a smile. Chang crossed to a mansion guarded by black-booted soldiers in high bearskins – elite guardsmen. The officer in charge had just given entry to a society lady with a beefy jawline and hair stained the colour of a tangerine. At Chang's approach the officer resumed his former position, blocking the way.

'Father.'

'Lieutenant. I require a word with Lady Axewith, if she is at home.'

'At home is not the same as receiving, Father. Your business?'

'The *Archbishop's* business is with Lady Axewith.' Chang was an inch taller than the grenadier and studied the man over his glasses, an ugly stare. The Lieutenant met it for perhaps two seconds.

'How do I know you're from the Archbishop?'

'You don't.' Chang reached into the cleric's coat and extracted a scrap of paper.

'This is a prison warrant.'

'Do you know how many criminals have been taken these last two days alone? Do you think the prisons can bear it?'

'What is this to Lady Axewith?'

'That's for *her* to decide. Your choice is whether thwarting an archbishop puts paid to your career.'

It would be an exceptional junior officer to withstand such rhetoric, and the way was cleared. Chang stumped into the courtyard, leaning hard upon his stick, wondering if the Contessa had already spied him from a window.

Born Arthur Michael Forchmont, Lord Axewith succeeded to his title only after a withering year had claimed the uncle, cousins and father standing in his way. Lacking opinions of his own, he happily accepted those of the Duke of Stäelmaere, and at His Grace's demise this tractability marked him as a reliable heir. Earnest, bluff, and blessedly disinterested in drink, the future Privy Minister had spent the bulk of his first forty years in the company of horses (even a fondness for stage actresses was affectionately tolerated by the public, as the assignations seemed limited to actual horseback riding). Upon his ascension to the title and entry to politics, Lord Axewith had chosen a wife and in turn that wife had doggedly given birth on a regular basis – seven births in near as many years, with four surviving. And for her pains, his child-ridden spouse now found herself the first lady of the land.

Chang could imagine the tide of flattery that had swelled around the wife of the new Privy Minister, bringing with it inclusion and isolation in equal measure. The Contessa di Lacquer-Sforza could hardly have found better circumstances in which to insinuate herself; too insignificant for any real interest at court, she would appear to be the safest soul in whom Lady Axewith might confide . . .

Two more guardsmen stood inside. A butler advanced with a tiny silver tray.

'I have no card,' Chang told him. 'Monsignor Lucifera, sent by the Archbishop – Lady Axewith will not know me.'

The butler indicated a well-proportioned parlour. Chang's eyes fell on a soft upholstered chaise. The prospect of stretching upon it pulled at him like a throbbing tooth. He shook his head.

'No doubt many suitors beg for Lady Axewith to intervene with her husband. I have come for the lady herself, on a most private – if you will understand me – and *intimate* matter.'

The word hung in the air and Chang wondered if he had gone too far. An 'intimate matter' first and foremost meant accusations of scandal.

'From the Archbishop?' asked the butler.

Chang nodded gravely. The butler glided off without seeming to move his legs.

Chang stood in silence with the guards. The well-made walls would have muffled a gunshot. He wondered if the furnishings resembled what Celeste Temple had desired for her house with Roger Bascombe. A house was the venue through which a young woman's every social ambition would be expressed. For the first time he realized that Celeste must have been well into the work before Bascombe had severed their engagement. Did her desk at the Boniface still contain those lists, the letters of inquiry to tradesmen, or had she burnt them, ashamed at those catalogues of outlived desire?

The butler returned, his voice as warm as old amber. 'If you would follow me.'

Cardinal Chang had been employed by his share of wealthy clients, but strictly through a veil of intermediaries. His presence in a fine home usually came about through a forced lock or an unguarded window – which was only to say that Chang's experience of the polite society of women was limited in the extreme. He knew there *was* a proper protocol, laid out with iron-bound rigour; yet, as he entered the foyer of Axewith House to call on the wife of the new head of the Privy Council, Chang might as well have been calling on the Empress of Japan.

'He told the *newspapers* that trains were not stopping because of the *rebels*. But his *diary* claims otherwise. In truth, the entirety of the line from Raaxfall to Orange Canal –'

Upon Chang's entrance the speaker went silent. He recognized the dress and hair – this was the lady who had preceded him through the gate – but the whole of her face, like that of the other eight women in the room, was concealed behind a mask of hanging tulle. What was more, despite the greedy cadence of gossip, Chang very much felt as if he had interrupted a formal *report*.

The butler murmured an introduction and slipped away. The women sat without any indication of precedence. Chang fell to a respectful bow. He did not know what Lady Axewith looked like.

'How kind of you to call, Monsignor.' This was a woman to his left, thick forearms poking from tight satin sleeves. 'I do not recall you amongst the Archbishop's retinue, though it seems a face one is bound to remember.'

She sniggered into one hand. Chang nodded in reply. At this the woman giggled again, along with several others.

'Would you care for tea?' Another lady, with a ribbon around her throat.

'No, thank you.'

'Then we shall go straight to your *intimate matter*. A provocative entrance.'

'And unpleasant, Monsignor.' The woman with tight sleeves shook her head. 'A pernicious preamble used to justify anything.'

'Even to put soldiers in one's foyer,' added the woman with the ribbon. 'For protection, of course. Have you come to protect us too?'

'Having met the Archbishop, I should not expect *charity*.' This was the woman with tangerine hair, whose voice had lost its lilt.

'Lucifera is a wicked-sounding name, for a churchman,' observed the woman with the ribbon.

'The name is from the Latin, meaning light.' Chang addressed the far end of the room, the women who were so far silent. 'As Lucifer is Lightborn, the first of the angels. Some say the Virgin Lucifera presides over executions, weddings and rebirth. An angel.'

'Presides how?'

This woman had not yet spoken. Her pale hair, the colour of sea-bleached wood, fell onto a sable collar. Moderately stout, not too old. Just above the collar, he saw a silver necklace with blue stones.

'Presides how?' she repeated.

'Some would call it alchemy.' A disdainful twitter danced around the room.

'I'm sure the Archbishop cannot have sent you to raise such forbidden topics.'

Chang silently crossed to her. He took the teacup from her saucer. He brought it to his nose – he could not smell a thing – and sniffed. 'That you hide yourselves shows you have some minimal awareness of the risk . . .' He emptied the contents onto the floor and then released the teacup. It landed on the carpet with a bounce, unharmed. The woman laughed.

'If you suspect the tea, I am already doomed. That was my second cup!' The other women laughed with her, their amusement falling suddenly silent at the realization that, as they had watched the cup, Chang had slipped a dagger from his stick. The blade hung inches from the chain of blue stones that ringed – Chang was sure – Lady Axewith's throat.

Chang kept his voice as courtly as before. 'With the confusion at the cathedral, how simple would it be for a man to bluff an entry and end this woman's life?'

He brought his heel down onto the teacup, grinding the shards. 'Are you so very sure of yourselves – your network of intelligence? Did she tell you *nothing?*'

Lady Axewith could not help but touch her throat. 'She?'

'Where is the Contessa?'

'What Contessa? Who are you?'

'Someone who has seen her face in a bride's mask.'

'What bride?'

'Tell her. She will see me – her life depends upon it.'

'I am afraid there is no *Contessa* –'

'Do not lie! Where is she? The Contessa di Lacquer-Sforza.'

Chang's fierce pronouncement of the name was followed by a sudden hushed silence. Then the entire circle of women erupted with laughter.

'*Her?* Why should anyone want *her?*'

'That vulgar Italian? She is no one at all!'

'Strackenz's lap dog!' called the woman with the ribbon, setting off a fresh cascade.

'Dirty *Venetian*,' said the woman with tangerine hair. 'Mind like a *monkey*.'

'Who gave you her name?' asked another. 'Pont-Joule? Some other rake with personal experience?'

'One of the *guardsmen*?'

'She skulks in the Palace as if it were an alleyway –'

'Rubbish through and through!'

'Low born.'

'Desperate.'

'Husbandless.'

'Stained.'

'*Diseased*. I know it for a fact!'

'Truly, Monsignor,' Lady Axewith observed acidly, 'who knew the Church contained such wits? I am in need of more tea – though you have robbed me of my cup! Byrnes!' A bald-headed footman arrived with a fresh cup and saucer and set to pouring around the room, a dutiful bee in a bed of overblown peonies.

Chang did not know what to do. Their response was not, he was sure, put on for his benefit. To these women, the Contessa's independence, her disdain, her association with outrageous figures such as the Comte or Francis Xonck, would inspire only resentment and ridicule. For the first time he understood that the women whom the Cabal *had* drawn to its inner circles – Margaret Hooke or Caroline Stearne – were not themselves high-born. Women of real social power had been targeted for *harvest* – their memories absorbed into a glass book – and then flung aside. But if he had guessed wrongly, if she had *not* organized these ladies to gather information for her . . . why *had* the Contessa gone to the Palace?

'Tea, Monsignor?' The servant hovered near, cup and saucer in one hand and a silver teapot in the other. The man was slender and the pot was heavy, his grip made unsure by pearl-grey gloves.

'No.' Chang restored the dagger to his stick, turning his gaze to Lady Axewith. Her eyes, above the veil, were animated, but the whites shot with blood. His gaze dropped to her fingers. Did they all wear gloves? No, only Lady Axewith.

'Perhaps our false Monsignor will confess the *true* reason for his visit . . .' This was the woman with the ribbon. 'Which is to serve notice that our enterprise is *known*!'

'Yes,' said the woman with tight satin sleeves. 'If we are to quiver in fear, should we not know by whom we have been *warned*?'

'Is it the Archbishop?'

'Is it the Ministries?'

'Robert Vandaariff?'

Lady Axewith shook her head. 'Those parties would never send such an agent.'

'Then who?' cried the woman with tangerine hair. 'Is he one of these rebels after all?'

She was on her feet and tugging on a hanging bell-pull. Chang met the prim satisfaction in her eyes, and spoke calmly.

'You take great pride in yourselves – and, no doubt, as an organ of intelligence, none can match you in the city. So, with respect, I tell you *this*. The explosive devices detonated across this city were packed with spurs formed of blue glass. These glass spurs were produced in quantities at the Xonck works at Raaxfall, a fortress – I assure you – your supposed rebels have *never* penetrated. The authorities know this. They have told no one. I leave you to your own conclusions.'

By the time he rose from his bow, the butler stood waiting in the open doorway.

At the end of the corridor, Chang bent his head to the butler's ear. The butler's silence transmitted disapproval, but he nevertheless led Chang to a tiny anteroom. Inside was a modern commode, and, above it, for ventilation and a touch of light, a transom-window. Chang stood on the seat. The window was hinged and he hauled his body through, finding handholds in the crevices of brick. He flicked the window shut with his foot. Any search would first be on the ground . . .

Chang crouched in an upstairs corridor, listening. Even if he *had* guessed correctly, there was little time. Voices rose from the foyer, women requesting their coaches. Chang hurried along the hall, opening doors – a bedchamber, a closet, another commode – and finally found one that was locked. His hand on the knob, he heard footsteps behind it, but then the sounds faded, rising upwards . . . a stairwell. Chang waited a count of ten, then forced the bolt. The sharp crack brought no cry of alarm. Was he already too late?

Two flights up Chang saw the butler knocking on a door.

'My lady? It is Whorrel. Answer me, please – are you well?'

Whorrel turned at Chang's approach, but Chang overrode any protest. 'Don't you have a key?'

'It is the lady's own retreat – the cupola room –'

Chang pounded with his fist. No response. 'How long has she been from your sight?'

'But how did you – the soldiers were instructed –'

'*How long?*'

'I cannot say! Only minutes –'

Whorrel sputtered as Chang once more forced an entrance. Again, the jarring snap was met with silence. Chang pushed inside and saw why.

Lady Axewith lay on the carpet, staring at a pane of swirling blue – a single page detached from a glass book. Her mouth was open and saliva dripped onto the glass. The nails on Lady Axewith's bare hand were ragged and yellowed, as if each fingertip had begun to rot. Unmasked, her lips were scabbed, gums blazing, nostrils crusted with a pink discharge.

Whorrel rushed for his mistress, but Chang caught his arm.

'What is wrong with her?' asked Whorrel.

'Pull her away. *Now.*'

The butler tried to raise his mistress to a sitting position, but she fought to stay near the glass. Chang drove his foot into the plate, snapping it to pieces. Lady Axewith wheezed in protest. He heard the clutch in her throat and stepped clear as she spattered vomit, first onto the broken shards and then, tumbling into Whorrel's arms, over the front of her own dress. Her eyes rolled in her head and her hands clutched at the air.

'Sweet Christ! Is it a fit?' Whorrel looked helplessly at Chang. 'Is it *catching?*'

'No.'

The window behind the writing desk was open. Atop the desk sat a box lantern, wick alight, next to a pile of coloured glass squares. The squares fitted across the lantern's aperture, tinting the light: a signal lamp, and it could even be used during the day, if the receiver possessed a telescope. Chang scanned the nearby rooftops, then – cursing his dullness of mind – set to searching the desk.

'I cannot allow any trespass!' cried Whorrel. 'Lady Axewith's private papers –'

But Chang had already found a small brass spyglass. He squinted into the eyepiece, easing the sections back and forth to find his focus. Foreshortened gables and eaves slanted up and down like theatrical scenery of painted waves. He wiped his eye on his sleeve and peered again. An uncurtained upper window . . . a desk, a table . . . and another lantern.

'What shall I *do*? Shall I call a doctor?'

The butler had dragged his mistress clear and wiped her face and front. Her eyelids fluttered. The silver necklace of blue stones gleamed below her throat. Chang wrenched it free, snapping the clasp. Lady Axewith screamed. Whorrel reached for the necklace, but Chang held it at arm's length, as if the man were a child after a sweet. He raised the necklace to the light, peering into a blue stone. His body met its delirious contents like a lover, and it was only Whorrel's touch on his shoulder that broke the spell. Chang shook his head, marvelling at the Contessa's raw practicality. The harvested memories of an opium eater were every bit as addictive as the drug itself, only more portable and easily hidden – so simply insinuated into the life of this respectable lady and in constant contact with her skin. His eyes caught the shattered plate of glass on the floor and he shuddered to think what extremities it had contained to deepen Lady Axewith's dependency.

He dropped the necklace on the floor and stamped on the stones, smashing each one to dust. Whorrel struggled to stop him and Chang shoved the man against the wall.

'The necklace is poison,' Chang said hoarsely. 'Search her things for the blue glass. Destroy it all. Do not touch it, do not look into it, or it will be *you* rotting to pieces.'

'But what . . . what of Lady Axewith?'

'Destroy the glass. Find a doctor. Perhaps she can be saved.'

Chang strode out and down the stairs, Whorrel's plaintive cry echoing above him. 'Perhaps? *Perhaps?*'

Chang walked wordlessly past the Lieutenant at the gate. Around the first corner he broke into a run for the front of St Amelia's. Cunsher dodged through traffic to join him, and in a few broken, huffing sentences Chang explained what had occurred.

'She was just there,' said Chang. 'I'm sure she saw me enter.'

'Constanza Street,' gasped Cunsher. 'Or such would be my guess.'

Constanza Street was blocked by another picquet of horsemen. Cunsher skirted behind the crowd waiting to cross. Chang had no idea where Cunsher was going, but followed – Cunsher was like a startled mouse that always managed to find a hole, no matter the circumstances of its discovery.

'The soldiers will block her progress as much as ours.' Cunsher's mutter was only half audible. 'So, what does the lady do? The further from Axewith House she appears, the better, thus – *ha* – she will exit from the *rear* –'

'And to the opera!' Chang groaned. 'Its cab stand is three streets away!'

They burst across the avenue in a desperate rush, dodging into the first narrow alley they found. Chang's longer stride took him past Cunsher at the first turn. The alley's end showed a narrow slice of the opera's stone façade. Cunsher careened into a side street, but Chang sped on, straight for a line of black coaches. The foremost coach, drawn by a pair of mottled grey horses, was just pulling away.

He raced after it, shouting at pedestrians to clear his path. The grey team had entered the wide roundabout in front of the opera, beyond which it would vanish into the city. Chang bowled into the roundabout, dodging horses and curses equally, and leapt to the island at its eye, a vast fountain. Funded by colonial interests, the fountain celebrated the splendours of Asia, Africa and America with three goddesses, each atop heaps of indigenous plenty – deities, beasts and native peoples all spouting water from their mouths with an equal lack of dignity. Chang hurried round the circle, pacing the coach – hidden now behind two tribeswomen riding a tiger – and readied himself to dash back into the road.

Quite suddenly the coach pulled short and the driver stood, slashing his whip at something on the coach's far side. Seizing his chance, Chang crossed the distance and leapt onto the door, reaching through the unglazed window. At the impact, the Contessa spun from the window opposite and swore aloud. She hacked at his fingers with her spike, but Chang thrust his stick through the doorway. The tip struck the Contessa like a fist and drove her

back to the corner of her seat. Chang swept himself in, kicking the spike
from her hand. Before she could find it Chang had his stick apart and the
dagger poised.

The coach had stopped. Through the far window Chang caught a glimpse
of a small figure in brown, just beyond the driver's whip. Cunsher had anticipated correctly, once again. In his hands were cobblestones, to throw. The
mortified driver called to the Contessa – was she in danger? Should he shout
for the soldiers?

The dagger touching her breast, Chang caught the swinging door and
pulled it shut.

'Drive on!' the Contessa shouted, her eyes never shifting from Chang's.
'And if anyone else gets in your way, run them down!'

'You will forgive me,' he said, and snatched up her spike, half expecting the
Contessa to attack him in the instant his attention was split. She did not
move. He felt the weight of the custom-made weapon, recalled its impact
near his spine. Chang threw it out of the window.

'Well, the highwayman in full daylight. Will you cut my throat now, or
after my ravishment?'

Chang settled in the opposite seat. They both knew that had his object
been her life, she would be dead.

'Who was your confederate, the gnome with the moustache? If I'd a pistol
I would have shot him dead. And not a word of protest would have been
raised – just as no one cares when a lady's coach has been waylaid.' She
cocked her head. 'How is your *back*?'

'I run and jump like a stallion.'

'The spine is damnably narrow – in the dark, one's aim goes awry. I don't
suppose you would remove your spectacles?'

'Why should I?'

'So I can see what he's done, of course. You'd be surprised how much one
can tell – the eyes, the tongue, the pulse – I do not venture to bodily discharge in a moving coach. Oskar would have made a fine physician, you
know, within his particular *realm*.'

'His realm is monstrous.'

'Ambition is *always* monstrous. You should have seen him in Paris – the house in the Marais, the *stench* – and that was just his painting!'

Chang slid the dagger back into his stick. The Contessa tensed herself as he reached deliberately to her and pressed a gloved finger on the exact spot, just below her sternum, where his stick had struck home.

'Do not doubt me, Rosamonde.'

'Why would I do that?' She dropped her eyes. 'That is tender.'

Chang was suddenly aware how simple it would be to turn his threat to a caress. She would not have stopped him. The woman's appetite was as flagrant as a peacock's feathers and as private as – well, as any woman's inner mind. She laid a hand on his wrist.

'I had words with Doctor Svenson –'

'Release my arm or I will hurt you.'

The Contessa restored the hand to her lap. 'Must you be so unpleasant – so stupid?'

'I am stupid enough to have you in my power.'

The Contessa sighed with exasperation. 'You carry the past like a convict carries chains. What has happened means nothing, Cardinal. Time may change every atom of our minds. Whose youth has not held a quaking fool, distraught, disgraced – a razor's edge from taking their own life? And for causes that, if one *can* call them to mind after even four months, are no more worth dying for than last year's fashions are worth ten pfennigs to the pound.'

'You speak to excuse yourself.'

'If you will take my life at the end of things, Cardinal, then you will, or I will take yours, or both our skulls will serve as Lord Vandaariff's finger-bowls. But until then – *please.*'

The Contessa laid a hand across her brow – her left hand, he noticed, remembering the gash across her right shoulder. Did she still favour it?

'I do congratulate you on the costume,' she said. 'The irony *sings.*'

Chang nodded towards the driver. 'Where were you going?'

'Does it matter? I'm sure you have your own plans for everything.' The Contessa shook her head and smiled. 'Now *I* am the sour cloud. Did you know Doctor Svenson nearly shot me dead? I trust his not being here means the child has *finally* spurred him to business. I do not recommend the use of children, in all truth. They whine, they forget, they are hungry – and the tears! Good *God*, every way you turn there is snivelling –'

'Where were you *going*?'

She glared at him, her cheeks touched with colour, then laughed – still a lovely sound, for all that the merriment was forced.

'Where we *can*, Cardinal. Every thoroughfare between the Circus Garden and the river is blocked and Stropping Station is its own armed camp. *Thus*' – she arched an eyebrow – 'the mighty Robert Vandaariff takes the city in his all-powerful fist.'

Chang nodded to the window. 'But our present path takes us straight *to* the Circus Garden.'

'I am aware of it, yet I think we have a few minutes to extend this *fascinating* talk.'

'You speak of Vandaariff's fist. According to Doctor Svenson, these explosions apparently elude your concern.'

'On the contrary, I am inspired to avoid large gatherings.'

'Is that why you quit the Palace?'

'The Palace is in actuality as dreary as a beehive – the buzzing of *drones* –'

'*Enough*. On every front where Vandaariff has extended himself, you have only ceded ground. The explosions, his control of Axewith, martial law, property seizures – you have opposed none of it.'

'How could I? Have you?'

'I have tried.'

'With what result, apart from Celeste Temple being blown to rags?' The Contessa reached for a small clutch bag at her side. Chang caught her hand and she disdainfully opened the bag to reveal a flat lacquered case and her cigarette holder.

'How did you know that?' he asked tightly.

'How do you think? From the wife of a deputy minister who heard it directly from Vandaariff himself – what else is that gaggle of harpies good for? I am at least *informed*.' The Contessa wedged a white cigarette into her holder. She set a match to the tip, shut her eyes as she inhaled, and then let the smoke out through her nose. 'Sweet Christ.'

Her momentary surrender to pleasure – or, if not pleasure, relief – brought the taste of opium back to Chang's mind. How simple it would have been to preserve just one of Lady Axewith's jewels. The Contessa waved the smoke from her face.

'Oskar was never like the rest of us. He truly *is* an artist, with the calling's every dreadful quality. He seeks no sensation for itself, but only to further his *work*.'

'But Oskar Veilandt is not Robert Vandaariff. You saw what happened at Parchfeldt – if you have tasted that book, you *know* what he's become. Whatever may have guided his intentions before –'

'I disagree – or, yes, he has changed his destination, but not the path. Not his *style*.'

'You cannot pretend this *chaos* is what the Comte d'Orkancz would have done.'

'Of course not, but neither does he care about it now.'

'I have seen him care for nothing else!'

'You are wrong. He stretches the canvas and sets his paints in order. He has not *begun*.'

'But the city –'

'The city can burn.'

'But Axewith –'

'Every lord and every minister can burn as well – to Oskar they are mind-less ants.'

'But how can you stand apart –'

'For the moment, I am trying to survive.'

Chang snorted with disbelief. 'The day you are content with mere scrab-bling –'

'Don't be a damned fool!' hissed the Contessa. 'That day has dawned. Ask the corpse of Celeste Temple if it hasn't.'

At the Contessa's instruction, the coach left them in a trim French-styled square of gravel paths and flowers. Chang helped the Contessa to the cob-bles, scanning the park for any sign of Vandaariff's agents. The Contessa thrust coins into the driver's hand, whispering in the man's ear. Before Chang could overhear she had broken off, walking along the square.

'This way, Cardinal, if you insist on coming.'

Many of the large houses bore brass plaques, some announcing a nation's diplomatic mission, in other cases an especially exclusive practice in medicine or the law. That the streets were empty seemed a strangely opposite reaction to the city's turmoil. Were these enclaves so protected? The Contessa paused at a narrow alley next to the Moldovar Legation. She took his hand, turning so as not to drag her dress against the wall, and held a finger to her lips for silence. He had assumed their destination to be the embassy, but instead it was the mansion next door, a servant's entrance, he would have said, though the alley was too narrow to allow deliveries. The Contessa rapped lightly, then looked past Chang's shoulder.

'Is that man watching us from the street?'

He turned, like an idiot, and then it was too late. He felt the edge against his neck – a blue glass card snapped raggedly along its length.

'I have not been entirely honest,' the Contessa confessed.

The wooden door opened, to Chang's utter disgust.

'Well, look who it is!'

Jack Pfaff gave the Contessa an adoring smile.

Pfaff relieved Chang of his stick and led them in. The ground floor of the house had been converted to the needs of a consulting physician, with examination rooms, surgery and a private study, where the proprietor awaited them.

'Doctor Piersohn, Cardinal Chang. We have little time – Cardinal, if you would remove your clothes.' The Contessa nodded to Pfaff, who pulled apart Chang's stick. She rummaged in her bag and set to fitting a cigarette to her holder. Chang had not moved.

'Your *clothes*, Cardinal. Piersohn must examine you. We must send an answer at once.'

'What answer?' Chang gazed coldly at Piersohn, who stood behind his desk. The Doctor was short and barrel-chested. His protuberant eyes were ringed with the faintest excrescence of dried plum: the fading scars of the Process. Piersohn's thick hair matched the surgical coat he wore over a patterned waistcoat, and shone with pomade. His hands were chapped like a laundress's. Chang wondered what sort of practice Piersohn actually pursued.

'To Robert Vandaariff, of course,' replied the Contessa. 'He has offered an exchange, and I must decide how best to *prepare* the one sent.'

'Prepare for what?'

'For God's sake – will you take off your coat at least? I promise you I have seen a man in his shirtsleeves and will not faint.'

Chang began to undo the red silk buttons of the cleric's coat. He glanced at Pfaff, measuring the distance between them. The Doctor, behind the desk, could be discounted, and the Contessa had made the mistake of sitting down. The dagger cane would be an unfamiliar weapon to Pfaff, and, once Chang's coat was off – their request put his best weapon straight in hand – it would be a moment's work to whip it across Pfaff's eyes and step past the blade. Two swift blows and Pfaff would be down. Chang did not even need to recover the dagger. He could snatch up an end table and dash out the Contessa's brains.

He slipped off the scarlet coat and took casual hold of the collar. 'If you hope to exchange me, may I ask what you will receive in trade?'

The Contessa blew smoke at the ceiling. 'Not what, but whom. I was not strictly forthcoming during our ride. Celeste Temple lives. Vandaariff has her, and offers her to me, in hopes that I will hand over Francesca Trapping. However, my *intuition* says he would be even more delighted to get *you*.'

Chang blinked behind his dark spectacles.

'That is a lie, to make me cooperate.'

'It is not.'

'Why should I trust you, of all people on earth?'

'Because our interests are one. Besides, Cardinal, can you afford *not* to believe me? Will you fail her yet again?'

The Contessa's face might have been made of porcelain for all he could penetrate her thoughts. He knew she viewed his compliance with contempt.

'Where do you gain in this? Celeste Temple is your enemy.'

'She remains useful – providing Oskar has not too much *despoiled* her, of course – another reason time is of the essence. Because I will *not* deliver Francesca Trapping –'

'As you've given her to Doctor Svenson.'

'I have done nothing of the kind. She is quite easily recovered.'

'You underestimate him.'

'The question is whether I have underestimated *you*. If you do not choose with speed, I must refuse his offer, and Miss Temple will surely die.'

'What would you have done had I not found you?'

'Something else. But once you did appear, I was able to oblige everyone. Our driver has carried word to Vandaariff.'

'Then take me to him and be done with it.'

'I said I was obliging, not that I was stupid. Take off your *shirt*.'

She tapped her ash into a dish of liquorice sweets. 'Near the base of the spine, Doctor. Any *adaptation* will be there.'

Chang draped his coat over a chair and set his spectacles atop it. He hauled his black shirt over his head, restored the spectacles and laid the shirt next to the coat. Piersohn had come around the desk, pulling behind him a standing tray of shining implements.

'So many scars.' The Contessa studied Chang's bare torso. 'Like one of Oskar's paintings. Sigils, he calls them – as if some ancient, lost god has scratched its name on your flesh. Isn't that a charming thought, Cardinal, fit for poetry?'

'Fit for a graveyard,' said Pfaff. He aimed the stick at a line along Chang's ribcage. 'How'd you get that one?'

'Do you mind, sir?' snapped Piersohn, waving the stick away.

Pfaff only lifted it out of reach and then, as soon as the Doctor's attention returned to his tools, darted it forward, tapping Chang's scar. Chang snatched at the haft, but Pfaff, laughing, was too quick.

'Please, Jack,' the Contessa called genially. 'The *time*.'

Pfaff grinned, his point made, and gave the Doctor room.

'If you would turn, and place your hands there.' The Doctor indicated a leather-topped table. Chang did as he was asked, leaning forward.

'Christ in heaven!' blurted Pfaff. 'Is it plague?'

'Be *quiet*, Jack!' hissed the Contessa.

Chang felt the rough tips of Piersohn's fingers palpate the perimeter of his wound.

'The original puncture just missed the spine on one side and the kidney on the other – a shallow wound, and lucky, as the blade pulled upwards –'

'*Yes*,' the Contessa said impatiently. 'But what has been *done*? That *colour*.'

Piersohn pressed against the object Vandaariff had placed in Chang's body. Chang clenched his jaw, not at pain, for he felt none, but at a queasy discomfort. Each time Piersohn touched the wound, Chang sensed more clearly the piece of glass inside him. Piersohn reached to feel Chang's forehead.

'The inflammation,' the Contessa asked, 'is it sepsis or an effect of the stone?'

'As far as I can determine, the discoloration is inert, almost a kind of stain.' Doctor Piersohn resumed his pressure on Chang's back. 'Is this painful?'

'No.'

The Contessa leant over the arm of her chair so she could see Chang's face. 'Did he say *anything*? You must tell me, Cardinal, even if you took it for nonsense –'

Chang stared at the table. He could feel the heat in his face and sweat under each eye. 'He told me I could cut his throat in three days.'

'What?'

'Just that. As if it were a joke.'

'When?' The Contessa shot to her feet. '*When did he say this?*'

'Three days ago. Today is the day. Believe me, I am perfectly willing to take him up on his offer –' Chang turned at the rattle of Piersohn taking something from his tray. 'If that man draws a drop of blood I will break his neck.'

The Contessa whispered in Piersohn's ear, 'Pray do not mind. He is deranged.'

'That seems all the more reason *to* mind, madam.'

'Is drawing blood strictly necessary?'

'All manner of tests depend upon it.'

'Derangement, Doctor, mere derangement –'

'But what threads bind him to reason? Without knowing the *programme* of his new master –'

'I have no master!' shouted Chang.

The Contessa nodded to one of the squat bottles. 'Very well, Doctor. Do what you can.'

The Doctor doused a ball of cotton wool from the bottle, staining it a pale orange. 'Now, let us see. If the inflammation recedes –'

'It won't,' said Chang quickly. Piersohn paused, the cotton suspended inches from Chang's lower back. 'Doctor Svenson attempted a similar procedure, with the same orange mineral, with drastic results.'

'Doctor Svenson?' asked Piersohn. 'Who is he? Did he even know how to apply –'

The Contessa grasped the Doctor's arm. 'Drastic how, Cardinal?'

'I was not in a position to take notes,' replied Chang. 'The inflammation deepened and spread. He also applied blue glass, with an equally dismal effect – a congestion in the lungs –'

'An imbecile could have foreseen *that*,' sniffed Piersohn.

'Shouldn't you cut him open?' asked Pfaff. 'If we want to see what it is, that's the simplest way.'

'Why don't I open up your head?' Chang growled.

'Hush. I have an idea of my own.' Chang felt the Contessa's slim fingers on his spine and tensed himself. 'Try the iron.'

Piersohn dunked another cotton ball from a second bottle. Chang inhaled sharply as it touched his wound, icy cold. He could not hear them speak for a hissing in each ear. He arched his back and broke the contact.

'A palpable reaction,' muttered Piersohn, 'but it fades already. Perhaps if we try the metals in sequence –'

'What in hell are you doing?' demanded Chang. It was as if he had returned to the table at Raaxfall.

'Isolating the alchemical compound, of course.'

Chang flinched again. The taste of ash curled his tongue.

'Why, look at *that*. Do keep going, Doctor . . .'

Chang shut his eyes, wanting to pull away, to thrash Pfaff to a pulp, to kick Piersohn across the room, but he did not move, knuckles whitening as he squeezed the table. Celeste Temple was alive. If he was not exchanged, there was no telling what Vandaariff would do.

The next application sent sparks across his vision. The one after that was like he'd been pricked with a hundred needles. The one following – against every bit of reason – sparked a vivid *scent*. Chang had lacked the ability to smell for more than ten years, but now he shook his head at the searing aroma of cordite. The next set off a fire in his loins and for the instant of contact he felt like a bull in rut, snorting air through each nostril with the shock of it. Then the cotton ball was removed and he gasped with relief, barely noting the Doctor's procedural murmur.

'And last of all, quicksilver . . .'

Each of the other applications had brought a sudden, specific reaction, but this last swallowed Chang's senses as wholly as if his head had been forced into cold water. His bearings were lost in a swirl of visions from the Comte's painting. His hands were black . . . his foot sank into the fertile earth of a new-tilled field . . . he was naked . . . he wore a swirling robe . . . he held a sword bright as the sun. . . and all around him faces, in the air like hanging lamps, people he knew – laughing, begging, bloodied – and then before him knelt the Contessa – blue teeth, one hand groping his thigh, and in the other, offered up, vivid red, visceral, oozing –

He was gasping, his face pressed into the leather table top. What had happened? *What had been done to him?*

'It is the worst result,' the Contessa was saying. 'All tempered into one.'

'That is impossible,' replied Piersohn. 'Whatever his intention, the chemical facts –'

'A moment, Doctor.' Chang felt her touch. 'Are you with us, Cardinal Chang?'

'Can you remove it?'

'I beg your pardon?'

Chang pushed himself to his feet, and called harshly to Piersohn, 'Can you *remove* it without killing me?'

Piersohn shook his head. 'I'm sorry, whatever has been implanted, enough time has passed that the seeding –'

'*Seeding?*' Chang kicked the standing tray, crashing it back into the Doctor's desk.

'That is the Comte's own term,' protested Piersohn.

'For *what*?' shouted Chang. 'What has he done?'

Piersohn glanced warily at the Contessa. 'He made many notes – untested theories . . . a procedure for the assimilation of glass within a body.'

'To make me his servant.' Chang pulled his shirt over his head.

'But are you, Cardinal?' The Contessa waited for Chang to restore his dark spectacles. '*Are* you his creature?'

'No more than I am yours.'

'Exactly. But Oskar is arrogant. He will believe his magic has worked. Do you see? If you are *convincing*, his hopes will blind him.'

*Had* Vandaariff's plan worked? What if the implanted glass was just another sort of timed device, ticking its way towards detonation? The third day was not finished. Chang thrust his arms through the cleric's coat and began on the buttons. 'And Celeste Temple will be freed?'

'She will.'

'And she is whole? Undamaged?'

'As far as I know.'

Chang looked at Pfaff, who wore a pale expression of unease. The stick had been restored to one piece, and Chang snatched it away. He turned to the Contessa. 'As soon as she arrives, you will deliver her to Doctor Svenson.'

'As you wish. And once *you* are with Robert Vandaariff, you know what to do.'

'Cave in his skull.'

'With the first brick that comes to hand.'

The Contessa led Chang and Pfaff back to the arid garden square. The streets remained empty, though in the distance Chang thought the sky had darkened.

'Is that smoke?'

The Contessa shrugged. 'Off you go, Jack. Find me when you have finished.'

'Finished what?' asked Chang.

'None of your damned business, old fellow.' Pfaff took the Contessa's hand, bending to kiss it. Chang could have kicked Pfaff's head like a ball, but took the moment to glance around him . . . the shrubbery of the park, brick gateposts, the shadow of an ornamental column . . .

Pfaff straightened, lifting the Contessa's hand to his mouth for another kiss, then turned on his heel, his orange coat-tails swinging dramatically. Chang stooped and took a stone from the gravel walkway.

'What are you doing?' asked the Contessa. 'We must —'

Pfaff had gone twenty paces when Chang threw the stone, perhaps the size of a pigeon's egg, striking square between the man's shoulder blades. Pfaff cried out, arching his back, and wheeled round, whipping a blade from beneath his coat, his face flushed red.

'God damn you, Chang! Damn you to hell!'

Cardinal Chang swept off an imaginary hat and waved with foppish deference. Pfaff snorted with rage and stamped across the square.

Chang straightened with a sigh. He only hoped he'd guessed correctly, and that his signal had been seen.

'I would ask if you are always such a child,' observed the Contessa, 'if I did not already have the answer. A child *and* a bully.'

'I would not say you are in any position to judge.'

'On the contrary, I am expert in each field.' The Contessa smiled broadly. 'That is why I find *you* so diverting — as much as any dancing, collared bear.'

'Even when your man takes the brunt?'

'Tish! Mr Pfaff is his own, or at least intends to be — his skills extend only so far, of course, a fledgling peeping from the nest.'

'He kisses your hand.'

'A hand is easily washed.' Chang frowned his disapproval and she laughed again. 'O I forget myself — it is not every day I stroll with Monsignor Virtue, beside whom I am the very Whore of Babylon. Dear Cardinal, do *you* want to kiss my hand instead?'

He took hold of her arm. She tensed, watching, mouth just open, daring him to act, though whether in violence or passion he had no idea — did the woman even distinguish?

'Such a shame . . .' she whispered.

They stood in broad daylight at the edge of the square, yet he could no more step clear than if they were trapped in the crush of a ballroom. Chang's voice was tight. 'Since when did you care for shame?'

Her words remained hushed. 'Afterwards . . . after you kill Vandaariff . . . after Miss Temple is redeemed . . . we must once more seek each other's life. It seems a terrible waste . . . two such well-matched creatures . . .'

'I am no creature, madam.'

Her eyes traced his jugular. 'And *that* is why I shall win.'

They walked beneath a canopy of trees on streets bereft of traffic. The Contessa's eyes became restless and distracted, scanning the fine house-fronts but seeing none of them.

'Have you ever been on a ship, Cardinal Chang? On the sea?'

'No. Have you?'

'Of course. I'm not a peasant.'

'I beg your pardon.'

'But I have never sailed any distance – for *weeks*.'

'Does that matter, aside from outlasting seasickness?'

'Have you not wanted to visit Africa? China? To feel the Indian sun on your face?'

'No.'

She sighed. 'Neither have I.'

'I fail to see the problem.'

'Did you ever hear Francis Xonck speak of Brasil?'

'Once, which was enough.'

'All Francis ever sought was excess.'

'Are you any different?'

'I never had to seek,' she replied tartly.

'Is this about Miss Temple?' Chang asked. 'You mention the Indies –'

'She is *from* the Indies. To her, *we* are the Dreamland – if more vaguely apprehended. But her obvious dissatisfaction here makes my point. One avoids Africa, Cardinal, because Africa will unfailingly *disappoint*. New horizons are always seen through one's old set of eyes.'

'But you *are* a traveller. When were *you* last in Venice? Or wherever you called home?'

'I am home every minute of the day.'

Chang bit off his reply. For the first time in his experience, the Contessa di Lacquer-Sforza was behaving like a conventionally galling woman.

'You are frightened,' he said.

'Of Oskar Veilandt? Cardinal, I am tired. And *hungry*.' The tone underscoring this last made perfectly clear that the Contessa was not talking of her dinner. 'Why, are *you* afraid?'

'Not for myself.'

'*Pah.* You are exactly as noble as a cart-horse.' She plucked the shoulder of Chang's scarlet coat. 'Did you actually murder a priest?'

'I did not need to.'

'Are you willing to murder Oskar?'

'Of course.'

'And if he promises to save your life?'

'I would not believe him. My life is forfeit – and along with me, how many others? The city? The nation?'

'When *I* am dead, Cardinal, cities and nations can go hang.'

Chang saw she was smiling and immediately became wary. 'Have we arrived?'

'Near enough . . . we are certainly observed.'

Chang saw only the same well-tended streets. 'Observed by whom?'

'To answer that is the reason I am here. I was not asked to accompany you – merely to deliver you to their hands.'

'If you had simply sent me off, I might not have cooperated.'

'If you were going to abandon Miss Temple, you would have done so earlier, when you could have pummelled Jack Pfaff raw. No, apart from the splendour of your company, I have come to see who else does Oskar's bidding.'

'And is this the house of someone you know?'

She looked at him quizzically, and then nodded towards a white-painted mansion at the end of the street. 'I thought you had been here. It was where he worked on Angelique.'

Chang sighed, recalling too vividly the abandoned greenhouse and its bloodstained bed. 'I did not realize we had walked so far. The house is improved – from the rear it looked a shambles.'

'Vandaariff money. And he *is* a resurrectionist.'

'What stops them from shooting us dead in the street?'

'How do you ever manage to feed yourself? If there are two people Robert Vandaariff is more keen to preserve than ourselves, I cannot name them. No, whoever he has charged will emerge, and then I will better know my enemies.'

'At which point you will saunter away? Why not take you as well, if he desires you so *ardently*?'

'Well, that is Oskar. I would end *his* life the first chance I had, but he will ever postpone. He has pretensions to *theatre*.'

'Like the Chemickal Marriage?'

She did not answer, for the white door of the mansion opened and a dozen green-coated soldiers poured forth. Behind them came a man whose Ministry-black topcoat belied his young face and fair hair. He stabbed an arm at the Contessa.

'That woman is wanted by the Crown! Seize her!'

Four soldiers broke forward. Chang only raised his hands.

The Contessa's nostrils flared with rage. 'I will cut off that man's –' But then the soldiers had seized her arms.

'The pride – the pride of it!' Harcourt's voice shook. 'Truly, madam, are you so brazen? So arrogant to think no one might withstand you?'

'Release her.'

Foison stood far away in the open door, but his voice stopped the soldiers cold. Harcourt stamped up the steps like a schoolboy.

'I beg your pardon! I am Deputy to the Privy Council – and this woman – *this woman –*'

'Release her.'

'Do you know Mr Foison?' Chang ventured.

'I had hoped he would be elsewhere,' replied the Contessa. 'But now I prize him above all other minions.'

It was clear that Harcourt was terrified of Foison, but the young man had

enough pride – at least for his office – to stand firm. 'This woman is a murderer, a spy, a saboteur –'

'There is an arrangement,' Foison corrected him, menacingly calm. 'If
that woman steps through these doors – I do hope you understand me – you
will answer for Lord Vandaariff's displeasure.'

Harcourt wavered. 'But – but surely she may be brought in – or if not
brought in – surely remanded to the Marcelline –'

'No.'

Harcourt wavered and in the silence his authority gave way. The Contessa
gently extracted herself from the soldiers. Harcourt wheeled to her, his slim
hands balled to fists.

'It is not finished, madam! You will be taken – you will be hanged!'

The Contessa whispered to Chang, '*Au revoir*. Remember your pledge.'

'Remember yours.'

'Celeste Temple will be delivered to Doctor Svenson.'

'Alive.'

The Contessa laughed. '*Stickler*.' She dipped her head and walked away.

Chang knew she was lying, and that Celeste would be delivered to whomever
the Contessa found most advantageous, or – in the absence of any advantage
at all – to a grave. It made managing his mission now all the more vital. He
noted with satisfaction a bruise below Foison's eye.

Foison relieved Chang of his stick, tugged it open and studied the blade.
Chang gestured at her receding figure. 'If only my stick were half as deadly.'

One corner of Foison's mouth twitched to acknowledge the remark.
Ignoring Harcourt, Foison nodded to the soldiers and Chang was escorted
inside.

The renovations were not limited to the exterior. The carpets had been
piled against a wall, and the floorboards were slippery with plaster dust.
Harcourt disappeared with Foison deeper into the house. Despite a slammed
door, their muffled argument reached Chang where he waited. He turned to
his nearest guard.

'A soldier cannot love taking orders from a rich man's secretary –
especially a man like that. An *Asiatic*.'

'Aren't you a Chinaman yourself?'

'That's why I *know*.'

The soldier peered more closely at Chang. '*Are* you a Chinaman?'

Foison reappeared, still carrying Chang's stick. 'Hold his arms. Search him.'

The findings were presented to Foison, arrayed on the green-coat's open palms like a tray: razor, money, key, the prison writ, the samples of glass from Pfaff's room, including the broken key.

'Dispose of it. Bring him in.'

A man had been bound to a high-backed wooden chair, a canvas bag over his head. His once-starched shirt was stained with blood, some dried rust-brown, some still a festive red. Whatever he had endured, it had spanned hours.

The man, whose head rose at their entrance, became more agitated at Foison's approaching footsteps, pulling on the ropes that held him fast. Foison's voice remained characteristically soft, with an absence of intent that nearly seemed kind.

'Someone to help you.'

The captive's bare feet kicked against the cords. His voice was smothered by the bag. 'Stop your torments! No one has come!'

'By God – you have won your way with Lacquer-Sforza, but here you do trespass, Mr Foison! That man is *mine*!'

Harcourt stood in the doorway with several Ministry men, reinforcements muttering at their superior's collar.

Foison nodded at Chang. 'And *he* is mine. Is it not possible they are acquainted?'

'Perhaps! Perhaps! And now that we are all present – well, go ahead and ask your best – but any attempt to exclude the Council will not stand. *My* prisoner is here only at Lord Axewith's personal instruction –'

'Your prisoner is here so *we* may learn what *you* could not.'

'If you throw them together they will only lie – you will be forced –'

'To take measures?'

'Exactly. And it will be no business of mine.'

'Though it was your business with this gentleman.' Foison sighed at the man in the chair. 'Rather crudely.'

'He is no gentleman!' Harcourt's eyes were hard. It was clear to Chang that the prisoner had been savaged precisely *because* of Harcourt's indecision – with the ferocity boiling forth in resentment at his dilemma.

Foison shrugged. 'He bleeds like one, but such distinctions are not my expertise. I do know that Cardinal Chang –'

'A criminal of the first water.'

'If by that you mean he will be more difficult to persuade, I agree.'

'Do not say that where he can *hear*!' Harcourt sputtered. 'You steel his purpose – now he will hold out even longer!'

'I tell the Cardinal nothing he does not know. Just as he knows, no matter his resistance, that I *will* break him. The only question is how badly broken he will be.'

'If you think we will spare you,' Harcourt called to Chang, deciding after all to support Foison, 'you are deeply mistaken. The nation is in peril. The *Crown*. And in setting yourself against us, you're nothing but a common traitor.'

Chang nodded towards their prisoner in the chair. 'Is he?'

Foison pulled the bag away. Mr Phelps flinched from the light as if it too might strike him. What Cunsher had endured at the Marcelline was nothing to the ordeal inflicted on Phelps. Dark blood smeared his face. One eye had swollen shut, and the other peeped through a veil of seeping fluid. His nose was broken and one lip split like a rotten plum.

Chang felt his stomach tighten. Phelps had been one of their own, and this is what they'd done. Foison gently turned Phelps's face to Chang. 'Do you know this man, Mr Phelps?'

Phelps nodded. His voice was a slurred croak. 'Criminal . . . ought to be hanged.'

'You just heard Mr Harcourt voice the same opinion. Perhaps you would explain *why* he should be hanged?'

'Outlaw . . . the Duke signed a writ on his life.'

'I don't believe he did.'

'Lost . . . never delivered –'

'Come, Mr Phelps. When did you last see this man?' Phelps shook his head at the question, as if such a thing were beyond his scattered mind, but Foison remained patient. 'At Parchfeldt? At Harschmort? This evening at the Palace?'

With a pang, Chang saw Phelps shake his head at this last suggestion, too vehemently. Harcourt pointed a finger, triumphant.

'He is *lying*.'

A tight, pleading gasp of distress escaped Phelps's throat. 'Chang is a killer . . . you know it yourselves –'

'Who did he kill?'

'I don't know –'

'Did he kill Colonel Aspiche?'

'I don't know –'

'What of Arthur Leverett? Or Charlotte Trapping?' Foison remained calm. 'The Crown Prince of Macklenburg? The Comte d'Orkancz?' Phelps gulped air, unable to reply. Saliva flecked his purpled lips. Foison rested a hand on Phelps's shoulder. 'So many deaths . . .'

'I would like nothing more than Cardinal Chang on a scaffold,' said Harcourt.

'*Why in hell are you here?*' Chang's voice was as dark as he could make it. Harcourt quailed.

'I – I – Lord Axewith – I am appointed, deputized, in the immediate crisis –'

'Do not speak to the prisoner, Mr Harcourt, he only seeks your discomfort.' Foison stepped away from Phelps, hands at his waist, near his knives. 'In truth, perhaps it would be better if you left.'

'Phelps is my prisoner,' protested Harcourt.

'But Chang is a different matter. I require this room free.'

Harcourt sniffed and took a pocket watch from his waistcoat. 'Very well. Five minutes. But then we will consult.' Foison said nothing. Harcourt nodded, as if they had agreed, and backed into his assistants. They left in a scuffle. The soldiers remained at either side of the door.

Chang spoke as brightly as possible. 'My turn?'

'I must deliver you alive. You understand the breadth of options I can exercise without compromising that condition. Whether I do so is up to you.'

'You will not break my teeth for your own revenge, then?'

'No.'

'Why not?'

'Because I know what awaits you, Cardinal Chang. Revenge enough.'

He was bound to a chair. When it was done, Foison crossed to the door, waving the green-coats out ahead of him. 'I will return momentarily – Mr Harcourt, for all his faults, is energetic and must be contained. You cannot escape – nor, if you value the young woman's life, will you try.'

The door closed and the room fell into silence, apart from Phelps's straining wheeze. Chang knew there was little time. He snapped his fingers

'Phelps! Wake up! Phelps!'

Phelps raised his head with difficulty, his one clear eye helpless and apologetic. Was he even in his right mind?

'Your friend is alive,' said Chang.

Phelps swallowed, blinked. 'Friend?'

'The one taken with you. He is alive and free.'

'Dear God. Thank heaven.' Phelps cast a wary glance to the door. 'The Doctor?'

'You need not worry. But there is little time –'

'No.' Phelps began to shake his head. 'No – I am so sorry – so ashamed –'

Chang dropped his voice. 'You had no choice. No one does. Listen to me – I must know what you said –'

But Phelps did not hear, still working to form his words. 'I did not know – you must believe me, Chang, I had no earthly idea. A failure from the start.'

'No one knows – and everyone submits. Phelps, there is no shame –'

Tears rolled lines through the blood on Phelps's shaking face. 'All this time, I had thought myself reclaimed –'

'They were bound to apprehend us –'

'But who *am* I, Chang? How much have I betrayed? Have I done so all this time?'

'Done what?'

'Betrayed everything!'

'But what did you tell them?'

'I don't know!'

Chang forced himself to stay calm. 'Phelps, they are about to set in on me – it will doom us both if I contradict you –'

'My soul is already taken.'

The man was useless. Chang changed tactics. 'Have you seen Celeste Temple? She is to be exchanged – have you seen her? Did they speak of her? Is she here?'

Phelps shook his head. 'Heard nothing. Seen nothing. If the girl is here . . .'

'What? What?'

'. . . she has already been consumed.'

The door opened. Phelps flinched at the sound and began to babble. 'I assure you – for God's sake – we said nothing –'

Foison smiled regretfully. 'Of course not. Still, one attempts what one can.' He took a third chair, facing Chang, but putting Phelps between them.

'Cardinal. Will you tell me of the Contessa?'

'By all means. She claims to be Italian, her figure is handsome, her personal habits are slovenly in the extreme –'

A knife appeared in Foison's hand, and he extended his arm until the tip pricked Mr Phelps's earlobe. Phelps gasped but kept still.

'No,' said Foison. 'Mr Phelps has divulged everything, or so I am convinced. Do you understand? I lose nothing in his disposal.'

'And I do?'

'Such is my *perception*. Start from the Customs House. After the explosion – how did the Contessa find you?'

'I found *her*.'

'She has sworn to kill you.'

'And I, her. It is deferred.'

'*How* did you find her?'

'I saw her coach and forced my way inside.'

'Another lie.'

Phelps gasped again as a whisper-thin line of blood formed across his earlobe. As Chang watched, a bead of red slid off the line and hung like a pirate's ear-ring, then dropped to stain Phelps's shirt. Chang had barely seen Foison move.

'Cardinal?' Foison tapped the knife against Phelps's shoulder.

'I guessed where she would be. She had hidden herself in the Palace, hoping to enslave as many highly placed courtiers as possible –'

'If you are referring to Sophia of Strackenz –'

'I refer to Lady Axewith.'

Foison shifted in his chair, the knife cradled in his lap. 'Do you have proof?'

'The lady's appearance, for one. But also the network of society women she has enlisted to gather information. They have been swarming Axewith House like bees a hive – all at the unseen behest of the Contessa.'

'Where is the Contessa now?'

'Laughing at you, I expect. Why did you stop Harcourt from taking her?'

Foison ignored the question. 'Where is Doctor Svenson?'

'We were separated after the blast.'

'Where is Francesca Trapping?'

'With Doctor Svenson.'

'How did he acquire her?'

'At the Palace. The Contessa had hidden her.'

'That isn't true.'

The words hung there. Phelps glanced desperately at Chang. Foison's grip shifted on the knife. Chang knew it was a test, exerting pressure to establish how far he would go to preserve Phelps. Chang kept his face empty. If he made up anything now, it would make matters worse. Foison flicked his head, flipping a lock of white hair from his eyes. 'Tell me about the painting.'

'Which painting?'

'You know very well.'

Another test – Chang had no idea what Phelps had already confessed. 'A

newspaper clipping. From the *Herald*, critiquing an art salon, especially a
painting of the Comte d'Orkancz entitled *The Chemickal Marriage* –'

'And you saw this painting yourself?'

'None of us did.'

'I will ask you once more. Did you see this painting?'

'No. The salon was in Vienna.'

The knife sliced through the earlobe. Phelps shrieked and hopped against
his bonds. The gash streamed blood, the severed nub of flesh somewhere on
the floor.

'The salon burnt down with the painting in it!' Chang shouted. 'The clipping came from the Contessa – if you want to know more, ask her!'

Foison ignored his anger. 'Again, please, how did you acquire Francesca
Trapping?'

'I didn't! We were separated in the Palace – when I found Svenson, he had
the child –'

'So Doctor Svenson had seen the Contessa?'

'If he had, she would have killed him.'

'She did not kill *you*.'

'Doctor Svenson would have given her no choice. She murdered the
woman he loved, Elöise Dujong.'

'So he stole the Contessa's property – this child – out of revenge?'

'You do not know Svenson. He rescued a child in danger.'

'Has the child been mistreated?'

'You saw her yourself, you damned ghoul. She's been poisoned by that
glass book. By your filthy master. Who's no more Robert Vandaariff than
I'm the Pope – or you're the God damned Queen!'

The door opened, and Robert Vandaariff tottered in. He had aged even
since the Customs House, his face grey and his bony fingers fiercely gripping
the head of his cane. His throat was wrapped in a neck cloth, but a red
bruise extended past its white border. Harcourt slipped in behind, eyes darting covetously between Chang and Mr Phelps.

'Time ticks on,' Vandaariff announced blandly. 'Close the door, Mr Harcourt. We have no need of soldiers.'

'But, my lord, your safety – Cardinal Chang –'

'Is tied to a chair. Mr Foison will preserve me. Will you not trust him, too?'

With a gesture somehow grudging and haughty at the same time, Harcourt sniffed at the grenadiers and shut the door in their faces.

'And the *lock*,' added Vandaariff.

Harcourt turned the bolt. A curl of dread climbed Cardinal Chang's spine. He had returned himself to this madman's power. Every impulse cried out to fight, but he'd thrown away the chance.

'Do you have . . . headaches?'

Chang did not answer, and then Vandaariff repeated the question, turning to Harcourt.

'Mr Harcourt? The pains – they grieve you, yes?'

'Beg pardon, my lord –'

'I think they must. Speak freely.'

Harcourt shuffled back a step, aware of everyone watching. 'Perhaps, my lord – but, given the crisis, regular sleep is impossible – much less regular meals –'

Vandaariff tapped Harcourt's forehead with a knuckled claw. '*There*. Is it not?'

Harcourt smiled awkwardly.

'And your eyes . . . have you seen your eyes, Mr Harcourt?'

'No, sir. Should I?'

'Take off your glove.'

Chang had not noticed the gloves: a self-important prig like Harcourt would naturally wear them. Harcourt squeezed his hands together.

'I know already that your nails are yellow, Matthew. That the cuticles bleed, that gripping a pen gives you pain.'

'Lord Robert –'

'Not to worry, my boy. I also know what to do about it.'

Harcourt gushed with relief. 'Do you?'

Vandaariff drew a handkerchief and laid it on Harcourt's open palm. Harcourt gently plucked the handkerchief apart. When a blue glass card was revealed, Harcourt went pale, licking his lips.

'You have met such an object before.'

'Excuse me, my lord – it is difficult – ah – it is extremely difficult –'

'Take it up, Matthew.'

'I dare not – I cannot – given the current –'

'I insist.'

Harcourt's resistance gave way and he sank his greedy gaze into the blue card's depths. No one spoke, and after a moment, like a dog in a dream, one of Harcourt's legs began to shake gently, heel tapping softly on the floor.

'The Contessa has no subtlety, no art,' Vandaariff muttered sourly. 'Yet she is effective, and through this fool has learnt far more than I would have liked.' He cocked his head at Phelps. 'But I'm afraid I interrupted your conversation, Mr Foison. Do you care to continue?'

'Not if Your Lordship wishes otherwise.'

'They spoke together?'

'Nothing you did not anticipate.'

'Too much to hope.' Vandaariff sketched a stiff bow in Phelps's direction. 'I thank you, sir, and regret your discomfort.'

'Mr Phelps,' prompted Foison. 'Late of the Privy Council.'

'Mr Phelps. It is a shame to make an acquaintance under such conditions.'

'Renew an acquaintance, you mean,' said Chang.

Vandaariff fluttered a hand near his ear, like a fop's handkerchief. 'I did not hear.'

'I said you *do* know Mr Phelps. He was the Duke's deputy.' Chang called to Phelps, hoping the man had strength. 'How many times did you visit Harschmort? A dozen?'

'At the very least,' Phelps muttered, rousing himself. 'But there were also private meetings at Stäelmaere House –'

Chang nodded. 'Perhaps Mr Foison was away on your business, my lord, but *you* cannot have forgotten the man who in your own chambers negotiated the Duke of Stäelmaere's rise to power.'

'Indeed.' The grey tip of Vandaariff's tongue wet his lips. 'I have been unwell. Even now, some . . . memories . . . they elude my grasp.'

'How do you not recall a man you've met above a *dozen* times?'

Phelps attempted to straighten himself in the chair. 'In the gardens of Harschmort, facing the sea – Your Lordship pointed across the water, to Macklenburg –'

'I do apologize, Mr Phelps,' Vandaariff cut in. 'If I have not, in our present dealings, been *mindful* of this past service. We need no longer trouble you.'

'I beg your pardon?' Phelps looked up without comprehension as Vandaariff tugged a slim leather glove onto one hand. 'You're setting me free?'

'I am.'

'My lord?' This was Foison. 'Without comparing the prisoners' accounts –'

'A question of balance, Mr Foison.' Vandaariff dug in the pocket of his waistcoat. 'You are not wrong – and yet, where is the right? Look at Mr Harcourt – ready to serve. Look at Chang, compelled to obey. But poor Mr Phelps . . .' Vandaariff sorted what seemed like coins in his gloved palm. 'I believe he has done all he can.'

Vandaariff raised what Chang had taken for a coin to the light – an edged disc glowing blue.

'My lord, with respect –'

Vandaariff jabbed the disc into Phelps's jugular, just enough to draw blood – which immediately crusted around the cut. Chang watched a vivid line crawl in both directions from the incision, up into his skull and under Phelps's shirt, to his heart. Phelps stiffened, but no sound escaped his mouth. Vandaariff wrenched the disc free and dropped it to the floor. He ground it to powder with his shoe.

Phelps slumped, lifeless. Vandaariff took another handkerchief from his coat and blew his nose. 'Mr Foison, inform Mr Harcourt's companions that they must report to Lord Axewith in his stead. He is unwell.'

'My lord.'

Foison left the room. Chang stared at Phelps's still-open eye.

'You gave me no choice,' said Vandaariff. 'And if you mention my memory again, I will shove a glass card between your teeth and force you to chew.'

With the croak of a carrion bird, Vandaariff began to softly sing.

My love is gone beneath the ground
though I was ever true
a dearer child would ne'er be found
until I first spied you . . .


Foison reappeared in the doorway. 'The coaches await, my lord.'

'Then let us be off.' Vandaariff patted Chang on the head. 'Everyone's ready.'

# SIX

# SOMNAMBULE

Chang had been right. A dusty, uniformed man leading a bedraggled child excited no comment and scarcely a glance of pity. Too much had happened to too many people. They passed bodies on carts, weeping women, men sitting stunned in the street, soldiers doing their best to clear the crowds – and it quickly became Svenson's task to shield the girl from the devastation. Victims reared up, roused to fury by the glass embedded in their flesh, and set to attacking whoever came within reach. After the first crazed assaults, the soldiers no longer scrupled in their response, and before their eyes had clubbed a shrieking woman to the ground with their musket-butts.

Svenson took Francesca in his arms and veered into a side street, itself a crush. The people around them did not speak – their faces, drawn, bloody, streaked with ash, made plain what they too had survived. Svenson shifted his burden and winced at the pain from his injured rib, sure he could hear the *click* of bone against cartilage. He mumbled soothingly and caressed Francesca's hair, and soon enough she settled into sleep, a heavy but tractable weight.

Celeste Temple was dead. Chang was determined to kill himself. Phelps and Cunsher were taken. Doctor Svenson was alone.

Or was that true? He could make no sense – no moral sense – of the encounter in the Palace. The woman had cut Elöise's throat . . . still he shuddered to recall the teasing caress of her breath.

The Contessa would be his task.

He kept on, beyond the Citadel, past the University, through the ugly brick of Lime Fields. At the corner of Aachen Street he set Francesca down and as she yawned – and his arms throbbed with relief – did his best to improve their appearance, sponging soot from their faces and brushing ash from their clothes.

Aachen Street was lined with old mansions that had been subdivided into smaller townhouses, and then – fashion and fortune shifting across the town – purchased anew and grandly recombined. In the centre of the block stood one such, with a tall iron fence that had been painted green and a guardhouse next to the gate. He had not recognized the address when Francesca had said where they must go, and it took a moment even now to interpret his sense of familiarity. It was the light – he had never seen the place during the day – but how many times had he been here to collect his Prince? The Old Palace had no sign advertising itself, but, as an exclusive brothel catering to the city's most powerful, he did not suppose one was required.

The man in the guard box waved them away, but Francesca called out shrilly, 'We have come to see Mrs Madelaine Kraft.'

The guard directed his gruff answer to Svenson. 'We are not open to visitors –'

'Mrs Kraft,' Francesca insisted.

'Mrs Kraft is not here.'

'She is so.'

'She is not well.'

'Mrs Kraft not being well is *why* we must see her. We were *sent*.'

Svenson saw a twitch at the front window's curtain. Before the child could speak again, he squeezed her shoulder. Francesca turned impatiently – with her pasty complexion and protuberant eyes it was the reproachful gaze of a piglet in a butcher's window – but Svenson held his grip for silence.

'The fact is, sir, we have walked far, through terrible disarray, with instructions to call on Mrs Kraft. If it is a mystery to you, it is also to me. I do not know who she is.'

The guard turned back to his box. 'Then I must say good day to you –'

Svenson spoke quickly. 'You say she is not well, good sir, but I will hazard more than that. I will hazard she has been stricken *insensible*.' The guard paused. '*Further*, I will surmise that no surgeon has been able to penetrate the cause. What is more – and if I am wrong, do drive us from your door – I say that Mrs Kraft was first taken ill during a visit to Harschmort House some two months ago – *and so she remains*.'

The guard's mouth had fallen open. 'You said you did not know her.'

'I do not. And you have kept her condition secret, yes?'

The guard nodded warily. 'Then how – who –'

'Permit me to introduce myself. Captain-Surgeon Abelard Svenson –'

Francesca threatened to spoil everything with an eager, dead-toothed smile. Svenson leant forward, blocking the guard's view. 'As the child said, we were *referred*. It may be I can do nothing . . . yet, if I can . . .'

A muffled *thud* came from the guard box, recalling the guard to his hut like a dog on its master's lead. Francesca squeezed Svenson's hand. The guard hurried out and unlocked the gate.

'Quickly,' he muttered. 'Nothing grows in the daylight but shadows.'


Standing in the lavish parlour holding the hand of a seven-year-old girl only complicated the Doctor's usual reaction to such establishments: disapproval of the architecture of prostitution – its tyranny, dispassion, degradation – and jealousy at his own exclusion – for his class, his poverty – from such rarified delights. Hypocrisy made both sources of discontent sting the more, but hypocrisy in matters of the heart was to Svenson no fresh wound.

The previous night's flowers were being replaced with fresh bouquets – orange-streaked peonies and purple lilies – by a serving girl scarcely older than Francesca. Svenson wondered if she was an apprentice to the brothel, and how soon she might expect to join the ranks of the Old Palace's wares. The little housemaid wrapped the dead flowers in her apron and gathered the bundle to her chest, but then she saw Francesca and stopped. The children stared at one another, but Francesca's haughty gaze held firm. The housemaid dropped her eyes to the carpet, dipped once in Svenson's direction and scurried out.

A rustle to their left revealed an alcove for coats and hats and sticks, and a pretty young woman waxing the counter-top. Before she could ask for their coats, Svenson shook his head.

'We are here for Mrs Kraft.'

The young woman nodded across the parlour, where another guard – despite his lack of uniform, there could be no other term – stood at a wooden rostrum. This second guard did not stir. After a lingering moment (during which, stupid from lack of sleep, Svenson could not recall if the twitching curtain had been from this level or the floor above), a *thump* echoed behind the rostrum, the exact sound that had come from the guard box. Svenson saw a pair of brass pipes bolted to the wall: pneumatic message tubes, allowing swift communication throughout the house. The shocking expense of such a system spoke to the brothel's prodigious backing.

The guard fished a scrap of green paper from a leather-wrapped tube.

'You're to be taken to Mr Mahmoud.'

'I'll do it, Henry.' The pretty coat clerk had already slipped from her alcove. 'You're not to leave the front, and I can be back in five minutes.'

'Make sure it *is* five minutes, Alice. No roaming off.'

'And why should I do that?'

'Mr Gorine's instructions –'

'Are exactly why you need to stay in the front. Now come with me, pet.'

She looked kindly at Francesca, her expression catching only briefly at the sight of the girl's sickly features, and led them out. Alice's hair had been pinned, but along her nape Svenson noticed a row of dense curls. She glanced back and nearly caught his stare.

'I've never been in the office myself. *No* one goes in the office, except Mr Gorine and Mr Mahmoud.'

'And who are they, pray?'

'Well, who are you, if you don't know *that*?'

They passed into an oval room. Come the night, it would be filled with exquisitely painted women – and painted boys – from which a visitor might choose. Now the only occupants were two women in their shifts, playing cards on a cushion between them, with a third, distressingly young, perched on an ottoman with a box of sweets.

Alice peered at Svenson, waiting for an answer. He stammered, too struck by the contrast between the gaily painted faces and, in flat daylight, the too-pale bodies.

'I'm sorry – I – I am no one at all.'

'Then who is *she*?' Alice winked at Francesca. Before Svenson could intervene, the child piped up, her voice disagreeably hoarse.

'I am Francesca Trapping. I am the oldest surviving *Xonck*. I will inherit the entire Xonck *empire* because my brothers are fools.'

Svenson squeezed her hand. 'I am sure Mrs Kraft must not be kept waiting –'

One of the card-playing women stifled a laugh. 'Mrs Kraft?'

'We have been *sent*,' said Francesca.

The girl on the ottoman spoke around the nougat in her teeth. 'Well, no reason to hurry on *her* account . . .'

'And why would the likes of you see *her*?' called the card-player.

'That is a secret.'

'A very *important* secret, to be kept by such a pair of beggars.'

'We are nothing of the kind!' Francesca cried. 'But you're a dirty thing. You're a pig's trough with a week of sloppings.'

Svenson seized the girl and marched for the far door, driving their guide before him.

'Surviving Xonck?' called an angry voice. 'That one looks like pickled fish on a plate!'

Francesca squirmed in his arms. 'Let me *down*.'

'You must hold your tongue.'

Tears had broken down the child's cheeks and her words burst out in gasps: 'But she *is* dirty. Her name is Ginny – she does wicked things! She did them with your prince!'

'My prince?'

'I know all sorts of things. He was *dreadful*!'

Svenson went cold in shock and the girl wriggled free. The Comte's book – she was a *child*. He went to one knee. 'Francesca, you poor thing –'

Francesca tossed her head. 'I am *not*. Stand up.'

But their guide's face had gone pale. 'Her name *is* Ginny. How did *she* know that?'

Svenson impulsively took Alice's hand. 'You can see the girl is ill. The

situation is delicate – she *is* the heir of Henry Xonck. Both of her parents
have died –'

'Died how?'

He turned. They stood in a long, expensively papered corridor, and
another party had appeared at its far end, foremost a soldier whose blue
jacket was rigid with gold brocade. Alice sank into a fearful curtsy.

'Colonel Bronque . . .'

The Colonel paid them no more heed than a hat stand, striding past.
Behind Bronque came a small, stout figure with a foreign-looking goatee,
wire-rim spectacles and pearl-grey gloves. His clothes were well tailored but
nondescript. Svenson's impression of familiarity was echoed by the man's
own surreptitious glance at the Doctor. The man vanished round the corner.

'Forgive me, Alice, but have these gentlemen called upon your premises
so early in the day, or do they depart after spending the night?'

'I'm sure I don't know, sir.' Her words were hushed and chastened.

'But you knew the Colonel. You must know the gentleman with him.'

'I'm sure I couldn't say.'

'Of course – the first rule of trust is discretion. But if I were to ask you
instead –'

She only bobbed another abject curtsy and hurried on.

Alice rapped four times upon a door sheathed in bright steel. A narrow viewing window was pulled back and then slid home just as fast. The door was
opened by a muscular man with skin the colour of cherrywood. Her desire
for diversion wholly extinguished, Alice dipped again and then fled down
the corridor. The large hand that waved them into the room held a revolver
whose oiled barrel seemed like a sixth finger.

This was quite obviously a room of business – ledgers, blotters, notebooks, strong box, and a large abacus bolted to a table. Gleaming pipes ran
down from the ceiling to another station for the pneumatic system. As Svenson watched, a leather tube rocketed into the padded receiving chamber.
The dark man ignored it. Svenson cleared his throat.

'You must be Mr Mahmoud –'

'A message came, we should expect you.' For such a large man, his voice was delicate, as sleek as an oboe, but the words were charged. 'And now you're here.' Mahmoud nodded coldly to a door on the far side of the office. 'So. Go see for yourself.'

Svenson released Francesca and the child tore off for the inner door. But at the threshold she stopped still, face frozen with wonder.

'O Doctor . . . she looks like a *queen*.'

He hurried to look. A woman lay on a chaise-longue, draped in silks, eyes closed, hands clasped below her bosom.

'Stay here, Francesca – *do not move*.' At the sharpness of his tone, the child obeyed.

Careful and thorough, the Doctor took the woman's pulse at the wrist and throat, peeled back both eyelids, opened her mouth, examined her nails, her teeth, and even, remembering the glass sickness, took an exploratory tug at her hair. Svenson's dispassionate eye put her age at forty-five. Her golden skin seemed sallow, but he did not suppose she'd seen the sun in two months. Was she from India? An Arab? He looked around the inner room, at the Moorish daybed and enormous desk, now cluttered with the detritus of a sickroom. This too was a place of *work*. Madelaine Kraft was no ordinary woman. The Old Palace was *hers*.

He saw no mystery as to why such a woman had been a target of the Cabal. A brothel-keeper possessed the means to blackmail thousands of rich and influential men – capturing Mrs Kraft's memory delivered them to the Cabal in a stroke. But why had the Contessa gone to such trouble to send Svenson to Madelaine Kraft *now*?

'Francesca, what else did the Contessa say? Surely there was some clue, some advice?' He peered behind the desk. 'Did she forward some parcel of supplies to help us?'

'There is no parcel.'

'Child, there must be. Her own experiments with glass –'

'There is *me*.' The girl wore a prideful smirk that turned his stomach. Before he could reply, an explosion of voices came from the outer room.

'They are strangers! What will the Colonel say?'

'What do I care?' This was Mahmoud.

'Damn you, we agreed –'

'*You* agreed –'

A sharp-nosed man with a moustache and long, oiled hair stormed in, his eyes leaping about to make sure nothing had been taken. Mahmoud waited in the doorway. The intruder tugged on his white shell jacket and then, glaring at the Doctor and the child, set to cracking his knuckles, one finger at a time.

'You are Mr Gorine?' Svenson offered. 'I am Abelard Svenson, Captain-Surgeon of the Macklenburg Navy, attached to the service of Crown Prince Karl-Horst von Maasmärck –'

Gorine pulled viciously on his thumb until it popped. 'And *you* will cure her? Is that what we are to believe? *Macklenburg?*' Gorine stabbed Svenson's chest with a finger. 'We have had enough of *Macklenburg* at the Old Palace!'

'If you refer to the Prince –'

Gorine slapped Svenson across the face. The blow was not hard – he did not think Gorine had much experience with slapping – but it stung. 'I *refer*, Captain-Surgeon, to two women abducted from this house, to seven more who wake screaming from unnatural dreams, to the collapse of our business, and lastly – *yes* – to Mrs Kraft. All because your worthless Prince came through our door!'

'If it is any solace, the Prince of Macklenburg is dead.'

'Why should that bring me solace? Does that bring back our women?'

'Michel –' But at Mahmoud's interjection, Gorine only gave the rest of his complaint directly to the dark man's face.

'Does that end the tyranny of our *occupation* – unable to come and go without leave from a gold-jacketed, stone-hearted –'

Doctor Svenson coughed into one hand. 'If your two women are Margaret Hooke and Angelique, I must inform you both are dead as well.'

Gorine turned on Svenson, his fury heightened. But while Gorine's back was turned, the Doctor had taken hold of his revolver and now pressed the barrel into Gorine's abdomen. Gorine's breath stopped.

'O well done, Mahmoud –'

'Be quiet.' Svenson's voice was calm. 'Ignorance makes a man angry, I know. The matter is larger than *us* – than all of us together. I *am* here to help – to help *her*. But I am entirely willing to blow you apart like a pumpkin beforehand.'

The pressure of the pistol caused Gorine's Adam's apple to bob like a

cork in a stream. The Doctor lowered the weapon that – he was quite sure –
no longer held any bullets. Gorine darted to the side, clearing the way for
Mahmoud to fire, but the dark man did not move. Svenson slipped the pistol
back into his greatcoat and addressed them both.

'The Prince of Macklenburg was as much of a dupe as your women, sacrificed to the ambition of a wicked few who are still driving this city to its
grave.'

Mahmoud stepped forward. 'Who? We have ten good men –'

'Save them – even a hundred is too few.'

'But their *names* –'

'The name that matters is Robert Vandaariff.'

Mahmoud cast a doubting glance to Gorine. 'But he was stricken with
blood fever – we assumed he was another victim.'

'Forty-seven people were taken ill that night,' said Gorine. 'Not one has
recovered, save Robert Vandaariff. Are *you* the one who cured him?'

'No. The recovery is false. His entire character is destroyed.' Svenson
rubbed his eyes. 'Would either of you gentlemen have any tobacco? I have
lost my supply and a touch of smoke would do wonders for my mind.'

At Mahmoud's nudge, Gorine took an ebony box from a desk drawer.
'Mrs Kraft's. Get on with your story.'

'The man is exhausted, Michel.'

'We are all exhausted,' Gorine retorted.

Gorine took a cheroot himself before offering the box to Mahmoud, who
declined. The squabbling intimacy of the two men was suddenly plain, especially to one who had spent years sailing in close quarters. Svenson shrugged
at the insight – it was nothing to him, after all – and took a tightly rolled
cheroot from the box and held it to his nose. Gorine held out a light and
Svenson puffed with a palpable greed.

Mahmoud waited, one hand still resting on his pistol-butt.

'So can you help her, Captain-Surgeon, or can you not?'

The Doctor began by asking questions, but the narrative of Mrs Kraft's care
only tightened his jaw. Nothing had answered, yet he could think of nothing
left to try. At last he stubbed out the cheroot – he must work or fall asleep.

'The attack was on Mrs Kraft's mind, not her body, and in her mind will be the cure.'

'Her mind is beyond *reach*,' replied Gorine. 'She cannot speak one word.'

'Yes. If I might impose for a supply of chemicals and then a meal – anything at all, though hot soup would be a treasure . . .'

Mahmoud went for food while Gorine found paper in the desk. As Svenson made a list of what he required, Gorine studied Francesca. She sat at the foot of the chaise-longue, and for the first time Svenson realized how quiet she had become.

'Heir to the Xonck empire, is it?' Gorine asked her.

'Once my uncle Henry dies.'

'And you're with this doctor? Alone?'

'Her parents,' said Svenson, 'along with her uncle Francis –'

Gorine plucked the list from Svenson's hand. 'Francis Xonck. One hopes she isn't heir to *that*.'

Gorine left the room. Francesca frowned at the carpet. Svenson had no idea how much the girl had heard at Parchfeldt between her uncle and her mother, or how much she had understood.

'Do not mind him. We are here to help this lady. As you said yourself, a queenly countenance –'

Francesca still stared at the floor. 'Did *you* like my uncle Francis?'

'I'm afraid your uncle did not care for *me*, my dear.'

'But he loved mother. He loved *me*.'

'Francesca . . .'

'He *did*.'

'Your uncle Francis loved to be happy, sweetheart – how could he not love you?' It was a feeble attempt, and Francesca Trapping wrinkled her nose. She fell silent again. 'What . . . ah . . . what did the Contessa say to you, about your uncle?'

Francesca snorted, as if the question was especially stupid.

Gorine hurried in. 'There is someone to see you –'

Svenson reached for his revolver. 'No one knows I am here –'

Gorine seized his arm. 'For God's sake – don't be a fool!'

Mahmoud appeared, and his added strength wrenched the Doctor's weapon away.

'There is no help for it,' the dark man said. 'He recalled your face.'

Colonel Bronque stood in the doorway. Black hair sat flat against his skull, a widow's peak accentuating his hawk-like nose. Gorine and Mahmoud retreated to either side.

'*Macklenburg.*' The Colonel spat it like a curse. '*Macklenburg.*'

'What of it?'

'You're Svenson. Surgeon. *Spy.*'

'Do I know you?'

'Obviously not. If you did, you would be more frightened.'

The Doctor's fatigue got the better of him. 'O no *doubt*,' he replied, and sat on the desk.

Colonel Bronque barked with harsh laughter. Svenson risked a glance to Mahmoud and Gorine – both nodding gamely along with the Colonel's amusement. Bronque came forward beaming. 'I did not think you fellows had any humour at all.'

'What fellows?'

'Macklenburgers – Germans. I knew your Major Blach. Tight as a drum head.'

'Indeed, a horrid man. Who *are* you?'

Instead of a reply, Bronque extended his arms, and his glittering eyes invited the Doctor to guess – a test. Svenson had no choice.

'Very well. Your name tells me nothing, nor – *a priori* – does your rank. You are seen in a brothel in full dress, with another man whose clothing is expensive but undistinguished. Judging by the poor crease of your trousers, you have spent the night. One guess says your charge is a high-born *personage* bent upon his pleasures, requiring an especially trusted chaperone in these troubled days.'

Bronque grinned with a wolfish satisfaction. 'But why should I bother with you?'

'Because, as a criminal, my presence opens your *personage* to scandal.'

'Nonsense.'

Svenson sighed. 'Indeed, you would simply kill me.'

'But I have *not*.'

The Colonel's intensity was oppressive. Svenson rubbed his eyes. It was early, and the better part of his mind was tangled with thoughts of blue glass. But then he had it.

'Ah. Because you are not *here* at all.'

'I beg your pardon?'

'You have not come for the brothel's wares. You have come for the tunnel.'

'What tunnel?'

'Under the Old Palace is a tunnel to the Royal Institute. At one point the Comte d'Orkancz used the Institute for his research, and employed the tunnel to ferry test subjects —'

The Colonel looked accusingly at Gorine and Mahmoud. 'Did *they* tell you that?'

'Of course not. But it explains why the Old Palace continues to operate — you have demanded access to the tunnel in exchange. Which sets your companion in an entirely new light — not a patron, but perhaps a Ministry official, an engineer, a Doctor of metals —'

Gorine could bear it no more. 'Doctor Svenson —'

'Silence!' Bronque's lips curled like a twist of uncooked meat. 'I apply the same logic to you, Doctor. You were attached to the Prince's party as a spy —'

Svenson shook his head. 'I am only here to attend Mrs Kraft.'

'I do not believe you.' Bronque stepped back, all amusement gone. 'The tunnel is watched. Consider yourself watched as well.'

The Colonel strode out as quickly as he'd come.

'Threaten away,' Svenson muttered. 'I already face a death sentence . . .'

Neither Mahmoud or Gorine replied. Both men were gazing intently at Madelaine Kraft, whose large brown eyes were open.

Despite the raised voices that had woken her, Mrs Kraft's attention was entirely taken with Francesca, and the child returned the woman's gaze with a directness ordinarily reserved for odd-looking insects or younger siblings.

'What will you do?' Mahmoud whispered to Svenson. He shook his head.

The girl gently patted Mrs Kraft's foot under the blanket. 'I am Francesca Trapping.'

'And I am Doctor Svenson.' He pulled a chair near to sit. The cost of her subordinates' well-intentioned treatments – extending to leeches and quicksilver – were etched on the woman. He laid a palm across her forehead. How long could anyone survive in such a cocoon?

As he had hoped, Francesca watched his every move. She glanced conspiratorially at the tray of chemicals. 'What did you send for?'

'Nothing that will cure her. We must search Mrs Kraft's mind.'

'Can she hear us?'

'Yes . . . but does she understand?' Svenson shifted his attention to the child. 'Now it is time for *you* to say what you know, Francesca.'

The girl covered her mouth with one hand, stifling a belch.

'How else am I to help her, dear?'

Francesca shook her head.

'Do you feel ill?'

'No.'

But her eagerness had fallen before her discomfort. That was natural enough – and as long as she felt sick, the girl would be afraid. Svenson patted the chaise-longue, inviting her closer.

'The Contessa has put us together, Francesca. Let us pool our thoughts. Now, everything *I* know of the glass tells me Mrs Kraft's condition is permanent. I met another lady with such a hole in her mind. She'd taken just a peek into a glass book – and in a trice some of her memories were gone. Nothing so serious as our patient here, but though she tried with all her strength, this lady could never recall them.'

Doctor Svenson placed Mrs Kraft's hand, heavy with metal rings, onto Francesca's lap. The girl began to stroke it, as if it were a kitten.

'When I asked what the Contessa had sent to help, you said she had sent *you*.'

Francesca's voice was thick. 'She *did*. But I do not –'

'And I believe you. You have absorbed some of the Comte's book – a frightening thing, I know, which you cannot think on without discomfort.' Svenson kept his voice easy and calm. 'However, the Contessa wastes no time on trifles. She believes Mrs Kraft can be cured – and therefore, my dear, *you* are the puzzle, not Mrs Kraft, and our task is to divulge your secrets safely. We must be clever and we must be brave. Are you brave enough to try?'

Francesca nodded, and clutched the hand to her stomach.

'Good. You need not fear.' Svenson forced a smile. The girl's dull teeth peeped back trustingly.

The Doctor peeled off his greatcoat, laid it over his chair and then rearranged the supply of chemicals. He felt their expectant eyes upon him as he crossed to Mahmoud's tray, bent to sniff and then poured the still-steaming black coffee into a mug. By the time the cup was drained – just the limit of his audience's patience – he had chosen his course.

'The Old Palace stands hostage to Colonel Bronque's use of your tunnel. What so commands his concern? Could the Institute be a staging area for the attacks upon the city?'

Gorine waved this away. 'The Institute is a gaggle of scholars in black robes.'

'Scholars like the Comte d'Orkancz?'

Mahmoud shook his head decisively. 'The Comte was only allowed on the premises at the insistence of Robert Vandaariff.'

'But the Comte is *dead*,' said Gorine. 'Without him Vandaariff is just a wealthy man.'

'Do you think so?' asked Svenson. 'Does Colonel Bronque?'

He used a handkerchief to extract the blue glass card from his greatcoat. Francesca's eyes were wide. Svenson ignored her and, keeping his voice gentle, addressed his patient.

'I am going to show you a thing, Mrs Kraft. Do not be afraid. Nothing will harm you.'

His patient did not resist when he gently angled her head, but she inhaled with force at first sight of the card, her pupils swelling black. Svenson eased the card into her fingers and they clutched it tight. Madelaine Kraft was completely immersed.

Svenson kept his voice low. 'Has either of you ever seen blue glass such as this?'

'Never,' said Gorine.

'Once.' Mahmoud knelt at the foot of the chaise-longue. 'Angelique. Mrs Kraft took it away.'

Gorine watched with suspicion. 'What does she see?'

'Dreams. Potent as opium.'

Immediately Mahmoud reached for the card. Svenson caught his hand.

'It *is* dangerous. It *is* deadly. But nothing you have tried has penetrated her mind. This will.'

Mahmoud threw off Svenson's arm. 'And cause her death? Michel –' Mahmoud appealed to Gorine, but Gorine stared at their mistress.

'*Look.*'

Madelaine Kraft's breathing had deepened and her face had changed – cheeks flushed with colour, with *life*. Gently, Svenson retrieved the card. Madelaine Kraft looked up. He took her hands, speaking softly.

'The Bride and Groom . . . did you see them?'

She blinked at him, and then nodded.

'Do you know those words now, Mrs Kraft? *Bride?*'

'*Bride* . . .' Her voice was tender with disuse.

Svenson nodded encouragement. 'You saw the faces . . . the angels . . . the feathered mask and the mouth below, you saw the teeth . . . the Bride's teeth –'

'*Blue.*' The word was a whisper. Mahmoud and Gorine pressed forward, but Svenson warded them off, fixing his eyes on hers, making sure.

'And the ball . . . the ball in the black Groom's hand?'

Madelaine Kraft's mouth worked, as if she were calling forth a key she had swallowed. '*Red.*'

Svenson sighed with relief. Her mind *could* make new memories, the harvesting process had not robbed her of that – she was no vegetable. Yet through her illness she had not spoken – why did only indigo clay etch its mark into her mind?

He patted Madelaine Kraft's hand. 'What do you think of that, Francesca?'

The girl had no answer, both arms wrapped across her middle. Was she that delicate, that susceptible? Suppressing the urge to comfort her, fearing it would only make things worse, Svenson turned to the others. 'I assume Colonel Bronque has gone?'

Gorine consulted his pocket watch. 'He has. But why?'

'Because we are going to need your tunnel.'

The bundle of chemicals lay at Svenson's feet. Francesca Trapping stood yawning and blinking. The girl had recovered, and though she showed a clumsiness descending the stairs, he ascribed this to exhaustion. At the end of the basement corridor lay an old iron door. Two uniformed soldiers crouched against the wall, bound and, though not cruelly, gagged. Gorine watched them with an unhappy expression and a pistol in each hand. Mahmoud sorted through a ring of keys. Behind, two servants gently held Madelaine Kraft upright between them.

'I hope you know what you're doing,' muttered Gorine. 'Bronque will summon his soldiers, the doors will be stormed –'

'You could take him hostage,' observed Mahmoud. From his tone, and Gorine's reply, it was no new suggestion. 'Allow him inside the house, have our men ready –'

'The Colonel will defend himself, and if he is injured or killed it is our lives – if *he* doesn't kill us outright to begin with –'

Sensing a tirade, Svenson broke in. 'If there was time to ask the Colonel to join us, I would. There is not. Mrs Kraft's only hope to recover her mind lies in defiance. Moreover, it is not the Colonel who controls your survival, but the man who comes with him.'

'We don't even know who he is!'

'I suggest you find out. Now which of you stays and which comes along?'

'Mahmoud knows the tunnel.' Gorine squeezed the pistols in his hands. 'If anything happens to Mrs Kraft you will answer. As we will answer to Her Majesty's displeasure.'

'I would expect no less,' said Svenson, noting Gorine's naive conflation of the Colonel with the Queen. 'Now who has a lantern?'

As a boy, Doctor Svenson had prided himself on his knowledge of the forest bordering his family's fields. In an adolescence of discontent, he made a practice of stalking at random into the trees, stopping only when the light had gone and darkness had instilled the place with shapeless dread. He made it his task to return by instinct. With each twig that popped beneath his feet or dragged across his night-chilled face, the stale misery of his days gave way to a deeper engagement, where his sacrificial determination echoed that of a knight sitting vigil in a cold stone church. In time he had seen the pride behind the romance, and the fear behind the pride, and these memories made him wince.

'Where have you been?' his mother would ask.

'Walking,' went his invariable reply.

He had always gone home – to light, to warmth – and his relief at being so recovered was a way of infusing his quotidian life, taken for granted, with value. But after so many years, was it not the dark wood that had held constant? What home was there to walk to now? In his rambles he had misplaced the life around him, but perhaps he had truly seen the world.

Mahmoud's lantern settled on stone steps beneath an angled doorway. 'This opens to the courtyard – the simplest entrance, but hardly concealed, given it is full morning.'

'Is there another way?'

'Do you have a specific destination?'

'I do. Across the courtyard is a brick roundhouse – rather like an iceberg, it extends a hundred steps below ground. The main chamber was fitted for the Comte d'Orkancz. Enough machines may remain to restore Mrs Kraft.'

'How?'

'That hardly matters if we cannot reach it.'

'As Lord Vandaariff once sponsored the Comte, so he now sponsors others, even offering his own men to guard the gates . . . still, there are other, older ways.' Mahmoud's teeth were bright in the shadows.

They followed the glow of the lantern to what seemed a dead end. Mahmoud pushed with both hands, and the entire panel of brickwork swung inward.

'It is an actual hidden panel!' enthused Svenson.

'Thus the King reached his mistress,' called Mahmoud, stepping through. 'Take care where you put your feet . . .'

The process by which a king's bedchamber became a dusty storeroom for scientific specimens – Svenson could see cephalopods in murky jars, geo-

logic samples, piles of bound notebooks – struck the Doctor as emblematic
of some larger entropic theory, one requiring a metaphor beyond his immediate wit. As he lifted Francesca over a row of bell jars, the lantern illuminated
the ceiling: a peeling fresco of a nude man in the sea surrounded by women.
Then the light was gone, Mahmoud playing it around the room, leaving
Svenson to wonder what grand tale had graced a king's most intimate hours.
The rescue of Jonah? Poseidon and his nymphs? Or a final crisis of the
flood – death in ecstasy?

'I do not like the spiders,' whispered Francesca, staring at a shockingly
large specimen under glass. Svenson picked her up again, to let the servants
pass with Mrs Kraft.

'No one likes them, sweetheart.'

'*He* does.' Her voice had thickened. '*He* thinks they are beautiful . . . he
makes me look, when I don't want to.'

'Look at Mrs Kraft instead.'

'Looking at her makes me sick.' Francesca belched. Svenson grimaced at
the foul smell.

'She did not make you sick before.'

'She does *now*.'

'Then we must drive the sickness from you.'

'How?'

'By following the Contessa's plan. You trust the Contessa, don't you?'
Francesca nodded.

'Well, then,' Svenson assured her. 'We will do nothing she did not intend.'


He sent off the servants with detailed instructions. It might not work – the
men might be seen, or his formula mistaken (was he sure of the treated paraffin?). Nevertheless, they crouched in silence, peering from a ground-floor
window, Francesca hunched next to Svenson, Mrs Kraft leaning with a glazed
expression against Mahmoud.

Directly across the courtyard stood the massive gate with its medieval
portcullis. A score of men in green uniforms lounged around it, bantering
with the Institute personnel. As Svenson watched, one black-robed figure was
pulled to the side and questioned by the guards before being allowed to pass.

Mahmoud used the disturbance as an opportunity to ease the window open. The brick roundhouse lay directly between their window and the gate. A single guard stood at its door.

'Stay as low as you can,' Svenson whispered. 'And run. Can Mrs Kraft do this?'

'A bit late for that question, isn't it?'

'Yes, of course – I only –'

Having made his point, Mahmoud cut Svenson off: 'It hardly matters.'

Across the courtyard, an iron door set into the ground was flung open – the courtyard entrance to the tunnel – and then a cloud of black smoke billowed up into the air.

'Where is the sound?' asked Mahmoud. 'There is no explosion – something has gone wrong.'

'Wait for it!' hissed Svenson. 'Listen!'

But something *had* gone wrong. The thunderclap he had hoped to achieve was absent, and in its place came only a roiling cloud. Slowly, painfully they watched, but not one of the guards took notice.

A voice cried out – finally! – but not from the guards. The shout came again, from the rooftop: sentries silhouetted against the sky. At last a man from the gatehouse jogged to the courtyard for a look. At his yell two more followed . . . and then in a blessed rush the rest of the guards ran to the tunnel entrance, calling for water, for axes, for everyone.

The man posted at the roundhouse hesitated, but at last set down his rifle and ran after his fellows. In a flash Mahmoud vaulted out. Svenson passed Francesca through and then did his best with Mrs Kraft, only to have Mahmoud pluck her easily from his grasp. Svenson clambered over the sill, all knees and elbows, and gathered Francesca. Mahmoud was already a dozen strides gone, his mistress over his back like a rolled carpet.

Svenson's side jolted with pain at every step. Mahmoud reached the roundhouse and slipped Mrs Kraft from his shoulder. Svenson thudded up next to them.

The door was not locked and they ducked inside. 'Down, my dear, fast as you can!'

Francesca gripped the rail and descended with a painful delicacy. The Doctor could not blame her – the merest slip on this high staircase meant a broken neck. Keeping firm hold of Mrs Kraft, Mahmoud gave the girl his other hand and made sure of them both. Svenson closed the door and turned the lock. Had they been seen? How long would they have? He dug out the revolver and rapped the open cylinder on the heel of his hand, scattering brass cartridges onto the landing. He pawed through the pockets of his tunic. Only three bullets. He slotted them in and told himself it was no shooting situation. If he needed more, he had already lost.

'Do not move.'

At Svenson's words, the laboratory's only occupant spun with shock, a glass flask slipping from his hand. The man yelped and hopped clear, batting at the greenish smoke that rose from the stone-flagged floor.

'Damn you, sir! Look at what you've done! What is this trespass?'

The indignant man was fair and unkempt, with a well-fed jaw blooming from his tight collar like a toad's. 'Do you *know* whose works these are? I promise you, when *Lord Robert* is made aware –'

'Professor Trooste,' Mahmoud called from the door.

The Professor swallowed nervously. 'Bloody Christ – I mean to say – hello. My goodness – and Mrs Kraft!'

'Professor Trooste is a patron of the Old Palace.' Mahmoud secured the door with an iron bolt. 'When someone sponsors his visit, of course. He's been travelling – haven't you, Professor? Research expedition?'

'Where?' Svenson demanded. 'Quickly – *where*?'

'Nowhere at all –'

'Polksvarte District,' said Mahmoud. 'And Macklenburg before it.'

'Damn your black eyes! Not that it matters – what are the rivalries of science to the likes of you? If you must know, I was advised of certain mineral deposits – utterly unprofitable, as it happens, waste of time all round –'

'You're a liar.' Svenson cocked the revolver. 'What does he have you doing?'

'He?'

'Robert Vandaariff.'

'Your uniform and voice, sir, suggest a foreign soldier. *I* am a patriot. Shoot me through the heart – threats mean nothing.' Trooste struck a noble posture, but then broke into a knowing cackle. 'In all candour, if I *were* to break my word, the Ministry would punish me tenfold –'

Svenson cracked the butt of the revolver on the Professor's forehead. Trooste fell with a cry. Before he could scuttle under the table the Doctor dragged him clear.

'Mahmoud – place Mrs Kraft on the table.'

'But what do you intend?' whined Trooste, both fat hands flat across his forehead. 'I am sorry this woman is unwell – but I am no physician –'

Svenson sought out Francesca. The girl stood staring at a little hut against the far wall.

'What is that room?' Svenson asked Trooste.

'The foundry.'

'For what is it used?'

'Smelting metals, what else?'

'Is there a door inside, to the corridor?'

'Of course not –'

Francesca coughed into her hands and sank down on a wooden crate. Her lips were dark and moist. Trooste squirmed to his feet. 'Is it plague?'

'It is not. Mahmoud, if you would prevent the Professor from leaving?' Svenson crossed to the child. 'What do you remember, Francesca?'

The little girl groaned, as if the disturbance in her body would not submit to speech.

'Try shutting your eyes. The memories will be less insistent –'

She shook her head with a whine. 'I *can't* – I can't look away.'

Svenson turned to find Trooste had edged near.

'She is sick with the genius of your master, through close contact with indigo clay.'

'Indigo clay?'

'Do not pretend you do not know it.'

'On the contrary . . .' Trooste studied Francesca like a fox eyeing a fallen fledgling. 'Close contact, you say?'

A sharp word from Mahmoud called Trooste to assist in situating Mrs

Kraft on the table. Mrs Kraft remained silent, gazing into the high, conical ceiling, an enormous brick beehive.

Svenson wiped Francesca's mouth with a handkerchief and left it in her hands. 'Once this is finished, you shall have anything. Back in your own home, safe with your brothers, all the tea cakes you can eat –'

Francesca nodded weakly, but her pallor forestalled further mention of food. The child had visibly deteriorated, the laboratory too resonant for her frail frame. It could not last.

'We need to align these machines,' he told Trooste. 'You will obey the child's instructions.'

'Obey *her?*'

'Exactly.'

'How provocative. That a child might possess such knowledge – one speculates . . .'

Svenson ignored him and began to take stock of each device, speaking aloud for Francesca's benefit. 'Copper wiring connects each gearbox to leads at the foot of the table, and runs inside these rectangular crates –'

'Crucibles,' interjected Trooste. Svenson glanced at Francesca, who nodded, pinching her nose. Svenson went on.

'More wires pass from the *crucibles* to the table and hoses, which attach to the subject's body – no doubt there is an esoteric meaning to each point of contact – and also, most prominently, a mask . . .' He found the thing hanging from a peg, rubberized canvas on a metal frame. 'The current is passed through a bolus of blue glass inside the crucible. I assume you have an adequate supply?'

This was to Trooste. The Professor nodded, adding in a crafty undertone, 'Lord Vandaariff assured me there was no rival inquiry in these subjects.'

'He is a liar. And I tell you here: every man to study indigo clay has paid with his life. Gray, Lorenz, Fochtmann, the Comte d'Orkancz himself – all of them dead.'

Trooste chewed his lip, shrugged.

'You *knew* this?'

'O yes. Lord Vandaariff was quite candid. But once I knew the details of each man's failure, I saw how my own efforts –'

Doctor Svenson dug into his tunic and came out with one of the glass spurs. He flung it at Trooste. The disc harmlessly struck the Professor's chest and dropped into his gloved palm.

'Packed into every bomb set off in the city,' Svenson announced. 'By the thousands. I trust you recognize the *provenance*.'

'But that's ridiculous –'

'Look *into* it, Professor!'

At Svenson's shout, Trooste raised the blue disc to his eye. An ugly grunt came from his mouth. Before the anger in the glass could fully insinuate itself, Svenson slapped the spur away.

'*Doctor Svenson.*'

With a cold horror, Svenson followed Mahmoud's gaze. From within the foundry came the rattling of a doorknob.

Mahmoud whipped a sheet of canvas over Mrs Kraft and shoved Svenson under the table. He plucked Francesca off her feet and carried her behind a tall cabinet, a hand across the child's mouth.

Trooste stood blinking, still confused by the glass and staring at the tip of Svenson's revolver beneath the hoses, ready to fire at the Professor's first mischosen word.

Mr Foison entered from the foundry. With the knife in his right hand he pointed past Trooste to the main entrance. 'Why is that door locked?'

'Is it?' asked Trooste.

Foison surveyed the room. 'What are you doing?'

'Nothing *objectionable*, I hope. I am *working*.'

'Lord Vandaariff is delayed. He will send word.' Foison flipped the knife into the air and caught it again, as if the action helped him to think. 'Did *you* lock that door?'

Trooste's voice hovered at the edge of a stammer. 'Perhaps I did. Lord Vandaariff said our work was extremely sensitive –'

'What sort of idiot locks one door but not the other?'

Trooste visibly fought the urge to glance at Svenson. 'I suppose an idiot like me.'

'The same idiot that dropped that flask?'

'Indeed, yes – an accident –'

'You are anxious, Professor. You have not been anxious before. No, I should have described you as singularly satisfied.' Foison's contempt entered his words like the surfacing eyes of a crocodile.

'Ah – well, perhaps – the state of the city.'

'I hadn't heard.' Foison flipped the knife again. Abruptly he stepped to the wooden crate where Francesca had been sitting. He drew a fingertip across the crate and flicked it at Trooste: a spatter of black across the Professor's pink cheek. Trooste dabbed a finger to his face and sniffed.

'A chemical residue – carbolic phosphate – I thought I had cleaned it all –'

Beyond Trooste, Svenson could just detect the tip of Mahmoud's shoe. He knew Mahmoud had his own pistol ready to fire. With a sickening dread Svenson saw Foison casually shift his stance to place Trooste between, blocking any clear shot.

'What you are *doing*, Professor?'

'I am assisting Lord Vandaariff –'

'And your guest?'

'Guest?'

Foison flipped up the canvas, revealing Madelaine Kraft's slippered feet. He pinched her toe and provoked a noise from beneath the canvas. 'I did not know your work at the Institute had graduated to . . . live subjects.'

'I do nothing save follow Lord Vandaariff's instruction.'

'I see. And – now your work *has* taken this turn – do you find Lord Vandaariff's instructions troubling?'

'Of course not.'

'Of course not,' Foison echoed.

'I – ah – ascribe them to his own f-fever – and – and his recovery. To be candid, we have all heard the rumours –'

'I have been abroad, until quite recently. *Rumours?*'

Trooste retreated into the table, rattling the hoses in front of Svenson's face. 'Lord Vandaariff's interest in Macklenburg – and the marriage of his daughter –'

'One explains the other, does it not? Where the daughter marries, the father invests.'

'Indeed. But his patronage of the Comte d'Orkancz, who had also been to Macklenburg – ah!' Trooste gasped at a sudden movement from Foison. Was the knife at his throat?

'You will not take advantage of Lord Vandaariff, because of his ill health.'

'Never. Christ above, I promise you –'

'No, Professor. I promise *you*.'

Foison stepped away, the knife back in his coat. 'Whatever happened to your face?'

Trooste touched his forehead where Svenson had struck it with the pistol-butt. 'Ah, that. One of the machines. Flay-rod. One's attention wanders –'

'And then you're dead.' Foison walked to the foundry door, but then paused. 'And Professor?'

Trooste forced a patient smile. 'Anything.'

'You wouldn't know how empty shell casings came to be littering the top of your stairs?'

'Shell casings?'

'From a revolving pistol.'

'I've no idea. I have no weapon.'

'That is wise. The way your day is going, it would only be used against you.'


As soon as Foison was gone, Trooste sagged against the table, pale with fear. 'I did what you asked – wait – wait! Where are you *going*?'

Mahmoud raced from his hiding place to the foundry room. Svenson hesitated, taking a step towards Francesca, but then followed the dark man. He found Mahmoud crouched at the second exit door. With silent care Mahmoud eased its bolt home, blocking any re-entry.

'That cold-eyed Asiatic will have my life.'

Trooste had joined them, but the Doctor paid no heed. Above the foundry's stone trough hung a metal rack, and there, like cakes from a baker's oven, lay three blue glass books.

'What in heaven . . .' whispered Mahmoud.

'O yes,' agreed Trooste. 'Aren't they glorious? Just made this morning, by Lord Vandaariff himself, every one untouched and pure –'

Svenson tried to control his voice. 'Mahmoud, take hold of the Professor. Do not touch or look into these books. A glass book brought your mistress to this pass.'

'But what *are* they?'

Against the wall lay a stack of leather cases. Svenson opened the topmost, noting with grim satisfaction that its interior was lined with orange felt. Equally to his purpose was a pair of iron tongs, wrapped with cloth. As the others watched, Svenson carefully lifted one of the books and set it in the case. He snapped the case shut. Mahmoud held another ready, but Svenson shook his head.

'Put it down. Turn away.'

'O no.' Trooste began to sputter. 'No, no – good God, the *effort*! He will kill me! I beg you –'

Svenson flipped the second book off the rack. It struck the edge of the trough and shattered across the stone floor. Trooste howled, and only Mahmoud's strength kept him from tackling Svenson. Svenson seized the third book.

'You cannot!' Trooste writhed. 'I swear – I will be hunted down –'

Svenson heaved the book onto the stone. He broke the shards under his boots. He stumbled. He was growing light-headed – there were fumes. He dropped the tongs and clapped a hand over his nose and mouth.

'Get out – hold your breath!' As the others fled, the Doctor stamped again and again on the broken books. He careened into the main chamber, slamming the door behind.

'Barbarian,' spat Trooste.

'You have no idea.' Svenson rubbed his stinging eyes.

'But, Doctor, I don't understand.' Mahmoud pointed to the leather case in Svenson's hand. 'If those books are so terrible, why keep that one?'

'Because the Professor is correct. We'll need a weapon.'

Svenson interrogated Trooste about the machinery, keeping one eye on Francesca – gauging the veracity of the resentful man's answers by the distress each nugget of information provoked in the girl. Caught between Svenson's bitter resolve and the spectre of Mr Foison, the Professor became more and more anxious. By the end Trooste barked his replies, flinching in advance at the child's grunts and soot-coloured drool.

But in that half-hour Doctor Svenson learnt more than he had ever desired about indigo clay: conduction, amplification, and the power Trooste termed 'reciprocal cognition'. He now perceived in the tangles of wire and hose a mechanical intention: the operative *essence* of indigo clay eluded him as much as ever, but laid bare were the physical means to translate memory into a glass book, to infuse a book's contents into an empty mind, to overwhelm a victim's will with the Process – each action a relatively straightforward matter of force and direction. The restoration of Madelaine Kraft, however, depended on knowledge Trooste did not have.

Svenson had seen the toxic effects of prolonged exposure and bodily ingestion, but Madelaine Kraft's affliction could not be put down to physical proximity – it was not as if blue glass had touched her brain. Moreover, she could form new memories – so how to explain her continued vacancy? Perhaps the chemical exchange wherein blue glass captured memory carried a charged violence, enough to leave the *psychic* equivalent of scar tissue. Could the power of these machines overcome that artificial barrier? And if so, would the action reveal her memory intact, like a forgotten city beneath a dam-formed lake? Or would the necessary intensity simply destroy her?

Svenson gazed down at Mrs Kraft and squeezed the woman's honey-coloured hand. Whatever he was supposed to find, there was precious little time in which to do it.

'She will be herself once again,' he said. 'Is that not right, Francesca?' The girl had brought her knees up to her chest and sat rocking, dirty ankles exposed. 'Perhaps you might tell Mrs Kraft yourself.'

Francesca shook her head, lips tightly shut. Hating the lie, he smiled encouragingly. The girl hiccupped and shook her head to stop him talking, but Svenson kept on.

'I know you feel ill, but you must trust the Contessa. Look at Mrs Kraft – or, even better, take her hand.' He lifted the child to the table, ignoring the worry on the faces of the other men. 'Excellent, now, think of what we know . . . when I look into a glass book, which is to say, when I *touch* it with my gaze, this contact allows its entrance to my mind –'

The child's hacking spattered black onto Svenson's sleeve.

'Doctor –'

'Please do not interrupt, Mr Mahmoud. Physical contact is different, Francesca, yes? For example, I was able to remove glass from Cardinal Chang's lungs with an orange liquid that dissolved the glass into phlegm, so it could be expelled. But even if we possessed that mixture –'

'Bloodstone,' Francesca croaked.

'Bloodstone?' Svenson had never heard the name.

'An al-alch . . .' She stumbled on the words with an unhappy squeak. '. . . *alchemical* catalyst.'

'Compounded out of what – what elements?'

Francesca choked again, spraying Svenson's coat. Mahmoud turned on Trooste. 'Do you have any on hand? Bloodstone?'

'Lord Vandaariff has procured a broad range of chemicals –'

Trooste indicated an apothecary's cabinet, a tall draught-board of tiny drawers. Mahmoud leapt to it, opening an entire row. Svenson carried the child over, so she might peer inside, but Francesca shook her head at each. Her eyes were wandering and wild. Mahmoud slammed the drawers as they went and wrenched at the next row.

'What does it *look* like?' he asked.

'The liquid was orange,' said Svenson. 'I have seen an orange metal as well, but that was refined, and no doubt an alloy –'

Francesca dismissed this row as well. Mahmoud set upon another and growled at Trooste, 'Have you *no* idea?'

'I am sorry, good fellow,' Trooste replied. 'Lord Vandaariff is not one to share a secret. Naturally I regret Mrs Kraft's condition – she has been a friend to the Institute – although, as a *regular* visitor, and I am not alone in this opinion, one might merit a *reduction* –'

Mahmoud squared on Trooste, but Svenson caught his fist before it could swing. The sudden gesture loosened his grip on the girl and she sagged forward. Francesca inhaled, nostrils flaring, and began to whine like a chastened pup. The nearest drawer was filled with brownish rock. Svenson held a chunk to her nose. She gagged and squirmed away, unable to breathe.

'You will kill her,' cried Trooste. 'Jesus Lord –'

Svenson ignored him. 'Francesca! What do we *do*? How do we use it?'

Francesca met his eyes, fearfully, plaintively, and opened her mouth wide, as if she were showing him a broken tooth. Black fluid poured down her chin.

'Dear God!' Trooste protested.

'It is nothing at all,' Svenson snarled. 'Mahmoud – bloodstone – mortar and pestle, grind it as fine as gunpowder –' He thrust a finger at one of the brass gearboxes. 'Professor Trooste, we will need *that* machine. Make it ready at once.'

'You have no idea –'

'Move, damn you!'

'The smell . . .' Francesca's voice was a stricken complaint. Svenson wiped her face.

'Do not mark it, my dear – two minutes more and we shall whisk you to clean air –'

'The smell . . .'

'Yes, I am so sorry –'

'The smell is *when*.'

Francesca's eyes rolled back into her skull.


The child lay shivering in Svenson's greatcoat. She would not revive.

'A terrible shock,' he muttered, 'a marvel she could help as she did. We will let the poor thing rest, and get her to safety as soon as possible.'

Mahmoud's silence was its own condemnation, but the steady grind of the pestle bespoke the man's determination. Trooste cleared his throat into a closed pink hand.

'I believe Mrs Kraft would be better restored with a garlic soup.'

Mahmoud merely lifted the mortar with the pounded bloodstone for Svenson to see.

'That is excellent, I'm sure. If Professor Trooste will deign to assist . . .'

Trooste did so, adjusting the brass knobs on a gearbox, though not without a glance at the door. Mahmoud's worry seemed no less acute.

'Why has no one come?'

'We do not know what has happened in the courtyard.' Svenson poured a handful of ground bloodstone into the gearbox.

Trooste frowned. 'If there were a crisis, Mr Foison would have told me.'

'He trusts you that much?'

'He trusts no one – but Lord Vandaariff has shown every confidence. Why not stop all of this and let me address him on your behalf?'

Svenson made sure of the hoses and wires. The black rubber mask left only Mrs Kraft's mouth exposed to breathe. Trooste inserted a heavy lozenge of blue glass into the crucible chamber. Svenson connected the copper wire to the crucible leads.

'Mahmoud, please step back from the table.'

'What will happen to her?' asked Mahmoud. 'All of this wizardry –'

'She will be cured.'

'She won't,' declared Trooste.

'Correct me if I am wrong, Professor. *This*' – Svenson pointed to a switch inside the wooden box – 'ignites the crucible. The initial charge sent through the glass is amplified by passage around the chamber and feeds back again into the gearbox. There the collected charge reacts with the bloodstone, and – when the gearbox valve is opened – infuses the subject with its properties.'

'That is the map of it,' replied Trooste. 'But a map is only half of the matter. How much bloodstone? You're only guessing. Just as you take the word of an incoherent child that it's bloodstone to begin with – or that bloodstone isn't fatal. How long do you wait before opening the valve? Not long enough, and the force is too weak. Too long, and the charge alone will kill her.'

Mahmoud looked to Svenson for an answer. He had none.

'That is the truth!' Trooste snapped.

'Why did that woman send you?' Mahmoud's question was a dagger between Svenson's ribs. 'Madelaine Kraft is nothing to her. I cannot believe in her kindness.'

Svenson spread his open palms. 'I do not ask you to.'

'Then you are here to kill her?'

'If that were true, why drag you all this way?'

'For your science.'

'Not mine, Mahmoud.'

'She will die on this table,' insisted Trooste.

'She will never heal as things stand,' said Svenson gently. 'She will waste to nothing.'

Mahmoud gazed helplessly at the woman, limbs bound and face obscured, only the red mouth visible. In an instant of clarity Svenson saw the isolated line of Madelaine Kraft's jaw exactly mirrored on Mahmoud's younger, darker face. He was her son.

'Do it.' Mahmoud's voice fell flat and hopeless. 'She would rather die than live like this. Do it now.'

Svenson pulled the switch. A rattle of current, like a rolling volley of musket-fire, leapt along the lines of copper wire, and the sharp stench of indigo clay burnt the air. The metal pipes that covered the walls took up the vibrations, escalating until the entire chamber throbbed with a deafening roar. Svenson clapped his hands over his ears, but it did not stop the pain. Like a fool he remembered the Comte's brass helmets – and there they were, across the chamber, in a row. If only either he or Trooste had known what they were doing! But it was too late to reach them. Madelaine Kraft's limbs tore against the restraints and her mouth gaped in an unheard howl. Mahmoud had a fist in his mouth, eyes fixed on his mother. Svenson lurched to the gearbox, ready to open the valve. Trooste tugged at his tunic, waving frantically. Svenson shook his head. Trooste tugged again. Madelaine Kraft arched her spine, rising off the table, higher, higher, until it seemed her bones must snap –

He almost missed it, between Trooste's attempts to shove him aside and the hammering noise, so loud he could scarcely link one thought to another. The current flooded the bloodstone, shaking the bolts that held the gear-box – then there it was, a burst of scent, bittersweet and musky, a rawness in his nostrils –

The smell is *when*.

Svenson opened the valve. The black hoses flared to life. Madelaine Kraft's twisting body went stiff, fingers splayed, jaw wide, the waves of force pouring through –

The current from the gearbox died as quickly as a candle flame, the blood-stone spent. Trooste leapt forward, closed the valve and groped in the box for the switch. The roar in the pipes fell away. The blackened wires snapped their final sparks and set to gently smoking.

Svenson fell to the table, ears pounding. Mrs Kraft's pulse was racing but strong. With a cry of relief he waved Mahmoud to him and together they peeled the mask from her face. She bore welts where it had pressed into her skin, but her eyes ... her eyes shone with a life Doctor Svenson had not previously seen.

'Mrs Kraft?' He could not hear himself, but it did not matter. She nodded. Mahmoud freed her limbs and raised her to sit.

'Merciful heaven,' she managed. 'I have been at the bottom of the sea. O my dear boy.'

She buried her face in Mahmoud's shoulder and his strong arms pulled her close. Mahmoud leant down, face to her hair, a spill of tears on his dark cheek.

'Now,' Mahmoud whispered. 'Now we pay them back.'

Svenson hurried to Francesca. The girl was cold to the touch, her breath shallow. He tapped her cheek to no response.

'Is she alive?' asked Trooste.

'Of course she is!' Svenson crossed to the still-open square drawer and heaped another load of bloodstone into the mortar. He sat on a bench and began to grind it furiously.

'Why do you need more?' asked Trooste. 'A child cannot withstand that current.'

'I am aware of it,' Svenson replied tightly. Mahmoud murmured to Mrs Kraft, yet her gaze fell on Doctor Svenson, to his discomfort.

'Then for whom?' Trooste pressed. 'Not one of us!'

'No.' Svenson filled a stoppered flask with the rust-coloured grains and tucked it inside his tunic.

'Then *what*?' complained Trooste. 'For God's sake will you not leave? They will think I have betrayed them – my entire prospects of advancement –'

'Are *bankrupt*. Lorenz, Fochtmann, Crooner – did you know Crooner?'

'Everyone knew Crooner – ludicrous fellow –'

'Crooner died with both arms shattered at the elbow, turned to blue glass.'

'Well, *exactly* – that is Crooner all over –'

'Don't be an ass!' The Doctor pulled on his greatcoat. 'Listen – we will climb these stairs. Mahmoud must help his mistress, I must carry the girl. We cannot drag you. But Vandaariff must not know what we have done.'

'Lock me in a cupboard, I will say I saw nothing –'

'You will divulge every detail.' Svenson pulled out the revolver. The Professor swallowed, his wide throat bobbing.

'B-but I have helped you –'

'And so I ask you to come with us. If you do not, I will shoot you or bury your mind in this last glass book.' The words were inhuman, but had he any choice?

'No. I would not wish it on a fiend.' Madelaine Kraft's voice carried an authority, however weak. 'If the Professor will not leave this business, Mahmoud could perhaps prove his resistance to our trespass . . . say, by shooting his leg.'

'Through the knee?' offered Mahmoud.

'Hardly sufficient,' she observed. '*Both* knees would be better.'

Trooste blanched, at which Mrs Kraft smiled, and the moment of violence was past. The ease of her intervention seemed from another world – as distant to Svenson as allowing himself satisfaction for her cure. The Doctor stuffed away the revolver and slung the leather case over one shoulder. He lifted Francesca and stumped to the door.

For once the height of a staircase did not disrupt the Doctor's thoughts, distracted as he was by the question of what to do next. They clustered on the upper landing, all save Mahmoud panting from the climb. Svenson put an ear to the door, but heard nothing.

'If the guard has returned, we must pull him inside – throw him down the stairs, anything for silence. If he has not, then I suggest we run for the same window we came from –'

'We will be seen from the rooftop.' This was Madelaine Kraft. Her tone carried no criticism, but Svenson felt nakedly at fault.

'Then I will charge the gate. While they surround me, Mahmoud runs for the window with you and the child –'

'They will shoot you dead, then the rest of us from a distance. Where will your mission be then? Or our revenge?'

Svenson could not think. He could not look down at the girl. He felt the grain of the wooden door against his forehead. 'I am open to suggestion.'

'I will go with the Professor. He is known, and if I am noticed, the reaction will at least not be immediately hostile. If he betrays me, I will cut him down. Mahmoud?'

Wordlessly, but in Trooste's plain view, Mahmoud passed her a short knife in a leather sheath. She gripped it with a turn of her wrist, so it appeared for all the world a folded fan. Mahmoud opened the door and ducked behind.

The light hit Trooste and Mrs Kraft and for a moment neither moved.

'Lord above,' Trooste gasped. 'My lodgings . . . my writings – O heaven!'

Trooste ran. Both Svenson and Mahmoud snatched after him, but Mrs Kraft blocked them with her arm. 'Let him go – look!'

Before their eyes an entire wing of the Institute stood shrouded in smoke and, licking from the billowing curtain, bright tongues of flame. Svenson shared a guilt-stricken glance with Mahmoud – how could this have come from their diversion of smoke? – but then a spatter of gunshots seized their attention. Trooste had been seen, and he shrieked as the grass around him kicked up in clumps. Hands over his head, the Professor reached the cover of an oak tree. Svenson saw sentries silhouetted above the gate – but who had given the order to fire, *inside* the courtyard, at a man they must recognize?

His eyes dropped to the gate itself. The iron portcullis had come down, and bodies littered the ground under the stone archway . . . what struggle had forced the guards to seal the way? Were these people from the *town*?

Mahmoud shook Svenson's arm. 'Listen!'

He heard nothing save the shouts of the men attempting to quell the fire – a poor handful, and all from the Institute, but the blaze had grown well beyond their ability. He saw men trapped by flames, others burdened with possessions, unsure where to flee. Still more huddled in the courtyard, like Trooste, unable to move for fear of rifle fire. A few sharpshooters aimed at them, but most faced the other direction, to the street . . . and then Svenson heard what Mahmoud had, beyond the walls, another roar to echo the inferno – a mob outside the gate! They had attempted to storm the Institute! Had the fire spread through the district?

A bullet chipped the brick above Svenson's head. They had been seen at last. Svenson plunged forward, Francesca in his arms.

'We will be trapped! Hurry!'

He cut to his left, tight against the curving brick, away from the snipers. A moment later Mahmoud and Mrs Kraft were there.

'I do not understand,' she gasped, out of breath. 'They have been ordered to keep people *in* as much as keep them out!'

A portion of the burning wing collapsed in a shower of sparks. Fresh jets of flame rose through the open hole.

'The Institute will burn!' Mahmoud cried. 'And every neighbouring building . . .'

'We must get out,' Mrs Kraft shouted. 'My people – I must know they are safe.'

A ricochet sent them further along the wall – at least one sniper had shifted for a better shot. Svenson saw Trooste dash from his refuge and into a gap in the wall. He boldly plunged after, Francesca bouncing in his arms. If anyone knew their way to a bolt-hole, it would be a conniving fellow like Trooste.

Bullets cracked through the branches over his head, but – perhaps due to the rising smoke – nothing found its mark and he reached the gap in the wall. Trooste had vanished, but the door he'd gone through hung open. Svenson charged on, into chaos: black-robed scholars fleeing with boxes, satchels, specimen cases. Svenson glimpsed Trooste through the mob and pressed after him, against the tide.

Mahmoud shouted over the tumult: 'He isn't leading us out! He wants his own papers –'

Svenson didn't answer. The Professor had spent a good minute cowering behind the tree, long enough to grasp the scope of the fire and the orders that had been given to the soldiers. Trooste was no fool.

'Where are we?' he shouted to Mahmoud. 'Which direction –'

Mahmoud pointed urgently. White smoke curled towards them from the corridor's end. Svenson wheeled round and spied a door ajar: an office whose window had been broken out with a chair. Beyond it bobbed the figure of Trooste, racing down an alley. Once through the alley they would be free.

'Mahmoud, as we did before – you first, I will help Mrs Kraft –'

Svenson paused. They stared at Francesca. He put an ear to the child's ashen mouth. Her breath was starkly uneven.

'The medicines you purchased for Mrs Kraft will answer – willow bark, and mustard to dislodge congestion – but we must get her out of this inferno!'

Fat flakes of ash filled the air like tainted snow. Improbably, the blaze had not yet leapt to the nearby townhouses, but their occupants had fled to the street. At the main road, Svenson and the others were swept into a jostling crowd. Any hope of locating Trooste was lost, and within seconds Mahmoud and Mrs Kraft were swallowed up behind him. Where *were* they? Francesca required immediate treatment, yet Svenson could not see which corners they were passing. He shifted his grip, despairing at the sickly flop of her hanging legs.

To either side stumbled figures in silk and fur, escaping within pockets of servantry. Surges of traffic tore at each little group as the smoke flowed over the rooftops: shoving, shouts, shrubbery trampled, a lamp-post torn from its place and crashing to the cobbles. Svenson wiped his eyes on the epaulettes of his greatcoat – if only he could *see*.

The people before him stopped short and Svenson piled into a wide man in his shirtsleeves. Before he could beg the fellow's pardon someone behind cannoned into *him*, and again it was all he could do to remain upright.

Trumpets. Hoof beats. Cavalry clearing the road for the fire brigade. The shirtsleeved man slapped at his neck, burnt by a cinder. The right side of the road – a single line of townhouses – was all that stood between the penned-in crowd and the growing blaze. A few water-carts would not stop its spread. In five minutes the street would be a deathtrap.

Black-jacketed lancers blocked the road. Beyond the lancers came the water-carts. Suddenly a wave of shrieking rose from the rear of the crowd. The fire had reached the townhouses. The mob swelled into the cordon of horsemen. Svenson stumbled to one knee.

'Back, damn you!' roared a sergeant of lancers, as if his throat were boiled leather. 'If these carts don't pass the entire district will burn! Once they pass you can go on!'

His voice was strong, and might have swayed the crowd if not for another eruption from the Institute. The sky bloomed to a rolling orange ball, showering the street with debris. The crowd surged without care into the horsemen. The Sergeant danced his horse away, but the troopers lacked his skill. Fearing for their lives, the lancers dipped their bloody points into the churning mob. People fell screaming – as those behind them screamed at debris and flame. A horse went down with a spastic thrashing of hooves, its rider pinned. The cordon broke and the terrified mass poured blindly through. In front of Svenson an elderly man fell and tried to rise – blood on his brow, pomaded hair flapping like a dove's broken wing – but his leather shoes slipped on the stones and he disappeared. For an instant the crowd parted around the obstruction – those who had seen him fall did their best to step clear, but those who had not tumbled heedlessly through the opening: a last ripple and he was gone.

Svenson ran as he never had in his life, past struggling horsemen, around an overturned water-cart, careening from the frenzy. He'd been kicked in the back, struck across the face and nearly skewered. He stood gasping with his back against a tattered sapling, upright in an otherwise trampled garden. The fire had entirely possessed the first line of houses and would certainly jump the road. Huddled shapes littered the street. Scavengers searched pockets and gathered trinkets and cutlery abandoned by the fallen and the fled.

The stitch in his rib sent a line of pain all the way to Svenson's jaw. He pulled Francesca tighter to his chest and did his awkward best to chafe the circulation in her limbs. Her breath came thick with congestion.

'Not much longer, my dear. The green guardhouse door and then hot tea and a bath – and tobacco for me, by God.'

The girl's hair stuck to her brow, curled with sweat and grime. He jogged her gently, hoping for a response. She blinked, the blue of her eyes clouded with an opaque film.

'You did very well, sweetheart – just wait until we tell the Contessa –'

A fresh chorus of trumpets. The lancers returning for more blood. He hurried in the opposite direction and, like a message from heaven, there was the signpost for Aachen Street.

'Thank goodness – sweet Christ, thank goodness –'

At a clatter of boots, Svenson stopped short. The Old Palace was untouched by the fire, but the guardhouse was smashed and the front of the brothel yawned wide. The garden was littered with debris, and as he stared, stupid with fatigue, two soldiers emerged lugging a wooden chest from Madelaine Kraft's office. Behind came two more, driving a gang of frightened women whose attire seemed as ill placed in the open air as a powdered wig in a poor house. Bronque's men had sacked the Old Palace as if it were their prize.

The Doctor turned to flee – if he could find Mahmoud and Mrs Kraft, if they had not been taken – but a firm hand shoved him into the iron fence. A burly corporal smiled grimly, his musket-butt ready to smash the Doctor's face.

'For God's sake,' gasped Svenson. 'I have a child –'

'Hold! Hold there!'

An officer stood across the road, where Bronque's men formed a cordon.

'His uniform, ass!' shouted the officer. 'That's the Colonel's German! Get him in the wagon – *now*!'

Before Svenson could address the officer, the Corporal heaved him into a panelled goods wagon. He landed awkwardly on his side, rolling to protect the girl, and just pulled his legs free of the slamming door. A rattle of iron caused the Doctor to start. Chained to the opposite bench – bloody, bruised and brutally gagged – sat Mr Gorine.

Svenson reached across for the gag, but paused when he noticed the horror in Gorine's eyes. He looked down. Francesca Trapping's head lolled in the Doctor's arms, her stained mouth yawning in the half-light. Her face was cold. Her eyes were sightless and unblinking.

He had no idea how long they rode, nor where their captors took them. A crippling guilt fixed Doctor Svenson to the bench and sank his mind. He wrapped Francesca in his greatcoat and fruitlessly rocked her body.

Somewhere in the midst of it he'd managed to prise the gag from Gorine's mouth; the chains were locked fast. In a ravaged monotone he had done his best to answer Gorine's questions. None of it mattered. He had known she was at risk. Willow bark, for God's sake! Francesca Trapping had been balanced on a gallows by the Contessa di Lacquer-Sforza, and he, Abelard Svenson, had kicked away the support.

'She was doomed already.' Gorine's voice was as gentle as possible above the creaks of the wagon and the pounding hoof beats. Svenson nodded dumbly. It changed nothing. He had lost himself, quite completely. He raised his face to Gorine's searching eyes. The man recoiled.

'You're not ill as well?'

Svenson's lips twitched reactively, a ghost of a smile, inappropriate, hideous. 'The damage does not signify.'

'But . . . your eyes, your *face* –'

'I'm sure it is only a lack of tobacco.'

'Have you gone mad?'

Svenson heard the question as if from a distance. Gorine stared at Svenson's hand, stroking the girl's hair. The Doctor carefully returned it to his lap.

'My apologies. Far too many tasks await before I can allow myself to expire.'

Gorine leant as close as his chains allowed. 'You're sure they were not taken? Mahmoud and Mrs Kraft – you're sure she is restored?'

'O yes.'

'Then where do they take *us*?' Gorine vainly attempted to look out through the ventilation holes. Svenson gazed at Francesca's shoe, sticking out from the greatcoat, marvelling at how small the foot, how fragile each toe.

'It was as you surmised,' Gorine went on. 'For three weeks we have suffered Bronque's trespasses – soldiers on the premises, arrivals at all hours – the Colonel and his *man*.'

Gorine's upper lip was bruised, and the swelling broke the meticulous line of his moustache. Almost like a cleft palate, Svenson thought, noting that Gorine now appeared less intelligent. What was it about disfigurement, however arbitrary the source, that led the mind to underestimate, even dismiss the victim . . .

'That fellow never said a word, you know. We offered rooms, choice of companions. Took us up, of course, but never let slip a damned thing. No papers or club cards, not even a mark in the fellow's clothes to show his tailor. Not one clue. Only his hands.'

'When I saw him he wore gloves.'

'At all times. But once I spied on them in the tunnel. This fellow's hands are *stained*.'

'A birthmark?'

'Are birthmarks *blue*?'

The wheels slowed, crunching into gravel. Gorine went stiff. 'What will they do? I am no soldier – I cannot withstand pain!'

Svenson shivered. The sweat of his flight from the Institute had gone cold. He worked a hand into his tunic and took out the blue card containing the Contessa's memory of the painting. He dropped it to the floor and broke it to shards beneath his heel.

'What are you doing? And what is that?' Gorine pointed to the leather case around Svenson's shoulder. 'Is it valuable? We should exchange it for our lives –'

'If they wanted to kill you, you would be dead. And since you've no idea where they are, you cannot betray your friends.'

'Bronque won't believe that!' Gorine's voice rose. 'They will tie me to a rack –'

'It is not as if racks abound. You are a hostage against Mahmoud and Mrs Kraft.'

The wagon came to a stop. An idea penetrated Svenson's gloom. 'Wait. What did Colonel Bronque say to you, on your arrest? When he learnt we had entered the tunnel –'

'He called me a whoremongering traitor, then I was kicked to the floor –'

'Nothing else? They will hunt Mrs Kraft and Mahmoud and they will kill them.'

The rattle of the lock echoed in the hollow space. Gorine shook his head. 'It wasn't Bronque – it was the *other*, and when we were outside, at the smoke –'

'Saying *what*?'

'That no man lights his own funeral pyre without reason.'

Canvas hoods were forced over their heads. Svenson pleaded for the soldiers to take care of Francesca's body, but they only pulled him away and bound his hands. The hood smelt of oats. After minutes of stumbling and barked shins, he was dropped onto a hard wooden chair.

'Let me see him.'

The hood was removed. Behind a table sat the gentleman he had passed in the Old Palace, Bronque's *personage*. A soldier set the leather case and Svenson's rumpled greatcoat onto the table.

'Wait outside.'

The soldier strode from the room without care. The man behind the table set to emptying the greatcoat's pockets. Svenson had time to study him: perhaps forty years of age, dark hair oiled and centre-parted, curled moustache, pointed goatee. He was thin-limbed but stout – a trim youth's thickening from lack of exercise, yet his dancing eyes, and the nimble movements of his gloved hands, showed a restless acuity.

The man set Svenson's revolver next to a crumpled handkerchief, a pencil stub, soiled banknotes, the mangled silver case. The leather case he ignored.

'Do you like the room, Doctor? Formerly a library, but there was damp – is there not always damp? – and so the books are gone. Abandoned rooms take what usage they can – like people – still, I so appreciate the cork floor. So quiet, so comforting, and with varnish just the colour of honey. Why isn't *every* room lined with cork? It would make a better world.'

He arched his eyebrows, plucked as thin as an ingénue's. The man's face was formed of potent details – ridged hair, wire spectacles, plump little mouth – creating a too-saturated whole.

'A more quiet world,' Svenson replied hollowly.

'Is that not the same?' The man shook his head to restore a more sober expression. 'I am sorry – I have anticipated our meeting, and it makes me merry, though the circumstance is most grave. I am Mr Schoepfil.'

'And you are acquainted with me?'

'Of course.'

'*You* sent Bronque to identify me, in the office.'

'Just to be sure. I had to be elsewhere.'

'The Customs House.'

Schoepfil chuckled ruefully. 'And only to discover but that *you* had been there too! How not, after all – how not, given our mutual *studies*?'

'Where is Colonel Bronque?'

Schoepfil waved a hand. 'Inconsequential. But you! You were on Vandaariff's dirigible! And at Parchfeldt! And the Customs House – and *now* the Institute! How I have waited to put questions to a man who *knows*!'

'You could ask Robert Vandaariff.'

'*That* gentleman remains beyond my purview.'

'What *is* your purview, if I may ask?'

'It would be such a pleasure to exchange tales, but there is no *time*. Would you like a cigarette?'

Schoepfil grinned at the mangled silver case and rang a bell. The soldier re-entered the room, one hand on his sabre hilt. 'A cigarette for Doctor Svenson. In fact, let us give the poor fellow half a dozen.'

The trooper measured six cigarettes into Svenson's shaking palm, then set a box of safety matches on top of the stack. He clicked his heels and was gone.

'Light up – light up!' urged Schoepfil. 'I require a man who can think, not a trembling ruin.' He slipped a pocket watch from his waistcoat and pursed his lips. 'To the task. How did Robert Vandaariff arrange for the dirigible to sink into the sea? Was a confederate aboard to trigger the descent, or had the machine been sabotaged before leaving Harschmort?'

Svenson inhaled too deeply and began to cough. 'I beg your pardon?'

'No shyness, Captain-Surgeon. I know of the alliance between Vandaariff, Henry Xonck and the Duke of Stäelmaere. I have identified their top tier of agents and a host of underlings. Their grand plan hovers at the very point of execution . . . and *then*, in one bold stroke, Vandaariff destroys his two rivals – Henry Xonck and the Duke – *and* launches his minions, their duties done, off to their doom. The entire Macklenburg expedition is but a red herring! Afterwards, to protect himself, he pretends blood fever, but in secret seizes control of Xonck Armaments, the Ministries, and – as is now plain to the simplest corner bootblack – reaches for the nation itself!'

Svenson tapped his ash into the matchbox. 'Lydia Vandaariff *was* a passenger on that dirigible.'

Schoepfil shrugged. 'I see you have little experience of men of high finance.'

'The circumstances of her death were appalling.'

'Just Lord Vandaariff's style – the others would believe themselves safe from his hand in Lydia's presence. What is more, his remaining enemies have been shown he will do *anything*! His own child! They cower in fear! But to my question. When did you realize the dirigible would sink?'

'When it struck the water.'

'You jest. Come, was it a triggered device, like those we have seen here?'

'Why is that important? The airship sank, nearly all aboard were killed –'

'Ah, and who was not? If there was a confederate, that confederate would have been most likely to survive.'

Svenson let the smoke enter his lungs, drawing strength. 'If you suspect I am that confederate, what use in denying the fact? You will believe me or you won't.'

'My reasons are my own. Could you answer?'

'Six people survived. Three are since dead – Francis Xonck, Elöise Dujong, Celeste Temple. Two others, Cardinal Chang and the Contessa di Lacquer-Sforza, may be dead as well – which leaves me.' He ground the butt into the matchbox. 'But it does not matter. You are wrong.'

'About you?'

'About everything. The airship went down through no pre-existing *plan*. Robert Vandaariff was defeated as much as Henry Xonck or the Duke. His resurrection at Parchfeldt only put a monster in his piece. Whatever Vandaariff once wanted in his life, he does not, I assure you, want it now.'

'Shocking statements! What can you mean?'

'He is insane. Quite literally of another mind.'

Schoepfil drummed the fingers of one hand upon the table. Then he rapped the table with his fist. 'It is no good, Doctor. The attempt is worthy, but I know *you* to be wrong as well!' A panel in the wall behind him popped open, and Schoepfil turned. 'Mr Kelling – already? Admirable dispatch.'

Kelling, a slim fellow with the angular features of an apologetic fox, edged in holding a wide tray laden with squat bottles. In each bottle floated an odd-shaped mass – tubular, sponge-like, ink-stained – like a collection of shapeless invertebrates. But Svenson could not hide from his own anatomical knowledge, and his throat tightened. Each specimen jar contained a different sample of corrupted tissue, excised from a child's body. Francesca Trapping. He leapt for the revolver.

With a speed belying his stoutness, Schoepfil snatched a wooden tray and swung it hard into the side of Svenson's head. Stunned, the Doctor took two more rapid blows, one to his reaching hand and another to his face, the last forcing him to stagger from the table. He looked up, blinking, furious, impotent. Schoepfil retained his seat – the revolver untouched but within reach. His expression remained cheerful.

'A surgeon and a spy, yet you retain this *sentiment* – as if ever there were two professions less suited to such a keepsake. The child is dead, sir. *Forbear.*'

Svenson felt his face burning. Schoepfil reached for the nearest jar. But Kelling had not gone, and whispered a private word. Schoepfil nodded eagerly.

'A reprieve! Though I *will* want your opinion, Doctor, for these samples appear to be *nothing* like those collected from the blast sites. One itches to speculate irresponsibly.'

He sniffed at Svenson's revolver. 'That stays here.' Schoepfil flung the greatcoat across the table for Svenson to catch. 'Though I should not wear it. On the contrary, you will wish to trade its warmth for an iced orange squash!'

Kelling waited in the corridor, next to an ovoid hatch, as on a warship. Svenson followed Schoepfil into a dark passageway that smelt of mould. He considered attacking Schoepfil – the way was so narrow that the man might not be able to turn – but hesitated, and in his hesitation felt the weight of his exhaustion and despair. If he did escape, where would he go? What would he do? Svenson felt as alone as he ever had in life.

The air was damp, smelling of rust. They walked on. Finally Svenson felt a single gloved finger impertinently touch his lips. He resisted the urge to bite it. With a gentle scrape, Schoepfil eased aside a tiny panel in the wall: a viewing window the size of a playing card. Through the opening came light and warm, wet air laced with the rotten tang of sulphur . . . and the echoes of water, splashing, slapping . . . the sounds of people in a bath.

A very *large* bath. Svenson dug the monocle from his tunic, wiped it on his trouser leg. He had seen bathhouses before, but rarely so opulent or so *old* as the one he was peering at now – as if the city's Roman bones had been overlaid with stucco flowers and birds, the brick archways enamelled with tile. Attendants crossed between pools bearing trays of refreshment and piles of thick Turkish towels.

A splash recalled Svenson's attention to the pool before his eyes. Along its far edge floated a line of women, rosy with heat, hair wrapped in turbans, bathing costumes of thin muslin plastered to their flesh. Svenson stared, dull-hearted, at bare throats and shoulders, at bosoms winking above the lapping pool. One lady raised a dripping arm, a signal. More splashes, beyond his view, and a new woman, grey-haired and fat, swam to the centre of the pool. She bobbed her head.

'The ladies you sent for . . .'

Svenson could not see whom she addressed – they were beneath the tiny window – but he stifled a gasp as another figure glided forward. A muslin bathing costume clung to her torso, and her bare limbs shimmered. The grey-haired woman made an introduction.

'Rosamonde, Contessa di Lacquer-Sforza, Your Majesty. An *Italian* gentlewoman.'

The Contessa shyly blinked her violet eyes. With her black hair wrapped away, she appeared disturbingly unadorned, almost innocent.

'I am much honoured by Your Majesty's attention,' she murmured, nodding to the space directly beneath Svenson's panel.

Svenson spun to Schoepfil, but the man eagerly nodded him back to the window. A second figure floated into view. Svenson could not breathe.

'And the Contessa's companion . . .' The speaker paused to suggest her disapproval. 'A Miss Celestial Temple.'

The scar above her ear peeped from the turban and fresh abrasions dotted her cheeks . . . but it was her. She was alive.

Alive and with the Contessa, and somehow here, at an unimaginable audience with the Queen herself. Schoepfil rocked with satisfaction, like a schoolboy.

'For God's sake,' Svenson whispered, 'who *are* you?'

Schoepfil shifted to better press his mouth to Doctor Svenson's ear.

'Who else could I be, Doctor? I am Robert Vandaariff's heir!'

# SEVEN

## THERMÆ

Following Colonel Bronque down a corridor of silver mirrors, Miss Temple was so taken with excitement at their destination as to forget the Contessa di Lacquer-Sforza walking beside her, until that woman reached out to flick Miss Temple's arm. Miss Temple snapped her mouth shut, abashed to find it had been open. The Contessa's expression had changed as well. Deference cloaked her animal confidence. Glancing back, Colonel Bronque appraised the women with a gaze that promised nothing.

They reached a bright room where well-dressed men and women gathered, palpably expectant. Bronque did not pause. Twice more their uniformed Virgil ignored similar weigh-points of privilege, delivering them at last to a strange oval door, made of metal and opened by a wheel at its centre instead of a knob. The wheel was spun by a footman and they descended to a shabby landing. Here waited a single man, whose broad face seemed a size too large for the wiry hair that gripped his skull. He consulted a pocket watch. Colonel Bronque came to a military stop and clicked his heels.

'My Lord Axewith.'

'Ah. Bronque.'

The Colonel waited. The Privy Minister, marooned, only sighed.

'My lord?'

Bronque followed the Minister's wary glance at the women, whose attention was dutifully turned – Miss Temple taking the Contessa's lead – to the peeling paint.

'I do not *require* Her Majesty's seal, Bronque, but Lord Vandaariff is *insistent*. Of course he is correct. Measures of *historic* consequence ought to be enacted by the monarch. But it leaves me waiting until I am a wilted stick.' Axewith – whose lantern jaw and spatulate nose suggested the face of a stranded turtle – tugged at his collar. 'And just when so many other pressing matters are . . . well . . . *pressing*.'

Bronque nodded to the satchel under Axewith's arm. 'May I wait in your stead, my lord, while you attend to business in a more congenial place?'

'Damned kind of you.' Axewith sighed sadly. 'But Reasons of State, I'm afraid. *Reasons of State*. And I cannot disappoint Lord Vandaariff . . .'

Another flick on the arm brought Miss Temple's attention to the arrival of an elegantly dressed older woman, of an age and grudging mutter with Miss Temple's Aunt Agathe. She addressed the Contessa without a word of greeting.

'You will remain silent unless spoken to. At a signal from the Duchess of Cogstead, who will make your introduction, the interview is terminated. Now, the attiring rooms are here . . .'

The older lady opened another oval door and lifted her dress, stepping over the sill. The Contessa went next, eyes darting once behind. Miss Temple glanced in turn, curious to catch Lord Axewith's reaction, but Lord Axewith was tapping at the clouded face of his pocket watch. It was Colonel Bronque who met Miss Temple's gaze, his eyes as dull as two tarnished coins.

'You will be collected. Do not forget the Duchess's signal.' Their guide's voice sank to a vicious warning. '*And do not stare*.'

As she stalked off, female attendants appeared, one for each of them.

'Stare at what?'

'At *whom*, Celeste. Pay attention.'

The attiring room's floor was yellowed marble, its walls pebbled with paint blisters. The air was moist and warm, as if they were calling upon the Queen at her laundry – an impression reinforced by the attendants gently guiding them to alcoves hung with linen curtains. Inside stood a wardrobe. A touch from her attendant had Miss Temple sitting on a wooden stool.

'If the lady would lean her head . . .'

Miss Temple did so and the attendant gathered up her curls. To her left, the Contessa's brilliant black hair disappeared into a deftly wound white towel that was quickly pinned up like a Turk's.

'If the lady would straighten . . .'

Miss Temple, her hair tucked tightly away, felt fingers picking down her back. In a trice her dress had been unlaced. The attendant tugged at the ties of her corset, and then removed her shift. The attendants unlaced the ladies' boots and peeled each stockinged leg until both women sat, apart from their turbaned heads, completely nude. The Contessa kept a grip on Miss Temple, squeezing hard.

'Do you recall what we spoke of, Celeste, in the coach?'

Miss Temple quite helplessly shook her head.

'We spoke of *redemption* – and a certain person you claimed to care for. You quite correctly assumed an ulterior reason for your visit to the tomb. My friend Oskar was new to this city when he received that particular commission. Given all he went on to achieve, the project seems but a trifle and even he – or *especially* he – may have dismissed his efforts. And yet – pay *attention*, Celeste – you should know that every artist is a cannibal, feeding relentlessly on those around them, yet feeding on *themselves* even more. Do you see? You went *there* because, if you will forgive the figure, those oldest bones may make a reappearance on our evening's menu.'

The attendants had gone, and each woman stood in a muslin bathing costume, sleeveless, their legs bare from the knee. Miss Temple rocked on cork-soled slippers. She tried her best to recall the details of the Vandaariff tomb, but her fragile concentration was undermined by the Contessa's nearness and her insidious frangipani scent. The tip of the Contessa's scar arched like a comet from under her shoulder strap. Miss Temple tottered closer, the muslin rough on the tip of each breast. Her breath touched the Contessa's skin. The Contessa was speaking. She could not follow the words. She could not stop herself from leaning forward –

The Contessa slapped Miss Temple hard across the cheek. Miss Temple staggered, but kept her feet.

'Wake up. If you ruin this, I'll have you skinned.'

'I am perfectly well.' Miss Temple swallowed. 'I will be the one skinning *you*.'

'Say nothing if you can help it. Respectful silence, pliant nubility – *listen*

to me.' She reached out and pinched Miss Temple's nipple. Miss Temple
squeaked. 'And don't *stare.*'

'Stare at what?' Miss Temple whimpered.

The Contessa turned to the opening door and slipped into a curtsy Miss
Temple just managed to echo.

'*Signora.*'

It did not seem that the portly, grey-haired woman in the doorway
approved of the Contessa, any more than she enjoyed her unflattering bathing costume, soaked through and dripping.

'Your Grace,' murmured the Contessa.

The Duchess of Cogstead exhaled without pleasure. 'Follow.'

The sanctum of squalid fairies, a cavern where gaslight laid a uric shimmer
across the surface of the water. Miss Temple's attention darted between the
women in the pools, floating with the stolid determination of pondering
frogs, and the hundreds more that stood along the walls, eyes lit with envy at
those immersed – young and old, thin and fat, pink, pale, mottled, brown
and veined. The mineral smell grew sharper as they walked, for the Duchess
took them to the thick of the steam, to a wide bath whose far side lay in a
cloud. She waded in, first down hidden steps and then, like a lumbering seal
finding its ease, gliding gracefully to the centre of the pool. The Duchess
stopped before a seat of mineral-glazed brass. Its equally substantial occupant – wide, fat, paste-coloured – was obscured by four servants, each
tending to one floating, bloated limb. As the pool's denizens watched, these
servants wrapped and rewrapped their respective arm or leg with strips of
cheesecloth, smearing between layers a greasy balm on their patient's putrid,
honeycombed skin.

The Contessa stabbed a nail into Miss Temple's palm and she obediently
dropped her eyes to the water. The Duchess spoke too quietly to hear – the
hissing pipes, the low voices, the lapping pools, all rebounded off the tile in
a buzz. Miss Temple leant closer to the Contessa's towel-wrapped ear. She
wanted to ask why she was here, why she had been saved, what the Contessa
hoped to gain from a despised monarch who, if one could credit popular
opinion, cared less about the state of her nation than Miss Temple, a keen

eater of scones, cared about grinding flour. But what she whispered instead was this: 'Why does everyone here *dislike* you?'

The Contessa replied from the corner of her mouth. 'Of *all* people, you should know that counts for nothing.'

'*I* have never cared.'

'Lying scrub.'

'She will not grant your request.'

'I request *nothing*.'

The Queen gave the Duchess her reply, a sibilant fussing that ended in a flip of one puffed hand, and the Duchess extended a formal wave to where they waited. The Contessa descended into the pool, allowing the water to reach her breasts before extending both arms with a pleasing smile and pushing forward. Miss Temple advanced more slowly. The water was very hot and contained an unexpected effervescence. She sank to her chin and pinched herself. The Duchess made the Contessa's introduction.

'Rosamonde, Contessa di Lacquer-Sforza, Your Majesty. An *Italian* gentlewoman.'

'I am much honoured by Your Majesty's attention,' the Contessa murmured.

The Queen's eyes in their leprous folds showed all the emotion of a toad.

'And the Contessa's companion,' continued the Duchess. 'A Miss *Celestial* Temple.'

Miss Temple bobbed her head, fixing her eyes on the floating basket that held cheesecloth and the greasy cruets.

'I do not see *why*,' wheezed the Queen in complaint. 'Why should I see anyone when I am not *well*.'

The Duchess gave the Contessa a dark glare. 'I am told the news is *important*.'

No one spoke. The water lapped against the tiles. The Queen huffed.

'Funny . . . thing.' The words came out in exhalations, as if the effort to form full sentences had been lost with her health, grammar perishing alongside mobility and hope. 'Always to mind with an Italian. Roman honey. Gift from Sultan. Arab? African? Poppy?'

'Her Majesty's memory is far superior to mine,' said the Duchess.

'Sealed jug. Inch of wax if there was a dab – common clay pot – came with ribbons. Velvet sack. African velvet must be rare. I hope no one stole it, Poppy.'

'I will consult the *inventory*, ma'am.'

'Everyone steals everything. Italy? *Italy.*' She poked a finger, thick as a gauze-wrapped candle stub, at the Contessa. 'Jar of honey from the bottom of the sea. Roman ship, sunk by . . .' The Queen paused, snorted. '*Whales.* Wicked. Whales eat anything. Still good. On account of the wax. Thousand-year-old honey. Ancient bees. My tenth year in the seat, or twelfth. Nothing like it on earth, rare as . . . rare as . . .'

'Milk from a snake, ma'am?' offered a lady clustered behind the Duchess.

'*Never,*' growled the Queen. 'Notion's absurd.' The servants took her subsequent silence as an opportunity to work, wiping the mottled skin with a sponge and spreading a new strip of cloth, the yellow oil seething through the weave.

'Did Your Majesty enjoy the honey?' the Contessa asked demurely.

'Ate it all with a spoon.' The Queen wrinkled one eye against a bead of sweat. 'Lady Axewith says I must see you.'

'Lady Axewith is extremely kind.'

'Bothersome scold. Husband should switch her raw.' The Queen grunted. '*Venice.*'

'Your Majesty's memory is very fine,' replied the Contessa.

'Should be Rome. One prefers Italians with *pedigree.*'

The Duchess cleared her throat. 'Lord Axewith waits, Your Majesty, for your seal. Lord Vandaariff is insistent, given the popular crisis –'

'Popular does not *last.*'

'No, Majesty. But Lord Vandaariff has made a most generous guarantee –'

'*Lord Axewith can wait.*' The Queen shifted on the submerged throne, slopping the water over her arms and draping her voice in a fuller malevolence. 'What do you *want?*'

The Contessa blinked her violet eyes. 'Why, nothing at all, ma'am.'

'Then you waste your time as well as mine! Lady Axewith shall no longer be admitted! Hellfire, Poppy, if every trivial foreign person –'

'Beg pardon, ma'am. I have come not for myself, but for *you.*'

At the Contessa's interruption the Queen's expression became fierce. Her wide mouth snapped like a pug's. 'You – you – this – *Poppy* –'

Steam rose up around the Contessa's placid face. 'My *errand* concerns Your Majesty's late brother.'

'*All my brothers are late!*' the Queen replied in a roar.

'The Duke of Stäelmaere, Your Majesty, who was Privy Minister.'

The Queen snorted suddenly, noting the Contessa's beauty as if it were an unpleasant odour. She waggled her over-fleshed throat. 'And one supposes you *knew* him.'

'Indeed, no, ma'am. The Duke had meagre use for any woman.'

'Then what?'

'Surely Majesty . . . you have heard rumours of the *irregular* nature of the Duke's passing.'

Moisture had pearled across the Contessa's upper lip. The Duchess was poised to end the audience. The Queen wriggled her nose, then turned for an attendant to wipe it.

'Perhaps I have. Who is *she*?'

Miss Temple felt every eye around the pool fall upon her.

'Miss Celestial Temple,' repeated the Duchess.

'Ridiculous. Name for a Chinaman. Girl should be ashamed.'

The Contessa slid forward. 'Your Majesty should know that the Duke, your brother, learnt of a plot against Your Majesty's health. Naturally he moved to expose it.'

Miss Temple knew this to be an arrant lie.

The Queen glowered. The whispers around the pool hushed. The Contessa continued.

'Your brother's death was an act of murder, Your Majesty, of the highest treason. And now others taken into the Duke's confidence have been attacked. Lord Pont-Joule, murdered yesterday. *Inside* the Palace.'

The Queen's voice fell to a throaty amphibian quaver. 'My Pont-Joule? No one has said!'

'I did not wish to disturb Your Majesty,' began the Duchess, 'on the advice –'

'Of Lord *Axewith*.' The Contessa shook her head knowingly. 'Who of course acts on the advice of Lord Vandaariff. *Lady* Axewith – who has been so kind to me – was another secret ally of the Duke. Her own sudden illness – for illness it *seems* –'

'I have heard of no illness! Lady Axewith?'

'Victim to the same poison that slew the Duke. But the good woman had the wit to understand the attack upon her for what it was, an attack upon the *state.*'

The whispers around the pool boiled into an urgent nattering. The Duchess cried out and splashed for quiet. In the turmoil the Contessa's hidden foot hooked Miss Temple's knee and drew her closer to the Queen.

'Majesty, I am dispatched to bring the only proof Lady Axewith could find. Celeste, tell Her Majesty what you know.'

Miss Temple had no idea what the Contessa desired her to say.

'Is the girl simple?' asked the Queen.

'Only frightened, ma'am.' The Contessa's hand slipped unseen to Miss Temple's waist, stroking gently. 'The *Duke*, Celeste. The Duke and the *mirrored room.*'

Miss Temple felt her throat clench as a memory rose up whole.

The Duke of Stäelmaere's recruitment by the Cabal had been planned to every degree, exploiting the cruelty for which the Duke was famous. Stäelmaere had duly arrived at Harschmort House and been taken by the Comte d'Orkancz to a secret viewing room. Hidden behind a wall of Dutch glass he had watched Lord Robert Vandaariff receive an apparently endless line of peers, industrialists, clerics and diplomats – all pledging their fealty in the case of an imminent, but unnamed, national crisis. Persuaded by the grovelling of such impressive minions, His Grace had joined the conspiracy, and soon after journeyed to Tarr Manor for a first-hand look at the glories of indigo clay – an expedition that had ended instead with a bullet through the Duke's heart, and his corpse's resuscitation, by virtue of the blue glass, as a walking, croaking puppet.

The Comte's recollections flooded Miss Temple's brain. She inhaled through her nose, the acrid steam clarifying her mind.

'By accident, Your Majesty, I became separated from my fiancé, Roger Bascombe, who, before his untimely death, was to be the next Lord Tarr –'

The Queen squinted – there were so *many* lords.

The Contessa gripped her waist. 'Her Majesty's *brother*, Celeste . . .'

'Just so. I was lost, you see, and the house so very large. I entered a strange room – and who else was in it but the Duke of Stäelmaere? He waved me to silence, and I saw that one entire wall was made of glass. We gazed into another room full of people, and not one of them paid the least attention, though we were as near as I to you. The glass was a one-sided mirror!'

'Wicked invention.' The Queen squirmed in her seat. '*Wicked*.'

'*Very* wicked,' agreed Miss Temple. 'And through the mirror we watched a *parade* of distinguished figures, bowing and scraping to the same person, as if he were a king. At each fawning suitor the Duke clenched his fist as if to say "Damn you for a traitor, Lord Whatsit!" When the last had gone, His Grace swore me to secrecy, promising justice would be done.'

The Queen furrowed an already layered brow. 'But who . . . who was the *person* in the other room?'

'I *do* beg your pardon,' said Miss Temple, doing her best to imitate the Contessa's tone. 'I was at Harschmort House, of course, and the man the Duke caught planning to overthrow Your Majesty's government was Lord Robert Vandaariff.'

The ladies at the pool's edge fell silent. 'My intent is to warn Your Majesty of the threat to your own person,' offered the Contessa. 'Until now, we had put our faith in Lord Pont-Joule –'

'And Lady Axewith,' added Miss Temple rather boldly.

'*Lady* Axewith, yes. Her husband, I fear, may be too naive for the role that has been thrust upon him. In his ignorance, the Privy Minister seems little more than Robert Vandaariff's confidential secretary . . .'

'Poppy?'

The Queen was querulous. The Duchess swam to her. 'You are safe, Your Majesty –'

'Won't see anyone! Won't talk to a soul! Won't sign a scrap!'

'Of course not, Majesty. But if we can get news of Lady Axewith –'

The Contessa tugged at Miss Temple's bathing costume, signalling their subtle retreat.

'Says she's *poisoned*!' hissed the Queen.

'*We* will send word, Your Majesty, and hurry to Lady Axewith,' the Contessa offered. 'But I do urge every precaution be taken with regard to your person. *The threat is grave.*'

The Queen groaned aloud and began to flail, her attendants moaning in choric sympathy. The Duchess pleaded uselessly for order. The Contessa hauled Miss Temple from the pool.

'Meet no one's eye, do not hurry, do not speak.' They had not reached the doorway before details of Vandaariff's plot echoed around them, rebounding in a dozen more dire variations. In the attiring room, the Contessa flung Miss Temple to an attendant and hurried to her own, the buttons of her bathing costume ripped free, dancing on the floor.

'My dress!' she barked at an attendant, and then to Miss Temple, 'Stop staring, you imbecile! Move!'

But Miss Temple could not move: too much was happening too quickly. Her bathing costume was stripped away and her skin chuffed to vigorous life by the attendant's strong hands – hands that thrust the towel without apology, like a dog's prodding nose, into every tender crevice. Again the Contessa stood nude, arms up, tearing the white turban and shaking her dark curls free. Her breasts shifted with the movement, a sketching measure of their soft weight, and with a whimper Miss Temple arched to her toes. Heedless of her distress, the Contessa primped with a practised economy, while the attendant worked the first stocking up her leg and towards the tangle of black hair.

'With luck, if your Mr Pfaff is not a total donkey . . .'

Miss Temple shut her eyes, yet in her mind she knew more, too much, the tips of her fingers tingled, a pearling cleft, her tongue –

In utter frustration Miss Temple slapped her thighs until the white skin burnt with the imprint of each hand. The attendant retreated, in fear. The Contessa caught Miss Temple's wrists.

'*Celeste.*'

Miss Temple turned her face, not wanting another slap.

'O good *Lord*.' The Contessa motioned her attendant to help the other. 'I will manage my own. Get her sorted.'

With both women tugging her to order, Miss Temple's shame overcame her stimulation and eventually she stood, corset tight and tied, dress restored. The Contessa pushed money at the attendants and waved them out. She met Miss Temple's hapless, tear-streaked face with an intolerant glare.

'Our survival depends on whether Lord Axewith still waits outside.'

'Why Lord Axewith?' Miss Temple's eyes burnt. 'I thought it was *Lady* Axewith –'

'Lord Axewith waits for Her Majesty's seal. His declarations do not *require* it, but – the crisis being what it is – he is frightened. Lord Vandaariff – who is rich and never wrong – has offered his aid and Axewith has leapt for it like a bishop in a choir loft. Yet, because these orders will spark new blazes of unrest – people displaced and their property claimed – Axewith, for he is weak, and Vandaariff, for he is shrewd, want the *Queen* to issue the commands, allowing Her Majesty – who is despised already – to take the blame. But *now*, because of *your* story, the Queen will refuse to sign any order coming from Vandaariff, whom she considers a traitor. The Queen's refusal will be a denouncement, which means the orders cannot be issued at all! Unless, that is, Axewith has lost patience, walked out and issued them himself!'

'But why should he? If he has waited so long –'

'O Celeste, why should a man do anything?'

'So if Axewith *is* gone –'

The Contessa pulled Miss Temple to the door. 'Then we, little piglet, are undone!'

The door was thrust open by a heavy woman with hair as bright as a Spanish tangerine. For an instant each side smiled in apology, but then the heavy lady's face went white with shock.

'*You*! How *dare* you! How dare you show yourself *here*!'

'Lady Hopton, how unexpected –'

'*Harlot!* I have just come from Axewith House!'

The Contessa stepped back, eyes lowered before the other woman's rage, hands submissively behind her back. 'Indeed? I trust Lady Axewith is well –'

'You *trust*! Lady Axewith is *dead*! But, unlike her physician, I am not blind to the cause!' Lady Hopton raised a fist. She shook it at the Contessa – still cowed by the woman's anger – then wheeled round with a snort for the far door. 'Out of my way, you filth! Once I speak to the Queen –'

The Contessa lunged, a cord in her hands. In a flash it was around Lady Hopton's throat.

Lady Hopton careened in a circle, straining for the door she'd come through. Her face went cherry-red, her mouth a garish, gasping hole. The Contessa tightened the cord with a convulsive snarl, dislodging Lady Hopton's tangerine wig. The hair beneath was thin and grey. But still the woman bulled forward, swiping at Miss Temple, her voice a terrified rasp.

'*Help* –'

'Stop her!' grunted the Contessa. 'If she opens that door we will be *seen*!'

Miss Temple froze, transfixed by the bulging eyes – this poor proud woman who had spoken to the Contessa just as Miss Temple had always wanted to. With a helpless clarity Miss Temple saw where she had placed herself, and how desolate her future had become.

She ducked Lady Hopton's arms and seized her dress, wrenching the woman from the door. Lady Hopton whined with dismay, but the Contessa twisted the cord and the sound soured to an ugly rattle. For five seconds the three of them hung suspended, then Lady Hopton collapsed. Without pause the Contessa knelt on the fallen woman's chest and, leverage improved, pulled the cord taut for another half-minute.

'Took you long enough.' The Contessa dragged the dead woman to the nearest wardrobe niche. 'Pick up her filthy wig.'

The attendants were told with a tactful nod that Lady Hopton required privacy for a *conversation*, and that any new arrivals might be shown to another attiring room altogether. Back on the mildewed landing, Colonel Bronque waited alone at the rail. The older lady who had shown them to the attiring room called with a knowing smile. 'Did you meet Lady Hopton?'

'I beg your pardon?'

The old woman's eyes glittered. 'I believe she took your same route to the baths.'

'We did not see her for the steam,' the Contessa answered blandly. 'No doubt Lady Hopton waits upon Her Majesty even now.' The Contessa turned to Colonel Bronque and raised an eyebrow.

'Lord Axewith was called away.' Bronque indicated the satchel at his feet. 'I am entrusted with his errand.'

'Called away?'

'The city is on fire.'

The Contessa wound an errant strand of hair around a finger. 'How *much* of the city?'

The old lady cleared her throat with a peevish determination. 'Not one to make your enemy, is Lady Hopton.'

The Contessa's reply was interrupted by a door opening behind them and the Duchess of Cogstead, wrapped in a robe, stepping through.

'*You!*' she called.

Miss Temple did not move.

'Colonel Bronque!' shouted the Duchess, with impatience. 'You have Lord Axewith's papers?'

Bronque clicked his heels together. 'I do, Your Grace –'

'Then you are required, sir! *At once!*'

Bronque rattled down the stairs and disappeared after the Duchess. The Contessa turned to the old lady.

'I am obliged for your kindness.'

The old lady glared. 'Kindness played no part in the matter.'

The Contessa grinned. 'It so very seldom does.'


Miss Temple's hands shook. Half the time it seemed as if her senses would overwhelm her – but when she *had* been in her mind and thinking clearly, what had she done but assist with outright murder?

'Why am I here?' she demanded recklessly. 'You are a terrible woman!'

They were hardly alone, and the well-dressed men and women passing in either direction turned at Miss Temple's angry tone. With a tight smile, the Contessa pressed her mouth to Miss Temple's ear. 'Once we are *alone* –'

'*Signora?*' An older man in a topcoat had approached the Contessa. She showed him a graceful smile, keeping hold of Miss Temple's arm.

'Minister. How do you do? May I present Miss Celestial Temple – Celeste, Lord Shear is Her Majesty's Minister for Finance.'

Lord Shear had no interest in Miss Temple. '*Signora*, you know Matthew Harcourt.'

'By acquaintance only, my lord.'

'Still, perhaps you can explain –'

'You know Robert Vandaariff,' Miss Temple blurted out, stinging at the memory of Lord Shear through the mirror at Harschmort, kneeling like the rest. 'If he asked it, you would lick his shoes. And then I daresay you would lick his –'

The Contessa spun Miss Temple to the nearest door and shoved her through. 'I beg your pardon – the girl's not well – father ruined, drink and gambling –'

She slammed the door in the face of the sputtering peer. The Contessa snatched a paper-knife off a writing table. Miss Temple backed away, arms outstretched. She opened her mouth, wanting to shout her defiance, but no words came. Her chest shuddered. She could not breathe. Miss Temple sank down to her knees, her words a half-voiced wail.

'What has *become* of me?'

She choked with sobs, cheeks wet and hot, half blind. The Contessa advanced. Miss Temple swatted at her, fingers splayed. But instead of an attack the Contessa knelt and extended the hand without the knife to Miss Temple's face.

'You are not so very pretty, you know, that you can withstand such fits. Round faces when they redden extinguish sympathy in a person. You are better served by disdain. Which I suppose is usually your own luck.'

Miss Temple sniffed thickly. Though soft, the Contessa's voice was not kind.

'There are two things I can think of to address your problem – you may well imagine what they are – but both will make you scream'– here the Contessa smiled and Miss Temple whimpered – 'and too many people are too near.'

'That woman – Lady Hopton –'

'Had to die, and at once. But half the court has seen you with me, and, while I may brazen out an ignorance of Lady Hopton, I can hardly do so for you – and so . . .' She tapped Miss Temple's nose with the paper-knife. 'I cannot take your life here. Unless, Celeste, you give me no other option.'

Miss Temple swallowed. 'But why did you bring me?'

'The Comte's memory, of course. You had seen those rooms. You spied on *me*.'

'But – but it was the Comte with the Duke, watching Vandaariff – I had to change everything –'

'Which you did.'

'But if the story had to be made up and changed, what did it matter that I knew it at all? Why didn't you tell it yourself?'

'O I could have, but never so feelingly. The Queen is highly suspicious of anyone seeking favour – by claiming no favour for myself, and by producing a witness without hope of advancement, the odds she would believe the tale were much increased. And besides, you *did* know the story. Even with the necessary embroidery, it did not sound a lie. And if the Queen *did* declare it a lie – always possible, she is as contrary as a mule – it was not *me* who'd done the lying.'

'But Lord Axewith is gone –'

'Axewith left his papers with Bronque. By now Her Majesty has flung those papers in the Colonel's face and the main goal of our visit is achieved. That Axewith is called to some entirely unrelated crisis only benefits us further. It keeps him from the tragic news at Axewith House, and also from Vandaariff. Now, will you stand?'

Miss Temple nodded and rose. 'Colonel Bronque is your lover.'

'Celeste Temple, how did you ever escape strangling?' The Contessa slipped the paper-knife into her bag and came out with a handkerchief. 'Yours to destroy.'

Miss Temple wiped her nose and eyes and then dabbed at her fingers, for the lace was too thin for its task. 'Why do all the Queen's ladies dislike you?'

'Why does everyone dislike *you*?'

'But – but I am not –' Miss Temple flushed. 'I am not beautiful.'

The Contessa's voice was flat. 'No. Beauty is more a danger than intelligence or wit. One becomes a living mirror for the inadequacies of others. Without the whip hand, which as a foreigner in the court is denied me, one proceeds in secret. Such constraints are exactly why unexpected encounters, such as Lady Hopton, such as yourself, are so gratifying.'

'But you have not killed me.'

The Contessa sighed wistfully. 'O *Celeste . . .*'

When she had stepped off the ship into the incomparably more complicated world of the city – a hailstorm of sounds and smells and people – Miss Temple's reaction, true to her nature, had been to retreat and, from behind a barrier of sceptical politeness, observe. The vectors of her relations were antagonistic, this new home defined by its otherness. When elements of her transplanted life *did* in time penetrate her reserve – a grudging familiarity with her maids, an appreciation for certain tea shops – the result was an expansion of her private enclosure to include these new pleasures, not a shift from her essential detachment. Now that enclosure, her castle's keep, housed only mortifying betrayal. Even her hate for the Contessa was blunted, first by the indiscriminate desire that ran in her blood like an infection, and, worse to admit, by Miss Temple's fear that the Contessa alone understood, however contemptuously, the truth of her polluted soul.

She wondered how many people the Contessa *had* murdered, and why *she* had been so many times spared? Certainly the Contessa had tried once or twice in earnest, but on so many other occasions the woman had refrained. Miss Temple believed that once a person was an enemy – horrible Cynthia Hobart, for example, whose plantation lay across the river – one worked against them without end. Moral sophistication – that one would not merely dissemble, biding time for a master stroke, but actually allow one's feelings to *change* – laid a chill in the pit of her stomach.

She shook off her thoughts. They had retraced their steps to the hall of mirrors, where they had first entered with Colonel Bronque.

'At *last*,' sighed the Contessa. 'If we can just find a coach – *che cavolo!*'

Blocking the way stood four soldiers and an unimpressive man with wire spectacles and a little beard, the tip of which he twirled between two grey-gloved fingers.

'Mr Schoepfil.' The Contessa released Miss Temple's hand. 'I had wondered if I would have the pleasure.'

'The pleasure is mine,' Mr Schoepfil replied. 'I insist.'

Miss Temple turned and ran, but another line of soldiers barred her way. She was taken to an empty room and left inside without a word.

Miss Temple disliked waiting at the best of times, and to do so without knowing where she was only made her feel more powerless, more like a child. She looked out of the window of the little room, wondering if she might simply smash the glass and climb through, but, while she did not remember having climbed so many stairs, the drop was at least thirty feet to an ugly gravelled courtyard.

She wondered if the Contessa would set the blame for Lady Hopton's death on her. And who was this Mr Schoepfil – *another* lover, along with Bronque? She thought of the indifference that ringed her own existence at the Boniface, where she was tolerated but hardly loved. And what of those people she had met in her romance with Roger Bascombe? Not all had been Roger's direct friends or family; there had been *some* who might have, had they desired, maintained relations with Miss Temple. Scarcely a single call had come.

Her handbag containing Roger's notebook had been taken by the soldiers without her ever having read it. Miss Temple wished she'd never seen the thing, hating her curiosity. She put her head in her hands and sighed.

She looked up with a dawning revulsion and walked to a knobbed wall panel. The back of her mouth burnt. Miss Temple pulled the panel wide. In the centre of a bare room stood a table covered with an oilskin sheet. A second, stained square of oilskin protected the floor beneath.

In the Comte's memories the horrid odour echoed necrotic tissue first encountered in a Parisian *atelier*, but Miss Temple's main recognition came from the pollution in her own body, from the tainted book.

She lifted the oilskin sheet. Her stomach seized. Whatever she had expected, it was not this. Saliva filled her mouth and she wheeled, willing herself to vomit, but nothing came. With a punitive determination Miss Temple reached again for the oilskin and, so as not to lose her nerve, flipped it wide. Francesca Trapping lay on the table like a forgotten doll, broken and tattered. The dress had been cut away and so had parts of the corpse, dark cavities opened with an unstinting cruelty. Miss Temple put her fist to her mouth and forced herself to look. She had abandoned the girl. She had triggered the explosion at the Customs House. This was *her* doing.

She felt her throat catch, aware of a stupidity she could not see past. The gaping holes . . . missing portions of the child's body. This was like the victims at Raaxfall, from whose corpses the knots of transformed flesh had been removed . . . but . . . but no, it was *not* the same. Those cavities had been ragged and irregular, formed by blue glass blooming into flesh. These incisions were precise and clean . . . surgical.

She stared down at the bloodless small hands, the feet turned in to touch at the toes – and realized the clothes *had* been cut away. The fabric was not torn or burnt, nor was it stained with blood – there was no sign of death by explosion or violence. What was more – she choked as the thought came home – the excavations in Francesca's body were not from any random blast. Through the Comte's knowledge of anatomy she saw what had been removed: kidney, spleen, lung, heart, thyroid, even the roof of the girl's open mouth . . . . Francesca had been dissected as deliberately as a hanged man sold for science. She had not been killed in the Customs House. Francesca had been poisoned by the Comte's book, her organs wholly consumed with rot.

How soon before Miss Temple succumbed as well?

It was not a generous thought, and she was ashamed. The murdered child lay before her. The small mouth yawned, slate-coloured lips gore-smeared from the extracted palate. How in the world had Francesca Trapping ended up *here*? Knowledge of the Comte's alchemy had been confined to an extremely small circle, and most of them lay in the grave. Francesca's dissection cast this Mr Schoepfil, who held both Miss Temple and Francesca's body in his custody, in an entirely more terrifying light.

Francesca's dress hung off the table like discarded wrapping paper. Miss Temple wondered when the dress had been purchased, and by whom, if it was a final memento from the girl's mother or something the Contessa had purloined for their stay in the tunnels. Sensible cloth, well sewn. Miss Temple cocked her head . . . several bits seemed of a double thickness.

The first pocket contained a tangled tuft of hair poorly tied with ribbon.

Miss Temple recognized its colour. This was Charlotte Trapping's, not taken from her head, but scavenged by Francesca from her mother's hairbrush. The child had kept it with her, from Mrs Trapping's disappearance right to the very end. Miss Temple put it back. The second pocket held a tiny leather sleeve, like a case for the Doctor's monocle. She prised it open and revealed, snug in an impression of orange felt, a blue glass key.

Miss Temple tucked the key sleeve in her own pocket and turned at a scuffing from the outer room. A tall man with a starched collar, whose pointed features were undone by coarse tufts of hair in his ears, peered past the panel with disapproval.

'Who are you?' Miss Temple demanded, before he could speak.

'I am Mr Kelling.'

'Why do you not keep such a door locked, Mr Kelling, instead of allowing innocent women to blunder onto so shocking a sight? It is disgraceful and cruel!'

Kelling studied her shrewdly. 'You were told to wait.'

'With that smell? Now I've been sickened. Now I just want some air.'

'Of course. If you would follow me.'

Kelling stepped aside. Under his arm was tucked an oblong box of dark wood. He led her into the corridor and locked the door behind him.

'Who was that girl?' asked Miss Temple. 'And what was that horrid stink?'

'An unfortunate orphan.' Kelling's voice was glazed with apology, like watered honey on a poor-quality gammon. 'The odour is regrettable.'

'I did not expect dead orphans in a palace.'

'One wouldn't.'

'What did she die *of*?'

'An inevitable question.'

A period of silence made clear it was also a question to which Miss Temple would get no answer. 'What do *you* do here, Mr Kelling?'

'Whatever I am asked.'

'So you're someone's spaniel?'

They reached another door. Kelling waved her through.

'Mr Schoepfil.'

Miss Temple stopped where she stood. 'I don't want to see any Mr Schoepfil.'

'He insists on seeing *you*.'

She was offered an upholstered chair. The only other furniture in the room was a little table on wheels, stacked with folders. Kelling gave Schoepfil the oblong box, then made a discreet exit. Schoepfil opened the narrow casket eagerly, pecking at its contents with the tip of one gloved finger, counting to seven. He snapped the box shut and impishly raised his eyebrows, inviting Miss Temple to share his pleasure.

'Your first *audience* with the Queen?' He nodded before she could reply, and rapped the stack of folders with a grey-gloved fist. 'I offer no refreshment – there is no time – as much as I would enjoy chatting at length with someone who, however inadvertently, might answer so *many* matters digging at my mind. I believe you even knew my cousin – I expect you saw her die! I imagine the event was *spectacular*.' Mr Schoepfil's hands flapped at either side of his neck and a wretched squawk came from his mouth, enacting – it took Miss Temple a moment to realize – Lydia Vandaariff's decapitation. 'Dreadful! Still, a stupid girl, and sacrificed with no more thought than a loaf of stale bread given to pigs. But *you* – you're a different fish. One gathers – one *sifts* – even within the lies! – and the name of Miss Celestial Temple *persistently* appears.'

He pursed his lips with a lemony expectation.

'I would like to leave,' said Miss Temple.

Schoepfil shook his head. 'No, no, no – think and move on.'

'What can you want with me?'

'Less by the second, I assure you.'

'Where is the Contessa?'

'Is she your patroness?'

'She can go hang. Where is Lord Axewith?'

'Why should a little thing like you care about *him*?'

'He was at the baths. His watch stopped working for the steam.'

'Lord Axewith was called to his wife, who is unwell.'

Miss Temple gazed back, blankly, knowing this was a lie – or, conversely, that it was the truth and Colonel Bronque was the liar.

'Is not the city on fire?'

'Yes, sometimes others are kind enough to manage things for you.' Schoepfil unexpectedly grinned. 'Most likely you should die here and now! What would you say to that? I am *nearly* in jest – but not all, because I *know* – and when one *knows*, one must always *fear*. Have you learnt that – learnt it enough? When did you last see the Trapping child alive?'

Miss Temple did not want to answer, but saw no value in the information. 'At the Customs House, before the explosion.'

'*Ah*. As I *suspected*.'

'But that's not where she was killed.'

'Of course not.' Schoepfil let out a frustrated huff, his torso compacted in a contemplative hunch. Again Miss Temple attempted to prompt him.

'Francesca's sickness –'

'Too fragile, could have predicted it ten miles away.' He tapped his thin lips with a thumb. 'But where does that leave *you*?'

'I have killed four men,' said Miss Temple.

'I do not doubt it. One's fingertips tingle. *Come!*'

He snatched up the oblong box and hauled her to the door, Miss Temple restraining an urge to kick. They passed Kelling in the corridor, and the servant fell in step.

'You asked to be reminded, sir –'

'There is no hope, Kelling – they must wait!' Schoepfil turned with an exasperated smile. 'Is there an hour in the day that might not be doubled and still found too brief?'

'Every last one of them,' she replied, not liking to be pulled.

Mr Schoepfil's eyes twinkled. 'You affect to be sour.'

'You are a ghoul.'

'The world is ghoulish. I do not see you hiding your head in a rabbit-hole!' Kelling darted forward to open a door, allowing Schoepfil to sweep through without pause. 'Figures such as ourselves do not *arise* without purpose.'

The door closed on Miss Temple's heel, Kelling outside. Schoepfil approached another table, piled not with papers but, to her dismay, a heap of metal tools.

'But *whose* purpose, Miss Temple?' Schoepfil sorted the tools with an extended finger. 'We navigate currents of *influence* as Magellan did the sea, and glean what? The source, if to address it thusly does not impugn the term, of *integrity*. In your own case, what *puppeteer* has hung you in my reach?'

'Since you saw me with the Contessa, I assume you've solved that mystery.'

'And whatever shall I do about it?'

'What you can get away with. But you had best make sure that woman's dead.'

Schoepfil gave her an indulgent smile and opened the oblong box. He peered at her above his spectacles. 'I suppose you know what I have?'

'Why should I?' replied Miss Temple. 'I am a puppet nobody.'

'O buck up.'

To her surprise Miss Temple bit back a retort that was palpably obscene. Was that next for her disintegrating character, the manners of a fish-wife? She nipped the inside of one cheek between her teeth. Heedless of her silence, Schoepfil again pecked at the contents of the box. Now his counting grew ever more complex, as if Schoepfil were attempting to solve a larger mathematical question. Miss Temple cast a wary eye at the iron tools.

'Who are *you* to have the free possession of so many rooms in the Queen's Palace?'

'Queer, isn't it?'

'Does the Queen even know?'

Schoepfil laughed and rapped the table with his fist, a gesture Miss Temple already found affected and odious. 'Why should she?'

'I don't suppose you slipped in with the tradesmen.'

'I did not. Those who do not belong here are *noticed*.'

'I was not.'

'*Au contraire!* Every bit as much as your dynamic companion.'

'Why would anyone notice me?'

Schoepfil nodded in agreement, a condescending dismissal. 'The *true* question was how so disreputable a figure as the Contessa managed an audience? It had to be you, her companion, however unimpressive, who bore some vital news. And *then* you mentioned Roger Bascombe, which changes *everything*.'

'You said I was of no genuine interest.'

'Was I wrong? You have killed, you say, four men – one of whom, unless I am a fool, was Bascombe himself.' He raised his eyebrows, waiting for her contradiction. When it did not come, Mr Schoepfil barked with satisfaction. 'To the business! What say you to *these*?'

Schoepfil spun the oblong box to her view. It was lined with orange felt, with eight indented slots made to hold glass cards. Seven had been filled, but the glass cards were swirled with different colours, only one of them properly blue. The last slot was empty.

What came to Miss Temple's mind, for the second time that day, was her former neighbour and rival, Miss Cynthia Hobart, the identification suggested by Schoepfil's fingers, flitting from square to square like indecisive bees, an exact mirror of Cynthia's hand above a tray of tea cakes. For years Miss Temple had been daunted by Cynthia in social matters, by the other girl's ability – no matter what opinion Miss Temple might express – to adopt a contrary and, it was disdainfully implied, superior point of view. Again and again the young Miss Temple had returned from teas or suppers or dances stinging with the hidden weals of Cynthia's condescension, victories well noted by everyone else in attendance.

But a day had come – brilliant, precious, a pearl. The matter was trivial: a pot of marmalade from the Hobarts' cook. The fruit had been coarsely cut and stood out by the spoonful in sweet gleaming chunks. At Miss Temple's demurral Cynthia had loudly announced a preference for firm, palpable fruit in her marmalade, an opinion shared by no less a personage than the Vice-Roy of Jamaica – who, it was implied, ought well to know. But Miss Temple, whose care for pastries and jams ran deep, knew that the finer the cut of the fruit, the more suffused the syrup became with juice. While she allowed, in the abstract, for a variance of taste, she did not consider variety a worthy excuse – and if the Vice-Roy of Jamaica felt otherwise, then he was a leather-tongued scrub. More to the purpose, she knew that Cynthia was *wrong*, and more – since her positions were only adopted to contradict Miss Temple's own – that Cynthia had no *idea*, and never, ever had.

When, at the pronouncement of vice-regal opinion, Cynthia turned with her customary sneer, Miss Temple, instead of retreating to cold silence, laughed outright. It was hollow, mocking, more fit for a bragging jay than a lady. The audacity stopped the table dead – and that silence provoked another triumphant and damning bray from Miss Temple. Never again had Miss Hobart given her trouble, though the poor thing had tried. Miss Temple had seen into her rival's heart and, to her great satisfaction, found it weak.

She was not fool enough to think that mere contempt would break Mr Schoepfil's control, but Miss Temple was sure of an essential similarity. Despite the impression Schoepfil projected of balancing a hundred facts at once, she marked his persistent reluctance to spell out exactly what he wanted to know. Hers was not a logical opinion, yet, even as Schoepfil studied the glass cards, it struck her as a performance – that, far from possessing a host of questions about the Comte's alchemy, Mr Schoepfil, who was unquestionably clever, sought to goad Miss Temple into asking questions of *him*, questions that would divulge her own knowledge – in this case, perhaps, the whereabouts of the missing card.

'Such colour,' observed Schoepfil. '*Brilliance*. I suppose you've never seen the like.'

He extracted a card for Miss Temple to see.

'Why is it green?' she asked.

'You may *well* wonder.' He raised an eyebrow.

'I expect it's ground-up emeralds.'

'Rather costly, don't you think? Besides . . .' He held it higher, so the light shone through. 'The *actual* colour cast is more yellow –'

'Then I expect it's dried lemon peel, lemons being less expensive than emeralds.'

'Do you tweak my nose?'

His voice betrayed a hint of steel – not *exactly* like Cynthia Hobart – but she kept on.

'How could a mere puppet do that?'

'You cannot. So you will tell me what you know of these glass cards.'

'I don't know anything.'

'I think you do.'

'Perhaps you should ask the Contessa.'

'Perhaps I already have.'

The menace of his last words, that he had forced the Contessa to his will, hung in the air. But Miss Temple did not take well to threats – that is, she took them to heart, and whenever a thing touched Miss Temple's heart, she answered resentfully in kind.

'All right, then, I'll tell you *this*.' She paused, allowing him to grin in anticipation. 'If you are the man who cut up Francesca Trapping, I'm going to make you number five.'

Schoepfil jerked his head back at the bluntness of her threat. He snapped shut the box. 'Mr Kelling!'

Kelling's head poked in. Schoepfil's smile was gone, and without it his face seemed a lifeless mask. 'This woman wastes my time. Get rid of her.'

Mr Kelling's grip fell painfully across Miss Temple's injured arm. She was pulled from the room and dragged into the open air to a wooden outbuilding. Kelling opened the bolt using one hand, levered the double door open with his foot – was it a stable? – and shoved her in. A moment later the bolt was shot and his footsteps were fading away. She held her arm, glad that the cut had not reopened, strode back to the door and kicked it. It was only then that Miss Temple realized that not once during all the time gazing at the oblong box and its glass cards had she felt ill. No echo of such a box came from the Comte's memories, nor of glass in those swirling colours. Schoepfil may have acquired his prize without understanding its function, but her own ignorance meant the cards, and the science behind them, had only come into existence *since* the Comte's demise, in these last months. But then Miss Temple frowned, for there *was* something . . . she tasted the bile on her tongue . . . an echo from the vast painting, *The Chemickal Marriage*. The different colours of paint were connected to the different colours of glass. The Comte had not realized the alchemical potential at the time, but – in the body of Robert Vandaariff – he must have done so since.

'Are you just going to stand there?'

She turned with a start. In the dying light she had not seen the figure slumped in the corner: a thin man in a white jacket and dark trousers. He had been beaten and his face swelled with bruises. Even as he spoke, his body did not move, as if to do so lay beyond him.

'Who are you?'

'Michel Gorine. Late of the Old Palace, now Her Majesty's guest.'

'I am Miss Temple. I'm not anyone's guest at all.'

'Forgive my not rising.' He raised his hands, bound about the wrists with knotted rope. 'Would you mind trying to untie me? My teeth will not do – our hosts knocked a few loose and I am loath to risk my smile.'

Miss Temple did not move. 'Is this the Old Palace, where we are now?'

'The Old Palace is a brothel. We are in a shed outside Bathings.'

'What is Bathings?'

'What everyone calls the Royal Thermæ. I wish you would untie my hands.'

Miss Temple pulled at the door, then kicked it again, without heat. She looked at the man in the corner. 'I suppose you told him everything?'

'I beg your pardon?'

'If you had not talked they would still be at you. Now they must be confirming what you said, in case you tried to lie. Did you lie?'

'About what?'

'I would be happy to know. The fellow I met was named Schoepfil. Stout and weaselly.'

Gorine shifted to a sitting position. 'Why would anyone interrogate *you*?'

'What did, or didn't, you lie about, Mr Gorine, and to whom?'

Gorine carefully touched his split lip. 'An iron rooster named Bronque.'

Miss Temple nodded. 'I *thought* he was wicked.'

'He has a wicked fist.'

'Why should he care about a brothel?'

'Who *are* you?'

'No one at all. I don't suppose you saw a beautiful woman with black hair and a dark dress?' Gorine shook his head. 'I can't think they killed her – how could they have killed her but not me? No, the real question is whether she is a prisoner or their ally. She's very good at getting people to do things. Did you see the dead girl?'

'What dead girl?'

'Francesca Trapping. A poor pale thing with red hair.'

Gorine shook his head carefully. 'How did she die?'

'That is the mystery. Those beasts have cut her to pieces to find out.'

'Good Lord,' cried Gorine. 'Why?'

'Because there is very little time – for anyone.' She crossed to Gorine. 'If you touch me I will do my best to hurt you, and my best is *keen*.'

'I recline forewarned.'

She tugged at the knots to no great success. 'You've bled into the rope.'

'My apologies.'

Miss Temple lifted his hands to her mouth, taking a knot in her teeth and tugging until the first strand grudgingly pulled loose. She spat it out and made quick work of the rest, until the sticky rope lay uncoiled on the floor. She snatched up some straw to wipe her hands. Gorine studied the raw bands around his wrists. 'You should wash that with salt and hot water,' said Miss Temple. 'It will hurt, but otherwise your hands will puff like a brace of adders.'

'I'll have my manservant boil some up directly,' muttered Gorine, but then he looked up at Miss Temple and caught her smile. He shook his head. 'You're an odd creature.'

'I suggest we escape, but I do not know where to go. My friends have vanished, if they are even alive.'

'My friends as well.'

'You have friends?'

'A shock, I know,' Gorine replied. 'A man named Mahmoud. A woman named Madelaine Kraft.'

'I do not know them.'

'Why should you, unless you have traffic with our business?'

'Which I do *not*.' But then Miss Temple sighed at an unwelcome thought. 'Unless you were acquainted with a woman named Angelique.'

Gorine leant forward. 'How in hell do you know of *her*?'

'Part of the same exceedingly long story. She died at Harschmort House.'

'By whose hand?'

Though she herself had fired the bullet, Miss Temple scarcely considered her answer a lie. 'The Comte d'Orkancz. He did terrible things to her body, with *machines*.' Before Gorine could give vent to his anger – anger that, she knew, would be fuelled to excess by the shame of his own imprisonment – she changed the topic. 'The fact is, I know all sorts of things – perhaps more about your own troubles than you. But if you expect me to help you must say what you divulged to Colonel Bronque.'

Gorine snorted with disbelief. 'How can you help me?'

'I have already untied your hands.'

'And I thank you. But tonight my place of business has been destroyed, my friends – my family – have disappeared, others whose welfare is my charge have been thrown to the law.'

Miss Temple crossed to the door. 'Obviously first we must quit this shed.'

'It is bolted from the outside – and made to withstand the strength of a horse.'

'But I am not a horse.' Miss Temple dropped into a far from ladylike crouch.

'One wonders *what* you are.'

Miss Temple smiled, for she took pleasure in being wrongly doubted. This was hardly the first time she had been shut in a stable. As a girl, being a routine nuisance, she'd often found the door bolted behind her by some resentful groom. When Kelling had pushed her in, she had noticed the similarity to her father's stable: instead of a wooden bar across the front, the doors were joined by an ostensibly stronger metal bolt, waist-high, which was further pinned in place by an iron pole sunk into the ground. Unable to shift the bolt, the young Miss Temple discovered that one *could* lift up the pole. Doing so while carefully pushing outwards opened the doors in tiny increments and eventually slid the bolt from its socket.

It took her a minute of grunting effort to raise the pole. She stood, wiping the rust from her hands and glanced over at Gorine. He had not moved. She began to rock the doors forward.

'What are you doing?' Gorine called. 'Where did you learn that?'

The door scraped free of the bolt. Miss Temple caught it before it swung wide and peered out. The derelict courtyard was empty as before. She looked back at Gorine.

'It's almost dark. With any luck –'

Miss Temple shrieked at the figure who appeared out of nowhere in the doorway. Gorine leapt to her defence, but Miss Temple had already turned with an outstretched hand. 'A friend – it is a friend!'

'I thought it might be you, mistress. We've little time.' Cunsher's voice was but a whisper, and Miss Temple was chagrined at her shriek, especially as she had been doing so well.

'This is Mr Gorine,' said Miss Temple, making it plain that she could whisper too.

Cunsher narrowed his eyes, then nodded. 'Mrs Kraft.'

'How do you know that?' asked Gorine.

'Mr Cunsher has my complete confidence,' she said pointedly, and then explained to Cunsher, 'I arrived in the custody of the Contessa, who may be either the prisoner of Mr Schoepfil or his ally. I believe she intended to depart with the contrivance of Mr Pfaff.'

'How I'm here, miss. Cardinal Chang set me on Pfaff, while he went off with the Contessa.'

'But the Contessa has been with me these hours. What happened to Chang?' Her voice had risen and she felt Cunsher's touch on her arm.

'I cannot say. Pfaff has a carriage. Beyond the southern wall, under a stand of trees. He creeps into the courtyard every few minutes, and even goes so far as to peer into the windows.'

'Did you see the German doctor?' Both Miss Temple and Cunsher turned to Gorine with surprise. He held up his hands. 'I am sorry, I should have been more trusting – I arrived in chains with Doctor Svenson. The child was with him – she was killed, in the fire.'

'Doctor Svenson is *here*?' hissed Miss Temple.

'What did Svenson say?' Cunsher demanded. 'Anything at all –'

'He went to the Institute, with Mrs Kraft. She has been without her mind – the Doctor knew of a laboratory at the Institute. He said she has been restored.'

Cunsher's sharp gesture brought them to silence. Miss Temple glimpsed a shadow flit past a window, far across the courtyard. Cunsher moved in pursuit, pulling the others after him.

The skulking shadow led them ably around a guard post and a strolling pair of gentlemen with cigars. Cunsher paused and motioned Miss Temple and Gorine near.

'There is a postern gate,' he whispered. 'His coach waits on the other side.'

Ahead of them Pfaff edged along the outer wall, in his orange coat like a fox skirting a farmhouse. Cunsher followed just as deliberately, with Gorine at his heels. Miss Temple let them creep away. Their attention fixed on Pfaff, the men had not noticed an unwatched doorway back into the Royal Thermæ. But Miss Temple darted to it, her business unfinished.

With the exception of her proper Aunt Agathe, Miss Temple had never met anyone who held the old Queen in the slightest regard. The image of Lord Axewith waiting in the mouldy vestibule spoke to how rarely the mechanics of government ever touched the monarch, and Miss Temple wondered at all the ladies in the baths – how their ambitions were tied to a sinking ship, how they must *know* this perfectly well. What kept them in such close attendance – Miss Temple shuddered anew to recall the Queen's skin – was it actual loyalty, or had they wagered all to extract a crumb of favour from the doomed woman's final testament? Miss Temple knew very little about the Crown Prince – only that he was becalmed in a lax sixth decade amongst actresses and wine – but guessed that he too carried a penumbra of hangers-on and hopefuls. No wonder active men like Harald Crabbé and Robert Vandaariff could manipulate the mighty with such ease, and with such relative anonymity. The courtiers they would formerly have served had exchanged actual accomplishment for comfort and prestige.

All of which was only to clarify Miss Temple's position. If she were a man, all she would have required to brazen any corridor was a Ministry topcoat and a scowl. For a woman, it was more difficult. She was in less danger of being named as a fugitive than of being cast out for inferior *couture*.

She followed the sound of water to a bustling laundry room, where harried, red-faced women stirred steaming tubs, and others wrung out linens and hung them to dry. Miss Temple emerged with a stack of fresh towels, hoping they would proclaim a legitimate errand. Managing several corridors without being challenged, she steeled herself to stop a young maid, who carried a covered tray.

'I beg your pardon. I am looking for Mr Schoepfil.'

The maid apologized for not knowing the gentleman.

'He may be with Colonel Bronque.'

Again the maid knew nothing. Miss Temple waited for a pair of older ladies to pass, aware of the maid's discomfort in their presence.

'They will be in their own part of the house, near the hall of mirrors,' she explained. 'I do not expect anyone else is allowed.'

The maid's mouth formed a knowing O. 'Is it . . . the *lady*?'

'It *is*,' Miss Temple confided. 'And she needs these towels *directly*.'

Rather proud of herself, Miss Temple followed the maid's directions, which happily took her to another servant's corridor, past locked doors and covered eye-holes. When she reached the proper door – seventh after the turn, painted yellow – it was with satisfaction that she set down the towels and rose on her toes to peek.

Mr Schoepfil sat at a table piled high with papers and books. The walls around him were covered with maps and charts, as well as three canvas squares of dense scrawls that, from a distance, formed pictures – flowers, a mask and two interlaced hands. Mr Schoepfil impatiently turned the pages of an ancient book until, not finding what he sought, the book was closed. The man held still, eyes shut, lips moving, as if in a private ritual of self-pacification . . . then he strode to the far door and made his exit. Miss Temple opened the servant's panel and crept in.

She went first to the far door and braced Schoepfil's chair beneath the knob. Three days of leisure would not have been enough to plough through everything the small room held. Next to the books were printed pages – newspapers and journals in many languages – and great piles of handwritten notes. Of the latter, each stack represented a unique hand. She identified notes by Doctor Lorenz, others by Mr Gray, and Marcus Fochtmann. At least seven piles came from the Comte himself, notes and diagrams and indecipherable formulae. On the walls were maps of the Polksvarte District

(Tarr Village and its quarry marked with pins), the Duchy of Macklenburg, the cities of Vienna and Cadiz, and finally an engineer's plan of the Orange Canal. Opposite the maps hung a star chart: black parchment pricked with white paint to spell out constellations. Miss Temple had always intended to learn the stars – one spent enough time staring at them – but, as she never had, she continued to the three squares of scribbling she had glimpsed through the spy-hole.

The back of her throat began to burn. The flowers were blue, the mask white, and of the two hands one was white, the other jet black. She recognized each from *The Chemickal Marriage*. Were these sketches to get the correct form? But what made any form correct? Just framing the question made her head throb – and, as she stared, each image seemed to swell, as if drawing life from her attention . . .

She rubbed her eyes. When she looked up Miss Temple gasped aloud. How could she not have seen it? It was no star chart at all! With the memory of *The Chemickal Marriage* bright in her mind, she saw every part of its composition – the Bride and Groom, the floating figures, each allegorical flourish – represented on the star chart by a mark of white paint. Schoepfil had found the Comte's blueprint for the entire canvas! Did he know what it was? Miss Temple tore the chart from the wall, rolling it tight. She looked about her and with a happy cry saw a cylindrical document case, sheathed in leather. She emptied the maps inside onto the floor, slid the parchment away, fitted the cap and then slapped the tube on her open palm, a diminutive boatswain ready to administer Sunday punishment.

Her smile froze for, until that moment hidden by the document case, her eyes fell across Roger Bascombe's notebook – taken from her purse and deposited, like any other bit of evidence, in Schoepfil's trove. Her regret at having lost it unread rose within her, but now Miss Temple thrust it down. That life was done. She would be free of it, by force of will if nothing else. She snatched up the notebook and wrenched at the cover. The fibres of its binding gave and with another tug came free. Miss Temple hurled both vanquished halves at the wall.

Abruptly she shoved a pile of Doctor Lorenz's notes off the table, where it exploded like feathers burst from a seam-ripped pillow. In quick order the rest of the papers followed. Between two stacks of books nestled a pair of fountain pens and bottle of black ink. With a grin she uncorked the ink bottle and flung the contents in wet bolts across the papered floor. She opened the books wide and heaped them together, tearing what pages she could on the way. She yanked the maps and canvases from the wall and balled them up atop the books. The painting of the hands she rolled into a tube and shoved its paint-clogged end into the gaslight sconce.

She glanced at the door. Were those footsteps? They were. The knob was turned, but the chair held, catching on the floorboards. The knob was worked again, and then the key tried. The tip of the canvas blackened and began to curl. The door was pushed with force. Flame crawled up the canvas, turning green and blue as it licked the coloured paints. Miss Temple stepped to the table, the door now rattling hard, and plunged the flaming tip into the pile of papers, maps, canvases and books.

'Open this door!' shouted Mr Kelling. 'Who is there?'

He flung himself against the door, the chair skidding back an inch. The flame leapt across the maps with a sudden hunger. Kelling's hand came through the gap, groping to dislodge the chair. Curls of white smoke climbed the wall. Miss Temple slipped into the servant's passage. Holding the leather tube in both hands, she began to run.

Her face glowed with the pleasure of mayhem. How long they must have searched to gather those artefacts together! Even if Kelling could smother the fire – she knew from childhood how hard it was to burn a book, especially a thick one – she'd ruined so *many* pages. She laughed at the hours needed to sort it back to sense – and who knew, perhaps it *would* catch after all!

She tumbled into the brightness of the main corridors. The danger of being recognized and denounced for Lady Hopton's death was as real as the prospect of Mr Kelling's appearing at her heels, yet exhilaration lent an air of invulnerability. What was more, something in the atmosphere of the Royal Thermæ had changed. The crowds seeking favour had dispersed. In their place were preoccupied individuals rushing in opposite directions. No one paid her the slightest mind, and when her path was crossed by officials or soldiers, they cared even less than the guests. What had happened while she'd been in the stable?

Shouts echoed behind her and a glance showed a gang of men in shirt-sleeves, faces black with ash. She prudently retreated to an empty reception room whose walls were hung with red draperies. The far door abruptly opened.

'*Stop!*'

Miss Temple froze. The uniformed man with his hand on the knob did not see her, his face turned behind him.

'What is it *now*?' called Colonel Bronque with impatience.

Miss Temple darted behind a curtain, flattening her dress and carefully angling her eye to peer out. The imperious voice that had called she recognized too well.

The Colonel stepped aside at the Contessa's entrance, and gave a grim nod to the two soldiers who were her escort, before closing the door in their faces.

'What has happened now?' Bronque's voice was wary, but the Contessa's reply was only plaintive.

'Where have you *been*?' she complained. 'I expected you this last hour, but have seen only that horrid Drusus Schoepfil. Such preening *satisfaction.*'

'Why should you care? If he has taken you under his protection –'

'I am his to deliver to the law at any time.' The Contessa caught the Colonel's hand. '*You* are my only friend. If you go, I am at Schoepfil's mercy.'

'Rosamonde, please. If you've been honest –'

The Contessa slapped the Colonel's face with an echoing crack.

'*Honest?*' she cried. 'There is a warrant for my life. Everything I know of Vandaariff's intentions I have told you both.'

Bronque said nothing. In the charged silence she traced the red mark on his cheek with an extended finger.

'Such indifference *humbles* a lady.'

'I have explained, once I return –'

'And if you don't?'

'Robert Vandaariff's hired brutes cannot stand against trained regiments.'

'But you've not said where you are going – or why.'

'You must make yourself content.'

'That's very cruel.'

Bronque caught her finger in his hand. 'Then you must be content with my cruelty.'

'Must I?' The Contessa ducked her head. 'May I ask just one more tiny, tiny question?'

'By God, you will press every advantage. What is it?'

'Were you a friend of Francis Xonck?'

Her voice retained the same shy lilt, but the Colonel's indulgent smile froze. 'Why in hell do you mention *him*?'

'Because you never said how you met Drusus Schoepfil, how you became of use.'

'We are *partners* –'

'Schoepfil is nothing to his uncle, after all – always the dog smelling supper from another room. Admittedly, a clever dog – no doubt why Vandaariff distrusted him. Smart animals make people nervous.'

Bronque sighed. 'We have spoken too long. You must go back, and be patient –'

'Blue Caesar blue palace ice consumption.'

She whispered the words and then stepped away. A shudder shook Bronque's body. His eyes went dull.

'Drusus Schoepfil is a boat that can venture only on the smoothest seas. He doubts. He trusts no one – which means he should not trust you . . . yet he apparently *does*. At first I wondered why, but then it was clear – *Francis*. I can imagine your relief at his death, silencing the secret of your corruption. But Schoepfil guessed, didn't he?'

'He'd seen me at Harschmort . . . knew I played cards with Arthur Trapping . . .'

'And so you secretly underwent the Process. Did you enjoy it?'

Miss Temple recalled Roger Bascombe on the dirigible, slumped against a wall, calmly confessing his own treachery. Every initiate of the Process was instilled with a control phrase. The speaking of this phrase, which the Contessa had deduced from her knowledge of Xonck, delivered the initiate into the power of the speaker, a passive state in which any questions would be answered and all commands obeyed. Colonel Bronque's reply was vacant and cool.

'*Enormously.*'

'You planned to betray me all along.'

'Of course.'

The Contessa slapped Bronque's face twice more, echoing blows that left a bead of red at the corner of his mouth. '*Tell me.*'

'Schoepfil will sell you to Vandaariff, forcing a meeting where Vandaariff will be killed.'

The Contessa's lips curled with fury. '*Why?*'

'We no longer need you.' Bronque's reply was distant. 'And Harcourt's warrant for your death absolves our action.'

'Where are you going now?'

'First to Axewith, so he knows the Queen has refused his writ, then to Vandaariff, to arrange your sale. After the Queen's denial, he will leap at the chance, and we will have him.'

'And where is Axewith?'

'At the fire. The longer he is distracted, the more time we have.'

'What weapons do you carry, apart from that ridiculous sword?'

Bronque unbuttoned his jacket and plucked out a horn-handled clasp-knife. 'I keep this for luck, it belonged to my father –'

The Contessa snatched it from his hand, opening the blade – a malignant flashing finger – then snapping it home. The doorknob rattled. She tucked the knife away and hissed at Bronque. 'You have not told me a thing. Wake.'

Bronque brought a hand to his cheek. He squeezed his eyes shut and turned to an agitated Mr Schoepfil, bustling in with the oblong box gripped tightly in one hand.

'What are you doing alone with this woman?'

'Nothing of your concern, I assure you.' Bronque's voice had recovered its strength, but his face still blazed with the impact of the Contessa's hand.

Schoepfil glared at the Contessa, who had retreated behind the Colonel. '*Someone* has set a fire in our rooms!'

'*Another* fire?' The Contessa bit her lip. 'Is the entire town tinderwood? Must we evacuate? Is Her Majesty safe?'

Schoepfil gave a derisive snort and quickly snatched her hands in his. He turned them to study each side, then lifted them to his nose.

'How gallant. Do you expect to smell paraffin or kerosene?'

He thrust her hands away and waved angrily to the two soldiers who had followed him in. 'Remove this woman.'

Schoepfil shut the door on the Contessa's heels and turned, fuming, on Bronque.

'A fire set in *our* rooms. Kelling will need hours to even divine the damage. And I find you with her here – alone! Please, Colonel! *Think!*'

'How could she be responsible? I distrust her as much as you do –'

Schoepfil reached to rebutton Bronque's jacket. 'What has happened to your face?'

'Nothing has happened.'

'You are very red.'

'From the steam. Wasn't the Contessa under guard?'

'But who else knew of our trove?'

'The German doctor?'

'He was with me,' said Schoepfil.

'The other prisoners –'

'Kelling locked them in the stable.'

'Then an agent of Vandaariff?'

'But Vandaariff wants my collection for himself. No, the Contessa is frightened, thus she has become desperate – perfectly natural . . . and *perhaps* even advantageous.' Schoepfil urgently dug under the cuff of one glove with the poking fingers of the other. 'Ah! The itching becomes unbearable – any excitement sets it off –'

He peeled down the glove and Miss Temple stifled a gasp of surprise. Mr Schoepfil's hand was a brilliant cerulean blue. He raised it to his mouth and nipped the flesh between his teeth, then tugged the glove back into position. Bronque watched with distaste.

'Drusus, I assure you. The woman means nothing. She's a monster – I *know* she's a monster. She'll get her comeuppance from Vandaariff or she'll hang. But what if we have another enemy entirely, perhaps one of the Queen's retainers? They cannot be pleased at your taking up residence, and they are not *all* fools.'

'Aren't they?'

'The Duchess of Cogstead, for example.'

'Is it possible?' Schoepfil frowned in thought, then abruptly slapped Bronque on the shoulder. 'I will consider – as I will continue to consider the Contessa. Go – to Axewith, then Vandaariff. Make the offer.' Bronque turned on his heel, but Schoepfil hopped after him. 'Wait! Do you credit this story about Madelaine Kraft – that she was cured?'

'Do you?'

'Svenson says so.'

'Svenson is a hero or a liar. Does he look like a hero to you?'

'I wouldn't know,' laughed Schoepfil. 'I've never seen one!'

Bronque marched out. Schoepfil stood staring at where Bronque had been. Then he lifted his nose and began to sniff the air. Miss Temple pressed herself against the wall. Schoepfil turned to her hiding place, but stopped sniffing as abruptly as he'd begun. He tugged his jacket into position and hurried after the Contessa.

Miss Temple crept to the keyhole. She saw the Contessa escorted away and Schoepfil, instead of following, disappear surreptitiously behind a Moorish screen. When he did not re-emerge, Miss Temple took a breath for courage and scampered down the corridor after him. The screen concealed another room. Schoepfil spoke into a copper funnel attached to the wall. He returned the funnel to its hook and shoved two fingertips under his glove, scratched, then briskly clapped his hands together, as if the sting might suspend the itching.

Beyond Schoepfil a door opened, his summons answered. At the distraction Miss Temple slipped in, as low as a spaniel, and dropped behind a sofa.

'*Doctor*,' called Schoepfil warmly. 'Enter, enter – so much to discuss, so little time. You have eaten – no? Well, hardly time now – you have been told of the fire?'

'I saw enough of it myself.' Miss Temple craned around a sofa leg. Doctor Svenson looked like a beaten dog. Schoepfil poked him playfully.

'Not *that* fire. Can you not smell?'

Svenson swatted at his greatcoat. 'I would smell smoke if we stood in a rose garden.'

'Yes, a shocking conflagration, by all accounts, and now that these accounts are arriving, thick as migrating crows – do crows migrate? – the Queen's court is a-boil with fear.' Schoepfil lifted a folder of papers from a table and raised a cloud of ash. 'Thus the extremely small blaze in my own quarters prompts a request that I *relocate*.'

'What caused this extremely small blaze?'

'Do you truly not know?'

'I have been locked in a room.'

'The Contessa di Lacquer-Sforza. She has provoked an abominable inconvenience.'

'I should say you came off lucky.'

'I did not count you amongst her admirers.'

'I am not. Where is Miss Temple? They were together in the baths.'

Schoepfil shrugged, as if the question were trivial. Svenson reached for the man, but Schoepfil's hand shot out and quickly twisted the Doctor's arm at the elbow. Svenson grimaced, but managed to repeat his question.

'Where is Miss Temple?'

'Perfectly safe – how you will squirm! – locked with that fellow from the brothel.'

'Let me make sure of her safety. I can as easily be locked up there as here.'

Schoepfil released the Doctor's arm. 'An extraordinary request. Does the Contessa care for her as well? What if I threatened to cut off her nose?'

'The Contessa would probably ask to eat it.'

Schoepfil sighed. 'Perhaps. Before I decide the fate of Miss Temple's nose, however, I must know more about Madelaine Kraft.'

'There is nothing to tell. She recovered. I cannot say how.'

Schoepfil reached into his coat pocket and removed a cork-stopped flask of brown dust. 'I believe this is called bloodstone.'

'Is it?'

'It was in your own tunic, Doctor. Gorine confirms that you employed *bloodstone* to effect the lady's restoration.'

'Mr Gorine was not present. He tells you what you want to hear.'

'What I want are Mrs Kraft's whereabouts.'

'She died in the fire.'

'Who taught you the properties of bloodstone? Vandaariff? He's resumed production of the Comte's *library*, as you know.' Miss Temple's eyes went wide at the sight of a leather case propped next to the papers. She bore a scar where another such case, containing the glass book preserving the Comte d'Orkancz, had nearly cracked her skull.

'With luck he's set a book aside for you.'

Schoepfil trilled with amusement and shook his head, too quickly, like a little dog shaking off sleep. 'You tweak me, Doctor Svenson – you *tweak* me because nothing has gone your way. I accept it – accept the *impulse* – though I insist on a serious response before we leave.'

'Leave for where?'

'Excellent question. And since I admire your abject determination, Doctor, I will tell you – well, tell you a *little* . . .' Schoepfil held up a hand, stepped to the archway and poked his head through. He re-emerged, smiled, and then without warning leapt behind the sofa. But when Mr Schoepfil's attention had been diverted at the archway, Miss Temple had crept to the cover of an over-stuffed *fauteuil*. Schoepfil lifted the sofa to glare at the carpet beneath.

'Are you quite well?' asked Svenson.

'Of course I am,' growled Schoepfil. 'Didn't you hear?'

'Hear what?'

'A *spy*.' Schoepfil returned to the archway, scowling out. '*Breathing*.'

Svenson sighed impatiently. 'If you refuse to tell me –'

'I will tell you when I want! And you will tell *me* – whatever I want – more than I want – you will beg for the chance!'

'No doubt,' agreed the Doctor blandly.

Schoepfil marched straight to Svenson and struck him across the face. Neither man spoke. Miss Temple dared not peek to see their expressions.

'I will not endure that . . . that *tone*,' hissed Schoepfil. Svenson's silence was excruciating. Schoepfil sniffed. 'Set the matter aside. What I was *going* to say – what I was going to *offer* – was a chance for your own skills to turn a

profit, Doctor. A chance to follow in the footsteps of greater men. Doctor
Lorenz, Mr Grey –'

'They were corrupt fools.'

'Better to follow fools than your neck in a noose, eh?'

'Follow where? Robert Vandaariff controls every such laboratory, does he
not? For heaven's sake, what is your *serious* question?'

Schoepfil hesitated, and his voice dropped to a nervous whisper. 'What
has my uncle *done* to this Cardinal Chang?'

A discreet cough announced Mr Kelling, soot-smeared but unperturbed.
'The Duchess of Cogstead, sir. She insists –'

Before Mr Schoepfil could welcome the lady or attempt to refuse, the
Duchess made her entry. Miss Temple hardly recognized the old put-upon
woman she had seen in the baths, for here was a high lady of court, wig and
powder perfectly applied, and her dress, in happy contrast to the clinging
bathing costume, a triumph of buttresses.

'Your Grace.' Schoepfil made an unctuous bow. 'As you see, we *do* prepare
our exit –'

'Where is that woman?'

'Woman?' Schoepfil fluttered a hand, a grey wren shaking its feathers, at
the leather case and papers. 'Kelling, if you could collect all that and bring
it to the coach?'

'The woman in your protection,' said the Duchess.

Schoepfil chuckled. 'I am no church offering sanctuary –'

'The Contessa di Lacquer-Sforza. She is in your hands. I want her. *Now*.'

'Goodness!' Schoepfil turned, distracted by politeness, to Svenson. 'My
apologies, madam, do you know Doctor Svenson? Personal attaché to the
late Crown Prince of Macklenburg. Doctor Svenson, Her Grace the Duchess
of Cogstead, Mistress of Her Majesty's Bedchamber and *de facto* mistress
of this entire facility –'

The Duchess shifted her voice, hard as a stone, to Kelling, who was gathering items as instructed. 'Put that down. Nothing will leave this room.'

Schoepfil raised his hands. 'First you tell me to go, *now* –'

'Until I have this woman your effects are impounded. You will not leave.

You will not communicate. Your moment – yes, I am aware where Colonel Bronque has gone, and where Lord Axewith has been diverted – your *moment* to engage with *events*, Mr Schoepfil, will *pass*. Unless I have that woman.'

'I'd no idea the Contessa held such value at court –'

'You have three seconds to reply.'

'Your Grace, I need only one. Of course you shall have her. At Colonel Bronque's suggestion, she waits in the custody of his soldiers. Allow me to escort you, and understand that I myself have no position on the lady. Apparently the Contessa and the Colonel are acquainted by way of the Duke of Stäelmaere . . .'

But instead of following Schoepfil, the Duchess only called to a group of courtiers who stood outside. 'Mr Schoepfil will take you to her. Once she is in your hands, you know what to do. Mr Nordling!' A grey-haired courtier came forward. 'Escort Mr Kelling and his crate of goods to the guardhouse. Nothing to leave until you have my word.'

Schoepfil pursed his lips. 'O Your Grace, I do assure you –'

'*Go.*'

Schoepfil disappeared down the corridor, waving both arms to hurry the pace of his escort. The Duchess and Mr Nordling watched Kelling put the last of the papers into the box. Before Kelling could prevent him, Doctor Svenson slipped a hand through the strap of the leather case and slung it over his shoulder. Kelling looked up with shock.

'I'll carry this,' said Svenson.

'No!' cried Kelling. 'You will give that back!'

Svenson switched the strap to his further shoulder, ahead of Kelling's grasping hand. He spoke to Nordling. 'It was mine to begin with, you know.'

'No!' insisted Kelling, but he was suddenly a mere servant in a roomful of his betters.

'Whatever takes the least time,' said the Duchess. 'To the guardhouse, Mr Nordling.'

Svenson clicked his heels to the Duchess and marched out. Mr Kelling snatched up the crate and hurried after. Mr Nordling bowed gravely and left his mistress alone.

The Duchess of Cogstead cleared her throat.

'That can't be comfortable, no matter how small you are. Come out, child, so I can decide whether you ought to hang as well.'

Miss Temple emerged on her hands and knees, meeting the Duchess's gaze as proudly as possible. She knew enough to understand that, while highly placed people expected deference, they did not respect it, and that, properly presented, confidence could serve as a compliment instead of an affront.

'Miss Celestial Temple?'

'Yes, Your Grace.'

'Your voice tars you a colonial. How are you here with the Contessa di Lacquer-Sforza?'

'Under compulsion, Your Grace.'

'Explain.'

'I am afraid it would require an hour.' Miss Temple batted her eyes to signal a lack of insolence. 'I doubt you will find her.'

'Schoepfil will defy me?'

'She is already gone.'

'That is impossible.'

Miss Temple shrugged. The Duchess folded both arms beneath her heavy bosom, a gesture of discontent.

'Are you acquainted with Lady Hopton? She has also vanished.'

'She is dead, Your Grace. You will find her in an attiring room. Hidden in a niche.'

That the Duchess did not blanch confirmed that someone had already done so.

'But *why* in heaven's name?' Beneath the Duchess's anger lay genuine confusion. She clasped her hands, the knuckles so thick it seemed to Miss Temple that the woman's flesh was but a pair of gloves, and the fingers beneath studded with rings. 'You saw it happen.'

Miss Temple nodded.

'Do your veins run with ice, girl?'

'No, Your Grace, it is simply that over the course of recent events –'

'Lady Axewith!' The Duchess grimaced at her own slow realization. 'Lady

Axewith persuaded me to grant the Contessa an audience with the Queen – I did not understand the urgency. And now Lady Axewith is poisoned. Lady Hopton must have known –'

'I expect she had certain conclusions to share with Her Majesty – or, more importantly with you, as you are Her Majesty's – well, I am not sure of the term –'

'*Friend*,' the Duchess stated, her flat tone an implicit corrective.

'Friend,' Miss Temple echoed softly. 'The Contessa and her allies discovered how to compel cooperation. I say compel, but the truth is closer to enslavement.'

'As *you* were compelled?'

Miss Temple shook her head. 'O no – I am not the Contessa's slave. I am her enemy.'

'But you helped her.' The Duchess fixed Miss Temple with a threatening glare. 'That story you told Her Majesty, was it a lie?'

Miss Temple felt the urge to make a clean breast of everything, but she knew the truth about the Duke, the glass, the books, Vandaariff and the Cabal – all necessary to impart before her tale to the Queen made sense – lay beyond her ability to persuade.

'No, Your Grace. That is the irony of it all. Lord Vandaariff *is* a traitor. The Duke of Stäelmaere *was* murdered.'

'Then why could not the Contessa merely deliver that message? Why did Lady Axewith and Lady Hopton have to die?'

'It is not the truth of the story, but the timing of its delivery. The Contessa is against Lord Vandaariff – and in that she is for the realm – but she is one who thrives on havoc, and in that she is the realm's enemy. Lady Hopton's arrival would have muddled the Contessa's plans when they brooked no muddling. Surely Your Grace knows the realm *is* under attack.'

'There is unrest . . .'

'If Robert Vandaariff has his way – O I cannot recall the name, but wasn't there a place – destroyed and forgotten –'

'At least by you.'

'They sowed the ground with salt?'

'That would be Carthage.'

'Would it?'

'Why should Robert Vandaariff seek another Carthage? How could he think such a result within his power? Is he insane?'

'O absolutely.' The Duchess stared at Miss Temple, a downwards tuck at the corners of her mouth. Well used to this, Miss Temple went on. 'What you ought to understand – and I don't know if it is worth the trouble to tell the Queen, that is, whether one actually tells her or tells the Crown Prince or even if one *did* whether it would make a bit of difference – I suppose that is why I'm telling *you* –'

'You are telling me because I caught you crouched behind a chair.'

'Yes, but in trusting Vandaariff Her Majesty's government has laid itself at the feet of a madman. The highest ranks of your nation are riddled with secret slaves, serving a master whose wealth insulates him from all reprisal.'

'But . . . but the *Contessa* –'

'You feel her acts more keenly being personally responsible for her presence here.' Miss Temple knew she'd found the heart of the Duchess's concern, and risked touching the woman's arm. 'You cannot blame yourself. I don't blame *myself*, because I know the Contessa. Even forewarned she would have found a way. You must not think you have betrayed your Queen – for here you stand, working to protect her.'

Miss Temple did not believe this at all. She blamed herself keenly for almost everything and knew in her heart that, however much she might, like the Duchess, assuage her complicity through effort, such actions would never shift the damage already done, nor, she was fearfully sure, alter the dark trajectory of her future. She gave the Duchess's arm another squeeze and ceased further argument. She had seen the look now inhabiting the woman's face on too many occasions to number: someone with her immediate fate in their hands attempting to gauge how much of what she'd said could be believed – which was to say, how much had been an inveterate lie. The Duchess stabbed a finger at the leather tube under Miss Temple's arm.

'Does *that* belong to Mr Schoepfil?'

'It does *not*,' replied Miss Temple, and then in a more honeyed tone, 'I do not mean to be forward, but will I be hanged?'

'Very possibly.' The Duchess took her hand. 'And myself along with you . . .'

On her father's plantation privilege arrived with possession, and those organs of advantage – servants of every role and function – were integrated into all the facets of her life with a blunt cruelty. What had been characterized since, by everyone from the staff of the Boniface to the greater Bascombe family circle, as Miss Temple's intolerant manner was but a natural inheritance. The subtleties that distinguished mere employment from outright property were no part of that landscape, and so escaped both her attention and interest. In a stroke of some irony, once Miss Temple had been catapulted into a life of adventure, which was to say a variety of social stripes and circumstances, her original notions of hierarchy and power had only been reinforced. Whether it was seeing the Prince's Own 4th Dragoons in service to Minister Crabbé, or Ministry officials doing the bidding of Mrs Marchmoor, or the hired rogues of the Xonck private army, Miss Temple's youthful assumptions of autocracy had been confirmed again and again as the model of the world's true working. Great power, like a swollen insect queen, was marked by a population of compliant drones.

Walking with the Duchess, Miss Temple perceived an entirely different mechanism. The Duchess presented no awesome presence, in beauty or violence or wit, but nonetheless provoked a willing deference from each soul they passed. Miss Temple compared this to her own arrival, trailing Colonel Bronque, and the relative disinterest with which the Colonel himself had been viewed, though the importance of his errand had been clear. The Duchess, despite her personal lack of affect, inspired unfeigned respect. And, while these courtiers, like Mr Nordling, sent off with Kelling and the Doctor, would have instantly done the Duchess's bidding, they did not seem to be her *minions*.

Was not the Queen's inner court the most stiffly hierarchical body in existence?

Miss Temple listened intently to her guide's mutters of greeting and her comments on a host of matters that seemed wholly trivial, given the crisis.

Why should anyone care about the milk delivery or invitations to next week's concert? She realized that the more trivial the task, the more agitated the person assigned to manage it had been, and that their entire progress had been one in which the Duchess – herself emotionally wrought, Miss Temple knew – had smoothed the disarray of the court like a tortoiseshell comb smoothed wet, tangled hair . . . and all without a threat, a slap or a single urgent word.

Miss Temple drew no conclusion, for when it came to a fight – as it seemed everything in her world, at the finish, must – she did not see how the Duchess could stand against Colonel Bronque's troopers. But she kept her eyes and ears open.

The prospect of violence returned Miss Temple's thoughts, as she supposed would be inevitable in the whole of her remaining life, to the Contessa. Assuming the woman had finally fled, why now? What had changed, or what had she at last achieved? Miss Temple admitted it was possible the Contessa had put her trust in Colonel Bronque and departed only at the news of his betrayal. But Miss Temple was not satisfied, and her dissatisfaction took firmer root as she realized the Duchess was leading her down damp staircases and past peeling walls, back to the level of the baths.

They stopped at another metal door with an iron wheel in its centre, flanked by two burly footmen. The footmen, white wigs drooping in the damp, came to attention at the sight of the Duchess, but her gesture to open the door was interrupted by an echoing cry. Miss Temple turned as a party of some dozen figures clattered down the stairs in their wake.

'Stand with them,' said the Duchess. Miss Temple was pulled behind the footmen with her back against the wheel, feeling like a weak but valuable chess piece.

Mr Schoepfil arrived first, anger evident in his ruddy face and strident tone. 'I will have answers, madam! I will have answers!'

After him in a jumble came Mr Kelling, still carrying the crate, leather case restored within it, then Doctor Svenson, sullenly rubbing his jaw, with Mr Nordling interposed between them. Miss Temple did not recognize the rest of the party – soldiers from Bronque's regiment, men in Ministry topcoats and several fellows who, like Nordling, wore more fashionable garments of different colours and were most likely to be courtiers.

Schoepfil gripped his oblong box in one hand and waved it for emphasis. 'Where is she, Your Grace? Where have you hidden her? Two men are dead at this woman's hands. But she has not passed the guardhouse. She has not passed any exit, nor out any window.'

'I dislike your tone, Mr Schoepfil.'

While the Duchess of Cogstead was taller than Miss Temple, this was no particular feat, and Mr Schoepfil – a man used to dominating conversations from below – met her eyes with disdain. 'You arranged today's audience. You and Pont-Joule have indulged her time and again.' He snorted once at Miss Temple. 'That you have *this* one with you is all the proof I need.' Schoepfil flicked his head at the iron oval door. 'You know where she's gone, and I demand you stand aside.'

The Duchess pitched her voice to the group. 'Mr Schoepfil has been commanded by royal writ to retire, at *once*. Any man that stands with him will pay the penalty.'

'What penalty?' demanded Schoepfil. 'Your city is burning and you're *here*, no more pertinent to its fate than a blood-stuffed tick is to a cart-horse.'

'Mr Schoepfil! No matter *whose* nephew –'

'My uncle will not survive this night. You do not want me for an enemy. Step aside.'

The Duchess did not move. The soldiers behind Schoepfil stood ready. Miss Temple sought Doctor Svenson, but Svenson's eyes met hers as if from a great distance – not cold so much as uninflected. She swallowed with dismay. Had he *given up*?

She went to her toes and whispered to the footmen. 'You must open the door and pull the Duchess through.' They did not reply, but one shifted his weight nearer the iron wheel.

'You cannot pass,' the Duchess insisted. 'Her Majesty is within.'

'O she is not,' retorted Schoepfil.

'Mr Schoepfil, your insolence paints no good prospect for your future at court.'

Schoepfil's eyes gleamed. The man found real delight in such contests of will, but hesitated to use force against the Duchess. However, though he would not attack, nor would he leave – and should the door open, he would push through. A soldier loosened his sword in its scabbard. The courtiers with Nordling inched backwards. Doctor Svenson looked at the floor, as if to confirm his altered heart.

What lay behind the oval door that could be so important?

That Schoepfil believed the Contessa could be within spoke to the woman having insinuated herself more deeply into the Queen's household than anyone had suspected. If Lady Axewith had employed the Contessa as a confidante, perhaps she'd managed a similar intimacy here, with this Lord Pont-Joule or – was it possible – even with the Queen? Why else had the Duchess come to this room but to answer her own fears? At once Miss Temple saw that to allow Schoepfil's entry – for he would take hold of whatever evidence he found – was to grant him unspeakable leverage: proof that a murderer had been granted favour by the Crown.

'This man should be under arrest!' Miss Temple pointed an accusing finger at Schoepfil. 'He is a threat to Her Majesty's person! Your duty is clear! Unless you are all cowards –'

Mr Kelling dropped his crate with a crash and reached into his topcoat. He yanked out a shining short-barrelled revolver, but no sooner had Kelling extended his arm than the weapon sprung from his hand and Kelling split the air with a shriek. Mr Nordling had pulled apart his cane and thrust its thin blade into Kelling's wrist. The Ministry men retreated, taking no side. Schoepfil roared with rage and struck Nordling three times across the face before the courtier could bring his weapon to bear. Kelling tripped over his crate and went down, holding his wounded limb. The soldiers swept out their sabres. The courtiers leapt to Nordling's defence and were struck repeatedly in turn. The footmen shoved Miss Temple aside and turned the iron wheel.

A shot rang out and Miss Temple flinched at the spray of plaster from the splintered ceiling. Doctor Svenson held Kelling's revolver.

Svenson aimed at the troopers, then swung the barrel at Schoepfil. 'The first to make a move will die . . . and probably the second.' He addressed the soldiers, nodding to Schoepfil. 'Perhaps this man is worth your lives – if so, you are welcome to come at me.'

'You wouldn't dare,' called Schoepfil. 'This is murder.'

Svenson ignored him. 'The case, Mr Kelling. Slide it across the floor.'

'Do nothing of the sort!' shouted Schoepfil.

Svenson extended the pistol towards Kelling and drew back the hammer with his thumb. 'Look at me, Mr Kelling.'

Kelling's face was white, and he turned guiltily to his employer, who sputtered and threw up his hands. 'Lord above, this cuts it!' Schoepfil protested. 'This cuts it fine!'

Kelling made to push the leather case to Svenson, but the Doctor nodded at Miss Temple. 'Not to me. To her.'

Kelling slid the case to Miss Temple's feet. Behind her the Duchess had passed through the oval doorway, but stood watching.

'Of all the idiocy,' declared Schoepfil.

Svenson returned his aim to the soldiers. 'Lay your blades on the floor . . .'

But the soldiers did not move. Instead, each took a careful step away from the other, and extended their sabres, measuring the distance they would need to cut Svenson down.

'Well, then,' said the Doctor. 'That's clear enough. Anyone who wants to leave, I would suggest it. Stray shots, you know.'

'Any man who leaves is dead,' cried Schoepfil, a smile playing again on his lips. 'At least to my favour.'

The Ministry men glanced at one another, but did not flee. The courtiers stood next to Nordling, who dabbed a bloody nose with his shirt-cuff. Svenson tightened his grip on the pistol. 'Celeste, please go. Seal the door behind you.'

'Come with me,' she whispered.

'Give my best wishes to Her Majesty. All of Macklenburg is at her service.'

She had not noticed Schoepfil moving – or he simply moved too quickly – but then the wooden crate was in the air. Svenson dodged and the missile smashed into the footman who had opened the door, a hammer blow that filled the air with fluttering paper and knocked the footman flat. Miss Temple jumped through the door. The Doctor's pistol roared, three rapid shots – cries of anger and pain – but before she could see, the second footman shoved the oval door closed and spun the wheel, sealing Miss Temple and the Duchess tight.

The room was silent, not a trace of the mayhem outside piercing through. Miss Temple found a heavy iron candelabrum and wedged it hard into the door's inner wheel. She turned to the Duchess, still stunned to immobility.

'Is Her Majesty truly here?'

'Of course not. These rooms belong to Lord Pont-Joule.' The Duchess led her into a strange octagonal room whose every side held another of the oval doors.

'They are tunnels,' declared Miss Temple. 'Spy tunnels to listen or watch.'

'With so many passages carved over the years for so many different baths, Pont-Joule thought he might exploit the fact for Her Majesty's safety.'

'Didn't the Contessa say Pont-Joule had been killed as well?'

'*Quelle coïncidence,*' the Duchess muttered drily. Both women spun to a wrench of metal at the entry door. The obstructing candelabrum held the wheel in place.

'It will not be long,' said the Duchess. 'The Contessa was Pont-Joule's lover. If she did not pass through any guard post, and I trust Mr Schoepfil's intelligence –'

'I beg your pardon,' said Miss Temple, 'but I believe it is more than that – that her audience with the Queen was at least in part an excuse to come here, to this very room.'

'Why? Just to escape?'

'No. I believe Lord Pont-Joule, without his knowledge, gave her a place to hide a thing she could not keep on her person.'

'What thing?'

Miss Temple set the leather case on a side table and snapped it open. The Duchess gasped at the shining blue glass book.

'Good Lord . . . I heard whispers . . .'

Miss Temple quickly shut the case. 'I do not know where Doctor Svenson found this, nor what it might contain, but the Contessa has in her possession another book, and her attempts to use it may kill us all.'

The door was jolted again.

'Where do the tunnels go?' asked Miss Temple.

'They all go to the baths.'

'No, where do they *exit*?'

'They don't. In one or two cases, there is an outlet elsewhere in the house –'

'She needs to *leave* the house.'

The Duchess nodded. 'I know. It makes no sense. Unless . . .'

An arm of the candelabrum snapped like a gunshot. The wheel lurched halfway round.

'Unless what?' demanded Miss Temple.

The Duchess indicated a door by a daybed. 'That way leads to the spring itself –'

Miss Temple was already across the room. She heaved open the door to find a red envelope on the tunnel floor. She tore it open.

'What does it say?' cried the Duchess. 'Is it from her?'

The rest of the candelabrum broke apart and Lord Pont-Joule's rooms echoed with the voices of men. Miss Temple leapt through, yanked the door closed and spun the wheel, leaving the hapless Duchess on the other side.

They would not know which door she'd used, but for how long? She groped in the darkness, knowing she must hurry. Would Schoepfil strike the Duchess down? Was Doctor Svenson still alive?

Her outstretched hand touched a wall and her feet found stairs. The blackness was leavened by a tallow stub, wedged into the rock. She stood before a hissing pool of black water, its surface seamed by blooms of effervescence. Miss Temple gasped. On the ground lay the Contessa –

She cursed her own credulity. Heaped on the ground was the Contessa's black dress. Miss Temple glanced back. She dropped into a squat, opened the case, pulled the star chart from the leather tube and folded it, wincing at the creases, until it fit atop the book. She took the small pouch holding Francesca's key and wormed it into the bosom of her corset. She stopped. She dug her fingers deeper. The handkerchief with Vandaariff's glass spur was no longer there.

There was no time. Without care, for she would never see it again, she ripped her dress to the waist and let it drop next to the Contessa's. A metallic scrape from the passage behind her. Had the Contessa left her petticoat? She had. Miss Temple thrust hers off and kicked free. A shaft of light in the tunnel. The door was open. She closed the case and set the red envelope onto the candle flame, where it caught and began to curl. Inside had been a single carelessly scrawled line: 'And so they shall be redeemed.'

Miss Temple inhaled as deeply as she could. Hugging the case to her body, she stepped into the black water and sank like a stone.

# EIGHT

## FONTANEL

When Vandaariff reclaimed the glass card from Matthew Harcourt, the young man dropped to his knees and, shaking like an opium eater, emptied his stomach onto the carpet. When the heaving subsided, Foison hauled the overmatched Interim Minister to his feet and marched him out. Vandaariff followed at his own slow speed, humming under his breath.

> Blood instructs us on the use of flame
> Fire's indulgence sings the end of shame

Chang had hoped to erode Foison's devotion to his master, and Phelps had paid the price. He watched in silence as the green-coats cut the corpse from the chair and took it away. When they returned it was with Foison, and for him.

His arms were bound behind his back with chain. Outside waited a large vehicle, unlike any Chang had ever seen. Sheathed in metal, the smaller front was like any rich man's coach, but was attached to a second portion, as large as a goods wagon.

Were the trains no longer safe?

Two lackeys led Chang into the long rear car and looped his chain over a hook in the ceiling. The height of the hook gave Chang no choice but to stand. They pulled forward, Chang balancing like a seaman on a heaving deck. He looked to Foison, slouched on a bench against the inner wall.

'The spur that killed Phelps,' said Chang. 'It wasn't like the ones we found at Raaxfall. It didn't hold rage, but something more like despair. He'd been cut with it before, under questioning, hadn't he, just nicks to help him along? The man was ruined.'

Foison waited, as if this required no comment.

'Blue glass in the throat. It's what killed Lydia Vandaariff. She was decapitated. Did you know that?'

Foison gripped a metal hook for support as the coach swept round a turn. 'Lord Robert was so informed, yes.'

'By whom?'

'Does it matter?'

'Only five people survived that crash. Francis Xonck is dead since. If any of the four – I include myself – had described that scene for your master, you would know it. I'll wager they have not, and yet he knows. How is that possible? Because those memories – memories of a dead man, also on that airship – have been placed inside his mind.'

A panel slid open and through a barrier of steel mesh loomed Vandaariff's haggard face.

'Such an interesting conversation, Cardinal. One is reminded of those Greeks, groping to understand the world – everything wrong, of course, the logic of intelligent children, fumbling in their mother's kitchen, rising on their toes in the hope of buttering bread. You observe – of course you do, you're a hunter – but do you comprehend?'

'I know you're going to die.'

'But not alone, Cardinal Chang. Do not let the news deject you.'

Vandaariff turned from the panel, but left it open. He resumed his hoarse humming.

> Love is a severance sure as any blade
> Flesh is a table where God's feast is laid

The carriage took another turn and the iron shackle dug into Chang's wrist. Foison watched him with a bone-deep readiness, and in the man's posture Chang recognized himself: at the Old Palace, present only by sufferance, waiting for a message from Madelaine Kraft – which would be his signal to depart. His eyes were ever fixed on Angelique, shining amidst the wealthy men who might at any moment signal the house manager, Gorine, and claim her for however long desire might last. Chang watched her, but what had he ever seen? Tiny hands holding a wine glass. Smiling lips. Black eyes. Scraps of whoever she might, truly, have been.

Even after so much time, so many *lives*, Chang preserved Angelique in his heart, but only – he knew – like a doll, a dream. What had all that longing served? Did his life merit survival? Had he punished wicked men? Of course. Had he done so within his own web of wickedness? Undeniably. Who spared a fowl-eating fox because it also dined on rats?

This was rhetoric and pity. Chang looked again at Foison – at his own futile past – and glimpsed what he stood to lose *now*.

She was not beautiful, not like Angelique. She was not kind. She was undoubtedly – in her heart, glass books be damned – an ignorant prude. She was a perfectly spoilt example of a class he despised. He did not honestly know if he could stand her presence for one entire sustained day. He did not know if she was alive.

But he thought of her in his arms, wading through the freezing surf. Her courage at Parchfeldt. Guiding them from Raaxfall, the acceptance of her doom. Against every instinct and all logic, these thoughts uncoiled like the sticky wings of a butterfly. He felt the rush in his soul. It was absurd. He could choose to suppress it – that was in his power. Yet he was dying too. He did not choose. He shut his eyes and let go.

Robert Vandaariff cleared his throat, a coach wheel crunching gravel. 'Wither your thoughts, Cardinal Chang?'

'How best to end your life.'

'I think not. No, you were far away.'

'What do you care?'

'All flesh may be cursed, but there are degrees. There are tigers and there are sheep. And tigers – though rare – can be anywhere in life. I am no snob, Cardinal. One finds as many sheep in a palace as in a poorhouse.'

'You seek to count my stripes, then? So I am remembered?'

'You'd prefer to be forgotten?'

'I'd prefer to set myself on fire.'

Vandaariff scowled. 'Posturing.'

'Not every man fears oblivion.'

'Not every man has tasted it.'

'Will you tell me where we're going?' Chang asked.

'Harschmort,' said Foison. 'You know that.'

Foison kept his gaze on Chang and did not see his master's disapproving look – though Chang did not suppose he needed to. The break in protocol had been deliberate.

Through the mesh loomed a line of lanterns, blocking the road. The panel slid shut. Outside came the sound of horses, and loud calls. The carriage slowed – a military roadblock.

'You were away,' said Chang. 'You returned *after* his recovery from blood fever.'

'Men change. The death of his daughter –'

'That man doesn't give a damn about any daughter.'

'You're wrong.' Foison's voice was soft, no longer needing to speak over hoof beats and wheels. 'I've seen the flowers in her bedchamber.'

'He's not the same man – the same *mind*.'

'He's dying. So are you.'

'And you with us, you ignorant monkey.'

Foison's eyes went cold. 'Unfortunate choice of word.'

'Woke you up, didn't it?' Chang leant to the end of the shackles' chain. 'Our world isn't theirs. Are you so well trained to forget it?'

The panel slid open.

'Mr Foison!' called Vandaariff. 'A change of plan. Disembark with your charge. And take care for his safety. We know the fellow's delicate.'

Chang stood in the street, a dog on Foison's lead. In the lantern light waited at least a company of elite grenadiers. Another knot of men clustered at the door of Vandaariff's carriage, chickens awaiting their handful of seed.

First amongst them – Chang squinted to be sure – was the Privy Minister, Lord Axewith. Chang thought of the man's wife, retching her guts out, another dupe led to the grave. Did Axewith even know? The Privy Minister's face was ashen in the torchlight, like a swine given its first whiff of the slaughterhouse. Next to Axewith stood Matthew Harcourt, sickly and pale. Chang pitied neither man – idiots who had naively passed their authority to

Robert Vandaariff to end their troubles. The old Robert Vandaariff might have done so, but the man in the armoured wagon had no care for anything save his own dark dreams.

A colonel of grenadiers in full glittering dress advanced to the carriage as if he had been summoned. Axewith himself stepped aside so the Colonel might lean into the coach. Chang half wondered if he would pull his head out again or, as if in a children's tale, the serpent in the cave would snap it off.

Foison lifted his face skyward, sniffing the air.

'A shift in the wind,' he said, assuming Chang possessed a sense of smell. 'Who knows where the fire will be halted?'

'Is it so severe?'

Foison flicked the chain as a sign for Chang to turn. The consultation had ended and the Colonel, bodily whole, strode towards them. He was a powerful, hawk-faced man, black hair flat against his skull.

'Colonel Bronque,' said Foison quietly. Bronque's eyes darted across them with distaste – Foison with his dandified clothes and Asiatic cast, Chang with his cleric's coat and scars.

'Chang, is it? Lord Vandaariff says you will help us.'

All three turned at the sound of the carriage door closing, sealing Vandaariff back in his protected box. Lord Axewith's men – save Harcourt, who was no longer visible – positioned themselves in a circle around several large maps spread onto the cobbles.

'I need to find someone,' Bronque went on. 'A Mrs Madelaine Kraft.'

'Why?' Chang asked.

'None of your affair. Say what you know.'

Chang smiled stiffly. 'She's at the Old Palace – or where her people put her. Left an imbecile. By a blue glass book.'

'She *was*.' The subject of blue glass gave Bronque no pause. 'She's been healed.'

'That's impossible.'

'That is the *point*.'

Bronque was serious. And that Chang, a prized possession, had been lent for the search made clear the cure had not come from Vandaariff's hand.

'The Old Palace has been ransacked,' Bronque went on. 'And its ashes raked. She has fled with an employee. An African. Where would he take her? Where would she flee?'

Chang glanced at Foison. 'Does your master have time for this? If this fire is as bad as you say –'

'You'll do what you're told!' Bronque bellowed at Chang, as if he were an insubordinate trooper. Without warning Cardinal Chang chopped his forehead into the Colonel's nose. Bronque staggered back with a cry of shock.

The soldiers around them leapt forward, weapons ready. The Colonel straightened himself, eyes blazing with hatred, blood seeping through his fingers.

'Calm, gentlemen.' Foison pulled the chain to place Chang nearer. 'Cardinal Chang will find this woman. But he is required – in sound condition – after the errand. At your peril, Colonel. Now I suggest you wipe your face.'

Bronque reeled away, shouting for water.

'I don't suppose you'd undo these chains?' Chang asked Foison. 'If I gave my word not to escape?'

'Your word means nothing.'

Chang turned at the creak of Vandaariff's massive carriage, pulling forward. Axewith waved his hat, an abject gesture. Chang had not expected Vandaariff to leave.

'But you won't escape,' said Foison, 'because you need to reach him, before the time. And without me you won't.'

'Then why this diversion?'

Foison called to Bronque, returning with a cloth pressed to his face. 'I have spoken to Cardinal Chang, Colonel. He will cooperate.'

The soldier clearly wanted nothing more than to hack Chang's head from his shoulders, but a man did not acquire so much gold brocade without learning to swallow his own desire.

'Very well.' Bronque sniffed wetly, to show he too was willing to begin anew. 'We've spoken to a Michel Gorine. He described Mrs Kraft's recovery.'

'And where is Gorine now?' Chang asked.

'He knows nothing he didn't say.'

Chang grimaced. 'Which probably means he said a lot of things he didn't know.'

'He had every motivation to confess.' Bronque dabbed at his nose. 'Under further questioning the story didn't change. I'm not a fool. The cure was managed by Captain-Surgeon Abelard Svenson. I understand you are acquainted.'

Mrs Kraft – *that* had been the Contessa's secret errand: to attain her cure. Could every other victim be so restored? Could Robert Vandaariff himself? This changed everything.

To Bronque, Chang only shrugged. 'Where is Svenson now?'

'Not with Mrs Kraft. They were separated in the fire. When Gorine met him, Svenson was caring for a child.'

'What child?' asked Foison sharply.

Bronque glared at the interruption. 'I don't know – a girl. Dead in the fellow's arms. Smoke, I believe.'

'The child is *dead*?'

'What can it matter? Do you know her?'

But Foison had already crossed to his green-coated mercenaries. He spoke low and rapidly. One man broke for a tethered horse, leapt into the saddle and clattered off.

'Is there a problem?' called Bronque.

'Continue.'

Displeased at Foison's evasion, Bronque snapped his fingers at an aide, who brought a map of the city. The soldier bent so the map could be spread across his back.

'We need to know where she'd go to ground.' Bronque traced a circle with his finger. 'Now, *these* districts are presently inaccessible because of the fire . . .'

Chang was astonished. The area was massive – a full quarter of the city. He tried to figure for wind, but Bronque was ahead of him, sketching the likely path of the blaze and filling in where the authorities – always before neighbourhoods of wealth – had entrenched their resources to prevent its spread.

'She can't have reached the river, and coach travel is all but impossible.

They are thus probably on foot, heading north or east. My own guess would put them *here*.' Bronque tapped on what Chang knew to be a nest of warehouses. 'She has wealthy backers – how else does a half-caste operate a place like that? One might easily hide her on his premises –'

'You're wrong,' said Chang.

'It makes perfect sense.'

'Only if she wants to hide.'

'Why wouldn't she?'

'Because she's been wronged. She'll want revenge.'

'Just her and a servant?'

'He's not her servant,' said Chang. 'He's her son. And he could snap your spine like a baguette. No, the question isn't where they've hidden; it's where they will attack.'

Bronque considered this, but shook his head. 'I still can't see it. I grant her intelligence, but how she can hope, even with this chaos –'

'It depends on whom she blames, doesn't it?' Chang turned to Foison. 'Assume she knows who formed the Cabal behind the blue glass. Any of those names could be a target.'

Colonel Bronque nodded, again admitting his awareness of this secret history.

'The Comte d'Orkancz is dead,' observed Foison carefully.

'And Crabbé, and Francis Xonck,' added Chang. 'Who else remains?'

'The Italian woman.'

'We don't know where she is,' said Bronque.

But Bronque knew *who* the Contessa was. 'Madelaine Kraft was invited to Harschmort along with a hundred other guests,' said Chang. 'That was where her mind was plundered.'

'Invited by Robert Vandaariff.' Bronque sighed. 'If you are right, their destination will be Harschmort House. Which isn't to say that reaching Harschmort won't be extremely difficult.' He peered at the map. 'I can post men at these crossroads –'

'Do you know Mr Drusus Schoepfil?'

Bronque looked up, but Foison's question was for Chang. Chang shook his head.

'With the death of Lydia Vandaariff, Drusus Schoepfil has become his uncle's heir. Do *you* know him, Colonel?'

'We've met in passing. Queer duck.'

'Indeed.' Foison traced a slim finger across the map. 'As you set your road-blocks, you might also post men to the Crampton and Packington railway stations. Any train to Harschmort must pass them both – that way we needn't bother with the madhouse of Stropping. We ourselves will visit Mr Schoepfil's home.'

'My understanding is that Mr Schoepfil and his uncle do not speak. Why would Mrs Kraft fix her revenge on him?'

'Not her revenge, Colonel, *theirs*. What the woman needs is an ally.'

Bronque hesitated. 'I've no wish to be indelicate, but, in all honesty, why would he betray his uncle *now*? If Lord Vandaariff's health is on the wane –'

'Will you join us or not?' asked Foison.

Bronque slapped the map hard. The aide grunted at the impact, then rolled it up. The Colonel gave his orders, detailing men to roadblocks and the railway stations, and others to accompany them on their search. Bronque's hand found the hilt of his sabre, gloved fingers curling around the guard.

'So. Let us see if this insight into her mind is sound.'

Foison extended a finger to Bronque's gold epaulette. 'Spot of blood.'

The path to Schoepfil's house, even accompanied by two dozen soldiers, required detours – around refugees, looting and roadblocks. The last they could have negotiated with Bronque, but the Colonel avoided the contact, preferring their errand to remain unknown.

'Why didn't you bring Gorine?' Chang asked. 'He could have been your hostage.'

'I didn't plan this,' Bronque replied testily. 'I came with dispatches from Her Majesty to Lord Axewith – this is at Lord Vandaariff's insistence. I should not have rated the fate of a brothel-mistress above a burning city, but he does, and now every other duty must hang.'

'You came all the way from Bathings?'

'None of your damned business.'

The chaos Chang had witnessed in his flight with Cunsher had grown worse. Each face they passed – whether helmeted soldier or stricken citizen – showed how beyond the grip of authority the crisis had become. Even the men he walked with – Bronque's soldiers and Foison's lackeys, ostensibly agents of order – passed through the city as if it were a place for which they bore neither responsibility nor affection. It burnt around them, and by all it was ignored. Surely these men had wives, children, homes – why hadn't they fled to save their own? Instead, every one did his best to save Robert Vandaariff.

Schoepfil's residence was a cube of soot-stained granite whose unadornment spelt out the estrangement from his mighty uncle's wealth. Bronque sent men to the rear of the house before mounting the steps. A servant welcomed them in and explained that Mr Schoepfil was not home.

'Do you know where we might find him?' asked Foison. 'Our errand comes from the Privy Minister.'

'I cannot say, sir.' The servant did not blanch at Foison's appearance or Chang's, not even at the leash of chain.

'The matter is extremely important. It concerns his uncle, and Mr Schoepfil's inheritance.'

'Indeed, sir. If I do hear from him, what message shall I give?'

'That Lord Vandaariff's health –' began Foison, but Bronque cut in.

'Tell him the woman and the black man were seen and his only hope is immediate surrender.'

The servant nodded, as if this threat was of a piece with everything else that had been said. 'Very good, sir. I will do my best to convey the message.'

Back on the street, Foison whispered. 'Do not apprehend the courier – we must follow.'

'I know my business,' the Colonel replied tersely. At a signal his men melted into the darkness. 'As you see, I am happy to provoke the man, though I remain unconvinced Lord Vandaariff's nephew will lead us to this woman. More likely, her own people hide her –'

'Madelaine Kraft is not *hiding*,' said Chang.

'You don't know that. Any more than I see how she's worth our time.'

Chang said nothing, yet the Colonel's comment raised a question as to the true – with regard to Robert Vandaariff – object of their search.

'What does Drusus Schoepfil *do*?' Chang asked Foison.

'Whatever he wants. A life of random expertise, a thousand tasks half done.'

'Another arrogant wastrel?' asked Bronque.

'If he was a wastrel,' said Chang, 'we should not be here. Is he capable of striking at his uncle?'

'Anyone is capable,' said Foison.

'Because he's threatened his uncle before?'

'No,' Foison sighed. 'Because he hasn't.'

One of Bronque's soldiers waved from the corner. The chase had begun.

Their quarry was a young man in a shapeless coat, hurrying from the rear of Schoepfil's house. Two of Foison's men, stripped of their jackets, made the nearest pursuit. The rest, including Bronque's grenadiers, came at a safer distance. Chang walked between Bronque and Foison, still chained. After a quarter-mile Bronque leant across Chang's chest to Foison, a sympathetic gesture intended to evince tact.

'Lord Vandaariff's rapid decline is most dispiriting. Is there truly no hope?'

'He does not entertain any.'

'But what of the nation?' Bronque ventured.

'Nations are vanity,' replied Foison.

The restive wanderers they passed echoed this fatalism, feral in the glare of bonfires. All his life Chang had seen inequity, implacable and institution-alized, and people bore it all, even their own children dead before their eyes. This night these desperate faces had found the spark of rebellion. But he knew their momentary gains – windows broken or constables driven off with stones – would only provoke harsher measures when law was restored.

Was this not the arc of any life – from oppression to revolt to still deeper servitude? He thought of Cunsher, how the man's competence was but a shell encasing a long-shattered heart. Who didn't nurse sorrow at their core? Chang's discontents were nothing new or precious. Had Foison lost a family, a lover, a language, a home? Of course he had – most likely all in one vicious stroke. And in exchange, offering his life to another man of power, he had survived . . . the doomed chain of service. Phelps, Smythe, Blach . . . and Svenson – perhaps the most miserable of them all. To a man they would be finished, and that he would be finished with them, Chang did not doubt.

The young messenger skulked to the gate of a livery yard and disappeared inside. The Colonel quickly positioned his men, then drew their eye to a line of gabled windows.

'With luck the woman has gone to ground. If we enter in force –'

Foison shook his head. 'If it is merely an agreed-upon place to leave word, such action will keep her away. Let us see if the messenger stays or returns whence he came.'

Bronque looked at Chang. Chang kept silent, allowing their disagreement to stand.

Gunshots echoed from inside the livery. All three charged for the door. On the floor of the stable lay the young man they'd followed, shot twice in the chest. Bronque's grenadiers crowded a far doorway, their officer holding a smoking revolver. Near the body lay another gun.

'He was trying to leave,' the young lieutenant explained to Bronque. 'Saw us, sir, and drew his weapon.'

Bronque knelt over the messenger – little more than a boy – pressing two fingers to the jugular. 'God-damned cock-up.' He thrust his chin at a staircase in the corner. 'Search the premises. No more killing. If the woman is here, we need her alive.'

The soldiers clattered off. Bronque exchanged a bitter look with Foison and set to emptying the dead boy's pockets. 'Idiots. Ruined everything.'

'Unless she is upstairs,' said Foison mildly.

Chang brushed the straw from around the boy's gun with his foot – it was a service revolver, heavy and difficult to fire.

'Lieutenant!' Bronque roared at the staircase. 'Report!'

The officer stomped back into view at the top of the steps. 'Nothing, sir. All empty.'

'Hang your idiocy! Get your men formed in the courtyard.'

The soldiers marched down the stairs and out. Bronque tossed the contents of the dead boy's pockets into the straw: a clasp-knife, a scatter of pennies, a dirty rag.

Through the boy's half-open lips gleamed a brighter touch of red, blood risen from a punctured lung. Chang cocked his head.

'What is it?' asked Foison.

'His cloak is untied.'

'What of that?' asked Bronque.

'It wasn't before, when we were following him.'

'So he untied his cloak upon coming in – that's natural enough.'

'Not if he wasn't going to stay. Not if he was attempting to leave through the rear door.'

Bronque's voice deepened. 'Are you saying he wasn't? Wait a moment . . .'

The Colonel slipped two gloved fingers into the messenger's boot and came out with a folded square of paper. 'A message, by God.'

He handed the paper to Foison, who opened it for them all to see: a page torn from an old book, a woodcut depicting a muscular black man in a turban, with an axe. At his feet lay an open casket, a jewel box that contained a human heart. But the woodcut had been freshly amended by its sender: with the crude stroke of an ink pen the axeman's eyes had been wholly covered by a thick black bar, like a blindfold.

Bronque frowned at the corpse, as if to doubt such a message could have come from such a courier. 'What can it mean?'

'The Executioner,' said Chang. 'From *The Chemickal Marriage*.'

'What does *that* mean?' demanded Colonel Bronque.

Foison sighed, almost sadly, and refolded the page. 'That Drusus Schoepfil must die.'


Foison sent another man into the night, this time on foot, with news of their discovery.

'But what *have* we found?' Bronque looked at them hopefully, then exhaled through his nose in the general direction of the corpse. 'We can leave this lot here, and I'll set my men to search the surrounding houses –'

Foison shook his head. 'You don't have enough men both to search and to establish a cordon. Anyone wary, and they are, would escape. Of course, with the messenger unable to speak and the message so obscure, we do not even know if it was meant for Mrs Kraft.'

'Who else?'

'Drusus Schoepfil – his people passing on your threat, no doubt to advise surrender.'

Bronque let this go. His men stood formed and ready. 'Well, what next? Are we finished or aren't we?'

'Perhaps we are.'

'Good.' Bronque did not bother to hide his relief. 'Where will you go? We can provide an escort –'

'Cardinal Chang and I can make our own way.'

'To Harschmort? On foot? It would take two days.'

'Perhaps Stropping, and an east-bound train.'

'Then let us walk together; Stropping Station is not so far from where Lord Axewith –'

'That won't be necessary.'

'But what will I tell Lord Axewith?'

'That we arrived too late. Our search was a fool's errand – and now you are relieved of it. Best of luck in the night.'

Foison flicked Chang's chain and began to walk, his three remaining men trotting across the courtyard to join him. Chang looked over his shoulder. Framed first by his grenadiers and then by the disaffected crowds, Bronque watched them go, a statue in the torchlight.

Around the first turn Foison stopped, listening. 'Will he come?'

'He must,' Chang replied. 'Once there are fewer witnesses.'

They had entered a walled avenue offering little cover. Foison stepped behind Chang to unwrap the chain. 'When did you know? Before the clumsy murder?'

'The interrogation of Gorine.'

'How so?'

'Svenson. If he cured Madelaine Kraft, we ought to be looking for *him*. We aren't – because someone already has him. And not Vandaariff, or you would know.'

Foison coiled the chain into a loop he could carry, then thought better of it and threw it to the side. 'Svenson could be dead.'

'Then why not say so?'

Foison set off without replying. Chang kept pace, rubbing his wrists. Two green-coats jogged before them, while the third hung back to guard the rear. At the cross street, the lead men paused, peering cautiously ahead. Foison and Chang stopped as well, waiting.

'The message was for Bronque,' Chang said, 'commanding our deaths. The Executioner's resemblance to Mahmoud was but a witty coincidence.'

Foison sighed. 'So Schoepfil was home when we called.'

'Who else could send such a message to Bronque, one that he would follow?'

'And if Madelaine Kraft was there as well – which would, as you say, inform the image – she is gone by now too.'

'The real question is the extent to which your master's been betrayed. Bronque has allied with Schoepfil – but who are they? Who pulls their strings – Axewith?'

'It makes no sense,' said Foison. 'He owns them all.'

The lead men waved them on, and they dashed across the open road. Once on the other side, the third man fell back and the lead two loped ahead.

Chang was aware of his own place in Foison's catalogue of men-as-property, yet how quickly his fortunes had changed – from free man to prisoner to fleeing through the streets – all of a piece with a city set spinning on a different and degraded axis. His first struggle with the Cabal had been a battle to gain control over institutions – Crabbé suborning the Ministries, for example, but the Ministries had been left intact. Now it seemed possible that anything could fall, any edifice could be torn down.

Chang sighed. If he lived, Svenson was their prisoner – as he was Foison's, as Celeste Temple had been taken by the Contessa. Was that what had become of their grand alliance – tethered familiars, each to a different demon?

The lead men signalled a stop. Chang bent over, still wary of the pursuit they had outpaced. Foison wiped the sweat from his neck with two fingers and then, in a disquieting gesture, licked them, an animal seeking salt. Their path had dead-ended near the sounds of a crowd, whose voices echoed over the rooftops . . .

'Two more avenues and we will find a coach,' said Foison.

'Or more empty stables.' Foison did not respond. Chang spat on the cobbles. 'Come – we're alone. No one will hear. What does it mean that the child is dead? What does it mean that Mrs Kraft is healed? Why did your master choose me over Celeste Temple?'

'None of that is my concern.'

'Someone might be saved. You can choose.'

'And follow your example – the nation of one man? Vanity.'

The blend of doom and duty drove Chang mad, almost as bad as the damned Doctor –

Doctor Svenson. Chang thrust out his hand. 'The message, from the stable!' Foison took the paper from his coat and Chang snatched it away. The black Executioner had been sketched like a gypsy's Tarot trump, in blunt strokes of a primitive, emblematic power – the axe in his hands, the casket at his feet . . .

'Explain,' said Foison.

'*Vanity. The Chemickal Marriage*.' Chang tapped the new-made slash of ink. 'The Executioner puts on the blindfold to kill – that mark is the order for Bronque, for our lives.'

'We know that.'

'Yes, but look at the image itself – torn from an old book –'

'So? Drusus Schoepfil has copied his uncle's esoteric habits –'

'Do *you* know the details of this story – *The Chemickal Marriage*?'

'Should I? My duties do not –'

Chang cut him off. 'Precisely the point. You know it exists, but only because of your master's interest.' Chang held up the paper. 'Schoepfil is no different. He knows the topic and pours himself into learning – from *books*. But the Comte d'Orkancz abandoned books to make his *own* versions – do you see? Schoepfil cannot know the Comte's vision of *The Chemickal Marriage*, because he cannot have seen the painting.'

Foison paused. 'And you have?'

'We all did – Svenson, Celeste Temple and myself. A memory from before the canvas burnt – preserved in blue glass.'

One of Foison's men hissed from the road ahead. Foison extended a palm so the man should wait, never taking his eyes from Chang. 'So you lied. Why raise the question now?'

Chang thrust the paper back at Foison. 'Because *this* is not from any book.'

A line of letters crossed the top and bottom of the image, so closely written as to appear decorative, like an engraved frame – yet without question recently added in the same black ink as the blindfold. Foison read the top line aloud. ' "Virgo Lucifera. No heart but goblet." ' He looked to Chang.

'In the Comte's painting,' Chang explained, 'there is no heart in a casket. The Executioner decapitates the Bride and Groom and their blood flows into a goblet. Don't you see? It's a message from someone who *does* know the painting, and who saw *me* in the foyer of Schoepfil's house. To anyone else the words are alchemical nonsense.'

'You believe Doctor Svenson inserted his own message into the one for Bronque?'

'Who else? That first line is to prove his identity to me. Now read the second.'

Foison rotated the page, for the letters on the lower edge had been written upside down. ' "Mother Child Heir . . . Virgin Lucifera . . . I'm sorry –" '

'The symbols!' Chang ran a finger along the text, as if he were schooling a child. ' "Mother Child Heir" is followed by two elemental signs taken from the Comte's work, for iron and wind. "Virgin Lucifera" is followed by signs for water and fire. Svenson had no time, so used code – look closely, It's not "Virgo" that's written but "Virgin". Virgin *and* Lucifera. *Two* people.'

Foison studied the paper, then nodded with an exasperated impatience at his own slow thinking. ' "Mother Child Heir" is Kraft, her son and Schoepfil. They are together, and – iron and wind – will travel to Harschmort by train. "Virgin" is Miss Temple, "Lucifera" the Contessa. Heat and water – since the Colonel is involved, this means the Royal Thermæ. Either they remain there in the Queen's protection –'

'Or?' asked Chang.

Foison returned the paper to his coat. 'Or the old stories are true.'

'What stories?'

Foison's face went still. Chang spun round to follow the man's gaze. The third green-coat, guarding their rear, was nowhere to be seen. How long had they been standing like fools?

With a drumming of boot steps, the darkness behind them filled with Bronque's grenadiers, bayonets fixed for silent work. Foison and Chang broke as one, waving the lead men on, racing blindly into the next intersection. A shot cracked out and the green-coat next to Chang staggered and fell.

The far end of the road had been blocked with overturned wagons. Chang ran towards them, weaving to present a shifting target, ready to hurl his body over the makeshift wall. More shots came from the soldiers, missing their mark but splintering the wagons.

The last green-coat reached the barrier first, caught hold and began to climb. As soon as his head cleared the wagon, a fist-sized lump of plaster potted him square on the ear. The man dropped hard to the cobbles. Chang and Foison veered, careening from both the bullets snapping around them and a hail of bricks and stones from the wagons – now topped by a line of angry faces.

He seized Foison's shoulder and they turned to see the crowd's fury directed at the grenadiers. How many errant bullets had torn into the unseen crowd? The grenadier lieutenant waved his sabre for order, but a brick struck the officer on the arm and his sabre rang on the stones. The soldiers answered with a ragged volley, plumes of smoke spitting forward. Another shower of stones. The Lieutenant flat on his face. From the wagons, shrieks –

Foison jerked free of Chang's grasp and ran. Chang followed, wondering what had happened to the world.

He caught an arm on a lamp-post and wheeled himself to a stop, ribs heaving. They had entered a warren of close lanes, but these were not streets simmering with discontent. Men in uniform stood scattered amongst the refugees, dismounted horsemen without their brass helmets, constables, even a priest, but no one claimed authority. Muskets cracked in the distance. A canopy of cloud hung over the city, its underside lit orange like an iron pot over a flame.

'Why do you stop?' called Foison.

Chang shook his head. These choked lanes led to the railway station. 'Stropping will be mobbed. And who's to say your master hasn't set off another device in the heart of it?'

Punctuating another grudging concession, Foison sniffed. 'Then what?'

'Schoepfil.'

'He has no army. He is but one clever man.'

'He may give us Svenson and Madelaine Kraft.'

'They are gone. More sensible to find Axewith – he can get us horses, escorts.'

'Schoepfil's house is on the way.'

A knot of children stared at them, two strangely dressed demons conversing under the lamp light. Foison grunted and reached into his coat. He flung a fistful of coins onto the paving. The children didn't move. Foison's flat nostrils flared at his useless gesture and he stalked off. Behind the children stood a fat man in a stained waistcoat with a heavy walking stick. Chang extended one arm and snapped his fingers. With a nervous nod the man offered up the stick – strong ash with a brass grip shaped like a bird. Foison glanced back, saw the weapon in his prisoner's hand, but continued on.

The cordon of soldiers had withdrawn, and with them the angry crowds, dispersing with the decision of Axewith and his engineers to abandon this district. The orange glow in the sky seemed no closer, but Chang wondered how many houses would survive the dawn. He snorted at the thought – that it had become a refrain – and focused his attention on the dark windows of Drusus Schoepfil's home.

'No one,' whispered Foison from the servant's lane behind. Chang followed to the rear door. The house had no rear garden or stable.

'No coach,' observed Chang.

'The allowance from Lord Vandaariff is small.'

'Why?'

'Schoepfil is Lady Vandaariff's nephew, no tie of blood.' Foison slipped a knife from his silk coat. 'Drusus Schoepfil is a parasite, his every gesture an imitation, of as little merit as a parrot's speech.'

'But if he has allied with more powerful –'

'*Allied.*' Foison spat the word. 'At a word from Lord Vandaariff each man would sprawl on his belly and beg.'

Foison wedged the knife in the lock, but Chang caught his arm. Foison twisted quickly and Chang released his grip, raising an open palm.

'Before we go in. The Royal Thermæ. You said the old stories might be true. What stories?'

'You're the native. I'm the monkey.'

'Don't be an ass. The Contessa and Miss Temple – where would they be?'

'With your old Queen, rotting in a pool.'

The discussion of Schoepfil had pricked Foison's loyalty back to prominence. Chang stepped back. The lock was as cheaply made as the rest of the house.

Having done his share of housebreaking, Chang was accustomed to inferring the character of a man from his furnishings, but the home of Drusus Schoepfil was as devoid of attachment as a hotel parlour. Foison lit a brace of candlesticks and passed one to Chang, who brought his to a mantelpiece topped with a line of identical Chinese jars, glazed with pagodas and bamboo. Likewise a case of silver showed no family pieces, only a tea service of middling value and cutlery purchased by lot.

The house was silent. Chang crossed to the foyer, smiling grimly at a viewhole behind a screen. Bronque's words – 'the woman and the black man were seen' – were spoken as a threat, but had been a warning from one ally to another, placing the decision of what to do next in Schoepfil's hands. Svenson must have watched from the window, but Chang discovered no sign of the Doctor's presence.

Deeper in the house they found a padlocked door. Foison passed his candlestick to Chang and drew a knife for each hand. The first kick rocked the bolts holding the padlock. The second sheared them from the frame.

'Worse than I'd feared,' Foison said quietly.

If the rest of the house adopted polite decor without feeling for use – for *life* – this inner room had been dedicated to another more strident imitation. Every inch of the wall was covered with alchemical scrawls, layered to create different shapes – flowers, bodies, planets – *almost* like one of the

Comte's canvases. But Chang had been to Harschmort, to Parchfeldt, and Schoepfil's room only made clear the actual *art* of the Comte's vision. This was the work of a schoolboy set to copy . . . markings of paint without passion, nothing insidious or disturbing or mad . . .

As Chang peered at an open mouth, the curving lips formed by an arching line of tiny glyphs, he thought of his conversation with Father Locarno, and *The Chemickal Marriage*. An alchemical narrative was less a story than a recipe: sequence, ingredients, actions. For the Comte, the art, the *grace* was all important – but was that, alchemically speaking, *necessary*? Granting any of this nonsense in the first place, did Schoepfil's vulgarity of vision make any difference if he had successfully captured the formula? With a growing chill, Chang wondered if Vandaariff's parasite nephew was unexpectedly dangerous?

'Schoepfil means to inherit more than his uncle's wealth,' he said. 'Alliances be damned, here is your enemy. You say he is no intimate of his uncle's. What of his uncle's associates – Francis Xonck or Harald Crabbé?'

'I have been gone these months. Not that I am aware.'

The words were an admission of neglect, and Chang sensed Foison's mind working, the urge to make up lost ground.

'What of Colonel Arthur Trapping?'

'A wholly negligible person.'

'Whose daughter's death was worth your sending a messenger.'

'I had standing orders –'

'And why was that?'

Foison's eyes loomed even blacker beyond the flickering candle. 'The approach of death is taken differently by each man. The actions of the powerful are naturally more . . . grandiose.'

'People are being sacrificed on its altar. That child. Lydia.' Chang rapped his stick against a lewdly painted rose. 'The girl had scarcely seven years.'

'Seven or seventy.' Foison walked from the ruined little room. 'Death is inevitable.'

They retraced their steps past the front parlour. Chang noticed a coat closet left ajar and looked to Foison before opening the door. He pushed the hanging coats aside with his stick to reveal the curled body of a soldier in green, bloodstained above the heart. The messenger sent to Vandaariff from the stable. Foison said nothing.

At a noise from outside both men blew out their candles. Foison peered through the slats of a wooden shutter. Abruptly Foison stalked to the foyer and wrenched open the door of Schoepfil's house, leaving it wide. In the shadows across the road loomed a band of tired refugees, who went still at the sound. When no one emerged from the house, a few of the braver souls crept forward. Foison retreated past Chang without a word, towards the rear door. The first of the crowd had reached the steps and begun to climb. Chang hurried after Foison.

'You're inviting them to loot the place.'

'I'm inviting them to do what they will.'

A hundred yards from Schoepfil's house Chang stopped. 'Enough of this wandering. Svenson's note gives us two choices – Schoepfil's train or the Contessa and Celeste Temple at Bathings.'

Foison glanced about with caution, but their immediate location, a modest, tree-lined lane, was silent. 'We cannot reach Stropping before Schoepfil leaves. The Contessa is long departed from Bathings. We have a third option –'

'Axewith?' Chang pointed with his stick to the west. 'The cordon has retreated beyond his command post. Given the fire's speed, we have little hope of finding him on foot before his place is abandoned once again.'

'We do not need the *man*,' countered Foison. 'If we walk north-east we will strike his troops, at which point Lord Vandaariff's name will get us transport.'

'It's no longer that simple.'

Foison gently shifted his stance. 'I thought you had agreed to come.'

Chang could not run. Foison would put a knife in his back – or more likely his leg – and drag him to the nearest horse. But Chang had come to his decision. He slipped into a defensive crouch. Foison drew two knives with an unpleasant ease.

'I will force you.'

'You will have to kill me. Perhaps you *can*, but it is against your orders. I, however, may kill *you* most freely.'

'You need me to reach Harschmort.'

'I disagree. And once I get there I will kill your master.'

'You won't get within ten yards of the door. How many men did Miss Temple send? How many dozens came from other rivals? Harschmort has changed. You *know* how they died.'

Chang extended the walking stick like a blade, the tip floating at the level of Foison's eyes. Foison sighed with impatience.

'This is madness.'

Chang feinted at Foison's abdomen, then swung the stick like a sabre blade, a cross-cut at the man's head. Foison deflected the blow with one knife, but his counter thrust was slow. They watched each other. Foison could not attack freely and risk the possibility of Chang's death, while Chang could attack and attack again, and finally – inevitably – strike home.

Foison retreated two steps. 'Stop this – I am willing to follow, as long as we leave. If you're not at Harschmort in time, Celeste Temple will be consumed.'

Chang advanced again, a jab to the face and then a swipe at Foison's knee. Foison parried, dodged, fell back.

'She'll be consumed anyway. You know full well.'

'I have no idea.'

'You lie.'

With a swift motion Chang cracked the haft of the stick across Foison's wrist and one knife clattered to the road. Foison brought the wrist to his mouth with a hiss, and fell back. Chang scooped up the knife, a weapon now in each hand. Foison flipped his remaining knife in the air and caught it by the tip, ready to throw.

'You change nothing. She *will* die.'

'She *shouldn't*.'

'We are all tested.' Foison's voice dropped to a whisper. 'And if I kill you here and now . . . so be it.'

Foison whipped back his arm and threw. Chang dived, taking the cobbles on his shoulder. He felt a sting at his hip, but Foison – still seeking to wound instead of kill – had missed. Chang rolled up, slashing the stick across the empty hands that reached to take him. Foison hissed at the pain, yanking both hands back as Chang lunged and stuck the knife into Foison's thigh. Chang brought the walking stick down hard on Foison's head. Foison fell and lay still.

The knife had pierced his coat, but the point had gone wide, scarcely a prick. Chang tucked a knife into his belt and glanced at Foison's wound. He would live. Chang began to run.

It was half a mile before he found the cordon: exhausted militiamen doing their best to tend to those displaced – handing out blankets and serving soup from a makeshift canteen. He presented himself to a weary subaltern as an emissary of the Church and was passed through. Soon Chang was running again, angling away from where he'd been directed – if Foison did attempt to follow, Axewith would appear to have been Chang's goal – and towards the train.

Not Stropping Station – there Foison had been right. The place would be a madhouse. But he recalled Foison's suggestion that Bronque post men beyond Stropping on the route to the Orange Canal. Now, because of Foison, Schoepfil would make his transit safely under the protection of the Colonel's men.

At the next checkpoint, further from the chaos, the troops again fed refugees from steaming pots suspended over open fires. He passed in easily, trading on the Archbishop's name to request transport. A sergeant directed him to a line of people pressing similar claims of urgency. He stood behind a dishevelled older man and woman, their rich clothing spoilt by soot and water. The woman's pleasure to see a churchman was visibly curdled by the Monsignor's scars.

'A terrible night,' she managed.

'We must reach our home,' explained her husband, shifting to maintain his place in line ahead of Chang. 'The grandchildren. The horses.'

Chang craned his head to the front. Despite there being any number of apparently free vehicles, no one moved. With a sigh of disgust he strode forward.

'We have to wait!' cried the old woman.

'Take us with you!' pleaded the husband.

Their calls caught the attention of others as Chang advanced, like a match to a trail of powder, igniting shouts of protest at his refusal to wait and calls of support from those attaching their frustration to his own.

Chang cared only that no one blocked his way – that they'd remained docile for this long showed how little destruction this crowd had really seen. At the head of the queue stood a major of engineers, looking up from a folding field table of maps at the growing cries. The weary officer raised his hoarse voice for everyone to hear. 'A system is in place, without favouritism – if you would just go back to your place –'

'I have urgent word for the Archbishop.'

The Major pointed with his stylus. 'And *that* man for the Admiralty, and *that* man for the Ministries, and *that* man for Lord Robert Vandaariff himself – unfortunately, everyone must wait.'

'Those coaches are unused.'

'They may be required.' The Major waved unhappily to his soldiers. 'Kindly escort the Monsignor –'

'That would be a mistake.' Chang spoke coldly enough to give the soldiers pause. He turned to a man the Major had indicated, fat-faced and fair-haired, laden with several bulging satchels. 'Your errand is with Robert Vandaariff?'

'I beg your pardon?' stammered the man.

'His errand is none of your –'

Chang's walking stick slammed like a shot on the folding table, directly between the engineer's two hands.

'What is your *name*?' Chang demanded, ignoring how his action had stunned everyone within earshot to stillness.

'Trooste.' The fair man's hesitation set a wobble to his chin. 'Augustus Trooste, Professor of Chemical Science, Royal Institute.'

Chang let his expression curl to a knowing sneer. 'Is that so?'

'It is! My research – to Lord Vandaariff, is of the *highest* –'

'When did you last see Madelaine Kraft?'

Professor Trooste blanched, swallowed, rallied. 'Why, whoever is that?'

Chang laughed aloud at the lie. The trade between the Institute and the

Old Palace was so thick that no resident scholar, whether he partook of her wares or no, could be ignorant of the woman who was its mistress.

'You'll come with me.'

'To the Archbishop?' protested Trooste, even as he bent awkwardly for his papers. 'But I have told you —'

Chang leant over the engineer's table, speaking low. 'Robert Vandaariff clings to life. The explosion at the Customs House – the news has been suppressed, but he will die tonight. His bequest of aid to the city has not been signed. He has no heir. Do you understand what that will mean to the city if his offer becomes swallowed in legal wrangling?'

'But – how does the Archbishop —'

'Who do you think arranged it to begin with? This man'– Trooste had joined him, breathing hard from the weight of the satchels – 'may be able to extend Lord Vandaariff's life. Can't you, Professor? If the matter is *blue glass*?'

Trooste baulked again, his shock evident, but the engineer, aware that the decision lay beyond his care, only shouted over his shoulder: 'Two to pass. A damned dog-cart if you've got it!' He glared sourly at Chang. 'All blessings on your task.'

Not a dog-cart, but small enough, a two-wheeled gig, given over at the soldiers' insistence by its whey-faced owner, who demanded – and was denied – an official chit to mark his property's requisition. Trooste drove, satchels crammed under the seat, as Chang, town-born and ever poor, had no skill with horses. He knew the city, however, and directed Trooste down unobtrusive roads where they made good time. The Professor was hardly calm in Chang's menacing presence, however, and it was minutes before he attempted conversation.

'Will we really go to Harschmort House? It seems cruel to the horse.'

'It's a cruel night,' Chang replied. 'Turn left.'

'But that takes us away from —'

'*Turn*.'

Trooste guided the trap into an unpaved lane. 'So, the Archbishop's own messenger —'

'The Archbishop can go hang. Do you know how Mrs Kraft was restored to her mind?'

Trooste stammered at the directness of the question, but then accepted he was not up to the task of duplicity. 'As a matter of fact I do.'

'Was it you or Svenson?'

'Well, I do not flatter myself —'

'Or the child?'

'What child?'

'The one who's *dead*, Professor.' Chang turned in his seat, making sure they'd not been followed. 'Left again.'

Trooste did so with some skill, for the road was littered with refuse that might well have broken a wheel. Chang wondered at the man's origins. Had he grown up with money, a horse-cart of his own, books and telescopes to feed his hungry mind? Judging by his modestly cut coat, that comfort had gone – gambled away? – though an attending air of privilege remained.

'Lord Vandaariff has not sent for you at all.'

'But he *will* see me.' Trooste beamed with confidence. 'He will want to hear what has been achieved – the actions of his enemies –'

'You mean Svenson.'

'Indeed I do.' Trooste shivered. 'A terrible figure. You should have seen that poor child writhe! *She* guided the machines – you guessed it, I don't know how – and the stench, the bile, like coal tar filling her mouth –' Trooste waved his hands at the memory, then immediately lunged back to recover the reins.

'Dreadful,' he muttered, 'simply *dreadful!*'


As the tale came out, Chang perceived the cruelty of the Doctor's dilemma: how to save Madelaine Kraft without destroying the child. Svenson had failed – or had acted with a coldness of which Chang had not thought him capable . . . yet who knew Svenson's mind or manner now? The horses of grief drove each man down a different, darkened path.

'We fled our separate ways in the fire, and that was the last I saw of them.' The Professor raised both eyebrows. 'That German is a madman, you know. A *killer*.'

'He refrained from killing you.'

'Not from kindness!' Trooste gave Chang a sidelong, crafty glance. 'You know, I think you want to see Robert Vandaariff as much as I – and intend that *I* shall get *you* through the gates with my treasure house of news!'

Trooste chuckled and went so far as to slap Chang's knee. Chang caught the hand as he might snatch a horsefly from the air.

'Tell me about Vandaariff's *new* glass. The different colours.'

'I'm sure I've no idea –'

Chang squeezed, grinding the bones. Trooste grimaced, and Chang released the hand, the puffy flesh pink where he had gripped it. Trooste worked his fingers, chastened, but his eyes remained bright. Usually force and pain were all that was necessary to contain a man unused to violence, but Trooste was more resilient.

'So that's where we sit, then? I had hoped for a more collegial –'

'Then do not *lie*. The different colours. Each with different alchemical properties.'

'Alchemical?' Trooste's sly look had returned. 'Surely *you* don't credit such nonsense?'

'I am not Lord Vandaariff.'

Trooste laughed. 'But that is just his genius! For every mention of alchemy, planets and spheres – the metaphorical brushstrokes, if you will –'

'Metaphorical horse droppings.'

'You may well say, but the science at play is as sound as a *bell*.'

'So. The coloured glass cards. What is their purpose?'

'No purpose at all!' Trooste insisted. 'Experiments in smelting, nothing more. The primary component of each card remains indigo clay –'

'But they are not infused with memory.'

'No! Each card is an amalgam of indigo clay with a different metal –'

'Why? Why *alchemically*?'

Trooste did not hear the question, for his attention had been taken by Chang's face. Chang wiped at his cheek, wondering if he'd been splashed with Foison's blood.

Trooste bit his plump lower lip, and dropped his voice to an eager whisper. 'My Lord, I'd no idea. And – sweet mercy – where is it *installed*?'

Chang seized the reins and pulled. Trooste fought to keep them – to keep the gig from spilling – but the horse came to a stop without incident.

'Of all the reckless – you could have broken our necks!'

'How the nation would mourn. Get out.' Chang reached beneath the seat and hurled one of the Professor's satchels to the street.

'What are you doing? I'm coming with you – you need me!'

Chang threw another satchel – aiming for the fetid gutter but landing short. Trooste lunged to stop him. Chang shoved him hard in the chest.

'Get *down*.'

The Professor did so, an awkward scramble as the final satchel struck the road. Chang vaulted down after him and walked off quickly. Trooste gathered his burdens and hurried to follow.

'But our gig! Someone will steal it!'

'Let them.'

'My papers are heavy!'

Chang called over his shoulder. 'Then let them burn.'

Trooste caught up at the corner, red-faced and gasping. 'You're a lunatic!'

'Is that so?' Chang gazed at the Professor over the rim of his spectacles. 'You see, I *know* Robert Vandaariff, and knew the Comte d'Orkancz before him even better.'

'You knew the Comte d'Orkancz?' Trooste's voice rose, like a dreamy imperialist speaking of Napoleon.

'I put a sabre through his guts.'

The Professor hitched his bundles higher on his chest. 'You are *not* a priest.'

Chang laughed and walked on. Trooste glanced back to the gig as they rounded the corner, the horse waiting docile in the empty street.

'Lord above!'

To Trooste's credit, the outburst was not so fearful as grim. Before them stood the Crampton Place railway station, the platform packed with so many waiting travellers that they spilled into the lane. Chang saw neither Foison's green-coats nor Bronque's grenadiers . . .

'We will never get through,' huffed Trooste. 'We should go back to the horse before it's taken.'

'One horse cannot get us there in time. You said it yourself.'

'In time for *what*?'

Chang stopped cold. Trooste slammed into his back and cursed as a satchel tumbled to the ground.

'Leave it!' Chang set off. '*Hurry.*'

'I cannot leave it! O damn you – will you not wait?'

Chang ignored him, sure of what he'd just seen. He plucked a satchel from Trooste's grasp and thrust it ahead, a battering ram to reach an alley that ran parallel to the rails.

Trooste gestured over his shoulder. 'Is not the platform *behind* us?'

Chang pointed the walking stick. Trooste extended his bulging neck to look – why did such men so often opt for constrictive garments? At the end of the alley, in a gap between tar-shingled shacks, appeared a squat line of green – rushes along the trackside . . . and through them came another wink of orange.

At the final shack, Chang knelt to wait. A far-off wail. The train.

'Who is the man in orange?' asked Trooste. 'A friend?'

'No. If he sees us, he may attack. You should flee.'

'Not you?'

Chang smiled. 'Let us say we share an outstanding wager.'

The train wheezed into Crampton Place like a massive metal ox, overburdened but stoic. A bell sounded from the station house and the air erupted with the tumult of hundreds attempting to board. Chang counted twenty carriages in all – a long train, extended to answer the fleeing crowds – and watched as Jack Pfaff broke from his hiding place and ran straight for the brake van. Chang slapped Trooste's arm and made for the nearest carriage, third from the rear. He vaulted the steps into the vestibule and brusquely pulled Trooste up. He whipped aside the curtain to the baggage compartment. 'Stay here.'

Trooste peered past Chang down the corridor. 'While you do what?'

'No.' Chang pushed Trooste into the compartment and whisked the curtain shut.

'What if this wager of yours goes sour?' protested Trooste. 'Where am I?'

'On a train to Harschmort, as you wanted. Don't make any noise.'

At the corridor's end he turned in time to see Trooste's head duck from sight. Chang sighed – there was nothing to be done about it now – and stepped through.

At a flash of white he raised his stick, blocking a forearm reaching for his neck, and dodged the other way, into the arms of a second waiting man. A hard elbow and this second man's grip gave way, and Chang chopped the walking stick into the first man's face, knocking him back on his heels. The man overbalanced, his back to the open boarding staircase. Chang thrust the stick into Michel Gorine's grasping hands, and retrieved him before he could topple out under the iron wheels. Behind Chang, Mr Cunsher exhaled painfully and rubbed his abdomen.

'A pair of fools!' Chang shouted over the noise of the wheels. Gorine jabbed his hand towards the rear of the train with the subtlety of a puppet show.

'Jack Pfaff! I know!' Chang waved them closer so as not to shout. 'Have you followed him, or were you on the train already?'

'From the Thermæ,' replied Cunsher. 'He hasn't seen us. No idea of his intentions.'

'Have you seen Celeste?' The question sparked an apprehensive look between the men. '*Tell* me.'

'Beg pardon – the noise is impossible . . .' Cunsher put his mouth to Chang's ear and with characteristic efficiency related his progress since Chang had thrown the rock at Pfaff in the square: following Pfaff, eventually to the Thermæ, Miss Temple's freeing of Gorine, Cunsher's intention to follow Pfaff, Miss Temple's wilful disappearance.

'We did not realize she was gone until it was too late, yet, with Pfaff likely to reunite with his patroness, he seemed actually the surest way to locate the young lady.'

'Headstrong idiot,' muttered Chang.

'Never met a creature like her,' agreed Gorine. '*Barking.*'

His smile of agreement wilted before Chang's grim stare.

'Resourceful young lady,' observed Cunsher.

Gorine nodded with vigour, then – wanting to appear useful – craned his

head to make sure no one was coming to disturb them, only to realize that
Cunsher and Chang had each already positioned their bodies to watch the
corridor without being seen. Gorine pulled back, chagrined. He smoothed
the lank hair from his eyes. Chang said nothing to alleviate the man's discomfort. How many times in the perfumed parlours of the Old Palace
had Michel Gorine kept him at bay, sending Angelique off with another
customer?

'What do you know of Drusus Schoepfil?' Chang asked.

'Vandaariff's nephew and heir,' replied Cunsher, as if it were a common
fact. 'Apparently *he* questioned Miss Temple at the Thermæ –'

'Wait!' Gorine cried. 'In the Old Palace, Bronque always had another man
with him – they used our tunnel to the Institute – we thought he was some
minor royal.'

'He'd be flattered to hear it,' said Chang. 'But it is with Drusus Schoepfil
that Madelaine Kraft has sought protection.'

'Impossible! They ransacked the Old Palace! Bronque nearly broke my
jaw!'

'She's a pragmatic woman.' Chang gripped Gorine's arm. 'What would
she offer Schoepfil in return?'

'Information about his uncle?' ventured Cunsher.

Gorine shook his head. 'Robert Vandaariff never went near the Old
Palace.'

Not Vandaariff, Chang realized, yet how many times had Mrs Kraft hosted
the Comte d'Orkancz? *Those* were the secrets to tempt Schoepfil . . . and
perhaps to fuel her own revenge.

He took hold of a wall bracket and swung his body down the open stairs,
face into the wind. Packington Station would not be far. Would Pfaff leave
the train? Would the Contessa board it? He pulled himself inside. 'In the
next baggage compartment you will find Professor Trooste, late of the Royal
Institute –'

'Augustus Trooste!' spat Gorine. 'That shameless fat sponge –'

'He was present at Mrs Kraft's restoration, and may be able to help. Hide
him. I will tackle Pfaff.'

'Is that wise?' asked Cunsher. 'If we interrupt his plans –'

'You mean if I kill him?' Chang reached for the door. 'I'll find you as soon as I can.'

'And if you don't?' asked Cunsher.

'Acquit yourselves well,' Chang replied. 'It's the end of the world, after all.'

He entered the rearmost carriage to find Jack Pfaff, in his orange coat and chequered trousers, slouched against the far door. Pfaff held up a finger for silence, and pointed to the line of compartments that lay between them. In spite of their earlier provocations Pfaff's sharp face showed a smile, as if they were allies, or at least men who shared a common goal.

Chang began to walk, stick held ready. He glanced into the first compartment: six men of business, cases gripped across their laps. Pfaff ambled forward as well, hands empty. Chang reached the second compartment: women of differing ages and too many children. The youngest boy lay cradled across the lap of a dark-skinned maid, his legs wrapped with bandages.

Pfaff came nearer. The third compartment held at least ten people, women in the seats and men standing. The curtains on the fourth compartment door were drawn. Pfaff halted at its other side, perhaps ten feet away.

'Joined the clergy, I see.'

'Where is she, Jack?'

'Which *she* do you mean?' Pfaff nodded at the walking stick. 'No room to swing. You're hampered.'

'Do you think?' Chang took a sudden step forward. Pfaff just as quickly fell back, though his teasing smile remained.

'Go in.' Pfaff's gaze darted past Chang, to the end of the corridor. 'While there's time.'

'You coming in with me?'

'I'll wait. Following instructions.'

'You always do, don't you, Jack? Until you stop following them.'

Pfaff's lips split in a childish grin. '*Precisamente.*'

Chang rapped the head of his walking stick against the fourth compartment door and entered. The occupants looked up, but Chang paid them no mind, stepping quickly from the doorway. He did not put it past Pfaff to have a pistol and fire through the glass. But no shot came. Chang glanced at Madelaine Kraft, then at Mahmoud, whose hand made a polished revolver look like a toy. The third man he did not know, crowded in the opposite row of seats, between boxes tied with rope.

'That is Mr Kelling,' explained Mrs Kraft.

'You're Cardinal Chang!' The angular Kelling pushed himself back into his seat, all elbows and knees. He wore the clothes of a clerk, but there was a bandage around his wrist and a deepening bruise across his jaw.

'Difficult day all round,' observed Chang; then to Mahmoud, at the window: '*Sit.*'

'Not while you –'

Before Mahmoud could finish Chang's hand was around Madelaine Kraft's throat. 'Sit or we'll start settling things the wrong way.'

'Mahmoud . . .' Mrs Kraft said gently. The dark man shoved the pistol into a pocket of his long coat and perched on the very edge of his seat, poised to fling himself onto Chang. Kelling did not stir. Chang released his grip. Mrs Kraft stretched her neck and studied Chang. He found the scrutiny unwelcome.

'Robert Vandaariff will die,' he announced, 'but without care his death will only deliver his world, everyone's world, to idiot children. Your desire for revenge risks disaster.'

Madelaine Kraft raised her eyebrows at his hard tone. 'You've changed.'

'Not at all. You no longer have anything I want.'

'I don't have the *same* thing.'

Chang let this go; there wasn't time. 'Tell me what you've planned with Schoepfil.'

She smiled at him. 'Who is that?'

'Are you so confident?' Chang asked. 'You were cast into a pit, and saved by the rarest chance.'

'Which is why –'

'Why you should realize your enemy is as strong as ever – no, far stronger, with the wealth of the world to ensure his safety. He searches for you, even now. Recovery makes you an especially rare species, to be displayed in a jar of spirits, post-dissection.'

'Take him in hand!' Mr Kelling whispered to Mahmoud. 'He is vital to Lord Vandaariff's plans!'

Chang slapped the metal head of the cane into a box, just wide of Kelling's hand. Kelling yanked the hand into his lap.

'Bronque and Schoepfil ransacked the Old Palace today,' Chang said. 'Michel Gorine is not two carriages away, beaten to pieces – he will gladly inform you of your error.'

Mahmoud made to stand, but Mrs Kraft only tilted her head. 'Michel's opinion is not mine and never was.'

'How did you sway Schoepfil?' Chang demanded. 'What do you know about the Comte?'

'Vandaariff is our enemy, Cardinal, and you need my help as much as ever. Each man braces his fear against his love. What you love may change. But if you love still, your fear remains.'

'Where is Michel?' asked Mahmoud. 'How badly is he hurt?'

Chang leant close to Mrs Kraft. 'I have seen it now dozens of times, people who think they can enter this arena and remain unscathed –'

'But I *don't* think that,' replied Madelaine Kraft. 'And I am not *unscathed* – any more than you. Lord Vandaariff's own ticking clock.'

Chang prevented himself from slapping her face. When he looked up – when he had controlled his rage – he saw Mahmoud on his feet with the pistol in hand.

'I saw her die,' Chang said to them both. 'I felt Angelique's mind. You gave her to him. If you think I do not blame you – if you think I will forget it – you are wrong. And if you think, whatever happens at Harschmort House, that I will lift a finger to save your cold-minded souls, you could not be more deluded.'

Chang turned for the door, then spun round, slashing Mahmoud's weapon to the floor. The dark man clutched his wrist.

'I have done this,' whispered Chang. 'I know. *This* was your one chance. It's gone.'

Upon exiting the compartment Chang once more darted to the side of the glass, but no bullet came. Pfaff smiled at Chang's seemingly unnecessary movement.

'And Mrs Kraft reckoned such a smart one. Well, she'll be dead again soon enough. Us too, unless we leg it. Come.'

Pfaff retreated down the corridor. At its end he hopped the coupling to the small brake van. In a corner, atop a trunk, sat a bent fellow in overalls, his lank greying hair like last year's rotten straw. With the coupling separating the brake van from the final carriage, there was no chance of being overheard.

'This is Downie,' said Pfaff, 'an old friend who permits my trespass.' Downie did not seem to hear. 'This is Cardinal Chang. Don't cross him, he's a hard one.'

Downie blinked his dull eyes and swallowed. An opium eater.

'We're nearly to Packington,' said Chang. 'The train will be crawling with soldiers.'

'Already is, in front.'

'What's your errand, Jack? You mentioned orders.'

'And betray a client's trust?' Before Chang could advance, Pfaff shook his head. 'You never did keep an ounce of humour.'

'You took her money. You broke your bond.'

'*Bond*. You have no idea what I have done, nor does she.' Pfaff's eyes gleamed. 'And nor does *she*, either.'

'You're a fool to cross either of those women, Jack. And a fool to cross me.'

'But I haven't! We're here, aren't we? What else would Miss Temple desire?'

'And today with that goblin of a doctor?'

'What else do you expect? If I am to play a part –'

'You're a liar.'

'I am not!' Pfaff sighed, like an actress preparing to sing. 'How can I convince you?'

'You tracked the Contessa from the bankside to the Seventh Bridge – you presented yourself, she enlisted you to her side –'

'She *believes* so.'

'And what do *you* believe, Jack? That you can find your own path? Against Robert Vandaariff? Against *her*?'

But at his hard tone Pfaff went cold. No matter where Pfaff's loyalty truly stood, jealousy formed a barrier he would never see beyond. Chang tried another tack. 'Two of the men you hired for Miss Temple disappeared at Harschmort. One died in St Isobel's Square wearing an explosive waist-coat – perhaps the other was shredded at the Cathedral. Vandaariff has turned Harschmort into a fortress. Obviously Bronque believes he can force an entrance with his men –'

Pfaff tossed his head. '*Bronque.*'

Chang was painfully aware of time. 'Jack, we reach Packington in minutes.'

Pfaff threw a knowing smile to Downie, whose gaze had not shifted from the floorboards, and then, as if this much delay had made his point, nodded agreeably. 'Right. You were exchanged for Miss Temple because he knew the Contessa would keep Miss Temple safe, and he'd get another crack at them both.'

'But why would the Contessa keep Miss Temple *safe?*'

'Why do cats play with mice before they dine?'

'Is that something you memorized from a play?' The words came out sharpened by impatience. Chang wanted to knock Pfaff to the floor and kick him to tears, yet whatever errand Pfaff had been charged with by the Contessa might well make the difference to Miss Temple's survival. Chang was stranded between enemies over which he'd no control.

And what did Chang have to match them? His own strength. The knowledge of Trooste, the hope that Gorine could sway Mrs Kraft – or Mahmoud – to sense, and the intelligence of Cunsher to get each to the right place when their skills might make a difference. But *every* arrow of antagonism streaking towards Harschmort must be allowed to continue its flight if there was a chance that Vandaariff and his works would be destroyed.

That the effort would cost his own life, Chang accepted, and with that acceptance felt a pang of such regret, such sorrow, that, still facing Pfaff in the swaying, crowded little car, Chang shut his eyes and sighed. Whatever impossible notions he might this day alone have begun to entertain would remain just that – phantoms, dreams.

'Listen to me,' he repeated. 'Whatever your errand – whatever you carry, whatever she's told you to do – I don't give a damn. I won't stop you –'

'No, you won't,' retorted Pfaff in a tight voice.

'But if you harm Celeste, Jack, I will kill you. I won't stop until I do.'

'*Celeste*, is it?' Pfaff met Chang's implacable gaze. 'Well, you're finished. Everyone knows it.'

'I may be.' Chang voice was soft. 'But I've *seen* the painting, Jack. He'll kill Celeste. And the Contessa too, whatever she believes.'

Chang opened the door, then called back above the racket of the wheels. Pfaff – and, strangely, Downie – listened with a fearful expectation. 'He'll kill us all.'

The corridor remained empty of soldiers. Chang strode past Mrs Kraft's compartment in time to hear the whistle. Packington Station. The platform was as crowded as Crampton Place, but fronted by a line of midnight-blue, Bronque's grenadiers.

The train came to a halt with a great hiss of steam. Chang leapt out and rolled beneath the carriage. He hauled himself onto the steel cross-braces, kicking his legs over and through. He positioned his hips on the cross-point and wedged the walking stick between the iron posts to support his shoulders, then extended a limb in each direction, along the struts.

The whistle echoed down the track bed and the train resumed its motion. At each station Chang relaxed his arms and legs, working the joints, careful not to let them hang where they might be seen by any passing eye. He heard Bronque's soldiers calling out, making sure no unknown persons gained access. That someone had already done so did not occur.

The only exception was Raaxfall. The Raaxfall Station had been burnt.

At last they reached Orange Locks, where the Colonel and his men would disembark. Chang remembered Foison's words: good men had attempted to reach Harschmort in stealth, only to be taken or killed. The surest way to reach Robert Vandaariff was to let Colonel Bronque clear the path.

Around him rose the shouts of men – orders to form up, whistles. Chang crawled between the wheels, away from the station, and rolled down a slope of gravel, out of sight. The whistle sounded and the train churned on. Chang scrambled up and lay flat in the cover of the rails. A company of grenadiers, at least a hundred men, formed ranks in the station courtyard.

Colonel Bronque trotted down the steps to join them. Chang traced Bronque's path backwards to the station house in time to see Madelaine Kraft make a dignified if fragile exit, supported by Mahmoud. Bronque's shouting, detailing men to stack wooden crates into a waiting wagon, brought his attention back to the courtyard. In the wagon stood Mr Kelling.

The rear red lantern of the train had passed from sight. Was Pfaff still aboard? Chang loped to the station and heaved himself onto the platform. He reached the station wall in a rush, his back flat against the brick. He peeked once in the window, then crept to the door.

He slipped out Foison's knife and burst inside. The nearest grenadier took the blade across his throat. The second soldier raised his rifle to fire, but Chang slashed it away with the stick and drove the knife into the grenadier's chest. On a bench, bound and gagged in a row, sat Cunsher, Gorine and Trooste. Chang yanked the rag from Cunsher's mouth and sawed through the rope around his wrists.

'They are marshalled for an assault on Harschmort.' Chang moved to Trooste. 'We have little time.'

Trooste spat a loose thread from his mouth. 'I have never experienced such cruelty –'

'The night is young,' muttered Chang. He slipped the tip of the knife between Gorine's wrists and ripped upwards, shearing the hemp, and left Gorine to extract his own gag.

'She did not listen, did she?'

Gorine's eyes were rimmed red. Chang returned to the door, peering out. The first soldier's guttural exhalations had finally ceased.

Cunsher cleared his throat. 'But she *did* listen, Chang, that is the painful fact. She knows who Bronque is, and Schoepfil – men who ought not hold the trust of a tea kettle, much less the secrets of indigo clay. She does not care.'

'She thinks it better.' Gorine wiped his lips on his sleeve. 'They will fall more easily in their turn.'

'Mrs Kraft was never so ambitious,' said Chang.

'No.' Gorine's voice had thickened. 'I did not know her.'

'What's natural is rarely kind.' Professor Trooste rubbed at the hemp strands stuck to his soft wrists. He met their inquiring faces with a shrug. 'Growth accelerates. Four cells become eight, eight become sixteen . . . in an instant there are thousands. Is it not the same with *licence*?'

No one spoke. Cunsher brushed Gorine's shoulder. 'That he could not act now does not mean he cannot soon. His mind is not hers. You know it.'

Gorine smiled weakly. 'So does she.'

The noise from the courtyard abruptly died. Something had happened that Bronque did not expect, but from his vantage Chang could see only the bearskin hats of the rearmost men.

'Arm yourselves. If I don't return, proceed as you can.'

'And Pfaff?' Cunsher passed a grenadier's bayonet to Gorine.

'He claims to still serve Miss Temple.'

Cunsher caught his moustache with his front teeth. 'The night will be full of fools.'

Chang slipped out, keeping low. Bronque's grenadiers were formed into neat lines. In front stood Bronque and his adjutants. Mrs Kraft sat with the wagon driver, while Mahmoud and Kelling perched amongst the crates, yet everyone's attention was focused on an elegant coach just entering the courtyard.

The coachman's face floated above his black livery. He rode alone in his seat, driving a team of four at an easy pace. A grenadier adjutant waved him to halt, and, in a confident gesture of compliance, the coachman veered his team into a sweeping curve, so the coach stopped directly in front of the adjutant with the horses facing back where they had come.

Two grenadiers moved to the bridles of the lead horses. The coachman paid no mind and tipped his black peaked cap to the officers.

'Good evening, sir! Is it Colonel Bronque? I am sent by Lord Vandaariff, who expects you.' The coachman turned his gaze to the lines of soldiers with an apologetic smile. 'Perhaps not expecting so very many, of course. I can only fit four, sir. Six if you're willing to squeeze.'

Cunsher, now carrying a carbine, joined Chang, the others close behind. Chang saw the logic – with every eye on the coach, this was the time to move.

He waved them to a line of scrub that would offer cover, but did not yet follow.

'If you'll come with me now,' continued the coachman, 'ample provision will be made for your men when they arrive. It is a march of perhaps two miles –'

'I am aware of the distance.' Bronque gestured with a pair of thin leather gloves – as if their softness made his intentions seem more civilized. 'You are Lord Vandaariff's servant – no harm will come, no charges laid to your name – do you understand, you will not *hang* – if you cooperate.'

The coachman's polite expression froze. 'I beg your pardon –'

'You will descend and describe every measure Lord Vandaariff has taken to secure Harschmort House. How many men, their placement, what weapons –'

The coachman stammered on his box, looking around him, though no assistance lay in sight. 'I – I assure you, sir, I know nothing – only Mr Foison –'

'And where *is* Mr Foison?'

'I had been told to expect him with you! Along with Mr Schoepfil –'

Bronque smiled. 'Doubly misinformed. Come, you have driven your team through gates and past guard posts –'

'But Colonel – are you Lord Robert's *enemy?*'

Bronque signalled for a soldier to bring down the coachman . . . yet the coach rocked ever so gently an instant *before* the first grenadier started his climb to the driving box. Before Chang could make sense of what he'd seen, the driver whipped out a pistol and put two shots into the grenadier. He furiously slashed the reins. The horses leapt to motion, kicking past their minders. Bronque began to shout, echoed by every officer and sergeant. The entire front rank of grenadiers shouldered their weapons and aimed for the departing coach –

The simplicity of the plan took Chang aback. In the split second before he'd flung himself face down he saw through the misdirection, how every eye's placement on the coach meant no one noticed the man behind it – the passenger whose exit from the coach's far side had caused the rocking Chang had seen: a man – no doubt the last of Miss Temple's missing hirelings – whose torso bulged with another explosive harness.

The passenger, suddenly revealed as the coach surged away, stood not ten yards from the heart of the massed grenadiers. He reached into his coat with both hands. Only then did Colonel Bronque see, far too late, and his scream of warning vanished in an unearthly roar.

Chang stumbled to the thicket of scrub. The entire night sky seemed to echo with shrieks and moans. He met the astonished faces of the others but angrily drove them on. 'Go! Go!'

'But what *happened*?' asked Gorine.

Chang caught Gorine's arm. 'They are alive. The wagon was too far away. *Run*.'

Only after fifty yards did Chang allow a look back. The Orange Canal Station was dotted with flame, even its shingled roof set alight.

Chang had glimpsed only a flattened mass, and enough bodies to turn a slaughterman's stomach. How many had been left standing – even as Vandaariff's damned coach rattled into the distance – perhaps three men in ten? But Chang had not lied to Gorine. The wagon, well off to one side, was intact, and its occupants apparently unhurt. As for Bronque . . . where the Colonel had stood was a seething heap.

In a stroke every contingency had changed. Chang had counted on Bronque's men forcing an entrance to Harschmort. He considered doubling back to join forces – and felt Gorine's pressing gaze silently urging that very path – but rejected the idea. The soldiers still standing would be only too delighted to find new targets on whom to vent their wrath. And Chang had already given Mrs Kraft her chance. He was damned if he would save her now.

They walked without the benefit of stars or moon. The chaos of the station gave way to rustling grass and the squelch of muddy fields. Trooste kept up a low litany of dismay, blundering into the muck and standing water the others always managed to avoid.

'Lost your papers, I see,' observed Chang.

Trooste looked up with a sour expression, balanced on one foot as he shook its dripping mate. 'Not lost at all! *Taken!*'

Chang looked at Cunsher, who scratched an ear by way of apology. 'The Professor's attempt to protect his possessions may have encouraged their confiscation.'

'And where are they now?' Trooste asked the meadow at large. 'Those papers were our only safeguard –'

'*Stop*,' said Chang. '*Listen*.'

Trooste paused, then turned to the sound. 'Is it *music*?'

The low grass would not hide them. Chang broke into a run. Twenty sodden yards brought an unpaved road. He vaulted the ditch at its edge and waved the others across, risking a look in the direction of the station. Led by a line of torches, a body of grenadiers gave full-throated voice to a regimental song of blood:

> Grind each foe beneath our heel
> Whenever duty calls
> Blood and iron, shot and steel
> Until the last man falls

Beyond the road the land grew sandy, rising to dunes. The grenadiers marched nearer, the crash of their boots like a bass drum to their song. The brazen advance – announcing their presence without care – spoke to a dark resolve. Once more Chang had no desire to be its object. The grass fell away, a slight depression but enough. He dropped flat and the others followed. Chang slid off his spectacles – the lenses would reflect the torchlight – and raised his head.

The Queen's elite regiment had been transformed to a medieval *danse macabre*, with every man – most showing visible wounds – bearing the weight of his own doom. Chang had not considered the screams and shouting that had followed the blast – he had been too busy gathering the others – but now he shuddered. These survivors had not been touched by the explosion. Their injuries were more cruel: suffered at the hands of comrades deranged by glass spurs. How many of their own had they been forced to put down like rabid dogs? A deadly bitterness constricted every face.

In front of the ragged column – Chang counted thirty men – marched

Colonel Bronque, bareheaded, gold brocade in tatters, left arm in a sling, singing louder than anyone. Bringing up the rear came the wagon, with Mrs Kraft, Mahmoud and Kelling. Chang ducked away from Mahmoud's higher vantage, and waited a full minute before risking another look. The column had passed like a funeral cortège into the darkness, the death song's echo like a trail of black crêpe.

Chang restored his glasses. 'We can follow at a distance on the road, but risk being caught up in their collision with Vandaariff.'

'Likely another blast,' said Cunsher.

'They're going to die,' said Gorine miserably. 'Every one of them.'

'Or we continue over open ground,' Chang continued. 'Easy enough to walk, but the closer we come to Harschmort the more dangerous it will be. In the past, the grounds were salted with steel traps.'

'*Traps?*' Trooste looked at the grass around him with an appalled suspicion.

Chang patted the Professor's knee. 'That would snap the leg off a bear.'

'We are caught between,' said Cunsher, 'while Vandaariff waits, a worm in its cave. The key element is *time*. He cannot wait for long. He needs you, Miss Temple, perhaps others.'

'Worm?' protested Gorine. 'He is rather more than that!'

'My apologies,' said Cunsher. 'I select the wrong word. Not worm, but *dragon*.'

'I see, yes, lovely.' Gorine frowned. 'But what does he intend?'

Chang tapped Trooste with the toe of his boot. 'Professor?'

Trooste sighed. 'He is dying. And believes he does not have to.' He gestured to Cardinal Chang, but thought better of saying more. 'In any event – he has made *plans*.'

'Like the Comte with Angelique,' said Gorine bitterly.

'And what do you know about that?' asked Chang, deadly cold.

Gorine shook his head. 'I *don't*. I swear to you. Mrs Kraft drove us from the room. But she and the Comte bargained for an hour, and then she gave him the Oyster.' Gorine saw their looks of incomprehension. 'The Oyster *Room*. Reserved for the highest quality – everything laid on, the most luxurious single chamber for a hundred miles.'

'But she didn't trust the Comte,' said Chang. 'Why show him that kind of favour?'

'He has already said,' said Cunsher. 'A room for the highest quality – kings, ministers, generals. It thus follows that clients were given this Oyster Room only to be *observed* by Mrs Kraft herself. And there her secret lies.'

The Comte d'Orkancz had been unable to avoid a simple sabre blade, and Robert Vandaariff would fall the same way if Chang could get near enough to land the blow. The larger task was not so clear. While the Comte had been the only soul in the airship with any understanding of indigo clay, now there were too many others – Trooste, Schoepfil, Kraft, even Svenson and, with her corrupted mind, Miss Temple. Must they all perish too?

Chang paused at the crest of a dune, saying nothing until Trooste, lagging and out of breath, reached the top. Chang extended an arm to the low line of lights. Originally constructed as the Queen's prison, Harschmort House was a large horseshoe-shaped structure, only three storeys tall but stretching from end to end as far as a parade ground. The flagged courtyard and forbidding gates looked north. The rear of the house, a hollow around which both wings curled (once an ornamental garden, since destroyed by the implosion of the dungeons beneath), faced south to the sea. To the east lay the terminal spur of the Orange Canal. The western approach, where they now stood, offered only dunes and fen.

'Surely Bronque has reached the gates,' said Gorine. 'We should hear shots.'

'I agree,' said Chang. 'One way or another.'

'What of these *traps*?' asked Trooste.

'We send the least essential man to test the way.' Chang smiled over his shoulder at Gorine. 'Since you failed to convince Mrs Kraft, the honour is yours.'

'Good God!' cried Trooste. 'Do not joke of such things.'

'He isn't,' muttered Gorine. 'In the past I have not been Cardinal Chang's good friend.'

Chang ignored this confession and pointed ahead: the bright line of windows was broken by rooms left dark, allowing the observers within to keep their night vision. 'His men are watching. If we run they will shoot us down. But if we advance, I believe their master's lack of time will dictate cooperation.'

'But why should they cooperate?'

'Because they will have seen *me*.'

As he stepped onto the mown grass that surrounded the house, a half-dozen men filed from it, looking in their green jackets and brass helmets like insects leaving a hive. Chang dropped to one knee to present a smaller target. The others, still in the high grass, did the same, so only their faces were in view. Vandaariff's men formed a line and, in unison, each reached into a canvas satchel slung over one shoulder, reared back and threw.

Chang was already in motion, dodging one of the hurled missiles. He heard the shatter of glass and felt a stinging in his eyes. He held his breath. Cunsher's carbine barked behind him and one of the six men fell. Glass burst at his feet in a cloud of bluish smoke – something flew past his head –

Then Chang was on them – slashing furiously, catching hands and wrenching them backwards, kicking at knees – above all staying in motion to prevent their greater numbers from pulling him down. The helmets limited their vision and made their movements awkward. Two retreated to the door, digging for weapons. Chang spun out of an attempt to seize his waist and saw Cunsher stagger from the meadow, carbine dangling from one hand, then fall, smoke swirling in his face. Chang drove his blade into an attacker's stomach and when the man doubled over slipped behind and wrenched the helmet from his head. The man fell, hands tight around his throat. Instead of putting on the helmet, Chang charged for the two men now guarding the door with wooden clubs. More glass shattered at his feet. He felt the pressure in his chest as he collided with them, viciously swinging the helmet like a studded mace. Chang broke through and to the door, which he slammed and bolted behind.

This air too was marked by curling smoke, and in the light he saw its bluish tint more clearly. He tore off his glasses and clapped the helmet over his head. The rubber seal gripped tight around his throat. He exhaled in a gasp . . . and on the inhale tasted nothing but air. The door rocked on its

Fontanel                                                                401

hinges, pulled from outside. More canvas satchels hung from hooks on the wall. Chang slipped one over his shoulder and ran.

Harschmort House had changed. Chang remembered the western wing (where he'd found Arthur Trapping's corpse, so long ago) enough to note rooms knocked through, walls stripped to prison stone. In two months this wing of Vandaariff's luxurious residence had been returned to its original state, as unadorned as a military barracks.

He opened the satchel. Carefully insulated in sewn pockets were a dozen blue glass spheres, the size of small apples. He eased one out with a gloved hand and raised it to the light, like a float from a fishing net but for the clouds inside, swirling like milk in tea.

Alerted by a shadow on the wall, Chang turned round and threw, the globe shattering between two bareheaded green-coats. With one shuddering breath they crumpled to their faces and lay still. Were they dead? Was there hope for Cunsher and the others? He did not go near to make sure. There wasn't time.

In the helmet he could just see straight ahead. At every room he was forced to spin like an antic dog to make sure he was alone. Three times he had not been – green-coats, servants, even a pair of housemaids – and a glass globe had preserved his liberty. Word of his penetration would spread, and Vandaariff's forces, no matter his attempts to twist and turn, *ought* to have converged by now. Instead Chang advanced unimpeded, past unplastered walls, lumber, copper piping bound together with rope. Obviously every resource had been devoted to construction – the creation of whatever arena this final alchemical rite required.

Chang did not have to search. As he bulled his way on, new figures appeared – always in rooms with multiple doorways, leaving one open path – guards and servants alike, never moving to apprehend him, or to sound an alarm. He was being herded along, like a sheep nipped on its flank. He could have burst free of the cordon, but the lives of his allies demanded a confrontation, and so he pressed willingly into his adversary's lair.

Chang's path stopped at a double doorway made of new-cut planks. Nailed to it was an envelope of parchment. Chang tore it open: a lock of auburn hair, tied with black twine. He knew the colour at once. Celeste had come, and whatever her hopes or the Contessa's plans, Vandaariff had claimed her.

Chang turned the iron knob, a glass globe ready in his other hand. On the floor inside lay an envelope sealed with blue wax. Chang tore it open and tipped a blue glass disc onto his palm. Words had been stamped round its edge. He had enough Latin from his student days, before his life had changed, but disliked the memory.

*Date et dabitur vobis*. Give and it shall be given to you.

White robes edged in green hung in a line on one wall. Below each robe waited a pair of felt slippers – as at the Raaxfall works, to prevent any hobnailed spark near the powder. Chang tucked the disc into a trouser pocket, with the lock of hair. Before him, extending for ten yards from wall to wall, a bed of gravel barred his way – like an ornamental path, save the rocks were dark as coal, and amongst them glittered hundreds of glass spurs. The black stones must be the concentrated explosive that had powered the devices, the same they'd set off on the dock. The gravel bed was too wide to leap, and from the felt slippers outside he assumed that to advance wearing boots such as his own risked triggering the charge.

But if the explosives showed what Vandaariff had pillaged from the Xonck arsenal, beyond them lay the first real sign of the Comte's alchemy. Between the explosives and the far doorway the floor was covered by seven rows of wide coloured tiles. A glance told Chang that the plates were not flush with the floor. Had they been laid atop the layer of explosives? Even if the felt slippers permitted a person to cross the exposed area safely, the first pressure on the metal tiles would create the same effect as his nailed boots and set off an inferno. As he stared he realized the tiles were made of the blended glass that Vandaariff had developed, each tempered by the infusion of different metals. Suddenly the puzzle was clear: the proper seven tiles – which lay atop inert material – would carry a person safely to the door. One only needed to know the alchemical order.

He kicked off his boots and shoved his feet into a pair of slippers. He carefully laid one foot onto the bed of explosive coal and sharpened discs, trusting the thickness of the felt. He took another step . . . then another . . . finally reaching the glass tiles. Could he put his weight upon them without the tiles breaking? What if it was only Vandaariff's joke? And if it wasn't – which tile to choose?

He let his mind return to the room at Raaxfall . . . the table . . . Vandaariff and the different coloured cards . . . 'We start with iron' . . .

The light in the horrid room at Raaxfall had been bad, and his eyes even worse. He could not recall what the cards had truly looked like. Chang pulled off his left glove and extended his hand over the tiles, gently touching them with the tips of his fingers. At the third tile the taste of blood filled his mouth, as had happened with the first glass card. He stepped carefully onto the tile. No explosion. Suddenly he wondered who else might need to follow this path. What if that person was Svenson or Cunsher? He took out Foison's knife and scratched an $x$ in the corner of the tile.

Next came gold, and a memory of a cracking heat inside his bones. This required an accurate hop of several feet, but he landed neatly. Another $x$.

He advanced two more rows, but each time the memory grew fainter, for the cards had begun to derange his senses. At the fifth row, Chang frowned. Past a certain point he'd shut his mind to the pain. Three tiles remained. He knew proper reasoning existed, that the metals in each tile carried associations with planets, the zodiac, the Hebrew alphabet, bodily parts –

Chang looked back. In the doorway stood four men in green, with carbines, but they did not shoot. Their task was to prevent retreat. Chang stepped – the very length of his long stride – to a tile shot with streaks of milky white. How he'd known it came next he could not say. He scraped the knife against the glass.

This very trial showed the ridiculous nature of the Comte's alchemy. It was not a question of whether it worked – something *always* worked – but if the choice between an infusion of mercury or silver was rendered consequential only by volatile explosives, their *alchemical* qualities meant nothing with regard to his reaching the door alive . . .

Still, he must suffer these trappings. What planet went with silver? He'd no idea. At the touch of his fingers on a tile of streaked violet his teeth ached sharply, as if his mouth had been crammed with ice. He stepped onto the tile, hacked an *x* in the corner, then jumped to a bilious tile in the seventh and last row that he knew he'd not yet used. No explosion.

Chang marked his *x*, then reached under the helmet and tugged at the seal, wincing as he pulled off the awkward thing. He shook his head, eyes bare and blinking, and faced the four soldiers. He gave them a sardonic nod, which was returned by their leader, whose eyes were ringed with scars. Chang straightened, then whipped a glass sphere straight at the man, so it burst against his chest. As all four crumpled, Chang slipped through the door. Only a fool kept an enemy at his back.

In the next room Chang found the Comte d'Orkancz – although not in body. Whereas the rest of the remade Harschmort had been expedient and raw, this was the man's vision to the last detail: sconces shaped like open wounds, murals of elongated Byzantine bodies, blue carpets with lurid orange beasts. Every carpet made a path from a doorway – one in each wall of an octagonal room – to its centrepiece: a fountain of clear glass, whose pipes and chambers looped in two intertwined but separate routes, not unlike a human heart. The fluid gushing through one chamber was blue, and through the other orange.

The fountain's rim was inscribed. *Imbibo frater vivo.*

Chang restored his spectacles. Drink, brother, and live . . . not damned likely.

He glanced at the other doors. Did each hide a corridor of explosives? Would others – Schoepfil, Svenson, the Contessa – be driven to their own particular trial? It seemed ridiculous. While proving oneself worthy might well be a tenet of an alchemical treatise like *The Chemickal Marriage*, here it could result in the deaths of those persons Vandaariff had already selected – and protected – for their participation. What if Chang had chosen wrongly, and blown off his own skull? Where would Vandaariff's great experiment be then? Was he so confident that his most desired guests knew the answers – and so willing to eliminate anyone else?

Chang worked quickly around the room. Every way was locked save the double doors on the far side of the fountain. These revealed a dim room with a squat rostrum studded with knobs and switches. Chang took a step and knocked his chin into a wall of glass, flush with the archway – the glass appeared to be built into the frame. He tapped it with his fingers, then his fist. The barrier was too thick to shatter without a hammer or axe.

On the far side of the small room was an identical archway, presumably sealed off as well, beyond which lay another large room, with an array of Vandaariff's machines connected to five large porcelain tubs.

Chang turned to the fountain. Did Vandaariff seriously expect him to choose between orange or blue, when the wrong choice meant death? And what in hell could the *right* one mean, apart from fulfilling Vandaariff's intent? In the room at Raaxfall there had been an eighth card, of bright orange glass, the experience of which had nearly killed him. For Vandaariff the orange card had represented a kind of completion . . .

Give and it shall be given. Chang fished the blue glass disc from his pocket, studying the pathways inside the fountain . . . and saw, right where the streams curled in a helix, two narrow openings in the glass . . .

He inserted the disc into the orange stream, and at once the flow was blocked; pressure forced the fluid up a previously unused tube of glass and into the air. In moments it filled a trough deep enough for him to dip his hand. Chang sighed. He set down the brass helmet, scooped out a palmful of the orange liquid and raised it to his lips.

He choked audibly and stumbled back, chin dripping, waving his wet glove as if it burnt. Chang's eyes tipped back in their sockets, showing the white. He fell, limbs extended like a fallen horse. His breath came ragged and he went still, eyes open to the ceiling.

'As tractable as a babe with an unknit skull. An object of desire dangles before it and all else recedes . . .'

The diminished voice of Robert Vandaariff. Somewhere behind Chang, a door had opened. Slippered footsteps. The orange fluid trickled in its trough.

'A common misconception . . . at birth the bones are soft, allowing passage of *essence* from one realm to another, the crucial, brutal *pressure* associated with *emission*. In time the gap closes and the seams calcify – or so fools would have you believe . . .'

Into Chang's peripheral vision came several figures in white robes, faces shrouded. A figure at his feet held a tray of corked bottles . . .

'But the skull of an adult bends every bit as much as the human spirit, and that same spot – the *fontanel* – remains in every esoteric system a *fountain* through which souls flow to the ether. Even as coarse a soul as this.' Vandaariff croaked with laughter. 'Little more than an animal in trousers! What is the time?'

The man with the tray replied, 'Near to the dawn, my lord.'

'And our other guests? Our royal party? Our Warden? Our Bride? The Virgo Lucifera?'

'All . . . mid-passage, my lord . . . save the ladies.'

'Feminine vectors. What of our *Executioner*?'

To this question there was no reply. The robed acolytes glanced nervously across Chang's body. A sharp sound brought them back to attention – Vandaariff rapping his cane.

'None of that! The contract will be signed. To the vessel – he must be readied!'

Chang waited for the hands to take his shoulders and each leg. He gripped the robes of the men at his shoulders and yanked down hard, driving their heads together with an ugly thud. Sharp kicks drove the men at his legs away and he was up. The acolyte with the tray retreated, protecting his charge. None of them appeared to be armed. Chang drew the silver knife and made for Vandaariff, ready to plant it in his chest.

'I am here, Cardinal Chang.'

Chang first turned to the voice – a metal grille, painted like a fresco of a blue-skinned maiden – and then to the glass barrier. Beyond it, in a white robe of his own, stood Vandaariff. The knobbed hand that gripped his cane was blackened, as if with burnt cork.

'So you did not drink the Draught of Silence after all.' Vandaariff's hood slipped back to show a smug rictus grin and above it a soft half-mask of pale feathers. 'I did not think you had.'

Chang snatched up the brass helmet and extended the knife to the acolytes.

'Show yourselves.'

Vandaariff nodded, and the five pulled back their hoods. Every face bore new scars of the Process, a raw-skinned loop around the eyes and across the nose – more souls sacrificed on the altar of ambition. He wondered what clothes they'd shed in exchange for these robes, what uniforms or vestments, fashionable stripes or silks. Chang slammed the brass helmet into the barrier with all his strength. It rebounded nearly out of his grasp, the glass barely scratched.

'Subdue him,' said Vandaariff.

Chang faced the acolytes. 'Keep away.'

'Subdue him!' repeated Vandaariff.

'You will die,' warned Chang.

Vandaariff cooed to his minions, 'You'll be reborn.'

Chang looked into eyes bright with belief and felt his stomach turn. His fist shot out, bloodying the nose of the foremost man and knocking him aside.

'You cannot win, Cardinal Chang. The spheres have turned!'

Chang clubbed down one man with the helmet and then another. The last of the four rushed him with both hands. Chang dodged to the side, as if he were in a *corrida*, and drove the acolyte face first into the wall. The fifth remained where he'd been, backed against the fountain, still holding the tray. Chang suddenly scoffed.

'I know your face. You're an *actor*. Charles Leffert!' Here was the leading man of the stage dressed like a eunuch in a comedy harem. 'Not enough roses after the matinée? Not enough wives to seduce in their husbands' carriages?'

'You must submit!' commanded Leffert in a heroic baritone. 'The ceremony has begun – you cannot prevent –'

Chang swung the helmet into the tray, sending the flasks and implements flying.

'O heaven!' wailed the actor, as if Rome itself had begun to fall. Chang dropped the helmet and seized Leffert through the robe. He dragged him to the fountain. Leffert caught the rim and pushed away. 'No! I am not given over! I am promised to ascend!'

Chang shoved the actor's head into the trough. Leffert struggled, holding his breath. Chang dropped a knee into Leffert's kidney and a spray of bubbles spat orange. The actor inhaled and swallowed. Chang lifted him, dripping, by the hair. Leffert's eyes were as blue as a songbird's eggs. Chang released him to the floor, the actor's mouth working soundlessly.

'The Draught of Silence?' said Chang. 'Not the best for his profession.'

'You have achieved nothing,' replied Vandaariff.

He rapped his cane on the floor. Another line of acolytes filed into the room of machines and tubs behind Vandaariff, one of them, again, with a tray of bottles. To Chang's horror the others bore the unmoving, naked bodies of Cunsher and Gorine. Both men were daubed with symbols in bright coloured paints, like savages from cannibal islands – or almost, for the skin beneath the paint was pale.

'What have you done to them?'

The acolytes lowered Cunsher and Gorine into coffin-shaped tubs. Their heads lolled. The acolyte with the tray emptied a flask of straw-coloured powder into Gorine's tub, and then Cunsher's. The tubs began to steam. The acolyte looked up, the fat face beneath the hood transformed with scars.

'You were acquainted, I believe, in my new initiate's former life. He will be more useful now – always clever, but now he will *transcend*.'

Chang watched helplessly as Trooste emptied more flasks. By the end both Cunsher and Gorine floated in a rusty liquid that foamed against their painted skin.

Chang shouted to the metal grille: 'What do you want?'

'For you to take the Draught of Silence, of course.'

'Go to hell.' Chang turned to the other doorways. 'I'll find a way through. I will cut your throat.'

'No, Cardinal. That is not your place.' Vandaariff's eyes shone brightly through the mask. 'You know the ritual, do you not, from Rosamonde's memory? I am in her debt, to be sure. So many *celebrants* now come prepared.'

'This cannot work,' called Chang. 'Even if you survive, into what world? The city burns. The Army rules the streets. The people have fled. The Ministries are silent, the bank vaults emptied –'

'Buzzing flies on a dunghill.'

'The *nation* hangs on the brink! Your nephew has allies in place. Every power will assist his accession, and your demise. You are unstable. Bronque is alive. His grenadiers –'

The words died on Chang's lips. The acolytes had returned with two more painted bodies – the angular man from the train, Kelling, and Colonel Bronque himself, whose flesh was marked with wounds. Chang recalled the silence they had noted in the dunes – what could explain it but the glass globes? Even a few of Vandaariff's men could overwhelm Bronque and his survivors before they fired a shot. Trooste stood above the Colonel, emptying a flask.

'Precious salts,' said Vandaariff, following Chang's gaze. 'Blood and sex, acid and fire – a sacred tempering, Cardinal. And so the flesh of life becomes the flesh of dreams.'

'Spare Celeste Temple.'

Vandaariff turned. 'I beg your pardon?'

'Spare Celeste Temple.'

'Why should I do that?'

'In exchange for myself, for my cooperation.'

'I will *have* your cooperation.'

'You won't.' Chang drew out the silver knife. He tore off the canvas satchel and his red coat. He lifted his silk shirt and reached behind, isolating the lump of scar near to his spine. 'I'll cut out your glass. Even if it kills me.'

Vandaariff studied Chang closely through his mask. 'It *will* kill you.'

'So be it.'

'*Stop.*' Vandaariff moistened his dry lips with a pallid tongue. Beyond him Trooste watched with an avid curiosity. 'I cannot spare her. She must act the Bride.'

'Use the Contessa.'

'She is the Virgo Lucifera.' Vandaariff raised a hand to the ceiling of the little room, which was formed of small open tubes, all of which had begun, ever so slightly, to *glow*.

'She is your enemy. She wants your head.'

'And I want her parts boiled down for *paste*. Nevertheless, ever we have found a way.'

Behind Chang, an acolyte had crawled to the canvas satchel. Chang stamped on the man's hand and felt the crunch of a glass globe giving way. The acolyte screamed at the pain, but kicked the brass helmet clear before he succumbed to the fumes. Chang went after the helmet, but another acolyte – they'd been waiting for their chance – caught Chang's leg, even as he too collapsed. The helmet spun beyond Chang's reach.

A muffled roar shook the room. Chang looked up, his lungs tight. Black smoke spewed in from a splintered doorway. Foul air would protect him as much as the helmet. Chang flung himself at the door and wrenched it wide.

Blackened figures lay on the buckled tiles – grenadiers, to judge by their singed and tattered uniforms. Then the smoky air parted and a soot-faced man cracked a rifle-butt into Chang's chest. Chang tumbled back, the breath knocked from his body. A sharp seizing took his lungs. His dark glasses were swatted away.

Vandaariff shouted from the other room: 'Excellent! Subdue him!'

Chang had lost the knife. He groped for the helmet. A kick into his ribs knocked him flat again. He saw the face above him and took it for Mahmoud – for Vandaariff's black Executioner – but this man was shorter and too lithe. Then he saw the white hair.

Foison fell onto Chang's chest, pinning an arm with each of his knees. He'd a leather case slung across his chest, and snapped it open.

'No, no!' cried Vandaariff. 'The draught – give him the *draught!*'

Chang arched his back but could not shift Foison's weight. His lungs were on fire.

One of Foison's hands sought Chang's battered eyes and peeled back the lids. The other slapped an open glass book onto Chang's face and pressed down hard.

For a blinding, screaming instant Cardinal Chang perceived the whole of his soul, suddenly naked, balanced on a precipice. Then every part of him was taken away.

# NINE

## INDENTURE

Doctor Svenson swung the pistol calmly between Bronque's soldiers, Kelling and Schoepfil. Any show of weakness would spark their attack.

'Give my best wishes to Her Majesty. All of Macklenburg is at her service.'

The words were meaningless. He was a criminal in Macklenburg and a criminal here. How many times would he fling himself at death before the black wings caught him up?

He saw Schoepfil move, but the man's damned speed was such that to stop him meant shooting to kill – and, while he knew Schoepfil to be a villain, the man *had* committed himself to bringing down Robert Vandaariff. Was this – lust apart – any different from his *détente* with the Contessa?

Schoepfil seized Kelling's crate of paper and hurled it like a stone into the chest of a footman, pages flying in the air. The soldiers charged. Svenson swore in German.

He shot one trooper in the thigh and the other, sabre raised to open the Doctor's skull, neatly under the arm. His third shot went to the ceiling as the falling soldier's sabre slapped Svenson across the forehead and knocked him to his knees. He looked up to see the door close behind Miss Temple, Schoepfil battering the second footman to the ground. The footman, with more than thirty pounds and seven inches on Schoepfil, collapsed, groaning. Schoepfil turned a raging gaze at Svenson, fists clenched.

'Why should I spare you? Why should you not die?' Schoepfil kicked Svenson's pistol away and spun round to Kelling. 'Open this damned door!'

Kelling barked at the Ministry men, standing off to the side, well clear of the struggle. Now that the prevailing wind of power was established, they willingly joined Kelling at the oval door – Kelling grunting at the pain, but heaving nevertheless – all straining at the iron wheel.

Svenson crawled on his hands and knees. Schoepfil hopped in front of him. 'Where the devil do you think *you're* going?'

'These men.' Svenson pointed to the soldiers. 'Someone must bind their wounds.'

'*And perhaps you should not have shot them!*' But Schoepfil stepped aside, then shrieked at the courtiers: 'And *you*! I will remember each of your names! *O I will remember your names!*'

Despite his patients' hateful looks, Svenson bent to examine each soldier. The leg would heal easily, bone and artery spared, but the arm would be a trial, for the bullet had pierced the shoulder joint.

'What's the old crone thinking?' Schoepfil asked, ostensibly to Kelling, but his secretary was hard against the wheel. Schoepfil thrust his face between the labouring men and shouted, 'I am not deceived, Your Grace!'

His searching little eyes found Svenson, his only audience. The courtiers had fled.

'The Duchess claims the Queen is within. She is a *liar*.'

'Is it some Eastern system of combat?' asked Svenson.

'Beg pardon?' Schoepfil chuckled. 'O! O no, not at all.'

'You move with an unnatural speed.'

'And I shall do something unnatural to the Duchess of Cogstead, you may be sure of it! I *know* who is there! Why should she protect the Contessa di Lacquer-Sforza – of all people? And *you*! You gave that colonial chit my *book*! My own glass book and you have thrust it into the arms of an empty-headed girl!'

'Only because I had no time to smash it.'

'O! *O!*' Schoepfil waved both arms at the ceiling. 'Artless! Crude! *Teuton!*'

'If the Contessa is inside, these few men will not take her.'

'*Pah!* I'll take her myself.' Schoepfil clapped his grey-gloved hands. 'So hard it *stings*.'

The wheel gave with a sudden lurch. Schoepfil bustled through, returning the pistol to his secretary as he passed. Svenson pushed after the Ministry men, but Kelling waved the pistol.

'Where are *you* going?'

'Put it away,' sighed Svenson. 'If he could spare me, I'd be dead. Since I'm not, I could shoot you in the head and he would only swear at the mess.'

'You're wrong,' Kelling snarled. 'He remembers – you'll pay!'

'You should bind that wrist.'

'Go to hell.'

Svenson found the others in a low octagonal room, with an oval door in each wall, like the engine room of a steamship. Schoepfil faced the Duchess with his hands on his hips.

'Well, madam? Your falsehood is exposed!' When the Duchess did not respond, he screamed again, waving at the doors: '*Open them! Open them all!*'

Doctor Svenson locked eyes for an instant with the Duchess. 'Whose rooms are these?'

'Not the *Queen's!*' crowed Schoepfil. Three doors were opened to utter blackness.

'They were given to Lord Pont-Joule,' said the Duchess.

'The *late* Lord Pont-Joule.' Schoepfil's voice echoed from inside a doorway. He reappeared to shove a Ministry man at the next door. 'Nothing – go, go!'

'He was charged with Her Majesty's safety –'

'I know who he is,' said Svenson. 'Or was.'

Schoepfil hopped back to the Duchess. 'These tunnels follow the springs!'

'Spy tunnels,' said Svenson. 'Just like where we observed Her Majesty's baths.' The Duchess gasped.

'O well done,' muttered Schoepfil. 'Blab every single thing . . .'

'You ought to have expected others. The rock beneath the Thermæ must have been honeycombed for a thousand years.'

Schoepfil sniffed at the next door. 'Sulphur – leading to the baths proper. Would the Contessa seek the baths? She would not.' He called to the Duchess: '*She* killed him, you know – Pont-Joule!' Schoepfil scoffed on his way to the next doorway. 'You arranged her audience. You aided her escape. He was her *lover*! Right in the *neck*!'

The Duchess put her hands over her eyes. 'I did not –'

'O I *will* see you punished. *Where is my book?*'

Kelling wrenched open the seventh door. Schoepfil sniffed the air. His face darkened. 'O dear Lord . . .'

'What is it?' asked Kelling.

'The *channel*.' Schoepfil spun to the Duchess. 'It's true after all! You knew it! And *she* damn well knew it! Of all the – O this takes the biscuit!'

Schoepfil's hand flew at the Duchess. Svenson caught the blow mid-air. With an outraged sputter Schoepfil's other hand delivered three rapid strikes to the Doctor's face. Still Svenson held on – giving the Duchess time to retreat – until Schoepfil wrenched his arm free.

'You presume, Doctor Svenson, you *presume*!'

Schoepfil's voice stopped with a guttural snarl. In the Doctor's hand hung his grey glove, peeled off while retrieving his arm. The flesh of Schoepfil's hand was a bright cerulean blue, nails darkening to indigo.

'Sweet Christ,' whispered the Doctor. 'What have you done – what idiocy?'

Schoepfil snatched the glove and wriggled his hand inside, glaring at Svenson with a mixture of abashment and pride, like a young master caught plundering his first housemaid. The instant the glove was restored Schoepfil turned on Kelling with a scream: '*What do you wait for? Inside and after them!*'

Kelling dived through, but the Ministry men paused. 'Is there a light?' one ventured.

Through the door came a crash and a grunt of pain. 'There are steps,' called Mr Kelling.

Svenson opened the doors of a sideboard and pulled out a metal railwayman's lantern.

'How did you find that?' asked Schoepfil.

'Pont-Joule must have used these tunnels for surveillance.'

'And look what it got him,' Schoepfil spat, then shouted at them all. 'A match! A match! *Light the damned thing up!*'

*

Kelling was waiting by a pile of clothing. Schoepfil stood at the black pool, glaring at the billowing effervescence. The Ministry men hovered, one, stuck between care and complicity, arm in arm with the Duchess, for Schoepfil dared not leave her alone. Another held the lantern high, but the cavern had no other exit but the pool.

Svenson gave the candle a glance, noticed the ash around its base and the tiniest curl of unburnt paper, coloured red. The Contessa had left a message, which Miss Temple had possessed the presence of mind to burn.

The riddle of the clothing was even simpler: one woman had followed the lead of the other, the clothing removed to swim. Svenson knelt at the water, swiped a finger through the fizz and put it to his nose, then in his mouth.

'Colder than the baths,' he said, 'though the minerals prove a mingling. This channel meets the river. Underground.'

'It was a secret way,' said the Duchess. 'Used for terrible things.'

He did not suppose any explanation was needed; they were beneath a palace, after all. 'The journey to air cannot be far. Do we follow?'

He plucked his tunic between his thumb and forefinger, as if offering to strip. Schoepfil scowled. 'Of course we don't. The ash there, Kelling – what was burnt?'

'A note. Unreadable, sir.'

'Blasted female. Shameless. Brazen.' Schoepfil pointed damningly at the clothes. 'Does she have a new wardrobe ready on the other side? Of *course* she does. And as soon as your little *beast* arrives she will also have my *book*!'

Svenson had thought Miss Temple dead, only to see her again in the baths – with the Contessa, of all people, and being introduced, of all things, to the sickly, costive Queen. From their concealment he and Schoepfil had heard the entire conversation, the Contessa's sly blaming of Vandaariff and Lord Axewith for the Duke of Staëlmaere's murder. Minutes later came Colonel Bronque's own audience, a litany of abuse received in place of Axewith, whose request for the Queen's seal was violently refused. Schoepfil had nearly exposed their hiding place, chuckling at this reverse for his uncle. Uncle! What but a life of envious proximity to power could explain this strange creature of a man?

From there Svenson had been passed to the odious Kelling, who – with two grenadiers – had shown him another cork-lined room stuffed with ephemera relating to the Comte d'Orkancz and indigo clay: books and papers, diagrams, paintings, half-tooled bits of brass and steel. Kelling hungrily noted where his attention fell, as if Svenson were a pilgrim in an alchemical allegory, presented with a table of riches, with his choice to dictate the course of his soul.

'Lorenz.' Svenson tapped a stack of that man's notes. 'Dropped out of an airship to the freezing sea.'

Kelling was silent. Svenson moved to the next pile.

'Fochtmann. Shot in the head at Parchfeldt.' He smiled at Kelling, as if in friendly reminiscence. 'Gray, killed at Harschmort by Cardinal Chang. And Crooner . . . everyone forgets him. Lost both arms – turned to glass and sheared off. Died of the shock, I suppose . . .'

'What about the *marriage*?' Kelling extended his knobbed throat like a buzzard.

'Do you mean the painting?'

'Do I?'

'Or the ritual behind it?' Svenson smiled pleasantly. 'A man like the Comte d'Orkancz would view the thing as a *recipe*. Since he was barking *mad*.'

Svenson fished out a rumpled cigarette and, not waiting for Kelling's permission, set it to light. He exhaled. 'Do you know what *happened* to the Comte?'

'He died on the airship,' replied Kelling.

Doctor Svenson took another puff and shook his head. 'No, Mr Kelling. He is in *hell*.'

He was taken by the grenadiers to another room, Kelling called away and, to Svenson's mind, happy to leave. Kelling was exactly the sort of court-bred toad whose dislike the Doctor had so often negotiated in protecting the Prince, men whose self-regard became one with their masters'. Svenson's refusal to be so *attached* had marked him a social leper.

But worse than the company of Kelling was that of his own untended heart. Left alone, the guilt Svenson had been able to suppress since his delivery to Schoepfil rose to the surface of his thought. Francesca. Elöise. The Contessa.

A soldier entered with a wooden plate of bread and meat, and a mug of beer. Svenson drank half the beer in a swallow and set the plate on his lap, forcing himself to chew each bite. The bread had gone stiff, sliced hours before, and the grey beef stank of vinegar. Still, he finished the plate, emptied the mug and carried them to the door.

As the guard took the empty dishes, Doctor Svenson looked out.

'Do you think I might stretch my legs?' he asked. 'I have had so little sleep, if I do not walk I will collapse.'

'Why not sleep now?'

'There is no time. Mr Schoepfil says we must travel. I require my wits.'

He took out his last two cigarettes, offered one to the grenadier, who – blessedly – declined. Svenson tucked it away, lit the other and indicated the small corridor. 'Just here?'

The guard did not protest and Svenson wandered to a window. Night had fallen and a movement outside caught his eye: a man in a white jacket, arms bound, dragged by soldiers towards a livery shed. A few steps behind came Kelling. Perhaps a minute later Kelling and the grenadiers returned alone.

In the distance came the sound of doors. Svenson ambled to the corridor's end in time to see the Contessa with an escort of guards.

'*There* you are!' She called with such self-importance that her soldiers allowed her to veer towards Svenson. He bowed as she approached.

'The Contessa di Lacquer-Sforza,' he said to his guard, 'a gentlewoman from Venice.'

The guard's reply, and her own guards' desire to interpose, was brusquely overridden. 'Doctor Svenson, thank *goodness*. I've just been with Her Majesty now' – this clearly for the benefit of the guards – 'and I *would* speak to Mr Schoepfil – yet I may not have *time*, you see. Because of Her *Majesty*.' She pointed past Svenson. 'Is that where you've been waiting? May we speak?'

'I am at your service,' replied Svenson.

'Mr Schoepfil wants you to wait,' managed one of her guards.

'Of course I'll *wait*,' she cried. 'But if the *Queen* requests my presence, what do you suggest? This way I may convey to Doctor Svenson – who also *waits* for Mr Schoepfil – my own account of the matter, so he may pass it on – *in case*. Don't you see?'

She strode down the windowed passage, unseen heels clipping the floor like the hoofs of a performing horse. 'I will knock when I am finished,' she told the guard. 'What is that, beer? Two more of the same. I am parched.'

She sailed inside and sat in the only chair. Svenson smiled apologetically at the guard and began to shut the door.

'The *beer*,' the Contessa snapped.

She flounced her dress into place. The knot of soldiers stared past him at the woman. Svenson accepted the beer and shut the door with his heel.

'What are you waiting for, trumpets?'

She snatched a mug from his hand and drank deeply, paused to breathe, then finished it off. '*Drink*. Drink or give it to me. There is very little time.'

He looked to the door. 'Surely everything we say is heard –'

The Contessa took hold of Svenson's belt and yanked him sharply to one knee. She took his mug and set it down, slopping beer across the varnished cork.

'We have unfinished business.'

'Madam, nothing between us –'

She jerked his belt to stop his rising. 'Speak *quietly*,' she whispered. She put her mouth near his ear. 'We have all *manner* of unfinished business, Abelard Svenson. Do not deny it.'

'I will not.' He swallowed. 'But this morning – I cannot –'

'Cannot *what*?'

'You took the life of Mrs Dujong –'

'Someone had to.'

The crack of Doctor Svenson's open hand across her cheek split the room. He leapt to his feet, furious, appalled.

Her eyes blazed. 'You'll pay for that.'

'I already have.'

The Contessa burst into a raucous laugh. The door opened and two grenadiers peered in, alarmed by the sound of the blow, but now confused by her laughter and the Doctor's shame-red face. The Contessa waved them away and, docile to *hauteur*, they went. She laid two fingers on her cheek. 'My lord.'

'Whatever you have to say, madam, *say* it.'

'Not until you kneel.' She raised her eyebrows. Svenson sighed and did so, reaching to shift the beer mug.

'I'll have that. If you're not drinking.' She took another long pull. 'I've been in the baths. No wonder her skin comes off in strips.'

'Immersion dehydrates the flesh,' observed Svenson. 'So does alcohol.'

'Not beer, surely.' She offered him the mug. He shook his head, and the Contessa tipped back the rest.

'Those soldiers will not wait forever. And Schoepfil not at all.'

'Nor Bronque. Do you know Bronque?' She gave him the mug, which he set down with annoyance. When he looked back she held a tightly wrapped piece of silk, plucked, while his gaze was diverted, from between her breasts. She tossed it to him, like a treat for a lapdog.

'I stole that from Celeste Temple. The handkerchief belongs to Robert Vandaariff.'

Svenson unwrapped the silk: a blue glass spur.

'I have seen these before. At Raaxfall – and in the square –'

'Everyone has seen them,' she said. 'Why give it to *her*?'

Svenson glanced quickly to the door. 'It must be different.'

'I have not time to investigate, but had I the time I do not think I would, as it was given to Celeste precisely before her delivery to *me*.'

'I am your enemy just as much as Miss Temple –'

Svenson began to stand. She caught his belt. 'Of course you are, lord – what does a woman have to do?'

'To do, madam? *To do?*'

She bit back whatever tart reply she was about to make and met his eyes. The moment stretched. 'You're not afraid of me, are you?'

'Of course not.'

'No. You're afraid of yourself.'

Svenson pursed his lips, shrugged. She relaxed her grip on his belt, and gently arched her wrist so her four fingers slipped inside the Doctor's trousers.

'Do you recall,' she asked, the back of her fingers slipping into his woollen undersuit, 'our *first* meeting? When we *first* spoke?'

Svenson's body tensed. 'The St Royale Hotel. I sought the Prince.'

'And I told you where he was.'

'Because doing so amused you. You later consigned me to death for the same reason.'

'But you did *not* die.' She studied him closely, *warily*. Her hand slowly slipped deeper, until her nails just traced his groin, then just as suddenly withdrew. She sat back in the chair. Her manner became brisk.

'Robert Vandaariff has exchanged Cardinal Chang, who was mine, for Celeste Temple, who was his. Now Celeste – and you – are guests of Drusus Schoepfil –'

'As are you.'

The Contessa let this pass as immaterial. 'She must be freed.'

He spoke bitterly. 'Because the child has died?'

'What child?'

'Francesca Trapping! And since Celeste is the other person with knowledge of your horrid book – and thus the Comte – you require her, to sacrifice her as well, to defeat him!'

'The child is dead?'

'You sent her to me!' he said savagely. 'You sent *us* to Mrs Kraft! What else could happen?'

The Contessa sighed. 'I did not know.'

'Did you care?'

'About what?'

'About her!'

The Contessa caught sharp hold of Svenson's chin and pulled his face to hers.

'Of course I didn't!' she hissed. 'She was an odious and unnaturally born cast-off. She was doomed, like every girl born to ruin. The world cannot withstand them grown. *Their kind makes the world pay.*'

She stood, forcing Svenson back onto his heels.

'I regret you bore the burden. And Madelaine Kraft?'

His mouth was dry. 'Restored.'

'Superb. If you survive, you may visit every brainless victim of Oskar's books and make a fortune reclaiming their precious minds. A grateful nation, lacking such a bounty of overlords, will grovel at your feet.'

'Did you know it could be done?'

She swept to the door. 'I do now, don't I?'

Doctor Svenson held up the handkerchief. 'And what of this?'

The Contessa lifted her dress and kicked the door. 'It's yours now, Doctor. Isn't that enough for you?'

The grenadier only just dodged from her path. He frowned with jealous disapproval at Svenson, still on the floor, and hurried after her.


Svenson paused to help the Duchess back through the oval door. Kelling had collected his papers. The footmen and the wounded soldiers had been taken away. Mr Nordling had returned with a dozen men of the court, and, though their presence had caused the Ministry men to retire – and then to join their number – Schoepfil paid them no mind. He told Kelling to be quick and sneered at Svenson's kindness.

'You must answer, sir,' called Nordling, sword cane in hand. 'You have transgressed, most gravely – and the person of Her Grace –'

'Let him pass, Mr Nordling.' The Duchess squeezed the Doctor's hand as she pulled away.

'Of course I'll *pass*!' cried Schoepfil. 'I'll leave the man who tries to stop me in tears!'

The Duchess spoke to the room. 'That girl, the colonial with the Chinese name – she said the realm was under attack. The *realm*.'

'O stuff,' muttered Schoepfil. 'On *and* on . . .'

'Robert Vandaariff is Our Majesty's enemy. I do not know who is strong enough to stand against him – hush, Mr Nordling, your loyalty is noted – save perhaps these criminals. Mr Schoepfil, and this Italian murderess –'

'And *that* German spy,' observed Schoepfil, 'awaiting the noose in two lands.'

The Duchess looked to Svenson with dismay.

'No tale is completely true, Your Grace. What can be done, will be.' Svenson tipped his head. 'And then – only then – will I consent to hang.'

*

'Leather-skinned valise,' growled Schoepfil. 'Interfering sheepdog. Did you see the hairs on her chin? In her *ears*? Less a duchess than a horse blanket.' He pounded on the ceiling and shouted to the coachman. 'Run them down! There is a curfew! *They* are in the wrong!'

They had extracted themselves from the Thermæ without issue, swift passage assured by the same duchess Schoepfil now hotly condemned.

'To call *you* a criminal, sir,' added Kelling. 'And in such company.'

'She will answer, Mr Kelling. Every last one will answer for every last thing. I have *friends*.' Schoepfil sniffed at Svenson, who sat next to the crate of papers. 'The way of the world, after all. Chemical equivalencies. Do you understand my meaning?'

'Alchemy?'

'You disapprove!' Schoepfil laughed. 'The fact is, so do I! And yet – *and yet*!' He twirled a hand with a flourish. 'My uncle is not, in fact, a fool!'

Schoepfil turned his attention to Kelling, who nodded with a professional deliberation, memorizing his master's commands. Svenson shut his eyes. His last cigarette had been sacrificed to calm his nerves after the Contessa's departure. A foolish indulgence, for he'd been desperate for another after studying the glass spur.

The grenadier had collected the mugs, scowled at the spilt-upon floor and come back with a rag, swabbing with an angry, protective zeal. Then Svenson had been alone. He had unfolded the square of silk, staring at the blue disc as if it were some faerie token that, wrongly handled, would serve his doom.

The spurs found at the Xonck works had been infused with rage, and it seemed reasonable that the simplicity of the content was determined by the small amount of glass. But here was a spur made for the specific target of the Contessa.

Such were both the Contessa's power and Vandaariff's invention that Svenson hesitated to touch the thing with bare flesh, much less gaze inside. He thought of Euripides' sorceress giving a poisoned gown to her lover's new bride, consuming the girl in flames . . . but that seemed wrong. The spur would never be so volatile, because of Celeste. Vandaariff could not depend on his messenger's lack of curiosity – thus, unless Miss Temple was its true target, which Svenson did not believe, the spur must be benign to Miss Temple yet deadly to the Contessa. Would it be safe for him as well?

He grazed the glass with a fingertip and felt a flutter at the back of his neck. He took a breath and pressed his finger onto the flat side of the disc. The hair rose on his nape and his breath quickened . . .

Svenson raised the spur to his eye.

A hollow lightness filled his chest. He was with Elöise, standing on the sand. He was with Corinna in the trees, her hand in his, knowing he must release it before their walk ended and they could be seen. Tenderness overwhelmed him. His eyes brimmed and then spilt tears down the Doctor's face.

Of course. The deadly spur held love.


They drove past soldiers and torches, angry crowds and noise, even the clatter of hurled stones bouncing off the coach. Doctor Svenson ignored it all. He was exhausted, disgusted by Schoepfil's self-satisfaction and sick with worry for Celeste. Chang had delivered himself to death to save her, not unlike Svenson himself in the Parchfeldt woods. He twisted into the corner of the seat and felt the pull of the long, puckered scar. Why her, of all people? Why he and Chang? A more unlikely trio would be hard to imagine. Yes, he was a spy, and Chang an assassin – yet Miss Temple remained unlikely in the extreme. But was she the strongest of the three? He recalled their morning in the abandoned tower, the awkward conversation after so long, her palpable distress. Could he or Chang have borne such a torment?

Schoepfil looked up from his papers. 'Are you uncomfortable, Doctor?'

'He drank two mugs of beer,' said Mr Kelling. 'The guard confessed it.'

'I do not enjoy beer,' observed Schoepfil in a tone that made clear, in the imminent domain of Schoepfil, no one else would either. 'A peasant's beverage.'

'Peasants also drink wine,' said Svenson. 'And make brandy.'

'Nonsense.' Schoepfil returned his nose to a battered notebook. '*Stuff*.'

The coach reached Schoepfil's home, passing through a cordon of militia. Schoepfil left the box for Kelling, who in turn heaved it into the arms of the first serving man they met. Svenson came last, and was commanded to wait in the main parlour.

'Would you, or any of your people, have tobacco?'

'Tobacco stains the teeth,' replied Schoepfil. 'Just look at yours!'

A traditionally dressed serving man, in a grey-striped jacket and gloves, eased into his master's range of vision.

'What can it be *now*, Danby?'

'Callers, sir. They insisted on being seen.'

'*Insist?*'

'An unusual pair of persons, Mr Schoepfil. The lady is most demanding, claiming that you *need* to see her. I have allowed them to *wait.*'

'A lady and a younger man?' asked Svenson. 'He darker than her?'

'Yes, sir.'

Schoepfil snapped his fingers in Danby's face as he marched away. 'He is not a *sir*. He is no one. *Need*, do I? We shall see. Kelling – everything for transport!'

Servants piled up more boxes taken from an inner room. When Schoepfil reappeared, all smiles, it was with Madelaine Kraft and Mahmoud. Doctor Svenson rose. Schoepfil ignored him.

'If there was but time!' He prised the lid off a box and peered inside. 'O yes – you will enjoy this!'

He offered a square of parchment to Mrs Kraft. Svenson met the eyes of Mahmoud, but the dark man's face was impassive.

'A woodcut, *aus dem Rheinland*, only one other copy, and that owned by my uncle! From the fourth day of the narrative. *Extremely* rare. The *Executioner.*'

Mrs Kraft nodded appreciatively, passed the page to Mahmoud. 'And how did you come to share your uncle's interest?'

'Let us say I follow the wind,' said Schoepfil. 'You know Doctor Svenson, I believe? One *might* say you were in his debt.'

'One might.'

'He is my captive. If either of you makes a single gesture of *aid* our bargain is null. If you wish to reach Harschmort, you will submit to my management in this and all things.'

'The girl died,' Doctor Svenson told them. 'Bronque stripped the Old Palace to its nails. Michel Gorine is their prisoner. This man, with whom you ally, has destroyed your livelihood and scattered your people to the law, or worse.'

Schoepfil raised both hands as if to take hold of Svenson's throat. The butler in the grey-striped jacket stopped him with a cough.

'Christ alive, what *is* it, Danby!'

'Men at the door, sir. And soldiers surrounding the house, sir. Grenadiers.'

'Grenadiers, you say?'

'Also members of an irregular unit, sir, in *green*.'

With an exaggerated care Schoepfil tiptoed to a latticed Chinese screen and put his face to a viewing-hole. At his signal Danby answered the door. Madelaine Kraft joined Schoepfil at the screen. He made room with a scowl.

It took a moment for Svenson to place the voice at the door: Vandaariff's white-haired captain, whose request for Schoepfil was deflected with a lie. Then a second voice, hard and loud, Colonel Bronque . . .

Svenson leant close to Mahmoud. 'They beat him very badly. Bronque himself.'

The door was closed and Schoepfil skipped from the screen to the shutters, watching his visitors go down the stairs.

'Who was there?' Mahmoud asked.

'My uncle's man, Foison,' replied Schoepfil. 'Ghastly fellow.'

'And Colonel Bronque?'

'O yes. Bronque slipped in that they search for you, they *know*. We must buy time. Danby – I'll need a messenger, no one *wheezy*.'

'And Cardinal Chang,' observed Madelaine Kraft. 'In chains.'

Mahmoud frowned. 'I thought Chang was dead.'

'No one dies when they ought to,' said Schoepfil, 'uncles least of all. So *that* was Cardinal Chang? Provocative . . .' He took the woodcut print from Mahmoud, and chuckled. 'Yes, this will do perfectly.'

Mr Kelling stood ready with pen and ink. Schoepfil dipped the nib and scratched a careful line across the woodcut.

'What is that?' asked Mrs Kraft.

'A message, of course. And misdirection . . .'

'What is this?'

Mahmoud had reached into the box of papers and lifted out a leather volume that, even as he handled it, began to moult paper and ash. Schoepfil
hurried to take it from his hands.

'No! That is an extremely valuable *grimoire*! Please set it down!'

For the briefest instant Mahmoud's eye caught the Doctor's, then the
dark man twisted away from Schoepfil, towards the light. 'Valuable? But so
much of it has been burnt –'

'Yes, yes – an accident at the Thermæ –'

Mahmoud innocently shifted further from Schoepfil. With the stealthy
ease of a cat Doctor Svenson took the pen and began to write, tiny letters,
quickly made. Kelling had joined his master in retrieving the precious book,
and Mrs Kraft chided her son to return it. By the time Schoepfil finally
snatched up the woodcut to fold and seal, the Doctor had retreated to his
seat.

An hour later Svenson sat across a coach from Mrs Kraft. Mahmoud was
beside her and Kelling next to Svenson, boxes between them and cluttering
the floor. Mr Schoepfil travelled with Colonel Bronque, a wedge of soldiers
clearing their way to Stropping.

'Mrs Kraft, what did you learn from being *healed*?'

She studied Svenson closely, and he saw with pity how every transaction
of her life must be a thing of leverage and guile. He did not doubt her desire
for revenge, her determination to wager all. That she was willing to risk
those around her should not have surprised him – what brothel keeper does
not rise on the destruction of others? – but that it would include her own
son took him aback. Had he misjudged her, or the hell to which she'd been
consigned?

'Your hands shake, Doctor.'

He raised one to his face and saw the thin vibration. 'I am in the habit of
consuming more tobacco than has been available. And I am tired. And . . .'
He met her eyes and smiled. 'I am sad.'

'*Sad?*'

'When I ask what you have learnt, it is not as physician or confessor, but
what you remember about the Comte d'Orkancz, as only that would be valu-

able to Mr Schoepfil. Something he did to one of your women? Or is your insight from another source – Francis Xonck? You must have known *him* very well –'

'Do not say a thing!' warned Mr Kelling.

The Doctor wanted to smile, for there was no better lever against Mrs Kraft's silence than a presumptuous underling demanding that she keep it. But either she was not so easily provoked, or Mr Kelling was too insignificant.

At Stropping, as they waited for the soldiers to clear a path, the Doctor had the presence of mind to put money into Mahmoud's hands and shove him to a kiosk, open to brisk business despite the hour. 'Anything – anything he has.'

Schoepfil glanced from where he stood with Bronque – letting the Colonel, who clearly relished the task, harangue the militia officers charged with keeping order – scowling at Mahmoud's departure, and then, having discerned the cause, wagging a finger in Svenson's direction. Svenson only looked away. The station echoed with every sound ten thousand desperate people could make. Whistles shrieked. Railwaymen laboured to add extra carriages to trains going in every direction.

'Turkish.' Mahmoud handed him a flat red tin. 'All that was left.'

'Bless you.' Svenson popped the lid with a thumbnail and inhaled. He plucked out a slender cigarette in coffee-coloured paper, tapped it twice on the tin and stuck it in his mouth. 'You have no *idea*.'

'Why do we wait?' Mahmoud asked Mr Kelling.

'Our special arrangements have been misplaced in all this nonsense. This *fire*.'

Svenson met Mahmoud's gaze over a flaming match set to the cigarette.

'Damned inconvenient,' added Kelling.

'I expect it spoils Lord Vandaariff's plans as well. He counts on our arrival as much as we do.'

'Not mine,' said Mrs Kraft.

'Of course yours – unless Foison and Chang are dead. He will expect us all.'

'They *are* dead. With all of the Colonel's men hunting them? Men like that are common enough, and they die commonly too.'

'I do not think you know Cardinal Chang.'

'I assure you, I do, Doctor. And his faults. Do you know of his feeling for Angelique?'

'Something of it. I was called to treat her, by the Comte.'

Mrs Kraft shook her head. 'Chang could have had her. Of course she was indifferent to him, as his behaviour was – almost *courtly*. But he could have *taken* her.'

'That is not Chang.'

'A man who indulges desire without acting to satisfy it deserves contempt. And that is Chang's doom.'

'What will be yours?' asked Doctor Svenson.

'*Stop*.' Mahmoud cut in, for they had both grown sharp. 'Where are *they* going?'

The bulk of Bronque's grenadiers jogged past, double time, a blue column returning up the grand staircase and into the night.

'The other stations.' Mr Kelling raised a knowing eyebrow. 'To make sure.'

'That means Foison and Chang still live, and we must take care.' Mahmoud reached for the red tin and helped himself to a cigarette.

'I do beg your pardon!' Svenson fumbled for a match. 'I did not think to offer.'

Mahmoud leant to the light, and then exhaled. 'People often don't. One would think I were invisible. Or small. Or – what is the word? – *property*.'

A weary conductor let them board the east-bound train, a motley group nevertheless given precedence over the waiting elite. In the third carriage Schoepfil pointed to a compartment. 'Here, Mr Kelling! And Mrs Kraft, with your man. To Orange Locks – as we have agreed.'

'We have not agreed on anything,' replied Mrs Kraft.

'Kelling has the particulars – I have considered your every wish! Do not fret, you will have the advantage of our numbers.'

'What if you and I need to speak?'

'We will not. I will be further up the train – quite impossible.'

'*Why?*'

'Now, now – I have given you sanctuary; you must give your *trust*. Doctor Svenson?' Schoepfil wagged his finger. 'With me, sir. You are *required*.'

The door to the front-most carriage had been augmented with a metal plate and a substantial lock that Colonel Bronque, leaving two men posted outside, turned once he, Schoepfil and Doctor Svenson had passed through. The compartment walls and seats had been removed, the draperies replaced with more sheet metal.

An array of machines took up the centre of the carriage – not the pipe organ of brass and steel that Svenson had seen at the Institute, but rather a modest scatter of brass canisters and tin-lined tubs, linked by copper wire and rubberized hose. Two much thicker bundles of cable ran to the far end of the car and out through holes cut in the wall.

'*Amazing*, yes?' Schoepfil clapped his hands. 'You have seen it before – Margaret Hooke, Elspeth Poole, even Angelique – marvels misunderstood and too soon gone! Now you will assist *us*!'

'Vandaariff must fall, Doctor.' Colonel Bronque turned a chair and straddled it. 'For the common good.'

'So you can replace him?'

Schoepfil removed his jacket and laid it on the table to avoid a crease. 'I *am* his heir.'

'Better us than that Italian hellcat.' Bronque gave a sour look to Schoepfil. 'You should not have allowed her to escape.'

'I did not *allow* a thing. She killed two of your men, neat as a snap! Besides, *you* – well, decency forbids me to say more.'

Bronque took a pull from a silver flask and exhaled. 'It was never the time.'

'You were her lover?' blurted Doctor Svenson. 'I thought it was Pont-Joule.'

Schoepfil blew air through his lips. 'The Colonel, Pont-Joule, Matthew Harcourt –'

'Not Harcourt,' Bronque cut in. 'There she only teased.'

'You see! He defends! O her hooks are in!' Schoepfil snorted at Svenson. 'I wonder she has not added *you* to their number!'

Bronque laughed and took another drink. Svenson felt his face redden. 'She may be beautiful, but her heart is black.'

'Spoken like a man never asked,' said Bronque. He tucked the flask away. 'Shall we?'

'I would prefer to be in *motion*,' replied Schoepfil.

'Why? You'll need to rest. And I'm getting out before you.'

'O very well.' Schoepfil sniffed, almost girlishly. 'Doctor, we take you into our confidence.'

'I have not agreed to anything.'

'But you *will* agree. Because my uncle, as my colleague says, must fall.'

'You forget Chang. You forget Miss Temple.'

'One cannot forget what one has never considered in the first place. The former is doomed through my uncle's science; the latter insignificant altogether.'

Svenson found the red tin and selected another cigarette.

'My *Lord*, Doctor,' sighed Schoepfil. Bronque laughed and held out a hand. Svenson offered him the box and struck a match for them both. The smoke touched his lungs like a perfume of nettles.

'If you need me, your disapproval can go hang. Now take off your gloves and show me what you've done, then tell me how you did it, and what madness I'm to help you do next.'


'Power, of course, comes from the engine. We sacrifice speed, but the duration is brief — has to be, or the same mistakes are made. No one understands the degree to which the Comte's achievement was determined by *aesthetics*. Three women turned to glass.' Schoepfil tugged at his goatee. '*Beautiful* — no doubt of it –'

'An abomination,' said Svenson.

'An opinion –'

'I knew the women.'

'The *point* is that *complete* transformation is neither necessary nor useful.' Schoepfil raised one bright blue hand, then rapped it hard on the table top. 'As you can see, still flesh, still mine to command. And *yet* . . .'

Schoepfil closed with Doctor Svenson and, showing the same preternatural speed as before, stabbed his hands in half a dozen places about the Doctor's body, well ahead of any attempt to block him. The blows became mere touches at the last instant, but the potential damage was unpleasantly clear. Red-faced again, Svenson raised his arms and stepped away.

'I have experienced your skill.'

'You did not know the cause.'

'But I knew there was one. You are no athlete. You have acquired only speed.'

'More than that, Doctor, speed is but the scent off the dish. The *advance* is in the mind.' Schoepfil grinned. 'Everything my uncle has acquired, I have plundered – he is betrayed by his own people, who already cleave to my inheritance.'

Svenson turned to Bronque. 'And were you a part of this? He can't have done it by himself.'

'But I did, Doctor! One hand at a time – the left is a touch less sensitive, but one learns!'

'We became partners after the fact.' Bronque clapped his hands. '*Drusus*. There is not time. And Doctor Svenson is not our friend.'

'No, he is *not*!' Schoepfil returned to the jumble of machines. 'I cannot *tell* you how much I wanted to throttle him at the Thermæ.' He peered at Svenson over his spectacles. 'The Kraft woman's cure is a miracle. You must dedicate the same knowledge and skill to our interests. Only then will you survive.'

'And if I told you I know nothing, that I merely followed instructions?'

Schoepfil laughed. 'The Colonel would dangle you from this train until your head met the wheels.'

After examining the paths through which the power flowed, how it was held and released in the different brass and glass chambers, the Doctor had to admit, and the admission frightened him, that Schoepfil was right. The Comte's alchemical creed had driven his discoveries to extreme forms, such as Lydia Vandaariff's pregnancy and the three glass women. With the exception of the glass books, the Comte had largely eschewed practical applications. Schoepfil's moderation – unburdened by ideology or belief – exposed a vaster and more terrifying danger.

'The speed of *thought*.' Schoepfil wiggled the fingers of both hands to mimic the energy coursing through the wires. 'The property of blue glass that touches the mind – that speaks in *thought's* chemical tongue. By lengthening time of exposure and lessening its intensity, the transformational effects are diminished – and, since I do not *desire* to be made of glass, there is no penalty. And, at the sacrifice of discoloration, what I *do* acquire is sensitivity. While Mrs Marchmoor could sift the thoughts of others, I am content to sense their impulses – their energy. And then respond with all of thought's speed.'

'Imagine an army,' said Bronque. 'Untouchable swordsmen. Accuracy of fire.'

'I do not know how much of the Comte's lore my uncle has digested, though it seems he feeds at the same alchemical trough, that he *believes*. If he's wrapped around visions of triple-souled births and exaltations of new flesh, we are halfway home!'

'Do not discount his practicality,' said Svenson. 'The explosions in the city, the spurs.'

Schoepfil pursed his lips. 'Well. Perhaps.'

Svenson nodded at the machines, the tin-lined tubs of water. 'And now?'

'My legs! I shall move like a ghost! The perfect *provocateur*.'

Schoepfil undressed to cotton underwear whose legs had been removed, so that he might undergo the procedure and retain his modesty. On the table lay what looked like an oversized bandolier. Each loop of leather was padded with orange felt and held a bolt of blue glass, larger than a shell for an elephant gun. Several loops were empty, but in one the charge of blue glass had been replaced with the flask of bloodstone Svenson had brought from the Institute. He fished out a handkerchief and prised loose a bolt of glass.

'This fits in the first chamber?'

'It does.' Schoepfil settled himself on a padded stool with each foot in a tub and flicked his toes in the water.

Svenson slotted the glass in place and fastened the chamber's hatch. He began to gather the black hoses. 'The Comte *did* attempt something like this, you know . . .'

'Well, his mind *was* exceedingly fertile. One entire notebook dedicated to *hair* –'

'Angelique, from Mrs Kraft's brothel. I was called in to consult, after the fact.'

Schoepfil shrugged, having no interest in a whore.

'The experiment went wrong. It was as if she were drowned, without ever going underwater.' Svenson strapped the hoses to Schoepfil's bare legs and fitted his feet with webbed leather slippers. 'His inability to reverse the effects led to her being substituted as the third glass woman, instead of Caroline Stearne.'

'What exactly went wrong?' asked Bronque.

'I never learnt.'

'Doesn't help *us*, then,' said Schoepfil.

The whistle sounded. The train began to slow. Bronque consulted his watch.

'Crampton Place. Once the train starts again we'll throw the switch.'

Through the next stations, from Packington to St Porte, every time the Colonel stepped from the carriage, two grenadiers entered to make sure Doctor Svenson did nothing to Mr Schoepfil, asleep on a straw pallet. Bronque had drawn a blanket around Schoepfil to his neck, as the last thing soldiers going into battle needed was to see a man with his limbs turned blue.

The procedure went smoothly. Svenson followed the mechanics of energy, his understanding augmented by the ordeal of Mrs Kraft. Well into the change Schoepfil could still converse, guiding Svenson through tight-clenched teeth until the blue colour began to saturate his skin. Bronque caught Schoepfil's head when he fell back insensible, but it was for Svenson alone to judge the moment when the power must be cut off, when going further risked the next stage of transformation, turning Schoepfil's flesh to glass.

Had he erred, he knew, Bronque would have taken his life. He wondered at the strange alliance between the two men, both possessed of a certain

talent, yet judged by their betters to be mediocrities. Were they kindred spirits of spite? Certainly they had staked their lives on this one throw. Without
Schoepfil inheriting his uncle's empire – that protecting influence –
Bronque's diversion of an elite regiment in a time of public crisis would
bring a court martial and disgrace, if not a firing squad. And if Schoepfil
failed, for his abuses at the Thermæ alone he would be banished or
imprisoned. For the next hours, however, both men remained free as lords.

With the second leg finished and Schoepfil collapsed into a stupor, Svenson was left alone with Bronque. He blew smoke at the rear of the train.
'How is Mrs Kraft here, after what you did to her people?'

Bronque laughed harshly and fished out his flask. 'If Vandaariff dies, she
won't care about a few sticks of furniture and some trollops.'

'You are an expert on women's feelings?'

Bronque screwed up his face and took a pull of whisky. 'Still brooding about the Contessa? Well, you may indeed. I've never had a more
*magnificent –*'

'No, Colonel, I am not *brooding*. Nor do I desire your narrative of con-
quest. But I am obliged to ask, are you so sure she did not conquer *you*? And
the details of this very campaign?'

'What in hell do you mean?'

Svenson said nothing. Bronque made to drink, but put the flask down.
'I would *know*.'

'Would you? She has learnt to make her own blue glass. With it, she could
have stolen your memories or persuaded you with new ones. Ask yourself,
Colonel, did you *ever* have her? Are you *sure*? I was there when she cut Pont-
Joule's throat. I did not know they were *en amour*, but it did not stay her
blade. If you think she would not ransack your mind like a trunk, then
you're an ass.'

Bronque flushed with anger but did not speak. Instead he pocketed the
flask and rubbed his face with both hands. He stood and stalked to the door.
Svenson heard him address his men, but not the words. Bronque came back
and reclaimed his seat.

'If there is coffee on this train we will have some.' Svenson nodded
blandly, for Bronque's sharp face still showed rage. 'And I'm a fool not to

allow for what you say. Which means that Mrs Kraft's *information* must be considered in an altogether new light.'

'Because she has only recently appeared,' said Svenson.

'And thus represents the one thing the Contessa categorically *cannot* know. And not only did that woman escape her captivity, by doing so she avoided a very specific fate. I planned to inform Vandaariff of the Contessa's location, and Lord only knows what he would have done to her. But somehow she chose *just* that time to get away.'

'As if she knew . . . or that you'd told her?'

'But why would I? It was *my* plan!' Bronque glared at Schoepfil on the pallet. 'If you tell him this I'll cut your throat.'

'Why should I?'

'Because you're as desperate as I am. And, because a damned whore-mistress knows something the Contessa can't anticipate, I must protect her at all costs. But, however important it might now be to reach Vandaariff before sunrise, that doesn't change our having to get through his front door.'

Colonel Bronque slapped his thigh with frustration. Doctor Svenson took that moment to palm the flask of bloodstone and drop it in his pocket.

They woke Schoepfil before Orange Locks, where Bronque and his men would disembark. Schoepfil exulted in his altered legs: vivid blue from the toes to mid-calf, with marbled streaks extending up each sparsely haired thigh.

'Did it *work*?' asked Bronque.

'O I do expect so!' Schoepfil rotated each ankle, then hopped from one leg to the other. He snapped his fingers – a command for his clothing – and the Doctor grudgingly passed Schoepfil his trousers.

'Do mind the crease!' Schoepfil chided, shaking them out and slipping one foot through. 'Anything in the meantime?'

'Nothing to change our plans,' Bronque replied. 'A few prisoners. Pretending to be bankers. Michel Gorine, for one.'

'*No!* That little nuisance must have set him free.'

'What matters is that he tried to see Mrs Kraft.'

'Very good of you to prevent it. Who are the others?'

'One I don't know – foreigner. The second is Vandaariff's man from the Institute. Augustus Trooste.'

Schoepfil paused between shirt buttons. 'With Gorine? Is it a *scheme*?'

Both men turned to Svenson. He sighed. 'I have been under guard with you.'

'Could be Chang,' Bronque admitted. 'Neither he nor Foison showed at any station, and the men sent after them did not return.'

Svenson made a point of balling up Schoepfil's waistcoat and tossing it across. Schoepfil caught it with a frown and stroked the silk to smooth it.

'Perhaps they are *all* dead. The violence in the town.'

'Perhaps.' Bronque snapped shut his watch. 'You know what to do?'

Schoepfil wormed into his jacket. 'Not to worry. I shall pass like a *shade*.'

Bronque gave Svenson a warning glance not to speak. 'We do not know what to expect. It may be that Mrs Kraft's knowledge –'

'Yes, yes, you are the *tactician*. I leave it to you, though Gorine may serve as leverage over the woman.' Schoepfil pulled on his gloves, as dapper a figure as he had ever been. He extended a hand to Bronque. 'Until the finish.' He laughed. '*Rebirth*.'

Bronque shook his partner's hand, but did not speak. He turned for the door.

'O do not be *dour*, Colonel! We will not fail!'

Bronque rapped on the metal panel. The door swung open, letting in the racket of the wheels. He nodded to them, without speaking, and stepped through.

Schoepfil sat on the table, legs dangling. Svenson had taken the Colonel's chair. On his lap Schoepfil held an oblong wooden box, the lid positioned to block Svenson's view. He ran a finger across its contents with a satisfied smile. The train rattled to its terminus.

'You're a soldier – of sorts, anyway. Are they all so superstitious?'

'Most people are, when it comes to death.'

'They should be *confident*.'

'Solitude lacks comfort. And there is no greater solitude than mortality.' Svenson rubbed his eyes. 'Your uncle who will not die, I expect you think him a fool.'

'The *biggest*.'

'You have given your body to his same foolishness – this alchemy.'

'I am not *dying*.'

'You might have died ten times today. I could have shot you through the head myself.'

Schoepfil smiled. 'You would not have!'

'I would have very well,' replied Svenson testily. 'But for the same reason you keep me – that you may prove of use. Another man would have spattered your brains –'

But Schoepfil had already burst into laughter. 'I be of use to *you*! O that is *prime*!' Schoepfil drummed a hand on his knee. 'You will be lucky to avoid the scaffold!'

The Doctor tapped his ash onto the floor, loathing the man, and even more the truth in his words. For a blessed moment Schoepfil did not speak. Svenson allowed his mind to touch upon the painful day he and Phelps had returned to Parchfeldt . . . the air wind-kissed, the clouds blooming white. He was no stranger to death. The medical habit of distance had run deep enough to let him search through the woods, and to at last identify the bundle of limbs – taken first for weather-beaten twigs – and the colour of the tattered dress she'd worn. Phelps had hung back with a handkerchief to his face, but Doctor Svenson could not. His hand had gently turned the corpse's face, no longer Elöise, and, yet, he could not un-see her, still the woman he'd loved in all her ruined parts. The gaping, gummy crease from the Contessa's blade, blackened with long-dried blood. The eyes cruelly sunken, glazed pale as milk. Her fingers in the grass, always so thin, now grey at the tips, puffed with bloat, foreign. He had spread the tarpaulin and so very tenderly eased her onto it, turning his eyes from the flattened earth where she had lain, the insects and worms writhing at the sudden light.

It is an illusion that we are not such objects while we still live, the Doctor had told himself. And in the time since, while Elöise mouldered in the garden of her uncle's cottage, where had time carried him – what achievement lay in his staying alive?

Small gestures with Phelps and Cunsher, meagre checks against their enemies. Preserving Celeste Temple's life, and Chang's – for a time. And his

own animal resurgence – the compulsion of *life* – had come at the provocation of an outright monster. Could there be any stronger proof of an
indiscriminate world?

He groped for the red metal tin. 'I assume we approach Harschmort by
the canal? Timed to coincide with the Colonel's arrival at the gate?'

'O more than *that*, Doctor.'

Svenson sighed, then asked, as was expected. 'How so?'

Schoepfil snapped the box shut and set it aside. 'I do not expect to be
*alone*.'

They disembarked at the Orange Canal Station with two grenadiers, the last
of Bronque's men, not a single other soul to be seen. The Doctor inhaled the
salt tang of the sea.

'I thought we would be joined.'

'Not *here*, Doctor. We must to the canal.'

So rapid was Schoepfil's pace that Svenson and the grenadiers were forced
into an awkward trot. The Doctor addressed them as they ran.

'Despite your orders, I wish to be civil – there is no telling what difficul-
ties may drive us together. I am Captain-Surgeon Svenson of the Macklenburg
Navy.'

Neither soldier spoke, so Svenson bent to the nearest, stripes on his
sleeve. 'Sergeant of grenadiers is no small achievement. Had I a hat, I would
touch it to you.'

At this the tall sergeant smiled. 'Barlew, sir, sergeant these two years. This
is Poggs. You don't want to cross Private Poggs.'

Svenson spoke across Barlew to Poggs, with a respectful gravity. 'I'm sure
I do not. But I am more concerned with your own safeties.'

'Not to worry, sir,' said Barlew. 'But very good of you.'

They nearly collided with Schoepfil when the man suddenly stopped. Sergeant Barlew muttered an apology but Schoepfil hissed him to silence,
peering around him in the gloom. Svenson saw nothing and heard only the
wind. Schoepfil flexed his hands, as if stroking the air for scent. He whispered to the soldiers, 'One of you stay here. Wait five minutes, then catch up
to us. Be careful. Keep your guard. *Come*.'

Trooper Poggs diligently stepped aside and the others hurried on until the dunes were replaced by the shining surface of the Orange Canal. Its walkways were empty, with not even a watchman's lantern. Schoepfil pointed away to a glow across the grass.

'Harschmort.'

Svenson turned to the canal. 'But is *this* not where we expect whoever will join us?'

'Be patient, Doctor. Who is this?'

Schoepfil darted to the side with astonishing speed. Footfalls came towards them from the dark. The Sergeant's bayonet was fixed and ready, but a whisper made clear it was Poggs.

'Report!' hissed Schoepfil.

'Someone following all right. I couldn't get him, sir. Kept hanging back.'

'But who *is* it?' Schoepfil squeezed his hands to fists. 'And are you sure it is a *man*?'

'Wouldn't be a woman, sir – not out here.'

Abruptly Schoepfil looked up, listening intently. With a pale, questioning expression he turned to Svenson. 'I don't hear a thing.'

'Ought you to?'

'Colonel Bronque should have reached the gate.'

'Perhaps he was delayed. Vandaariff has his own men –'

'No, we should have *heard*.'

Sergeant Barlew cleared his throat. 'There was the fire, sir.'

'What *fire*?'

'We saw it behind us, from the train. The Colonel must have burnt the station. Didn't you see? We were told not to disturb you –'

'There was no plan to burn any *station*!'

'I'm sorry, sir. We must have it wrong, then.'

'Of all the blasted idiocy! Follow me and *watch* – beware what traps I avoid – pay attention! Our purpose is stealth, not confrontation. Colonel Bronque is the broadside of cannon. We are the stiletto in the ear. Do you understand?'

'Why do you need us at all?' asked Doctor Svenson.

'I need *them* to watch *you*. I will need *you* to preserve my life.' Schoepfil darted away, his short, thin legs as brisk as a bird's.

'And why in hell should I do that?' called Svenson.

Schoepfil's reply echoed off the still canal. 'Because otherwise she wins!'

The nearest Svenson had seen to it was watching men such as Chang, whose instincts had been thoroughly etched onto the most primitive portions of the brain, where action preceded thought. In Schoepfil's case it had nothing to do with experience.

Running at full speed, Schoepfil abruptly jumped in the air. When Svenson and the soldiers reached the same point, they found black wire stretched between two huts, tied to an explosive charge. Carefully they stepped over and kept on – past more wires and beds of glass spikes hidden in the path. Veering around the last, Svenson glanced back and caught a glimpse of motion. Someone *did* follow, and aped Schoepfil's safe path as well.

Muffled cries and the crack of breaking glass reached them with Schoepfil's warning.

'Stay back! Wait for the wind!'

Svenson perceived a cloud of smoke and watched it break apart, towards the sea. He advanced to find two men in green on the ground, their heads encased by brass helmets. Each carried a canvas satchel of apple-sized glass balls, several of which lay broken at their feet.

'Hurry!' called Schoepfil, already well ahead.

More traps and men – so many that Barlew and Poggs, wading in with their bayonets, reached Schoepfil before he could finish the last. Svenson, without a weapon, hung back, hoping to snatch something off one of the fallen men, but Barlew took the Doctor's arm before he could.

They joined Schoepfil at a set of glass garden doors. This was the eastern wing of Harschmort. Schoepfil's face gleamed with perspiration but he smiled.

'Now we are to it! Follow some steps behind, weapons ready. The new construction has been concentrated in the western wing –'

Schoepfil whipped his head towards the outbuildings, then lunged for the door. Svenson heard the explosive pop of breaking glass as Schoepfil hauled himself through. Poggs and Barlew sank in a cloud of smoke. Schoepfil slammed the door even as the panes shattered, smoke rising around them from the shards.

Svenson clapped a hand over his mouth and ran – for an instant after Schoepfil, but then veering wildly away. He heard Schoepfil's cries of outrage, but still more glass and smoke prevented any pursuit. Svenson crossed the ballroom floor before risking a look back: a distant figure like a tall tropical insect, all orange and brass, with two pitiless glass eyes that marked the Doctor as he fled.

Construction in the western wing, Schoepfil had said. Svenson gathered his memories of Harschmort as he ran, but the carpets were gone and the furniture covered with white sheets. He brought himself to a panting stop when the floor changed to black-and-white chequers. This was near the kitchens – at the corridor's end had been the staircase descending to the Comte's underground chamber. Chang had described it destroyed, collapsed to form a vast crater. And yet . . . renovation. Svenson began to trot in that direction.

At a swinging wooden door he paused and peered into a scullery. A heavy steel cleaver stuck up from a butcher's block, and Svenson wrenched with both hands until the blade came free. A woman in dark livery watched from an inner doorway. Past her more servants gathered around a teapot.

'Everyone all right?' whispered Svenson.

The woman nodded.

'Excellent. Stay here – you've all been told, haven't you?'

The woman nodded. Svenson turned for the door, then craned his head back. 'Beg your pardon – so much has changed – the western wing?'

'No one goes there, sir.'

The cook was joined by the others, the increase in numbers heightening the dubious nature of his uniform, his accent, his filthy appearance.

'That's my cutting knife,' said one of the men.

'I will not abuse it.' With an afterthought Svenson sketched a bow of thanks. 'Not to worry. I do serve the Queen.'

The disapproving man only pursed his lips. 'Queen's an old haddock.'

*

Where the staircase had stood was a wall of new-laid brick, unplastered and without a door. This route blocked, Svenson followed the path of recent construction and eventually met voices, coming near. He scrambled behind a cloth-draped statue of an Eastern goddess (nearly putting out his eye on a finger of her fourth arm). The voices went past: two men in green with carbines guarding a half-dozen shambling, bandaged grenadiers.

He walked on, gripping the cleaver. The corridor was gritty with plaster and sawdust, and ended at a wide, high foyer. He had reached the front of the house. Svenson flattened himself against the wall.

The foyer was filled with bodies: grenadiers. Unlike the Customs House, these men were not dead: they stirred and moaned, slowly regaining their senses. A group of six, standing shakily, was bullied to order by Vandaariff's militia.

More of Vandaariff's men marched through the main door carrying the same boxes that Kelling had so assiduously cared for. These men wore brass helmets, and dropped the boxes without ceremony. There was no sign of Kelling, or of Bronque. Perhaps they were still outside. Perhaps they'd been killed.

The western wing lay beyond the foyer, but Svenson could not cross without being seen – any more than he could remain where he was. The group of grenadiers began to trudge towards Svenson's arch. He retreated to a squat piece of cloth-covered furniture and ducked under the sheet, only to find a solid Chinese trunk. Svenson curled into a ball. The footfalls passed by, endlessly, but finally he tugged the cloth from his head. Not ten yards away on the opposite wall, similarly peeking from his own shroud, was a young man Svenson did not know.

Carefully the young man slipped free of his hiding place and Svenson recognized the figure who had followed from the canal – orange coat, brass helmet, canvas satchel. He pointed deliberately to the floor.

'We must go *down*,' he whispered.

Svenson nodded. 'First we must cross the foyer.'

The young man reached into the satchel, coming out with a pair of blue glass balls. He offered one to Svenson, but the Doctor shook his head, leaning close. 'They have helmets – more than enough to stop us. Still, I have an idea.'

'What is that?'

The Doctor carefully laid the cleaver on the young man's throat. 'That you are my prisoner, Mr Pfaff.'

The last grenadiers were being roused with kicks. Svenson's quick count of Vandaariff's men stalled at fifteen, four or five in helmets. Keeping to the wall, he and Pfaff advanced nearly halfway to the far wing before they were seen. The curiosity of Svenson holding a knife to Pfaff's neck prevented an immediate clash. Instead, Vandaariff's men formed a line to hem them in, carbines raised. Svenson addressed them as calmly as he could.

'I am here for Lord Robert Vandaariff. If prevented, I will take the life of this man. Since Lord Vandaariff desires him *whole*, whoever amongst you provokes my action will pay the penalty. I will speak to Mr Foison.'

'You'll speak to me,' replied a senior guard, shouldering through the line.

'I am Captain-Surgeon Abelard Svenson of the Macklenburg Navy. This man is named Pfaff. He has information vital to Lord –'

'*Svenson?*'

'That is correct – and I assure you, unless you allow . . .'

The Doctor faltered, for the senior guard had taken a paper from his pocket and, upon consulting it, signalled to his men. The four in helmets strode forcefully towards Svenson and Pfaff, then knelt to lift two panels in the floor, exposing a staircase leading down. The drone of machines echoed from below.

'The Warden. You are expected,' said the guard. 'Leave the satchel and the helmet.'

The carbines snapped back to readiness. Pfaff eased the satchel and helmet to the floor.

'And the knife.'

Svenson dropped the cleaver with a clang. The guard motioned them to the stairs. The soldiers who'd opened the stair doors stood just out of reach . . . but they did not spring.

In a moment of strange calm, Doctor Svenson reached into his tunic for the red tin, took a cigarette, tucked the tin away and struck a match. He exhaled, and tossed the match aside. Still none of the green-coats attacked.

Still mystified, Svenson descended, boots rapping the steel steps like a pair
of mallets. Pfaff came after, and his head had just cleared the edge when the
panels above them were unceremoniously slammed shut. Both men flinched,
Svenson groping for the rail.

'What did he mean, "Warden"?' asked Pfaff.

'I have no idea.'

Their shadows danced above them as they went, elongated demon shapes
with twisting limbs. At its base the staircase vanished into black water, like a
pen in a massive inkwell. Across the dark pool, too far to jump, awaited a
brick wall and a door of unpainted oak.

'Do you think it's deep?' asked Pfaff.

'I do.' Svenson knelt and cupped a palm. The water beaded on his skin
like oil. 'It's warm . . . and filthy from the machines. I should not drink it.'

'I had no desire to.'

Svenson thrust his hand into the water and shoved forward, sending small
waves at the door. He stood. 'Come.'

'Where?'

Svenson extended one foot deliberately over the pool and stepped down.
The water did not rise above the ankle of his boot. He used his second foot
to kick another wave.

'Look where the ripples break. There are stones beneath, in a path. Simple, really.'

He picked his way to the door, Pfaff following only after having rolled up
his precious chequered trousers. 'Why would anyone do this?' Pfaff muttered. 'Take all this trouble?'

'To keep people like us out. And I suppose stepping stones instead of a
path because the water needs to flow freely.'

'*Why?*'

'To power the machines.' Svenson reached the door and turned. 'But it
isn't salt water.'

'What does *that* mean?' Pfaff balanced on the last stone, waiting for him
to open the door and make room. Svenson did not.

'It means the river. Where is the Contessa, Mr Pfaff?'

'How should I know?'

'Of course you know.'

'Open that door.' Pfaff filled his hands with a slim knife and a brass-knuckle guard.

Svenson nodded across the black water to the stairs. 'You should go back. The soldiers will not harm you if you do.'

Pfaff spat in the water. So answered, Svenson opened the door and stepped into a scene of his own hell.

Copper wire had been strung around the room on hooks, well away from the floor, which was awash with filthy water like a slaughterhouse with blood. Around a medical table stood a dozen figures in white robes. A large man lay strapped to the table, his face obscured by a black rubber mask that bristled with tubes and wires, his skin the colour of cherrywood.

A robed acolyte knelt to insert a bolt of blue glass into a brass box-stand, one of several strung together. Another acolyte fitted wire inside a wooden box lined with orange felt. Each discarded box cluttering the corners of the room meant another convert, and the faces looking up at their entrance, eyes peering through red livid rings, lacked any expression save cold will.

'Get away from him,' called Svenson.

'We will not,' replied an acolyte at the head of the table, gripping a brass handle.

'I am named Warden of this ritual, by your master. This one is not to be reborn.'

'How do we know you speak the truth?' asked the man with the handle. His hood hung loose around his shoulders and Svenson glimpsed a grenadier uniform: one of Bronque's adjutants, captured and already made Vandaariff's slave.

'Do you *presume*?' Svenson replied haughtily, but felt his ignorance. Nowhere did he recall any *warden*. What was he intended to do? 'Where is the Executioner?' he demanded. 'Where is the Virgo Lucifera? Where is the *Bride*?'

The adjutant of grenadiers only shook his head.

'Then find them!' shouted Svenson. 'How else can we continue? *Hurry!*'

He stabbed a finger at the exit – a curtain, he saw – and the acolytes retreated, bowing and bobbing . . . all except the adjutant, who remained, still ready to throw the switch. Svenson approached, looking stern.

'Why do you delay?'

The adjutant swallowed, fighting some inner command. 'I . . . I have surrendered my will, in order to be free . . . my desires have been redeemed . . .' His mouth groped for words. 'The – the –'

'Where is Colonel Bronque?' Svenson asked gently.

The adjutant shook his head.

'Where is Mrs Kraft?'

'Consumed. Consumed. *Every last soul shall be –*'

Pfaff's brass-bound fist shot into the adjutant's jaw. Svenson leapt for the handle as the man toppled, luckily, backwards.

'Good Lord! If he had fallen the other way –'.

'Is he dead?' asked Pfaff, looking down at Mahmoud.

'He is not. Untie him, wake him – we must know what happened.' Svenson prised the mask from Mahmoud's face, wincing at the clinging layer of gelatin, smeared to conduct the electrical charge. Instead of helping, Pfaff crossed to the curtain.

'Where are you going?'

'Why did they listen to you?'

'Because obviously Vandaariff left instructions –'

'And you made a bargain,' Pfaff sneered.

Svenson pulled at the restraints. 'Everyone has made bargains. While Vandaariff holds Miss Temple or Chang, he is convinced he can command my aid – and so names me Warden to put me near him, where I can defend him against Schoepfil . . . or you.'

'That's what I thought.' Pfaff ducked through the curtain and was gone.

No doubt because of his size, more of the blue glass balls had been employed against Mahmoud to bring him down, and Svenson could not rouse him. The large man was too much to carry. Svenson could only leave him where he was.

Outside the curtain waited a second, wider moat, churning and black. On the opposite side rose another flight of iron steps. The wall behind the staircase bore a line of square embrasures, one of which had its metal grille bent aside. Pulses of water – translucent and clean – slopped over the embrasure's lip and into the pool.

Svenson carefully negotiated another set of hidden stones. No wet prints from Pfaff climbed the steps – had *he* bent aside the grille? Svenson was tempted to follow, but reasoned that the sooner he reached Vandaariff the better. The stairs rose to an open trapdoor. He climbed through and gazed about in wonder. If Schoepfil's makeshift arrangement in the railway carriage had been a pencil sketch of Vandaariff's prowess, here was a full work executed in oil: more machines with more wires, more hoses, and two large medical tables in the centre. Around the tables, instead of paltry footbaths, hulked five massive coffin-shaped tubs, with space for a sixth. Each tub perched atop a brass-legged dais, like giant, gleaming scarabs. At the beetle's mouth lurked an ugly crucible chamber, each primed with a bolt of blue glass.

The walls were painted in the style of Oskar Veilandt, though Svenson felt the execution differed . . . another artist, or the same artist with an older and unsteady set of hands? Much of it echoed the massive painting from Vienna . . . but as much again had been changed, reimagined. Had Vandaariff's practical knowledge deepened? Or had his desires changed? Or had a scrap of the old financier's practical mind remained to assert itself?

Doctor Svenson cupped his hands around his mouth and called: 'Robert Vandaariff! Oskar Veilandt! I am here!'

'So you are, my Warden. *Welcome.*'

Framed in a small archway, Robert Vandaariff stood wearing a white robe, with a half-mask of white feathers over his haggard face. One blackened hand lay on a squat rostrum that sprouted a mix of knobs and handles. A second archway was at Vandaariff's back, through which Svenson glimpsed a fountain swirling orange and blue. From the reflections Svenson perceived that Vandaariff was sealed away by protective walls of glass. Vandaariff turned a knob on the rostrum and a door closed, blocking off the fountain room.

Svenson wondered if he could use one of the smaller machines to smash the glass. 'I am not yours. If you do not surrender I will do my best to sabotage every piece of equipment you have.'

Vandaariff shook his head. 'But, Doctor, surrender is exactly what I intend!'

'Then enough of this nonsense. Too many people are in danger, and your fortune –' He checked himself. 'Robert *Vandaariff's* fortune – cannot be passed to dangerous fools.'

'We agree again. It is a shame we have not taken tea.'

'It is a shame I have not shot you through the heart.'

'Don't play-act a man you are not. Do you imagine I have not divined your *nature?*'

'And what is that?'

'Enough words. See those souls you – you *alone* – protect.'

With a sudden chill, Svenson turned to the line of tubs.

'Protect or sacrifice, dear Doctor, whichever you choose.'

The acolytes Svenson had driven from below – and that many more again – returned to the room hauling a sixth porcelain tub with its brass undercarriage. Black hoses were attached and dark fluid poured inside.

The sixth tub contained Madelaine Kraft, her honey-coloured skin covered with painted symbols, as senseless as she'd been in the Old Palace. Now she floated naked in a rust-red fluid.

An acolyte approached the glass wall with a bow. 'All is ready, my lord.'

Svenson gaped at Professor Trooste's red-scarred face. 'Dear God.'

'Very well!' Vandaariff did not hide his pleasure at Svenson's dismay. '*Proceed.*'

Trooste clapped his hands and several acolytes followed him out. More attended to the tubs, wary of the Doctor's interference, but he was too stricken at seeing whom they held: Mr Kelling, Colonel Bronque, Matthew Harcourt, Michel Gorine and, last of all, poor Cunsher, his lank hair suspended in the viscous liquid.

'Abate your concern, Doctor – worse decisions await. *Nothing* is forbidden. Habituate yourself to that fact.'

Svenson did not reply. Any attempt to save them now would fail – he could not, unarmed, defeat so many – and cast away any chance of saving them later. That every tub was fitted with a glass-charged undercarriage meant that a vast amount of power would be channelled into each: the thought of a well-seasoned *broth* came foully to mind. These were living beings, laid out like stew-meat in a kitchen. The entire enterprise, every lusciously fashioned, brass-bound inch of it, was obscene.

'It won't work,' he shouted to the glass. 'I see the sepsis in your hands – you're rotting from within. That you can stand is a miracle.'

'No miracle, Doctor – deliberately timed. Though time *does* run short . . .'

Svenson followed Vandaariff's eyes. Mr Foison limped into the room, a bloody bandage wrapped around his right thigh. Vandaariff's dapper captain had become as dishevelled as the Doctor. In one hand he held a silver knife and in the other a leather case. With a horrible certainty Svenson knew it was the same case he'd passed to Miss Temple in the Thermæ.

On Foison's heels bustled Trooste and his acolytes, bearing Cardinal Chang, naked to the waist and senseless. Before Svenson could move, Foison raised the knife.

'Is – is he . . .'

'Dead? No.' Foison nodded to the leather case. 'But neither, would I say, is Cardinal Chang at *home*.'

Chang was strapped face down on a table, head in a padded frame, as if for surgery. An acolyte carefully cleaned the scar at the base of his spine. Svenson grimaced at the increased inflamation.

'Mr Foison has been impetuous, but the *vessel* has arrived.' Vandaariff broke into a gurgling cough, groped for a shallow bowl and then retched into it, a clot of curdled aspic. 'I am . . . unclean – not meant for such a fragile basin . . . yet to be rid of it is to die.'

'You will find no relief.' Svenson called. 'Robert Vandaariff was a healthy man at Parchfeldt, before contact with that book, and in a few months his body's been destroyed. Though Chang is healthier still, the same will happen. No matter how you may try to *prepare* him alchemically, you will find only the same unstoppable decay.'

'Contact with a book?' murmured Vandaariff. 'What *book*? I have consulted physicians by the score. The precipice I occupy is due to consumption aggravated by an especially grievous bout of blood fever. With no other avenue available, I have turned to the late Comte's intriguing research.'

He shrugged at Foison, as if to apologize for Svenson's offensive theories.

'That is a lie,' Svenson said to Foison. 'He needs you to protect him.'

Trooste took a beaker of red liquid from Mrs Kraft's tub and raised it to the light. An acolyte stood ready with a tray of flasks. Trooste poured the beaker back into the tub and selected a flask, sprinkling its contents judiciously . . . bright flakes gleaming gold. The flask was capped and they moved on to Mr Harcourt. Another beaker to the light, and another flask, but for Harcourt it was a sprinkling of dark pellets.

The Doctor pressed at Foison. 'Today, at the Institute, you asked the Professor if he found Lord Vandaariff's interests *troubling* –'

'A test, obviously,' said Vandaariff.

'*Obviously*,' echoed Trooste. Foison said nothing.

Svenson's voice rose to a shout. 'These are good men – Cunsher, Gorine! They do not deserve this barbaric treatment! This is *cannibalism* – forbidden by every sane precept – Lord, how can you not *see*?'

Foison said nothing. Vandaariff tapped the glass with his stick.

'If your outrage can bear it, Doctor, I have a question for Mr Foison myself. Actually I have two. The first from the confession – upon initiation to the Process, secrets will out – of Professor Trooste. He swears that Doctor Svenson destroyed two glass books at the Institute today, and kept one for himself. Somehow, the Doctor lost that book, most likely at the Royal Thermæ, as you have obviously found it. Yet, in the tumult of Cardinal Chang's arrival and subsequent harvest, I have not had the details of that acquisition. One winnows the list of those who might have taken such a book from the Doctor – Drusus Schoepfil? The Contessa di Lacquer-Sforza? If you had bested any of these enemies I should expect to hear of it.'

'Forgive me, my lord.' Foison's thin voice held not an ounce of contrition. 'It was my intention to report whenever you had time to hear. I found the book in the house of Drusus Schoepfil, in a secret room painted in the man-

ner of the Comte d'Orkancz.' Foison glanced, impassively, at Svenson. 'Mr
Schoepfil is a dangerous man. As his people occupied the Harschmort train,
I was forced to find my own transport, and entrance.'

Vandaariff waved away this inconvenience, along with Foison's concern.
'I well know of my nephew's painted *room*, and that he has collected every
artefact of the Comte he could find. Who do you think made them available?
Who instructed those powerful men to promote Drusus Schoepfil as a fig-
urehead in the first place? Though he credits his own ludicrous destiny, he
remains as he ever was, an insignificant worm.'

'You underestimate the power of his belief,' said Doctor Svenson.

'The man believes nothing. His heart is inert.'

Svenson had given the book to Miss Temple. Foison must have had it from
her, have *seen* her. But why had he hidden that from Vandaariff? Not from
any weakness or wavering of purpose – Foison had used the book to reduce
Cardinal Chang to a mindless husk, after all – a fact Trooste's examination
had just confirmed. Had Foison taken the book from the Contessa instead?
Was *that* the alliance? Was Miss Temple even alive?

Foison cleared his throat. 'There was a second question, my lord?'

'Indeed, for Doctor Svenson. You were given entry in the company of
another man. A Mr *Pfaff*. Where is he now?'

'We parted ways.'

Foison cut in, softly but insistently: 'Pfaff is an ally of the Contessa, my
lord. He collected Miss Temple from the tomb. A criminal for hire, like
Chang.'

'Are *you* in league with Rosamonde, Doctor Svenson? I should find
that . . . *amusing*.'

'I am not.'

'I wondered if you had forgotten poor Mrs Dujong so very soon.'

'Burn in hell.'

'I have a better notion – why don't you come join me?'

Leaving nothing to chance, six acolytes escorted the Doctor past three different locked doorways, the last edged with a band of black rubber to make an

airtight seal. Brass helmets hung on pegs, two taken by acolytes and a third given to Svenson. The door was opened and, the seal of the helmet pulling at his neck, he followed the acolytes through.

In the corners of the room stood copper braziers, each heating a bowl of orange-coloured oil, a tonic for Vandaariff's condition, and evidently fatal for anyone else. The ceiling was honeycombed with small holes, aglow with growing light.

Vandaariff waited at a table, blackened fingers tracing the edges of a blue glass key. An acolyte with gloved hands set a gleaming book before him. Vandaariff carefully inserted the key into its binding, lengthwise from the base, and the bright glass clouded, ever so slightly. He opened the cover and ran a fingertip down the first page.

'*Delicious.*' He gently closed the book. 'Time enough . . . time enough.'

The braziers with their oil, the glass balls with their somnolent gas, the explosions and the sharp-edged spurs – in how many other ways had Vandaariff expanded the Comte's initial discoveries? Schoepfil was a fool to underestimate him. And where *was* Schoepfil? If Vandaariff's men had not brought him down like Bronque, they must have sent word of his intrusion . . . but the fact did not appear to perturb.

At a touch the key emerged from the book and Vandaariff tucked it away. The acolyte reverently restored the book to a case holding a score of others – most only partially extant, their bindings cracked.

Vandaariff sighed. 'It was a second Library of Alexandria. Now so much is lost, and so thoughtlessly.'

'These are not the tragedies of Agathon. Chang deserves to live, in his own skin.'

'Chang is forfeit.'

'As are you. The rot in your body proclaims it –'

'Please, we have been down this road. You are not here to lecture.'

'Then why? To witness my friend's place in your *collection*?' Svenson glared angrily at the books. Both acolytes moved to block his way.

'Doctor Svenson, you cannot hold a single thought much less two or three. I have brought you to my person through deliberate steps, knowing your preference for my death. Why? Because, plain enough for a cat to perceive, in exchange for your aid I offer you something you desire, available nowhere else on earth.'

'That Chang will survive, of course, and Miss Temple –'

Vandaariff shook his head. 'No. No, they are gone. Their consumption is required.'

'I will not be party. I will do anything in my power –'

Vandaariff rubbed the skin beneath his feathered mask and groaned with impatience. 'Doctor, I beg you, *think*. What have you *done* today? Beyond all sane probability?'

'Madelaine Kraft was healed. As Chang might now be –'

'*Not* Chang! *Never* Chang! Chang has become raw goods. No, Doctor Svenson, who else? What else in the world would prick your virtue like the balloon I know all virtue to be?'

Another glass book was set on the table. Vandaariff inserted the key and, resting a fingertip lightly on the glass, turned the pages to the clouded leaf he sought. He rotated the book so that it faced the Doctor.

'*Taste.*'

'I won't.'

'You will not regret it.'

'Damn you.' Svenson stabbed his forefinger onto the glass.

The first impression was too sharp, like whisky on his tongue, a pungent whirl of hair and scent, of softness and weight, tenderness, doubt, carnality –

He yanked up his hand. Vandaariff fed on his reaction with an ugly leer.

'O . . . do take a little more.'

Svenson swallowed. 'How . . . how in all hell –'

'You know yourself! You were *there*!'

'Tarr Manor,' Svenson whispered. 'Her memories were taken. Only a few, still, she almost died –'

'A singularly aggressive reaction – and the only reason these memories survived! Set aside for study – the actual information, once Arthur Trapping was dead, bore no interest. But *now* it bears all manner of interest – for you! And, through your inevitable compliance, for me!'

Svenson shook his head. 'I won't. I won't. She is *dead* –'

An acolyte hooked an arm around the Doctor's neck, while the other caught his hand and pressed it, palm down, upon the glass. Svenson bucked against the contact. Yet, at its bite, he could not but drop his gaze . . .

. . . and enter the memories of Elöise Dujong, the whole of her relations with Arthur Trapping from innocent affection to shame-filled lust. The Doctor gasped at intimacies he himself had never shared, her body in gross and sweet detail – assignations, fervent, guilty, compulsive. He swam in her tears, sank in her self-recriminations, thrilled to the touch of kisses down her neck, Trapping's fingers tracing the inner sweep of her white thigh –

Svenson blinked, in tears, the confinement of the helmet unfamiliar and strange. The acolytes had pulled him free. Vandaariff stood at the glass wall, shouting.

'*No!* This must not occur! Stop him! Mr Foison! *Mr Foison!*'

Mahmoud held a length of copper wire and swung it like a whip at an acolyte foolish enough to have gone near. The wire slashed through the white robe and the acolyte dropped screaming. The big man took the acolyte by the scruff of the neck and hurled him down the trapdoor stairs, a sheer drop of at least thirty feet. Several acolytes lay on the floor, and who knew how many more had taken that plunge. Foison, armed with only a silver knife, had retreated behind Chang's table with Professor Trooste.

Mahmoud reached into the sticky red fluid to raise up his mother.

'Do not!' cried Trooste. 'You will kill her! The essential liquor is all that keeps them alive!'

Mahmoud hesitated, not trusting Trooste, yet not daring to risk her life. Vandaariff rapped his cane against the glass.

'*Enough!* If you care for that woman, you will listen to me!' He gave Svenson a haughty snort and when he spoke it was as much for the Doctor as for Mahmoud. 'Six chambers, for the first six compounds, each reduced in turn. The seventh will infuse the final coupling. The vessel itself constitutes the eighth – *tempered* metal, the rebirth. The ordure of death will be shed like a serpent's skin, peeled like a malignant husk, *passed on.*'

'What in the name of all hell –' began Mahmoud. Vandaariff rapped on the glass.

'*I* hold that woman's life in my grasp. The dawn has come!'

Vandaariff waved like a tragedian at the honeycombed ceiling. Each round tube glowed brightly, the shafts of light landing, Svenson saw, directly on the rostrum. Vandaariff ran dark fingers along six identical brass knobs. 'What do you say, Professor Trooste? Iron, to start?'

'Yes, my lord.'

'Matthew Harcourt,' Vandaariff intoned, 'I initiate your sacred journey . . . *now.*'

'No!' shouted Doctor Svenson, but the acolytes held him back. Vandaariff slipped the brass cap off one knob to expose a lozenge of blue glass. The light from the ceiling fell upon it and the glass began to glow. A moment later, the wires leading to Harcourt's tub coughed sparks into the air. Mahmoud raised a hand to shield his eyes . . .

Nothing else happened. No surge of energy came through the machines. Vandaariff was speechless. He slipped the brass cover on and off. More sparks, then nothing. Mahmoud roared and went for Trooste with both hands.

'*Stop.*'

Foison knelt over Gorine's tub, the silver knife at the floating man's neck. 'Down on your knees or he's dead.'

Slowly, Mahmoud did just that. Svenson saw the heaviness in the large man's limbs, that his body still fought the effects of the blue smoke.

'What in heaven, Professor Trooste!' shouted Vandaariff. 'What has gone wrong? Examine every coupling, every cable! This cannot be allowed! Send men below! The time, sir, *the time*!' Vandaariff turned from the window, mopping his mouth with a sleeve.

'Already your plan fails,' said Svenson.

'Momentary malfunction is not failure,' barked Vandaariff. 'Why was that black fellow not *redeemed*?'

'Because I saved him,' said Svenson.

'*Saved?* You have doomed him altogether.'

Mahmoud looked at the glass wall with a baleful hatred. Svenson spread his fingers on the glass, anything to urge patience.

'Why preserve *me*?' Svenson asked. 'Why any warden at all? You offer me Elöise – but merely her shadow, a sliver of her mind –'

'A taste of heaven is still heaven, Doctor.'

'But *why*?'

'Because I will be forced to trust you.'

'And if I refuse?'

'Then everything dies. And every person with it. The chaos in the city goes unchecked and my work will be scattered like African diamonds, treasure waiting for the worst of men to use for the worst of purposes.'

'What is that to me?'

'Because I see who you are. What is your answer? For Elöise?'

'No. Never. No.'

Vandaariff gurgled with pleasure. 'O Doctor. Such a terrible man with a lie. *Excellent*.'


By the time Svenson returned to the machines, Mahmoud's arms had been bound behind his back, copper bands digging into his dark skin. Trooste kept well away, moving from tub to tub, adding pinches of different powders. Foison guarded Mahmoud, favouring one leg, knife held listlessly.

Svenson rubbed his neck where the helmet's seal had pinched the skin. He nodded to the second, unoccupied medical table, and called to Vandaariff behind the glass: 'Is that for Miss Temple or the Contessa? Or does it matter?'

'Such cynicism – everything *matters*.'

'We should find Pfaff,' Foison called. 'We should locate Drusus Schoepfil.'

'You should let me examine your leg,' said Svenson.

'Thank you, no.'

'Doctor Svenson has been tempted to save the innocent,' called Vandaariff. 'He has refused. He has been tempted by his own heart and refused again. He is a man of *duty*.'

Mahmoud spat at the Doctor's feet. 'That's for your duty, if these two die.'

'I'm sure Doctor Svenson's assistance is welcome,' Trooste muttered from Chang's table, a pair of callipers measuring the expanded inflammation. 'If not altogether required – earlier today, for example –'

Abruptly the curtains over the far door were torn free, pulled to the floor by a flailing acolyte. Another two reeled in, turned and flung themselves back at a figure Svenson could not see. Each man's body was arrested in three different spots, jerking like puppets, and both dropped senseless. Hopping past them with a mincing precision, Drusus Schoepfil beamed with a cold intent.

'Doctor Svenson – you *did* survive – well met indeed!'

Without breaking stride Schoepfil twisted his torso and slashed the air with his arm, deflecting Foison's thrown knife so it rang against the wall like a bell. He pulled a sheaf of papers from his coat and waved them imperiously.

'Uncle Robert, do not think to avoid me! I have searched your papers! The payments to my supposed allies! Your *new will*! I know it all!' He hurled the papers at Chang's unmoving form. '*That* man – that *criminal* – will not inherit. I will prevent it with my own two hands!'

Even with an injured leg Foison cut Schoepfil off, blocking his way to the table. Schoepfil only smirked.

'Mr *Foison*. I apologize for not receiving you earlier when you called. I'd just had the place swept, you see, and simply couldn't bear to admit my uncle's trained baboon.'

Foison did not react to the insult, so Schoepfil's arm shot out and slapped him hard across the face. Foison staggered and Schoepfil came on, swinging. Foison managed to block two blows, but a third, so fast that Svenson only heard it strike, left him weaving.

'Do not fight him!' shouted Vandaariff. 'Mr Foison, retreat!'

But Schoepfil would not allow it. He feinted from side to side, while his fists, not strong but precise and persistent, pummelled Foison's face and body. Foison's skill was on full display, for he stopped more blows than struck home, but his counter-strokes found nothing but air. Schoepfil grinned fiercely. He darted about, teasing Foison with the final strike – but then, as he finally came near, Foison hurled himself, arms wide, and pinned Schoepfil's arms to his body. He lifted Schoepfil off the floor, and squeezed.

Schoepfil gasped – with surprise as much as pain – and kicked his legs and swatted with his forearms.

'Good Lord! Release me! Release me now and I – *ah* – I will – *ugh* – spare –'

Foison squeezed tight, tottering with the effort. Schoepfil's eyes locked on Svenson.

'Doctor – our agreement – *gah* – please –'

Svenson did not move.

'*Doctor* –'

Mahmoud staggered past Svenson. The wire still held his arms but a swinging kick behind Foison's knee brought all three men down. In a flash Schoepfil was up, stamping at Foison's head. Foison did not rise. Schoepfil stamped again for spite. He swept his angry eyes around the room until he found Svenson and screamed.

'*You! Snake! Judas!*'

'Calm yourself –'

'*Calm myself?*'

Schoepfil stalked in a ragged circle, glaring at the line of tubs, before stopping short at the sight of Bronque and Kelling.

'Good Lord! This is not the ritual! What is this?' He bellowed at the glass wall. 'What have you done to Colonel Bronque? Uncle! What . . . wait – *wait*! *Who in hell is that?*'

Svenson followed Schoepfil's gaze. Vandaariff stood unmoving behind the glass, a bright blade at his throat. Holding the knife was a woman, her head hidden by a brazen helmet, her filth-stained dress hanging heavy, soaking wet.

'Uncle Robert?' asked Schoepfil.

'Do your duty, Doctor Svenson,' croaked Vandaariff. 'You know what can be yours.'

'Be quiet, Oskar,' buzzed the voice from inside the helmet. 'Doctor Svenson is of absolutely no importance to anyone.'

The Contessa gave the blade a sharp tug. A ruby jet splashed the glass and rolled down, fed in gouts as Robert Vandaariff slumped into the window and sank lifeless to the floor.

# TEN

## SEVERANCE

Swimming itself Miss Temple enjoyed, for she was small and water offered a freedom of movement that air never could. She kicked her legs like a frog – a lovely feeling – and pulled with one arm. Bubbles nibbled her skin like the mouths of tiny fish. The water was cold, but as she went deeper she met plumes of different temperature. The warmest water fed the baths, but the colder moved more quickly. Was that the river? She kicked to the cold, her lungs beginning to pinch, and felt her hand slap rock. Miss Temple held on as her body, paused, sought to rise. She felt a current . . . was there a channel in the rock? Her searching hand grazed a soft tendril – a bit of grass? She caught it and felt the bump of a seam: a strip of the Contessa's petticoat, looped around the rock.

Miss Temple groped lower, into a pocket of cold, then wriggled through an opening well wide enough for her body. Her lungs were painfully tight. She kicked up into a faster current. Now that she wanted air the seconds grew unbearable.

She broke the surface with a gasp, still in the dark, and immediately swallowed a mouthful of water. She choked and almost lost hold of the leather case. Her loud breath echoed. A current carried along. Miss Temple swam to the side, and eventually her hand struck not rock but slippery brick.

She floated there, easing her breath, then felt her way along the bank. She'd begun to shiver. Her hands found a protrusion in the brick – it took her a moment to realize it was a ladder of inset rungs. Miss Temple climbed onto a dank but dry landing, but did not stand.

She turned to the sound of creaking wood. The formless dark took shape with the glimmer of a candle, well away but coming near, an oval face just glimpsed beyond its glow.

'At *last*, and what a fright you look. Hurry up.'

'The problem, of course, is that we may need to swim again.'

Miss Temple shivered under a heavy wool blanket, too chilled for her nakedness to cause disruption. Her teeth chattered and her bare knees pressed cold against her breasts. The Contessa, hair wrapped in a towel, wore a white robe and cork slippers, all purloined from the baths. She poured brandy into a teacup and passed it across.

'Drink. *Slowly*.'

Miss Temple took small, burning sips, hating the taste but grateful for the warming glow.

'Now, will anyone follow?'

Miss Temple shook her head. The Contessa glared, this not being enough of an answer, and so Miss Temple provided a brief account of Mr Schoepfil's assault on propriety and her own escape. At the end her cup was empty and she held it out for more. The Contessa poured for them both, tucking the robe about her knees. Behind the Contessa, in an untidy pile, lay several open hampers. Miss Temple's arrival had interrupted smoked oysters in sauce and the Contessa restored the jar to her lap. She dipped a finger in the sauce, frowned at the taste, dribbled some brandy into the jar and resumed her meal.

'You should eat. The passage will take hours.'

Miss Temple sniffed. 'What passage?'

'Channel between royal premises,' replied the Contessa, chewing. 'Enabling duplicity and outright crime. In a spasm of conscience the way was bricked up – those habits being *impure*. An astute adviser of this present queen made it his business to uncover the legend – in secret, opening the passage enough for one or two very sodden individuals, an *expedience*. And I made it my business to uncover *him*.'

'Lord Pont-Joule.'

'Would you like an oyster? They aren't very good.'

Miss Temple shook her head and the Contessa tossed the jar at the far wall. She frowned at the nearest hamper. 'Cheese?'

'No, thank you.'

The Contessa brought a white-moulded *toque* to her nose. 'It's very ripe.'

'Where does the channel lead?'

'Well, that was the value of Pont-Joule. An older man, desire and capacity so rarely in twain, but philosophic and not sour. A life dedicated to nothing of course – to that moulting cow – but he saw the wind's way. Can you?'

'Royal premises,' said Miss Temple with a sniff.

'O who *is* a good pup?' The Contessa broke the cheese with her hands and took an exploratory nibble. She raised her eyebrows with approval and then filled her mouth.

'I expect they sent people to prison in secret,' muttered Miss Temple, for the Contessa was no longer entirely listening. 'Sent them all the way to Harschmort, underground.'

Once the brandy had done its work, however, Miss Temple's old troubles returned. The Contessa had wiped her fingers on the robe and gone to another hamper, this filled with clothing, her squatting hips an unwelcome gust across the embers of Miss Temple's desire. She looked away, down at the brick.

'Perhaps I will eat after all,' she managed. The Contessa waved vaguely.

'It is for you or the rats. Or, with that straggling hair, you as the largest rat . . .'

Miss Temple forced herself to swallow a water biscuit and a lump of cheese, taken from where the Contessa had not chewed. Though it stuck in her throat, she reached in the hamper for more. But, as she reached, the Contessa flung an armful of various garments and the blanket was knocked from her shoulders. Miss Temple turned, covering herself with her hands. The Contessa laughed.

'I had not planned for two, much less two of such differing sizes. With a corset to wrench it all in, you may be presentable. Probably not.'

'I will wear my own things,' said Miss Temple, pulling the blanket up.

'A mere corset and shift? You will freeze. They will hear your teeth from St Porte.'

'I do not care.'

The Contessa dropped her robe and stepped into a pale silk shift. She pulled it over her hips, smiled, and then, as Miss Temple could not but look, slipped one arm and then the other through. The Contessa paused.

'Celeste, I believe you are biting your lip.'

Miss Temple only swallowed, wet hair in dark ringlets on her nape. 'You know what has become of me.'

'But do I know it well enough?' The Contessa did the last button and tugged the shift against her breasts, as if for comfort, but primarily to drag the silk across her nipples, knowing that Miss Temple could not look away.

'You are very cruel.'

'Not *only* cruel. What would you like?'

Miss Temple rocked on her heels. 'That's a horrible question.'

'Only if you have a horrible answer.'

'You amuse yourself. You will kill me.'

'I thought *you* were going to kill *me*.'

'I *am*,' whined Miss Temple.

'Stand up, Celeste.'

'I won't. I can't.'

The Contessa came forward and caught the hands Miss Temple raised to put her off. Miss Temple was lifted and the blanket fell away, her pale skin tight with the cold. The Contessa looked at her. Miss Temple trembled.

'I am ashamed,' she whispered. 'I am not myself.'

'Few people are.'

'But you –'

'We are not talking about *me*.'

Miss Temple persisted. She forced out the words. 'But I – I am not kind. I am not pretty. I want things. I want *people*. I –' She shook her head. 'I am so hungry . . . so *angry*.'

The Contessa set a hand on Miss Temple's breast, squeezing it with the dispassion of a farmer judging ham. 'You are not *ugly*. Besides, that matters very little.' The hand took in the soft pinch of Miss Temple's waist and the turn of her hips. 'The person who isn't angry is a stone. And the person without desire is in the grave.' Miss Temple squirmed, for the Contessa's hand had dipped between her legs. An extended finger pushed without warning past hair and skin to wetness and slipped in. Miss Temple gasped.

The Contessa looked her in the eye. 'We have done this before. Do you remember?' Miss Temple nodded. The Contessa eased her hand into motion. 'In the coach, with Oskar. To shame you. To derange your little heart. Did it work?'

Miss Temple shook her head. The motion was already luscious.

'No. That was my mistake. But what did you learn?'

'That I am my own,' whimpered Miss Temple.

'O that's a lie, isn't it?'

Miss Temple did not speak. The Contessa gave her hand a twist and employed a thumb.

'I said that's a *lie*, isn't it, Celeste? You admitted as much just now, this close to tears . . . because you want a world that isn't yours . . . because your pleasure is unbounded . . . because in your heart you are the biggest *whore* in all Europe.'

Another turn of her hand stopped Miss Temple's objection.

'Or is that wrong? Are you not? Or are you? What other word would you use?'

'Why – *O* – why are you –'

'Because someone has to die, Celeste. It won't be me. For this – your demons? Banish shame. Accept desire. Most men *deserve* the whip. You are what you are *now*.' The Contessa dropped to her knees. She met Miss Temple's eyes. '*Yes?*'

Miss Temple could not move. Sure as the strike of a snake, the Contessa's tongue shot home. Miss Temple cried out. She writhed, but the Contessa held her hips fast and the crest was already imminent, a swelling of unbearable sweetness. Her fingers found the Contessa's head and pulled it close.

Miss Temple had tumbled panting onto the blanket. The Contessa gave her a cold-eyed smirk. 'And what do you know *now*?'

Miss Temple's voice was small. 'That this changes nothing.'

'*Precisamente.*' The Contessa took a corner of the blanket to wipe her face. 'Get dressed and help with my corset. I'm damned if I'll meet Robert Vandaariff without proper underpinnings.'

In the end, the Contessa's clothing *was* too large, even the undergarments, and Miss Temple took back her own. She had carefully hidden the glass key upon disrobing, but still hoped she might find the silk-wrapped spur, that it might have slipped lower into her shift. She searched as unobtrusively as she could. Nothing.

'Is something wrong?'

'No.' Miss Temple saw the leather case now lay near the Contessa's foot.

'Mine,' the Contessa said. 'Fair exchange.'

There being no dress to fit her, Miss Temple tied the Contessa's cotton robe over her corset and shift, and walked in cork slippers with her hair in a towel. The Contessa wore a dark dress and simple shoes, her combed damp hair hanging past her shoulders. She held the leather case in one hand and the candle in the other. A small hamper was Miss Temple's to carry, contents unknown. A short tunnel took them back to the embankment and a trim, narrow craft, not unlike the skiff Miss Temple had taken from the Raaxfall dock.

'In the front,' said the Contessa. 'Try not to tip in and drown.'

The hamper went first and then Miss Temple, scrambling to the foremost thwart. The Contessa hitched her dress about her waist and settled in the rear of the skiff, stowed the leather case under her seat, and came up with a small box of glass and metal. She lit the candle inside it and wedged the box into a stand, then reached behind her for the tiller.

'There is a pole, Celeste, beneath your feet. We should not run into the bank, but, if we do, you will use it to push off. I will steer. If you think to use that pole on *me* you may discard the idea now, for it will not reach. Are you ready?'

Miss Temple extracted the pole, which was indeed not very long, and turned to face forward. The Contessa cut the rope tethering them to the landing with a knife. While the weapon was no surprise, it was nevertheless bracing to see. The current caught the skiff and they shot into the dark.

For the first part of their journey, Miss Temple's attention was fixed on the half-moon of light preceding the tip of the skiff, watching for dangers of all sorts. Large patches of the ceiling had fallen in, and from those spots dangled ropes of black moss. The banks were smooth rock save for the very occasional appearance of another landing. Miss Temple peered at these relics as closely as the light allowed. Sometimes the Contessa would announce their location, 'the Citadel' or 'the Observatory'; but other times, and Miss Temple was convinced it was because she did not know, a landing passed without comment. Soon they flew on in silence and, at last, Miss Temple's wilful concentration was undermined.

The act had been obscene and unnatural, with regard to Church teachings (which she dismissed) but also to Miss Temple's understanding of loyalty, of virtue. Of course she had known *those* sorts of girls – everyone knew them – but in her own person the urge had been absent, or at least unconsidered. That had changed dramatically upon the invasion of her mind by the blue glass book. If a memory held a man's relish of a woman, then Miss Temple's experience of it quite *naturally* located that pleasure, that appreciation, in her own body. And many of the memories *were* perverse: women with women, men with men, and more, in such a profusion of incident that her body, if not her moral mind, was taught at last only ripe possibility. And so Miss Temple decided that, while she did not *approve* of the Contessa, or her tongue, it was plain enough that one tongue was much like another. Given that she could not, with her present knowledge and appetite, abjure tongues whole, whether it be a man's or a woman's seemed to make no matter at all.

But loyalty was something else again, and here her thought snagged. The Contessa was her enemy – it was as complete a fact as might exist on earth. How could even the highest claim of expedience justify such . . . *abasement*? Wasn't it abasement? Wasn't it compromise? Betrayal? It was – she *knew* it was – and yet she had done it! And in another circumstance of degrading need she would do it again! Miss Temple gripped the pole with both hands, hating the woman behind her, but loathing herself even more. In the coach, the Comte d'Orkancz had seized her throat – she was unable to resist . . . on the landing the Contessa's hands had but cupped her thighs to bring her near.

Did it matter that it was her desire instead of theirs? Miss Temple scoffed at the hopeful phrasing – as if the teeming contents of the glass book were *hers. Her* desire was long gone – with bitterness she recalled the filthy words of Mr Groft, her father's overseer – like piss in a stream.

And that was that. With nothing to be done, Miss Temple's practical mind shoved the issue aside. She could not help what had happened, nor – for with the abating of need came clarity of mind (probably the Contessa's exact intention) – did she regret it. And, besides, she was wrong: it would *not* happen again. Soon – and soon enough – either she or the Contessa di Lacquer-Sforza would be dead.

They travelled without significant conversation aside from an observation that Miss Temple could move less clumsily or move not at all. Miss Temple pushed away the wet strands of moss, which seemed to dip nearer as they went.

'The water has risen,' said the Contessa, both by explanation and by complaint.

'What if we run out of room?' asked Miss Temple. 'What if Pont-Joule built another stop-hole further on, to keep people out?'

'He did not.'

'Have you been here?'

'No one has been here.'

'Then you don't know.'

'Be quiet. O stinking hell –'

The Contessa ducked as they plunged through an especially sodden curtain of moss that swept the towel from Miss Temple's head. She squealed with disgust, forcing her body flat. But then they were through and the skiff slowed into a lazy spin, the channel opening to a deeper pool. The ceiling rose, vaulted, the crusted tiles in different colours, a mosaic.

'We have reached St Porte.'

Miss Temple followed the Contessa's gaze to an entirely different sort of landing. Where the others had been simple brick, this was carved white stone, with a wall of once-elegant glass-fronted doors, opaque with filth.

'What was in St Porte?' she asked.

'A woman who was not the Queen.'

Miss Temple considered this. The Contessa, in unacknowledged curiosity, had turned the tiller to slow their way. No one, not even the disrespectful young, had ever found the doors, for each heavy pane remained quite whole.

'Who was she? Who was he?'

'A king with a fat foreign wife.'

'But what happened?' Miss Temple looked back as the current carried them away.

'She died. The King did not return.'

'I suppose he couldn't,' said Miss Temple.

'Of course he couldn't,' said the Contessa. 'She died of *plague*. The rest of the place – above the ground – was razed flat.'

After St Porte the landings became few and far between, the last but a stand of rotten pilings. The Contessa changed the candle, which had sunk low.

'That is the final station before Harschmort, though we've still far to go. Harschmort was placed well away for a reason.'

'What will we find there?' Miss Temple asked. 'What sort of welcome?'

'How should I know?' The Contessa tossed the old stub in the water with a *plonk*.

'It is your expedition.'

'The train was impossible, and our situation at Bathings precluded a coach.'

'That is a lie. You had this route planned.'

'I have many plans. But, as I had not seen the channel landing at St Porte, I have not seen the one at Harschmort either – because of Oskar's construction, his great *chamber*. The foundation of the place was walled off, even as he exploited the channel itself for power.'

Miss Temple frowned. 'But that chamber was destroyed by explosives. Chang said so.'

'Yes, I know.'

'What if there *is* no landing?' The Contessa did not reply. Miss Temple turned to look at her. 'I am hungry.'

'You should have eaten before.'

'Did you bring food or not?' Miss Temple reached for the hamper.

'*Celeste.*'

'If you try to stop me it will tip the skiff.' Without waiting for a reply she flipped back the wicker lid. Inside were three squat bottles sealed with cork and a layer of black wax. Miss Temple plucked up the nearest and held it to the light.

'Damn you to hell, Celeste Temple, put that *down*.'

'Tell me what's in it or I'll throw it overboard.'

'You would not. You would not be so *stupid* – O damn you. It is a liquid you have seen before, derived from something called bloodstone. It is orange, and in most instances *very* harmful.'

'In all three bottles?'

'All three, you little pig.'

Miss Temple leant into the hamper. The open space inside showed a glimpse of blue beneath the bottles. The glass book the Contessa had taken from Parchfeldt. The book that held the corrupted essence of the Comte d'Orkancz. Miss Temple replaced the bottle.

'I am *not* a pig. But I would have thrown it.'

'Of course you would have.'

'As long as we know each other,' said Miss Temple.

The rest of their journey passed in silence, Miss Temple brooding again, bitter that, with the exception of some sofa-bound groping with Roger Bascombe, which she dismissed, and a single misguided kiss at Parchfeldt, her body's charms had been sampled only by the worst of people. Kings and mistresses were nonsense, she knew full well. Most people made horrid marriages, mismatches of beauty and temper that only provoked a person to imagine the couple conjoined, as one hearing of an accident imagined the wounds. Was it so strange that her legitimate affection – if any such thing existed, and this was, the more she thought, the exact matter for doubt – had settled on a man such as Chang, suspect and unpresentable in every way?

She glanced back. Earlier, when the Contessa had stepped into her shift, a new scar, on her thigh, had come into view, a knife-cut by Miss Temple's own hand from their fight at Parchfeldt. She remembered the other scar across the Contessa's shoulder, from a train window in Karthe. No doubt there were more – no doubt there were scars *within* – and she wondered at the woman's continuing beauty. How long would it last? Would some rash plan finally be met with disfigurement or death? She thought of Chang's face – did not the Contessa deserve the same? Did not Miss Temple herself?

How – and, honestly, why – could the woman so *persist*?

'You said before we'd swim again,' she called. 'Does that mean you've lied and you *do* know where we'll go?'

'Eyes ahead, Celeste. We ought to be near.'

'How do you *know*?'

'Eyes *ahead*, Celeste. I cannot see past you.'

Miss Temple turned, pleased to have pricked another nerve, then sat up straight.

'*Celeste!* You cannot just *move* –'

'Do you hear the water? Listen! The sound has changed.'

The channel had gone glassy calm, but, as their circle of light reached out, Miss Temple detected a shadow, an oddly shaped depression pointing *down*. She frantically waved her arm. 'To the left, quickly!'

The Contessa pulled on the tiller and the skiff shot to the side, but not before the stern crossed into the glassy oval. Their motion was checked. They were being pulled.

'It's sucking the water down!' cried Miss Temple. 'Like the drain in a tub!'

'The pole, Celeste! Use the damned pole!'

Miss Temple plunged the pole into the water to try to push them away but found no bottom to push against.

'The *landing*!'

The Contessa strained on the tiller as the skiff spun stern-first towards the sink-hole in the centre of the pool. For it *was* a pool, Miss Temple now saw, flowing underground instead of further on. She stabbed at a piling with the hooked end of the pole – she had not actually believed the thick hook was for fish – and it caught fast, then she squealed as the weight of the skiff nearly tore it from her gasp.

'Hold on! Just a moment . . . *there*!'

The skiff swung to the landing wall. The Contessa looped a rope around a rusted stanchion and tied it off.

'You can let go.'

Miss Temple sat back and shook her fingers. 'How do you know about boats?'

'I am a Venetian.'

'And I'm from an island. Ladies don't sail boats.'

'Then *ladies* should be careful getting out, because if they fall in they'll get sucked down into the gears.'

Miss Temple again bore the hamper while the Contessa kept the leather case and the candle-box from the skiff. Harschmort's platform was littered with broken masonry.

'It does not seem as if Robert Vandaariff knew about this landing at all.'

'No,' agreed the Contessa. 'Perhaps it wasn't on the plans . . .'

'How can something *built* not be on the *plans*?'

'Celeste, how do you even eat breakfast?'

Miss Temple followed her to a door that had once been formidable, iron-bound planks four inches thick. Now the wood was eaten by worms and hung by a single hinge. The Contessa lifted her dress and kicked with the flat of her foot, turning her head at the dust blown up when the thing fell in. She let the cloud settle and stepped over the mess.

'Why did you say we had to swim?' asked Miss Temple.

'Because we may. Or I may.'

'Why not me?'

'Perhaps you.'

'Perhaps I'll go my very own way.'

'Perhaps that is my intention.'

'Your intentions can go hang,' replied Miss Temple. 'This leads nowhere.'

The ceiling had collapsed, blocking the passage with debris. The Contessa set the candle-box on the leather case and bent for a tumbled stone. She lifted it with a grimace and heaved it behind them.

'Put down that hamper and help.'

'You cannot be in earnest.'

The Contessa raised a second stone. 'If you do not help me I will club out your brains.'

Miss Temple snatched up the light and climbed the pile, dislodging bricks and gravel where she stepped. At the top, she poked an arm between two beams and then wormed her head to follow. Threads of dust traced the air around her.

'Celeste, you are just making more work.'

'There is a way.'

'You cannot fit. *I* cannot fit.'

'You're wrong. Come see.'

The Contessa gamely scrambled up, holding her dress with one hand and groping with the other until she could reach a beam to steady herself – an action that launched another spray of brick dust. She spat it from her mouth.

'Look!'

Miss Temple raised the light. Perhaps ten feet above, the darkness opened to black space.

'But where does it lead? We could be trapped in a hole.'

'We *are* trapped in a hole.' Miss Temple handed the candle-box to the Contessa. 'Keep it steady. I will do my best not to bury you as I go . . .'

It was just like climbing a monkey-puzzle tree, not that she had done that for a decade, but Miss Temple's limbs remembered how to wriggle from one branch to another. Only one of the beams gave way, a heart-stopping moment when – in the midst of a cascade of pebbles and dust and, from below, Italian profanity – the light went out. Miss Temple clung to where she was in the dark, waiting for all the debris to settle.

'*Goffo scrofa!*'

'Are you all right?'

A snap of a match and the light returned, to show the Contessa covered in dust, black hair like an old-fashioned powdered wig. '*Climb.*'

The distance was not far, and once she had a solid brace for her feet Miss Temple raised her head to the edge of a floor. 'Half a moment . . . shut your eyes . . .'

She pounded the broken lip with a fist, breaking away weakened brick until she was sure that what remained would take her weight. Then Miss Temple writhed up over the edge. The air was warm and dank. She could not see, but the sounds around her – water and machines – echoed from a distance.

'Pass everything up,' she whispered. 'We are inside.'

The Contessa joined her with an extremely sour expression, her person filthy, and shone the candle around the room: a barrel-shaped ceiling, a door cracked off its hinges and a line of furnaces, all cold.

'You'll be happy for a swim now, I wager,' said Miss Temple as they padded on.

The Contessa did not reply and Miss Temple realized that they must be silent now, that around any corner might be a foe. They continued on, past standing pools and buckled plaster, finally reaching a gas-lit spiral staircase. They climbed one turn to a door. The Contessa faced her.

'Put the hamper down.' Miss Temple did, warily. The Contessa held out the leather case. 'Take it.'

Miss Temple did, then backed away. 'Why?'

'Because I cannot carry everything. Because now I do not need it. I took it from you so you'd have no weapon.'

Miss Temple glanced at the hamper, wondering if she could snatch that up as well – and, with both books, run.

'I thought you needed me. I thought I would be *used*.'

'And did you *want* that?'

'Of course not.'

'What *do* you want, Celeste?'

'I want to stop him,' she said boldly. 'Stop all of this. I want to save Chang. And Svenson.' She hesitated. 'And myself.' The Contessa pursed her lips, sceptical. Miss Temple wanted to kick her. 'What do *you* want?'

'To find Oskar.'

'*What?*'

The Contessa was silent. The knife was somehow in her hand.

'But *why*?' Miss Temple did not understand at all. 'And *how*? Oskar is dead. And he wants to *consume* you. You've seen the painting. Those people get boiled down – they get killed and cooked in tubs and what's left is given to him, to revive.'

'Reincarnate. There's a difference.'

Miss Temple remembered, quite vividly, the Comte's last moments on the airship, his rage at the death of Lydia Vandaariff. His intention to wring the Contessa's neck had been stopped only by Chang's sabre. 'You do not understand. He is mad. He was *dead* –'

'But what if he wasn't any more? What if he was just wicked old Oskar?'

'*He isn't.*'

'Then you can kill him, if I'm wrong. And become his little Bride if I am not. You'll want to go upstairs. And don't *confront* anyone. Stay alive to the end.'

'Where are you going?'

'Into the works, of course. Do you remember the tomb?'

'What?'

'Really, Celeste, try not to be completely stupid.'

'I am not stupid. If it wasn't for me you'd still be on the landing.'

'As ever, Celeste Temple, you underestimate *everything*.' The Contessa picked up the hamper and slipped through the door.

Miss Temple stood, undone at being suddenly alone and resenting the feeling extremely. She had not underestimated *anything*. She could sense the Comte's death in the back of her throat. Why would the Contessa risk her life to restore him? She narrowed her eyes, anger building now the woman had gone. If she could not save herself, she would be damned if their two fates would be any different.

She climbed to another door. The landing was damp and wet footprints climbed the stairs. One of the prints, the right foot, carried a swirl of red. Against all reason she wondered if this was Chang. She stopped herself from calling out. The prints continued up, past the next door, which she tried to open out of curiosity. The door squeaked – it was locked – and at the squeak Miss Temple heard a noise above her on the stairs. She did not breathe. Then faint footfalls, coming down. Miss Temple retreated in silence until she was out of sight. The footfalls stopped on the platform, and she heard the same squeak of the door being tested, then the sound of a key. The door was opened . . . then closed again . . . silence. The man had gone through. If she moved quickly she could get past without, as the Contessa warned, *confrontation*.

She hurried around the turn to find Mr Foison on the landing. He leapt at her like a cat, grunting with pain as he landed and snatching at the tail of her robe. She dashed away and down, fumbling for the door at the next landing, but it was only half open before Foison was there. She swung the case at him. He dodged the blow and took her wrist.

'How are you here?' he hissed. 'Where is *she*?'

'Where is Chang?'

'Chang is lost.'

His cold voice brought Miss Temple back to the Raaxfall works. She kicked at a bandage on his right thigh and yanked her wrist with all her strength. Foison's grip broke, but then his fingers caught on the case. For an instant they strained against one another, but he was too strong. She let it go. He toppled back and Miss Temple raced away.

She burst through the next door down and ran until the corridor met another pool. She looked back and realized that Foison hadn't followed. Of course not: he'd opened the leather case and seen what she'd been fool enough to lose.

Back on the floor where she'd started, Miss Temple stopped to think. What had Foison been doing *here*? A man like Foison did not repair machines. Had he been chasing someone? And what explained his being so *wet*?

Across the pool she saw water pouring through an open grate, forced from above. She peered upwards, shading her face from the spray, and her heart quickened. Had Foison followed someone into Harschmort on such a dangerous route – someone like Chang?

But if Foison had been following Chang, he would not have come after her, and he would have shouted for help. For some reason she did not understand, Mr Foison had made his own secret entry into Harschmort, through the guts of his master's new construction.

Steeling her courage, she returned to the stairwell. Foison was gone. In that case, Miss Temple told herself, she would chase *him*.

The bloody prints continued to climb, despite – and Miss Temple's heart leapt to her throat each time she slipped past – the noisy presence of Vandaariff's men behind each successive stairwell door. Foison's errand *was* his alone. But at the top of the staircase her search was foxed, for the bloody trail vanished into a long runner of carpet.

She kept walking. This was Harschmort. She would meet someone – and *confront* them. The Contessa was wrong about that too.

When the shouts came she hurried towards them, and the explosion that followed. Ahead, a woman careened through a smoking archway, gold-skinned and frail, black hair around her shoulders. She saw Miss Temple but did not pause.

'Hurry!' she cried. '*Run!*'

Without thinking Miss Temple took the woman's hand and fled. A cork slipper flew from her foot, and after three awkward steps she kicked off its mate.

'All of them – every last one taken –'

Cries and the sound of breaking glass came from behind. Miss Temple saw shadows wrestling in blue smoke, and brass-helmeted men charging into the cloud with clubs.

The woman watched with too wide eyes, hand to her mouth. 'My son –'

Miss Temple tugged her on. 'You can do nothing. *Run.*'

'Who are you?' the woman demanded, out of breath. 'How did you escape?'

'I have not escaped. I have entered. Wait.'

They had reached a doorway left ajar, and Miss Temple peered through. Four green-coated men lay on the floor, though they bore no wounds. The air stank of indigo clay, and Miss Temple's eyes stung.

'Wait,' gasped the woman. 'In case. My name is Madelaine Kraft –'

'There is no "in case" if we keep moving,' said Miss Temple.

'I cannot run. You will be taken with me. Listen. You don't know who I am. Please. I heard him once explain a thing –'

'*Who?*'

She squeezed Miss Temple's hand in a feeble request for patience. 'The Comte d'Orkancz. The secret is light. "The chemical value of light" – as if it were as solid as earth or water, or active like fire or cold. He put a disc of glass – do not be shocked – a *disc of glass* on a woman's body and opened a curtain so the sun hit it. She fairly sang with pleasure –'

'What woman?'

'That does not matter. Her name was Angelique –'

Miss Temple pulled her hand away. '*Ah.*'

'*Light.* The character of blue glass –'

'You mean it will not work in the dark?'

Madelaine Kraft shook her head. 'We are already too late – the dawn has come! The only hope now is to know – to understand his *thinking* –'

'His thinking is as scrambled as five eggs in a bowl. Do you know Cardinal Chang?'

'Of course I know Chang.'

'Where is he?'

'I do not know. I have misjudged him. I have misjudged myself and lost my son.' Abruptly Madelaine Kraft pushed Miss Temple through the door. 'I will lead them away. *Go.*'

She closed the door, and through it Miss Temple heard her shouting to attract the guards.

Miss Temple pulled a revolving pistol from the holster of a fallen man. She waited, bracing the weapon with both hands, ready to shoot the first man through the door. The sounds outside went quiet – Madelaine Kraft had been taken away – and no guards returned to search. Still, for some minutes Miss Temple did not move. The men at her feet, asleep or dead, lay in a heap like the bones outside an ogre's den. She had managed an entry to Harschmort, but this room marked another degree of danger. Newly constructed for the ritual of this night, here was the true beginning of her battle with its master.

Blocking her path was a bed of black gravel mixed with blue stones: blue glass spurs. She could not risk the spurs in bare feet. On the wall hung a line of white robes edged with green, with a pair of felt slippers at the foot of each. She exchanged the Contessa's cotton robe for that of a Vandaariff acolyte, and helped herself to the slippers, noting how filthy and dark her feet were.

Between the gravel and the far door lay a mosaic of large tiles. A noxious resonance in her throat warned her not to simply walk across, though she'd no idea what would happen if she did. Each tile was made of a different coloured glass, but the Comte's memories brought only confusion. Then Miss Temple laughed aloud, for in the corner of one tile she saw an $x$, quite freshly scratched.

'Well, thank you *very* much . . .'

A series of hops brought her to the far side, thinking very little of the entire challenge. Like so much learnt thinking, to Miss Temple it was just another obstacle to avoid – or, like the fellow with the knot, hack through.

She threw the hood over her face and opened the door. Here was the same acrid smell . . . now augmented by gunpowder. Across the room three robed acolytes lay huddled in death. Another doorway had been blown open. Miss Temple padded to it, but quickly turned from the burnt, twisted bodies. It was now clear what happened if one stepped on the wrong tile.

She forced herself to approach the robed corpses, examining each as carefully as Chang or Svenson might have done. One man's face was stained orange. Though the Contessa had taken such pains to bring her own supply, here was a bubbling fountain full of the stuff, from which this poor wretch had drunk. His lips were stretched and his empty eyes wide in a carnival mask of fear. The other two acolytes had been beaten and stabbed, but, judging by the blood smeared on the floor, there had been more men, hauled away. Again, she did her best to sort the passage of each one, diligence rewarded when her eyes at last caught a particular blot in a sooty footprint. These prints emerged from the blasted door and followed the drag marks leading out. She'd found Mr Foison . . . and he'd found someone else.

She started at a skittering noise: a metal grille, painted to blend with the distorted figures that decorated the walls. Miss Temple went to her toes and turned the knob. Through it came voices she knew.

'You underestimate the power of his belief,' said Doctor Svenson.

'There was a second question, my lord?' asked Mr Foison.

The doors next to the grille had been pushed closed, but remained ajar. Miss Temple cautiously craned her head. Robert Vandaariff stood with his back to her, the only occupant of a strange little room sealed off by thick glass. Beyond him, and more glass, stood Svenson and Foison in what was obviously Vandaariff's new laboratory.

'Indeed, for Doctor Svenson. You were given entry in the company of another man. A Mr *Pfaff*. Where is he now?'

'We parted ways.'

'Pfaff is an ally of the Contessa, my lord . . .'

They kept talking. Miss Temple paid no attention, for at the sight of Chang on the table her heart went cold.

She kicked off the slippers and ran, following Foison and the drag marks, only to reach a crossroads and more damned carpet, where the trail disappeared. Without a thought she dashed left, reached the end of the carpet and cried out as her toe caught on a new-laid plank. She hopped on one foot, picking at the splinter. Staring at Miss Temple with an imperious distrust was a band of acolytes in white robes.

'Sister?' ventured one. 'What brings you here?'

'I must find Mr Foison!' cried Miss Temple. 'Where is Mr Foison?'

But her hood had slipped off. The acolyte pointed at her face. 'She has not been consumed. She has not been redeemed.'

'*Tell me!*' Miss Temple raised the revolver. 'Where is Mr Foison!'

Her threat meant nothing. The acolytes charged. Miss Temple pulled the trigger. The pointing acolyte fell, clutching his leg. Miss Temple bolted, snapping another blind shot behind. She careened around a corner. A door ahead of her opened and another white robed idiot peeked out. She raised the pistol, her aim bouncing wildly. The acolyte threw out his arms.

'*There* you are!'

She did not break speed, each step narrowing her aim.

'It's me! It's me! It's *Jack*!'

She saw beneath the hood and did not shoot. Pfaff pulled her in and slid the bolt home. Fists pounded on the far side of the door.

'Well, well, little miss –'

'I must reach Chang! They're going to kill him!'

Pfaff flashed a confident smile. 'Then you must follow me.'

He pulled her to an unfinished staircase, little more than a hole in the floor. She noticed his chequered trousers were wet from the knees down.

'Where have you been, Mr Pfaff?'

'Not Jack?'

'It was never Jack. Do not bother to lie. *She* sent you here. You met her, and she set you a task.'

'Miss, I came to find *you*. I *have* had dealings with the Contessa – had to convince her, didn't I? But here I am, and I *will* take you to Chang.'

'Do you know what they have done to him?'

Pfaff stopped and turned to her. He took a deep breath. 'Miss –'

'We must hurry!'

'I do not like to tell you, but someone must. They took his mind, Miss Temple. Snatched it with a blue glass book, so Vandaariff can exchange himself into Chang's empty shell. That has been his intention all this time.'

Miss Temple heard the words as if from a distance.

A part of her heart went away, a cloud pulled to pieces by the wind.

'Who?' Her voice was calm. She realized Pfaff had taken her hand, to comfort her. Miss Temple gently reclaimed it. 'Who did this?'

'Old Foison.'

'With a glass book.'

'Who knew that there were any left? I heard them talking, the ones in robes. But they're all in on it. Even your German doctor. You'll see for yourself. I'm the only one with you now.'

Pfaff nodded, as if her silence confirmed his last words, and walked on. Miss Temple followed in silence. Pfaff glanced back, with a wary look.

'The Contessa is all that's left, you know. Everyone else plays his game.'

'Please stop talking, Mr Pfaff. Just take me to them.'

Instead, he stopped at a metal panel studded with iron wheels and numbered gauges. Pfaff consulted a pocket watch she did not recall him owning, then shot a white cuff from his coat, marked with numbers. He peered at the scribbles of ink and turned the wheels accordingly. These were controls for the turbines, she guessed. He winked at her.

'Couldn't let him get too far without us!'

The pipes behind Miss Temple's head began to vibrate. Pfaff pointed to an open, square embrasure, its metal grille prised back. Pfaff threw off his robe.

'No more need for these!' He gathered his coat-tails and scuttled in. Miss Temple hiked up her own dripping robe, then discarded it as well.

The metal passage was hot, despite several inches of water. She waddled half bent, aware that only the Contessa could have instructed Pfaff on the workings of Vandaariff's machines. Whether Pfaff had betrayed Miss Temple outright or somehow sought to serve both women and survive, the overweening optimism of the man sickened her. She could shoot him in the back this moment.

Pfaff clambered out. Miss Temple followed, aware of extending her bare legs.

'Do not *look* at me, Mr Pfaff.'

'Just making sure you don't fall in, miss . . .'

He nodded to a roiling moat of black water. A tattered streamer of white rolled to the surface and then, with a tug, shot back to the depths . . . an acolyte's robe.

They picked their way to an iron staircase, leading up. At its foot lay another acolyte, neck broken from the fall.

Pfaff leant close to her ear. 'Take care now. We may come up in the middle of everything.'

She tightened her grip on the revolver and began to climb.

Another acolyte's corpse blocked the stairs halfway up. Pfaff extended a hand to help Miss Temple over the corpse. They crept the final steps bent double, then paused to listen, hunched below an open trapdoor.

'You have done nothing, madam!' This was Mr Schoepfil's mannered tenor. 'Nothing save deliver all into my hands!'

'How is that?' The Contessa's voice was far away. 'You are disinherited, are you not? You are officially, legally *nothing*!'

Schoepfil laughed. 'I have the will in my hand – once it is burnt, I reclaim my rightful place. You have slain the source too soon! His precious empty vessel will remain so – as if such a man, a known *criminal*, would ever be permitted such a legacy! No matter what this piece of paper may declare, my own array of supporters, powerful men –'

'They are not yours,' Doctor Svenson broke in. 'Robert Vandaariff arranged it all. Just as he made sure you bought the Comte's papers, and had the money to do so. Those men are loyal to him, and they will be loyal to his wishes.'

'O what a tale!' Schoepfil's amusement trilled on. 'His intentions, yes – I have read the strategy. But why should he engineer my support? What *service* do I provide him as an antagonist?'

'By exposing your true self,' replied Svenson. 'With your own horrible behaviour *you* – and you alone – have made it possible for a criminal like Chang to inherit. Do you doubt that the Duchess of Cogstead, with the entire court behind her, will not intervene on his behalf if it means damning you?'

Schoepfil was silent, then abruptly erupted in petulant screams. '*No! No!* The court is *nothing*. And now that he is gone, those men will follow their own sense – they will throw their support behind the man they know! And mark me, Doctor, I won't forget a *word*. After I burn this will – *then* I would like to see –'

'O *think*, man,' called Svenson. 'Do you imagine there are no copies – lodged at his bank, with the law? He will have foreseen every objection. You cannot do a thing.'

'*No?*' Miss Temple heard a scuffle and Doctor Svenson grunted in pain. 'I can punish every one of you. And take this criminal's life right now. With him removed, the estate must revert to me, no matter how many damned wills there are!'

Miss Temple charged past Pfaff to the light.

'*Get away from him!*' Her voice came as shrill as a pipe. Schoepfil's hands – his *blue* hands – hung above Chang's neck. Miss Temple pulled the trigger, but the gun was too large and kicked, the shot flying high to shatter a mosaic. Miss Temple aimed again, bracing with her other hand, straight for Schoepfil's heart.

'Celeste,' gasped Doctor Svenson, on his knees.

'Wait!' This was an enormous dark man with a soiled silk waistcoat, rubbing his arms where he'd been bound. On the floor behind him, bloody and still, lay Mr Foison. At the sight of *him* Miss Temple's temper flared. She pulled the trigger, but Pfaff had reached around and the hammer snapped on his thumb, preventing any fire. He swore with the pain and wrenched the weapon free, extricating his hand with a wince.

Miss Temple kicked Pfaff in the shin. He cursed and hopped away, looking at the window. For the first time Miss Temple saw the blood, and the dead man in the feather mask.

'Celeste Temple, do not move!' The Contessa's voice was doubly distant, by virtue of the helmet she wore and the glass barrier in the wall. 'Mr Pfaff?'

'All ready down below, Your Ladyship.'

'This is nonsense,' declared Schoepfil. 'I *will* kill Cardinal Chang, and then I will kill the rest of you.'

Pfaff raised the revolver, taking charge of the room. 'Now, now then –'

Schoepfil simply ran at him, faster than Pfaff could aim, and chopped the weapon to the floor. Pfaff swung with his brass-knuckled fist, but Schoepfil dodged and drove Pfaff back into the glass with a flurry of blows. A final kick and Pfaff collapsed wheezing. Schoepfil set his foot on Pfaff's neck.

'You will surrender, madam, or your man will die.'

'That is *your* man, in the tub next to Harcourt, is it not?'

The Contessa's voice was polite, as if she were asking about his tailor. Schoepfil turned. 'Yes. Mr Kelling. A very useful person – and this disgraceful treatment –'

'I wonder if he is more useful to you than Colonel Bronque.'

'What? Colonel Bronque is my good friend.'

'You have no friends. You are a mole.'

Schoepfil's face reddened. 'Come out at once! Or I promise you, this man will pay.'

The Contessa stepped to the rostrum. Her hand danced above the brass-covered knobs.

'It does not work,' Mahmoud called to her. 'Vandaariff tried. The machines –'

'Were disabled, yes, at my command – but now they are reset, and the sun has risen.' The Contessa faced them all. 'The question is one of *attachment*. One speculates in every direction . . . but I don't suppose any one of you gives a damn for Matthew Harcourt. I'm the only person here who might, I suppose. And I do *not*.'

She pulled off the brass cap. Light fell from the ceiling onto the exposed glass lozenge and set it to gleaming. The copper cables leading to Harcourt's tub sparked high into the air and the hoses along the tub shot stiff as they were filled. The liquid in the tub leapt to a hideous boil.

'Stop!' shouted Doctor Svenson. 'God in heaven –'

The Contessa uncovered another knob and sparks leapt up round Mr Kelling's tub. Schoepfil stepped towards his man, but already the liquid spit and steam billowed, the figure within obscured. Miss Temple covered her mouth and nose. With a slithering rush the hoses connecting the two tubs to the undercarriage of Chang's table vibrated with the transfer of some gruesome *reduction*.

The power switched off. The noxious steam dispersed. With a sickening compulsion Miss Temple joined the others, stepping near enough to see. The red liquid had sunk to an opaque inch of crimson mud. Apart from lump-like shadows beneath the scum, no sign of either body remained.

Miss Temple turned, her gorge rising. No one moved to help her, not even Svenson, stricken dumb. She bent over, but nothing came . . . nothing save jumbled visions of bright paint and cold machines.

'I trust my point is made,' called the Contessa. 'From now on you are responsible for one another's good behaviour. Drusus Schoepfil to protect his *friend*. Mr Mahmoud doubly for his mother and his spouse.' She laughed at Mahmoud's expression of surprise. 'O come, Bronque told me everything. And you, Doctor Svenson, will want to protect *everyone*, as ever, especially the gnome. The only one of you who might not care – care enough to submit – is poor, puking Celeste. I leave it to you gentlemen to compel *her* cooperation.'

'And what do you intend?' asked Doctor Svenson. 'If it is anything like what Vandaariff had planned, these poor people are already lost. Kill them now and be damned!'

'Why, Doctor, why should I follow Robert Vandaariff's plan?'

'Then what *are* you doing? What do you want?'

At last Svenson came to Miss Temple, a hand on her bare shoulder. She shrugged herself free, her eye falling upon the revolver near Pfaff's feet, and dashed towards it.

'Stop her!' warned the Contessa. 'Or someone else turns to soup!'

In a flash Schoepfil had his arms around Miss Temple's waist. Mahmoud was only a step behind and snatched up the gun. His finger found the trigger as he looked to the glass.

'Do try.' The Contessa reached to the rostrum. 'Will you break the glass in time to stop my hand?'

Mahmoud lowered the gun. Her hand did not retreat. He tossed the weapon through the trapdoor.

'Bloody idiot,' snarled Miss Temple. 'She's going to kill you all.'

'That is not true,' replied the Contessa. 'Poor Celeste. I'm only going to kill *you*.'

A dozen acolytes entered from the open doorway and through the trapdoor climbed green-coated lackeys, three with carbines and a fourth, with a wry smile, holding the revolver Mahmoud had just thrown down. The two groups surveyed the chamber with a menacing aspect, but the Contessa addressed them with an easy confidence.

'Welcome. As you can see, your master, Robert Vandaariff, is dead. His legacy is not. The man on that table is his legal heir. It is your duty to protect him. This is the will of Robert Vandaariff. If any one of these people attempts to interfere, take their lives. Faithful service will be handsomely rewarded.'

Schoepfil stammered with outrage. 'That – that – woman – *she* has killed Robert Vandaariff. My uncle! *I* am his heir! *I am his only heir!* She is the villain!'

The Contessa's hand floated warningly above the rostrum. 'Mr Schoepfil . . .'

'She *killed* him!' protested Schoepfil desperately. 'Use your eyes!'

Miss Temple knew it was the Comte d'Orkancz who would be restored, but the soldiers and acolytes had all sworn allegience to Harschmort's lord.

The acolytes did not move, but the four soldiers took in the blood and the corpse and exchanged a look between them of great suspicion.

'Perhaps I might speak – for the benefit of those others present *in belief*?' An acolyte who had been crouched behind Chang's table came forward, slipping the hood from his face. His Process scars carried an authority inside

Harschmort, and the acolytes and soldiers listened closely. 'My name is Trooste. I was redeemed this very night. The woman speaks the truth. She did take our master's life. It was his intention that she do so. *He* commanded her admission to his chamber. He *knew*.'

The green-coat with the revolver pointed it at Vandaariff's corpse. 'But why?'

'Yes!' cried Schoepfil. 'It makes no earthly sense –'

'Only bear witness, gentlemen,' replied Trooste. 'And you will have your answer.' He whispered to a pair of acolytes and they hurried away. Trooste bowed to the Contessa, who dipped her brass-bound head in return. Then she flicked the cover off a third glass knob.

'Now, then, since, by Mr Schoepfil's resistance, there is no love for Colonel Bronque . . .'

Schoepfil screamed his useless contrition. Bright sparks leapt up to burn the air.


The acolytes returned with a wheeled rack of blue glass books and a wicker hamper Miss Temple knew well. Trooste carefully extracted the book from the hamper and slotted it into the rack. He then emptied the three squat bottles, one by one, into rubber reservoirs that hung from the undercarriage of Chang's table like bloated, black fruit.

The other acolytes confidently tended the machines. The four soldiers adopted positions of fire: two at the main door, one by the glass wall, and their leader behind Schoepfil, the revolver pressed to the man's back. Schoepfil had fallen to his knees, his pinched face red and wet with tears, unable to turn from the horrid remains in Colonel Bronque's tub.

The Contessa watched from the window, but her gaze most often returned to Miss Temple, who stared right back. This was the Contessa's promise from Parchfeldt, a slow death after extinguishing all hope.

Doctor Svenson stepped casually between them, facing Miss Temple.

'My poor Celeste,' he whispered.

'Chang and I are lost. I saw what happened to Francesca. Save yourself.'

'I will not allow it.'

She looked into his blue eyes, despising his decency, even as she knew Svenson's care was the only mirror that might show her as she had once been. She took his hand and glanced at the machines. 'The star map. It shows every coupling, every wire and box.'

'Star map?' asked Svenson, fumbling his hand into a pocket.

'In the leather case with the book. It does not matter. How much of this do you understand?'

'Enough – perhaps as much as Trooste.'

'Good.'

'It isn't *good*. Vandaariff showed me a book. Elöise – a scrap of her. God help me. In that rack, not ten yards away.'

Miss Temple's voice was cold. 'Elöise would be ashamed. Destroy everything.'

With that she pushed past him, to the glass. She pointed to the enclosed room's blazing honeycombed ceiling. 'That is a *technique* from the Vandaariff tomb. Each shaft draws light from the surface, passing it through different layers of treated glass – each shaft with its own alchemical recipe. The tempered light generates a reaction, and the turbines amplify it. Why did you want *me* to know?'

'In *case*, Celeste,' replied the Contessa. 'And because you might have made something of the knowledge. Did you? No – only a sweet knot of regret in your stomach. But that is enough for me.'

'How can such an insignificant person as myself command such malice?'

'You have earned it ten times over.'

'Why do you risk everything to restore a man who wished your death? Are you so lonely? Are you so old? Are your lovers sickened by your scars?'

The Contessa called with impatience, 'Professor Trooste, we are past time. Strap the Bride to her marriage bed.'

Acolytes secured Miss Temple to the second table, next to Chang. She did not fight them.

The Doctor shouted to the Contessa: 'This serves no purpose, madam – her participation is completely unnecessary!'

'On the contrary, Doctor, it serves several aims in one thrust. Shall I explain? First, Cardinal Chang dies. Second, so does Celeste Temple. Third, Robert Vandaariff is restored.'

'You know very well that Vandaariff is long gone.'

'Robert Vandaariff will be *restored*.'

'And you will become the next lady of Harschmort? Is it that simple?'

'*I* am Robert Vandaariff's heir!' Schoepfil insisted, wiping his face on a sleeve. 'Not that inert felon –'

Miss Temple did not mark the rest of his complaint, nor anyone's reply. She turned her gaze to Chang. His face was wedged into a gap in the table, but his naked back offered its own portrait, muscles, nicks and scars. His strong arms were sheathed in black rubber, sprouting wire, like a bird's wings stripped of feathers. Her heart ached for him, as it had never done for herself. Professor Trooste worked between them, connecting hoses and wires from Chang's table to Miss Temple's body at the hands and feet. He brought up the rubber mask, dangling cords.

'Please,' she whispered. 'I want to see him.'

'You will know him inside yourself, to every detail, before you succumb.'

Trooste smoothed her hair aside and cinched the mask in place, so hard her eyes began to tear. With a lurch the table was tipped to the same angle as Chang's. She could look only forward through the narrow slits, straight at the equally faceless Contessa in her den. The room fell silent. Trooste came forward, dipped his head to the Contessa and began to speak.

'The tale of *The Chemickal Marriage* is ancient, a true account of the defeat of corruption and perfect rebirth. A band of chosen guests make possible through their faith a resurrection. First, the royal party is sacrificed. Then the King and Queen, the Groom and Bride, are reborn. Some of this is metaphor. Much more is fact.'

Trooste bowed again to the Contessa. 'Lord Vandaariff named you Virgo Lucifera, angel of light, the heaven-sent overseer – the celebrant of this most sacred rite. He knew a certain volume would arrive in your possession, madam. He *relied* upon it.' Trooste indicated the glass book he had taken from the hamper. 'Now death is immaterial and the marriage can begin. The ritual will remove the taint of corruption that consumed his body, and thus enact a new covenant. The flesh of life is remade to the flesh of dreams.'

Trooste's last words were echoed by acolytes as if it were part of a liturgy.

The Contessa nodded gravely. 'As he was ever the most mighty, so shall Robert Vandaariff be first redeemed.'

Trooste laid a hand on Chang's scar. 'The vessel has been prepared, seasoned through the progress of metals. As his essence is restored from the book, our master's soul will pass through infusions of six sacred alloys, and so by each be *cleansed*.' Trooste knelt at an empty slot beneath the table. 'The glass volume is placed in a chamber charged with quicksilver, the seventh metal. An eighth metal, tincture of bloodstone, protects the vessel himself, serving as an alchemical sieve. The soul will take root in its new home.' Trooste indicated the hoses that linked Chang to Miss Temple. 'While the corruption of death is *passed on*. Into the Bride.'

Miss Temple's throat burnt. The more fully Trooste detailed the path of violent energy, the more the Comte's memories confirmed her doom. Trooste moved to where Miss Temple could see his earnest expression. 'Thus she becomes the embodiment of pure love.'

'It will kill her,' declared Svenson.

'Not immediately. We should have several hours for study.'

'Wait.' Mahmoud stepped forward, eyeing the metal tubs with suspicion. 'Six metals? You're not going to kill anyone else.'

Trooste blinked and said nothing.

'You are *not*,' repeated Mahmoud, 'going to kill *anyone else!*'

'Of course she is!' bleated Schoepfil. 'Don't be a damned fool!'

'I'll do it this instant if you don't be quiet,' said the Contessa. She called to Trooste: 'And his mind will be whole again? The corruption, the madness –'

'All cleansed, madam. Purity. Rapture. Eden.'

Mahmoud began to protest but Svenson touched his shoulder and addressed Trooste: 'How do *you* know this? Today, healing Mrs Kraft, you had no more idea than I.'

'Lord Vandaariff instructed me, this very night.' Trooste was a priest describing a revelation. 'Just as his *incarnation* informed the child. And all has come to pass as he foretold. The Vessel returned for consumption, the

Bride to accept the sin, the Virgo Lucifera to enforce heaven's will. He *knew*. And he will know again.'

Trooste raised his hands like the conductor of an orchestra. A snapping sound came from Doctor Svenson's hands. In a stride he reached Trooste and plunged the broken tip of a blue glass key into his neck. The blood around the wound stiffened to glass, cracking as Trooste's throat filled. The wound bulged and his face darkened to purple. Trooste's gasp of shock was swallowed in a gutteral crackling and he fell. Svenson stepped away and lifted his empty hands, three carbines and a revolver aimed at his chest.

'*You bloody imbecile*!' shouted the Contessa. 'You – *you* –'

Svenson's voice cut through her anger like a sword. 'If I am killed, this *ends*. None of you know enough about the Comte's science. Without me nothing can continue.'

The Contessa snarled with frustration. She nodded the helmet, ruefully it seemed and, despite her fury, with a certain appreciation. 'And, let me guess, you refuse to do so?'

The Doctor reached into his tunic for a cigarette. 'Not at all. But there will be conditions.'

At once the weapons shifted to Mahmoud and Schoepfil, each of whom had moved towards Svenson. Svenson blew smoke from the corner of his mouth, eyeing them coolly.

'I'm sorry, gentlemen. At some point a man's just had enough.'

With a feeling of dread Miss Temple watched Svenson approach the rack of books. His eyes were as absent of feeling as they'd been in the Thermæ. She had passed him Francesca's key, as they discussed the star map, in the hope that he could somehow open the book and save Chang's memory, but he had thrown away the tool to secure his own freedom. She had told him to save himself . . .

Svenson took a handkerchief from his pocket to protect his hand. He pointed to one of the volumes in the padded book rack and looked at the acolytes.

'This volume has been lately brought by the Contessa – I'm sorry, the Virgo Lucifera?'

The acolytes nodded. Svenson pointed to another book, near it. Despite their disapproval, the acolytes did not prevent his reach. He carefully slid the second book from its slot, keeping a layer of cloth between his skin and the glass.

'I will want *this*.'

'And what is that?' the Contessa sneered. 'Lost love?'

'It is my business, madam.'

'Is that all?'

'No. Safe passage – let us say a ship sailing east – and a supply of funds. As Lady Vandaariff in all but name, I doubt this is beyond your power.' He broke off to address the acolytes sharply. 'Is the quicksilver alloy prepared?'

When they did not immediately reply, he called to those attending Chang. 'The quicksilver for the book! Has it been compounded?' He turned back to the acolyte slipping the Contessa's book from the rack, his hands insulated by the thin silk robe. 'By God – not with your *robe*! Get away!' He tucked his own book under one arm and used the handkerchief to lift the book containing the Comte. A properly gloved acolyte came forward to assist, but Svenson simply strode to Chang's table. 'Where is the mercury?'

'Be *careful*!' shouted the Contessa.

'The interior of the chamber is already *bathed*,' explained an acolyte, indicating the book-sized slot beneath Chang's table. 'A *sheath* of compounded glass plating –'

'I must examine it . . .'

'We have obeyed every instruction –'

'And I do not care! You – every one of you – before this day wore other clothes! What were you – a banker? A shiftless second son? Parrot all you want – but I must *know* what has been done! I believe *trust* has been proven quite bankrupt in *this* enterprise!'

Svenson went to his knees, squinting at the brass undercarriage. He shifted the books from arm to arm as he changed position and probed gingerly with his fingers into the slot where the book would go. Finally he stood and thrust a book into the hands of the gloved acolyte. 'It will need cleaning. There cannot be the slightest blemish or smear.'

'Doctor Svenson,' called the Contessa. 'I admire this zeal for survival, but your demands? Is that all?'

He glanced at Miss Temple. The Contessa clucked her tongue.

'You cannot save them. Chang is gone already. Celeste will die at your own hand.'

'Better mine than someone who does not care.'

'I'm sure she values the distinction. Can you hear us, Celeste? Have you gone to sleep?'

'Robert Vandaariff was your enemy.' Miss Temple was ashamed at the quaver in her voice. 'His restoration will mean your ruin.'

'Celeste, while you *persist* in refusing to see yourself, I do not. I am very good at some things, and not at others.' She laughed. '*Spelling*, for example. Robert Vandaariff will be wise enough to see the many advantages I can offer. It is a circle returning to its start, for he and I began this whole affair. Doctor, what are you doing?'

'I am protecting my charge.' Doctor Svenson crouched near the rack of books, and for the first time Miss Temple saw the leather case, the same she had lost to Foison. The Doctor swivelled it to the Contessa. 'I do not want *my* book broken in any disturbance.'

But before Svenson could place his book in the leather case, he had to remove the one that lay inside. He slipped it out and then juggled the two books arm to arm, for he'd only the one handkerchief with which to shield his skin, even as he also awkwardly moved the cigarette from his fingers to his mouth.

'Doctor, please, what is that *other* book?' called the Contessa impatiently.

Svenson raised it to the light, squinted, shrugged. 'Mr Foison could tell us for sure, but I *believe* this book holds Cardinal Chang.'

'Is Foison alive?' asked the Contessa. 'I thought not – rouse him! Rouse him! And rouse that idiot as well.'

This last was to the green-coat at her window, who gave a stiff kick to Jack Pfaff's inert form. Acolytes hurried to Foison, turning his body and tapping his face, and the man rose stiffly to a sitting position.

'The book in the leather case,' Svenson explained. 'Cardinal Chang?'

Foison nodded. 'What has happened?'

'Your master is dead,' Svenson replied. 'And about to be reborn.' He knelt and set the other book into the case, standing again with the one Foison had agreed held Chang.

Svenson weighed it in his hands. 'Perhaps I will take this too, as a condition.'

'No,' said the Contessa.

'Why not?'

'I do not trust you, Doctor.'

'Then we are matched.' He turned to Miss Temple. 'Forgive me, Celeste. I did try.'

Without another word Doctor Svenson heaved the glass book into the air, straight past the green-coated guard and through the open trapdoor, where – to everyone's ear – it burst to pieces on the iron steps.

The Contessa exploded with anger – the book was hers, the waste, it could have been reused – but Miss Temple only closed her eyes. When Pfaff had told her Chang's mind was gone, she had been stricken, but at the book's destruction he was finally, truly lost. With a dreadful relief Miss Temple exhaled, expelling with her breath all hope and all despair. For the first time in what felt like years, her mind was clear.

And the men before her were fools.

'Would Colonel Bronque stand so idly by? Would your mother?' The words were thick in her mouth, but she did not care. 'She's going to kill them all. She's going to kill *you*.'

Mahmoud looked at Schoepfil. The Contessa's cold voice cut in: 'I *can* kill them now. But I will not, if I do not have to. *Do* I have to, Doctor Svenson, for the procedure to work?'

Svenson had returned to Chang's table, bending low to peer beneath. 'I am examining the Professor's work – obviously he *intended* that they should be consumed –'

'*All* must be consumed!' warned an acolyte. They stood in a menacing ring around the machines.

'Indeed. However,' Svenson went on blandly, 'art is not science. As

Mr Schoepfil has taught me, what satisfies alchemical symmetry *may* be superfluous to the desired result.' He indicated the tubs with distaste. 'Mr Harcourt gives us iron . . . Mr Kelling copper . . . poor Colonel Bronque lead. Now . . . iron serves the blood, of course . . . '

Miss Temple's head swam. The more Svenson spoke, the more the Comte rose within her. She coughed wetly through the mask. Each insight felt like a knife turning inside Miss Temple's chest. Was this what had happened to Francesca? She pictured the ravaged corpse, each ruined organ excised –

'What is going on?' asked Jack Pfaff. Miss Temple saw him stand through a haze. He was looking at her. 'Is she being made to talk?'

'She's being made to die,' said the Contessa. 'Do not intervene.'

Pfaff said nothing, but his face was pale.

'What report from the gates, from the perimeter outside?'

This was Mr Foison, hobbling to the green-coat with the revolver.

'The party at the gate was taken in hand, sir.'

'That was an hour ago. What since?'

'There is nothing *since*,' called the Contessa.

'Bronque brought but one company. If the remainder of his regiment follows –'

'The *remainder* is occupied in town. Besides, do you not have a strategy in place?'

'Not for that many men.'

'Mr Schoepfil, where is your late *friend's* regiment?'

Schoepfil pulled his brimming eyes from the gruesome tub. 'What?'

'Where are the grenadiers?'

'Aren't they dead?'

'What is wrong with him?' asked Foison.

Schoepfil's voice was small. 'She has killed the Colonel.'

'One is *amazed*,' muttered the Contessa. 'We need not worry, Mr Foison. Lord Axewith has given orders that no one should come near Harschmort. That the Colonel disobeyed with so few only describes the limits of his power.'

'I would prefer to see for myself –'

'And I would prefer you to remain.' Without waiting for Foison's reply – for he gave none, even when one of the soldiers came up with a three-legged stool for him to sit upon – she called, perturbed, to Doctor Svenson. 'Are you not finished? Can we not *proceed*?'

'We can.'

Miss Temple erupted in a spasm of choking, her mouth filled with the taste of rotten flesh.

'Good Lord,' said the Contessa. 'Even at a distance, it's disgusting.'

'It will only worsen.' Svenson stood before Miss Temple. 'You know as well as I, Celeste. Like Francesca, you *do* see what will happen – and, like her, your sickness is a measure of my success with these machines, what I'm sure you see as my betrayal. The more I correctly arrange the fate of Chang and yourself, the more you plunge into distress.'

He met her eyes, took a puff on the cigarette. Miss Temple let fly a stream of dark phlegm that splattered near his boot.

'That's for your damned betrayal,' she rasped, scarcely able to form the words.

'Doctor Svenson,' groaned the Contessa. 'May we *please* –'

Svenson raised his hand in acquiescence, but his expression clouded as he saw the hoses and wires connecting the two tables. He called sharply to the acolytes standing at either side. 'What is this? Who is responsible? These are wrong!'

'They cannot be wrong,' protested an acolyte. 'Professor Trooste –'

'I don't give a damn about Professor Trooste.' Svenson was on his knees, pulling at the undercarriage of each table. 'Celeste! Look at me! Celeste Temple!'

She looked down, ready to spit again, though her eyes were swimming. He rapped his hand on the brass fittings that connected the black hose. 'The direction of force is incorrect, Celeste? Is it not? It must pass through the tubs' – he indicated the line of rubber reservoirs – 'then through the mineral compounds and into the book. The whole reaches Chang and the bloodstone. The discharge, the corruption, is strained off and sent to you. But if these are misaligned, the bloodstone will come into play too soon – *look* at me, Celeste!'

He shoved aside the acolytes and with a few rapid tugs flipped a line of brass switches, toggling the flow of the hoses. Then, pivoting on his heels, cigarette pinched in his lips, the Doctor took a glass flask from his tunic and poured the raw bloodstone – with a spasm of pain Miss Temple knew it on sight – into a chamber beneath her own table. But she perceived within her fog of nausea that the Doctor's actions bore no resemblance whatsoever to his words. There was no call for bloodstone on her table, and the brass switches now sent the purifying energy to *her* instead of Chang.

'What are you doing?' called the Contessa.

'Exactly what you want, damn you!' Svenson stood. 'Ask Celeste!'

On cue Miss Temple began to froth and spit. She did not know what he intended, but knew what was required.

'You're a bastard,' she croaked.

Svenson stepped back and wiped his hands on an acolyte's robe. He waved for the acolyte with the Contessa's book to join him. 'On second thought, I should prefer my book to be cleaned as well –'

He quickly knelt and extracted the book from the leather case. As he extended his hand for the one book and offered up the other, the Doctor's gaze fell on Mahmoud.

'Wait – watch that man!' he shouted.

Mahmoud had indeed stepped nearer to the tubs and at the Doctor's cry every carbine swung its aim to his chest. Mahmoud went still, staring at the Doctor. Then, his arms raised, he slowly sank to his knees. Svenson cleared his throat to regain the acolyte's attention and handed him a book. '*Gently,* please – and when you've finished, put it back in that protective case.'

'Damn you to hell,' growled Mahmoud.

'I am sorry,' Svenson told him. 'I cannot help you more than I have. You must make your own choice. I know it is an impossible position.'

Svenson slid the glass book into the brass machine and stood.

'My Lady Lucifera, at last, all is prepared.'

Miss Temple did not know what the Doctor had done. He stood with his cigarette – his last, perhaps – and brushed the hair from his eyes with thin fingers. She would not escape. Once the Doctor had been shot for his impudence, the Contessa would try again – or simply cut Miss Temple's throat. But that he had done something, that he had tried to the last, touched

Miss Temple in her sick isolation, like a rope snaking down into a well. She would never be pulled up, but even a glimpse of a world beyond her fate eased her heart.

She was not afraid. She had been exhausted by corruption and fever – she did not desire that *life*. She did not want to live without Chang either, and Chang was gone. And, since she did not imagine he would reciprocate her feelings, that they might perish together without her being subject to his rejection was perhaps an inadvertent benefit of the Contessa's victory. Miss Temple smiled, and bile burnt the corners of her mouth.

The Contessa stood with one hand hovering over the brass knobs controlling the tubs, the other on a larger knob, the size of an apple, at the centre of the rostrum.

'You must do it all together,' explained Doctor Svenson. 'Secondary cables will begin the rendering of the remaining metals. The minerals will advance in the proper sequence and temper the incarnation. The infusion of *identity* will travel directly to Chang. The *corrupted* essence will burn apart and flow to Miss Temple. Do you understand? Are you ready?'

The Contessa spoke to the green-coated guards. 'If he has done anything, shoot him. Be ready, in fact, to shoot anyone. Your master's survival is at stake. Doctor?'

Svenson nodded, glanced once at Mahmoud, and then stepped away.

The Contessa slid back the brass caps on three of the knobs, and then uncovered the largest, a blood-red ball of glass, like the one they had found in the Contessa's abandoned laboratory, which had so nearly claimed Chang's life and her own. This new red sphere was undamaged and whole. The light struck the glass and the glass transformed, glowing with heat. With a shriek the cables leading to Chang's table rattled to life. The hoses went taut and the machines took up their escalating drone. Miss Temple jolted against the restraints as the current met her limbs. Without volition sound came from her mouth, air from her lungs.

In the same instant, sparks leapt from the three tubs. With a decisive lunge Doctor Svenson brought his heel down hard on the coupling at the front of Cunsher's tub. A grisly crack and the coupling gave way, spitting smoke and fire. Miss Temple saw Mahmoud hesitate – the Doctor's warning, she now realized – before flinging himself at the tub of Michel Gorine. He seized the coupling with both hands, screaming at the contact, and with a brutal wrench tore it free. Sparking smoke spewed from the broken connection. Mahmoud's body vibrated cruelly, his fingers locked around the cable, and he fell. Both Cunsher and Gorine remained as they had been, unharmed, but the tub containing Madelaine Kraft, like the others before her, erupted with a cloud of horrid steam.

Miss Temple could no longer see for the shaking of her eyes. The machines became deafening – or was the roaring in her blood? She braced herself for the flood of cold corruption – but what she felt instead was heat, a clean consuming fire that scored each bone and every lineament of muscle and vein . . . and, with the agony of its passage, she felt the whole of her body reclaimed.

The corruption of the Comte d'Orkancz had been scoured away. Her eyes streamed, and with her tears went his memories . . . from this much of her burden, at least, she was set free.


The air reeked of burnt flesh and indigo clay. Mahmoud and Doctor Svenson lay on the ground, a guard with a carbine over them. Madelaine Kraft was gone. The Contessa's hands were pressed against the glass. Every acolyte had gathered. Foison had come forward, along with Pfaff. Every one of them was looking at Chang.

The scar on his back had lost its flaming shade, was now white and smooth like so many of his older wounds. Chang's muscles strained as he fought to rise.

He was alive . . . and awake.

'Is it him?' cried the Contessa. 'Did it work or not?'

Acolytes lowered the table to a horizontal position and loosened the restraints. Six together lifted Chang gently and turned him on his back. Then they bowed their heads. Chang groaned.

'We require an answer! Are you these men's master come back to life?'

Chang raised a hand against the light. His voice came raw.

'Who is there? What is this place? What has happened?'

The Contessa raised her hand so that no one else might speak. 'You are at Harschmort. Are you Robert Vandaariff restored?'

Chang turned and met Miss Temple's gaze. What had the Doctor done? His final changes had redirected the flow of power, and the bloodstone had effected her cure. But what had he done to Chang?

'What is your name, damn you?' This was Mr Schoepfil, still on his knees. 'Do you know me?'

Chang pushed himself up, his eyes narrowed to slits. 'Drusus Schoepfil. *Nephew.*'

'And do you know *me*, Lord Robert?' called the woman in the brass helmet. 'Can you name my *role*?'

'I know your voice . . . Rosamonde.' Chang hesitated. 'My Virgo Lucifera.'

The acolytes erupted with praise, fairly singing their master's return. Mr Foison, Miss Temple noted, said nothing. Nor did Jack Pfaff. Chang held out a hand.

'Something to drink. To return from so far away is thirsty work . . .' The acolytes helped him off the table. One offered a white robe that Chang refused, another a bottle that he scrutinized and then accepted. He clutched the table for support, his body not yet under full command. His gaze fell on Svenson and Mahmoud. 'Are those men dead?' He turned again to Miss Temple, without expression, and her blood went cold. 'Does this woman live?'

'This is not my uncle!' declared Schoepfil, edging closer. 'I do not believe it.'

Chang ignored him, drinking deeply. 'Come out, Rosamonde. If I owe this delivery to your kindness, I would thank you.'

'Are you truly healed?' she asked.

'In every particular.'

'Then you cannot be offended by a *test*. Much depends upon it. Poor Mr Schoepfil's inheritance, for one.'

'Does he *have* an inheritance?' asked Chang drily. 'Surely new provisions have been made. As for tests . . . try me as you see fit.' Chang inhaled deeply and drew his fingers along the canvas hoses, the blackened hanks of wire. He gazed into the porcelain coffins. 'What a provocative arrangement . . . what *sacrifice*.' With a shiver Miss Temple saw his gaze fall on a small table of metal tools. He nodded to it and addressed the acolytes. 'Take that woman down. She ought to be *examined* while the infusion is fresh . . .'

The acolytes leapt to the task. With two successive jerks Miss Temple was brought flat on her back. As the straps were loosed and the mask none too gently peeled free, she heard more questions fly at Chang.

'How did Harald Crabbé perish?' asked the Contessa.

'What do you know about Ned Ramper?' called Pfaff, who had pulled the tray of sharp tools from an angry acolyte.

'When did we last speak?' demanded Schoepfil. 'The two of us alone?'

'Excellent questions . . .' Chang approached Miss Temple's table. She felt the exposure of her bare limbs and a helplessness in her heart.

'What would you have me do now, my lord?' asked Mr Foison.

Chang ignored the question and brought his scarred face up to hers. With his thumb Chang wiped the black drool from Miss Temple's chin. An acolyte offered him a cloth.

'The Bride has accepted the corruption, my lord. Consuming the flesh of life –'

'To make the flesh of dreams. By whose command?'

'By your own,' answered the Contessa.

'I do not recall it.' For the first time Chang noted the corpse of Robert Vandaariff. 'But I am apparently indebted for your . . . assistance.'

'There will be ample time to discuss debts.'

'I would expect no less.' Chang's arm slipped and he fell back, catching himself on the table, his mouth near Miss Temple's ear. His words were scarcely more than a sigh. 'Remember the rooftop. *Stay alive.*'

Miss Temple did not move. '*Rooftop.*' Happily – so *very* happily – she saw the Doctor had exchanged books – his fussy juggling, his insistence that the glass be cleaned, the leather case turned for an instant from all eyes. And the Contessa's book had shattered on the iron stairs. If nothing else, the Comte could never return.

Acolytes moved at once to help him up. Chang pushed them away. He faced his audience and snapped his fingers. 'I am perfectly well – but *under-clothed*. A shirt. For the rest of you, Harald Crabbé died on a dirigible, slain by that woman's hand. You and I, nephew, have not spoken alone for *years*. As for this Ned Ramper, I confess to never having heard the name.'

'A lie!' Pfaff smacked a fist into his palm. 'He was your captive in this very house!'

'I do not *recall* it,' replied Chang. 'But neither do I recall the changes made to this room. So many beautiful machines. Have I been . . . asleep?'

Before any of the acolytes could reply, the Contessa spoke forcefully: 'Unfortunately the procedure was not completely successful. The blood fever has clouded Lord Vandaariff's memory of recent events.'

'Then have I answered you? Or is there more?'

Chang smiled thinly, as if his patience had been exactly spent. He held out his arms as an acolyte returned with a crisp white shirt and allowed himself to be dressed.

'What I would have you *do*, Mr Foison,' he went on, gesturing to the bodies on the floor and in the tubs, 'is to gather these men up. If they are dead take them away; if they live, let them wake and receive judgement. Assuming I command my own house, of course. Do I?'

The acolytes bowed at once. After a moment's hesitation, the green-coats came to attention. Chang turned his gaze to the glass.

'And you, *Signora*? Will you not join us?'

Miss Temple rolled her head slowly from side to side, as if in delirium. She counted, to her right, four acolytes bending over Mr Cunsher and Mr Gorine, and one guard at the trapdoor. Directly before her two acolytes stood between the still bodies of Svenson and Mahmoud, and with them the sentry from the Contessa's window. To her left stood Chang, with Foison, Pfaff and Schoepfil – in the excitement no longer meriting his own guard – and at least six more acolytes. Beyond them all were the last two green-coats at the main door.

The Contessa ignored Chang's invitation. Instead, her fingers tapped restlessly on the rostrum. Chang could do nothing without revealing himself. Once that happened he would be assailed by all.

Miss Temple leant to one side and retched, an act whose vulgarity stopped conversation. Very little foulness remained in her mouth to void, but she covered the lack with an ugly croaking. She looked up with wild eyes.

'Poor Mr Schoepfil. The Duchess will have her revenge. As least Colonel Bronque is spared the disgrace of being shot.'

Schoepfil's mouth worked, and his goatee shuddered like a small mouse in the cold.

'And Mr Foison,' Miss Temple called, 'are you a child? You *know* whom that book held.'

'He is *not* my uncle,' cried Mr Schoepfil with a rising zeal. 'My uncle is dead and this man is nothing – a criminal! An assassin!'

Pfaff – more warily now – stepped back from Schoepfil. Miss Temple located a new supply of drool and let it fly.

'And do you think she will lie with you, Jack Pfaff? With *you*?' She heaved herself up to a sitting position. 'What have any of you won? If she – *she* – is still in *there*?'

The words hung in the rancid air, and the acolytes and soldiers – for their loyalty determined the power in the room – shifted their attention back and forth from Chang to the Contessa.

'I will come out,' the Contessa at last replied, 'but I will not be fooled.'

'What else would you have me do?' Chang asked.

'I want you to choke the life out of her. Kill Celeste Temple in front of us all. *That* will convince me. And nothing less.'

'And if I prefer to study her condition?'

'You cannot. It is my price for your restoration.'

Chang smirked. 'That alone? I expect your *price* to extend well into infinity.'

'It is my price *now*.'

'Or what?'

The Contessa cocked her head. 'Don't you know?'

Chang looked at the glass book in its slot. 'My restoration does not extend to these latest days. The exact details of this chamber elude me.'

'That is a pity. Watch.' The Contessa slipped the cover from another knob and the light struck a glow inside the glass. From the ceiling dropped a small

glass globe, bursting into a bloom of blue smoke amongst the acolytes minding Cunsher and Gorine. In an instant all four toppled senseless. The guard
at the trapdoor retreated, his hand over his mouth and nose, waving his arm.
But the Contessa had chosen her target deliberately: the men were far
enough apart for the fumes to disperse before reaching anyone else.

'The entire chamber may be so *fumigated*,' warned the Contessa. 'After
which it might also be required that I come amongst you and cut a few more
throats. In the interests of our higher purpose, naturally.'

'Naturally,' replied Chang.

'*So.* Will you kill her now, Lord Robert, or am I to feel . . . *unappreci-
ated*?'

Pfaff turned with a pained expression. 'Come now, whatever her offence –'

'Be quiet, Mr Pfaff –'

'But she's already going to die –'

'Then a quick death is a *mercy*.'

Miss Temple laughed. 'The most powerful man in the land, forced to murder a woman, by a woman! There's restoration for you! There is transcendence!'

'*Do it!*' shouted the Contessa.


In the mansion of Miss Temple's heart, pity was consigned to a very small
pantry nook, and so it was with a cold eye that she watched Jack Pfaff
exhaust his disapproval with a tight-lipped slap on his thigh.

Chang advanced to Miss Temple and she braced herself for his touch –
but then behind him came a blur of movement. Chang spun round, but that
did not stop the blow that turned his jaw.

'*I* am master here!' Schoepfil cried. 'Harschmort is mine! Every last
stick!'

He fell on Chang in a fury, battering his chest, his face. Two acolytes, loyal
to their new lord, hurled themselves at his assailant. Schoepfil easily dispatched them and returned his attention to Chang, who had stepped back
and stood ready. Schoepfil feinted, several blows in sequence, and Chang's
arms moved in instinctive response to block them. Schoepfil's face darkened
with a strange mixture of rage and glee. He raised his arms to the ceiling and
crowed.

'Questions be damned! Come and see – all of you! This cannot be Robert Vandaariff! Robert Vandaariff does not *fight*! Robert Vandaariff could not kill a sleeping rat with an axe!' Schoepfil aimed an accusing finger at the Contessa. 'Your enterprise has failed, madam! We have been duped! This is no one but Cardinal Chang! Nothing but criminal slime!'

The spinning leather case struck Schoepfil's head and bounced off, splitting open as it struck the floor. The glass book inside flew free and shattered directly before the knot of acolytes. The robed men tottered and fell, screaming and clutching their ruined legs. Svenson called from his hands and knees, off-balance from throwing the case, his face a mask of blood.

'Run, Celeste! Run!'

Chang launched himself feet-first into Schoepfil, sending the small man sprawling. Miss Temple leapt off the table. Glass balls dropped and burst across the chamber. Miss Temple held her breath. She saw Chang in a swarm of bodies, Doctor Svenson wrestling with Jack Pfaff, and – with a shock – Mr Foison, limping directly for her. Broken glass blocked her way to the trapdoor. She could only run for the main door, where two green-coats stood guard.

'Stop her!' shouted the Contessa.

Miss Temple ducked the swinging carbine of the first man, but the barrel of the other's caught her on the shin and tripped her flat. She clawed for the doorway but a guard caught her waist. She kicked out, lungs on fire, eyes watering chemical tears. The second guard had his carbine high to strike when Mr Foison, not one for mincing matters, drove a knife into the soldier's back. The second guard dropped Miss Temple to grapple with Foison.

'*Go!*' He put a fist into the guard's abdomen, then bashed the knife hilt across his jaw, but speaking even that word brought the gas into Foison's lungs. He clutched his throat and sank to the floor. Miss Temple scrabbled to the corridor and ran.

Past the first corner she took deep breaths, forcing herself to think, to see. This was where she'd been before – when she met the party of acolytes and let loose with the revolver. Now she needed the other direction. Her bare feet pounded down the corridor.

She burst into the fountain chamber and rushed straight to where she'd first come in, hopping like a schoolgirl across the tiles back to the band of gravel. With desperate fingers Miss Temple snatched up lump after lump of the black explosive stone and heaped it onto one of the robes, fast as she could, heart pressing at her throat. Not after regaining herself, not after regaining him. She would not see him perish.

Each second was agony – she could bear it no more – it must be enough – and Miss Temple gathered the robe like a tramp's bundle. She returned over the tiles – stepping now, never a hop – and to the open room.

Two soldiers in blue stood in the charred doorway that had been blown wide, bayonets fixed – Colonel Bronque's men, bloodied and bareheaded.

'Help me!' she hissed, before they thought to run her through. One had stripes on his sleeve. 'Sergeant – I beg you –'

Miss Temple flinched at the crack of his rifle. The doorway to the carpeted hall was crowded with green-coated men. One flew backwards at the Sergeant's shot, and then another from the second grenadier's. Both men raised a terrifying shout and charged past Miss Temple. The green mercenaries could not withstand such ferocity – despite their greater number no two amongst them wanted to receive the bayonets – and broke away. The grenadiers thundered after, bringing down the rearmost with a shriek.

Miss Temple let them go. She dashed to the doors covering this side of the Contessa's cell and swung them wide.

She retreated quickly as the Contessa leapt towards her, behind the glass. Miss Temple swept the bundle round her head, for momentum.

'Celeste Temple – what in all hell –'

She gave her improvised explosive its release and dropped to the floor. The bundle struck the glass and every particle of air roared into smoke and flame.

When her mind returned her skin ached and it felt as if her body had been showered with sharp stones. Smoke hung low in the room, thick and grey. Her right side was painfully tender. She touched a sharp protrusion with terror before her slow wits told her the corset had absorbed the worst of the blow, that these were shafts of broken whalebone poking through the rips. She pushed the scraps of her shift between her legs to preserve her decency, coughed thickly and sat up.

The Contessa's room no longer existed. Both walls of glass were blown clean through, the rostrum obliterated. The ceiling of light lay in chunks of twisted piping on the floor. Of the Contessa, Miss Temple saw no sign.

She stumbled forward, stepping over fallen pipes, searing hot to the touch, and finally into the far room. Her foot recoiled at the touch of something soft. She looked down to see Jack Pfaff, the orange coat shredded and his naked back, even up to the base of his skull, studded with daggers of glass. His face lay twisted to one side, lips curled in an expression of endless dismay. Beyond Pfaff, shielded from the blast by their grappling, Doctor Svenson lay rolled on his side, spitting dust. The blast had dispersed the blue smoke. The brass machines sparked and steamed, toppled and tipped, black hoses spurting like severed limbs.

He looked up and saw her. 'Celeste . . .'

She passed Svenson by, her foot sliding in the blood of an acolyte. Another body lay across a tub, face down in the dregs – she extended a fearful hand and felt the rough wool of a guard's green coat. She stumbled on to the tables. A hand caught hers, gripping, strong. She flinched and saw it was Chang. He lay on his back. She sank to her knees. He rose to meet her.

'Celeste –'

'You cannot die.' Her tears poured out. 'I could not bear it – not again –'

He squeezed her hand and reached to cup her cheek with an indelible soft care. She fell upon him, kissing his face until at last her lips found his, and there she stayed, sinking her need and her fear into his mouth, moaning, sobbing. Her fingers snaked through his hair and she cradled his head. At last she lifted her mouth to breathe.

'I am so sorry,' she gasped.

'Do not. You are superb.' Chang coughed and blinked. 'Forgive me – the gas –'

More coughing came from behind them and Miss Temple turned. Svenson on his knees, hacking into one hand.

'O dear Doctor . . .'

He waved vaguely to her, turning unsteadily towards the smoke. Miss Temple followed his gaze to the case of glass books, blown over, every felt-lined slot emptied. The shards of every book lay jumbled in a vast shining bed.

Abruptly Svenson doubled over and fell.

'He is wounded!' Miss Temple cried and struggled to rise.

'He will *die*,' Mr Schoepfil corrected her, emerging from the cloud, stepping over the groaning Svenson. Blue flesh showed through the tatters of Schoepfil's clothes. 'You will *all* die. Harschmort will be mine.'

He struck Miss Temple and she went down. Schoepfil glared at Chang with hatred.

'*You*. You are no one at all.'

His swift hands dropped fast around Chang's throat. Miss Temple scrambled up. She tried to break his grip but again Schoepfil thrust her away.

'You can *have* Harschmort!' she screamed. 'You can have it all!'

Schoepfil laughed – then grunted as Chang jabbed a knee into his stomach. Chang thrust out his leg, shoving Schoepfil back over one of the tubs. In a flash the small man regained his feet. He rubbed his belly tenderly and licked his lips.

'I can have it, can I? Well . . . well, perhaps –'

'You can have nothing,' said Chang, standing. 'Harschmort will drown, and the Vandaariff fortune with it.'

'O no.' Schoepfil shook his head. 'Never heard anything so absurd in my life. *No*. If you imagine – that anyone – that *this* world would *allow* – good Lord, such sums do not *vanish* – especially – *ha* – not – O *mercy* – not at the behest of the likes of *you* –'

Schoepfil's amusement got the better of his words and he tipped back his head to laugh. The blade shot through his neck clean as a needle, emerging with a crimson spray in tow. Schoepfil gargled his surprise, eyes as wide as two eggs. The strength left his body and the Contessa shoved him down in the debris.

*

Without doubt the brass helmet had preserved her life, for her body was burnt, and she bled from a dozen oozing lacerations. Even with its protection, the Contessa's face was divided by blood dripping from her hair.

'Well.' Her voice was as dry as sand. 'Inevitably.'

Chang came forward, standing unsteadily before Miss Temple and Svenson.

'I'll kill you first,' the Contessa said. 'And then I'll kill them.'

'You should run,' said Chang.

'No one's running.' The Contessa brushed a blood-wet lock of hair from her eyes.

She swept the blade at Chang's face, but she was not near enough and the tip stopped short. Chang tried for her wrist, but she twisted the knife so the tip nicked Chang's forearm.

Miss Temple gasped. Neither Chang nor the Contessa reacted at all. The stakes were clear: if the Contessa won, Chang would die. If she missed, if he took her arm, then he would take the weapon from her and drive it home, or simply end her life with his hands.

Miss Temple could not bear it. She looked about her for a weapon, but did not see a thing. Then her arm scraped on the broken corset. She plucked a broken strip of whalebone from its sleeve.

The Contessa jabbed at Chang and set off a vicious clockwork of blows between them that ended with the Contessa's blade shooting past Chang's throat and her wrist pinned in his hand. She dug for his groin with a knee but he blocked it on his thigh. She clawed his face with her free hand, but he caught that too. The Contessa lunged to bite his face. Chang thrust her back at arm's length.

'Stop this –'

'*Never.*'

The Contessa turned to Miss Temple's stumbling arrival, bloody lips curled in a sneer, but Miss Temple's arm was already in motion and the Contessa, hands held by Chang, could not move. Like a sharp stick of toast into the soft yolk of an egg, the slip of whalebone broke the surface of the Contessa's right eye and then messily ripped free so all within spilled wide, onto her face and in the air.

The Contessa shrieked and – Chang releasing his grip in shock – tripped backwards and crashed down. Miss Temple did not move. The scream dipped just long enough for the Contessa to draw air and then blazed out again, a blistering klaxon of pain and rage.

Doctor Svenson pushed past Miss Temple, on his knees at the Contessa's side. She thrashed against his attempts to touch her, spitting curses in her native tongue. Then a handkerchief was in Svenson's hand. From the silk he withdrew a spur of blue glass. With a sudden force the Doctor pressed it hard into the exposed flesh, below her throat.

At the contact the Contessa arched her back, suspended in sensation. Her legs shook. One hand seized Svenson's arm. Her cries gave way to the laboured pants of an agonized animal.

'O . . . O God damn you . . . what – what . . . O damn you to hell . . .'

Her words collapsed to a devastated whine. Doctor Svenson's hands moved gently to her face. 'Let me see . . . just let me see –'

In a scramble of limbs the Contessa broke free and crawled. She somehow stood and careened back through the shattered room. She tripped on the pipes, fell with a grunt of pain, staggered up again and vanished in the smoke.

Doctor Svenson remained on his knees. Miss Temple said nothing. Chang collected the Contessa's knife.

'I'm sorry, but – should I not – should not *someone* –'

Svenson's words were drowned out by a clatter of boots. Through the main doorway marched a crisply uniformed cavalry officer at the head of a dozen hussars. The officer waved the smoke from his eyes and viewed the carnage with a pinched dismay.

'This house is under royal writ. All present will disarm themselves and be detained.'

Chang dropped the knife. The officer advanced to the sound. He bent his face to Miss Temple, sniffed, and took in the two men with an equal dismay.

'I am sent for a young lady. She is wanted by Her Grace the Duchess of Cogstead. A Miss Celestial Temple. If any of you know what has become of her –'

'I am Celestial Temple.'

'Dear God. Indeed?'

'The Duchess will know me. She will know my companions.'

The officer considered this unlikely promise, then opted for discretion and stepped aside, offering Miss Temple his arm.

'Her Grace waits outside with the rest of the regiment. Come.' He wrinkled his nose and looked at the wreckage that now embodied Harschmort House. 'This circumstance cannot be pleasant for you.'

# EPILOGUE

Captain-Surgeon Abelard Svenson tapped the ash of a black cigarette into a brass dish bolted to the arm of his chair, which itself had been secured firmly to the cabin floor. His uniform was crisp and his new boots shone like black glass. He was clean-shaven, blond hair parted neatly, and nearly every bruise or laceration on its way to mending.

As he spoke his voice did not shift tone, so that Miss Temple, who had retreated to her inner room, might not infer that the two men talked about her – although of course she did assume it and of course they were, however indirectly.

'You are well?' The Doctor exhaled at the inadequacy of his words. 'I mean to say, you seem hale. But, yes, of course, all of this. Departure – and, I apologize, what word to use . . . alliance?'

Cardinal Chang glanced at the damp ring of coffee in his white bone-china cup. He reached for the flute-nosed pot and poured, offered to Svenson, who demurred, returned the pot to the tray. He did not drink.

'I have no earthly idea.' Chang rubbed his eyes, pushing up the spectacles. He matched Svenson's sigh, his lips unable to prevent the twitch of a smile. 'I know that, from all appearances, the arrangement is absurd.'

Svenson, less than helpfully, did not reply. Chang took the tiny cup in both hands.

'Such constructions cannot exist in the world. In *this* world. She is impossible. I am impossible. We could not meet. Exist. There is no *place* for it.'

'And so you hope to find one?'

Chang shook his head. 'Every land is the same. Every village has its order. I will be a criminal and Celeste a whore.'

'You are too severe. Money changes minds.'

'Not mine.'

'Then marry.'

Chang sniffed. 'She will not.'

'She?'

'*She.*'

The Doctor glanced towards the other room, where the tinkering of jars and tins spoke to Miss Temple's persisting occupation. 'So you will be tied together, but only by will. Can that last?'

'I have no earthly idea,' said Chang. 'I will not be *kept*.'

'She could not keep you. Nor does she need to – the Vandaariff estate, however entailed – despite everything, there is a quite valid claim, at least for a substantial settlement, and since there is no active rival claimant –'

'Let it rot,' Chang said coldly. 'Let it burn and sink like the house.'

Svenson reached the end of his cigarette and ground it out. He found his cup, half filled and cold. Chang leant forward to pour, self-conscious of the china, the chairs, carpet, brass, his own new boots, creased red trousers, silk waistcoat, white shirt and, hanging behind them on a peg, a newly made long coat of red leather. Small expenses all, yet the whole of his former life had been reclaimed with a scatter of gold coin. Chang set down the pot and now it was he who looked into the other room.

'I understand,' said Svenson. 'About the fortune. I even agree.'

'Thank you.'

'So you will keep one another. On a ship without destination.'

'She cannot be alone. Your trick took away the corruption that would kill her, but not the other memories, those that derange her . . . needs.'

'She's told you?'

At Chang's pointed silence the Doctor reddened and fumbled his slim fingers for another cigarette.

'She will need protection. Wherever in the world she goes. She will need a man like me.' Chang raised his gaze to the ceiling. 'But she will drive me mad.'

'Only as you will need her,' observed Svenson. 'And you were mad already.'


Miss Temple, certain she had given them more than enough time, sailed back into the parlour with the tissue-wrapped box and settled beaming in the seat near to Chang. Her dress was aubergine wool and her boots again dark green. Despite the nicks and scrapes that still marked her skin, Celeste Temple – Svenson could not but notice, indeed could scarce but look away – glowed with an almost obscenely evident sensuality.

'So,' he said, smiling. 'Tenerife?'

'I *believe* so,' replied Miss Temple, 'but there are so *many* choices. East or West, the Indies or Recife, Zanzibar or Sarawak. And rather several places in between, as you know. Is there only coffee?'

Chang took up the fatter pot that she knew very well held tea and poured. She watched with pleasure as he then slopped cream into the cup and stirred and passed it to her. She sipped and wrinkled her nose. 'Lovely. Too long steeped, but that's what I get for being *busy*. Doctor Svenson, please, this has just arrived, for you.'

She held out the little box. Svenson set his cigarette in the dish. He tipped the box to see each side.

'I worried it would not come in time – but, as I let the man know I saw *no reason* why it should not, it did!' She laughed. 'Open it!'

Svenson pulled at the paper. Miss Temple glanced conspiratorially at Chang, but he watched the Doctor's face.

'O Celeste.' Svenson lifted a silver cigarette case. 'Thank you so much. My other was lost, you know.'

'Of course I *know*,' she said. 'And there is an inscription. "*Zum Kapitänchirurgen Abelard Svenson, vom C. T.*"'

Svenson smiled, somewhat sadly, she saw, to read it. 'That is almost what it was. But now from you. Thank you, my dear.'

'I did not know the German myself, of course, except from memory.'

'It will mean the world to me. Let me fill it now.'

She smiled to see him take the tin of cigarettes from his pocket and carefully fill the silver case. She turned to Chang. 'Cardinal Chang has a new walking stick. Very handsome.'

'I'm sure it is,' replied Doctor Svenson, somewhat drily.

Miss Temple smirked at this, for she was no longer so shy, or shy at all. She began to think about when she and Chang could next be together, if there would be time after the Doctor departed – if she would in fact ever see

Doctor Svenson again – and what piece of furniture to employ in exactly what manner.

'Did they find her?' she asked. 'The Duchess's men?'

'I do not know,' said Svenson. 'I have not heard.'

'You would think, with an entire regiment surrounding the house – and going *through* the house. One injured woman, screaming like a witch?'

'It was the fire,' said Chang. 'The fire drove them out and stopped the search.'

'She *set* that fire,' said Miss Temple.

'I'm sure she did,' said Chang. 'And I would guess she fled to the lower depths, to the river, where no one could follow.'

Miss Temple sipped her tea, and once more looked at Chang.

'What did you *do*?' she asked.

Svenson closed the case with a snap of its clasp, and tucked it into his tunic pocket. He realized that Chang had not spoken and that the question was in fact for him. 'Beg pardon?'

'When you went to her, Doctor. Why did she stop screaming and then damn you to hell?'

'I believe it was a general curse, aimed at us all. I could do nothing.'

'I thought you had a bit of glass.'

'What? No, no.'

'Well.'

For a moment no one spoke, the only sounds echoes from outside the cabin, the muffled creak of the vessel, distant voices on the pier. Miss Temple sipped her tea.

'*That* is not why we are leaving, I assure you. I am not afraid of her, no matter where she is or what she tries to do. I will never be afraid of anything again. I have had enough of it.'

'Then why *are* you leaving, Celeste?' asked Chang. He cocked his head. 'All has been forgiven. You could do here what you would.'

She cocked her own head to mock him. 'For reasons you well know – as I have told you in your ear. But since you ask, for the Doctor's benefit, I am happy to explain. You see, Doctor Svenson – I *cannot* stay because it would be impossible to *live*. Cardinal Chang and I would be driven apart. I know it, and I would be alone. I do not wish to be alone any more – I can no longer bear it. But neither can I go *home* – were I able to go home, I never should have left, if you follow. Perhaps when I am an old woman of eighty-nine I will reclaim my father's seat. Until then the only alternative is travel. Constant motion.' She looked at Chang and finished her cup of tea. 'It is the one sure way to ensure mutual occupation and mutual protection. And mutual dependence, if I may say. It's actually very sensible. I've thought it through.'

'I see you have.'

'And of course Chang's agreed, because I'm right. What would he do here? Die in a year – senselessly. You know he would. And what would I do? Fall under a train. This way we won't. Or not immediately. I can always fling myself under a train in the Malay Straits, if the Malay people *have* trains. What of you?'

'How will I die within the year?'

She laughed. '*No*. If you do I shall be angry.'

'I will bear your wrath in mind.'

'How is Cunsher?' asked Chang.

'Well, I believe,' replied Svenson. 'I have not seen him.'

'Mahmoud and Gorine are recovered,' said Chang. 'The Old Palace is to be rebuilt. Along with half the city.'

'Invest in brick.' Svenson smiled. He finished his coffee and set down the cup. 'I'm sure it is near your time.'

'What will you do?' Miss Temple asked again.

'O Celeste. My reprieve puts me at liberty – at least while I am here – so here I will stay, at least for a time, waiting to go home.'

'Do you *want* to go home?' asked Chang.

'Not in the slightest,' said Svenson. 'That being the rub. Ah well.'

The Doctor stood and collected his greatcoat and peaked cap. Far too quickly and with a disturbing ease, he shook hands with Chang and bent down to embrace Miss Temple.

'I will never forget,' she whispered.

'Nor I.'

He squeezed her tight and shook hands a second time with Chang. The low cabin door closed and his boots echoed down the passage. Miss Temple stared after him, as if she could see through the wood. Chang held out his hand. She took it and dug her nails into his palm.

Cunsher waited unobtrusively amongst the draymen, around the first corner. He fell in step with the Doctor, refusing a cigarette with a shake of his head. Once Svenson had tossed away the match, Cunsher passed him a slip of paper.

'Passage booked to Cadiz,' he said, 'sailing in two days.'

'Are you sure?'

'There cannot be so many ladies thus disfigured.'

Svenson studied the address of the rooming house: inexpensive and near the riverside, and therefore thronged with the displaced, and – so many of those displaced having been injured – all but anonymous. It was possible. Cunsher coughed discreetly.

'Mr Foison might supply some fellows, if asked – his recent willingness –'

'No, thank you. I am in your debt. All the more if this remains between ourselves.'

'Of course.'

They reached the end of the lane and stopped, for Svenson would proceed alone.

'How will I know you have returned?' asked Cunsher.

'You won't. One way or another, you see, it's quite impossible.' Doctor Svenson sighed and clapped Cunsher on the shoulder. 'But there's an end to everything, my friend. And then – somehow, somewhere – going on.'

# G.W. DAHLQUIST

## THE GLASS BOOKS OF THE DREAM EATERS

In *The Glass Books of the Dream Eaters* three most unlikely but nevertheless extraordinary heroes become inadvertently involved in the diabolical machinations of a cabal bent upon enslaving thousands through a devilish 'process':

Miss Temple is a feisty young woman with corkscrew curls who wishes to learn why her fiancé Roger broke off their engagement . . .

Cardinal Chang was asked to kill a man, but finding his quarry already dead he is determined to learn who beat him to it and why . . .

And Dr Svenson is chaperone to a dissolute Prince who has become involved with some most unsavoury individuals . . .

An adventure like no other, in a mysterious city few have travelled to, featuring a heroine and two heroes you will never forget.

'Fantastic. Somewhere between Dickens, Sherlock Holmes and Rider Haggard. I was in seventh heaven' Kate Mosse, author of *Labyrinth*

'A page-turner, a rollicking ride. As stupendous as it is stupefying' Giles Foden, *Guardian*

# G.W. DAHLQUIST

## THE DARK VOLUME

On a barren coast, young heiress Miss Temple awakes from a fever to discover herself friendless, alone and having shot her fiancé stone dead. Fleeing from suspicious villagers and attacks by 'wolves', Miss Temple finds herself with a most unlikely travelling companion in the shape of the seductive and deadly Contessa di Lacquer-Sforza.

Meanwhile, assassin Cardinal Chang and surgeon Dr Svenson are following an orgy of destruction and corruption, involving books of blue glass, to the ruins of Harschmort House, where a mysterious and vile volume is being hunted by a diabolical cabal bent on world domination.

As Miss Temple, Cardinal Chang and Dr Svenson uncover further devilish treachery, so the terrifying secrets contained in *The Dark Volume* are revealed one by one.

'Fans of a ripping yarn will find it hard to resist' *Metro*

'Undeniably moreish . . . curl up with this under a rug' *London Paper*

www.penguin.com

# He just wanted a decent book to read ...

Not too much to ask, is it? It was in 1935 when Allen Lane, Managing Director of Bodley Head Publishers, stood on a platform at Exeter railway station looking for something good to read on his journey back to London. His choice was limited to popular magazines and poor-quality paperbacks – the same choice faced every day by the vast majority of readers, few of whom could afford hardbacks. Lane's disappointment and subsequent anger at the range of books generally available led him to found a company – and change the world.

*'We believed in the existence in this country of a vast reading public for intelligent books at a low price, and staked everything on it'*
**Sir Allen Lane, 1902–1970, founder of Penguin Books**

The quality paperback had arrived – and not just in bookshops. Lane was adamant that his Penguins should appear in chain stores and tobacconists, and should cost no more than a packet of cigarettes.

Reading habits (and cigarette prices) have changed since 1935, but Penguin still believes in publishing the best books for everybody to enjoy. We still believe that good design costs no more than bad design, and we still believe that quality books published passionately and responsibly make the world a better place.

So wherever you see the little bird – whether it's on a piece of prize-winning literary fiction or a celebrity autobiography, political tour de force or historical masterpiece, a serial-killer thriller, reference book, world classic or a piece of pure escapism – you can bet that it represents the very best that the genre has to offer.

## Whatever you like to read – trust Penguin.